DAVID JONES
THE MAKER UNMADE

DAVID JONES
THE MAKER UNMADE

JONATHAN MILES & DEREK SHIEL

seren

Seren is the book imprint of Poetry Wales Press Limited
38 Nolton Street, Bridgend CF31 3BN, Wales
www.seren-books.com

First published 1995
Reprinted 2003

British Library Cataloguing in Publication Record
for this title is available from the C.I.P. Office

ISBN 1-85411-134-5

Book designed by Catherine Louveau at FICHE L'ÉCRAN® – Paris
Design planned in consultation with Jonathan Miles and Derek Shiel
and with Mick Felton and Simon Hicks at Seren.
With a very big thank you to Éric Martini of Biotem

Cover painting: *The Garden Enclosed* (detail), The Tate Gallery, London.
Cover photograph: David Jones in 1934, en route to Cairo

Printed in Gill Perpetua by HSW Print, Tonypandy

CONTENTS

FOR CATHERINE LOUVEAU AND LILLIAN SHIEL

AND FOR STANLEY HONEYMAN AND ANTHONY HYNE

SHIFTS OF FOCUS

Sufficient time has elapsed to allow a more objective consideration. David Jones grew up at the centre of a vast world-wide empire and he died on an offshore island undergoing an extensive re-evaluation of its history, rôle and internal relationships, in a society increasingly affected by American modes and dithering over the question of whether to become part of a larger political grouping, not of its own making. During those first three quarters of the twentieth century, behavioural codes which had been designed to manage an empire efficiently changed. Monarchy and sovereignty had lost much of their grip and the church seemed ill-equipped to respond to the increasingly fundamental questions that people were posing in order to probe more deeply into the pains and power structures of their lives. By the mid-1970s, the thinking person in the West had thrown off the shackles of a monocular vision and was facing the puzzling doubts provoked by relativism. Part of Jones's 'dis-ease' as he grew older resulted from these shifts, shifts which he perceived but which his circumscribed beliefs gave him limited ability to negotiate. He was agonized by what he considered to be a decline in sign-making, whereas, towards the end of his life, there was an explosion of sign-making on a scale which could not have been possible in a less technologically advanced society. Jones's inability to respond to the poetry of electricity instead of candle-light perhaps resulted from his being born in a place and at a moment which he experienced as an interface between the country and the city, the nineteenth and twentieth century. A child born in 1895 will become an effective member of the twentieth century but will trail into maturity many modes and traditions which held sway at the time of his birth. Jones remembered that 'as a small child' he felt a 'vague sense of loss when the postal address was changed from *Kent* to *London S.E.*' He considered this to be a child's instinctive 'reaction against the encroachments upon site and locality and the inevitable and ubiquitous sprawl'.[1] He saw the event not only as unfortunate: 'encroachment', 'sprawl', but also as 'inevitable'.

In his thinking about art as well as in the use he made of themes and styles, Jones straddles centuries, not just the two in which he lived but the many centuries in which human beings have made artefacts. Yet, during his lifetime, agencies of cultural continuity such as the church, limited access to learning, pervasive ignorance, chronic discrepancies in the distribution of wealth and unquestioned patriarchy were challenged. While attentive to the formal possibilities of modernism in painting and poetry, Jones remained ideologically trapped in the tradition that had been forged by church and state, even if his own biography lent an intriguing eccentricity to his reconstruction of that tradition.

Artefacts can become popular because they suit a technology capable of re-producing them or distributing them. Bold, saturated colours reproduce reasonably well, whereas the ethereal delicacy of a Jones watercolour does not; as the artist himself put it, 'my technique defies the camera … in my case the better the picture the worse the photograph'[2] - hence the decision to reproduce as many works as possible in black and white rather than to restrict selection to a limited number of colour plates which would inevitably prove unsatisfactory and deceptive. The reproductions function as reference points in relation to the text and are no substitute for seeing the paintings themselves. Jones's work is often completely unknown to the serious art lover today and even if one or two of the more frequently reproduced images are recognized, the scope of his entire endeavour has remained obscure. While this is not a *catalogue raisonné*, there is an attempt at a kind of thorough-ness in respect of treating the breadth of Jones's visual work. We have seen, during the course of research, well over a thousand images of which only a portion can be reproduced or discussed. There is, furthermore, the sheer hazard of the search - as Jones himself put it, 'titles get changed and what was owned by Mrs. Bloom is now owned by Miss Calypso Trotter'.[3]

The fact that David Jones does not use modes which have, by and large, domi-nated twentieth century painting - abstraction, formal solidity and saturated colour - does not render his visual work irrelevant or unworthy of attention. In different decades, two of America's most perceptive critics, Harold Rosen-berg and Robert Rosenblum, have recognized Jones's importance. The sum total of his visual and literary achievement is prodigious but in literature his work is often opaquely allusive and visually his effects are intimate; he hasn't produced big oil paintings that can be sent hurtling across the globe to satisfy the increasing voracity of the international exhibition circuit. Neither the recent bias of museum curators for works off paper nor the fact that artists produce works off the wall should persuade us to neglect him in considering that often embarrassingly self-apologetic subject, British art in the earlier part of the twentieth century. In the context of that history, Jones is *sui generis* and yet his rôle is important; John Russell remarked in the early seventies that Jones 'fits nowhere in today's canons, but it is a wonderful thing to have him'.

How to fit in the odd man out? It would be unfair and negligent to isolate Jones or to consider him purely in terms of English art; many of his early efforts are clearly influenced by a partial, imperfect and difficult-to-acquire knowledge of contemporary European practice. It would also be unjust merely to neglect much of his work because it was anchored by a religious world view that may not any longer be intellectually fashionable or comfortable. It is necessary to understand his intentions and to place those intentions in relation to the time in which he lived and against the drama of his personal story. It is commonly held that Jones led an uneventful life, a view based on the fact that no account of his work, neither in poetry nor in painting, has considered how internal pressures affected his output. What we see on the wall is ultimately what counts but history and art history contextualize the work and biography can explain the pattern of making. When René Hague, in the years after Jones's death, assembled *Dai Greatcoat*, offering an autobiography of the painter and poet through his own letters, he privileged the literary over the visual because he chose to include correspondence to people predominantly concerned with literature; he also felt inclined 'to omit any account of David's attachment to the women he fell in love with'[4] and this gave rise to an imbalanced view of the pressures affecting the artist. Furthermore, some of Jones's correspondence has been destroyed - letters held to be of too personal a nature - letters from Prudence Pelham and from Valerie Wynne-Williams. Letters like these may or may not be considered relevant to painting *per se*, yet when an emotional life so affects the artist's ability to work either at his best or even at all, then perhaps such biographical elements will prove pertinent, shedding light upon the nature and quality of production. An artist goes public by exhibiting or publishing and if, as was the case with David Jones, he felt frustrated by being misunderstood, then he deserves an earnest and comprehensive attempt to understand him.

In tracing the work of a man who followed so many and various undertakings it would be difficult to keep track of these in a merely linear fashion so we have decided to keep the broad sweep of the book chronological but, for the purposes of the integrity of study, to treat different media or genres in different chapters. While we introduce the various genres at an appropriate moment in the chronology, certain activities were obviously concurrent. Jones began making serious landscapes while working as an engraver but as the bulk of the most important landscapes were made in the last years in which he was engraving or just after he stopped, it seemed logical to treat landscape after engraving. Overlap occurs, but not unneccessary repetition. The reader will see Jones from different perspectives and within different contexts than have hitherto been proposed. By treating his work generically and yet broadly chronologically, we have the chance to revisit certain themes and examine them from different or more penetrating points of view.

David Jones was a complex figure, full of paradoxes and puzzles. He was a man programmed to poverty who would habitually take taxis. Friends would arrive with all his daily needs to ease what appeared to be an endless financial predicament and yet he would purchase clothes from Gieves and Hawkes, Harrow-on-the-Hill. He was shy and apparently self-effacing but he would sign, as if for posterity, the annotations he made in the margins of the books he owned. His drawings are generally regarded as tender and fragile but, in fact, as one astute reviewer has noted, they are also often 'ferocious'.[5] He touched many circles, meeting painters like Sickert and Braque as a young man. Later in life the fiction editor of Cape wrote asking if he could bring Allen Ginsberg out to visit him. He also struggled against many internal pressures; in the 1960s he awoke from a dream to find that he'd scratched a cross on his chest, provoking questions about what religion had done to the psyche and vitality of the man. Much earlier on Caldey Island, visiting the religious community, Jones was seen sitting silently at his meal, stroking the red hair of the young milkmaid who sat beside him. He then turned his face to the wall and hit his head slowly against the stone again and again and again.

I

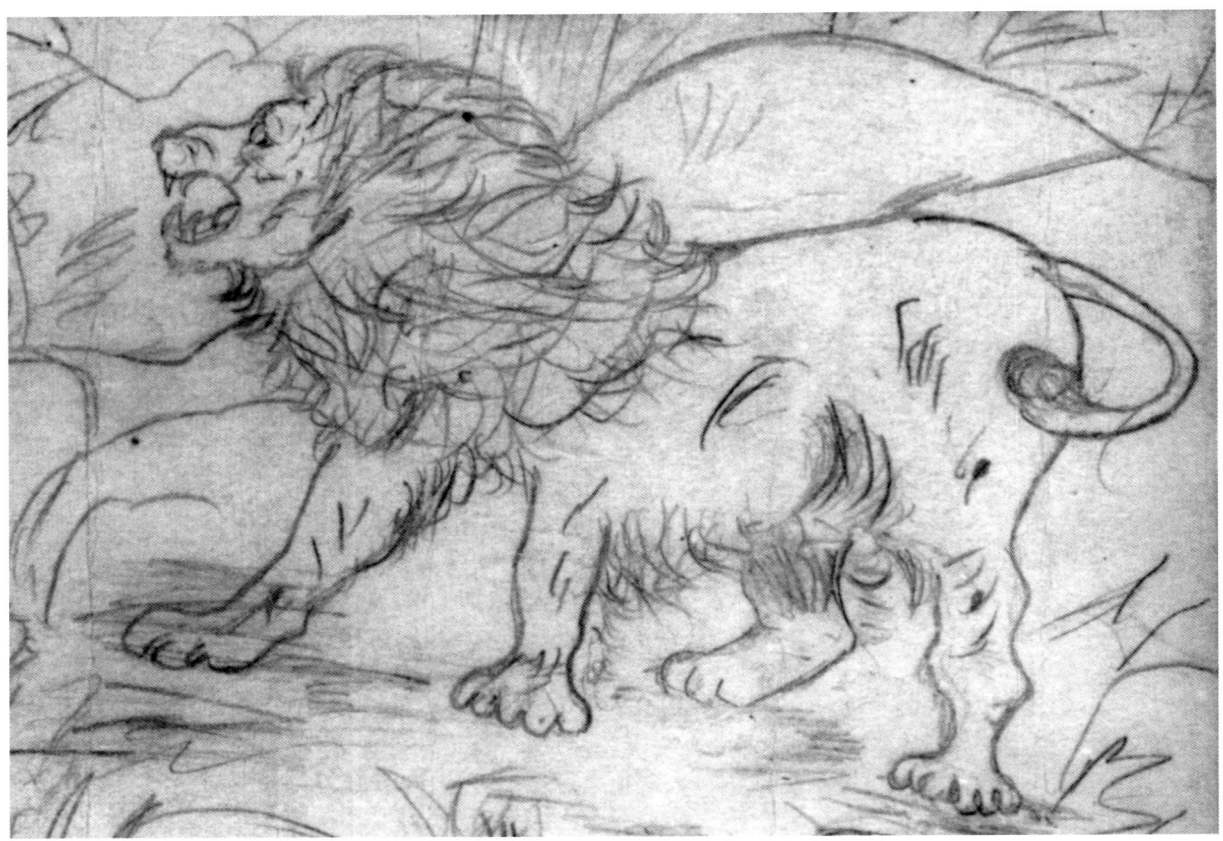

1. The Lion (detail), 1902

THE EARLY YEARS

'It shows a kind of freedom', observed David Jones, talking about a drawing made so early that he could not even remember doing it.[1] In 1902, 'aged seven', as his father wrote in the bottom right hand corner, David Jones drew *The Lion* and, indeed, it has a vivacity that animates the illustrational image on which it was quite probably based. It also, and more remarkably, demonstrates a compositional finesse which belies the youth of its executor.

It is rare to begin an exploration of an artist's œuvre by considering paintings and drawings done during childhood, and yet, in David Jones's case, it would seem not only justifiable but necessary. Leaving aside for a moment the inherent merit of these works, we find that Jones chose to draw animals and historical subjects and that he had a very early inclination to paint looking out of a window; there is, therefore, a continuity between the instincts of the boy and the preoccupations and habits of the man. Moreover, Jones himself is responsible for our taking his childhood work seriously; when in 1963, Stephen Spender took Igor Stravinsky and his wife out to Harrow-on-the-Hill to visit Jones at the composer's request, *The Lion* was the first drawing which the painter chose to show to his visitors. It had initially been exhibited in 1903 at the Royal Drawing Society for the Encouragement of Youthful Art in Queen Anne's Gate, and later the same year, at the Cork International Exhibition. It reveals a natural aptitude; the sweep of the mound on the right, curving downwards into the extended forepaw, throws the head up into a snarl against the scribbled hill. Emotionally, the scene makes an impact; the energetic marking of the landscape in which the lion stands echoes the wildness of the beast.

By the time of the artist's birth in 1895, his father, James Jones, had been promoted from Compositor to the position of Printer's Overseer and he would eventually become Production Manager of *The Christian Herald*. He took much care and interest in his son's early attempts at drawing and painting; the nature of his job helped to create a home environment which 'took the printed page and its illustration for granted', and this, as Jones observed, most probably had an influence on his 'early preoccupation with drawing'.[2]

David Jones's mother, Alice Ann Jones, of Italian descent on the maternal side, had worked successfully as a governess and teacher before her marriage and she had 'drawn well as a young woman'.[3] One of the painter's earliest recollections was of seeing three of his mother's drawings, 'one of Tintern Abbey, another of a Donkey's Head, and a third of a Gladiator with curly hair'.[4] Alice Jones's range of subject matter: an animal drawing, a landscape with religious ruins and an historical subject, prefigures, in a quite astonishing manner, her son's later

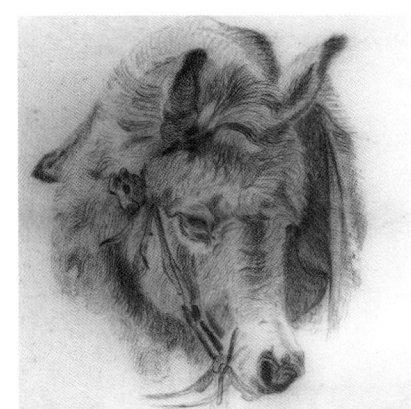

2. Alice Jones, Prize Shetland Pony, 1880

13

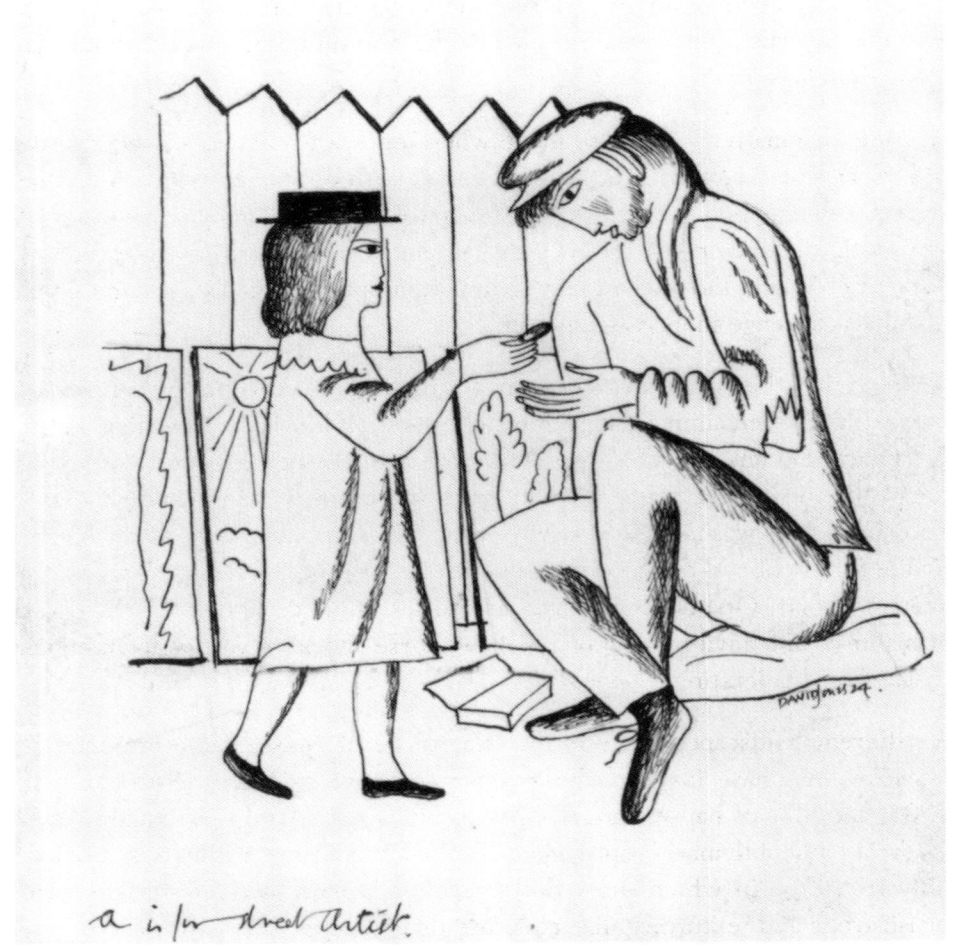

a is for dreed Artist.

3. A is for Artist, 1924

preoccupations. While Jones might have remembered these in particular because they were of some interest to him, it is also possible that they may have been influential. When he asked his mother why she no longer drew, she replied that her drawing had been done a very long time ago and 'when one gets married there's no time for such things as drawing!'[5] Her remark may have inadvertently planted the idea that married life and the making of works of art were not necessarily compatible. She used to drop a few pence into the cap of any pavement artist that she passed. When quizzed about 'why they all got a few pence, irrespective of the merit of their work', she would reply that that was 'her business'. Later on, Jones discovered that 'she feared' that her spoilt and special son 'would end in the gutter' if he gave his 'entire attention to drawing and remained so backward' at his lessons.[6]

Mr. and Mrs. Jones would take their family to the London Zoo. When a periodical published some children's drawings, the proud James Jones wrote enclosing 'a few sketches done by my little boy ... who is not yet eight years old.' He 'went to the zoo and when he came back he drew these clever pictures'[7]. Among the drawings inspired by visits to the zoo was *Elephant and Baby* which, although childish in overall appearance, wittily reveals the young elephant's need of its mother as well as demonstrating the boy's capacity to use a strong, decisive line to describe the larger elephant's back and hind leg. As a mature artist, Jones would return to the Zoo on numerous occasions and make drawings on the spot.

A more imaginative work, also made when Jones was only six or seven years old, is *Tiger and Leopard*. The leopard cub is both delicate and ferocious; the tiger has an enigmatic expression, a mixture of bafflement and alarmed pugnacity. As in the drawing of *The Lion*, the simple landscape is important; the line of the hill behind the leopard cub almost mimics that animal's back and head, giving its challenge an increased power.

Along with the loose drawings and paintings a sketchbook survives, containing sixteen animal, landscape and historical drawings. As well as works of imagination and sketches inspired by the zoo, the book records aspects of life at the turn of the century when Jones was a boy. During his early childhood, Brockley was not yet part of Greater London but truly in Kent, within a mile or two of real country, with its own open spaces, and a lot of trees and a farm of sorts. One of Jones's vivid memories 'is of going to watch the smith at his forge and anvil making or repairing horse-shoes',[8] a vestige in an epoch marked by accelerating change.

A different landscape, and one that was to be of considerable importance later on, may have inspired the imaginative painting *Winter*. Round about 1904, the first of happy annual visits to his father's family in North Wales made 'an indelible mark'[9] on the boy. The painting shows a solitary house in a hilly landscape in which snow floats across a stormy sky and variations of brushstroke and texture vitalize a picture that is compositionally enhanced by the odd inclusion of the gate in the lower left hand corner.

A small painting in black and white was made after 'witnessing a bonfire on Nov. 5th from the window'.[10] It gives the spectator the feeling of being part of the event; with the foreground figure running towards the bonfire, the spectator is carried into the scene; an inversion of the spreading flames of the fire, his arms are outstretched, thus uniting the two groups of children.

The Jones family was not only artistic but musical. Alice Jones's singing made a great impact on her youngest son and the title of one of his childhood paintings, *The Race for Life*, was taken from a song that Jones's older sister used to play on the piano. The animals were depicted from a slightly raised angle, which involved a sophisticated foreshortening of their bodies. Although Jones's father wrote 'Imagination' beneath the painting, it is hard to believe that so complicated a viewpoint could have been achieved without the assistance of a visual source. Certainly, Jones later recalled that as a boy he 'did drawings of imaginary medieval Welshmen on hillsides with wolf-hounds; of Russians surrounded by wolves in snow-storms, all imitative of illustrations in boys' magazines'.[11]

James Jones, moved by his son's ability to depict animals, wanted him to 'draw missionaries encountering lions'.[12] This early encouragement to paint religious stories is not surprising; Jones recalled that his father had not been '"artistic"' at

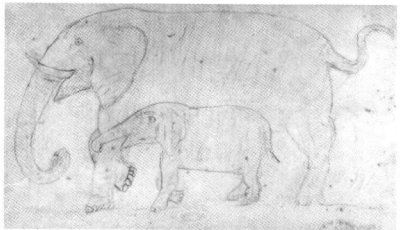

4. Elephant & Baby At London Zoo, 1902

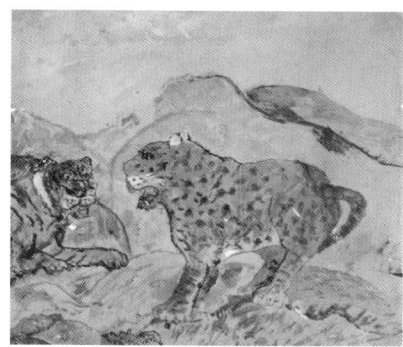

5. Tiger and Leopard, 1902

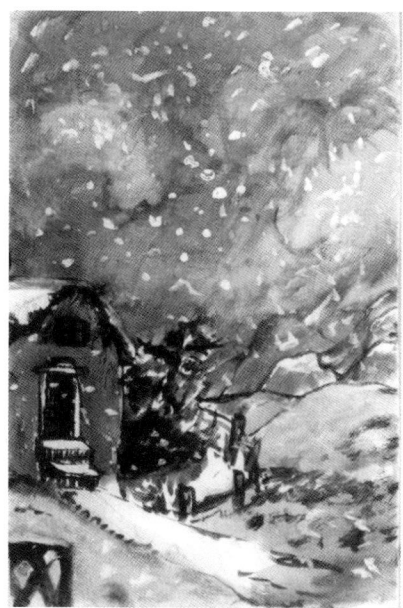

6. Winter, 1904 (?)

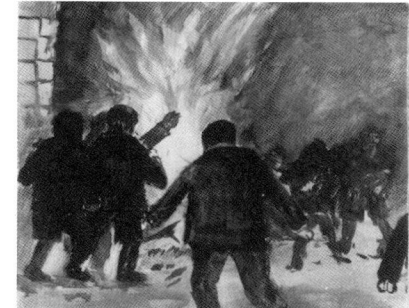

7. Bonfire, 1904 (?)

15

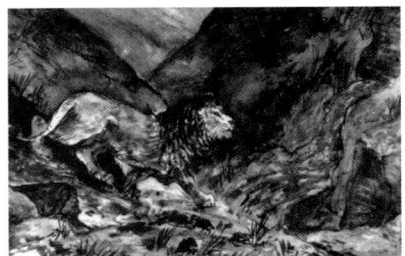

8. Lion Prowling in Ravine, 1905(?)

all, nor '"literary"' but that 'he was very religious, a Protestant of the Low Church of England school and a lay-preacher'.[13] There is no religious presence, however, no chomped missionary in *Lion in the Valley*. The alert beast moves resolutely through the dark ravine. As with the earlier *Tiger and Leopard* the astute relation of beast to landscape can be seen in the repetition of the angle of the striding front legs and of the diagonals behind, so that the hills themselves seem to participate in the mighty stride of the lion.

John Rothenstein's general observations about Jones's childhood work in his *Modern English Painters* seem unjust; far from offering 'no indications of exceptional talent',[14] we have already observed an astonishing instinct for the visual. When Rothenstein criticizes *Wolf in the Snow* (1906) for being 'without merit'[15] he appears churlish. Emotionally and compositionally, *Wolf in the Snow* shows both accomplishment and promise. As with *Winter*, the child has a feeling for the qualities of snow though, in this case, a blanket fall has created a lonely landscape which condemns the solitary wolf to a forbidding environment. The hungry animal is stopped in his tracks near a Calvary of three trees - two bare and one broken. The scene suggests an instinctive inclination towards the imagery of northern Romantic painting. The composition is, again, adroit - the line of the hill descending from the left in relation to the placing of the wolf's snout, and the overall simplicity is significant rather than empty. Curiously, Rothenstein's father, William, in his 1918 oil, *Blasted Trees, Western Front*, made a metaphorical statement about the war using a similar tripartite grouping of trees; Jones's painting is the work of a child and his theme is not so charged but, nevertheless, there is a poignancy, a feeling for lonely animals perhaps stimulated by Jones's sensitivity to the single robin in the snow in the song *The North Wind Doth Blow*, that his mother sang and which made the child cry.

The first drawing that Jones, later in life, could positively remember making was of a dancing bear seen in Arabin Road, Brockley, where his family was living. He recalled that 'there was until I was seven or eight or maybe older a

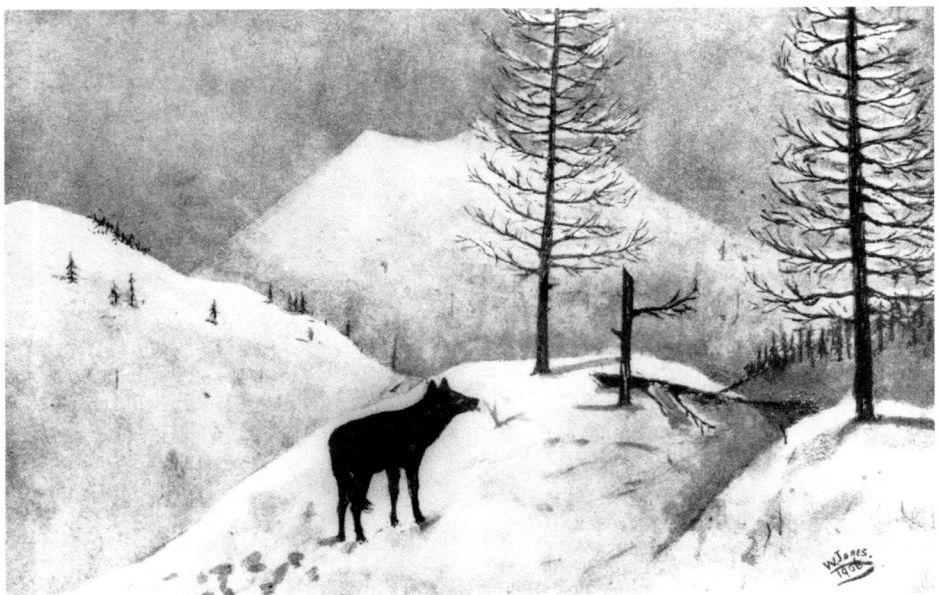

9. Wolf in the Snow, 1906

16

builder's ... yard with wooden railings, immediately opposite the house, and it was those railings that appear in my drawing of the dancing bear made when I was seven...'.[16] Jones, who later observed that 'it was a horrible thing to see a dancing bear in the street',[17] rendered the weight of the animal, the perilous, almost hideous deftness of its forced and undignified dance with great sympathy. Erratic markings which indicate the fur of the bear give the drawing a quality of movement; the eye is animated and excited by these marks, and such sensitivity to the creaturely gained Jones the 1903 'Art for Schools Association Prize'. Throughout his life, like *The Lion*, the drawing was cherished.

When he treated a marine subject, at about the age of eleven or twelve, it is evident that the process of growing up was taking its toll on the 'vitality of the drawings' done earlier; these youthful flashes rapidly became 'vitiated under the influence of contemporary magazine illustration - old Royal Academy catalogues, and the general dead weight of outside opinion, until quite destroyed by this pressure, about, I suppose 1907-8 - or earlier, yes, a good bit earlier.'[18] The stiffness of a studiously painted steamship is typical of an older child's attempt to record things as accurately as possible instead of remaining content to tap the spirit of the subject. Jones later acknowledged his belief in the destructive pressure

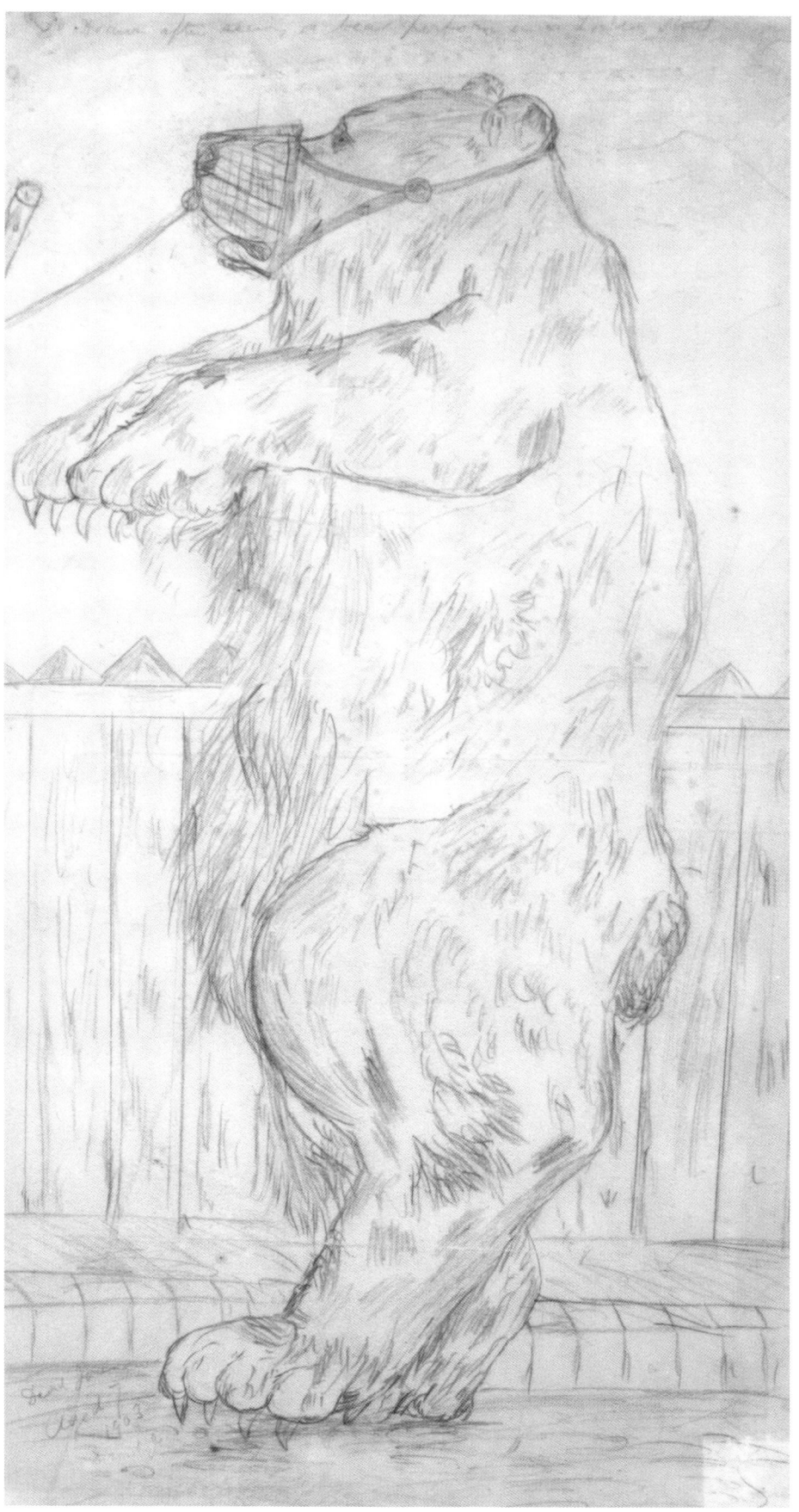

10. Dancing Bear, 1903

17

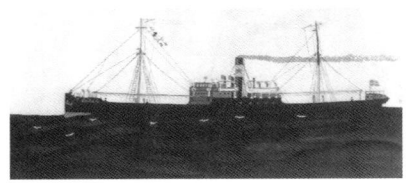

11. Steamship 'Severin', 1907 (?)

of adult know-how when he confessed, in his mid-sixties, that whenever a child wanted him to draw something he felt, 'as though one were being asked, unwittingly, to teach them a really *bad* thing.'[19]

The watercolour in *Landscape with Houses* is handled fairly crudely, the sky is lightly painted but the composition is representative of the maturing but as yet untutored child. The buildings are situated, and a sense of distance is secured, by the accenting, at intervals, in a vertical line that descends from the white chimney on the left of the house to the lone plant in the foreground.

Despite the range, energy and precocity of his work, Jones had to beg to go to art school, his 'requests' becoming 'sufficiently tedious' to ensure success[20] and so, at an early age – not quite fourteen – he was allowed to go to Camberwell School of Art. Indeed, Jones later recalled that 'both my parents, though of very limited means, did everything they could to encourage me to follow my bent as an artist.'[21] As well as being close to Brockley, the choice of Camberwell was cautious; the purpose of the school was, according to its Prospectus, 'to provide instruction in those branches of design and manipulation which bear on the more artistic crafts and trades.'[22] Jones's training would therefore have been ordered towards a trade and his mother's fears about the impecunity of the fine artist would have been allayed.

Even before entering the art school in knickerbockers and Eton collar, Jones was given, in March, 1908, *Landmarks in Artistic Anatomy* by Robert Colenso, a perhaps somewhat off-putting, technical and serious manual for a 13 year old. However, when Jones started at Camberwell, he was not allowed to attend the Life Class because of his age. His access to that class would further be delayed by a 1910 Board of Education Inspection Report recommendation that, at Camberwell, 'a short course of study from the Antique' should be interpolated between the drawing of 'details of casts' and the Life Class. So Jones spent a good deal of his first years 'drawing stuffed rabbits' and 'Voltaire's death mask'.[23]

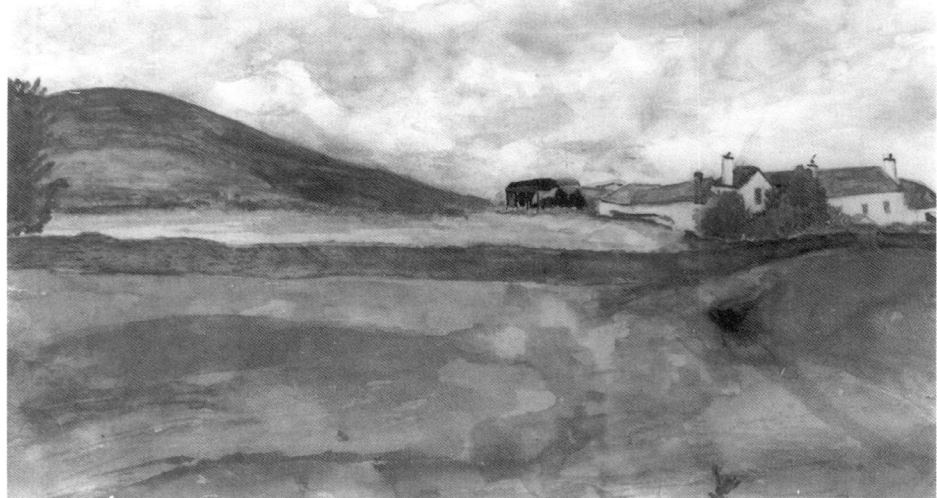

12. Landscape With Houses, 1907 (?)

18

Among the scant records of the school dating from this period, there is only one mention of David Jones; it concerns an incident that occurred on 19 January,10 1911:

> W.D. Jones after alighting from a tram-car outside the school was, whilst in the act of crossing the lines to pass into the school, knocked down and injured by another tram-car. After receiving medical assistance he was sent home to Brockley in a taxi-cab accompanied by members of the school staff for which an expenditure of 6/- was incurred.[24]

When one of his tutors, A.S. Hartrick, recalled in his autobiography, *A Painter's Pilgrimage*, that Jones was 'fortunately uninjured' by the accident, Jones, the hypochondriac, wrote at the bottom of the page in his copy, 'This is inaccurate, for I had a rather nasty cut in the head and nearly lost the sight of one eye. - D.J.'[25] The event perhaps excited Jones's appetite for the fuss and attention lavished on the sick as well as initiating a taste for travelling by taxi.[26]

At Camberwell, Jones studied under Reginald Savage and A.S. Hartrick, the former teaching book illustration and the latter teaching drawing from the figure, a course he shared with Niels Lund, who had studied in Paris under Bougereau. Hartrick had only been teaching at Camberwell for one year before Jones became his pupil.[27] As a young man he had studied in Paris where, Jones claimed, he had known 'Van Gogh, Gauguin, … Degas … Toulouse Lautrec … and was intensely interesting about them and that age'.[28] Jones's early training would therefore have been informed, not only by the classical tradition and recent indigenous trends, but also by certain developments in French art during the late nineteenth century. However, the litter of classical poses in the photograph of the life modelling room from the 1912 Camberwell Prospectus leaves us in no doubt about the pervasiveness of the classical in Jones's early training. Jones recalled that he made

> drawings of plaster casts of such works of classical antiquity as the Aphrodite of Melos (that most serene and gracious of works in the academic tradition), or that confounded Disc-Thrower … of the Dying Gaul from Pergamon, with his typical oblong Celtic shield and his torque. I naturally liked him, for he epitomized for me so much of Celtdom, or what little I knew of it in 1909-10.[29]

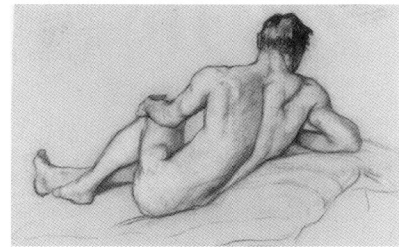

13. Male Nude for Niels Lund, 1913

Hartrick had been a student of Alphonse Legros at the Slade. Although Legros appeared in the progressive company of Baudelaire, Whistler and Manet in Fantin-Latour's *Hommage à Delacroix*, he was rather conservative and a not altogether 'stimulating' teacher, for, as Hartrick noted, 'in the first place he did not speak English'.[30] A further indication of the somewhat plodding conservatism of Legros is that Pissarro, seconded by Degas, advised the young Lucien Pissarro not to study with him at the Slade. However, under Legros, who was a considerable draughtsman, Hartrick had learnt to draw with the pencil point thus insisting 'on drawing by the character of the contour rather than the mass' which was 'the method of the old masters'.[31]

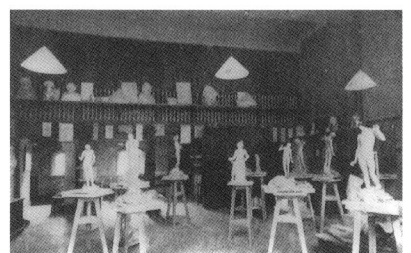

14. Camberwell Life Modelling Class, 1912

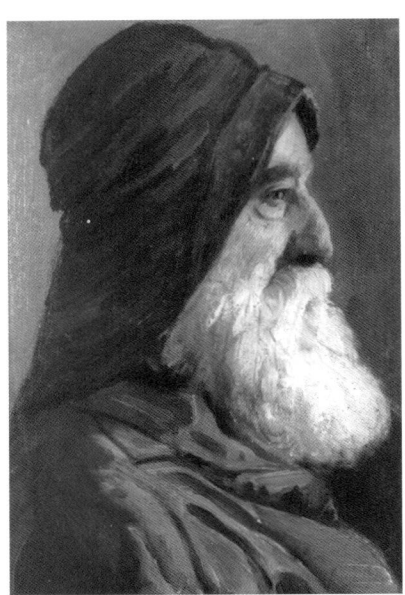

15. Portrait of Fisherman, 1912 (?)

In *A Painter's Pilgrimage*, Hartrick recalled his duties at Camberwell: 'I was engaged to give instruction in drawing and painting from the head, and drawing from the costume model for illustration or poster work, the latter being in connection with lithography and commercial art generally.'[32] From the Prospectus, it is clear that Hartrick also gave a still life class in water-colour and oil in addition to those classes that he himself remembered. For David Jones, the partly Welsh Hartrick was clearly one of his most influential teachers; in a letter of 1943 to H.S. Ede, Jones credits Hartrick as having awakened in him 'the nature of drawing and so recovered (eventually)' some quality of the 'earliest drawings'[33] though Jones's work from this period reveals the inevitable academicism that such an art school, particularly in the early stages, inculcates. Much later, in a draft of a letter to *The Times*, replying to the Art Critic's notice of Hartrick's memorial exhibition at the Royal Watercolour Society, Jones wrote that:

> when I first met him in 1909 he was regarded rather as re-presenting something a little 'advanced' and 'impressionist' for an English art-school of that period, but by 1919, with post-impressionist theory & practice infiltrating the English front, he was already regarded as somewhat out-moded, which is understandable enough ... The nature and limitations of his work, did, as your critic suggests, preclude him from being a 'major artist' but he was an artist ... At his best, and now & again, he did drawings - very directly felt drawings, which put him into a separate category from what is usually meant by 'English illustrator'.[34]

He was, as Jones noted elsewhere, 'vastly superior to the ordinary English art school master of that date'.[35]

Reginald Savage, who introduced Jones to the nineteenth century illustrators such as 'Pinwell, Sandys and Beardsley',[36] taught Figure Composition and Book Illustration which included 'line or chalk drawing ... tail pieces, initial letters'[37]. These offered the boy the chance to develop techniques that would be most useful to him later on. Savage's intention to keep before the students 'the best examples of black and white work'[38] would have had some effect on Jones's engravings in the 1920s. Earlier in his career Savage had been part of the circle of Ricketts, Shannon, Sturge Moore and the poet John Gray but he had become discontented with a fine artist's meagre income and had become an illustrator who eventually took refuge in teaching.[39] It was Savage whom Jones credited with giving him 'the "civilizing thing" in a general way - "history", the pre-Raphaelites & Co.'[40] Under Savage, Jones's attempts at figure composition nearly always included 'some medieval subject introducing a vested priest'.[41]

One surviving portrait from this period demonstrates the level of academic proficiency that Jones achieved before leaving his first art school; the subject of the oil is a Camberwell sardine vendor that Jones painted, under encouragement from his father, for a competition to find a new label illustration for Skipper's Sardines and it is quite unlike anything else that remains of his early work.[42]

A particularly interesting and progressive element in the curriculum at Camberwell was the English Literature class. This, together with his home environment, could explain why Jones, who had given up his scholastic studies at fourteen, developed a love and certain knowledge of literature. In Eric Gill's *Letters*, one of the first mentions of David Jones is of his 'reading *Twelfth Night*' to Gill's daughter Petra;[43] even if this was in an era when people had to make their own entertainment, and even if it was an amorous ploy, it suggests a real delight in literature. During Jones's years at Camberwell, the courses included Shakespeare, ballads, lyrics, as well as some Chaucer and Coleridge - all favourite areas of reference or borrowing for David Jones's own poetry.

Despite the influence of his father's work, David Jones was determined to avoid becoming a 'commercial artist',[44] and so, in the first instance, illustration was closed to him. Also, having avoided courses that would have qualified him for teaching,[45] Jones faced that first and great dilemma for the person who wants to practise a pure art: finance. Yet, leaving Camberwell 'completely muddle-headed as to the function of the arts in general',[46] Jones did not have to confront this problem as his ambitions were turned, quite suddenly, towards serving in the 1914-18 war.

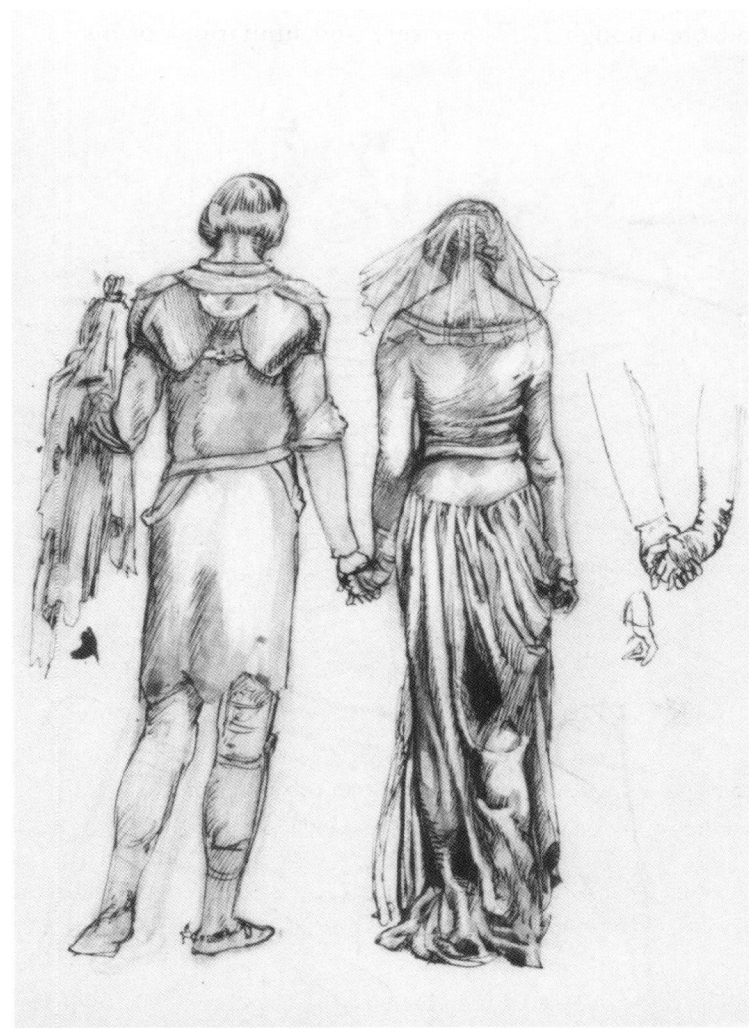

16. Knight and His Lady, 1913 (?)

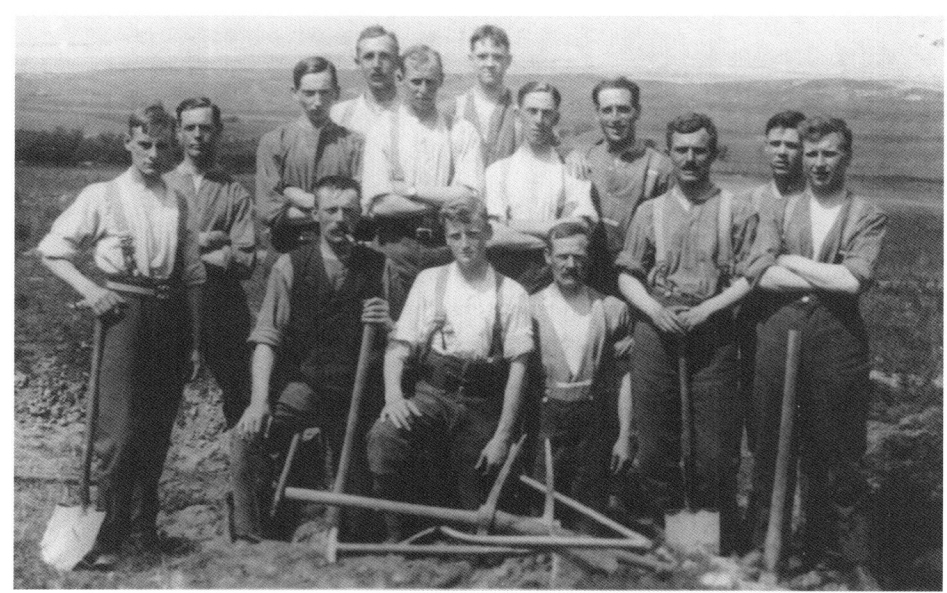

1. Anon., David Jones (back, right) on a Working Party on the Creuddyn Peninsula, 1915

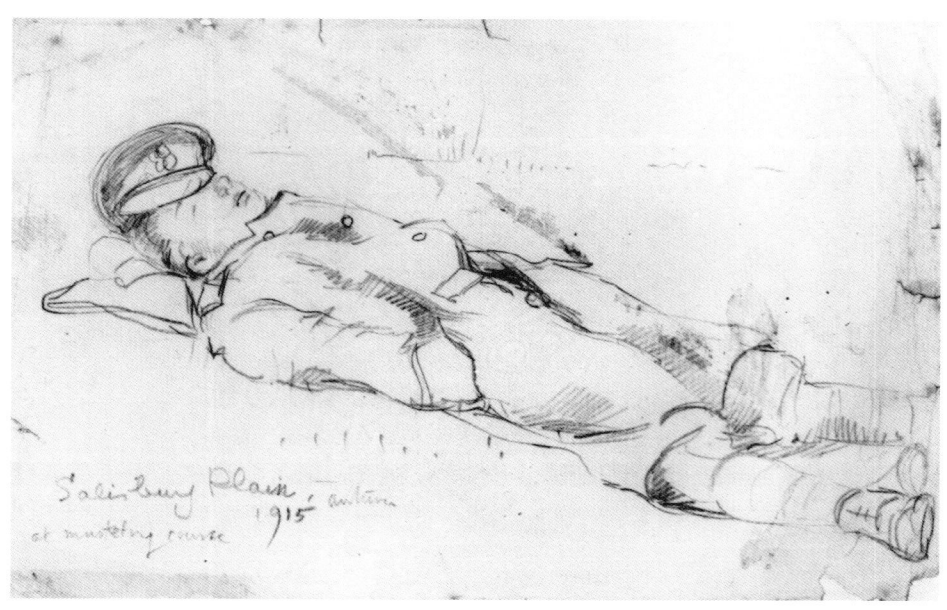

2. Soldier Lying – Salisbury Plain, Autumn, 1915

TRAINING AND THE TRENCHES

THE SKETCHBOOK RECORD

The First World War made an impact on David Jones that he himself was slow to understand. His experience of the Western Front resulted, at length, in his great literary work, *In Parenthesis* (1937), but it did not provoke a large number of visual compositions. One has to look more deeply at how the war became a factor in Jones's subsequent imaginative resource in order to perceive its full effect on his creative output, how he used the war's paradoxical manifestation of destruction and cultural continuity.

Jones was attracted by the idea of serving with the Artists' Rifles, but he was not accepted, being 'deficient in chest measurement' and therefore considered 'physically unfit for military service'.[1] The regiment had, in the past, included the cream of the Pre-Raphaelite painters and poets and Jones was later delighted by a passage in Gaunt's *Pre-Raphaelite Tragedy* which observed that William Morris, when on parade, inevitably turned to the right when the order 'Left' was given.[2] As Jones, somewhat disingenuously, liked to claim a similar incompetence, it suggests his affection for and attraction to human fallibility within the ordered world of the army.

Despite his rejection by the Artists' Rifles, Jones used to trot through the streets of Brockley and Lewisham in order to 'build up his slight but resilient physique'[3] because his father was beginning to explore the possibility of his son joining the Welsh Division which Lloyd George wanted to create. In fact, James Jones wrote to Lloyd George 'personally asking him when the Government were going to make official the proposed formation of a London Welsh battalion, as his son was anxious to enlist'. When Jones found the Secretary's reply among his papers after his father's death it struck him 'as bloody amusing, for it sounds as if Mr. Jones's son was anxiously waiting to be given some post of High Command, instead of merely, along with everybody else, attempting to enlist in the ranks'.[4]

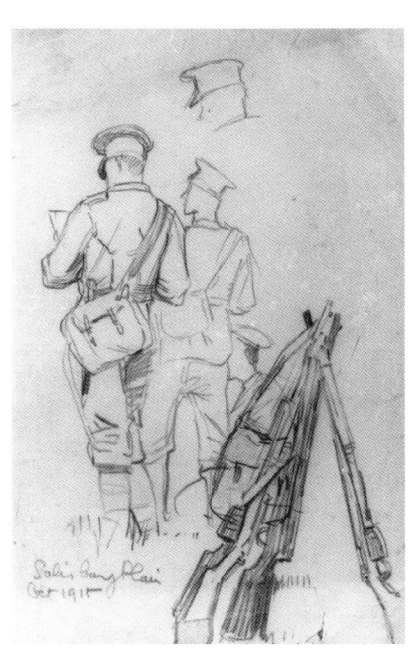

3. Officers from Behind with Rifles
Salisbury Plain, 1915

On 2 January, 1915, Jones, recruited to the new London Welsh Battalion, found himself drilling with brooms and walking-sticks in Hyde Park while still living at home.[5] After a short while, domestic substitutes for arms gave way to mock artillery; old telegraph poles mounted on bus wheels and sub-standard rifles with wooden bullets were issued to be used in dummy attacks on landmarks on the north Welsh coast where the division spent the first half of 1915 in training.

Jones's extant visual record of his time in the London Welsh Battalion of the Royal Welch Fusiliers seems to have begun in the three and a half month

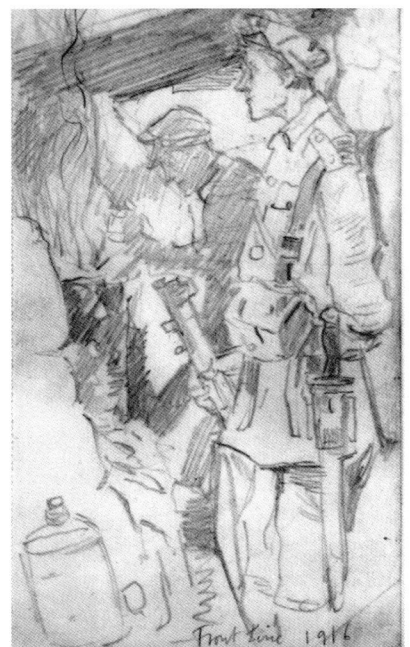

4. Front Line, 1916

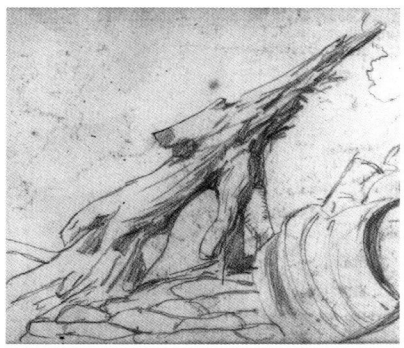

5. Dead Wood, 1916 (?)

period of final training on Salisbury Plain where the tedium of waiting fully manifested itself as an intrinsic part of the private soldier's life. Jones's drawings of men at rest reveal the skills developed at art school for they are drawn with ease and competence. These qualities are also visible in sketches done in the trenches, many made in the front line possibly against standing orders.[6] Although Jones described the sketches as 'Bloody art-school stuff',[7] he obviously considered some of sufficient quality to allow eleven of them to be shown as 'records only' at the R.W.S. Gallery in June, 1965.

The loose sketches in various private collections, those hanging on the walls of the Royal Welch Fusiliers' Museum at Caernarfon and the sketchbook preserved in the Imperial War Museum are the records of an infantryman. The five-by-seven Reeves sketchbook, which Jones began during the period covered by his long prose poem *In Parenthesis*, reveals not only the habits of a sensitive ex-student but also, quite surprisingly given the vastly different circumstances, the re-emergence of the preoccupations of the childhood sketchbook: landscapes, an historical drawing, animal drawings, one of which was done from memory of London Zoo in Ploegsteert Wood in 1916 (see p 85). The sketch which bears the earliest date,[8] 'Nov. 1916 Belgium', made in the Boesinghe Sector, north of Ypres, is a charcoal landscape of Ploegsteert that shows obvious traces of Hartrick's teaching in its Impressionist handling of trees (see p 95). Another such Impressionistic scene records, as Jones notes, 'The Mill at Neuve Eglise which was used as an observation post ... the building in the foreground ... the estaminet'.[9]

In a more intimate study of nature, Jones inadvertently anticipates the surreal natural object, by making the association between this broken deadwood and the form of a gun.

In the drawing of equipment hanging in a trench, Jones seems to have moved beyond a mere sketch. He frames the image on the page and flattens the

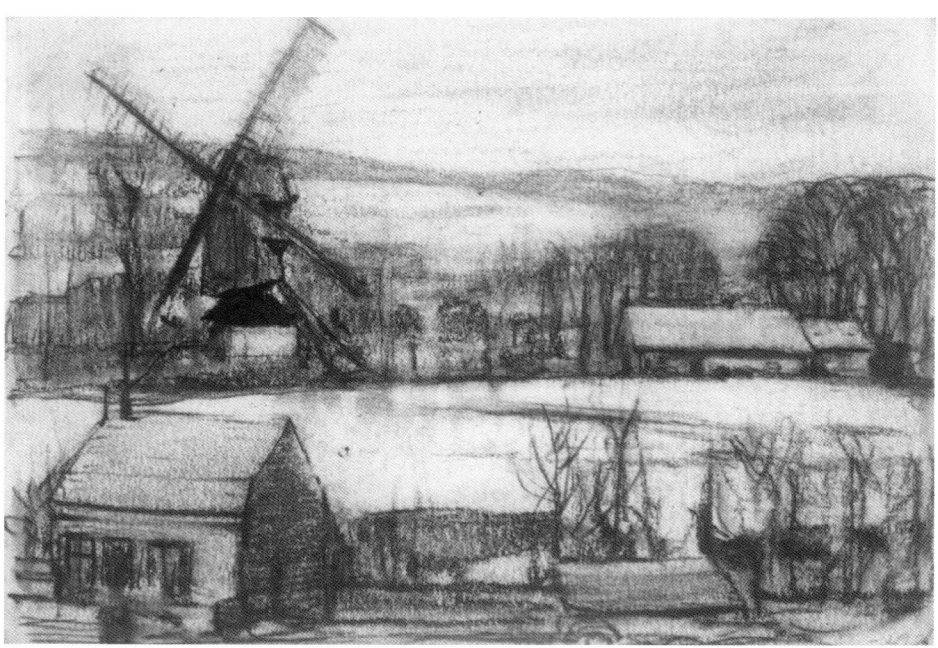

6. Mill at Neuve Église, (?)

24

drawing with an emphatic tonality. Another instance of his interest in the representation of military objects is the *Apparatus, Observation of Fire, Instrument Mk. 1*[10] drawn, with a sense of scale and a preoccupation with mass and reflection, somewhat in the manner of commercial illustration of the day. In a third drawing of equipment, made in 1917, Jones's handling of objects is less obviously descriptive, more delicately linear and more expressive.

Jones remembered that 'until the Somme battles there had been a feeling of some sort of optimism however foolish'.[11] There were also moments of beauty and stillness despite the usual smell and din. Dawns could be particularly impressive; Jones wrote of how he liked the moment 'when the sky is dark and the stars still out in the west and the dawn coming up in the east.'[12]

On 10 July, 1916, during the battle of the Somme, in the attack on Mametz Wood launched by troops in a state of 'all but total exhaustion',[13] Jones was wounded by a bullet which passed through the muscle of his calf. He was returned to the beautiful and very English village of Shipston-on-Stour to convalesce. Immediately after being wounded, he remembered lying with a 'terrible thirst',[14] a sensation which provided a potent image to consolidate his later equation of the Western Front with the wasteland. The attack was chosen by Jones for the ending of *In Parenthesis* because, as he remarked, when he returned to the battalion at Ypres in October, a new and more mechanical form of warfare had begun. Interestingly, the German writer, Ernst Jünger likewise recorded that on the Somme 'chivalry disappeared' and gave way to 'the new tempo of battle and to the rule of machine.'[15] Jones seems not to have been much interested in making a visual record of the war's machinery, unlike those Vorticists who went to the front; only a very few of his drawings include tanks or study the armaments in any detail. Censorship, of course, may have intervened as with the interdiction on

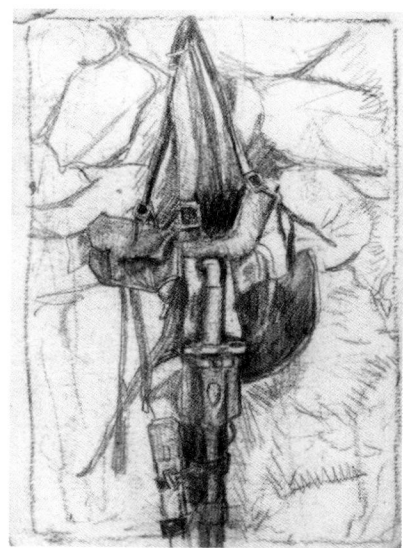

7. Equipment Hanging in Trench, 1916 (?)

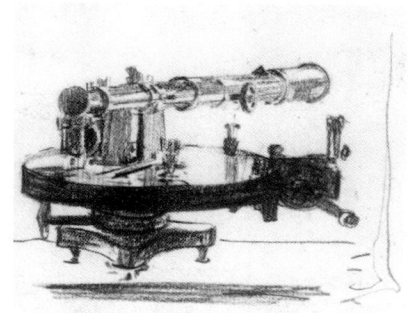

8. Apparatus, observation of fire, Instrument Mk 1, 1916

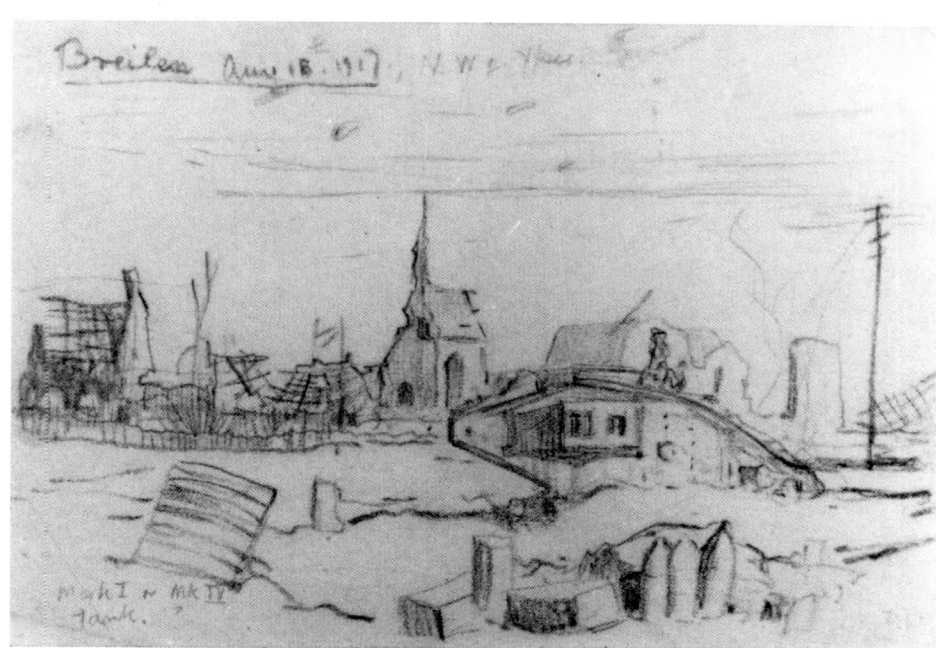

9. Landscape with tank, 1917

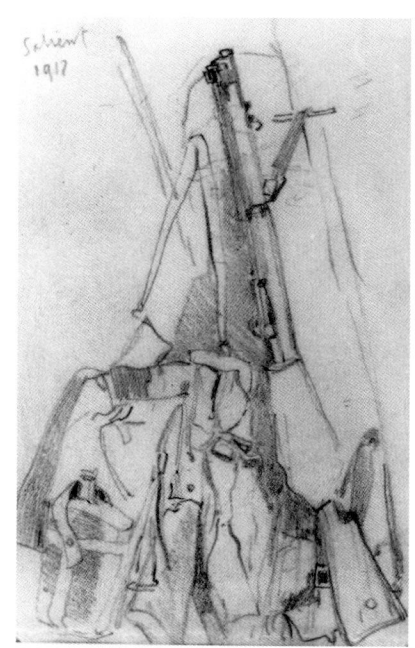

10. Rifle and equipment 'Salient 1917'

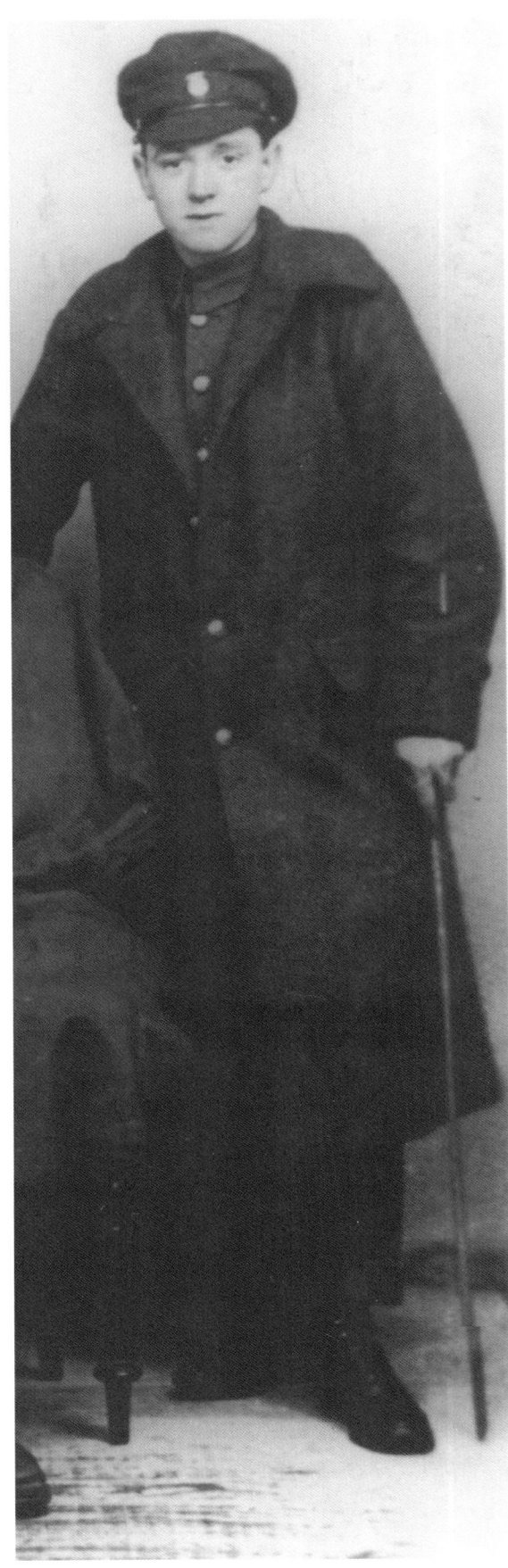

drawing dead or wounded men.[16] Life in the trenches gave Jones the opportunity to make studies of the non-human inhabitants; he made drawings of rats shot during the pulling down of an old dug-out in Ploegsteert. These are not the elegantly tailed, almost decorative rats of the *Frontispiece* to *In Parenthesis*, but rather reveal Jones's exceptional sensitivity and sympathy for the creaturely; the rats may be dead but the studies exhibit no morbid curiosity, these heads possess a lively sniffling rat-ness.

Writing much later, Jones maintained that 'I don't recall that we felt any very great revulsion with regard to most of our ordinary duties as infantry soldiers - not, for example, anything like the shock and distress felt by many at home in contemplating the wastage ... we took most of this for granted - rather as though it were part of some unavoidable natural calamity'[17] and yet the stricken aspect of Jones's youthful face *(11)* discloses a certain shock and distress.

Jones felt that the greatest impression which the war made upon him was the 'extreme *tenderness* of men in action to each other';[18] so much so, in fact, that the 'ill-treatment of a prisoner' could seem 'repellent'.[19] The sketch on the bottom of the post card on the opposite page could well be a study of a prisoner. The hardening effect of war, so visible in the drawings of contemporary German artists like Otto Dix, can be seen in this tiny sketch.[20] Whereas the figures on the top of the post card are, as is usual with Jones, just young men in uniform, the face at the bottom communicates something of the war's brutality.

Although just out of art school, Jones shows that he would not have been out of place in the company of older, official war artists sent to the front. *The Dug-out* compares favourably with

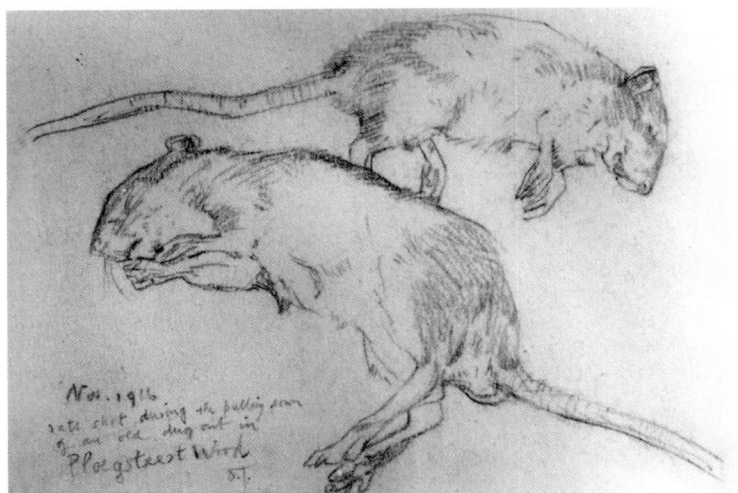

11. Anon., Jones in uniform, 1916 (?)

12. Rats Shot in Ploegsteert Wood, 1916

OBITUARIES

Richard

ON THE WEB
Download obituary archive
telegraph.co.uk/obits

Sir Kyffin Williams

Artist told he could not draw who went on to celebrate the landscape and people of his native Wales

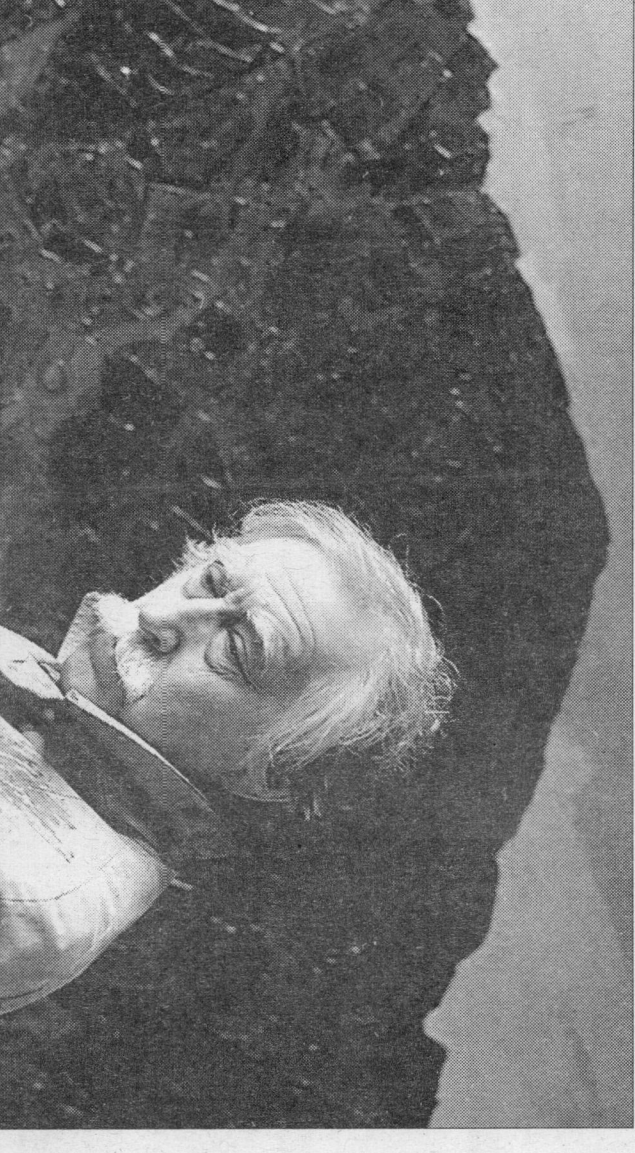

NICHOLAS SINCLAIR

S IR KYFFIN
WILLIAMS, who
died yesterday aged
88, was one of the
great figures of
Welsh art in the second half
of the 20th century.

His paintings of the North
Wales landscape and the
people who lived and
worked there were executed
in a bold and idiosyncratic
palette-knife style, and
became enduring and
instantly recognisable
images; meanwhile, his
unselfish and energetic
contributions to the artistic
life of Wales did much to
enhance its sense of
distinctive cultural identity.

John Kyffin Williams was
born on May 9 1918 at
Tregefni on Anglesey. His
family had long historic and
landowning connections on
the island; so many of his
forebears were buried in
Llansadwrn churchyard that,
he was to say, "but for the
Williams bones the east end

so mysterious. His brief
employment as a land agent
before the war had made
him very familiar with the
landscape of Snowdonia and,
more specifically, with the
hill-farmers who lived and
worked there and had
helped shape its present-day
appearance.

Nothing better captures
Williams the man than his
friendship with the great
natural history artist Charles
Tunnicliffe. A near-
neighbour of Tunnicliffe on
Anglesey for many years,
Williams persuaded the
Royal Academy to put on an
exhibition of Tunnicliffe's
unique collection of
measured drawings and
sketchbooks of birds in 1974.

The show was a great
success, and when
Tunnicliffe died in 1981 the
family decided to sell all the
work at auction. An
elaborate catalogue was
produced by Christie's, and
the collection which

Telegraph 'ShareCheck' real time share prices: Dial 0906 004 0000 and after the prompt key the 4-digit code, listed every Monday. Calls are charged at 60p per minute at all times. For more details call the **Telegraph 'ShareCheck' Helpline on 020 7412 3782**

GOVERNMENT SECURITIES

52 week High	52 week Low	Stock	Price £'s	+ or −	Yield Flat	Rm@
		%				

@ Yield to Redemption. Source: HSBC Bank

- On Mondays, we also carry a list of other gilts which are widely held by private investors, but are less often traded.

10-year Government Bonds

	Yield%	Spread vs Bunds T-Bonds	Spread vs T-Bonds
France	3.76	−0.97	
Germany	3.63	−2.13	−3.10
Japan	1.81	−0.62	−3.22
Great Britain	4.51	+0.75	
United States	4.73	−0.97	

AEROSPACE & DEFENCE ⇧ 1.01%

52 week High	Low	Stock	Price pence	+ or −	Yld	P/E
449¾	314	BAE Systems	372¼	+13¼	2.8	20.3
195¼	589	Chemring	145	−28	b0.7	45.3
187	135	Cobham Gp	175½	+3	1.9	20.1
1433⁄	45	Hampson Inds	143½			
38214	273	Meggitt	320	+54	2.4	20.8
2191⁄2	1603⁄4	Qinetiq Gp	1643⁄4	+7		
490	831	Rolls Royce	443½	+1	b2.0	22.1
1052	826	Smiths Gp	1019	+12	b3.3	22.2
535	42014	UMECO	428	−7	b1.6	23.2
5001⁄2	323	VT Group	4921⁄2	+14	2.2	20.5

AMERICANS ⇧ 0.23%

		Stock	Price	+ or −	GrsYld Cvr
1996	1264	Alcoa	1511	+19	2.1
4462	3756	Altria Gp	4425	+28	3.9
3283	2644	Amer Express	2762	+47	1.2
4023	3101	American Intnl	3360	−6	1.0
2785	2330	BankAmerica	2708	−9	4.0
4877	3488	Boeing	3959	+12	1.6
1845	1074	Bowater Inc.	1194	−7	3.7
4442	2745	Caterpillar	3501	+71	1.1
3699	3055	Chevron Texaco	3399	−1	3.3
2882	2383	Citygroup	2592	−5	4.3

The Alternative Investment Market is for young and growing companies. Shares may carry higher risks than those with a full quotation, and may be difficult to sell.

HEALTHCARE ⇧ 3%

HOUSEHOLD GOODS ⇧ 1.01%

INFORMATION TECHNOLOGY ⇧ 0.77%

Indexed Lnkd projected inflation: 5% 3%

RETAILERS ⇧ 0.81%

TRAVEL & LEISURE ⇧ 0.83%

AIM ⇧ 0.48%

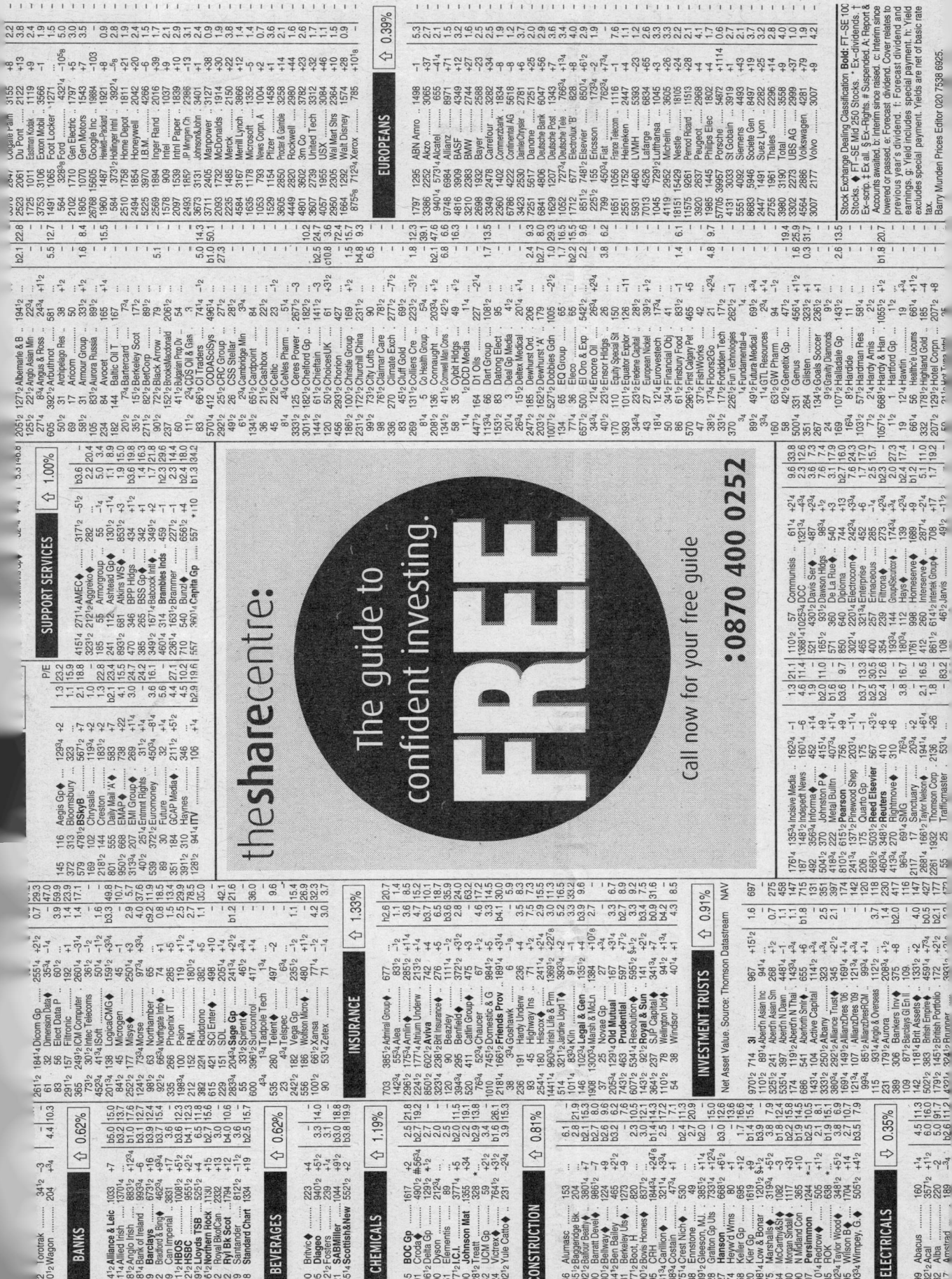

thesharecentre:

The guide to confident investing.

FREE

Call now for your free guide

:0870 400 0252

probably collapse".

Kyffin's childhood did not presage a career as an artist; aged four he was soundly spanked by his mother for drawing what was deemed a "nasty picture". His father (who managed a bank at Chirk on the Welsh borders) arranged for him, when he left Shrewsbury School, to become a land agent at Pwllheli. This Williams did for a brief period before war intervened: looking back, he saw in this work the beginning of his passion and understanding for the landscape of North Wales.

Commissioned into the Territorial Army in 1937 in the 6th Battalion Royal Welch Fusiliers, Williams was about to be sent overseas in 1941 whenhe was diagnosed as epileptic and declared medically unfit. The doctor then added: "As you are, in fact, abnormal, I think it would be a good idea if you took up art."

A friend suggested he tried the Slade School of Fine Art, of which, at the time, Williams had never heard, and which was based during the war at the Ashmolean Museum in Oxford. "The old Prof said I couldn't draw," he later recounted. "I was told I could come for one term only. There were few men around because of the war, so he let me stay for another two terms and then a year."

In fact, he stayed for three, and the young man who had arrived drawing nudes that looked more like trees ended up winning the Slade Portrait Prize and the Slade Leaving Scholarship. The turning

point had been an encounter with a Piero della Francesca drawing for "The Resurrection" in the Ashmolean Print Room; the compassion Williams saw in Christ's eyes made him understand what art could be about.

Nonetheless he had, as yet, no great ambitions, something he always saw as an advantage to the way his work was to develop. "My greatest fortune was that I was ordered to take up art for the good of my health," he wrote later in his autobiography Across the Straits. "This presumed that I was not a born artist and therefore was able to paint naturally, in an uncomplicated manner, free from the pressure of the man who knows he is an artist and has to live up to it."

His main aim on leaving the Slade was thus to find a job as an art-master at some comfortable and undemanding public school,

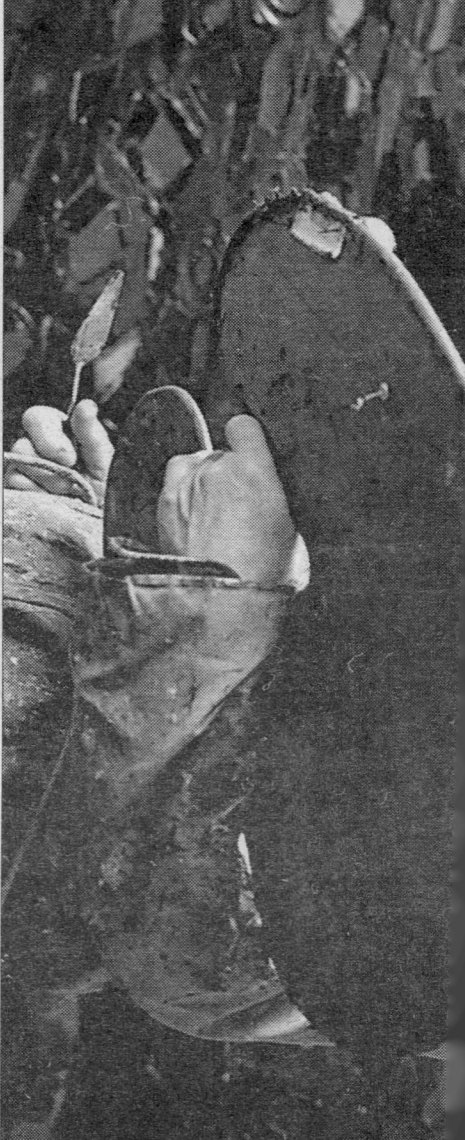

Williams: an Army doctor told him, 'As you are, in fact, abnormal, I think it would be a good idea if you took up art'

but he had been slow to achieve even that until, unable to pay his rent, he was thrown out of his lodgings in St. John's Wood. This crisis not only had the effect of his getting a job at Highgate School but also made him realise that art was his vocation. For the next 30 years (1944-73) the post at Highgate provided Williams with the perfect base to develop his highly characteristic work, "free from the pressures of fashion and the contagious influences of art schools".

The school, it has to be said, was extraordinarily tolerant. Williams's increasingly frequent truancies on nearby Hampstead Heath generated only gentle rebukes from the headmaster ("By the way, you didn't turn up for a lesson. You know, it is awfully difficult if you don't"), and he was actually appointed senior art master; over the years he was much

loved by his pupils, and he produced some outstanding students, among them a fellow Royal Academician, Anthony Green.

His first exhibition was at Colnaghi's in 1948; at the opening he watched excitedly as two elderly ladies walked round with an attentive air, only to hear one mutter, "Oh dear, much too Chekhov", before they departed. At another gallery a millionaire chose the most expensive picture, returned to his car to fetch his chequebook, and dropped dead on the pavement.

Williams was fortunate in that, despite his medical problems, he had extraordinary physical energy. He could fulfil his teaching duties while producing something like 100 paintings a year.

The evolution of his characteristic style is something of a paradox. By temperament very much a conservative, Williams was

always in a state of war with the authorities promoting contemporary art in Wales — he wanted to found a gallery for the history of Welsh art, but wanted it to stop at 1950 when, in his view, all the problems of modern art began.

But the manner in which he began to paint owed a great deal to just those aspects of modern art with which he professed to be so uncomfortable. With his bold palette-knife application of paint, sombre tonality and considerable degree of abstraction, Williams pursued an artistic path far removed from the kind of well-mannered, painterly sub-Impressionism in which such attitudes usually resulted; it was a path closer, in fact, to the dark-hued Expressionism of the early 20th-century paintings of peasant life by the Belgian artist Constant Permeke. Williams's choice of direction was not, perhaps,

up. Williams, ensuring the support of his friends and landlords, the Marquess and Marchioness of Anglesey, and of Anglesey County Council, put together a complex last-minute bid and an "in lieu" tax relief package that forestalled the sale.

Then, with no building in which to show the works, he became involved in the successful fund-raising efforts that led, some 15 years later, to the building of the museum of Anglesey history, Oriel Ynys Môn at Llangefni.

Williams's energy in the cause of Welsh art saw him serve as president of the Royal Cambrian Academy from 1969 until 1976, and then again from 1992 until his death; he also served on many committees, including those of the Contemporary Art Society of Wales and the National Museums of Wales.

He was elected RA in 1974, appointed OBE in 1982 and knighted in 1999. Awards from his native country included the medal of the Honorable Society of Cymmrodorion.

Williams published two volumes of autobiography, Across the Straits (1973) and A Wider Sky (1991).

He once described himself as "an obsessive, depressive, diabetic epileptic, who's apprehensive, selfish, intolerant and ruthless". It is a harsh self-assessment from a man who was not only warm and funny but also extremely generous of his time and energy on behalf of other artists.

Kyffin Williams never married.

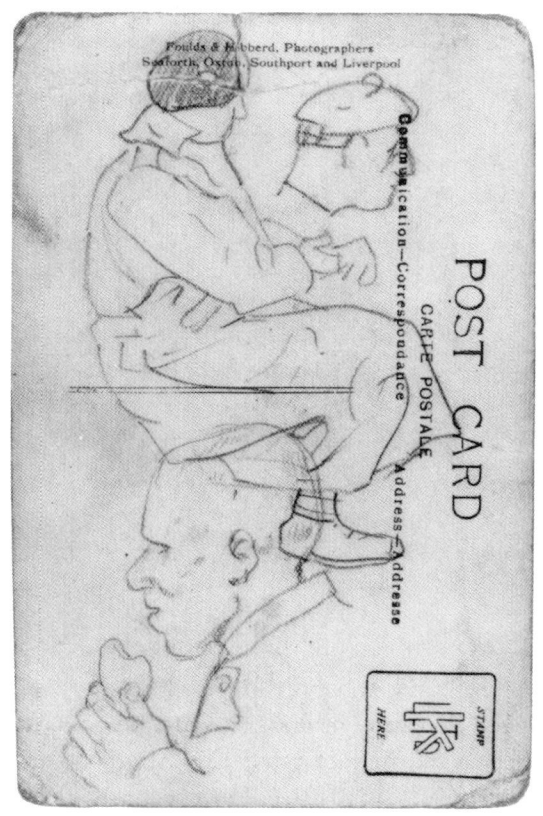

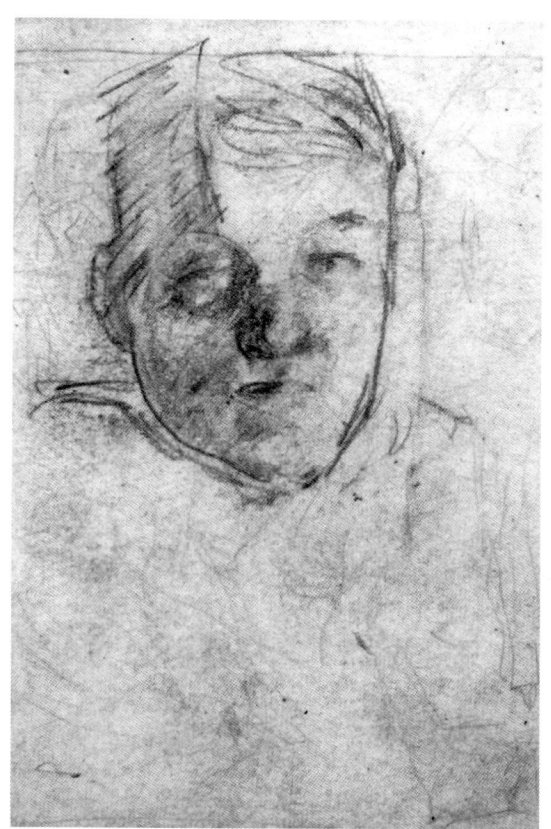

13. Postcard – Soldiers, 1916 (?)

14. Soldier's Face (Self-Portrait?), 1916

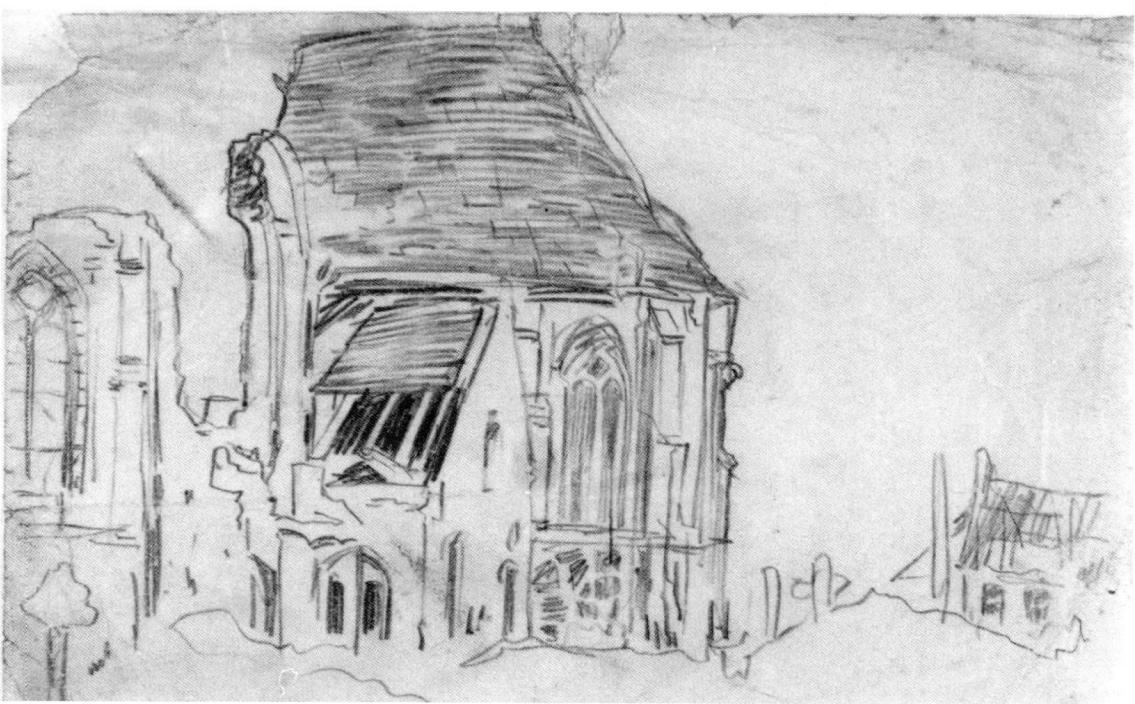

15. Ruined Church, Flanders, 1917

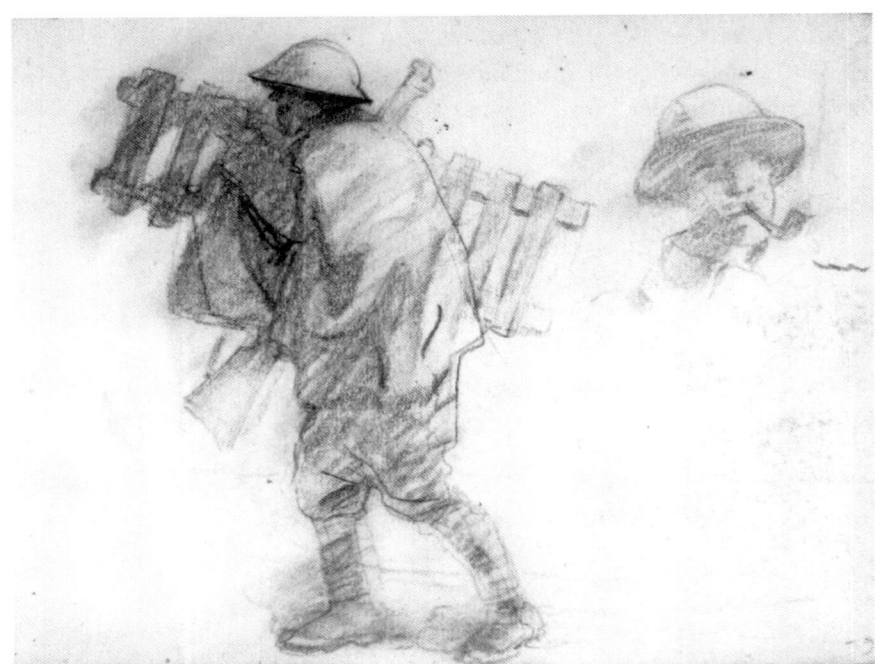

16. Soldier Carrying Duckboard, 1916

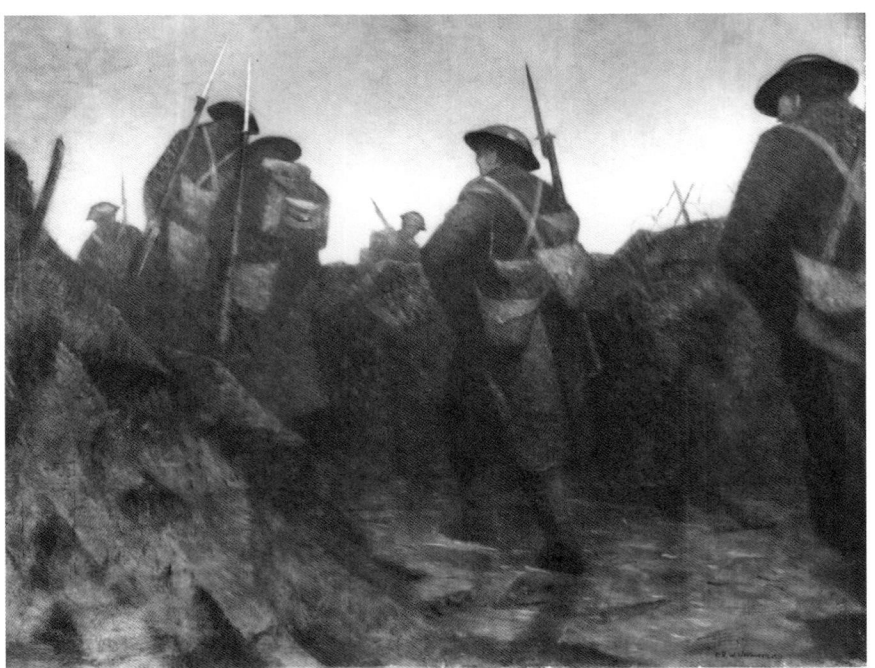

17. C.R.W. Nevinson, Reliefs at Dawn, 1917

similar sketches by artists such as Borlase Smart, who saw active service as a subaltern and whose paintings and drawings were shown in his 1917 exhibition *From Vimy Ridge to the Somme*. Jones's sketch of the figure carrying the duckboard has an emotional charge at least equal to the figures in Nevinson's painting, *Reliefs at Dawn*.

Jones's unit was involved in the extensive preparations for the Battle of Passchendaele but he missed the attack on Pilckem Ridge, which opened the offensive, because of a posting to 'battalion nucleus'. In February, 1918, he was returned to England with severe trench fever and so his actual sojourn on the Western Front ended. Later chapters will show how the war infiltrated his imagination in varied ways and consider how Jones, as a mature artist, and in relation to others, treated this broken world.

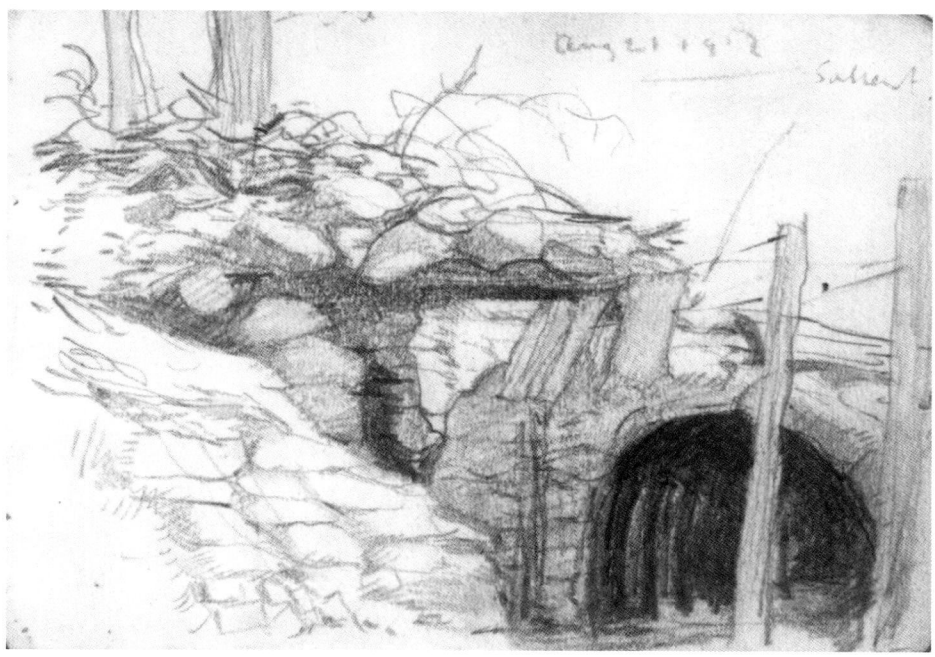

18. A Dug Out, 1917

WESTMINSTER SCHOOL OF ART

His time in the army was later described by Jones as 'a parenthesis'[1] and from the point of view of his art training so it was. Wisely counselled by his father against joining the campaign to aid the White Russians, and eligible for an ex-serviceman's grant, Jones enrolled at the Westminster School of Art. He was 'full of hope', returning to his training with an 'open mind', 'enthusiastic with the possibility of starting painting again',[2] and he felt knowledgeable enough to allow himself liberties with traditional themes. In a squared-up drawing of the Crucifixion, with its unusual and seemingly un-dramatic concentration on the activity of the soldiers, he displaced the obvious focus. Though compositionally very different, attention to the variety of human incident and, more particularly, to the dice players, suggests a knowledge of Tintoretto's *Crucifixion* in the Scuola di San Rocco; indeed, a reproduction of the central portion of that painting was found among the artist's early portfolios.[3] Probably done in 1919 during his first year at Westminster, the *Crucifixion* is one of the most finished drawings for a religious composition that remains from this period as Jones later burnt, in the fire of his mother's washing-copper at Brockley, a good number of the 'pre-1925 drawings and watercolours that he could lay his hands on'.[4] Strikingly, even at this early date, there is an attempt by Jones to establish a contemporaneity: the soldiers are in shorts, several wear tin helmets, and one has his hair cut in the current fashion, pudding-bowl style, like Stanley Spencer and the artist himself.

The treatment was the upshot of something deeper than the art student's need to engage with art history. Jones had begun to think about the Roman Catholic Church in 1916-17 in talks with the Catholic Chaplain, while serving in the Ypres sector when he was returned to France after recovering from his wound at Mametz.[5] During this period, in foraging for fire-wood, Jones had his first sight of the Mass when he stumbled on a ruined outhouse where he thought he might find a dry stash. He peered through a chink in the wall of this building and marvelled at the sight of a priest 'in a gilt-hued *planeta*, two points of flickering candlelight ... white altar cloths ... and a few huddled figures in khaki'.[6] The impact of this visual experience forged a vivid link between wood, for which Jones had been searching, and the chalice which was being used to re-present Christ's death on the wood of the cross. It was a connection that would be intellectualized for him after the war by Maurice de la Taille's insistence on the relation between the sign-making with the Chalice at the Last Supper and the Crucifixion itself.

Nevertheless, the apparently pious act on the left of the crucifixion drawing is somewhat problematic; the position of the latreutic figure suggests that the legs and feet in the upper right-hand corner belong to Christ, but the women at the base of the fully visible and tilted cross suggest that this is where Christ hangs, as one would expect, in the central position. In Tintoretto's San Rocco *Crucifixion*, the bowl contains the vinegar that quenches Christ's thirst, but here one may suppose that the figure with the upraised bowl is praying to a thief for good luck in his game of dice. In any case, what is significant is that Jones concentrates on the soldiers who are detailed for the crucifixion, a focus which would preoccupy him in early visual works as well as in his late poetry. In *The Fatigue*, finished in 1965, he described such soldiers as

> those who handle the instruments
> who *are* the instruments
> to hang the gleaming Trophy
> on the Dreaming Tree.[7]

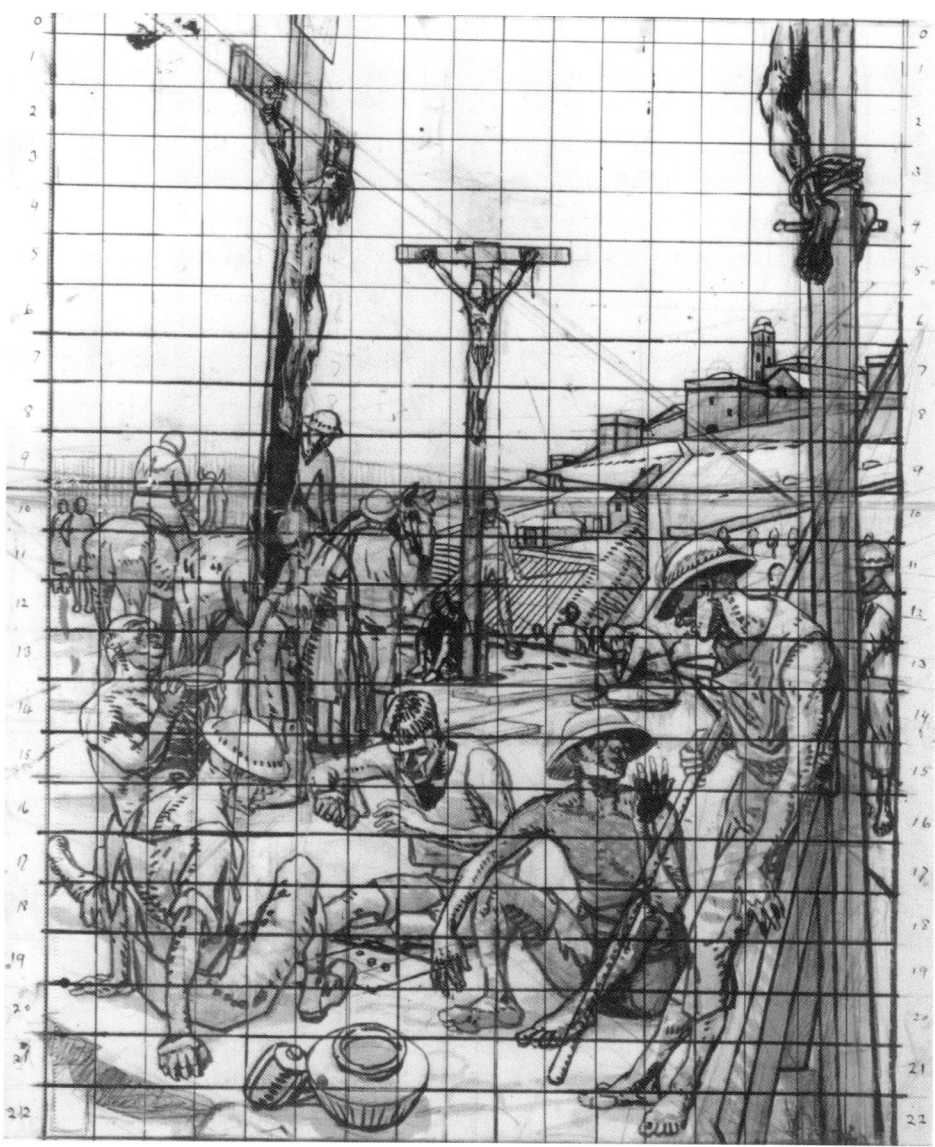

1. Crucifixion, 1919 (?)

31

The soldiers are 'instruments' certainly, but in their resemblance to First World War Tommies, they are also victims. When he considered the roadside crucifixes of Northern France in relation to the sacrifices of soldiers under his command, Wilfred Owen wrote that 'One ever hangs where shelled roads part', suggesting that his men, like Christ, were asked to 'lay down their life'.[8]

Jones noted of his student years at Camberwell and at the Westminster School of Art, that not only were 'the last dregs of the Classical tradition … implanted in me' but also 'Impressionism and the earlier years of Post-Impressionism'.[9] The latter had become a cult-word around 1912 and it was Roger Fry's intense 'enthusiasm for the "old masters" of the modern movement, Cézanne, Van Gogh and Gauguin'[10] and his mounting of two important Post-Impressionist exhibitions which gave artists and an interested public the chance to study the works of modern French, British and Russian painters.

For Roger Fry and Clive Bell, Post-Impressionism was 'nothing but the reassertion of the first commandment of art - Thou shalt create form',[11] and form rather than content was understood by them to be the most important element in a painting. The great good of Impressionism was, according to Clive Bell, that it had 'taught people to seek the significance of art in the work itself'.[12] However, the impact made by Fry and Bell was limited and sporadic; a decade later, students at Goldsmith's, Graham Sutherland included, found work by Cézanne and Matisse incompetent and superficial when it was shown to them by an enthusiastic instructor.[13]

Because of his awakening enthusiasm for recent French painting and for the Catholic religion, the relationship of David Jones's development to such ideas and to those which had been circulating in France toward the end of the nineteenth century is important. Writing about 'abstract art' in some notes drafted in the 1960s, Jones stated that

> I suppose I first heard the term just before becoming a soldier in the 1914-18 War. I seem to recollect a Post-Impressionist exhibition round about 1912, but it was not until after demobilization and my return to an art-school … that I became aware of the deep and ubiquitous implications inherent in Post-Impressionist theory and in the insistence on the abstract in the arts … What struck me about this 'Post-Impressionist' *theory* and what is implicit in the *notion* of 'abstract art' is that men make *things* which exist in their own right and … not 'impressions' of other things.[14]

Precisely because Jones rapidly came to believe that a made 'thing' was 'a *signum* of reality' the artistic challenge became more complicated than a question of mere formalism. Certainly, in the climate of the resurgence of religion and the proliferation of alternative spiritualities at the end of the nineteenth century, questions about the nature and function of the arts were legion. The painter and critic, Georges Aurier, writing in an article on Gauguin in March, 1891, suggested that

> The normal and final goal of painting, as of all the arts, cannot be a direct presentation of objects. Its ultimate aim is to express Ideas by translating them into a special language. To the eyes of the artist objects are meaningless as objects. They can only appear to him as *signs*.[15]

So beyond purely formalist considerations lay the question of the intellectual charge of forms. Indeed, Fry had reservations about Bell's notion of 'significant form' and its ability to move us without extra-formalistic elements.[16] As far as David Jones was concerned, it was extra-formal signification that would eventually preoccupy him and provoke his mature work in the visual and literary arts. However, in the paintings and woodcuts that he produced upon leaving Westminster, while often religious in character, there is a compositional strength that registered the impact of the formalistic nature of Fry and Bell's enthusiasm for Italian Primitivism, Byzantine art and Cézanne. As Eric Gill wrote of Jones only a short time later, 'Already in 1920 (it might have been earlier but for the five years' interim of the war) he saw that the substance of a work of art was an intellectual construction and not a similitude - it was realistic and representational only by accident.'[17] As Jones himself later put it, the aim of the Post-Impressionists was 'to make a "thing" - let's say a mountain … *under the form of paint*, and not an impression of a 'mountain' … this idea was … similar or analogous to what, I understood, the church held with regard to the Mass.'[18]

For Jones, during his second period as a student, aesthetic and religious questions were converging, so it was convenient to find Westminster Cathedral only a few steps from Vincent Square, where he attended, 'rather irregularly',[19] the Westminster School of Art. Indeed, the school's proximity to the Cathedral provided him with 'a temptation to put aside' whatever he 'was supposed to be doing and spend half an hour or more at Solemn High Mass'.[20] Once, when he was praying alone in the Cathedral, some people drifted in and one started the Rosary and then left, asking the young art student to carry on.[21] While Jones struck the dignified mother of one of his art school friends as no 'gent at all but clean and well mannered and fervent',[22] to one of the students the shy ex-soldier seemed 'a very holy young man'.[23]

The Westminster School of Art had been started in Tufton Street in 1876, became a government school in 1893, and moved eleven years later to new premises on the upper floors of the London County Council Westminster Technical Institute in Vincent Square. It had counted among its pupils Duncan Grant and among its teachers Fred Brown who, before going on to be Professor at the Slade, had 'built up classes for drawing and painting from the nude that gained Westminster a high reputation among English artists'.[24] Although Henry Tonks, who was assistant to Brown at the Slade, wrote that the Westminster School was a 'truly comic and dirty little studio',[25] it became 'a powerful centre of reaction against the established institutions of the day',[26] the Royal Academy, the Royal College of Art and the Slade. Compared with these, Westminster, according to Walter Bayes, its Principal during Jones's time, was 'the smallest, the least official, the least endowed'.[27]

While 'no individual records of students or staff are now extant', prospectuses do survive from the period during which Jones was a pupil and these describe Westminster as 'essentially a school for Drawing and Painting'[28] and hence more focused on fine art than Camberwell had been. When he arrived at Westminster, although Walter Sickert had been replaced by Bernard Meninsky, Jones records that Sickert's 'influence continued and he used sometimes to come and talk to us.'[29] He

> would take us out to draw on our pads. He made us draw what we saw before our eyes. Back in the school he made us square the drawing up, and make a larger ... one. The squaring had to be exact to the millimetre. 'There you are,' he would say, 'isn't it easy? Some learn to be accountants and you are learning to be artists. Easy!' But we weren't all Sickerts![30]

Jones, as a Westminster student, could have attended such day and evening courses in the 1920-21 session as 'Drawing and Painting from Life' with Bernard Meninsky, who did 'Figure' three times and 'Costume' twice a week. Jones remembered how the students, before this class, 'scrambled for pegs and easels and donkeys'.[31] The 'Antique and Elementary', led by Meninsky, involved 'drawing and painting from casts of antique figures'. In 'Figure Composition and Decorative and Narrative Design', led by Walter Bayes and Mervyn Lawrence,[32] the teaching was based on 'an acceptance of three-dimensional space, and hence a study of the principles of perspective, and their practical application'. Bayes, who described himself as bristling 'with principles like a porcupine' wrote that at Westminster the science of perspective was regarded 'as the inevitable basis of Western drawing'.[33] 'Drawing and Painting from the Antique', was taught in collaboration with Lawrence in the evening and Meninsky during the day. 'Still Life' was taught by Bayes and Lawrence and 'Drawing from plants and other natural objects' by Miss Collin.[34] The sensitive young Jones must have found the atmosphere congenial, for, by comparison with the severity of the Slade which Paul Nash remembered as 'a typical English Public School seen in a nightmare',[35] at Westminster 'they didn't believe in grief and tears', there were never 'any suicides amongst the students'.[36]

Walter Bayes had studied under Fred Brown and also for a spell at the Académie Julian in Paris, at which the progress from antique cast to life room was the accustomed method.[37] Bayes was a founder member of the Allied Arts Association, the Camden Town and London Group, and was regarded by his colleagues as an intellectual, excelling 'in what has been called the science of picture making, including perspective and the proportions and balancing of colour';[38] the Crucifixion drawing discussed at the opening of the chapter was most probably produced for Bayes's class. The teacher's 'workman's attitude'[39] gave Jones a foretaste of the unaffected approach to making which he encountered later with Eric Gill.

The most pronounced stylistic influence on Jones while at Westminster was made by Bernard Meninsky whose tastes somewhat coincided with those of his pupil, combining, in the tradition of Fry and Bell, a lifelong devotion to Italian painters of the early Renaissance such as Masaccio and Piero della Francesca with an interest in Cézanne, Derain and Picasso.[40] When David Jones attended Meninsky's life class,[41] the tradition of the great Italian masters was passed on to him with its emphasis on the line which produced a self-contained figure.[42] Years later, in a draft of some notes on painting, Jones elucidated this technique:

> Try to contain the *volume* of any object by the use of line because this will help you to register the subtle changes of direction of the so-called 'outline', which at first sight may seem a relatively simple curve in one direction whereas it is in fact composed of a very great variety of directions, being the line of division between the complex of planes ... which form a three-dimensional solid body and the space in which that body stands.[43]

Meninsky had been a Medical Orderly during the war and although shy of personal publicity was, by the early 1920s, somewhat of a name to reckon with. He taught in order to pay the rent and preferred his job at Westminster to the post he held at Central because the students were older and therefore more advanced and interesting.[44] Despite being compelled to teach for financial reasons, Meninsky's classes 'were eye-openers and sources of inspiration to countless young artists' and 'all his drawings had a wonderful firmness, apparent simplicity and weight'.[45] He would reduce a subject to pure construction, demonstrating his method on a student's drawing. He was a strict teacher but Jones remembers that he found him 'very helpful' in making him 'feel the recession in drawing'.[46] In some notes on painting, written in the 1940s and showing the continuing influence of Meninsky, Jones suggested that

> ... 'outline' *must never* be thought of as an end or termination, it must be thought of, on the contrary, as expressing a *continuation*, i.e. it *must* express the uninterrupted continuation of the surfaces and planes from the front and side to the unseen surfaces and planes at the back.[47]

When Westminster was shut on Saturdays or in the holidays Jones went to an 'old-fashioned atelier in Kennington near the Oval ... one just walked in, gave a chap a bob or something, signed a register ... tried to get hold of an easel or at least a stool and started to paint, after saying "good evening" all round'. From time to time, Sickert, whom Jones found unassuming and 'very friendly and accessible',[48] would look in.[49] Jones later remarked that

> We used to argue a lot - and we used to think we were going to be terrifically great artists! The model used to undress behind a torn bit of curtain hanging from a ramshackle bent curtain-rod, if I remember aright ... I wish I had gone there more ... But I really went only to get work done when it was not possible to go to the regulation place. I must say we were pretty single-minded, we just did drawings and paintings all day, every day, except Sunday.[50]

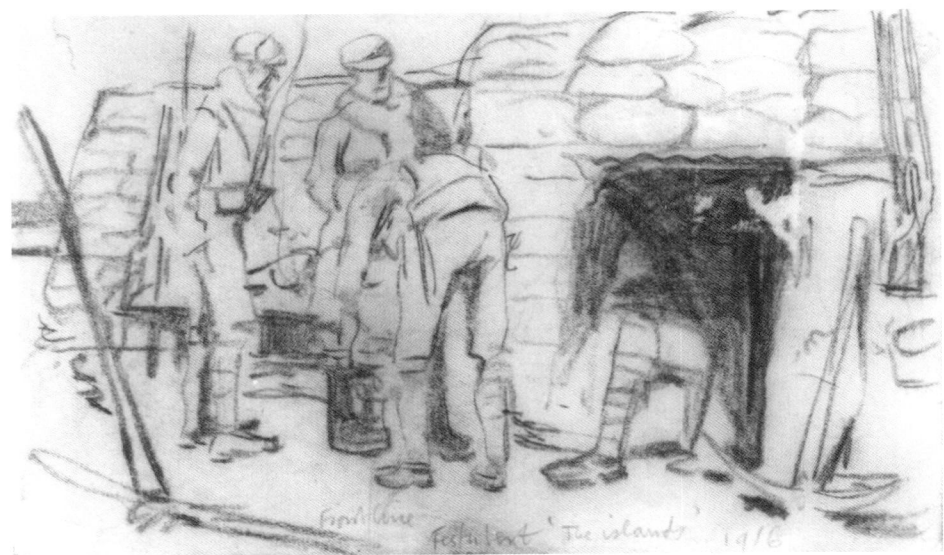

2. Front Line, Festubert 'The Islands', 1916

But it was not only discussions with other students, the controversies of the art world and the example of his instructors that exerted an influence upon David Jones during this period. It is clear that he had been deeply affected by his time as a soldier in the trenches and the relation of the First World War to Jones's development as an artist can be seen in the use that he made of experiences and sketches done in the trenches. He displaced the traditional focus in that squared-up crucifixion composition in order to make the soldiers of central importance. An impromptu drawing made in the 'The Islands' or grousebutts, the walls of sandbags in the marshy region around Festubert in 1916, relates to the more classically composed art school exercise for which Jones chose the activity of men in the trenches as his subject matter. Apart from the similarity of the sandbagged scene, there is a resemblance between the figure in the sketch, seen from behind, bent over his dixie, and the stooped figure in the squared-up drawing. In this student work, the sense of space and largeness of scale are achieved by placing the soldiers, all of similar medium height, in the upper half of the drawing. It is a well ordered study of men existing where, as Jones puts it in *In Parenthesis*, 'a culture' is 'already developed';[51] the carrying figures are placed so as to suggest depth and, along with the standing harmonica player, lead the eye to a glimpse of the blasted landscape in the top left hand corner. Bayes advocated a 'training in the ordering of spacial relationships' which he remarked had been undertaken by painters such as Perugino,[52] and so it is understandable that many of the postures in Jones's study owe a debt to Italian Renaissance artists such as Mantegna or Perugino although there is a modernity about the work secured by the cubed and figureless foreground. While Jones explores aspects of a burdensome existence interspersed by hours of inactivity, the drawing remains an art-student's exercise rather than registering his own reaction to the war. Jones tended to suppress the drama in his visual treatments of the subject whereas William Roberts, who had also been at the Front, embraced the violent impact of modern warfare.

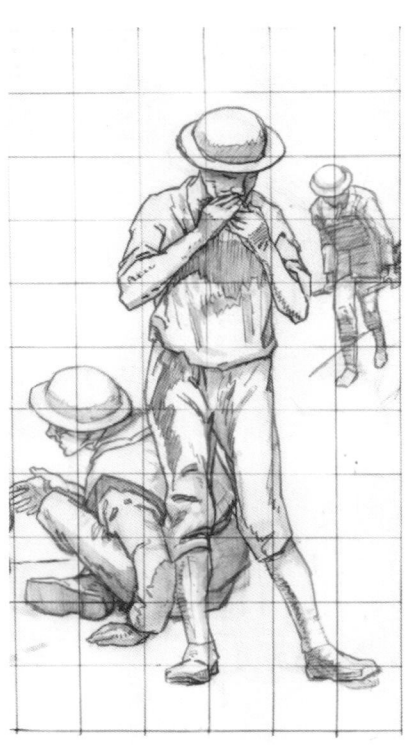

3. Trench Drawing, 1920 (?)

Jones later found in the modes of speech of the First World War Tommy a vital way to bring to life the soldiers of the Roman Empire, using the lingo of

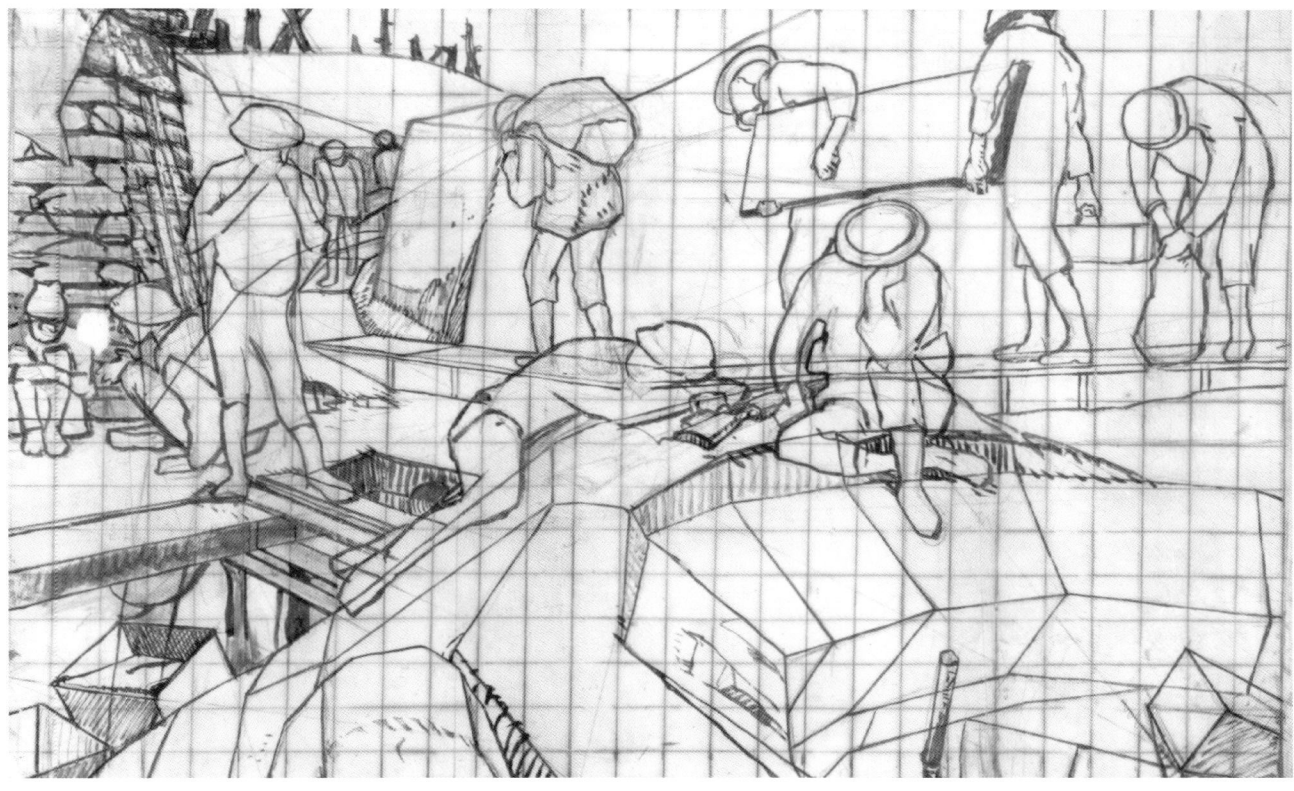

4. Trench Drawing, 1920 (?)

the present to animate the past; in the poem, 'The Fatigue', the fact that soldiers, who talk and behave like Western Front Tommies, are set the task of crucifying Christ gives that story a renewed vigour, a freshness and accuracy deriving from the actually seen and remembered. Likewise, the soldiers in the preparatory drawing made at Westminster for *The Betrayal* have that relentless and mechanical modernity that might be found in a Futurist war picture by an artist such as Nevinson. The drawing divides into sections: Peter, the group around Christ, the NCO and the marching soldiers. Peter, standing sword in hand, has just cut off the ear of the sitting figure. A curiously proportioned NCO counterbalances the disciple, his extended left arm following one of the perspective lines that relate the feet of the tramping 'Tommies' on the right to the vanishing point behind Christ's head. Thus he

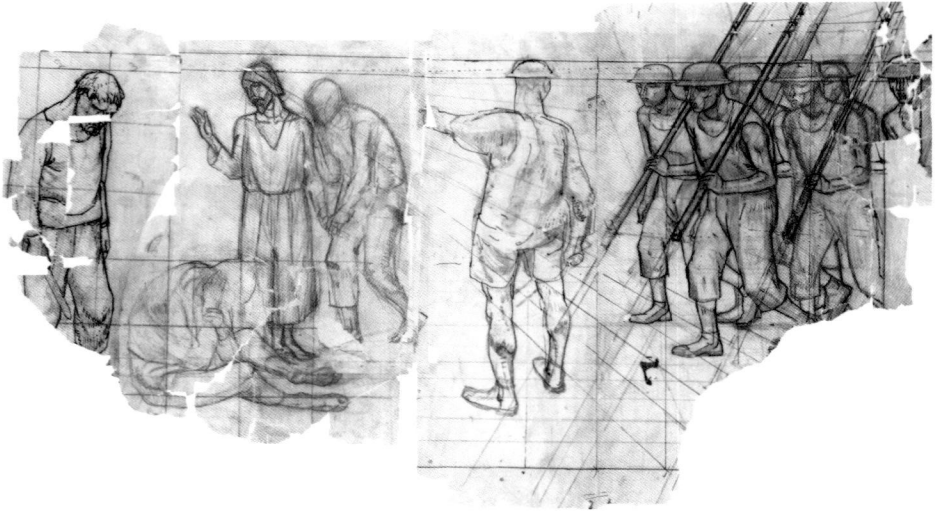

5. The Betrayal, 1920 (?)

mediates between the chunkier modern side and the more Italianate grouping on the left. Jones's experience of soldiery informs his imagining of a Biblical scene and he obviously considered the result successful for he had a more finished version hanging in his room late in life. What is more, Walter Bayes reproduced *The Betrayal* in his defensive article about the teaching at Westminster School of Art in *The Architectural Review*. Bayes observed that the feet of the marching soldiers, which repeat one pose, demonstrated 'the variety that perspective gives to any monotonous repetition … they are placed in absolutely symmetrical fashion: thus we are conscious of them only collectively'.[53]

An oil sketch for the same incident marks a step towards Primitivism as Jones deliberately jettisons the formal and finished techniques of art school training and goes in search of a manner in which to revitalize old religious scenes and stories. It was to be the example of Gill's attempt to escape from the post-Renaissance world that would somewhat legitimize or at least contextualize such expression which harked back to earlier examples of formal vitality. While the stylistic debt here is more to the Italian primitives, the idea of painting soldiers coming to arrest Christ was probably suggested by El

Greco's *The Lord's Agony in the Garden*, which Jones remembers viewing with 'intense feeling'[54] after its acquisition by the National Gallery in 1919.

In *Gardening,*[55] Jones picks up on Millet's theme of people in relation to the land; as with the figures in the *Gleaners,* that mid-nineteenth century vision of rural poverty, the man with his shovel is held below an imposing horizon line. The sprawl of the city encroaching on the life and traditions of the countryside was something that Jones, in his own childhood at Brockley, had experienced at first hand. But the suburban inhabitants seem to be resisting that trend in this ambitious study in perspectival composition, terminated in the middle distance by the broken silhouette of church and railway - two elements positioned to mark the challenge of different ways of life, the older agrarian way, punctuated by Church festivals, and the new and relentless industrial rhythms. Their presence poses the question of what relation the age-old activities of digging and delving have to the new suburban circumstances. There are fifteen figures arranged in planes and the muted painting treats a peaceful and restorative scene on an early spring evening after the war; the bent man who punctuates the skyline with his umbrella resting on his shoulder in the manner of a rifle recalls the conflict. Prominent elements like the ample woman, the tree in leaf and the church seem to offer emotional anchors. The seated woman clasping her knees is a pose that Jones uses at the extreme left of the squared-up trench drawing. The subject acknowledges Millet, but the style owes something to British Post-Impressionists such as Bayes or Robert Bevan, who had also studied at Westminster, but earlier, under Brown. Most interestingly, however, Jones is displacing the vision of the New English Ruralists of the late nineteenth century onto an emerging suburban middle class who have little intrinsic relation to the land. The choice of subject results in the most contemporary or socially pertinent painting which he made at Westminster.

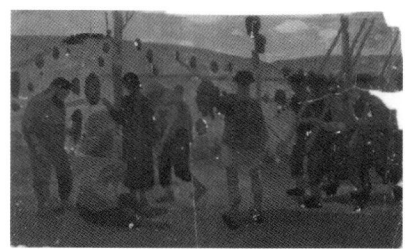

6. The Betrayal, 1920 (?)

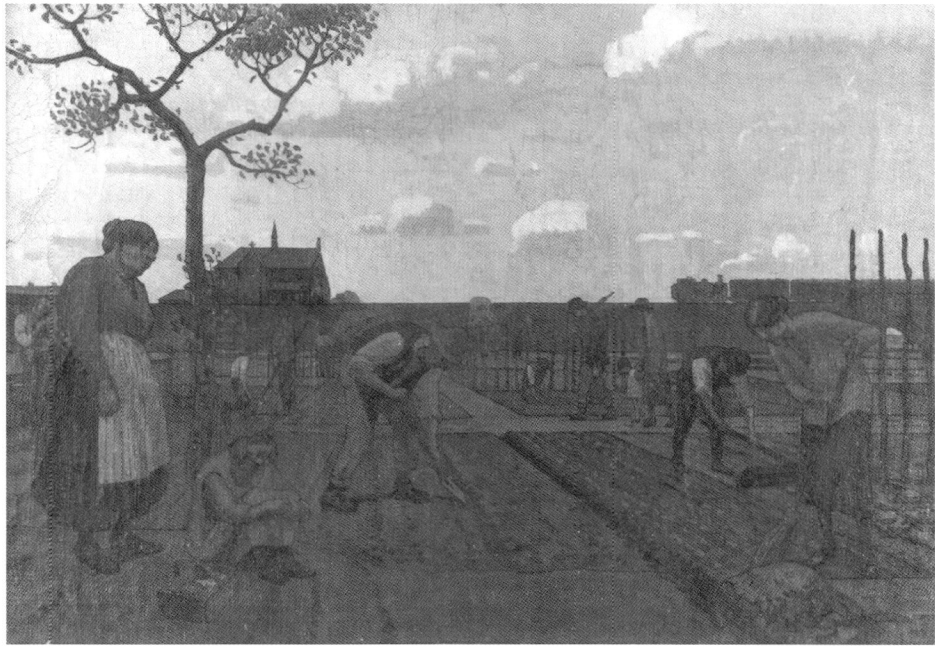

7. Gardening, 1920

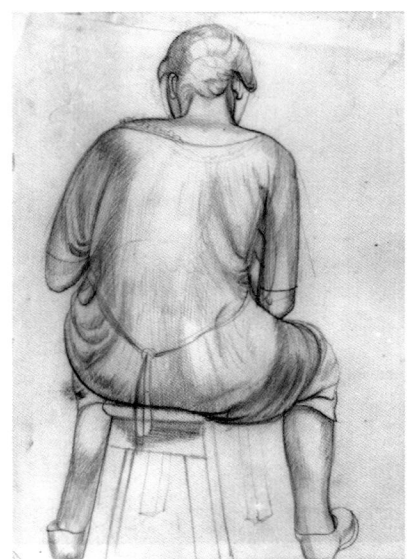

8. Seated Woman, 1921 (?)

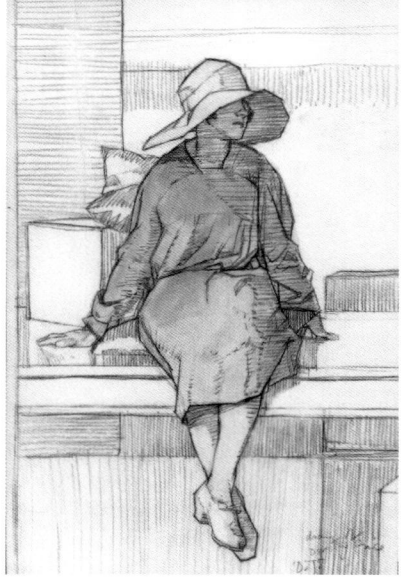

9. Dorothy Price, 1920 (?)

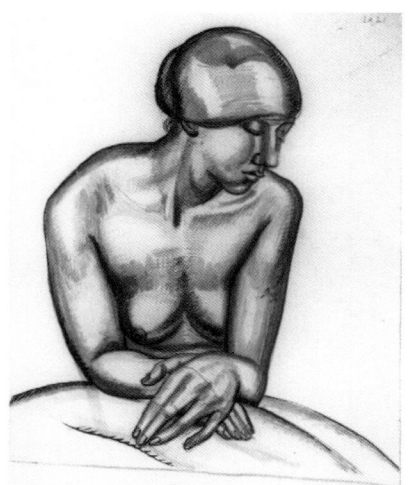

10. Torso, 1921

The influence of Meninsky's teaching can be seen in the full, rounded forms of the pencil study, *Seated Woman*. When drawing *Dorothy Price with a Hat* all the curves have been broken into a series of straight lines, flattening the image, more in the manner of his teacher Bayes or of Bevan. In *Torso,* done in 1921, Jones pushes formal simplification further and, in a style that begins to explore the geometry of the body, hints at the decorative possibilities which Meninsky, or more particularly Duncan Grant, pursued.

Sickert's habit of getting the students working outdoors is reflected in Jones's Westminster Sketchbook of April, 1921, which has been preserved in the Tate Gallery Archive. It contains twelve sketches in pencil, ink, and coloured crayon of landscapes and animals, as well as ideas for compositions including one of Christ at the foot of the cross. While not from this sketchbook, the landscapes shown here are typical of Jones's work at this time. In the 1921 ink and pastel, *An Afternoon in the Park - Greenwich*, Jones sets out a composition in a three-dimensional manner but flattens it with the shading of the foliage using a technique similar to that in his drawing of Dorothy Price.

In 1919 Jones walked from Orpington to Canterbury 'on the track that runs most of the way on the southern slope of the North Downs'.[56] Whether the sketch of that sweeping landscape *(12)* was made then or whether it was drawn during later forays into the Kent countryside it is impossible to say, but it reveals the beginnings of that rhythmic approach to landscape which Jones explored during his years with Eric Gill, first in Sussex and then in the more dramatic terrain of the Welsh border country.

The surviving drawings and paintings done at Westminster reveal a devotion to the study of art and Jones's ability is particularly evident in the versatility of his approaches as a draughtsman. His imagination often fixes on the unusual in a scene, stimulated by the work of earlier artists and by the originality of his budding transhistorical vision which had been provoked by the war. His imagination had certainly been struck; years later, Dr. Stevenson, treating Jones at Bowden House for a nervous breakdown, said, 'You must have been a bloody sight more frightened in the First World War than you realized at the time'.[57] Westminster was a period when the intellectual questions, which were about to determine the basis for his life's work, began to trouble Jones. He was in the process of turning to religion as the source of succour and replenishment and it became pivotal to his whole understanding of the need, purpose and practice of art. There were also fashionable and sympathetic secular notions about what was involved in making a painting and these seemed to give support to his own intimations concerning art and religion.

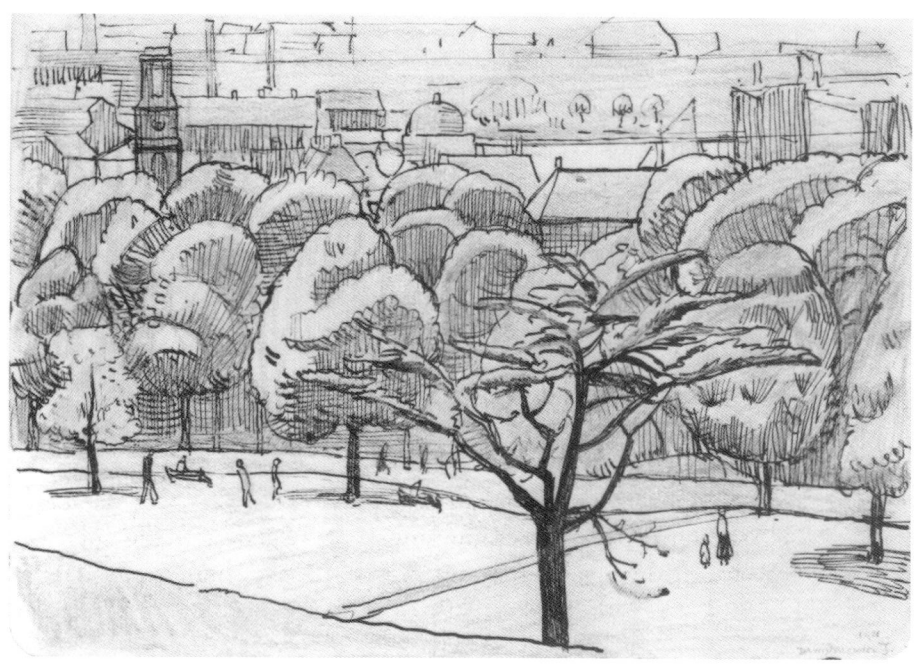

11. An Afternoon in the Park – Greenwich (London), 1921

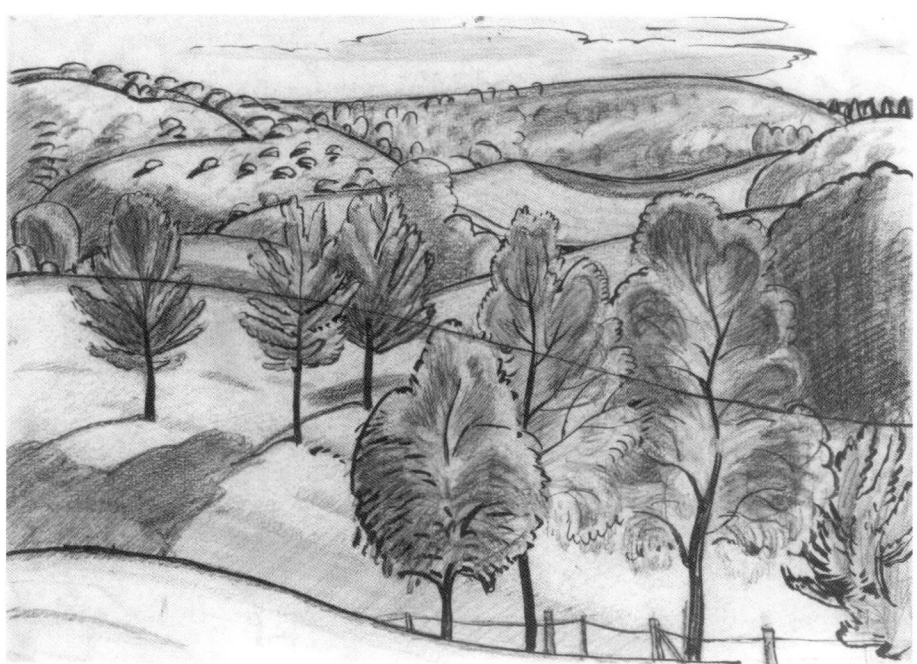

12. Landscape in the Downs, 1920

THE YEARS WITH ERIC GILL

From James Jones to his son, David, 24 August, 1921:

> I am amazed at the contents of your letter re. your joining the Romish Church. It baffles my understanding how any well-balanced mind can be brought to accept such teaching. I always gave you credit for insight and common sense. To link yourself with a Church ... that is and always has been the enemy of progress and enlightenment; ... By joining such a church you are limiting your loyalty to your King, for his Highness the Pope claims first place ... You become an idolator like the heathen in worshipping idols of wood, stone and brass ... [1]

From Eric Gill to David Jones, a little earlier in the year:

> you describe your present state of uncertainty very lucidly. I hope you will soon find it possible to take the leap for in my own opinion it is not necessary that a person should feel himself absolutely convinced on every point of faith. [2]

Two extracts which suggest sympathetic understanding shifting from father to father figure. James Jones praises his son's judgement, wisely appeals to his patriotism, but misjudges the situation when he calls the church an 'enemy of progress' and designates it the haven of idolators. The Roman Catholic Church was, at the time, attempting to refresh, revitalize and modernize its teaching under the inspiration of Neo-Thomism. It had the desire, not only 'to defend the stability and permanence of traditional thought' but also to guard against immobility. [3] As for the importance placed upon the use of significant artefacts in religious ceremonies, such a practice would certainly appeal to a young man who was not only absorbed by religious questions but who was, above all, dedicated to the making of works of art.

Between Jones's parents there was a difference of religious inclination; the artist recalled his father, the low church Protestant, arguing 'in his own sitting room' with a curate of 'advanced views' and commenting that 'Alice, my wife ... is smiling just a little, for she is, at heart, a bit of a Puseyite'. [4] David Jones inclined towards his mother's sympathies derived, perhaps, from her Italian antecedents. Instinctively, he felt called to make religiously charged objects and gestures; one Good Friday afternoon when he was about six, he fashioned a cross from two rough pieces of wood used to section flower beds and marched around the garden with it held aloft. Upon his return, Jones's father was furious; not only had his garden been disturbed but his son, as he explained to him, had performed an action associated with Catholics who substituted external manifestations of devotion for true Christian faith. The child had merely been acting on the instincts which similarly inclined him to kneel during the Creed[5] or which had confounded the bugles of a mounted detachment of the City Imperial Volunteers, heard from his bedroom, with 'a detachment of the heavenly armies' of 'Angels ... which Daddy says can't be proved from the Bible, but that someone called Dr. Pusey got ... from what he calls Papists'.[6] Some kind of association between the military and the religious, centering upon the celebratory act of bugling, was therefore made half-consciously at a very early age.

In Catholic France, during the late nineteenth century, a religious industry had proliferated in swift response to accelerating capitalism and decades of social turmoil; the cults of Lourdes and Lisieux and Joan of Arc were begun and the new cult of the Sacred Heart gave rise to the basilica of the Sacré-Cœur on Montmartre, crowning the Paris skyline in bold retaliation to the secular engineering of the Eiffel Tower.[7] A number of Post-Impressionists and more particularly certain Symbolists and Nabis were absorbed by religious resurgence and their resulting work is instructive both in its achievements and shortcomings. Gauguin managed to meet the challenge of well-worn Christian subject matter by re-invigorating it with what was immediately 'to hand'[8] in the lifestyles and landscapes of Brittany and Tahiti. He also assiduously explored new possibilities in painting and gave old themes a new vision. Van Gogh was consumed with the charge and intensity of epiphany which he too expressed by daring and misunderstood effects of paint and colour. The paintings of Jan Verkade *(1)* and Maurice Denis testify to some of the difficulties and possible pitfalls of trying to make explicitly religious works in an increasingly secular western world. A painter like Denis, influenced by the example of Filippo Lippi and, adversely, by a tendency towards sweetness in certain paintings by Fra Angelico, produced a good deal of work which somehow never matched his ability to theorize.[9] However, Denis, with his demand that 'a painting ... shall look like paint' was an important figure for the Gill circle. Jacques Maritain, in *Art et Scholastique,* which was used as a basis for debate at Ditchling and Capel-y-ffin, quotes frequently from his writings. Denis also instructed Dom Theodore Bailey in painting when the Englishman went to Paris to study. Later, Bailey, with his artistic training and clerical knowledge, was a key contributor in discussions on art between Gill, Jones and René Hague at Capel-y-ffin in the mid twenties.

With only isolated exhibitions such as *French Art 1914-19* at the Heal's Mansard Gallery or *Picasso 1903-1920* at the Leicester Gallery in 1921, Jones did not have much opportunity to study exciting recent artistic innovation. So, neither ignorant of nor particularly well informed about continental developments in art, Jones was in a dilemma over questions of artistic form, style and content; perhaps certain new strategies for making a painting could be placed at the service of some traditional sign system, if significant form was not to be allowed to remain, ultimately, insignificant. Eric Gill's *Stations of the Cross* in Westminster Cathedral, finished in March, 1918, attracted Jones

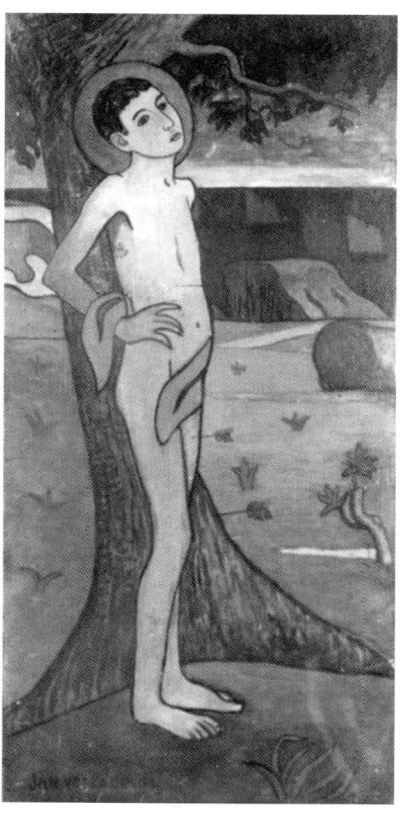

1. Jan Verkade, Saint Sébastien, 1892

43

during his time at Westminster; their example of 'cool restraint', their blend of Byzantine and the modern,[10] suggested to Jones that there might be a possibility that his religious inclinations could find expression through his art. Jones found the *Stations*, such a potentially boring project, - 'fourteen things, all roughly the same'- to be 'the best of all' Gill's public commissions (see p 52).[11]

While there is ample evidence in his work in the early 1920s of an acquaintance, not only with Post-Impressionism, but also with the earliest phase of Cubism, Jones appeared indifferent, certainly isolated, quaintly parochial and somewhat eccentric in the choosing of his artistic models and masters. Gill, irritated by a concept like *significant form*,[12] was in ways an odd, but as it transpired, supremely important choice; for good or bad, nearly everything that Jones did and everyone whom Jones met was the direct or indirect result of his association with Eric Gill.

By the time of his conversion to Catholicism on 7 September 1921, Jones had visited, worked and corresponded with Gill.[13] On the advice of Fr. John O'Connor, Jones had made a day trip to Ditchling in January of that year and what he had found there was an artistic and religious guild which sought, not only to transmit to its members and apprentices particular skills, but an entire way of life. As Gill put it in *The Game*, an occasional and sometime monthly magazine published between 1916 and 1923 at Ditchling, the Guild was 'primarily a religious fraternity for those who make things with their hands'. Jones later observed that apart from worship, there 'was no other community life except what might be expected of families of the same religion living in close proximity and sharing like views.'[14]

Soon after Jones's first day visit, Gill was writing to the young art student in his favourite tone of mentor:

> It is true that it is no more reasonable to begin again with a Byzantine manner of work than with the manner of Francesca. The only sensible thing is to go back to the beginning or whatever seems to be the beginning …

> With regard to the question of representation I think that neither you nor I need concern ourselves about it. Our customers will certainly see to it that the things we *do* bear a passable likeness to the things they *order*. Our concern, first of all, is to make things as well as we know how, and as well as we know how means *'how'* rather than *'why'* or *'what'*.[15]

Jones, who subsequently confessed that 'I thought and I still think that art schools are pretty hopeless',[16] was, at the time, under the somewhat mistaken impression that he 'felt the need for the workshop rather than the studio', but much later he acknowledged that 'inwardly my desire remained what it had been since my childhood, i.e. to draw and paint'.[17] Instead of staying in London, however, and working in bohemian studios such as the one visited by Sickert, he was attracted to this religious community of artisans on Ditchling Common. Such a community in which devoted men were directed

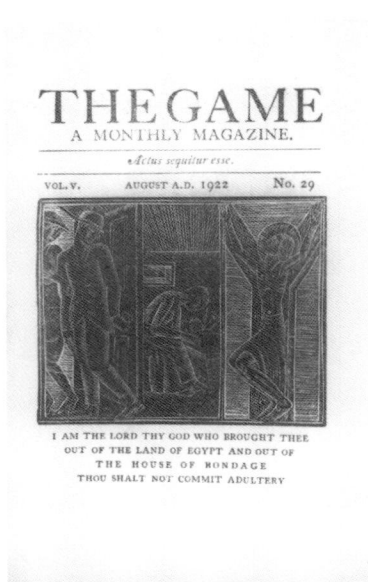

2. *The Game*, No. 29, August 1922

to some common purpose recalled something of the fraternity which Jones had experienced in the trenches, but Ditchling offered more than that, it offered the comfort of a family.

Above all, Jones the ex-soldier was received and cared for to a quite extra-ordinary extent by Gill. The theme of tending and adoring the wounded man appears in Jones's work: Christ in a watercolour Deposition of 1925, *Lamentation*, or in a drypoint of 1930, the wounded knight of Malorian literature seen as the symbol of the wasteland rather than its redeemer. In both cases the stricken man is in the healing arms of a woman. Although Jones found it ultimately impossible to embrace such solace, clearly the warmth of the Gill family and the love of Gill and his daughter Petra were of great importance to him. The sheer familial fun of being at Ditchling and at Capel-y-ffin should not be underestimated; Jones, in the more casual woodworking jobs which he undertook, has left a testimony to this in the form of toy villages, some animals and deal puppet heads, based on the three Gill girls and adopted son, and carved perhaps for Hilary Pepler, who was developing an interest in puppetry and mime. Without doubt, Gill's qualities of kindness, humour and simplicity were a source of comfort and succour to a young man whose senses had been bombarded on the Western Front.

In relation to art, Gill reveals himself, even in that early letter to Jones, as too pragmatic in his thinking about purpose and procedure to be much worried about complex and burdensome questions rationalizing the activity; the emphasis in the letter quoted above was very much on 'how'. As the engraver, Philip Hagreen, later put it: 'Eric regretted that there was no tradition within which to work or from which to advance. David rejoiced that for the first time

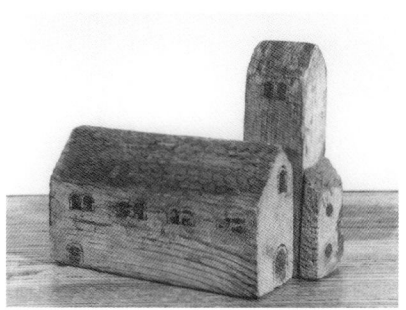

3. Church for Toy Village, 1922 (?)

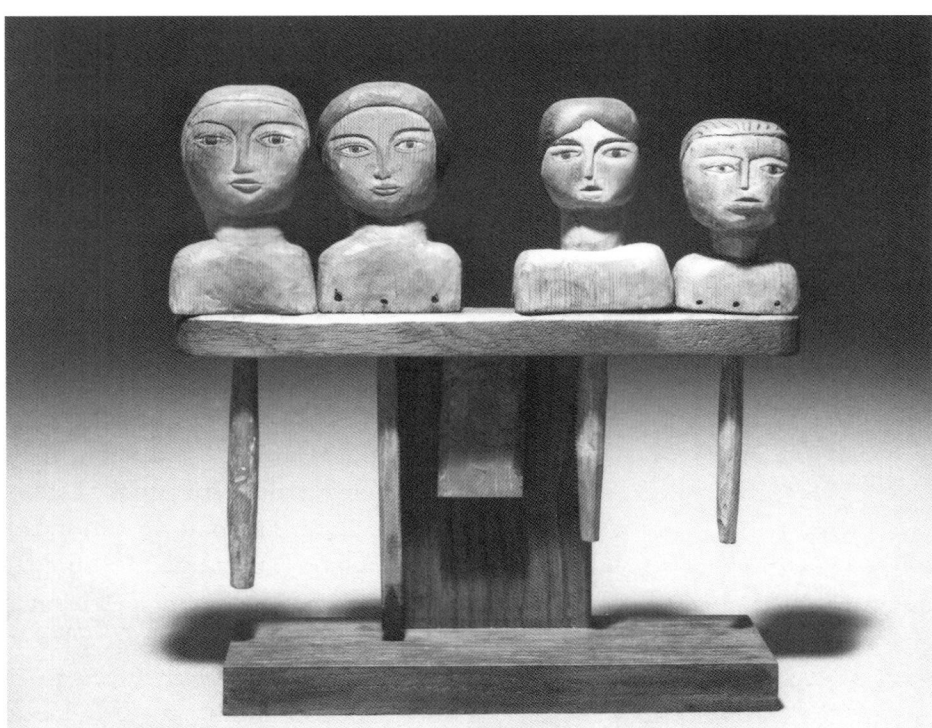

4. Four Puppet Heads, 1922 (?)

45

in history the absence of tradition left the artist free'.[18] Similarly, the American critic, Harold Rosenberg, writing much later in *The New Yorker*, observed that Jones took pleasure in the questions raised by the twentieth century, daring it to knock him down.[19] Of course, an absence of tradition is as perplexing as it is tantalizing, so perhaps what initially attracted Jones was a certain security and impersonality in Gill's hieratic approach to art:

> It is not that artists should endeavour to reproduce this or that antique hieratic form (sham byzantine is no more to be sought after than sham gothic), but that they should, as becomes Christian men no less than Christian artists, endeavour to rule out from their work all that *personal idiosyncrasy and emotionalism* which, however interesting and delightful it may be in private life, is out of place in public worship.[20]

To a young man suffering the after-effects of shell-shock, but who, as we have already seen, was unable to admit the impact which the war had made upon him, such escape from emotion offered, if not ultimate relief, at least a timely evasion of the problem. Petra Tegetmeier remembers Jones talking about the war in a light-hearted manner[21] and Hagreen remembers that there were things about the conflict that were deliberately left unsaid.[22] It is a tendency that becomes apparent in Jones's life, the reluctance to register the gravity of events as, or just after, they happen.[23] Like Eliot's idealized poet in 'Tradition and the Individual Talent', Jones was already feeling the desirability of not 'turning loose … emotion', of 'an escape from personality'. Eliot, of course, went on to point out that 'only those who have personality and emotions know what it means to want to escape from these things.'[24] Jones deflected emotional issues with questions about the relation of art to religion and these not only allowed him to escape, at least temporarily, from the self, and make of making an almost self-conscious ritual, but also provided him with an insoluble problem for the rest of his life. He decided, during the Gill years, to be not only a practising artist, but also somebody who would constantly try to understand the nature and purpose of the activity.

As there had been several shell-shocked young men at Ditchling, Gill was quick to appreciate Jones's emotional condition and set him to work doing physical tasks such as painting windows.[25] He was apprenticed to the carpenter and wheelwright George Maxwell in January of 1922, an antidote, Gill hoped, to too many years of art school training.[26] Jones proved inept as a carpenter - 'more of a bloody nuisance than anything else',[27] yet his skill in producing certain wooden fittings for Maxwell's house, such as latches capable of securing the doors from within[28] reveals a sensitivity in shaping wooden forms that would manifest itself more fully in the small boxwood carvings which Jones produced during the following years from used or abandoned engraving blocks.

Living conditions on Ditchling Common were almost as grim as they had been in the trenches; as Philip Hagreen remembers, Jones was lodged 'in a stable that was one brick thick and had a sloping brick floor. Around and

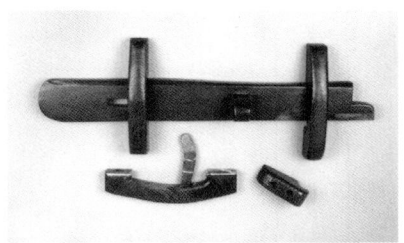

5. Door locks, 1921 (?)

under it clay - the dregs of Noe's flood not yet drained'. The 'workshop was without lining or ceiling' and the 'wind blew between the weatherboards and floorboards'.[29] Such a spartan existence was hardly surprising when one considers that the Ditchling experiment was set up in reaction to modern civilization and its palliative, comfort, which was held by Gill and his associates to be mere compensation for wage slavery. Under industrialization, artistry had been replaced by mechanical production and workmen had become machine minders; they lost the opportunity and thus the capacity to use tools and to work as designer craftsmen. Art, which traditionally had been practised by all men who made things, was suddenly prohibited to the workman and came to be thought of as a superfluous and specialized activity that odd, and to a certain extent, parasitic people 'went in' for. To make a stand against this situation was to take up the ideas of nineteenth century writers like Ruskin who had urged the re-birth of man-the-maker. Such a creator materialized an idea, added impromptu and gratuitous elements which issued from his imagination, and thus both brought joy to, and expressed joy in, his labour.[30] William Morris echoed Ruskin's position, claiming that a fundamental principle of making was that it was 'direct communication between a man's hand and his brain'.[31] These wooden spoons which Jones carved and gave to Petra Gill suggest the artisan's loving intelligence. Many years later, taking issue with Berenson's hierarchical distinction between 'art' and 'artefact', Jones wrote that 'I can see no difference of kind, but only of infinite degrees, between … a wooden spoon carved by a Welsh peasant for his sweetheart … or Picasso's *Chandelier, pot et casserole émaillée*.'[32]

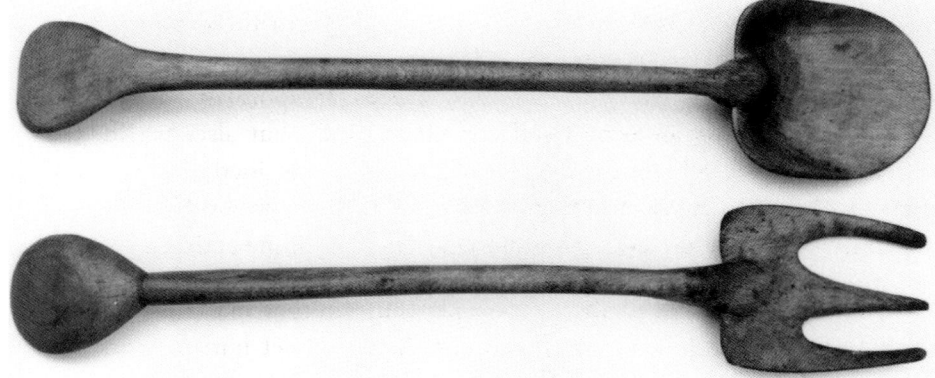

6. Wooden Salad Spoon and Fork, 1924 (?)

Philip Hagreen later remembered that at Ditchling 'we talked endlessly about work and religion - mostly we heard Eric talk'.[33] Certainly, the ever enthusiastic Gill was fired by the rich brew of ideas that he assimilated and accommodated to his particular concept of Roman Catholicism: Fabian, Socialist and Distributist notions. Also at Ditchling, Guild members were inspired by the social idealism of Fr. Vincent McNabb who had introduced Gill and his associates, Hilary Pepler and Desmond Chute, to the idea of becoming Dominican Tertiaries who were lay people, living under the guidance of the Order, and undertaking more rigorous religious obligations than those of ordinary Catholics.[34] Philip Hagreen

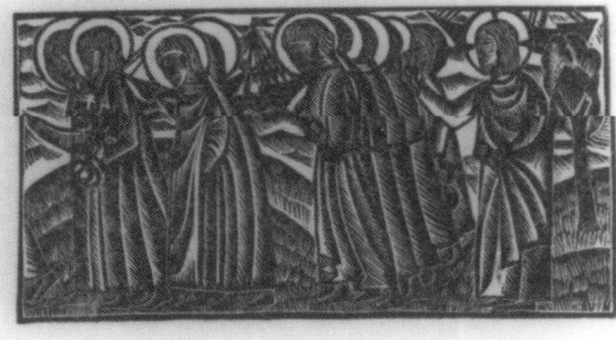

St. Dominic's Press

DITCHLING   SUSSEX

BENCH BOOKS

PHILOSOPHY OF ART   Being
'Art et Scolastique' by Jacques Maritain
translated into English by the Rev. John
O'Connor, s. t. p.   10s. 6d.

WOOD-WORK   A. Romney Green,
illustrated.   7s. 6d.

SCULPTURE   An Essay on Stone
cutting with a Preface about God.
Eric Gill.   5s. 0d.

VEGETABLE DYES   Ethel Mairet
Fourth Edition   5s. 0d.

WOOD-ENGRAVING   Practical
instructions in, with a Preface by E. Gill,
John R. Beedham.   5s. 0d.

VERSE

THINGS UNSEEN   By the Author
of *A Soul Cake*.   2s. 6d.

IN PETRA   A sequel to *Nisi Domi-
nus* (out of print), by the author of *Concerning Dragons*, engravings D. J.   5s.

SONGS TO OUR LADY OF SILENCE
Second ed. engravings D. Chute, 7s. 6d.

7. St. Dominic's Press Bench Books, 1925

believed that McNabb wasn't much interested in the artistic side of the endeavour; he couldn't recall that Fr. Vincent ever looked at their work. He came into the workshops to talk:

> His chin threatened like the toe of a hob-nailed boot. He never paused to listen or ask a question. All his talk was about himself. I suppose he had been taught to examine his conscience and had become an addict ... Tho David and I found Fr. Vincent futile and a bore, others thought him wonderful.[35]

The Community debated 'Usury, Private Ownership, Beauty, Goodness, Truth'[36] and aesthetic matters were elucidated by relevant Neo-Thomist ideas which were set out in Jacques Maritain's *Art et Scholastique*; this was translated by Fr. John O'Connor, at times in Gill's workshop while the sculptor backed up the translating work with dictionary consultation.[37] Although a more accurate translation was produced seven years later, the publication of this book at Ditchling in 1923, in a print run of 400 copies, was important to the thinking in Gill's establishments at Ditchling, Capel-y-ffin and Pigotts as well as to David Jones's thinking about art. As René Hague later wrote, 'the Post-Impressionist attitude to the arts fitted in very well with Maritain' and 'Thomism'.[38]

In the tradition of Aquinas, Maritain stated that art is a habit of the intellect[39] and Jones followed this, maintaining that there was 'no surrogate for being "on the job"', insisting that art, and he had the experience to support the statement, 'is an infantryman's job'.[40] The habit of art is

> *a virtue*, that is to say a quality which, triumphing over the original indetermination of the intellective faculty, ... raises it in respect of a definite object to a *maximum of perfection, and so of operative efficiency*.[41]

And it is this habit that sets about controlling the form of a work of art; form, not only the shape and determination of an artefact, but the cause of its coming into being, a reflection of the idea in the mind of its maker. So a picture could be seen to be the subject itself under the form of paint if the painter eschewed the tendency towards imitation in favour of the re-creative vigour of re-incarnation in his or her chosen medium.

The philosophy of Maritain explored two related questions that are of importance for David Jones: signification and epiphany. By rigorous habit, the artist would not only be able to reveal this or that object under the form of paint but also make an epiphany, make the universal shine out from the particular. Thus, what is re-presented also becomes a sign of something else and if that something else is significant of something divine, then the art can claim to have a sacred character or function, a sacramental vitality. Maritain wrote that the joy or delight of a work of art is in proportion to its powers of signification:

> ... the more there is of knowledge, or of things presented to the understanding, the vaster will be the possibility of joy; this is why Art, in so far as it is ordered to Beauty, does not, at least when its object permits, stop at forms or at colours, ... but it takes them also as making known other things than themselves, that is to say *as signs*. And the thing signified may itself be a sign in turn, and the more the work of art is laden with significance ... the vaster and the richer and the higher will be the possibility of joy and beauty.[42]

Here was an acceptable complement to the insufficiencies of Bell's 'significant form'. Here were Jones's reasons for shying away from abstract art. Here were the seeds of the development of Jones's overloaded historical and mythological vision, for whenever he allowed 'knowledge of things presented' to take the place of transubstantiation and *anamnesis*, he encountered difficulties.

'*Anamnesis*' or re-presentation, is a notion tied to the institution of the com-munion rite by Christ at the Last Supper. According to Maurice de la Taille, another important influence on the Gill circle, Christ's execution could only have become a meaningful sacrifice because he pledged himself as victim before the fact. The Priest at the Mass makes that Offering - he re-presents it under the form of bread and wine - just as, according to Jones, a Post-Impressionist re-makes a landscape in paint.

If the comforts were few and the life demanding, Ditchling provided Jones with another intense visual experience of religious celebration:

> I shall always retain memories of the little white interior of the chapel at Ditchling with the bunched children and others holding small lights during the mass ... You can't beat whitewash can you, and whitewash and candle-light is about as good a thing as you can see in this world I reckon. That luminous thing about whitewash is so wonderful ... It makes the obscure corners of rooms full of reflected light - I don't know anything else that does it.[43]

In that chapel at Ditchling, on 24 April, 1924, David Jones became formally betrothed to Petra, Gill's second daughter, with the unusual blessing of a possessive father. On one level it is an indication of how dearly Gill had come to feel about Jones and perhaps, on another, sub-conscious level, a realization that Jones posed little or no sexual threat.

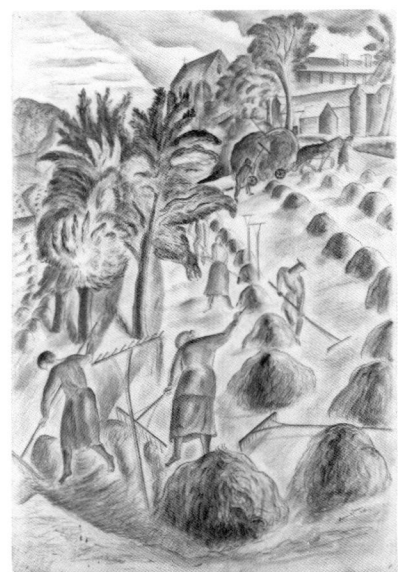

8. Mr. Gill's Hay Harvest, 1926

By this time, as a power struggle had developed between the two remaining founder members, Hilary Pepler and Eric Gill, the general situation at Ditchling was no longer convivial. Ostensibly an argument about financial methods, a clash of character and differing 'notions of an organized community' were at stake.[44] Shortly afterwards, the Gills departed with the Hagreens for the disused monastery at Capel-y-ffin, near Llanthony in the Ewyas valley on the English-Welsh border. It was an isolated spot, an enormous distance from London, and Gill saw the venture as a challenge and also as an opportunity to make a stand. As he wrote in his *Autobiography*, 'we were compelled by mere geographical circumstance to live in a way which would have been fantastically heroic and unnatural and pedantic in any place less remote from industrial civilization.'[45] Life at Capel afforded the opportunity for its inhabitants and visitors to pursue their work in a condition of holy poverty, which is not to say in a state of deprivation, but governed by a sense of what was materially necessary to their creative and religious pursuits. The effect was undeniably yet undeliberately medieval, a quality captured in Jones's watercolour, *Mr. Gill's Hay Harvest*; while the rest of the family and other visitors energetically set to work with the harvest, Jones, with his reluctance to help very much about the place, painted it.[46] Jones was a frequent visitor to Capel-y-ffin, staying there for extended periods, but it is essential to note that by 1924 he was not bound to Gill or his attempts to set up a new community;[47] there was no question of discipleship and yet, significantly, Jones later remarked that he was with Gill 'a much shorter time really than I think I was'.[48]

By the end of 1924, Gill's stylistic influence on Jones was diminishing. There is a feeling of airiness in Jones's best Capel, Caldey and French pictures that shows him throwing off the constrictions of being an explicitly religious artist and allowing nature to glorify God. Aspects of Gill's example would, however, haunt him down the years.

Dramatically, at the beginning of 1927 the emotional harbour of the Gill household was to some degree destroyed by the breaking-off of Jones's engagement to Petra Gill. The second half of the twenties marks the beginning of the peripatetic life that the artist led for over the next twenty-three years, a style of life which contributed to his feeling of not quite belonging anywhere, of waiting to be assigned.

Gill was a highly methodical man. His need for a right or wrong, either/or solution hampered his work as an artist. Robert Speaight suggested that 'He quite lacked the ... capacity for resting in uncertainty ...; he believed in too many rules and he thought that all one had to do was to follow them.'[49] Jones, on the other hand, clearly realized that no

> amount of true philosophical or metaphysical definition will aid *one bit, necessarily*, the painting of a picture. The ability to paint a good picture does not come through philosophy or religion in any direct manner at all. They could only indeed have a damaging effect on the making of things if thought of as providing some theory to work by - a substitute for imagination and direct creativeness.[50]

Donald Attwater recorded that Jones was 'a disciple of Eric's mind' but 'not of all his ideas',[51] and in fact, Jones recalled that he 'disagreed' with Gill 'over all sorts of things.'[52] Hague gave an accurate picture when he stated that Jones took 'many fundamental principles from Eric Gill', and summed it up excellently when he wrote that 'Eric had an enduring influence on David's thought - if little or none on his work'.[53] Jones himself noted, 'I don't think' Gill 'was a great artist ... I think he was a great man'.[54] Philip Hagreen observed the relationship from another perspective: 'Eric was not David's master as he was mine, but he was Petra's father.'[55] These all give indications, but when we consider the total impact of Gill on Jones it is clear that it was nothing short of colossal. Few modern artists have been so loved and nurtured by an older master and Gill's estimation of Jones was more than encouraging; once, around a crowded dining-table, Gill said, 'We have been talking a lot about art but there is only one real artist in this room', and he pointed to David Jones.[56] The Gill household gave refuge and Gill himself spun an endlessly proliferating web of important friendships, contacts, and introductions to galleries. So much so that many choices of subject, the opportunities to engrave and carve, habits of writing and attitudes to work were the results - direct and indirect - of that visit by a young, uncertain art student and ex-soldier to Ditchling Common one wet January day in 1921.

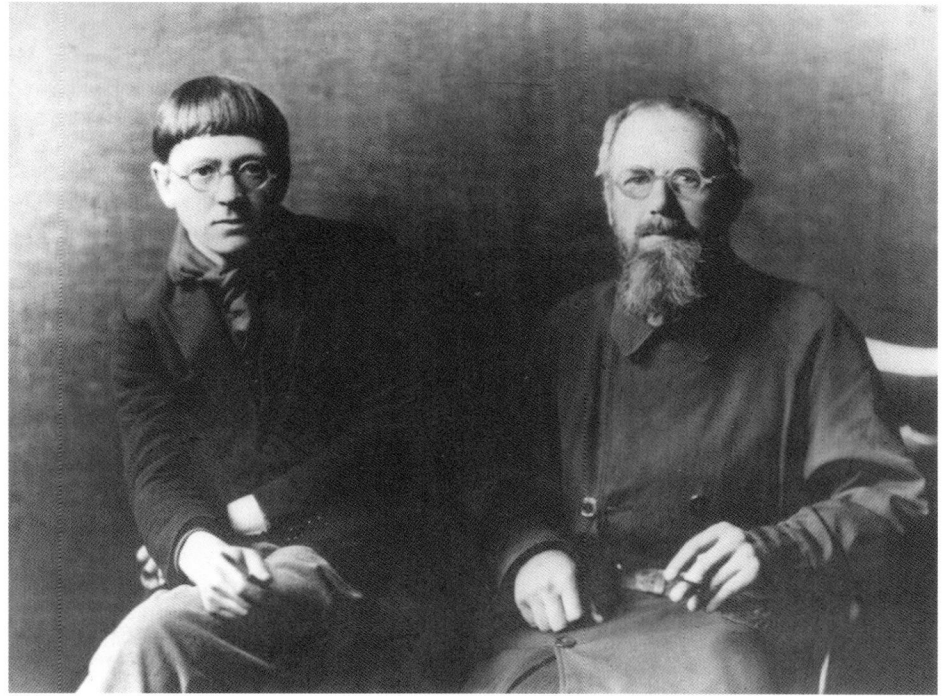

9. Anon., David Jones and Eric Gill, 1927 (?)

HIERATIC EVASIONS:
CHRIST AND THE SAINTS

With the post-war boom degenerating into massive unemployment, and depression and slump on the way, the shelter of an incongruous artistic community was not such a bad option for a young artist. Charles Harrison observes that in the 'post-war years … English art as a whole was withdrawn and convalescent'.[1] What is more, art and religion were not, as Clive Bell noted, 'occupations for which men can be paid', they were rather two roads by which men could escape from circumstance to ecstasy.[2] What, in the uncertain world of the twenties, could be more auspicious than to retreat to a community where these two roads converged?

If we compare *Christ Before Pilate*, which Jones did at Ditchling in 1922, with his Westminster Art School work we can see immediately how far he has discarded a tendency towards the illustrational and has submitted himself to the hieratic style of Eric Gill. Indeed, both subject-matter and square format, no less than its manner, show that Jones was thinking of Gill's *Stations of the Cross* which had so impressed him when he was a student at Westminster. Nonetheless, the soldiers are Tommies with corporal's stripes and First World War helmets, figures that are already embedded in Jones's imagination.

What is particularly educative about the drawing is to note how some fine compositional ideas have been compromised. The faces of the soldiers crowded ominously behind Christ in the upper right hand corner have been cluttered by the positioning of the vicious spear and yet its form echoes the thorn-like points on the inside of Christ's halo and the V in the drapery of Pilate's robe. While this sets up, intellectually, a nice causality, pictorially it disturbs the eye-line which has been drawn between the protagonists and which is underscored by the blue belt of Pilate, the strongly coloured red belt of Christ, the line behind the kneeling boy, and the horizontal arms of the soldier and the Procurator. The stairway linking the two groups is, like the halo, unnecessary, for the space created by exclusion would have been expressive. Jones, inexperienced and under the new-felt pressure of religious iconography, ignores the modernist *credo*, 'less is more', and we are left with what we see so often in Gill's work, an eerie and stilted emptiness embellished by religious business. Nevertheless, there is an attempt at modernity which Gill eschewed in his *Stations*. The particular kind of modernity in *Christ Before Pilate* might be identified by considering a blend of the classicized primitivism of early Frank Dobson sculpture and the work of William Roberts, whose frieze-like paintings with their expressive, 'Tubist', distortions of the human figure offer a well-ordered if not always unfussy

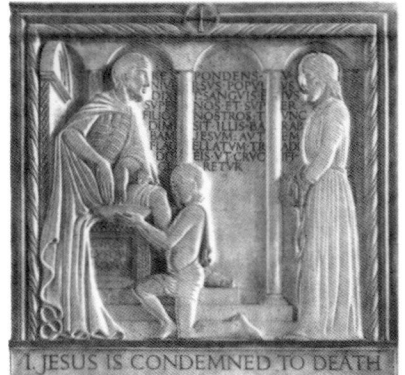

1. Eric Gill, Christ Before Pilate, 1918

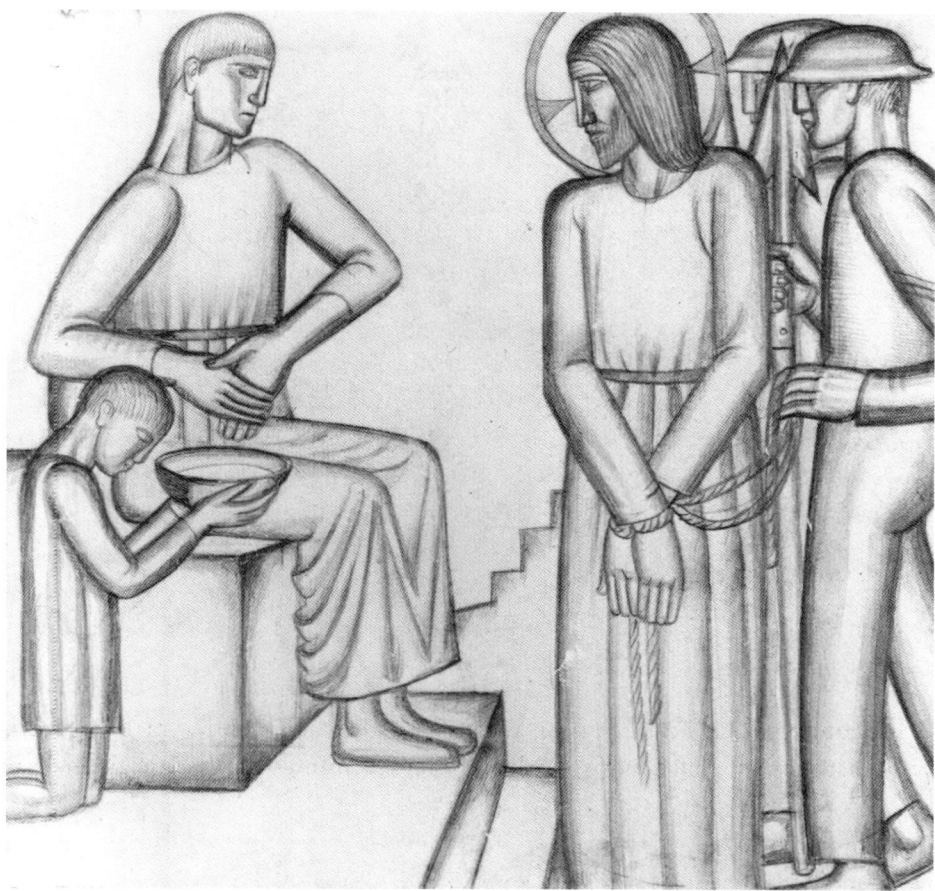

2. Christ Before Pilate, 1922

design.[3] Roberts, who was born in the same year as Jones, was, by the early twenties, working on a large scale; he received the dubious compliment from *The Times* reviewer of his 1923 one-man exhibition of being 'the ideal decorator of a municipal or commercial building'.[4] Jones, on the other hand, had begun to work on a smaller scale during these years. The big schemes at Westminster Art School gave way to small drawings and with the loss of scale there was, at first, a loss of challenge, accompanied by the intrusion of words, haloes and other religious labels.

Impressive exceptions to the small scale works were those painted in oil on tongue-and-groove board in what were, for Jones, bold forms with striking colours: alizarin, ultramarine, umber and black. These panels originally formed part of the inner walls of the Ditchling woodwork shop and the themes of the paintings were obviously religious. The bold style bridged the gap between Italian Primitivism and aspects of the modern.

In *Jesus Mocked*, there are four soldiers in provocative posture around the stillness of Christ, although the kneeling figure, to whom Christ directs his gaze, appears more devotional than taunting. The force lines of the soldiers, particularly those on the left, are cunningly placed to add rhythm and move-ment to their threatening gestures and the overall dance-like effect of the mockers seems to owe something to the sprightly configuration of Meninsky's

53

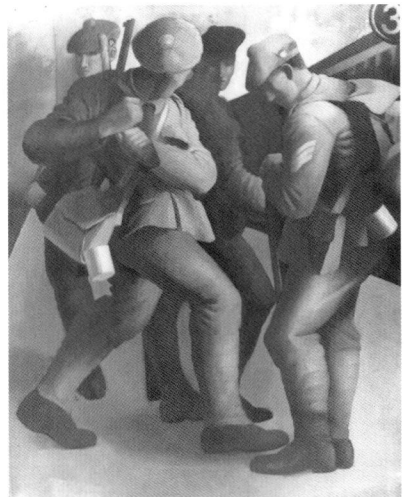

3. Bernard Meninsky, *Soldiers on a Platform*, 1918

Bruegelesque soldiers on a platform which, as it was painted in 1918, Jones may well have seen as a Westminster art student.

Interestingly, Christ is placed off-centre in relation to the niche behind. There is a tilting of the confined space and a changing viewpoint such as may be found in Cézanne; we seem to be looking down on Christ, which gives him an increased feeling of vulnerability and yet the two soldiers in the background appear on the spectator's eye level. Christ's body is flattened and hardly seated and while this may remind the spectator of primitive art it is also disposed in the way that Gauguin ambiguously situates a seated Javanese female model in a position that is half-sitting, half-flattened on the picture plane.[5] Christ's apparently vertical feet suggest the crucifixion and nail holes in the tongue-and-groove provide pre-emptive stigmata. The tongue-and-groove itself is used to clever effect; the vertical slatting punctuates the scene with a counter-rhythm, both sectioning-off dynamic areas and participating generally in the upward thrust of the composition. Only two of the heads are fully developed whereas, in a drawing of the same subject, the soldiers are more literal, closer to the style of that student, squared-up trench scene, though Christ's torso is finely formalized and his eyes more expressive of the broken man. Bayes reproduced another preliminary drawing in his article in *The Architectural Review*, calling Jones a 'deserter' from the Westminster training but, nonetheless, admiring the study.[6] With the presence of the tin-hatted Tommies, this scene further explores the position of the soldiers in relation to the crucifixion of Christ: they are innocent members of a chance fatigue-party and representatives of a worldly, martial power that opposes the whole order of heaven.[7]

There is something that resembles the rapid effects achieved by Duncan Grant and Vanessa Bell in their decoration of Charleston in the wood panel paintings done by Jones at Ditchling. A similar spontaneity characterizes the work as well as a mixture of primitivism and the modern; in *The Crucifixion*, Cézannesque houses stand behind figures that are part modern, part Italian primitive and part Romanesque in a way that does not appear incongruous according to the Bell-Fry aesthetic. The composition seems to be somewhat casual when one considers the off-centre placing of Christ in relation to the tongue-and-groove divisions; but studied more carefully, the actual positioning allows increased space and importance to the penitent, whose crimson robe appears to move the figure forwards to act as a mediator between the spectator and Christ.

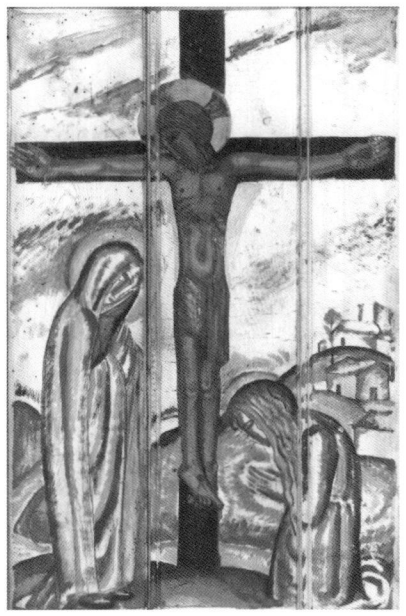

4. *Crucifixion*, 1922-3

The life and work of the people at Ditchling were punctuated by the routine of religious devotion; the day started with *Prime* in the tiny Chapel, mid-morning the work stopped for *Terce* and again, before lunch, for *Nones*. In the late afternoon work stopped for *Vespers* and then *Compline* was sung in the evening.[8] As a Tertiary, Jones participated in this routine although he never advanced beyond his postulancy in the Guild. Because Ditchling was Dominican, it was quite logical that he should paint, on the wall of the woodwork shop, the figure of St.Dominic himself in a bold, simple style with an iconic presence. Again, there is a modernity about the figure: the cloak

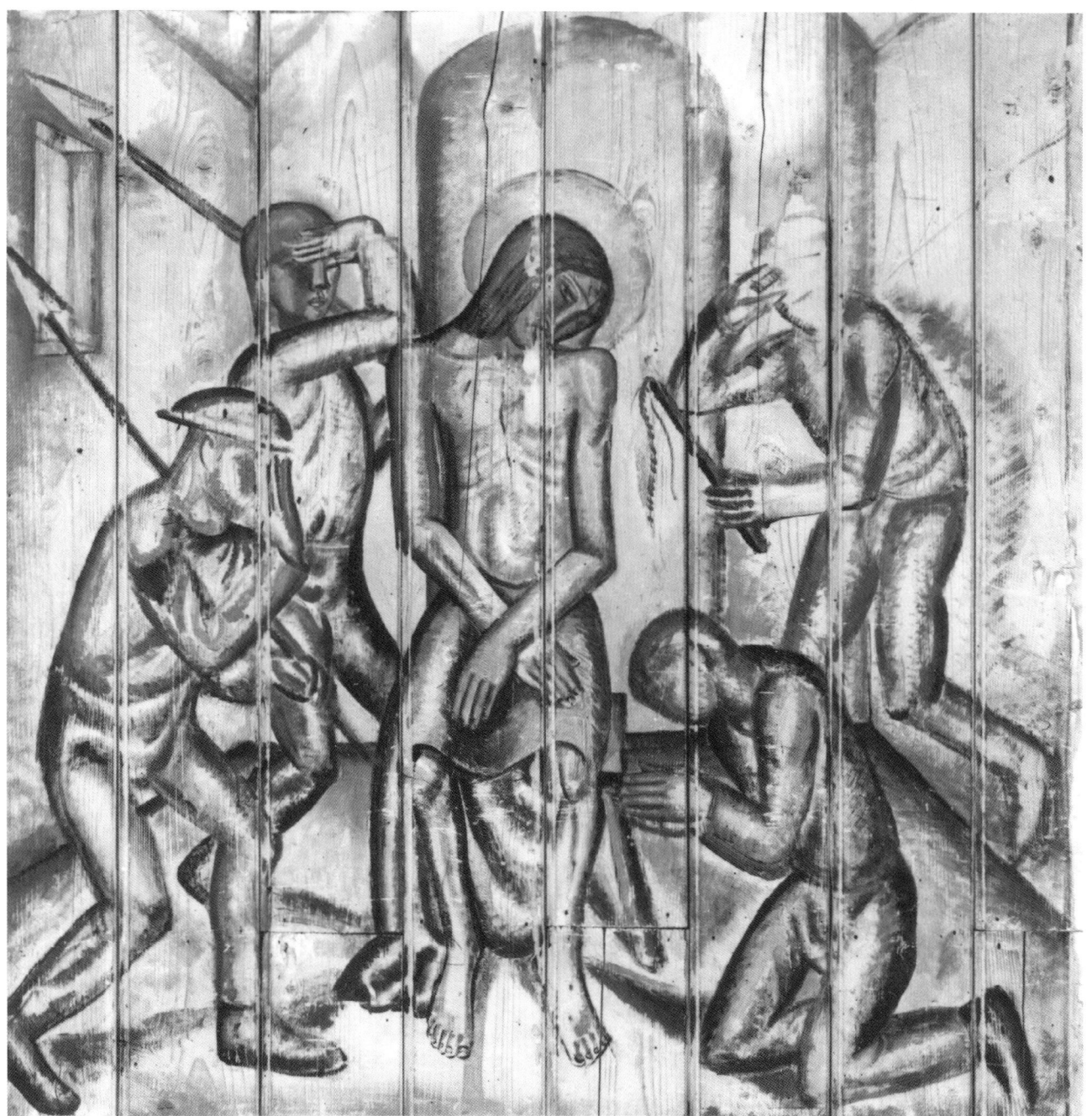

5. Jesus Mocked, 1922

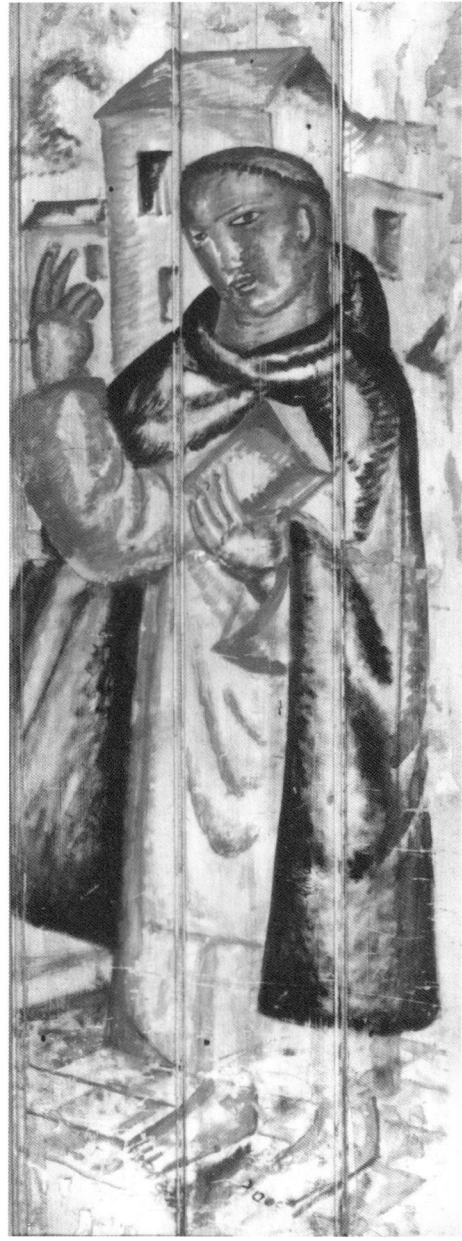

6. St. Dominic, 1923

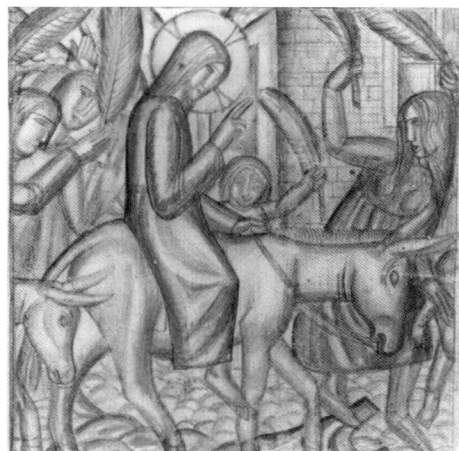

7. The Entry into Jerusalem on Palm Sunday, 1923

owes something to early Cubism and the upraised arm emerges seemingly from the centre of the torso at some distance from the thick neck which has already become a feature of Jones's style. The loss of the cape at the left-hand side perhaps suggests that we are not seeing the whole image and the presence of hinge marks in the top right corner indicates that this may once have formed a door panel or shutter that has been carelessly cut.

> The term 'Sorrowful Mysteries'[9] was used for the misfits and rolling stones that drifted to Ditchling. Mostly, they had been sent by Fr. Vincent McNabb. Some were broken men and some were cracked. Eric was invariably kind … Some were given shelter in the stable, which thus got its name.[10]

It was in this damp appendage to Chute's house, Wood-barton, that Jones painted his *Entry into Jerusalem (Cum Floribus et Palmis)*. According to Philip Hagreen, this 'moved Will Rothenstein to tears'[11] and today, worn by the passage of time, the detail of the frieze of faces *(8)* seems like a moving relic of twelfth century Roman-esque mural painting *(9)*.

In the sketch for the mural, the composition is flattened and the sensuous walk of the animals is deftly echoed by the undulating palms; their rhythm and plume-like quality is somewhat lost in the mural itself as is the drama of the eyeline between the sensual, Magdalene-like girl and Christ.

It is unclear why Jones began his mural on the short stretch of wall beside the door; perhaps the original intention was to decorate the entire room. In any case, the crowding of the figures in the corner does give a propulsion to the procession and a sense of space to the area around Christ. Cleverly, the brick itself is used to suggest the walls of the houses in the painting. Although the effect of the mural is primitive, the event seems im-mediate as if these are Ditchling houses and the children members of the Gill and Pepler entourage. Jones, who was prescribed the workshop by Gill as an antidote to 'art nonsense', seems unable to have resisted painting - even on the workshop walls.

Small pictures from this period demonstrate that the ready availability of a fund of Christian incidents was a solution to one of the foremost problems for the twentieth century artist - the question of what to paint.

56

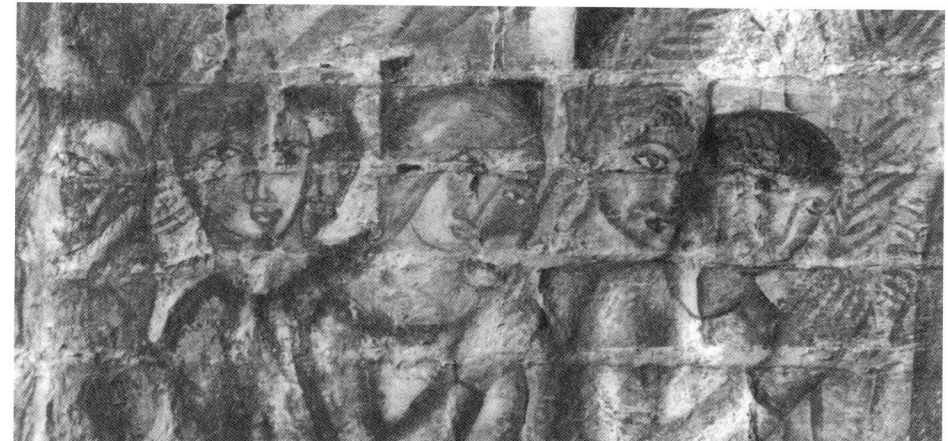

8. Mural of Christ's Entry (detail), 1923

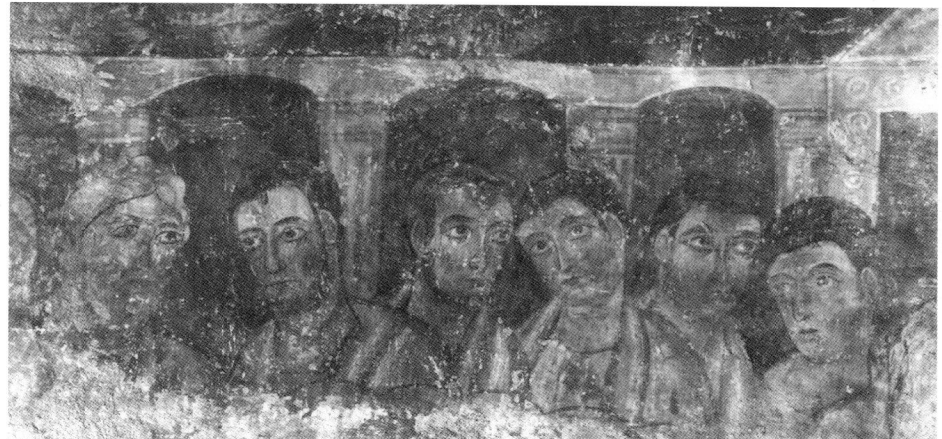

9. Anon., Apostles at the Last Supper, c.1180

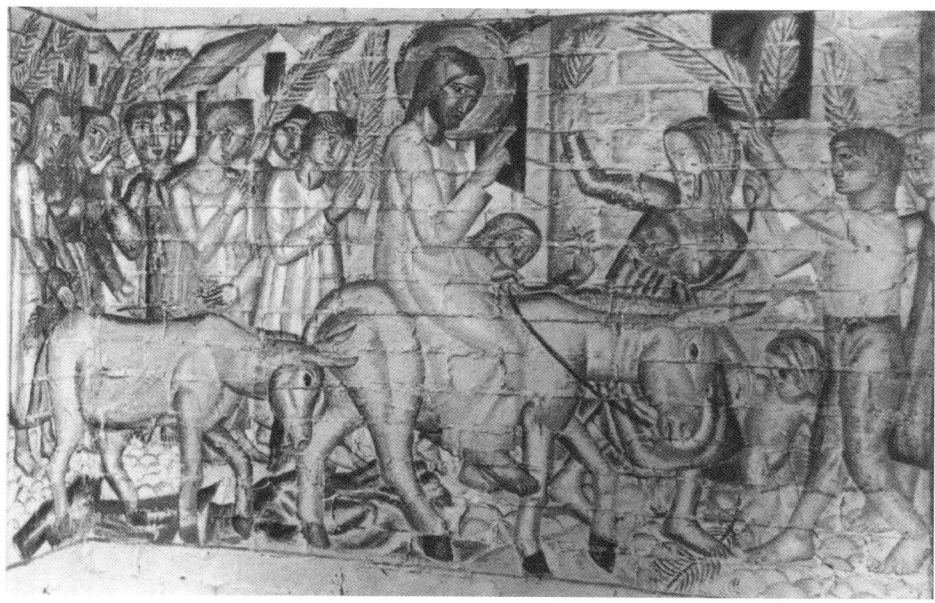

10. Mural of Christ's Entry (Cum Floribus et Palmis), 1923

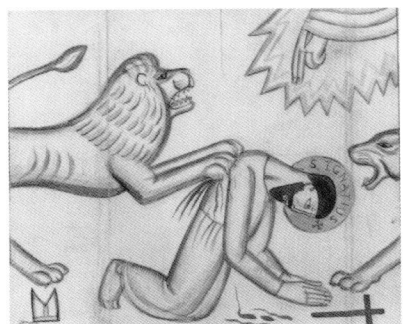

11. St. Ignatius, Bishop of Antioch, Martyr, 1922

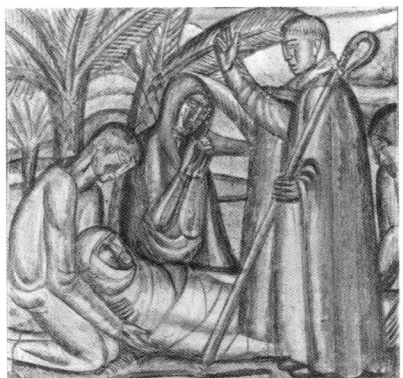

12. St. Hilary Raising a Man from the Dead, 1922

Despite the short-lived souring of relationships over his conversion to Catholicism, Jones produced this diagrammatic watercolour of a saint being mauled by lions, a subject which his father had suggested to his son long before his art studies began. Religious subjects provided Jones with pretexts for formal essays and the results reveal a degree of gentle eclecticism as well as one or two emerging idiosyncrasies such as the tendency to freeze figures in their youth. In *St. Hilary Raising a Man from the Dead*, painted on card, the flat, foreground plane gives the image immediacy. The dead man recalls the stone figure of a medieval knight on a tomb, whereas the fragment of the figure at the extreme right has a modern primitivism about it and the landscape is no more than a simplified evocation of the middle east.

There are two treatments of St. Gregory. The first is a triptych in which, in the left-hand panel, St. Gregory may be seen blessing slaves. In a weaker central section, a ship, warded by a dove placed against a wafer-like aureole, brings St. Augustine to England. On the right hand side, Augustine can be seen blessing the English King and Queen. A relentless patterning unites the three segments and the clouds in the central panel mediate cleverly between the downward movement of the blessing gesture on the left and the upward movement of the benediction on the right.

The *St. Gregory* made a little later is, at first sight, one of the most charming and considered of these early religious paintings and yet there is a certain frailty or facility creeping in; the young child is given no face, another is completely hidden and the features of the saint are crudely stylized, all limiting power of expression. It lacks the robust quality of *St. Hilary Raising a Man from the Dead* or the vigorous clumsiness of *Sts. Peter and Paul* which is one of a number of religious crayon drawings that Jones did during these years. And yet *St. Gregory* is enchanting and jewel-like: the crushed, spectating Roman townscape, the writing on the halo which sorts with the detailing of the brickwork, the elongated figure of the boy carrying the cross, owing something to eleventh century Romanesque wall painting or to the Novgorod school of icons, the modernistic re-ordering of the kneeling figure facing the spectator, the distant echo of Masaccio's *Expulsion from Paradise* in the Brancacci Chapel, all these are enriching aspects of the work.

Jones most probably adopted the habit of working on a small scale during this period because his principal endeavour was the making of engravings, but in the works on paper, he did not achieve the expression of the life of the spirit. Jones's response to saints' lives is often formally inventive but a quasi-naïvety or the weight of religious baggage often dulls the image; in a good number, for instance, the haloes tend to dominate. Cézanne, distracted by the haloes in the paintings of the Italian primitives, remarked to Gasquet, 'The fact is one doesn't paint souls. One paints bodies; and when the bodies are well painted, damn it all! the soul, if there is one, … blazes out and shines through!'[12] Van Gogh had another solution: 'I want to paint men and women with that something of the eternal which the halo used to symbolize, but which we now seek to counter through the actual radiance of colour vibrations'.[13] Serious artists were seeking new expressions to replace worn iconography. It was to be in his reaction to nature, to his civilization, in his simmering obsession with the war and in his wrestling with his eros that Jones would begin to give expression to the life of his soul.

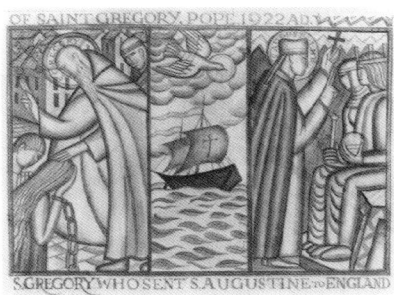

13. St. Gregory who sent St. Augustine to England, 1922

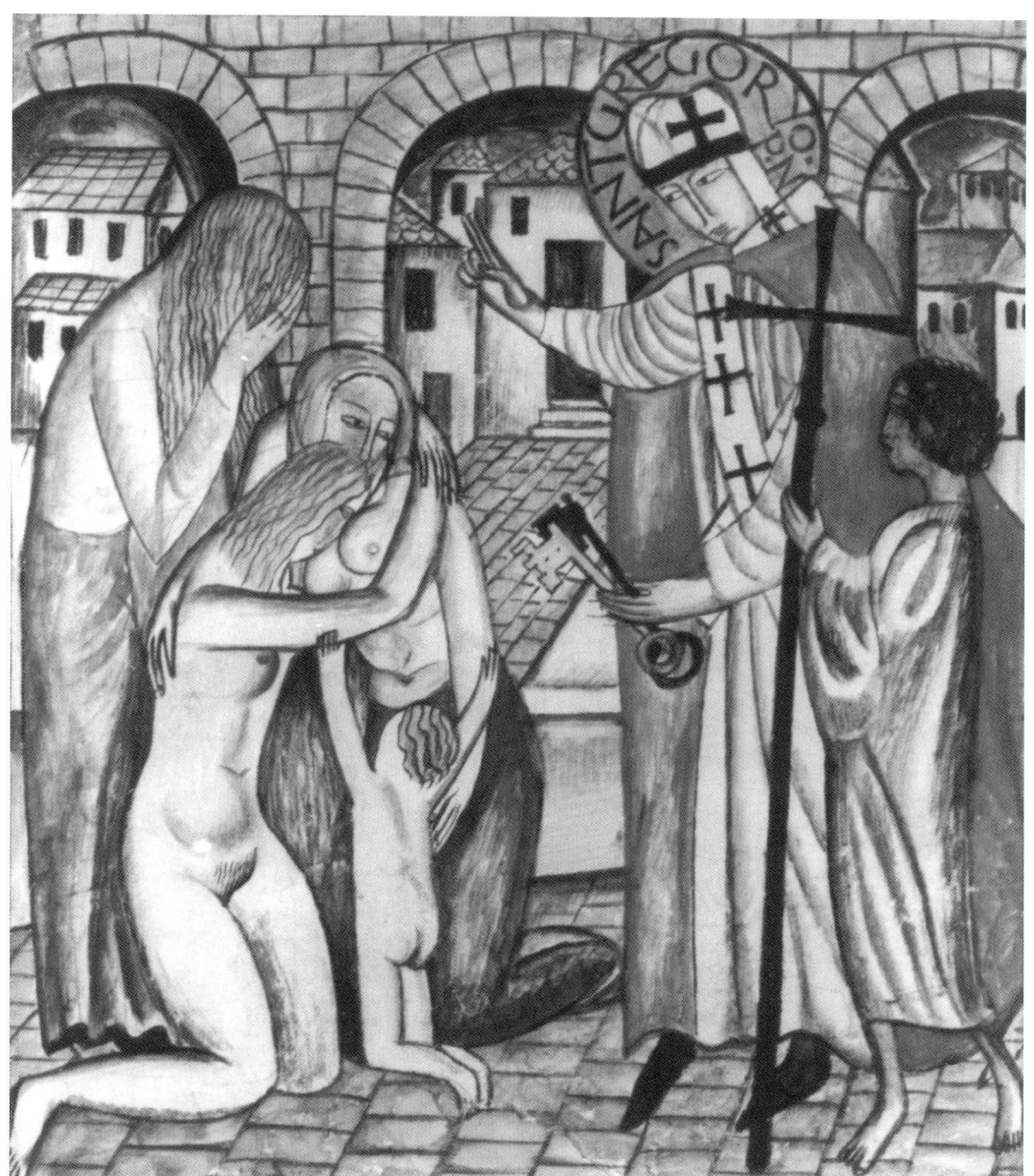

14. St. Gregory, 1924

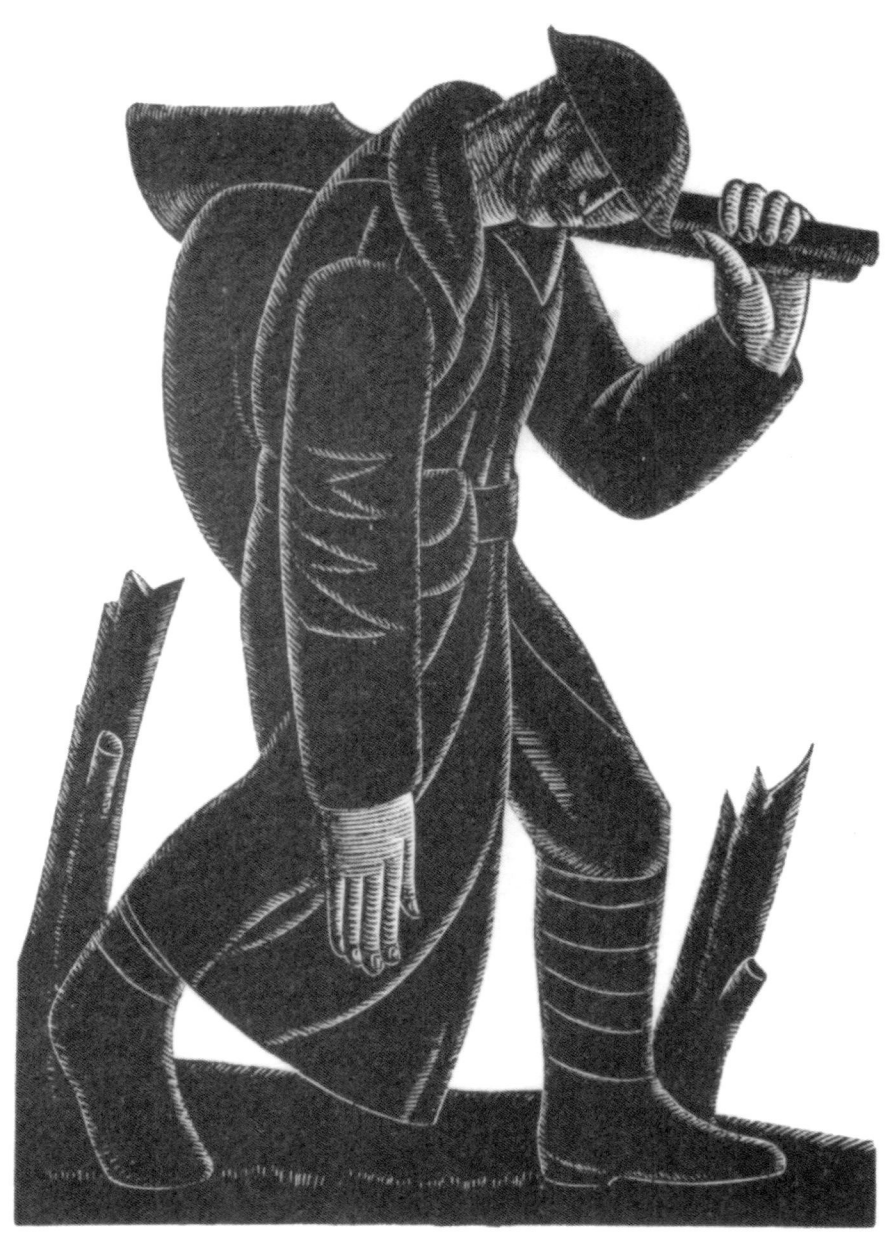

1. David Jones and Eric Gill, Westward Ho, 1921

ENGRAVINGS AND ILLUSTRATIONS

Eric Gill spent All Saints Day, 1921, engraving *Westward Ho*.[1] Although David Jones had not by then become a permanent resident at Ditchling, he was a frequent visitor throughout the year, spending part of the summer outside Pepler's print shop colouring the lettering which Gill and his assistants had been cutting for the New College War Memorial;[2] it was quite possibly during that time that Jones drew the design on which this engraving was based because Gill, having called for help with the soldier in greatcoat and tin hat, incorporated it into his sketches for the projected Trumpington War Memorial which he despatched in September.[3] At Ditchling, during the late summer Jones had taken some instruction in wood-engraving from the ex-Slade student, Desmond Chute, but was, by the time Gill came to produce *Westward Ho*, still too much of a novice to be capable of realizing in wood the subtleties inherent in his design. Jones's conception was given expression by Gill's experience, for the latter had been engraving seriously for over seven years.

The subject-matter reflects the fact that Jones was involved, as many artists and sculptors were, with the creation of War Memorials. The composition attests to Jones's preoccupation with the soldier's equivocal position as saviour and victim, often explored in his work in situations related to the figure of Christ. If soldiery had given Jones, as Saunders Lewis suggested, a feeling for 'the normal human male in Western Europe through most of its history',[4] it also gave him some feeling for the rôle of the scapegoat who carries away the ills that have been affecting a people, ills traditionally invested in a god who is thereafter slain.[5] Wilfred Owen, writing to Osbert Sitwell about training troops saw his recruits as such:

> I was at work - teaching Christ to lift his cross by numbers ... I see to it that he is dumb, and stands at attention before his accusers. With a piece of silver I buy him every day, and with maps I make him familiar with the topography of Golgotha.[6]

In *Westward Ho,* the soldier is framed significantly by three pieces of dead wood: two tree-stumps and the wood of his rifle butt which is a burden as heavy, it seems, as Christ's cross. The idea of a crucifixion or of a victim is not fanciful considering that the strong vertical of the foreground arm and the right-angled horizontal of the rifle create roughly cruciform axes on which the burdened figure is 'hung'. The anonymity of the soldier lends an archetypal quality to the idea of the man 'gone west'.

The finesse of Jones's design skillfully realized by Gill is, however, somewhat atypical of the style of much of the wood-engraving executed at Ditchling which had a homely, rough-and-ready aspect. When, in 1916, Hilary Pepler had acquired an ancient Stanhope hand press and two founts of the popular Caslon Old Face, he set up St. Dominic's Press in a disused stable in Ditchling village, at first using home-made printer's ink. Wood-engraving evolved in order to embellish texts expediently without involving expensive and scorned mechanical processes. The advantage of this reaction against the dissociations effected by commercial procedures was that it forced the artist into a position of almost complete responsibility for the image. Apart from polemical works, poetry and practical tracts such as Ethel Mairet's *Vegetable Dyes* (1916) and Ralph John Beedham's seminal *Wood Engraving* (1920), there were psalms, hymns, children's stories, a magazine, Christmas cards, Broadsheets, and Rhyme Booklets printed at Ditchling, many of which demanded illustration. Indeed, it was the cover of the October 1921 issue of *The Game* which bore David Jones's first published engraving, *The Most Holy Rosary*.[7] Made only weeks after he had begun to engrave, technical incapacity forced the novice into a simplicity which resulted in a sensuous boldness.

As a mode of subtle representation, white line engraving, where delicate lines are incised on a largely untouched block of boxwood, was developed in England at the beginning of the nineteenth century by William Blake and, more commercially, by Thomas Bewick who took advantage of the expressive and exploitable potential of hard and durable boxwood, imported from Turkey, the Crimea and the Caucasus; this was cut across the end grain and the wood's durity meant that an engraved block could withstand thousands of impressions. This increased delicacy and sensitivity in the rendering of light

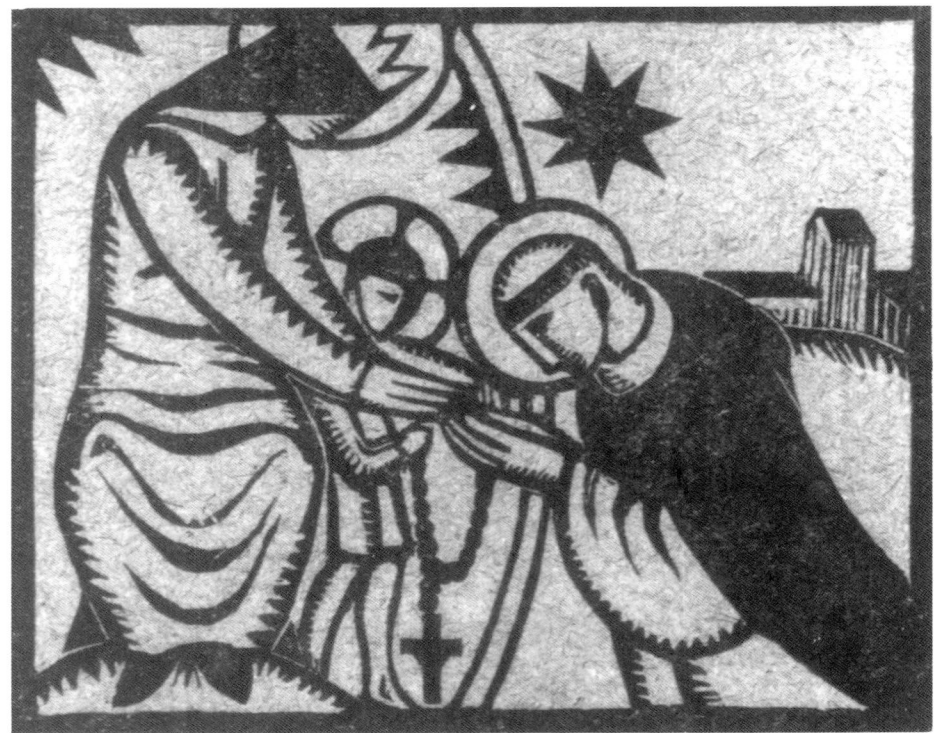

2. The Most Holy Rosary, 1921

facilitated by white line engraving meant that the technique flourished during the nineteenth century as a medium by which to reproduce mechanically drawings and paintings as well as to produce illustrations for journals. Only thirteen years to the day before Jones's birth, Van Gogh wrote to his brother, Theo, about his enthusiasm for English wood-engraving. As a child, David Jones had visited his father's printing office at *The Christian Herald* and had been impressed by how the blocks for illustrations and advertisements were engraved on boxwood in reverse.[8] The commercial use of boxwood engraving would have been in decline by the turn of the century; the process used at *The Christian Herald* had been considerably speeded up by the invention of a system of bolting blocks together so that several engravers could work on a composite illustration at the same time.[9] However, as a result of the challenge of other techniques such as the zincograph, wood-engraving lost its commercial viability and re-emerged as a creative activity in its own right; by 1898 a show entitled *The First Exhibition of Original Wood Engravings* was mounted by a group which included Charles Ricketts, William Nicholson, and Jones's Camberwell teacher, Reginald Savage.

With the demise of wood-engraving's commercial application, the medium, along with woodcut, became an original means of expression in the hands of continental artists such as Gauguin, Kandinsky, Munch and the German Expressionists. Exciting Vorticist woodcuts using powerful, bold forms were produced in England prior to the First World War; Wadsworth exhibited at the Twenty One Gallery in 1914 at the same time as the 'blunt, thick and brutal'[10] woodcuts of German artists such as Pechstein and Marc were on show. Edward Gordon Craig, who had appointed another of Jones's instructors, Bernard Meninsky, to teach at his school for art in the theatre in Florence, asserted the expressive potential of wood-engraving if purely formal values were applied to the medium. Undoubtedly, the English heir to many of these tendencies was the artist Paul Nash who, in engravings like *Black Poplar Pond* of 1922, revealed the influence of German Expressionism. In works like *Genesis* (1925), Nash took wood-engraving into the realm of abstraction in order to dramatize the awesome events of the origins of the universe, thereby producing an unequivocally twentieth century response to a religious subject.

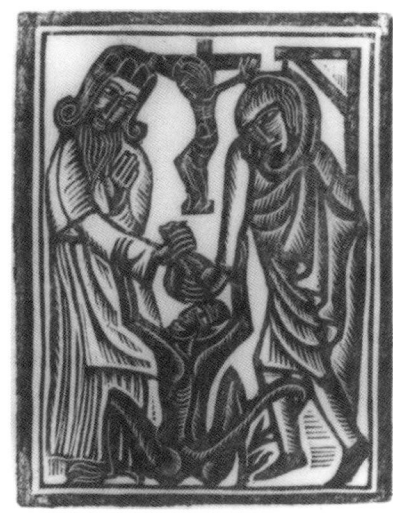

3. Judas, with Caiaphas and the Devil, 1924

By comparison with such modernism, wood-engraving at Ditchling harked back to the primitivism which characterized the earliest European prints on paper, images from the life of Christ or the Saints, often crudely carved by monks in order to be sold to the innumerable pilgrims travelling to various shrines. Reminiscent of such images is Jones's *Judas with Caiaphas and the Devil* (1924) in which the Apostle's suicide gibbet is placed beside the crucifix which dominates the scene. The noose is already around the traitor's neck and the thirty pieces of silver changing hands are, as with the treasure in Chaucer's *Pardoner's Tale*, thereby equated with death. The engraver clearly demonstrates a formal and notional sensitivity towards medieval expression. *Nativity With Ox and Ass* is a striking devotional image. Particularly effective is the framing, by the animals and baby, of Mary whose broad neck and large forehead were inspired by Petra Gill's physique which had already become, by 1923, Jones's archetype of female beauty.

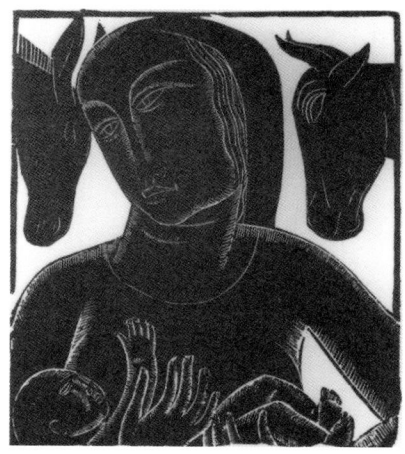

4. Nativity with Ox and Ass, 1923

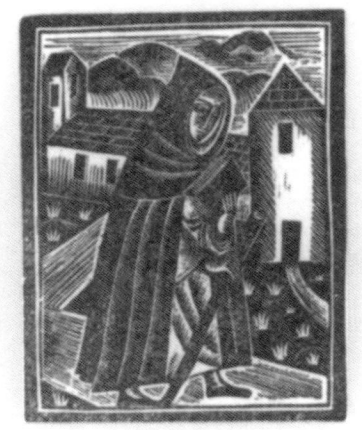

5. Dominican Friar, 1924

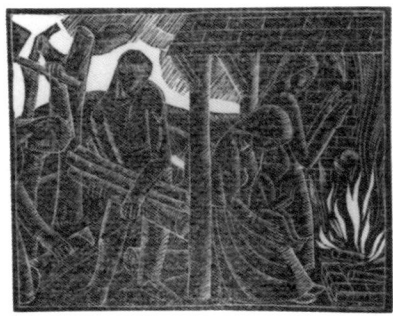

6. Family at the Hearth, 1922

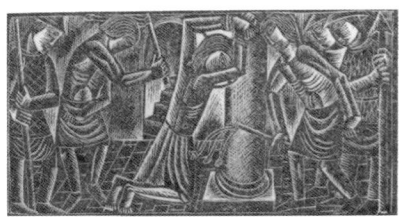

7. The Scourging at the Pillar, 1924

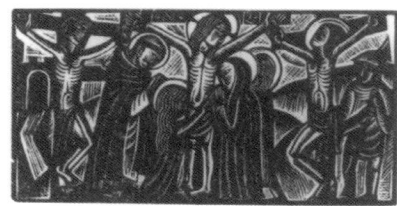

8. Crucifixion, 1924

While the Ditchling engravings could be looked on as mere apprenticeship there is a steady and rapid technical improvement in Jones's use of the medium which results in some powerful depiction. A decorative quality is evident in the small engraving, *Dominican Friar*, which was used frequently in the publications of St. Dominic's Press over the years. It is an intelligent, charming design and the figure, larger in relation to the total area than is often the case, takes on a personality and a sense of story which is not often found in Jones's figures. Hilary Pepler later wrote that at Ditchling Jones loved

> the wood and the feel of it; all his work has that fine quality of
> co-operation between artist and material. Eric Gill imposes his
> will on wood or stone alike, but David Jones discerns the nature
> of the substances he handles and brings their life into his own.[11]

Although, as Pepler later admitted, Jones's covers for *The Game* were 'handicapped by the idea of propaganda we imposed on him',[12] there was, nonetheless, a developing expertise evident in *Family at the Hearth* which appeared on the cover of the final issue published in January, 1923. The fascinating posture of the log carrier, contrived in a style reminiscent of William Roberts, expresses a timid appreciation of the splendours of the hearth although his job forces him to remain out in the rain. While progress is evident and while the tacit overtone of the religious allusion is welcome after the explicit nature of other *Game* covers, elements such as the insistently literal brickwork and roof tiles clutter the image.

A Child's Rosary Book, the first volume entirely made up of wood-engravings by David Jones, was printed at Ditchling in 1924. The images are a mixture of rhythmical sensitivity and a rather lumpen, uninspired mock-medievalism. The cover, printed on grey paper, featured two of the fifteen engravings which Jones produced for the publication: *The Visitation* and *The Finding in the Temple*. The poor relation of typography to image on this cover is typical of the haphazard manner of production at Ditchling. In *The Visitation*, Joseph, returning home with the tools of his trade slung over his back, finds the Angel Gabriel embracing Mary. There is evident cunning and a great degree of excitement in the splitting of the space, but somehow the drama in the room is eclipsed by the staggered pattern of the whites on the staircase at the left and by the particularly airy landscape on the right. In *The Finding in the Temple* we can observe Jones's interest in the tiny variations in repetition that can sophisticate the building of a design. Interest in the setting up and breaking of rhythms is likewise visible in *Christ Sending Forth His Disciples* (1924), not a part of the *Child's Rosary Book* but an image which appeared at the bottom of the *St. Dominic's Press Bench Books Broadsheet* (see p 48), where Judas breaks the movement between the despatching Christ and his emissaries by turning, sack of silver in hand and surrounded by a black nimbus, to confront the spectator.

The Scourging at the Pillar and *The Crucifixion* are among the most powerful images from *A Child's Rosary Book*, a work which appears to have been marked by a declining enthusiasm on the part of the engraver.[13] *The Scourging* gives an angular version on a much smaller scale and in another medium of *Jesus*

Mocked (see p 55). While soldiers are prominent here and in *The Crucifixion*, there is interest in the caring women who almost seem to crush Christ and in the angular path, first seen in the squared-up Westminster crucifixion drawing, which now terminates in an ominously dark doorway.

Jones's delight in repetition to build design and the playfulness of another 1924 project, *Libellus Lapidum*, probably inspired Harold Munro of The Poetry Bookshop to commission him to illustrate Eleanor Farjeon's *The Town Child's Alphabet*.[14] In engravings for the *Libellus Lapidum* such as *The Natural Law* and

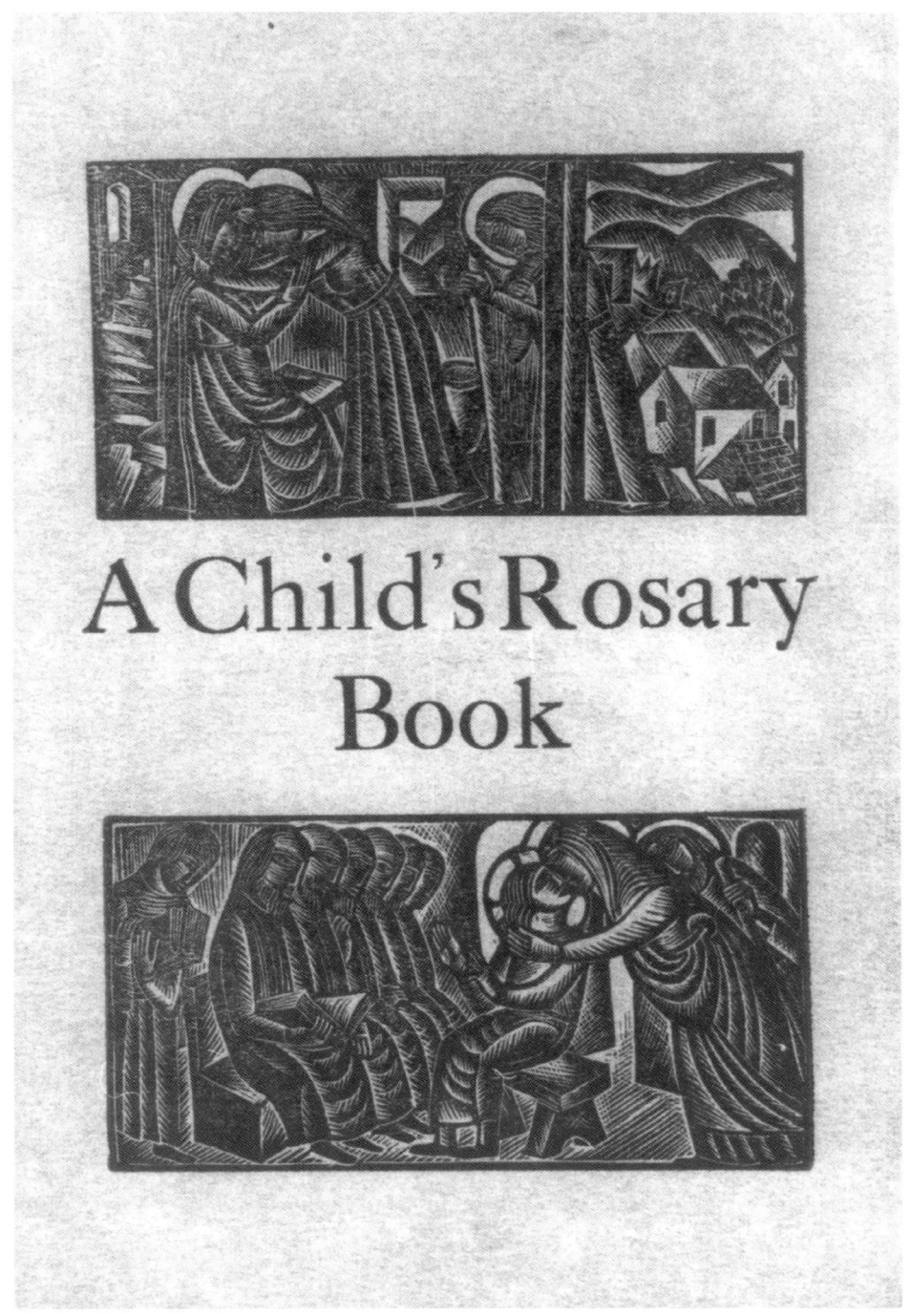

9. Child's Rosary Book, 1924

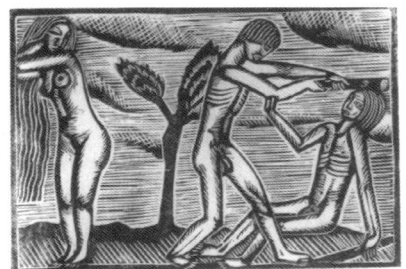

10. The Natural Law, 1924

David Jones and Hilary Pepler Mounted on Pegasus a certain exuberance which had been largely suppressed in the earnest religious work of the preceding years was allowed to emerge. Other images, produced in response to Hilary Pepler's impromptu verses, also permitted a reassertion of some modernist traits which again had been almost overshadowed by the mock-medievalism of the Ditchling religious aesthetic. Philip Hagreen, who was impressed by Jones's engravings from the outset, speaking of their 'speed and assurance',[15] felt that through his work on *Libellus Lapidum*, Jones acquired 'wood-engraving as a living language'.[16] The stylistic range between two images from that short booklet is enormous: the strongly striated, primitive *Natural Law* and the hard-edged decorative wit of writer and engraver who hold respectively outsized quill and burin and who are mounted on Pegasus stamping and snorting to create Hippocrene, the fountain on Mt. Helicon which became sacred to the Muses. From Philip Hagreen's account of how the book came about it is clear that by mid-1924 David Jones had achieved a great dexterity in the medium:

> Hilary thought to print some of the sly foolery that was peculiarly his own. Working at the press he would think of a rhyme. Then he would come into our shop, which was next door, and tell us. David without fail would produce an appropriate block, ending with the splendid big one for the cover.[17]

Jones had already begun to work on *The Town Child's Alphabet* when, on 13 August, after months of growing estrangement between Gill and Pepler, the Gills, the Brennans and the Hagreens left Ditchling for a new home at Capel-y-ffin. Jones returned to London to finish the drawings for the two colour line blocks, near enough to enjoy the company of his eighteen-year-old fiancée, Petra Gill, who stayed behind in Ditchling to learn weaving with Ethel Mairet.

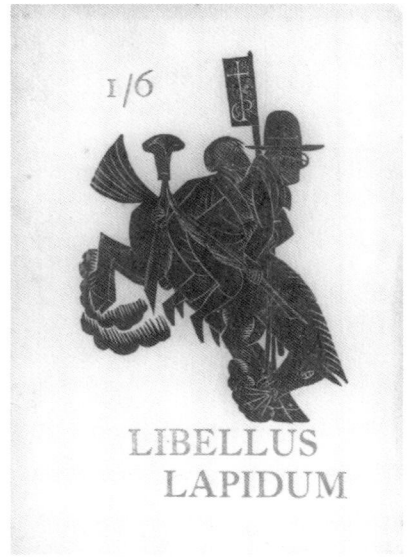

11. Libellus Lapidum, 1924

Most of the drawings for *The Town Child's Alphabet* are delightful; a very few, however, are disappointing and as the illustrations for X, Y and Z are less inspired than for the earlier letters, it seems that Jones once again ran out of steam towards the end of a series. As it was unlike him to be able to produce 26 drawings in the space of a few short months without much fuss, it was perhaps the levity of the project which released a sense of freedom in him. Again there is an admirable range, from the Penny-Plain, Tuppence-Coloured world of *J for Jazz-man* to the Léger-like rhythms of the well articulated curves in *D for Dustman*. Jones could bring to bear his knowledge of Cubism and concentrate on purely pictorial values without being much concerned about any message. Yet illustration was a realm in which he was too comfortable to be wholly comfortable; his childhood urge to become an illustrator had, after all, been supplanted by more ambitious aims. But, as 1924 marks the beginning of a turning point for Jones, not only in engraving but in painting, we should perhaps not underestimate the importance of the freedom of visual exploration opened up by these charming, witty and usually inventive designs. Certain liberties allowed by modern art were aptly destined for the eyes of children not yet blinded by lessons in conventional one-point perspective.

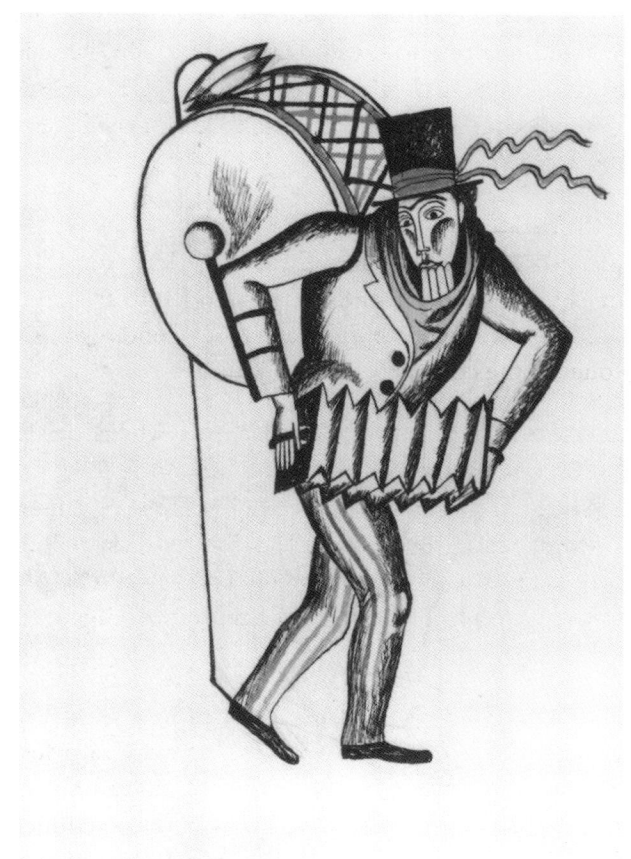

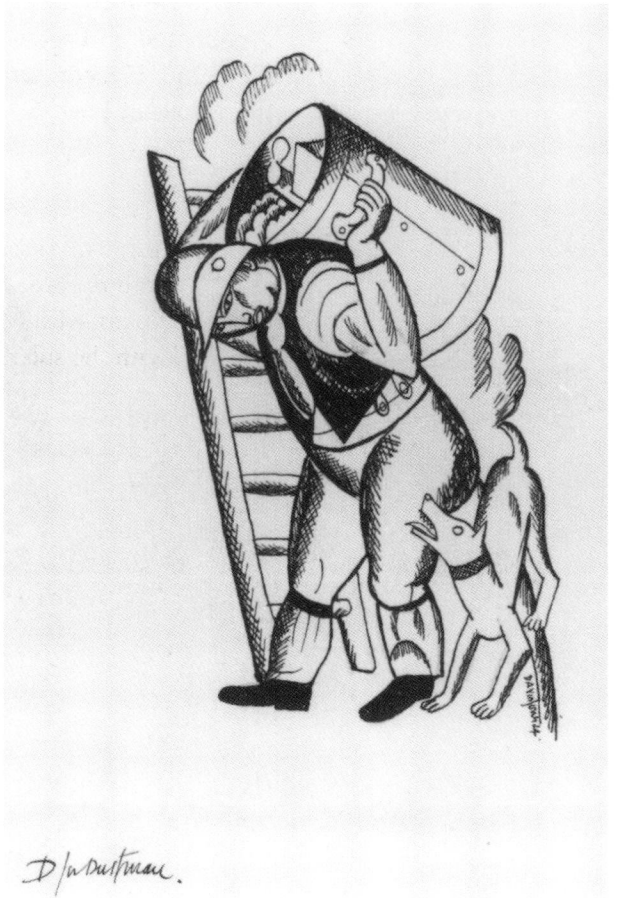

12. J for Jazz-man, 1924

13. D for Dustman, 1924

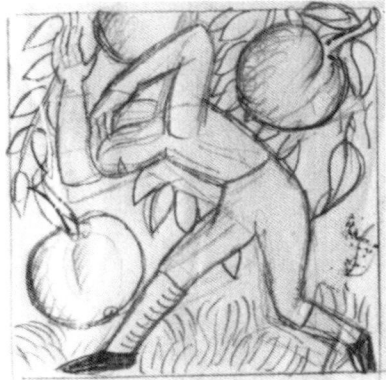

14. Gulliver is Knocked Down by the Apple, 1925

It was Philip Hagreen who, in 1920, had 'brought together the artists who were to found the *Society of Wood Engravers*'.[18] While Gill had had reservations about the dangers of snobbery and aestheticism in such a society, he was also quick to perceive the advantages of setting standards, facilitating labour exchange and creating a market through exhibitions.[19] The artists assembled by Hagreen at his studio in March 1920 to form what was initially to be called *The Bewick Society* included Lucien Pissarro who had been an exhibitor in that seminal 1898 exhibition, Robert Gibbings and Noel Rooke and these were joined by artists like Gill, John Nash, Gordon Craig and Gwendolen Raverat. Their first exhibition in November, 1920, drew a largely positive reception from the press and the following year Paul Nash and Ethelbert White joined the group. In 1925, the engravings of Gertrude Hermes and John Farleigh were added to the list of exhibitors at the Redfern Gallery as were those of David Jones who went on exhibiting with them until 1930, although he continued to be listed as a member until 1936.

Many of the most talented of these engravers were commissioned to provide blocks for books published by the Golden Cockerel Press; as Gill wrote in a letter of 1928, 'Book work is, and always has, and always will be the *raison d'être* of wood-engraving'.[20] The Press, whose name was inspired by *Le Coq D'Or* which its founder Harold Midgely Taylor had seen performed by the Russian Ballet, was created as a co-operative in the same year that *The Society of Wood Engravers* had been established. As the idea for a co-operative swiftly proved impracticable,[21] the Press turned to fine printing and when Taylor's health deteriorated it came under the direction of the engraver Robert Gibbings, who guided it to a position of prominence in which it was particularly renowned for the quality of its engravings. Gibbings claimed that a good deal of the engraving done for the press 'is experimental' and that the 'artists who design … are chosen on account of their work considered as Art'.[22]

Eric Gill produced several books with the Golden Cockerel Press, and became a close friend of Moira and Robert Gibbings. Indeed, they participated in many erotic adventures in the 1920s; Gill hardly visited them at Waltham St. Lawrence without some sexual experimentation occurring such as fondling or dancing nude with Moira, or being initiated into the pleasures of fellatio by Robert.[23] It was Gill, of course, who introduced Jones to Robert Gibbings. In visits to Waltham, while Jones did participate in concocting naughty limericks and drawings,[24] it is unlikely that he shared more generally in the sexually raucous atmosphere; whereas Gill notes in his Diary that on 30 November 1925, Robert and Moira 'fucked one another … M. holding me the while', on the following day, after Jones's arrival, Gill records a more sober activity, the discussion of 'books etc.'[25]

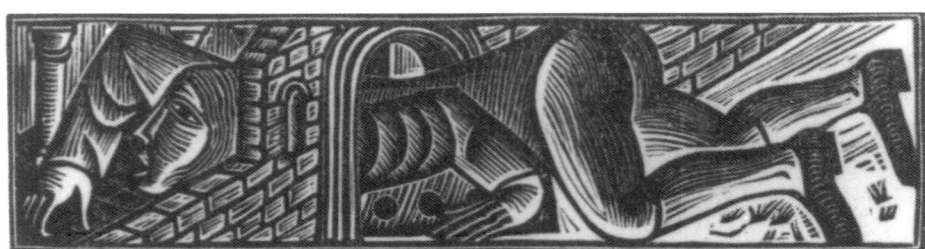

15. Gulliver Creeps through the Gate in Lilliput, 1925

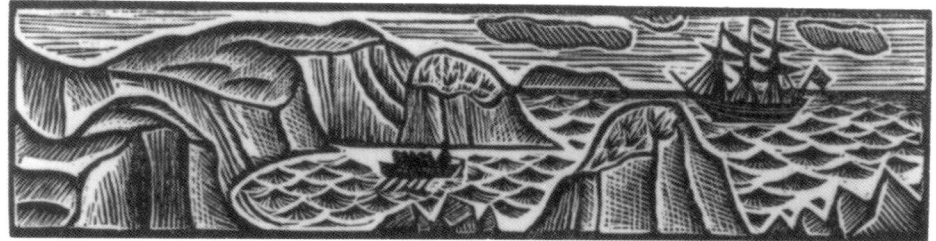

16. Ship and Long-Boat in Bay, 1925

Gibbings commissioned Jones to engrave thirty-seven illustrations and five maps for a two volume Quarto edition of *Gulliver's Travels*. While Jones found the book itself boring, there is an inventiveness and ingenuity in the often small engravings which he produced. The slightly crowded relation of image to text helps to draw attention to a recurrent theme in *Gulliver*, the question of size in relation to perception. Gulliver is seen cramped and gigantic, stretching to crawl through a minute gate in Lilliput, tiny and threatened when seized by a monkey, or when knocked down by apples in Brobdingnag. The project hung over Jones when he wanted to be painting watercolours on his first trip to Caldey Island, but because of 'the kindness of the Prior' he was at least able to 'use their Scriptorium'[26] in which to do his engraving, and the *Ship and Long-Boat in the Bay of Brobdingnag* has obviously been inspired by a Caldey bay.

Jones's first instructor in the medium, Desmond Chute, wrote to Gill praising *Gulliver*: 'His technical achievement amazes me, knowing him'.[27] Certainly some of the extreme situations in the book made Jones go to the very fore-front of artistic experimentation in order to produce telling images (see pp 145,147) so it is unjust for Douglas Cleverdon to dismiss the *Gulliver* engravings as being of no great importance.[28]

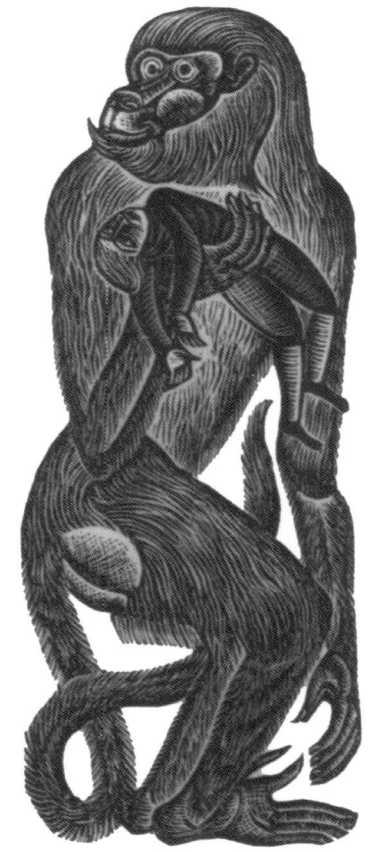

17. Gulliver is Seized by a Monkey, 1925

The printing was completed by 17 November 1925 and Jones must have begun work almost immediately on thirteen wood blocks for *The Book of Jonah*. While this involved a certain return to a Gillian manner of stylization - 'pure Eric' as Jones later commented[29] - he was nonetheless able to incorporate more daring elements such as the fragment of Nineveh which we see in the first image appearing like some Futurist metropolis. Indeed, this block is particularly interesting as it utilizes the two different wood-engraving techniques: the angel and Jonah, who is being touched by the word of God, are cut by the traditional black line technique, whereas the earth and the wicked city of Nineveh appear dark, engraved by the white line technique. The dramatic split caused by the use of two contrasting methods cleverly represents the two orders of heaven and earth.

The Times review of an exhibition of engravings at the St. George's Gallery in 1927 spoke of 'the harmonious relation between typography and illustration'[30] in Golden Cockerel books and that is certainly evident in the effective relation between the figures and the text on page 12 of *The Book of Jonah*. It was one of the fundamental premises of the Press that 'the size and shape of the type determines the space left for decoration, and not until the type has

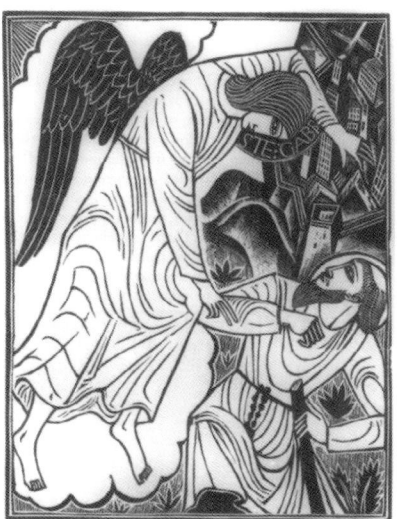

18. Archangel Gabriel Appears to Jonah, 1926

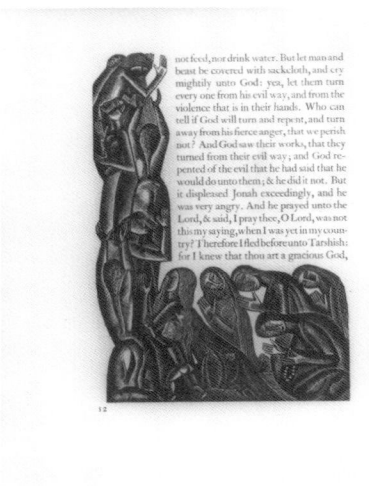

19. The Repentant People of Nineveh Praying, 1926

been set and the page proofed does the artist begin his work.'[31] While it is perhaps a little fanciful to suggest that this would always be possible when the artist working for the press was as slow as Jones could be, Gibbings maintained that 'Wood engravings for books are not ends in themselves, they are ornaments for the *Book*'.[32] Gill observed, in a letter to his sister, that 'engravings … don't merely illustrate the text, they also decorate the book'.[33] On page 12, Jones strikes the ideal balance between an engraving, important in its own right, and a successful border.

Whereas *Gulliver* had appeared in an edition of four hundred and eighty, some of which were hand-coloured by art students,[34] *Jonah* appeared in a much more limited edition of 175. The printing was completed by 11 June 1926 and prints of four of the engravings were offered for sale at £1.10.0 each in the Catalogue of *The Seventh Annual Exhibition of The Society of Wood Engravers* in November 1926.

There is skill in the decorative texturing of *The Whale Vomits Out Jonah*, a sense of drama in *Jonah Seized by the Sailors* which presages something of the shipboard dramas of *The Rime of The Ancient Mariner* and, much later, the watercolour and drawing, *Trystan ac Essylt*. Yet 'pure Eric' is not an unfair assessment inasmuch as Jones's work brings increased address in the medium to an aesthetic which, by the time the book was published in 1926, he had all but shed. In fact, Jones's vision was developing in a direction that was not altogether compatible with the medium of wood-engraving. Yet he was undertaking a good number of commissions such as the frontispiece and title page for the 1927 Gregynog Press edition of *The Book of Ecclesiastes* in Welsh, *Llyfr Y Pregeth-Wr*, (see detail on p 146). Technically Jones had made enormous progress. In early Ditchling days, both Gill and Pepler had attempted to make Jones more workmanlike; Philip Hagreen recalls that

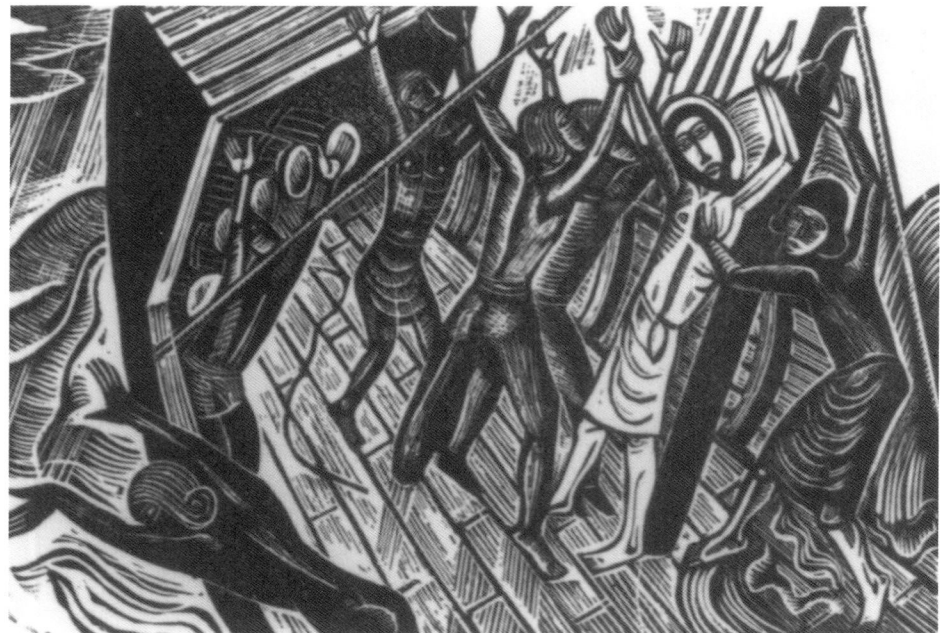

20. Jonah is Seized by the Sailors, 1926

70

When David had taken a trial proof he was apt to stuff it into a pocket. At some later time he would take it out and consider its qualities, noting how they were enhanced by the crumpling of the paper. Hilary caught him thus chewing the cud and said: 'A proof is to let you get on with the block, knowing what needs doing. It is not to be lifted up, carried about or adored.'[35]

Jones's ability for intricate organization is revealed in *The Artist* which he engraved as a frontispiece to Gill's pamphlet *Christianity and Art*, published at Capel by Gill's friend and neighbour, Donald Attwater. There is a fluid and graceful articulation of forms that is the hallmark of Jones's mature engraving. The figure of the artist which, Hills suggests, is 'modelled on evangelist portraits from Early Christian and Romanesque manuscripts such as the *Lindisfarne Gospels*'[36] is foregrounded by the ambiguous space he inhabits. Discarding perspectival notions enables Jones to re-order, an activity intrinsic to the artist.

The subject matter of Gill's essay is the enslavement of the maker by industrialism, and the pamphlet also considers the relation of the Church to artefacture, crediting the institution with 'maintaining the ideas and the attitude of mind in which alone any great art is possible'.[37] Again, however, it appears to be the polemical aspect of a composition which weakens Jones's visual expression; like the nimbuses in the religious paintings of the period, the area above the roof of the artist with its guiding hand of God is the weakest part; blocked out, the rest becomes tighter and the spots on the wonderfully feline leopard resonate more powerfully with the dotted ceiling of the artist's shelter. While *Christianity and Art* also contrasted modern individualism with medieval anonymity, there is, in the frontispiece, a discreet assertion of individuality as the artist appears to be making a design which resembles the plan of the Ark that Noah receives from God in the second of the *Chester Play of the Deluge* engravings, a sequence on which Jones was concurrently at work.

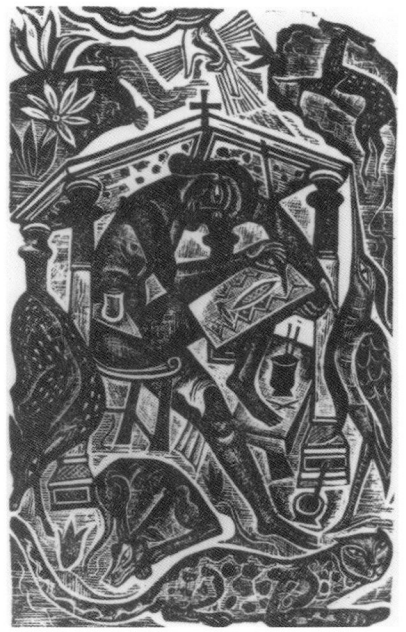

21. The Artist, 1927

Decades later, in a letter to a young friend who was in the process of teaching himself the art, Jones wrote:

> in wood-engravings in general the most satisfactory kind are those where the blacks and the whites and the greys are so 'organised' or managed as to give ... unity. In *one* way old Bewick has never been surpassed in knowing how to get the best advantage out of the greys and whites very subtly set off against *very* small areas of solid black.[38]

To the engraver, Reynolds Stone, he wrote, 'Bewick could do miracles with greys - and no one has done it so well since'.[39] Happily, in many of the ten engravings for the Golden Cockerel Press edition of *The Chester Book of the Deluge* Jones achieved a unity of blacks and whites and greys.

The Flood is powerfully dramatic with its diagonal deluge, its animals thrown into desperate poses, that tellingly isolated open mouth near the bottom

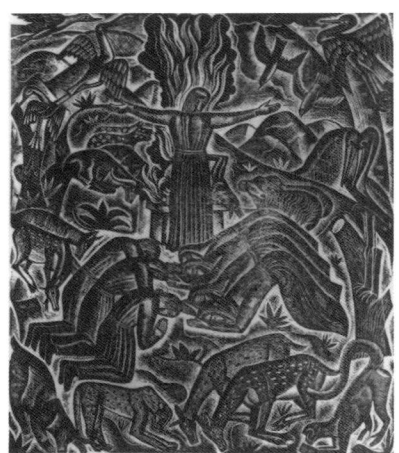

22. Noah offers a Sacrifice, 1927

right-hand corner, crying for help and evoking the peril of ingesting water and drowning. The central group, impossibly balanced in the fork of a tree, recall the misplaced hope of the figures in Géricault's *Raft of the Medusa* and, at the same time, appear like a propitiation offered up to God. The Ark, serene in the background, acts as a sign of God's presence without the engraver resorting to a tired religious symbol.

Noah Offers a Sacrifice reveals the importance of the illumination streaming through these woodcuts. The wit, softened only by those oversweet and docile eyes of deer, is evident here as it is in the *Animals Approaching the Ark* (see p 87). Throughout the series the characterization of the animals is adept and Jones wrote, much later in life, that the 'only drawings of animals that I can recall making for the purpose of using later in another medium are some I made in 1925-26, in the London and also Bristol Zoo, when I was about to make a series of wood-engravings as illustrations to *The Chester Play of the Deluge*'.[40]

The paper used by the Golden Cockerel Press, made specially by Joseph Batchelor & Son, was a pure rag paper which 'by reason of its hardness must be dampened before use';[41] in the case of *The Chester Play of the Deluge*, in order to meet a publication deadline, such dampening was omitted and the blocks printed on dry paper.[42] So Jones, who had been paid £100 for the project and who was justifiably pleased with his engravings, writing to Douglas Cleverdon about his 'sumptuous work' and believing that 'it will really look good - if I may be allowed to say so',[43] was, inevitably, disappointed by the result.

Aesthetically, the results are again uneven. The best engravings are tight but graceful, intricate but not overloaded, vibrating with movement. However, the depiction of water, which during that period was troubling Jones in the medium of watercolour, was even more difficult to realize in wood-engraving, and waves curling in *The Drowning of the Wicked* appear like something between the frills of a petticoat and creeping algae. The treatment of the foreground water in *The Flood* results in a distinctly neo-Romantic effect with its heavy, bio-morphic shapes. Although a Gillian mock-medievalism persists throughout, for the most part the images are supple, intricate and intelligently organized when compared with those of Gill; religious iconography such as the wounded Ram of the first engraving is, for the most part, blissfully absent.

Douglas Cleverdon was brought to visit Capel-y-ffin in the summer of 1926 by Desmond Chute and during his stay, in lengthy talks with Gill, it was decided that the young bookseller should take over the distribution of Gill's pamphlet *Id Quod Visum Placet*. In October, when Gill was staying in Bristol lettering the signboard for Cleverdon's shop, he came down with the flu and spent several days idly sketching out letter designs, which were later seen by Stanley Morison of the Lanston Monotype Corporation, a powerful force in the typographical renaissance of the 1920s. For Gill these events led to his designing some important type faces including *Gill Sans* and *Perpetua*; for David Jones the connection was also important. Cleverdon was impressed by

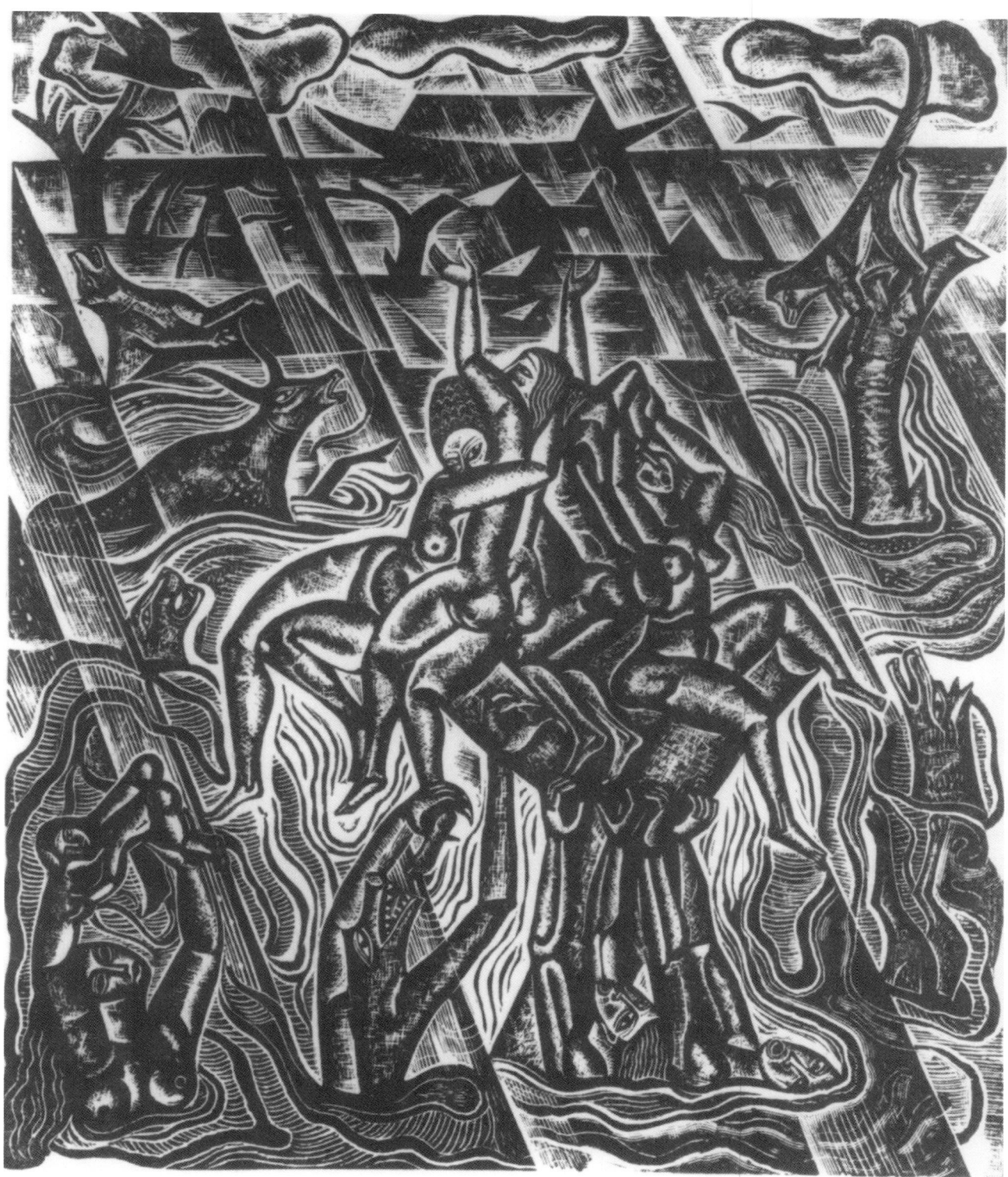

23. The Flood, 1927

Jones's first attempts at copper engraving (limited editions of *Ponies on a Welsh Hill Slope, Reclining Cat, Puma* and *The Crucifixion*), and he considered embarking on a publishing project: 'greatly daring, I asked David to engrave on copper eight illustrations with headpiece and tailpiece, for Coleridge's *The Rime of the Ancient Mariner*.'[44] Jones was still working on the *Deluge* when talk of the project started and he wrote from Brockley in June, 1927, expressing his enthusiasm and suggesting a fee of £5 per engraving.[45] He was already very busy and, in a year which had begun badly with a broken engagement, he sounded as if he was thrilled to be in such demand; from Brockley in August, Jones wrote:

> I will do specimen as soon as poss - Morison wants a specimen plate at the same time for *Aesop* and Donald [Attwater] also. All clamouring for things within the next three weeks.[46]

Jones also spent a week that month in Bristol staying with Cleverdon, doubtless discussing the project, and making a watercolour each morning from the studio window above the bookshop. By 1927, while his chief source of meagre income was still engraving, he was working very hard at painting and an exhibition of watercolours earlier in the year at the St. George's Gallery, which he shared with Gill, had been particularly successful for Jones.

The 'specimen plate' to which Jones referred in that letter quoted above related to a commission from Stanley Morison to do a series of seven copper engravings to embellish *Seven Fables of Aesop*, a specimen book of *New Hellenic Greek* type designed by Victor Scholderer of the Monotype Corporation. A comparison between the drawings and engravings for *The Lion and the Farmer* reveal not only how subtleties of design changed when Jones began to engrave but, more importantly, how the fluidity of his pencil line persisted in the engraving; the copperplate is a sure development with an increased sense of space and a greater finesse in the treatment of the animal. The fable concerns a lion who falls so hopelessly in love with a farmer's daughter that in order to have access to her he agrees to have his claws cut and his teeth pulled, only to be cudgelled out of the house by the angry father who has rendered him defenceless.

Being busy with *Aesop* and other activities and having the chance to go to the south of France with the Gills in April, 1928, it was some time before Jones was able to make a start on more than 150 preliminary drawings for *The Rime of the Ancient Mariner*. In any case, the artist was worried by his inexperience with copper engraving and suggested that wood-engraving might prove appropriate. Cleverdon, however, had copper in mind, and so Jones, considering his lack of experience, decided that 'nothing elaborate should be attempted'[47] and found, furthermore, 'a deceptive surface ease and facility and a simplicity of artistry'[48] in the poem which he had 'enjoyed from childhood'.[49]

Jones stayed on in the south of France in order to visit the Hagreens who were living just outside Lourdes. During this brief period, Gill wrote to Jones: 'Don't stay out there much longer "England hath need of thee"'. He mentions particularly the predicament in which Cleverdon found himself over

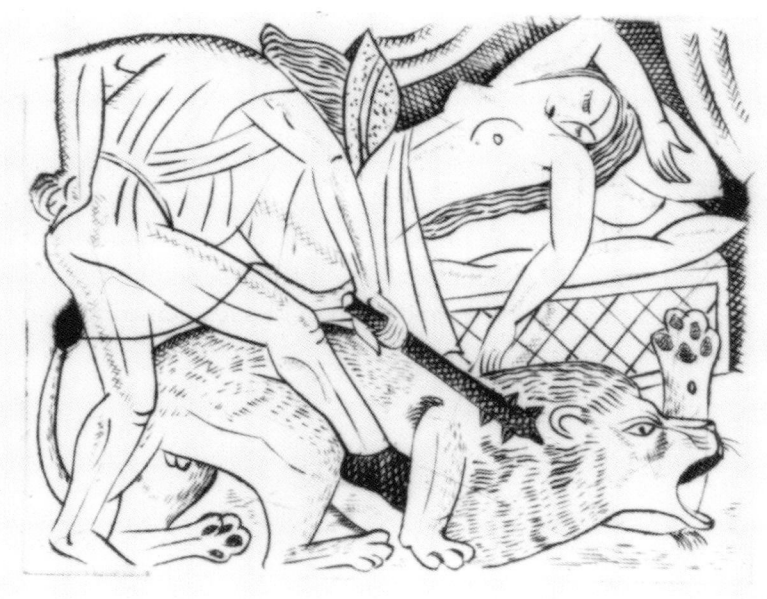

1. Λέων καὶ Γεωργός.

Λέων ἐρασθεὶς θυγατρός τινος γεωργοῦ ταύτην ἐμνηστεύσατο· ὁ δὲ μὴ ἐκδοῦναι θηρίῳ τὴν θυγατέρα ὑπομένων, μηδὲ ἀρνεῖσθαι διὰ τὸν φόβον δυνάμενος, τοιοῦτόν τι ἐπενόησεν. Ἐπειδὴ συνεχῶς ὁ λέων αὐτῷ ἐπέκειτο, ἔλεγεν, ὡς νυμφίον αὐτὸν τῆς θυγατρὸς δοκιμάζει· μὴ ἄλλως δὲ αὐτῷ δύνασθαι ἐκδοῦναι, ἐὰν μὴ τοὺς ὀδόντας ἐξέληται καὶ τοὺς ὄνυχας ἐκτέμῃ· τούτους γὰρ δεδοικέναι τὴν κόρην ἔφη. Τοῦ δὲ ῥᾳδίως διὰ τὸν ἔρωτα ἑκάτερον ὑπομείναντος, ὁ γεωργὸς καταφρονήσας αὐτοῦ, ὡς παρεγένετο πρὸς αὐτόν, ῥοπάλοις παίων αὐτὸν ἐξήλασεν.

24. The Lion and the Farmer, 1928

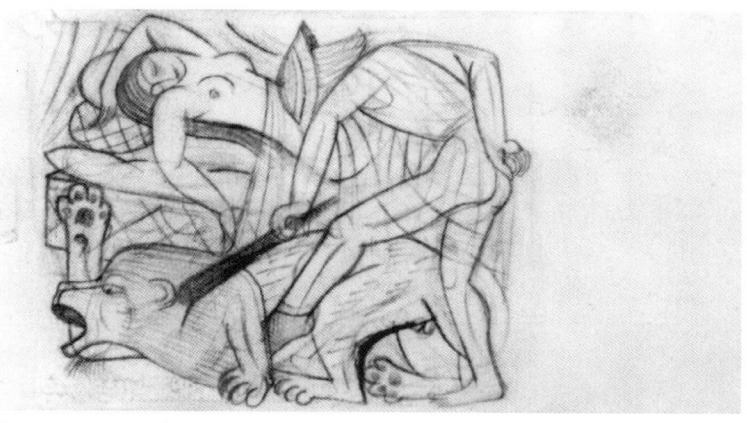

25. The Lion and the Farmer – preparatory drawing, 1928

the engraving project: he had 'borrowed money from his father to enable him to publish *The Ancient Mariner* … he professes not to be anxious to hurry you on, yet he's really pretty anxious about it and not very happy in his mind because of his father'.[50] Only a week later Jones was writing to Cleverdon from Brockley: '*I have returned*. - don't abuse me too violently for staying away so long. I forthwith proceed with Mariner. I was working violently in France trying to get watercolours done for a show I hope to have in the autumn - how to keep pace with things I do not know.'[51] Yet Jones was about to embark on an activity that would prove to be more demanding than he could ever have imagined, a writing that would become, after four years of furious activity, *In Parenthesis*.

For *The Mariner*, Jones decided

> that simple incised lines reinforced here and there and as sparingly as possible by cross-hatched areas … was the only way open to me. I decided also that these essentially linear designs should have an undertone over the whole area of the plate, partly as an aid to unification. This is easily and naturally achieved in copper-printing by not wiping the plate totally clean of ink before putting it in the press … the designs … fall to pieces … without it.[52]

Jones 'designed and redesigned, eliminated and eliminated' until he got 'the kind of drawing sufficiently simple … to tackle on copper'.[53] Despite the lengthy process, in the best of the engravings all the vigour of the preliminary drawings is kept in the final image. The arbitrary hatching that runs like stress lines through a composition such as *The Mariners* reinforces the disturbing sense achieved by the dramatic angles of mast and rigging. The figures are here, as elsewhere in the series, disappointing, but it is clear that Jones was far more interested in the technical nautical questions posed by the project. A tendency which, decades later, could predominate and deteriorate into a kind of numbing pedanticism was already at work; Jones wrote to Douglas Cleverdon from Brockley in August:

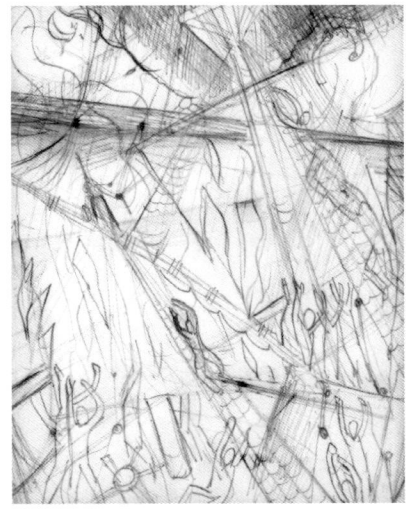

26. The Mariners – preparatory drawing, 1928

> N.B. Do you happen to have a book or know of a book dealing with sailing vessels and rigging, management of sails - anything with diagrams - or pictures of details of ships … - It is not that one cares about 'correctness' at all but one does need to know *how things work* or what is typical, especially in detail … I'm so utterly at sea with the principles of seafaring things! … and there is a plate I'm doing which I think will require - or would be fuller in content if I could get, a bit more information especially about the heaving up of sails and the possibilities of a ship's deck when men get busy hauling ropes.[54]

There is also a sketch of a 'museum model' of a sailing ship dated 'DJ c.'28' which, given Jones's dating, most probably relates to work on this project.[55] Perhaps such preoccupation with nautical exactitude accounted for the fact that Michael Ayrton, reviewing a 1944 exhibition in which *The Mariner* engravings

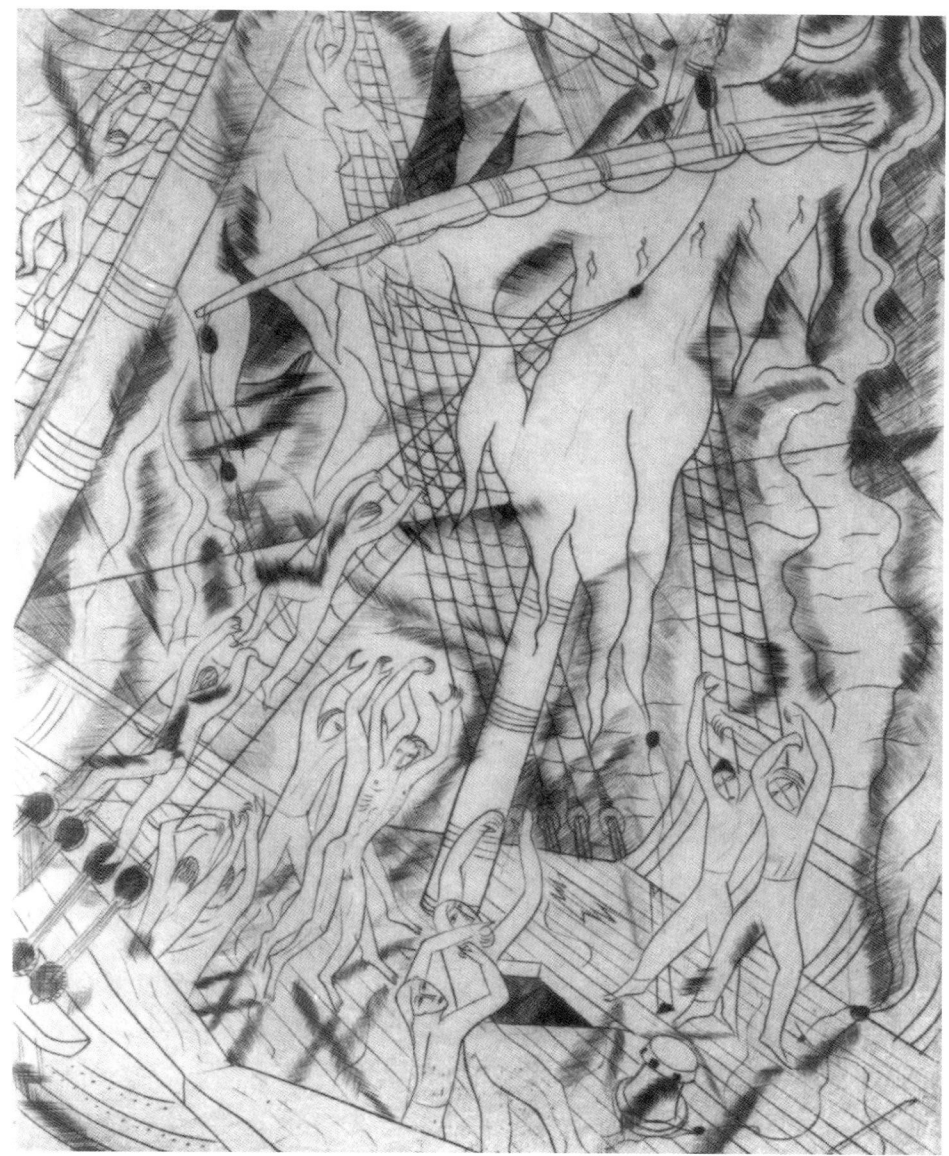

27. The Mariners, 1928

were on display, found that they possessed 'the refinement and subtlety always associated with the work of David Jones' and yet that they seemed 'to lack the sinister force demanded by the poem'.[56] Or one might say that the truly powerful images, *The Albatross* (see p 88) and *The Mariners*, are those in which the structure of a ship is used to most dramatic effect: horizons, decks and masts that tilt, result in a loss of vertical orientation and give energy and movement, qualities which the artist always sought. Jones also managed to get away completely from the mixture of the bogus medieval and the watered-down pre-Raphaelitism of the pen drawings which had been done by his Camberwell teacher, Reginald Savage, to illustrate *The Ancient Mariner*;[57] it was that kind of 'historical' quality which made him anxious when Cleverdon suggested that he might like to engrave an edition of Malory's *Morte d'Arthur*:

> I hate to feel not equal to a decent task - but there it is! It re-
> quires almost a 'life work' for a modern person to extract what is

77

'essential' and external from the *Morte d'Arthur* & free it from Chain-mail - sword - knight - lady - pennon - castle - serf - romance - gothic - Cloth of Gold - Chess-board business.[58]

Upset that Beardsley had tackled the *Morte d'Arthur* as it 'was not a world he understood',[59] and while, on the other hand, he was deeply attracted by the Arthurian project and, as becomes clear from his late watercolours, was unable to let go of certain aspects of the cycle, Jones nonetheless, for reasons of health and deteriorating eyesight, declined the offer. After his work on *The Mariner*, Jones produced less than a dozen engravings, odd commissions for covers, frontispieces and Christmas cards for friends. But weakened eyesight appears to have been somewhat of a pretence; although his eyes became periodically 'worse', a condition which prompted him to consult his family doctor who became 'pessimistic' and said that he 'should not engrave',[60] when he consulted an eye specialist just over a year later, the opinion was that there was 'nothing fundamentally wrong' with his sight.[61] More telling than health, for that had by 1929 become a habitual excuse, was the statement that he didn't see 'how one can keep any "live" ideas on the same theme for three years - anyway in my present *very* experimental state.'[62] And it was a particularly exciting time for Jones, consolidating his reputation as a watercolour painter with a joint exhibition with Gill at the Goupil Gallery, participating in his first exhibition with the 7&5 Society, making his first visit to the home of his collector and eventual patron, Helen Sutherland, at Rock in Northumberland. He was also hard at work on the writing of what was to become *In Parenthesis*; his friend Harman Grisewood remembers walks along the beach near Portslade, where Jones's parents rented a house and where the artist went to paint, when the two friends discussed the burgeoning project. After the retreat at Ditchling and periods of calm at Capel and on Caldey, the pace of life was intensifying; Jones was concentrating on watercolour and on writing, and the short engraving career of the man who H.S. Ede later called 'the best engraver'[63] in Britain, was by 1929, to all intents and purposes, over. The intrinsic tendency towards neo-Romanticism that characterizes a good deal of twentieth century British wood-engraving, a tendency reflecting its direct lineage from Blake and Calvert, would find an outlet in the historical and religious works which Jones started around 1938, just after his association with engraving ended where it began, when he made a drawing from which Eric Gill would engrave an image. Jones wrote to Gill from Sidmouth in May, 1938:

> No don't tell people I did the design - anyway I'm sure when you've engraved it it will become as though you had designed it, don't you think? I tried to avoid any of my idiosyncrasies. It is in a kind of scheme I learnt so largely from yourself.[64]

SMALL CARVINGS

Somewhat surprisingly recalling a Japanese *netsuke*, *The Bear* appears to have been the earliest of Jones's small carvings that he fashioned from used or abandoned boxwood or pearwood engraving blocks.[1] The sober, restrained, yet sensual stylization and the minimal markings are qualities that could suggest a non-European tradition although the carving has an affinity with work by Gaudier-Brzeska. Jones has tried to maximize the block and the semi-relief gives us the sense of the original, uncarved wood. The high polish and simple curves suggest a more exotic medium and the status of a treasured artefact. There is tension; the bear, while possessing a tight, introspective quality, is also segmented by the incisive lines of its haunches which cut the body into three parts and by the unification of the front legs and paws, resulting in the sectionalizing of the head. *The Bear* was made in 1922, the year in which Eric Gill was engaged in much boxwood carving and, according to Douglas Cleverdon, it was fashioned from the 1921 block which Jones engraved of a bear.[2] Certainly, the respective dimensions suggest that this is so, but, interestingly, the economical rhythm of the wood engraving, so expressive of the creaturely, is at a far remove from the mysterious self-consciousness expressed by the hieratic little carving.

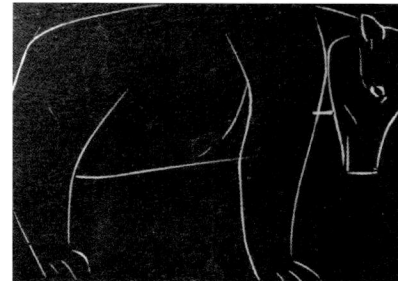

1. The Bear, 1921

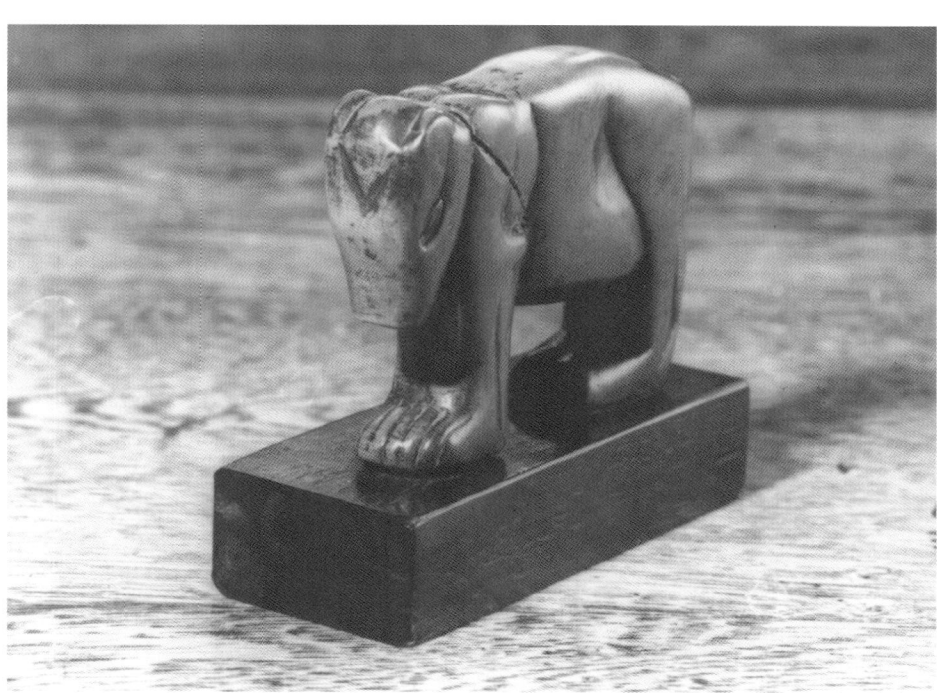

2. The Bear, 1922

79

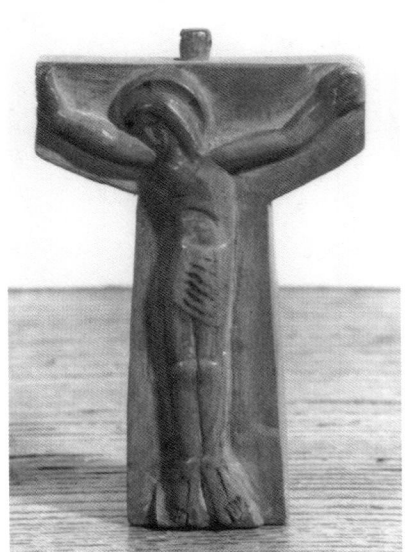

3. Crucifix Pendant, 1923 (?)

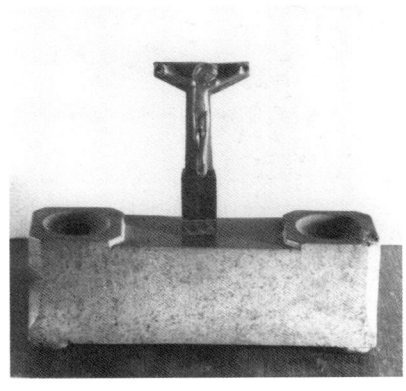

4 David Jones and Eric Gill,
Crucifix on Gill's Base, 1926 (?)

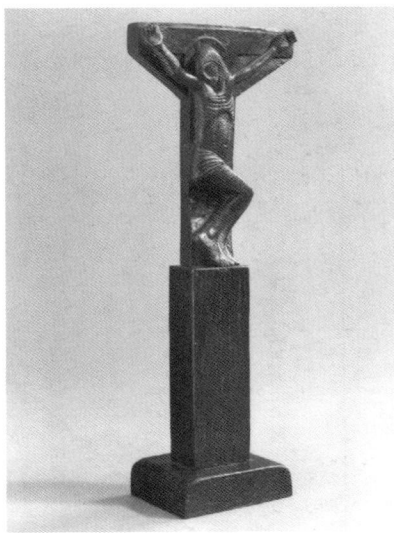

5. The Crucifixion, (?)

The smoothness of *The Bear* carving resembles the polished finish of the door latches which Jones produced under the guidance of George Maxwell. More deliberately crude is the powerfully primitive *Crucifix Pendant* with its swollen right arm pillowing the head of the crucified Christ. The poignant, rough economy of the off-centre body gives a sense of scale that belies the fact that the pendant is only eight centimetres high. Felicitous generalization turns the halo, often intrusively dominant in the works on paper made during this period, into an expressive element of the overall design, echoing hair and rib-cage, and mirroring the top of the loincloth.

Despite the insensitive scale of Gill's stone plinth and the inappropriate decorative flower incised on the overlarge wooden base, another small *Christ* has, again, a size as well as a finesse which would have been effective if it had been cast. Hanging on a wing-like cross it seems as if Christ is indeed capable of embracing all the sins of the world and the size of the supports, in some ways, only emphasizes the greatness of such a task.

The worn and beaten look of a crucifixion and communion group gives it a sense of age that is commensurate with its style. A relief rather than a sculpture, it was carved from two joined pieces of boxwood which in no way seems to have inhibited its sensual fluidity. R.L. Charles suggests that it is indebted to Carolingian art[3] but there is a rhythmic insistence that derives from Celtic examples, not so much through stylistic resemblance but through an understanding of the capacity of flowing rhythms to induce a kind of reverie or hypnosis. A sort of slow dance takes place about the God from whom blessings, quite literally, flow. While the halo and hair of Christ again direct the eye down into this supple world of redemption and blessing, the up-angled, straight arms lift the eye towards a proclamation of the brutal fact of the crucifixion. Charles interprets the figures on either side of Christ as representing the *Old Testament* (carrying the scroll of the law) and the *New Testament* (the chalice catching the blood of Christ)[4] but the figure on the left also seems to be in the act of censing Christ so that we have a condensed image of act and re-enactment; we see the crucifixion and also the ritualized re-presentation when the blood is in the cup and the censed altar locates the presence of the Holy Spirit. The associated elements of the sacrament of the Mass as Jones understood them from his reading of Maurice de la Taille are thus embodied in this small work; Christ 'placed himself in the order of signs'[5] by pledging his body at the Last Supper and making a commemorative act of his death before being broken by the executioners. In his poem of 1952, *The Anathemata*, which starts with the Mass, dissolves into its institution at the Last Supper, and ends with the Mass merging with the crucifixion, Jones wrote that on Maundy Thursday, 'Already they have put wood into his bread'.[6] The actual offering or crucifixion is physically made one with the anterior ritual offering of bread-breaking. Perhaps Jones's interest in that image which he took from *Tenebrae* on Maundy Thursday was quickened by the Post-Impressionist idea of 'under the form of'; here wood is carved becoming wine.

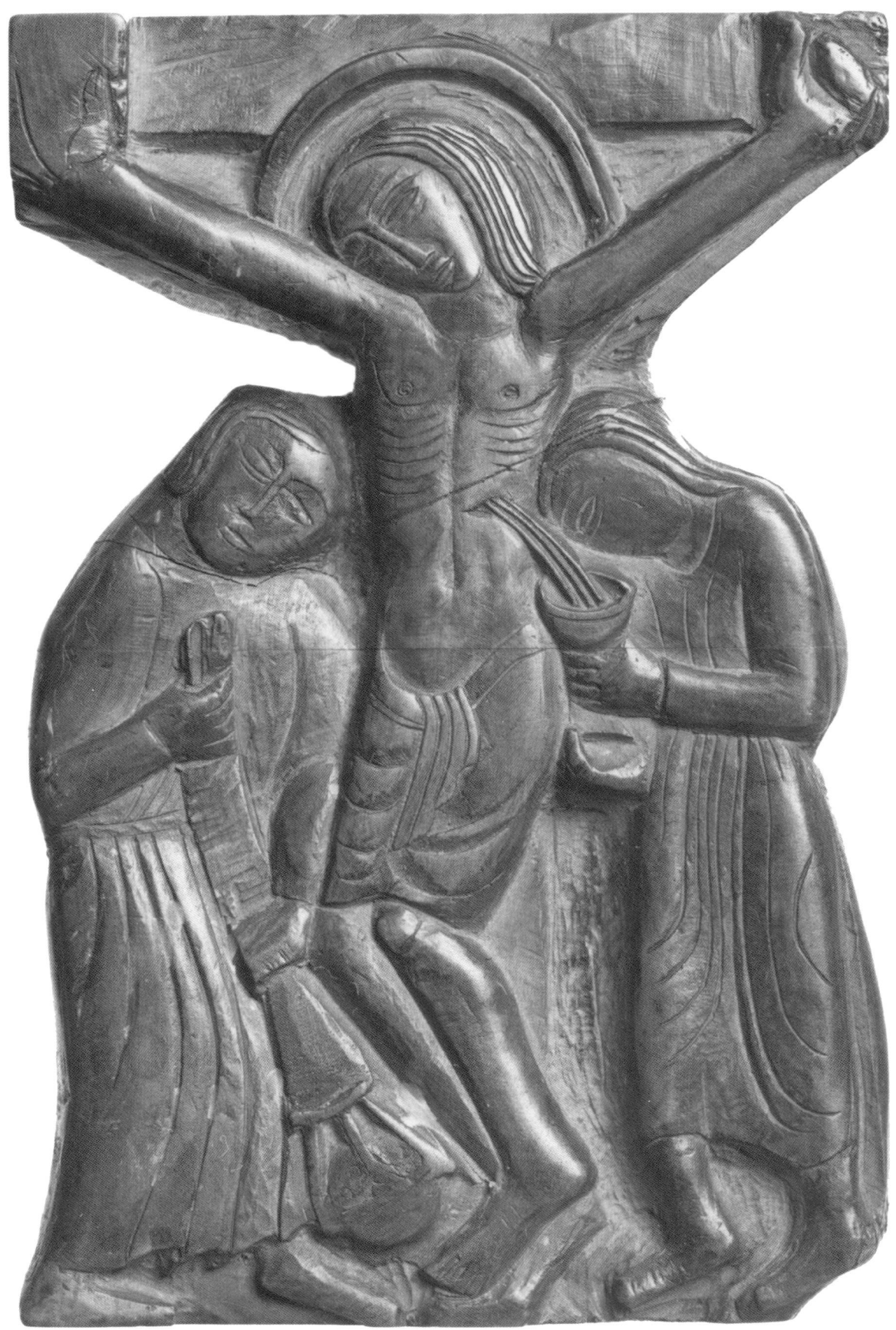

6. Crucifixion, 1925 (?)

In a passage in the poem, *The Fatigue* (1965), based on his understanding of these relationships, Jones wrote:

> (where the stripped *mensa*
> is set up
> where the long *lancea*
> obliquely thrust
> must drain the Cup
> for here
> is *immolatio oblata*.)[7]

In a footnote to what he took to be a difficult 'hinge-passage' in the poem, Jones identifies the cross as 'altar': 'the term *immolatio oblata* is used to describe the actual bodily immolation on the unlit Altar of the Cross of what had already been oblated at the lighted and festal board in the Supper-Room'.[8] De la Taille's insistence on the importance of Christ's gratuitous yet efficacious ritual in which he pledged his body as a sacrifice, set up for Jones a lifelong preoccupation with the fundamental importance of the making of a work of re-presentation, the making, in fact, of a work of art. Elsewhere Jones wrote, somewhat romantically, that it was de la Taille's 'French understanding of an artistic wholeness' that 'made his theological propositions so coherent'.[9] By contrast, it was the clergy's incomprehension of that venerable work of art, the Mass in Latin, which caused Jones so much anguish towards the end of his life. It was the significant form rather than the content or development of the religion which seemed to preoccupy the artist.

Unequivocally religious in intention is the *Mary and Christchild* which is starkly incised as if in stone rather than carved in wood. Indeed, the techniques of engraver and sculptor are often, in Jones's case, close to one another with the block being considered frontally and left virtually intact rather than being chiselled away from all sides in the manner of true sculpture. Any iconic detachment is discarded in a secular treatment of the theme of *Mother and*

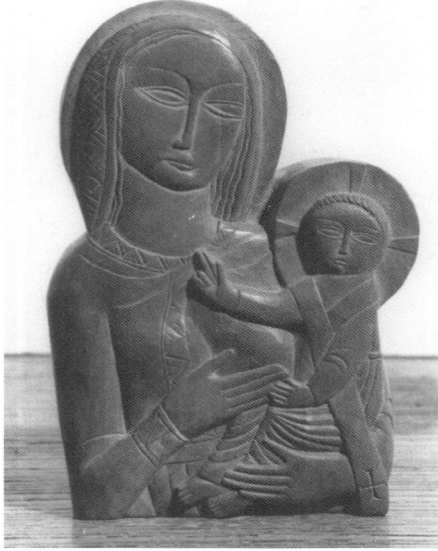

7. Madonna and Child, 1924 (?)

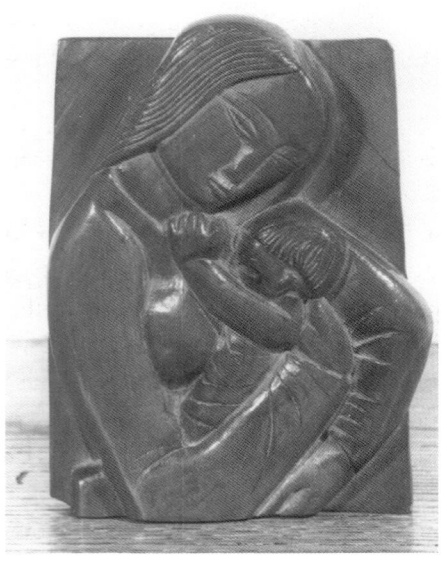

8. Mother and Child, 1924 (?)

Child. The gentle seesaw cradling of the mother's action is asserted by her left elbow breaking from the block. Yet maternal intention and the baby's need so simply and evocatively suggested do not disguise the sense of the male child being overwhelmed by the mother. The somewhat smothered baby would seem to be almost struggling against the mother's need, and perhaps some of the appeal of the Christian scheme for Jones is the distance which Christ is able to put between himself and his mother. Jones's own rather 'pushy'[11] mother had an inclination not to let go of her son, a need perhaps exacerbated by the death, in 1910, of Jones's older brother, Harold.

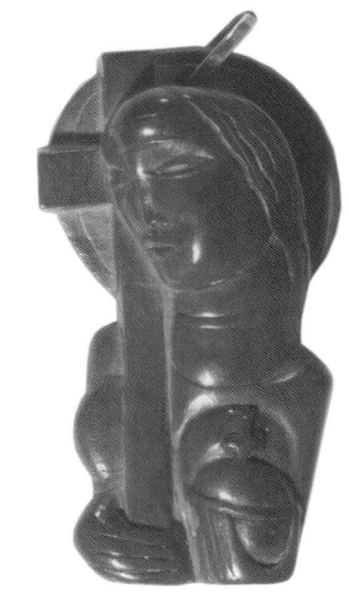

9. Sancta Helena O.P.N, 1926 (?)

Petra Helen Gill was mythologized by Jones in his treatment of Mary in an early engraving, *Nativity With Ox and Ass* (see p 63). Here, she is associated with the accoutrements of St Helena, the mother of Constantine the Great and the alleged discoverer of the wood of the Cross.[10] The fact that such an identification was made in this pendant carving, almost certainly executed during their engagement, suggests a love token of a rather impersonal nature. Yet despite the distancing sanctification of the love object, there is a gentle accumulation of round sensuous forms which rise from orb, breasts, cylindrical neck and a brow made more prominent by the flattening of the back of the head which is in turn thrown into powerful relief by the halo. The sensuality of the figure is in some sense diminished by the *crux nuda* which has been cut in severe relief; less pronounced it could have added an element of mystery to the figure's sensual reverie.

An oddity among these private carvings[12] is *Torso*, a work that marks both Jones's affinity with, and distance from, the boxwood sculptures of Gill. Jones is more preoccupied with sensually formalizing and less with either facile stylization or an unmitigated obsession with the sexuality of the female. Only the fussy detail of the hair at the back weakens the intelligent organizing of forms and accents. Atypical not only because of the subject matter but also because its medium is sycamore, this 'round, deliciously round and most worshipful'[13] carving is unusually three-dimensional. Later, friends observed how Jones would use his hands, slicing the air with frustration or describing sensual contours as he spoke; many of his carvings are of a size to be held in the hand, caressed by a man who had a severely inhibited but naturally tactile nature.

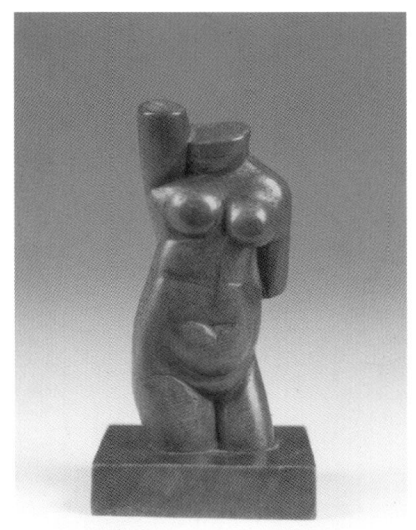

10. Torso, 1925 (?)

The standing *St. Dominic (11)*, at seventy-three centimetres high was obviously not fashioned from an abandoned or used wood-engraving block. If *The Bear* had something of the *netsuke* then this figure has something of Celtic or Innuit carving. The lily branch for the faithful[14] and the Bible are merely suggested and the body so slightly carved that it has an almost entombed quality and yet the head, more fully stated, stares hypnotically, commanding the attention of a totem. Such a rôle is suggested by the fact that Jones placed flowers before this object and pierced its base with a candle-holder in his room in Harrow much later in life. Indeed, the status of most of Jones's small carvings is that of votive object and that is one reason that he conceives them frontally rather than in the round in the manner of Renaissance sculpture; they provide evidence of how seriously Jones was taking his new religion and, with St. Dominic as his patron, his status as a Tertiary.

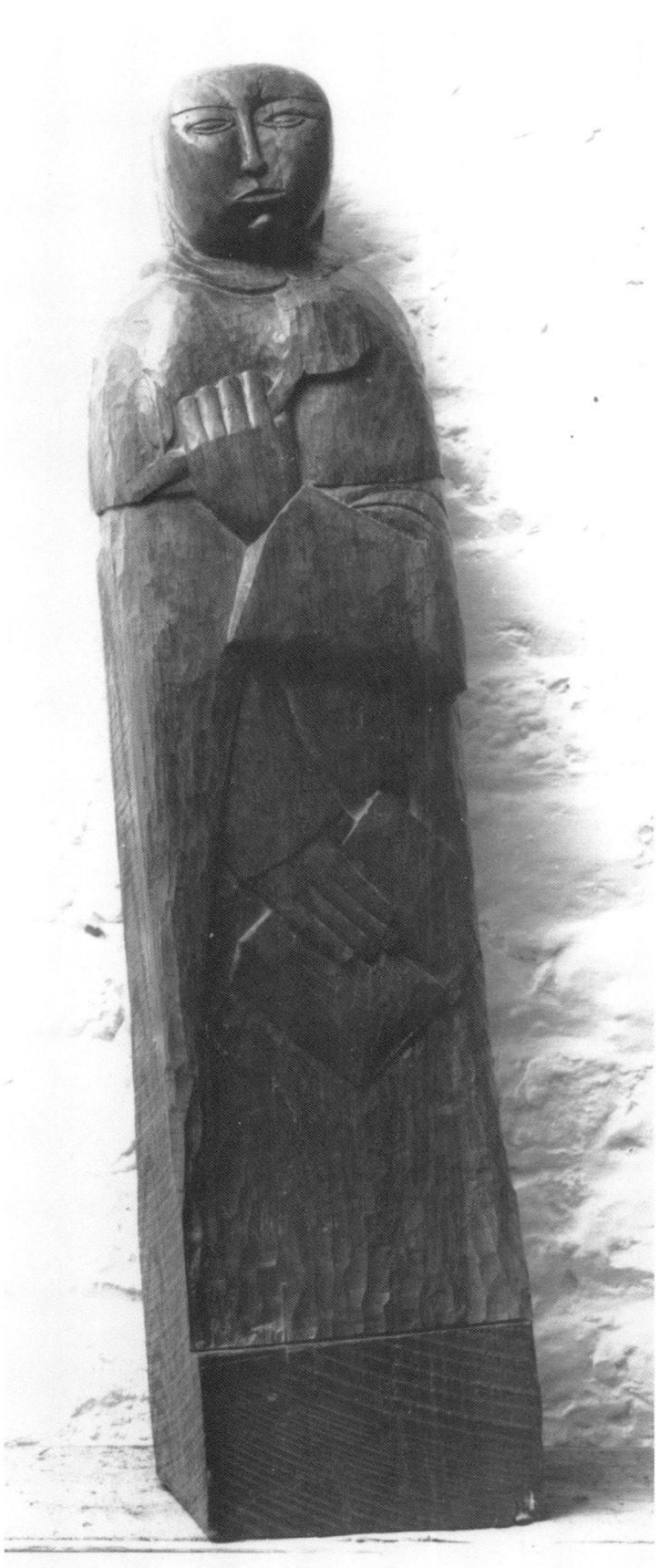

11. Carving of standing figure (St. Dominic), 1923 (?)

It is not surprising that Jones carved for such a short period because the work was related to his activity as a wood-engraver and that was also of limited duration. Any development into larger projects would have been prohibited by the fact that Jones never had a studio; sculpture is hardly an activity for the peripatetic. But when elements of religious iconography such as the blood flowing from Christ's side, which often appear blatant and uncomfortable in his paintings, were so successfully accommodated in the wood carvings by virtue of the homogeneity of colour and the vigour of their form and resolution, it is sad to think that Jones relinquished a medium in which he could realize so effectively a re-presentation of the more miraculous incidents of the Christian story. While these carvings owe stylistic debts to earlier periods, they appear as genuinely and urgently felt expressions of a spiritual intention and devotion. During the years of excitement and stress which followed the departure from Capel, Jones turned away from the direct expression of religious themes and when they re-emerged in his work over a decade later, his religion, like the man himself, was in a considerably imperilled condition.

ANIMALS

Visible behind the precocious child's response to an alert rabbit and the unusually inexpressive head of a cat is the outline of a standing bear, perhaps a first attempt at what became Jones's favourite drawing, *The Dancing Bear* of 1902. Animal drawing was important to Jones as a boy and throughout his life he felt a love and sympathy for the creaturely. He had an early desire to ride a horse, perhaps spurred by the childhood vision of the mounted detachment of City Imperial Volunteers, those 'angels' on horseback. An obvious opportunity presented itself when what certain strategists considered would be a cavalry war started in 1914; sadly, Jones's attempt to join a unit known as 'The Welsh Horse' was thwarted. When he went to enlist, a monocled officer suggested that as the young volunteer confessed to knowing nothing about horses, he should join the infantry; in the cavalry, the officer admitted, 'we see to the care of the mounts first and the men second'.[1] Serving as an infantryman in the trenches, Jones drew those creatures which eventually became most associated with the conflict, rats. In *In Parenthesis*, rats are seen by Jones to mimic the activities of the troops; the 'scrut scrut sscrut' of the 'rat of no-man's land' is seen redeeming 'the time of our uncharity', sapping 'his own amphibious paradise' with 'carrying-parties' and 'at night-feast on the broken of us'.[2] Animals from the well-groomed horses of the central command to the literary 'speckled kite of Maldon' make appearances in the poem. And such was Jones's affection for animals that in the trenches he made a surprisingly accurate drawing from memory of a cat which he had seen at the London Zoo.

In a sketch, *Calves*, done during his second period at art school, it is noticeable that a child's empathy has given way to the art student's earnest attempt at learning how to draw. Nevertheless, there is a sensitivity in both versions of the calf's head, a quality also preserved in the finished drawing of *The Goat* despite the choice of such a hard pencil. Somewhat crude cross-hatching and gentle stylization owe something to Gill's manner of drawing around 1926, the period of *First Nudes*. The undulating line of the spine, a powerful feature of many quadrupeds and one to which Jones had responded with a confident instinct even as a very young child, is elegantly delineated.

During childhood, animals were often placed in imaginative landscapes but while at Capel, another period when he could have realized his ambition to ride, Jones made several paintings of groups of animals in actual settings.

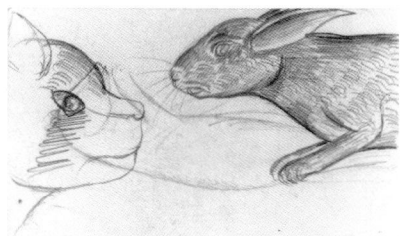

1. Cat and Hare, 1904 (?)

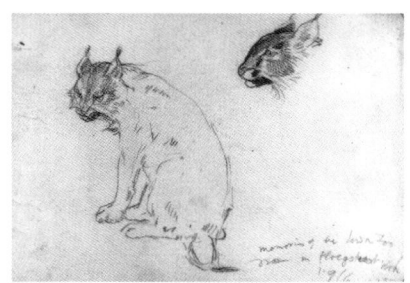

2. Animal Drawn in Trench, 1917

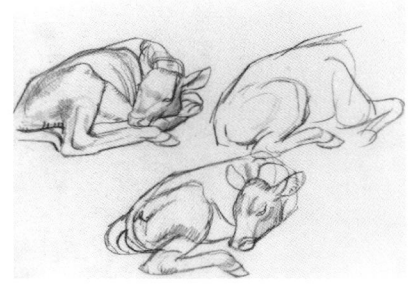

3. Three Calves, 1921

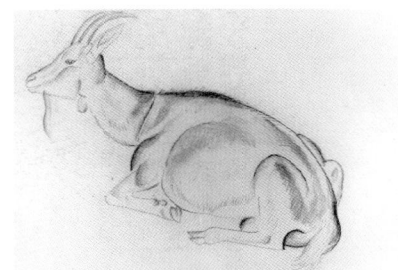

4. Goat, 1925

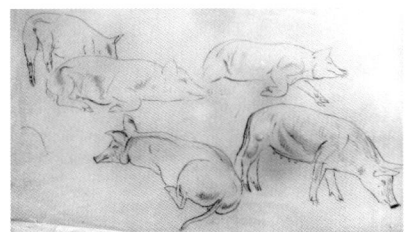

5. Pigs at Capel-y-ffin, 1926

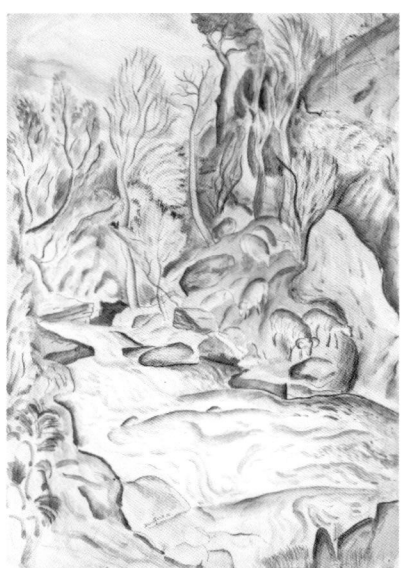

6. Pasture by Water, 1926

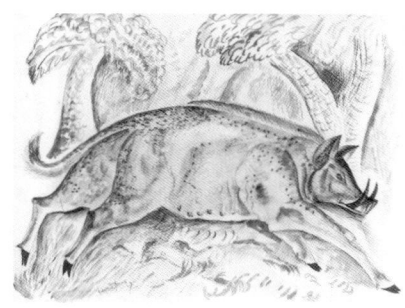

7. Wild Boar, 1927

None of these achieves the same degree of perception, wit or charm as the engravings or casual sketches like that of some delightful smiling pigs.

Romantic artists such as Delacroix, Géricault and Ward had been eager to use the energy of animals emotively in their work but Jones, except when he uses animals as symbols in his mythological pictures, has more in common with artists interested in creatures for their own sake such as a painter like Stubbs, an engraver like Bewick or, in the twentieth century, artists like Bonnard, Marc and Chagall. *Horses in a Meadow*, a chalk and pencil composition, includes no less than seven horses and a dog, and the suffused nature of the delicately applied chalk gives the work a quality of wonder which distantly resembles a Chagall or an early Franz Marc, when the latter was not abstracting from or splintering animal forms into landscape. Among Jones's compositions of grouped animals there is even a rare, though not very successful oil, *Resting* of 1928, a predominantly grey and brown painting of three sitting deer reminiscent of the style of Marie Laurencin.[3]

Jones remembered 'how very *big* little ponies looked when grazing on a hill opposite', going on to note that there were '*always* graceful but primitive looking horses standing still on Welsh hill-sides'.[4] In his animal paintings done at Capel there is an initial clumsiness in making the creatures too large within the scene. Unable or unwilling to muster the formal vigour of an artist like Marc, it is only when he recesses the animals in a timeless landscape that the paintings begin to succeed. One such success, *Pasture By Water* of 1926 was noticed by a perceptive contemporary reviewer who suggested that 'If Mr. Jones is not yet represented in the national collections' this painting 'might well be secured as giving a fresh turn to a persistent strain in English landscape'.[5]

Over and above his delight in creatureliness, what is distinctive about Jones's interest as he comes to maturity is that, in the manner of a late-medieval artist, animals are seen to be an essential part of the created world. As is the case with medieval illustration or tapestry, scale can be at odds with expectation in Jones's work; in a watercolour made at Rock a bird tugging a worm from underground appears unnaturally large in relation to its surroundings. Later on, the inclusion of many animals in the mythological works would make of his empathy with the creaturely an echo of medieval abundance where beasts are often allowed to mark the wonder of creation, as well as, at times, its grotesque or frightening aspects.

Lively and idiosyncratic is an impromptu treatment of a wild boar painted for the three-year-old daughter of a very close friend from Westminster School of Art. The girl was doodling when Jones arrived one day and asked her if she would like him to draw a picture. As there are some marks on the paper in the child's hand it suggests that Jones drew directly over her scribbles. Subsequently hung in a toy garden house, it is miraculous that the *Wild Boar* survives in such good condition. Jones was eager to delight children with the seemingly spontaneous magic of an image appearing on a page; once while staying with the Cleverdons, he made some animal drawings with the charred end of a stick which had been burning in the fire.[6]

The man responsible for reviving white line engraving in England, Thomas Bewick, was also an enthusiastic observer of animal life and perhaps this inclination as well as his technical skills endeared him to David Jones. The engravings for his *General History of Quadrupeds* and his *History of British Birds* presented such sympathetic studies that in 1843 one ornithologist ventured to name a new species a 'Bewick's Swan'.[7] The animals in the fifth and sixth blocks of *The Chester Play of the Deluge*, images pulsating with syncopated rhythms, abundant activity, and witty characterization are among the best of Jones's engraved beasts, particularly the leopards, cats and bears; the horses, however, show how slick simplification can mar expression. The cunning articulation of animals in the crowded engravings for the *Chester Play* demanded an increased awareness of the physical being, of the expressive contours and poses of each creature, and this entailed careful study at the zoo.

Revealing his versatility, it is a totally different and linear expertise that is visible in Jones's treatment of the shooting of the Albatross, the second image which he engraved for Cleverdon's edition of *The Rime of the Ancient Mariner*:

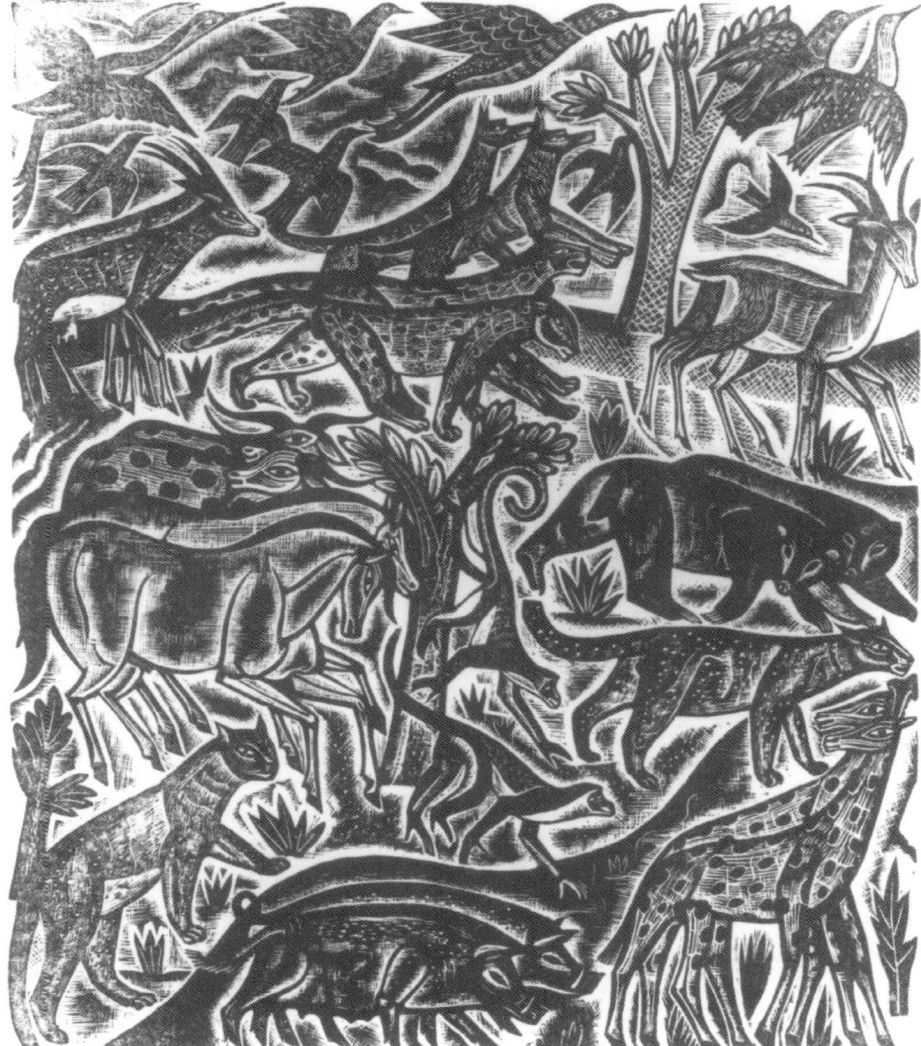

8. Animals Approaching the Ark, 1927

God save thee, ancient Mariner!
From fiends, that plague thee thus!-
Why look'st thou so?' - 'With my cross-bow
I shot the ALBATROSS'

The choice of positioning the innocent victim against the cruciform mast leaves little doubt about the metaphorical potency of this image for Jones. It is also a fine example of his control of the linear which is likewise visible in certain sketches. In the first of these, the lower dog has been drawn with a single line like Picasso's cover illustration for Stravinsky's *Ragtime* and is also reminiscent of the style of some early wire animal sculptures by Calder. Jones is enjoying the contemporary idiom of free line drawing: economy of expression achieved by a simple line is also evident in the sketch made on a prospectus for Gill's engravings. In its placing, the drawing appears almost like a border

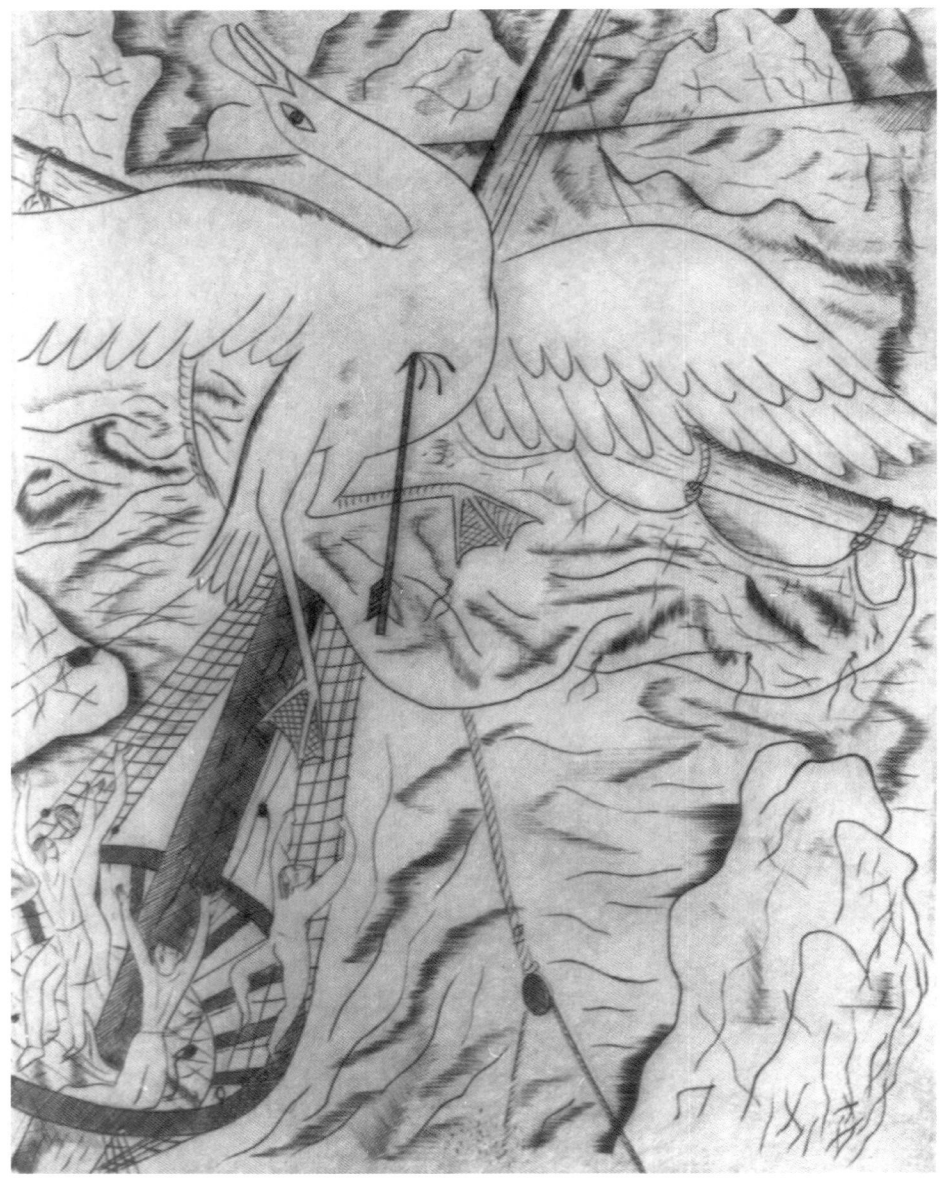

9. The Albatross, 1928

decoration for a medieval manuscript. Jones's impromptu animal sketches can turn up in the most unlikely places; there is one on the verso of a sketch of a cunnilingual couple drawn by Eric Gill, now securely lodged in the British Museum.[8]

Among twentieth century British artists Sutherland and Moore have been particularly interested in animals. Moore produced impressive sculptures and Sutherland, in his paintings, used beasts in a surreal and symbolic manner. Jones's preoccupation with animals results from his understanding of their importance in mythology, in history and as a source of delight in the created world, a delight more cherished in the face of the mechanical and urban pressures of the twentieth century. He felt his creaturely affinity with 'hairy ass and furry wolf',[9] lamented the ecological disaster of the 'dying gull' stricken by oil slick,[10] and, towards the end of his life, kept a photograph in his room of Laika, the little dog which travelled in Sputnik II.[11]

Although Jones had a slight fear of dogs, including the one owned by his parents, he drew them. One study, somewhat in Picasso's 'Ingrian' style, of a sleeping dog sensitively depicts the animal's shaggy hair with a minimum of marking, and its elongated, outsized paw cleverly extends the sweep of the line of the back. Jones's distinct preference for cats results in the sophistication of his treatment in a detail from an interior of 1930, *Cath Gartref* which means 'cat's home'. We can see that the side of the bowl on the window sill, the curtain ruffles and the echoes of the chair's arms with their paw-like scrolls create abstract rhythms which, as Hills puts it, act as 'a perfect pictorial metaphor for the spell a cat casts upon its territory.'[12] The painting is lyrical and appropriately dream-like, but there is also a clever manipulation of space; the cat's back is flattened in keeping with the abstract aspect of the image but its head and front paw are more three-dimensional so that it appears to move out towards the spectator.

Between 1926 and 1932 Jones often went to Regent's Park Zoo to draw and he also visited the Zoo in Bristol while staying with Douglas Cleverdon. So interested was he in observing the animals that he suffered the crowds, the odours and the unsympathetically cramped space in order to depict them. This interest in studying caged animals persisted; even during the Second World War Jones 'went to the zoo for a treat' after a friend's wedding, 'there was a raid on at the time (nothing dropping however) and the animals seemed all the same to sense some of the insanity of man'.[13]

The artist maintained that 'the better animal drawings' were made in the early thirties, they

> were more 'free' than the previous ones - maybe I had by then developed a 'technique' of sorts which conveyed more the feeling I wanted. I used to make them in much the same way as my landscapes, 'still-lifes' etc. of that period, using a bit of colour here and a pencil line there to try and get the feeling, rhythm etc., of the creatures. I mean that they were made like that while looking at the animals and never touched afterwards ... .[14]

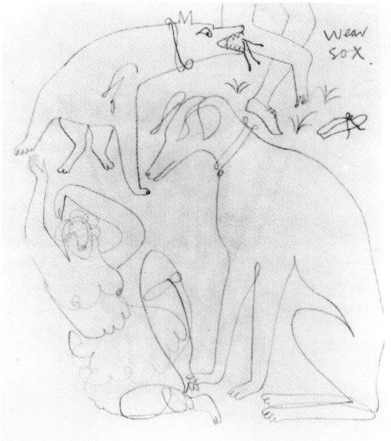

10. Wear Sox, (?)

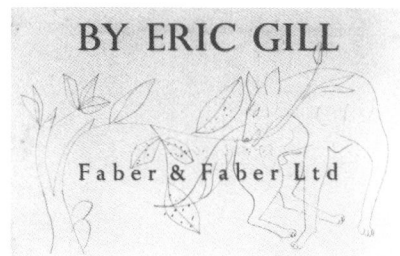

11. Dog Biting Branch, 1933 (?)

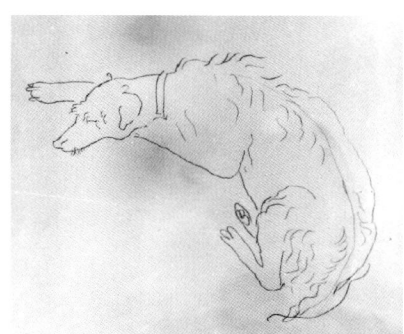

12. Dog sleeping, 1927

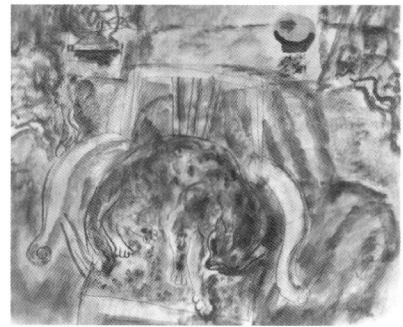

13. Cath Gartref (detail), 1930

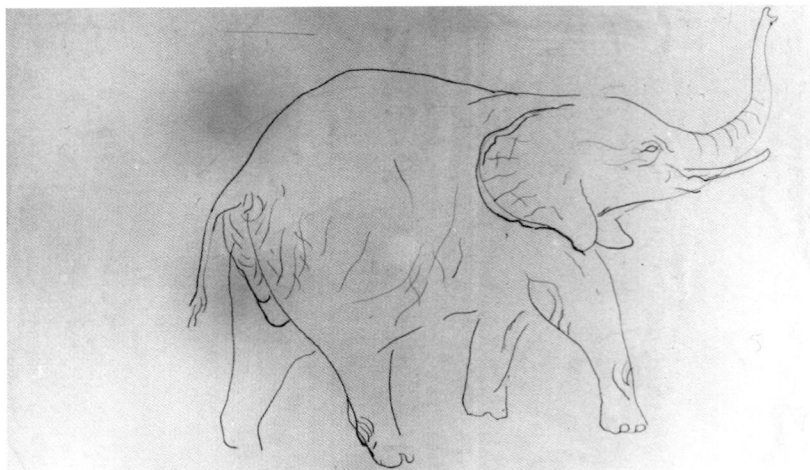

14. Elephant, 1927

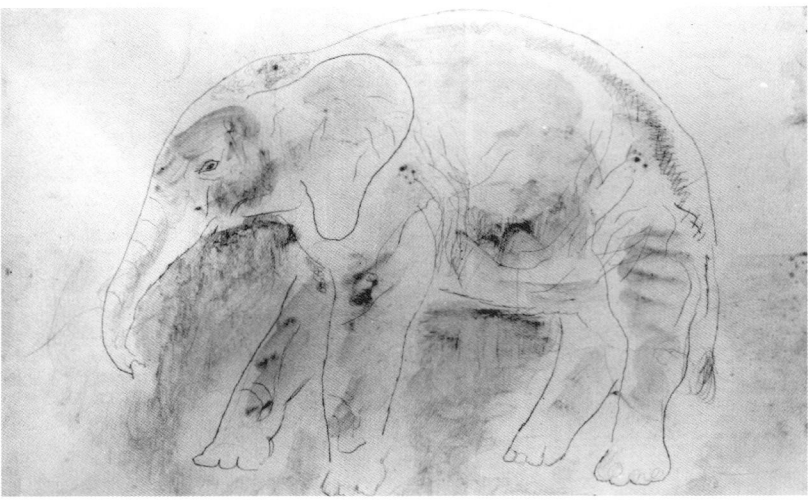

15. Elephant, 1927

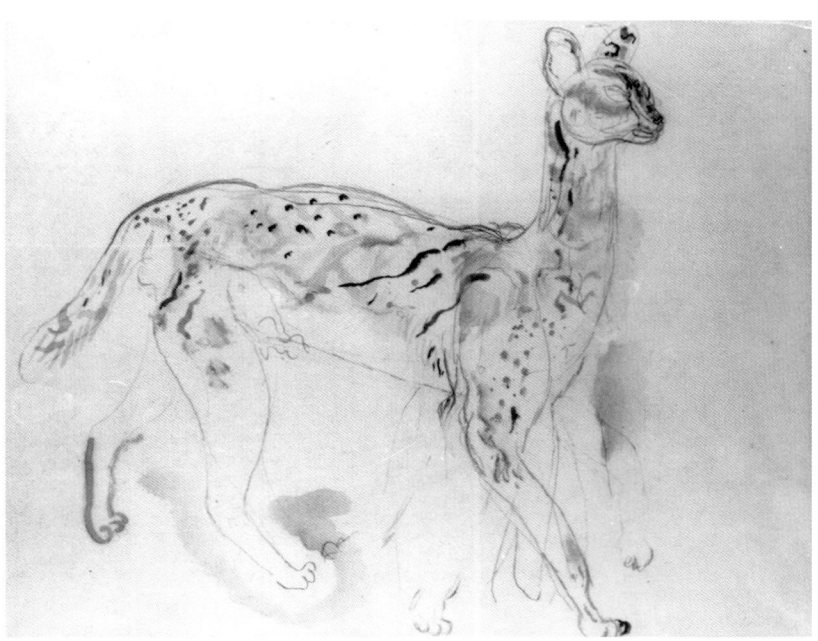

16. Agag, 1930

Despite the economy of the line, *Elephant with its Trunk Raised* from a sketchbook used in London Zoo in 1927, reveals the bulk and motion of the elephant. Jones made many elephant drawings and one sequence, a study with a more generalized ear *(15)*, was taken further and developed into an oil of 1928 that was exhibited with the 7&5 Society which Jones had been invited to join in the same year by Ben Nicholson. Nominated at the Society's Annual General Meeting in the studio of Cedric Morris in January,[15] he became an exhibiting member at that year's exhibition. In the thinly washed oil, *Elephant*, the composition, despite its lightweight and humorous quality, takes on an almost Surrealist aspect because of the discrepancy between the enormous, audaciously pink body and the apparently cramped space.

In 1930 Jones shared an exhibition with another 7&5 artist, Ivon Hitchens, at the Heal's Mansard Gallery which he considered to be an 'important' show from his point of view because it included 'quite a lot of animal drawings'.[16] *The Times* reviewer, in comparing the two artists, suggested Jones to be 'more ingenious and complex in rhythm of line'[17] and a rhythmical finesse is visible in *Agag (16)* of 1930 which was considered by Jones to be 'one of my best'.[18] The ghosting of Jones's attempts at placing the front legs sets up a rhythm which gives the animal a mobility and yet the wash that surrounds the hind leg successfully counterweights the repetition of those multiple choices. What appears delicately undecided in the placing of legs is offset by the proud and purposeful head.

Jones wrote, in the draft of the letter to the Assistant Keeper of the Walker Art Gallery quoted above, that in drawing the 'great cats', 'I was concerned only to get the feel of them as they turned and traipsed to and fro.'[19] This is captured by the length of the body which appears so exceptional in Jones's *Leopard (17)*. The sinuous line that curves across the paper like the rounded hills of a landscape articulating the arching back, powerful shoulders, and lowered neck expresses the lithe power of feline energy. Line is the predominant means of expression but there are patches of ochre, burnt umber, black and gray wash which help the eye to slither across the page; the colour falling from the cheeks and the odd accentuation of the right forepaw only detain the spectator for a moment. As first attempts at back, legs and tail remain visible, again the viewer is witness to the process of making a drawing.

One monotonous result of the restrictive circumstances in which Jones drew his animals is that most are viewed from the side; it is therefore welcome to see this *Lynx* from a foreshortening, three-quarter position, its bony, yet evanescent body appearing and disappearing like a Chinese landscape. For a shy man such as Jones it was brave and ambitious to produce drawings and watercolours of such complexity at the zoo with its evident distractions. People would watch him at work, something he detested, and cockney schoolchildren would disturb and amuse with their chatter:

> - Ask 'im to draw yuh.
> The pal, glancing at the giraffes under consideration:
> - He wouldn't draw me, m' neck ain't long enough![20]

The Old Animal From Tibet seems to inhabit its natural domain rather than the restricted confines of the zoo; the contours in the background appear like hills, or, with that line cutting across the linear animal in the background, they could be seen to owe a debt to apparently random cave markings like those at Lascaux. The female in the bottom right-hand corner takes us into the scene which has a depth of space more akin to the fully realized animal paintings made at Capel than to the flatter studies such as *Leopard* made at the zoo.

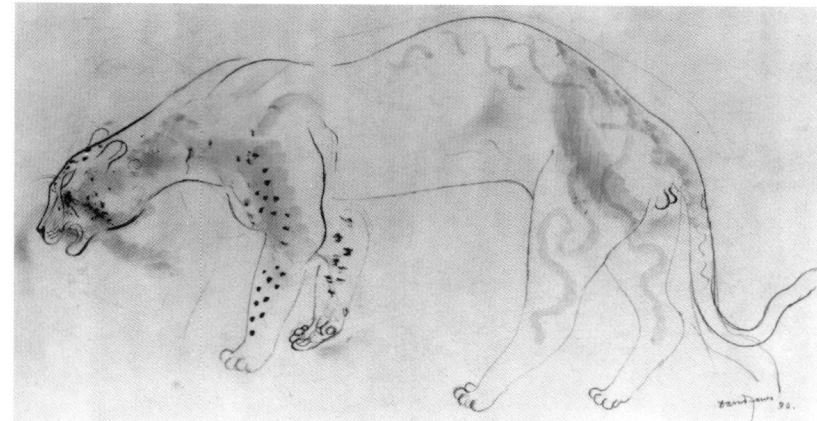

17. Leopard, 1930

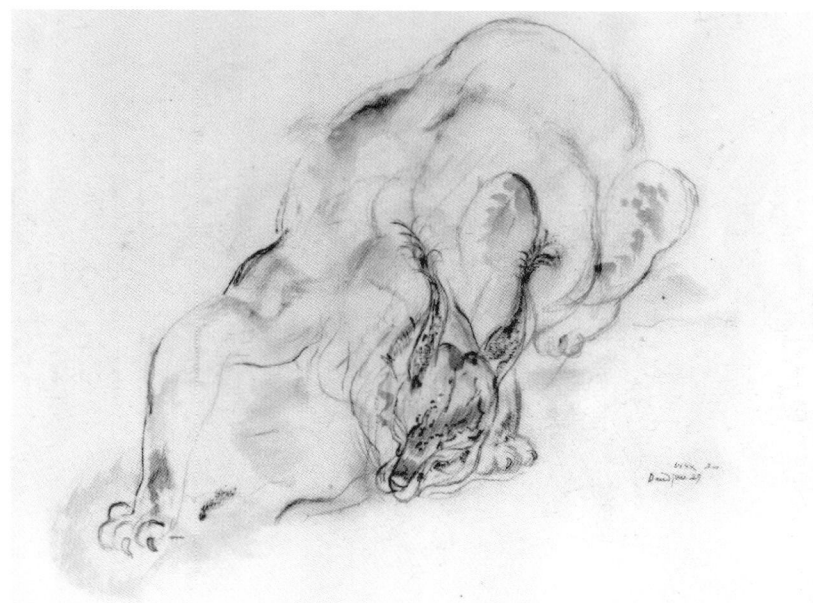

18. Lynx, 1929

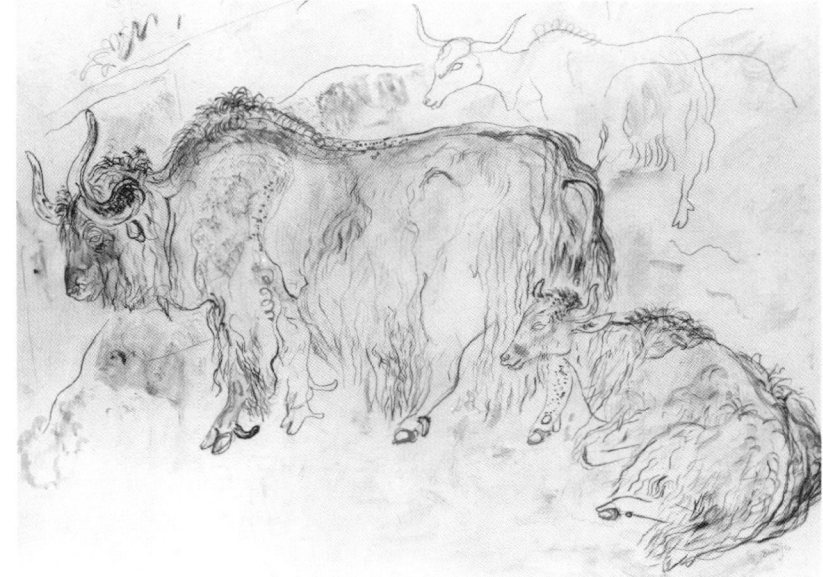

19. The Old Animal from Tibet, 1930

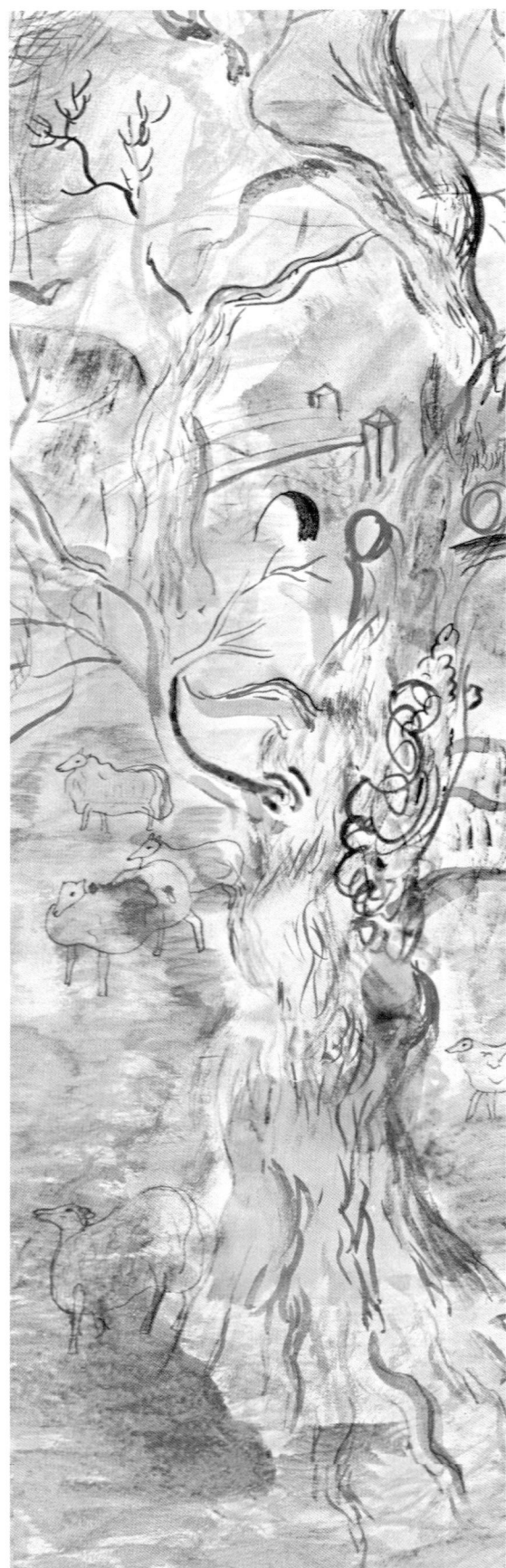

20. Chapel in the Park (detail), 1932

After Capel, animals continued to be included in landscapes, notably those done at Pigotts and at Rock. In the detail of the 1932 drawing and watercolour, *Chapel in the Park*, Jones produces *faux-naif* modern equivalents of prehistoric scratchings to re-create sheep economically but expressively. Such an echo complements the transhistorical dimension that Jones was beginning to suggest in his painting at this time through the use of allusive titles.

The allegedly linguistically retarded schoolboy, who nevertheless won *Birds I Have Known* as a school prize for Grammar in July 1907, was, fifty years later, marvelling at the variety of birds which came to his window in Harrow:

> 'even a sea-gull … but four blue-tits seem the most constant - well, apart from sparrows and a robin and some damned starlings … and a lovely green woodpecker with his red head often perches on the tree a few feet away.'[21]

He occasionally sketched such birds in rare and rapidly drawn works like the chalk and pencil *Brief Record of a Bird on a Bough* of 1948,[22] or *Flower Piece With Yellow Bird*, a pastel and watercolour of 1950.[23] He also filled his later paintings with animals. The Welsh ponies which had graced the Capel hills came to be associated with the post-Roman period and with a type of horse used by the mobile forces of the ancient Britons. These can appear ambiguously as actual horses or Celtic hill carvings such as in the landscape behind *The Four Queens* (1941). Animals seen decades earlier were included in late drawings. In a mythological illustration of 1961, *Fontana Perenna*, the 'herons in the sky are the two herons' Jones used to see when he 'lived in Wales'.[24] Jones's admission somewhat contradicts his claim that it is necessary to work from a thing itself and not from imagination and possibly accounts for the degree of generalization in the details of later works. Even in the the last big watercolour and drawing that Jones made, *Y Cyfarchiad I Fair* (*The Annunciation in the Welsh Hill Setting*), there are, as well as a positively medieval array of animals, countless varieties of bird flying about Mary and Gabriel. Animals which had earlier been placed in imaginative settings, studied in their own right, engraved and even carved - for Jones made animals for a toy Noah's ark as well as producing engravings for *The Chester Play* - are integrated into the warp and weft of his exhaustive mythological and Christian celebrations.

In his *British Drawings* of 1946, Michael Ayrton considered Jones's work as 'a symbol of the continuity of tradition'. Yet, despite tradition, animals in Jones's mythological pictures more often than not express disturbance. Horses twist in erotic frenzy. Ilia, the she-wolf subject of Jones's drawing and watercolour of 1942, *The Mother of the Nest*, which presides over the wreckage of a war-torn world, was first envisaged in a sketch where ghoulishly distorted wolves, stricken and lost, scavenge in an uninviting landscape. What an image like this so powerfully evokes, and what is lost in the obsessive finish of the mythological works, is brute dismay. Distortion, perhaps, best characterizes cultural plight.

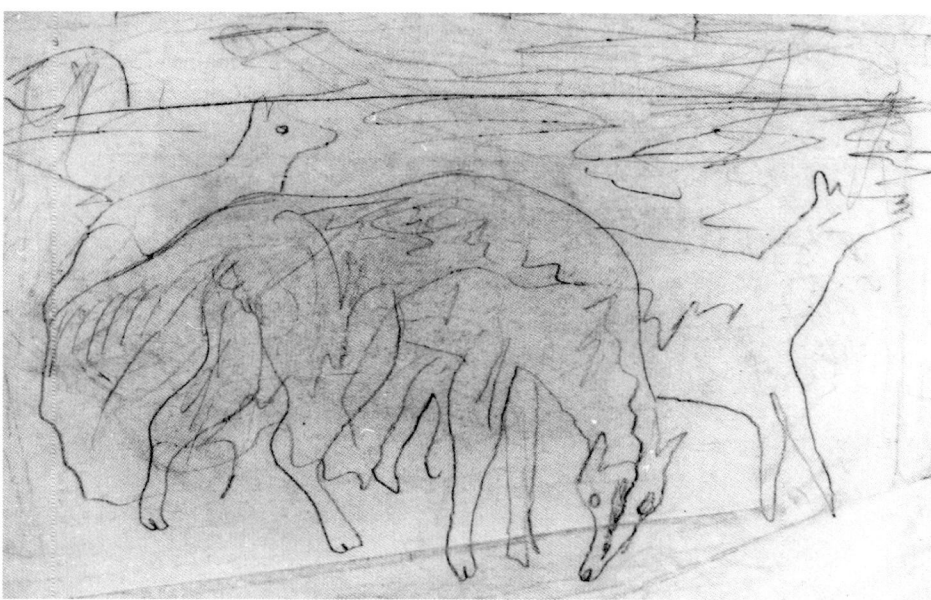

21. Sketch of Wolves, 1942 (?)

APPROACHES TO LANDSCAPE

At the end of the eighteenth century, and with the emergence of the British watercolour landscape, Wales attracted painters with its 'Fertile and Romantick Country'. It was so designated by Paul Sandby, a founder member of the Royal Academy and early champion of the use of watercolour, in the title to his set of *Views* produced from his 1771 tour of the country.[1] Prior to that period, Richard Wilson had painted Wales and Paul Hills suggests that it was the great 'bowls of space' found in Wilson's landscapes which interested Jones.[2] In a letter to Arthur Giardelli, Jones suggested that the

> great master, Turner, did not, in his *Welsh* landscapes catch quite the spirit of the place as did Wilson. The watercolourist Julius Caesar Ibbetson caught it, I think, especially in a watercolour of Conwy Castle.[3]

During the nineteenth century, curiosity in the landscape shifted from an excited response to awe-inspiring uplands and moved in two diverse directions: either towards a scientific concern with the secrets of nature or towards a growing nostalgia in which landscape was increasingly perceived as the repository for traditions threatened by industrialization. In the second half of the century when interest in landscape declined, Wales, unsustained by an Academy, exhibition spaces or art schools declined in artistic importance.[4] By the time David Jones, aged seventeen, set off on a painting holiday in the summer of 1913 with a fellow art student, the Welsh landscape was once again attracting native artists such as Augustus John and James Dickson Innes, who, in the company of Derwent Lees, cut a colourful path through the countryside in search of landscapes and in drunken pursuit of women. By contrast, Jones and his friend in a pony and trap, armed with a copy of Borrow's *Wild Wales*, visited Cardigan, the ruins at Strata Florida, and Tregaron, which Jones painted in an early oil. The square church tower at the extreme right is perhaps the one which Jones remembered painting during the trip, selling the resulting canvas to a friend of his mother's.[5] Despite its sense of space, *Tregaron* is a dauby, slightly indecisive and sketchy example of English Impressionism, reminiscent of a painter like Steer.

Studying in an art school in South London obviously limited Jones's chances of making landscapes and it is clear from the scant evidence of *Winter* and *Tregaron* that Wales, as well as acting as an emotional magnet for the boy's developing interest in history, provided an opportunity for such activity. Yet in 1915, stationed at Llandudno with its striking coastline Jones did not, it seems, take the opportunity to draw the landscape. In the sketchbooks of his training, he is preoccupied with recording his fellow soldiers and officers. Subsequently, the Western Front imposed its restrictions in terms of scale and medium but the

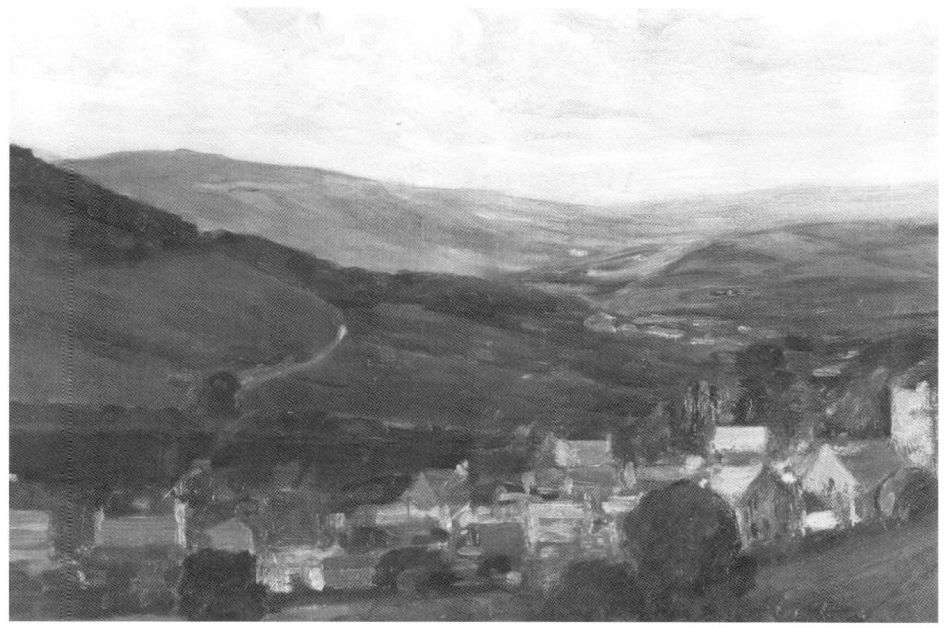

1. Tregaron, 1913

interminable hours of inactivity gave Jones the chance to sketch. In both the documentary impression of the wintery Richebourg St.Vaast and in the impressionistic charcoal drawing made in Ploegsteert in the Boesinghe Sector, north of Ypres, Jones reveals that he is capable of producing fine and generally people-less topographical studies. After the war, however, he showed little interest in the topographical watercolour; although a sense of place and site became intellectually important to him, accurate geophysical description did not. Landscape became a pretext for formal experiment, but as form is the reflection of an idea in the artist's mind, the artist's feeling about a place will necessarily affect his formal choices; as Jones puts it, 'An appreciation of natural beauty, a feeling for some specially beloved *patria* - this hill, that sea-coast or whatever it may be, will not, *in itself*, be of avail to the artist *qua* artist'[6]; it is rather an understanding of the formal nature of the art itself which is relevant.

After a war which had pulverized the landscape of northern France and Belgium, a number of British artists, who had been involved, turned to un-touched landscapes in order to recuperate: Matthew Smith went to Cornwall in 1920 when his health collapsed and he was anxious and depressed; Paul Nash went to Dymchurch on the Kent coast to tend what was diagnosed as 'war strain'; David Jones, after a second spell at art school, spent a good part of the twenties in rural situations tackling usually empty landscapes. If certain painters immediately before the war had treated an industrial world and its relation to the human figure, was there not a feeling of escape or avoidance in the paintings of artists such as Nash or Jones? There was insularity and comfort in the British landscape enabling such people to efface, for a moment, the fact that something as horrible as the war had ever happened. Furthermore, landscape and still life were 'aesthetic categories'[7] and were, therefore, blissfully sealed off from the failure of civilization manifested by the war and the subsequent slump. In August, 1926, Nash stated that 'My anathema is the human close-up'.[8]

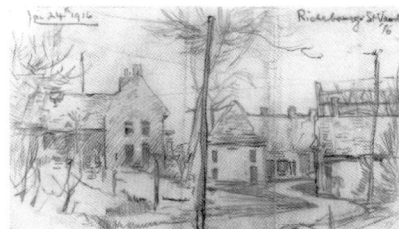

2. Richebourg St. Vaast, 1916

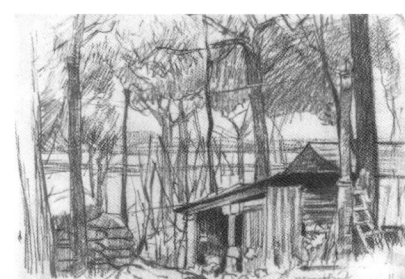

3. Ploegsteert, 1916

95

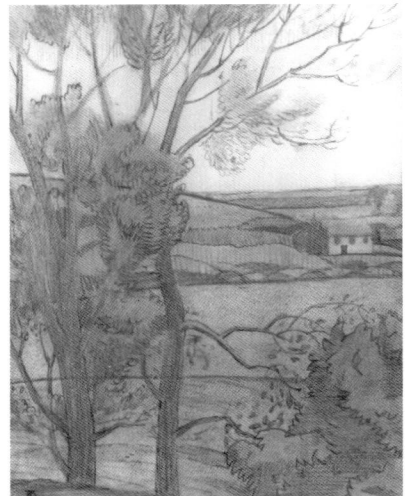

4. Kent Landscape, 1920

During his second period as an art student, Jones became increasingly interested in the countryside. *Kent Landscape*, in coloured pencil, is one of several intelligently organized drawings which survive, its recessive horizontal bands suggesting the influence of Bayes's teaching. Considerably more dramatic, and one of the few existing finished art school paintings is *Landscape in Kent*. Its formalizing tendency reveals, as does the contemporary *Madonna and Child*, executed in the same style and set in a similar rolling landscape, Jones's readiness to submit himself to conceptualization. The sizeable *Landscape in Kent*, taken from a sketch (see p 41), was painted on a shelf in the room at Westminster where students used to wash their brushes and where they 'used to boil the gelatine to make the priming for the canvas'.[9] Jones laid the paint on a surface of cooked gelatine and powdered white applied to the hessian,[10] the texture of which was allowed to appear through the painting despite a thick application of powdery colour. The style owes something to Meninsky and the effect of the empty, modelled landscape with its boldly placed horizon, its dull viridian, ochre, yellow-greens, and muted tonality is decidedly eerie. While the triple grouping of trees in the mid-ground appears crude, branches appearing like bunches of bananas, the left foreground tree, placed centrally on the canvas, with its luminescent area around its upper trunk, seems to possess a 'magic' core.

Before giving it to an art school friend, Jones submitted this large picture to the London Group, at that time dominated by Fry's enthusiasm for paintings reflecting French influence.[11] It was turned down for exhibition and Jones was understandably depressed,[12] though during this time as a student he had a slight measure of success when pictures were accepted for the Goupil Gallery *Salon* from 1919 onwards.[13] At first, the outrageously high prices he attached to these works (*The*

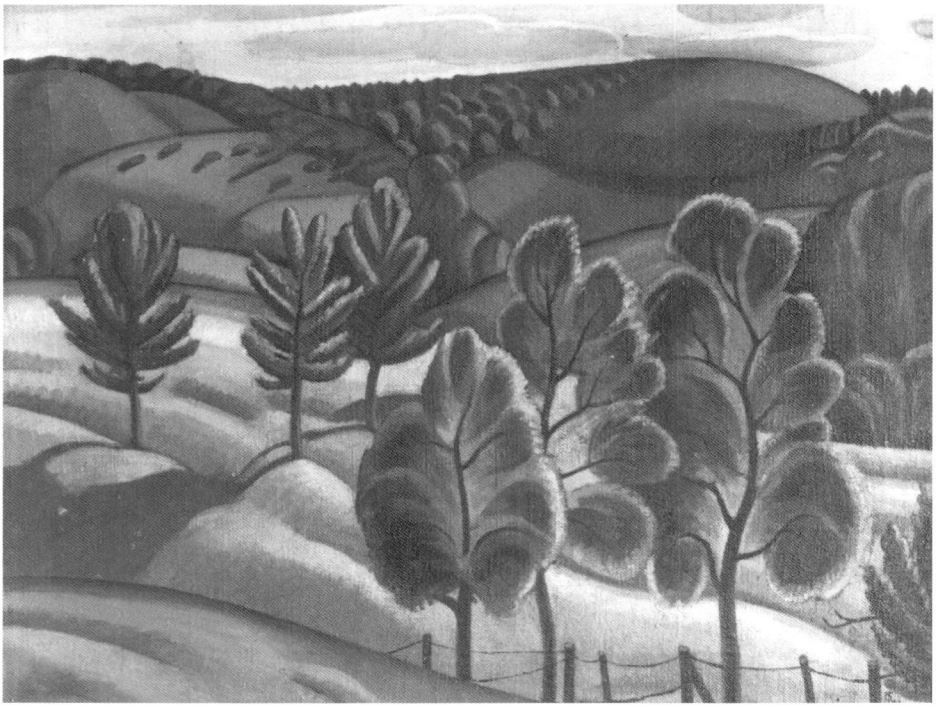

5. Landscape in Kent, 1921

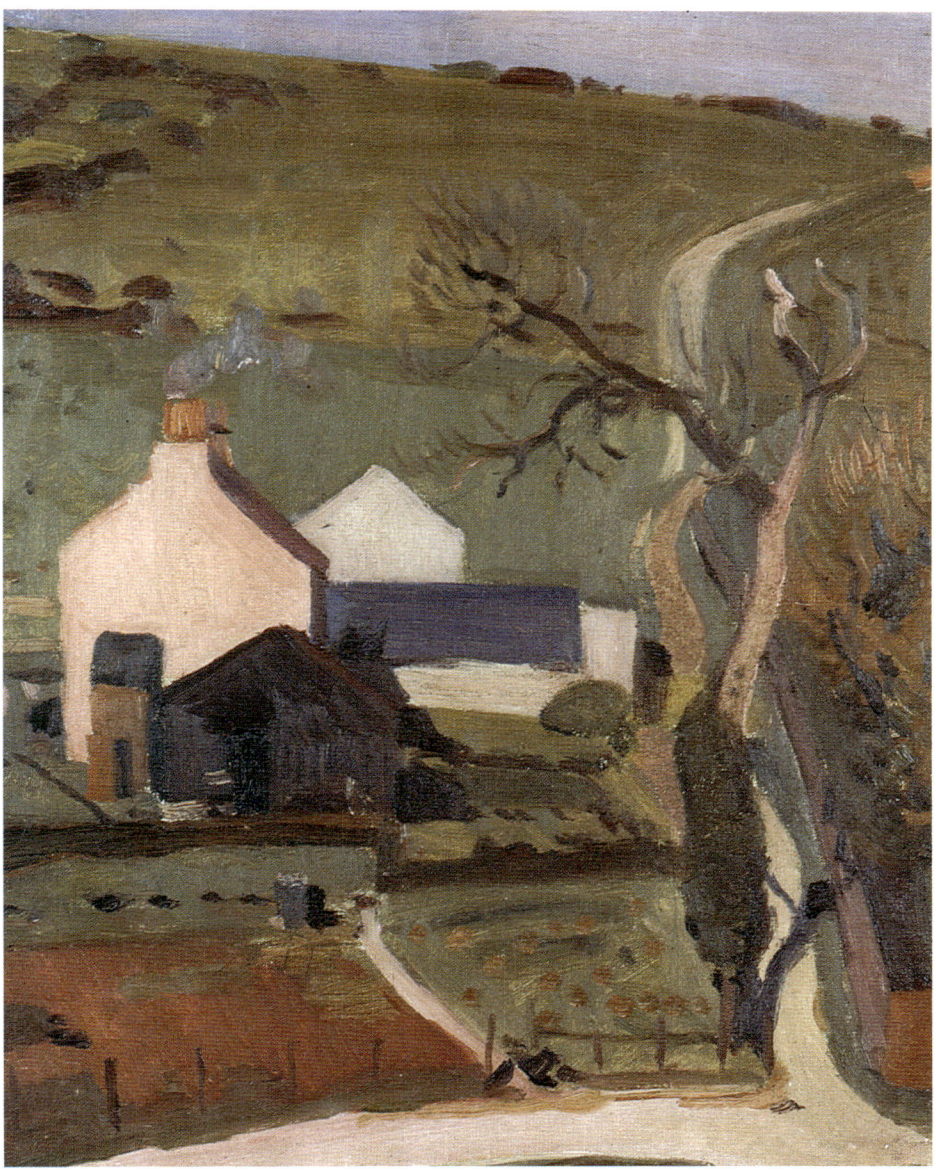

6. Landscape (South Downs), 1921

Military in 1919 and *The Reclaimers* in 1920 - both at £63 while Bayes, the Principal of his art school, was pricing works at between £40 and £100) suggested that even at this early stage, Jones was reluctant to sell paintings. Although the prices at the *Salon* dropped during the twenties to the more commercial range of £5-£20, the artist never sold at these exhibitions.

In *Landscape - South Downs*, with its selective strokes and planes of colour, Jones adopts a more liberated approach which could be designated as English Post-Impressionism. He secures an interesting tension; the landscape is flattened on the right by the path running up the canvas. This becomes involved with the foreground tree trunk and branches, so that both are at odds with the path that leads to the farm and so into a sense of depth which fixes a middle distance. But such spatial illusion is further defeated by the slab of pink wall, the blue roof and by a stroke of umber on the upper path as it nears the horizon line.

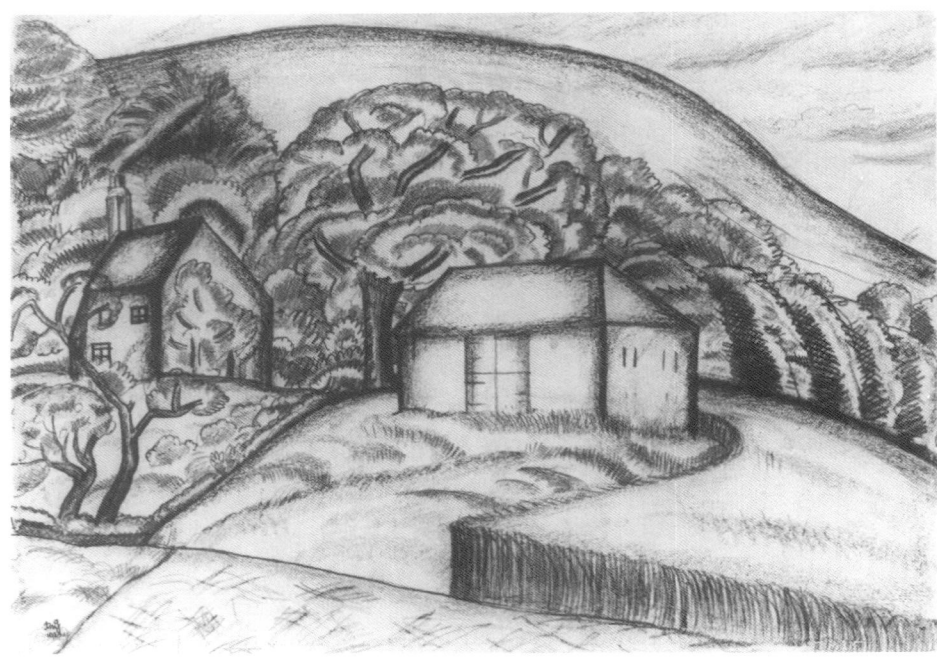

7. Ditchling Landscape, 1924

The regrettably small pencil and crayon drawing, *Ditchling*, dated 1924, is deceptively simple. The background vegetation is arrayed in a series of decorative generalizations not so very far removed from the patterning which animates *The Town Child's Alphabet* on which Jones was working at the time. By using a childlike medium and apparently childlike forms, Jones disguises his sophisticated organization. The parallel of rising smoke and of the border between the buildings leads the eye up to the sloping hill which sweeps us towards the open and emptier right hand side, where a field bends expansively around a flattened barn end towards the spectator. Because of its relation to the trees behind and the sweep of the cornfield, the barn appears continually to recompose itself, yet the triangular roofs on both buildings echo, holding the two sides of the drawing together. Colour, which is only placed on the edges of the forms, gives them a neon-like heat, a potential to expand.

Strikingly rhythmic, and in a much more modern idiom, is *Garden Path, Ditchling*. To see two such different attempts at landscape juxtaposed indicates that Jones was coming to maturity under the excitingly varied options of vastly different styles. Here the scene has been re-ordered with almost Cubist violence and it is a good example of what Jones believed a painting ought to be: 'A "thing" having abstract qualities by which it coheres and without which it can be said not to exist' yet which 'shows forth something ... representational.'[14] Certainly, the path, terminating abruptly at the centre of the image and transforming itself into an apparently barren tree which has been lopped, is of more than formal significance. About the time that Jones became engaged to Petra Gill he made several paintings in which a garden path fails to reach a domestic destination but stops instead abruptly in the centre of the work or obtusely at the corner of a building. Philip Hagreen later observed that, 'All that is meant by home - warmth, trust, privacy, a fixed point on the map - all this was not for David ... He could only be a guest

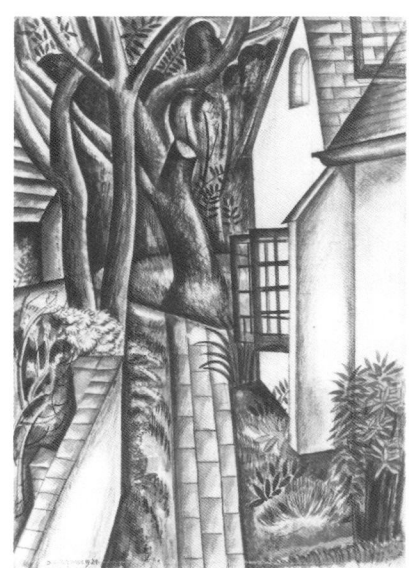

8. The Garden Path, Ditchling, 1924

or a lodger'.[15] In 1924 Jones made the engagement as a vow[16] and yet for a dedicated young artist perhaps the sheer impossibility of starting a family without any guaranteeable income was registered in works like *The Garden Enclosed* (see p 247).

For all the strength and tension between the curves of the trees and the sharp angles of house, garden walls, and path, the painting is weakened by the generalized incidentals of the vegetation; comparison with a *Landscape* of Autumn, 1908, by Picasso shows how the jettisoning of such detail allows abstracted form and space to resonate. Jones, like so many other English artists, seems unable to let go of trivial details.

More conceptually successful is an elegantly formalized *faux-naïf* early Capel-y-ffin landscape painted in the year before Douanier Rousseau's first one-man show in London in 1926. It is, moreover, suggestive of the kind of simplification and stylization that Ben Nicholson adopted later in the decade after his chance discovery, during a trip to St. Ives, of the works of Alfred Wallis who, aged seventy and completely untutored, had begun to paint for company.[17] The contours, bold and decided, create strong rhythms: skillfully, the sweep of a hill curves down across the top of the picture into a row of trees that leads into a path which, in turn, descends into the top of a tree and through that tree into the stump of another at the bottom of the canvas. The lonely dwelling, rather like the path which doesn't lead to an entrance, is a feature of Jones's paintings of this period and the U of trees or bushes towards the upper right hand corner with a contour bisecting it is an interesting anticipation of the *agelastos petra* often to be seen decorating the ancient hill sites in Jones's later mythological works. The *agelastos petra* was the 'laughless rock' at Eleusis where a rock cleft was symbolic of female genitalia. Interestingly, this painting was given to Petra.

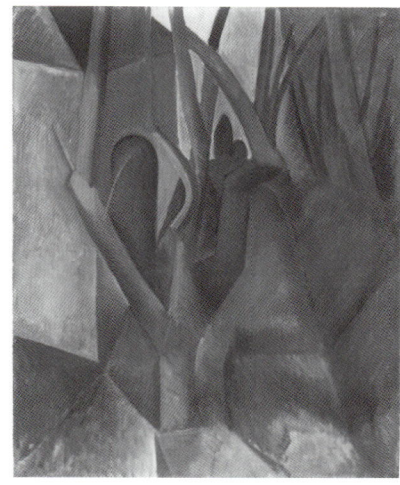

9. Pablo Picasso, Landscape, Autumn, 1908

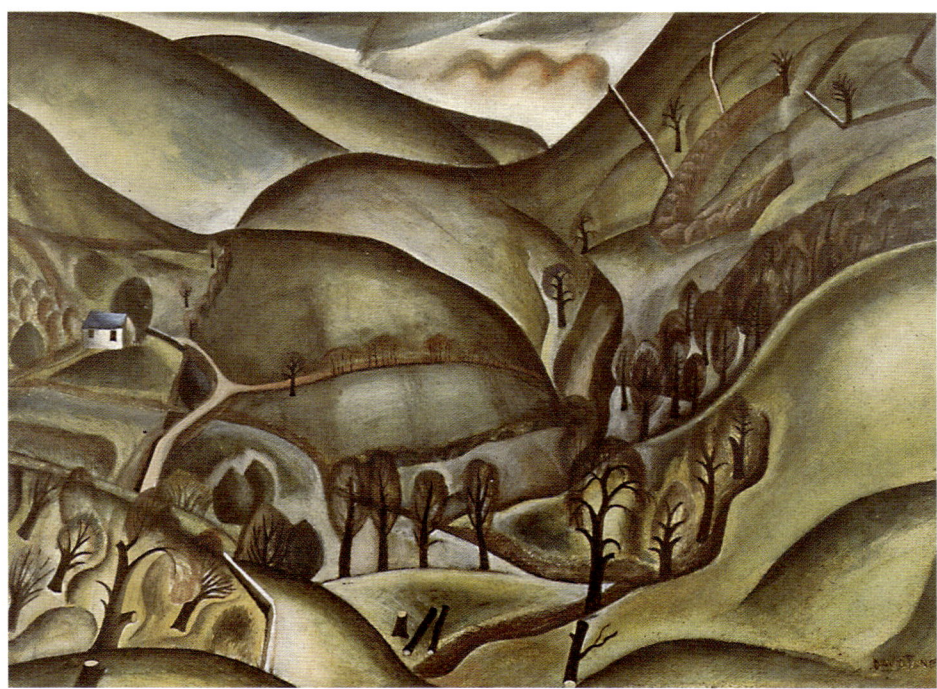

10. Capel Landscape, 1925

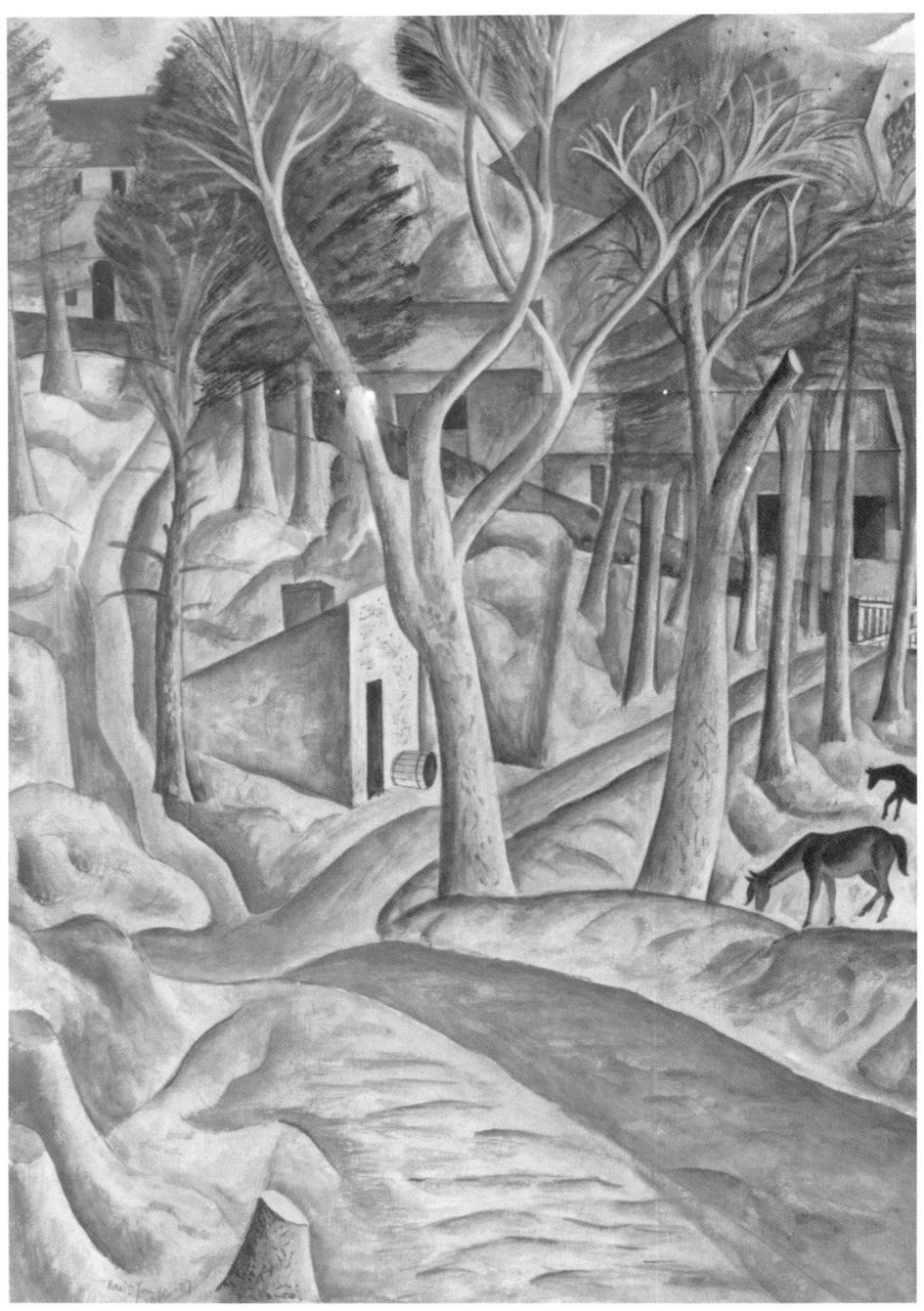

11. Capel-y-ffin, 1926-7

Paul Nash had an exhibition at the Leicester Galleries in November, 1924 and it is possible that Jones may have seen this before going to Capel-y-ffin in December. Stylistic similarities in their work register a common precursor, Cézanne, rather than direct influence and it should be noted that Jones did not mention Nash as being among his closest contemporaries.[18] Hills observes that Jones comes nearest to him in work of 1925-6.[19] Certainly, *Capel-y-ffin* of 1926-7 exhibits an affinity with Nash in its dry stylization, in the clarity and overall sameness of light, crispness of form and unsettling emptiness. It can be seen hanging on the wall in Jones's watercolour of Petra and Joanna Gill sitting before the fireside at Pigotts, evidence of Eric Gill's enthusiasm for the young painter's work. It is also not unrelated to *Capel-y-ffin* of 1925, a detail of which appears on the dust-jacket of this book, but in the later work, inter-relations of trees, hills and buildings seem less formalistic and the painting is harmonized by a light that suggests autumn giving way to winter. The out-of-scale horses can, only for a moment, hold the eye against the myriad rhythms which reverberate in a Cézannesque manner across the background. Peopleless and with a stagger of dark doorways, it is marked by another feature that pervades Jones's work, the lopped-off branch - echo of a war-torn landscape, an unconscious symbol of arrested development, and a side-glance at the Cross.

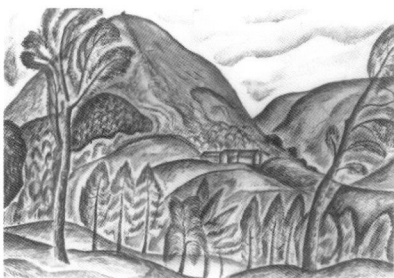

12. Y Twmpa with Conifers, 1925

Y Twmpa, because of its dominating position on the opposite side of the valley from Gill's home, was a favourite subject for Jones during this period. He treated it so many times and in such differing manners that it became for a short while like a Cézannesque motif, an assertive shape able to act as an anchor for the artist's aesthetic researches. In *Y Twmpa With Conifers* of 1925 the bulk of the hill itself interests the painter for the foreground trees are dismissed with a decorative simplification. It is the bumpy sweep of the hill that travels right across the paper, the modelling with economically applied, feathery watercolour, the negative spaces and dark outlines delineating the successive hillocks that range towards Y Twmpa which impress. Jones is not concerned with atmosphere but rather attempts to distil the essence of the landscape. Derain, whose work was on exhibition with other French painters at the Lefevre Gallery in November, 1924, may have exerted some influence on Jones. *The Church at Vers* (1912)*(13)* with its stiff, formalized and compart-mentalized landscape, from a period when Derain appeared to be helplessly casting about for a style, has elements in common with aspects of different Jones landscapes of the mid-twenties.

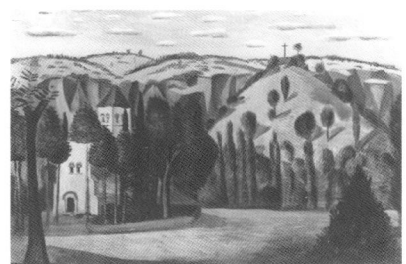

13. André Derain, The Church at Vers, 1912

Y Twmpa overlooks the empty mid-ground of the tiny *Nant Honddu* which, Douglas Cleverdon suggests, because of its 'rather hesitant line', may well have been Jones's first attempt at copper engraving in 1925.[20] The halting quality produces an effect more like dry-point where the metal burr thrown up by the engraving is left to trap ink and this gives a fragile feel to the flat-tened and simplified fairytale image with its lost house.

A more expressionistic and immediate response to Y Twmpa is visible in an energetic landscape, *Y Twmpa*, of October, 1926, in which the colours are heightened and unrealistic. The fact that it has been kept in a folder whereas many of his contemporary watercolours have been hanging in full light since the 1920s perhaps provides some indication that Jones's colours were less muted than is often thought. Watercolour is vulnerable to light, and between 1920 and 1940, there were many fugitive colours which would eventually upset the tonal and chromatic balance of a painting: crimson lake, carmine, chrome-based lemon yellows and mauves were unstable.[21] What is interesting is that Jones, who so often relies on an engraver's style of cross-hatching to evoke the multi-textured landscape around Capel, can also rely on colour to mark the form. With preoccupations similar to those of contemporary American artists such as Marin and O'Keefe, artists doubtlessly unknown to Jones at the time, it shows us yet another possible avenue that Jones was opening for himself.

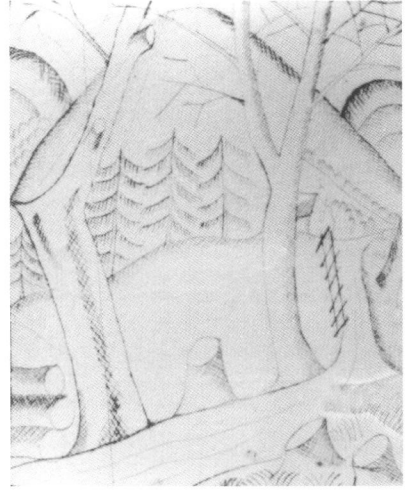

14. Nant Honddu, 1925

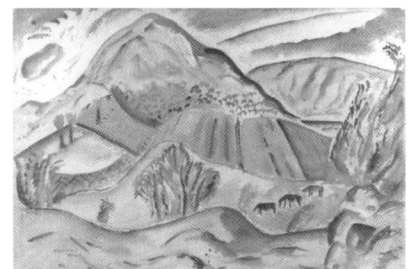

15. Autumn Landscape, Capel, 1925

With the move to Capel-y-ffin, landscape painting began in earnest and Jones had started to work almost as soon as he arrived in December, 1924. Living conditions were better than at Ditchling but not comfortable; John Rothenstein, visiting Capel, found the house damp and without hot water and the food 'spartan'.[22] The winter of 1924-5 was a hard one but René Hague remembers Jones working outside 'muffled against the cold in scarf and tightly lashed trench-coat.'[23] According to Philip Hagreen, Jones didn't much like painting out of doors, dreading

> the discomfort ... but he heroically endured it at Capel, on Caldey and at Lourdes. We discussed the matter and he said that to design landscape from imagination gave only easy lines and rhythms. He needed to struggle with unwilling material to produce the tensions and stresses that make a live painting.[24]

Overtly religious subjects were also tackled such as the large crucifix (1m.80 x 1m.20) painted on whitewash in what had been Fr. Ignatius's Bible Cloister and was at the time, the Gills' first chapel. Jones also painted a metal tabernacle and it is unlikely that the small religious paintings were stopped when he left Ditchling, but it was predominantly the rough landscape of the border country that spurred his imagination during this period.

In a 1926 view of Y Twmpa, the hill seems diminished by the mid-ground clump of trees about the bend in the river. This clump of vegetation takes on a mysterious or magical quality with light emanating from its interior. The idea of the magical grove or wood was one that appealed to Jones but here it is only hinted at as form and texture are explored rather than the numinous or the poetical charge of the landscape.

While many views of Y Twmpa were painted from a position close to Gill's establishment, Jones did cross the valley on occasion and paint the view looking back towards the monastery. He also walked up the valley following the stream and in *Afon Honddu Fach (18)* of June 1926, he allows smaller and more conflicting rhythms to create a qualified Expressionism. An energy swirls through the charged terrain and only the mundanity in the drawing of the bridge and fence anchors the spectator amid fluid and dislocating ructions. The stream is given considerable size as it curves around those sharp jagged rocks, reminiscent of Jones's treatment of the cliffs on Caldey Island during his first trips in 1925 and 1926. The landscape is sectionalized as it so often seems to be in Capel watercolours but here the usual feeling of a tapestry gives way to the abrupt clippings of a *collage*-like effect, where one section or element cuts across another. It is an intense work by a young artist whose eyes struck John Rothenstein when he was visiting Capel as having 'in their depths a little touch of fanaticism'.[25]

Jones never stayed at Capel for a period longer than about three months and he punctuated his stays with painting trips to Caldey Island and time in London, using his parents' home in Brockley as his base. Eric Gill occasionally accompanied him and in the October prior to Jones's arrival at Capel, Gill spent no less than eight days with Jones's family, whom he had

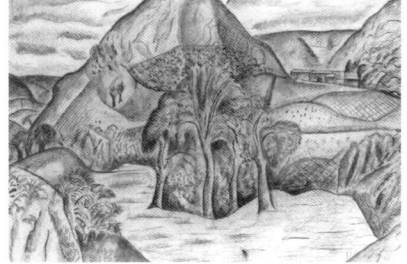

16. Y Twmpa - Capel, 1926

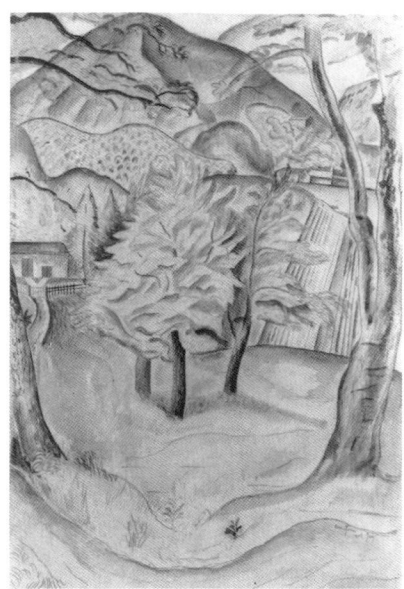

17. Landscape at Capel, 1926

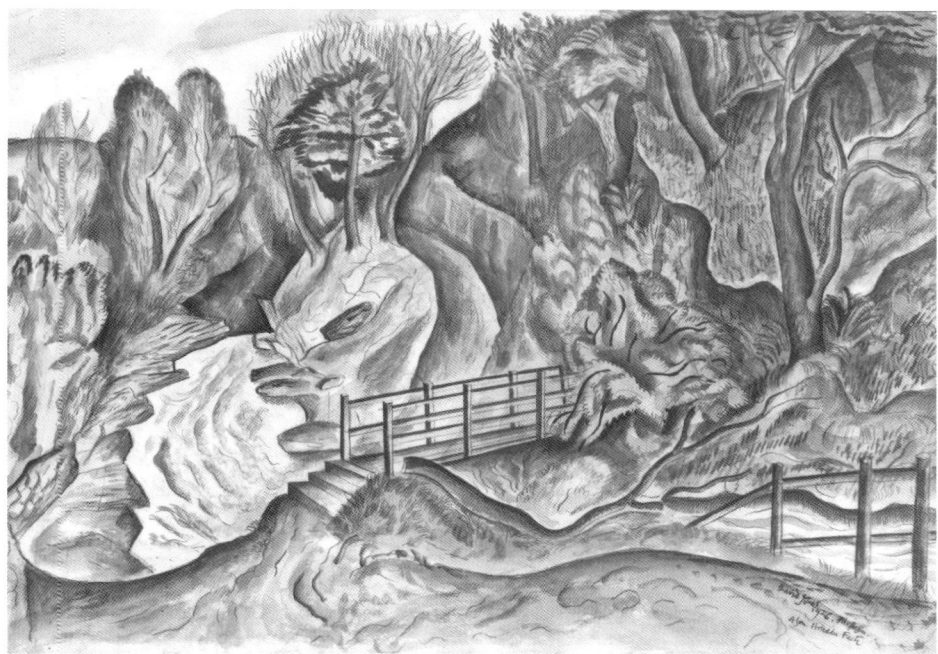

18. Honddu River Fach – 'Afon Honddu Fach', 1926

found on a previous occasion 'kind and hospitable'.[26] During Gill's stay in London he offered the young Jones a helping hand for on 12 October, 1924 he notes that he spoke with William Marchant of the Goupil Gallery 're D.J.'.[27] The talk bore fruit in March 1929, when Jones exhibited thirty-eight paintings at the Goupil. But, in 1927, Gill and Jones shared a joint exhibition at the St. George's Gallery, (Gill exhibiting 'by arrangement with the Goupil'). On that occasion, Jones showed twenty-seven watercolours largely made at Capel, Caldey or in Brockley. Titles were often grandly poetic, *The Dolorous Mountain*, *Castle and a 1000 Hills* or *The High Mountains of Israel*, but others were given the simple titles by which they are known today: *The Suburban Order* or *The Dog on the Sofa*. Most of Gill's rather simple sketches were priced at three or four guineas and Jones's watercolours at between 8 and 20 gns.

Gill wrote to Jones from Salies-de-Béarn before the exhibition with a touching humility that clearly demonstrates the high regard in which he held the younger man:

> I am most grateful for all you have done in the matter of choosing drawings for our show. I am perfectly certain you have done the thing well - I wish I were as perfectly certain that the things were worth choosing and worth selling … in most cases the price should be low because the value is low. But then I come up against Howell and the Goupil who have an entirely different view of the matter. It seems to me we can't help it. It's their galleries we're showing in and so they must be arbiters of prices. I suggested a uniform rate of 10/6 except for a few more obviously careful or successful drawings, but they are indignant! So the minimum is to be £2.2.0 (framed) … You know I don't profess to draw well … so please accept my apologies and let us both pray that the collaboration won't harm you.[28]

It did not. On 29 May, Gill wrote to Desmond Chute that the exhibition had been 'quite successful, especially from the point of view of David who sold nine',[29] a third of the paintings exhibited. Jones received a favourable review, quite possibly from a friend or acquaintance of Gill's, in the Catholic *G.K.'s Weekly*:

> This is the first show of Mr. David Jones, though as a wood engraver he must be well known ... to those who care for the best modern woodcuts. In his watercolours, an individual vision is combined with a formal quality of expression ... breadth and simplicity of treatment ... strong sense of design and charm of colour.[30]

The St. George's Gallery was particularly interested in the work of up-and-coming artists such as Henry Moore, Frances Hodgkins, Edward Bawden and Ceri Richards. The owner Arthur Howell's account of how the Gill and Jones exhibition came about is most entertaining and illuminating and worth quoting at length:

> David Jones had been sent along by Eric Gill: this he told me. He brought a portfolio with him.
>
> Would I see his watercolours? Certainly! I asked him to sit on a settee and to spread them out, two or three at a time, on the floor ... What he took from his portfolio was entirely new in style to me. While objective in character, the representation of the objects before which he had worked *in situ* was loose even to distortion, and had been subjected to considerable elimination.
>
> I then said, 'What do you want of me?'
> He replied, 'An exhibition.'
> To which I quickly rejoined, 'Oh no! you have never sold publicly any of your work, have you?'
> 'No'
> 'Then,' I added, 'I can tell you exactly how many pictures you will sell and what will be written about them by any critic who might come to see them.'
> 'What will happen?'
> 'None will be sold and little will be written!'
> There was a silence. He turned to me, 'What would you suggest?'

Howell's advice was to put one or two into the September Exhibition of the Modern English Water Colour Society.

> Of the many critics who reviewed the show, little encouragement was offered to David Jones. P.G. Konody in *The Observer* wrote, 'I cannot see eye to eye with Mr. David Jones, whose tortured forms - haloed with aureoles of light in the case of his landscapes - do not seem to spring from any particular conviction, but rather from a desire to 'go one better' than the Washes.'

While the *Morning Post* published these words, '... and Mr. David Jones ... owing to their impoverished content, are only of temporary value ...'. No other notice was taken of his work ... in the following July, he reappeared carrying the same portfolio.

The St. George's Gallery consisted mainly of a single exhibiting room reached from George Street through a long passage, the walls of which were spacious enough on which to hang many pictures ...

'Do you re - member me?' he asked.
'Very well', I replied.
'And do - you remem - ber saying you would like to be my a-gent?'
'Oh yes.'
'Would you still ... like ... to be?'
'Let me see, may I, what you have in your portfolio? ... Yes, alright.'
'Is there anything to ... sign?'
'No, just give me your word that you will bring everything you do in to me. I am to handle all your work.' This was agreed to... .

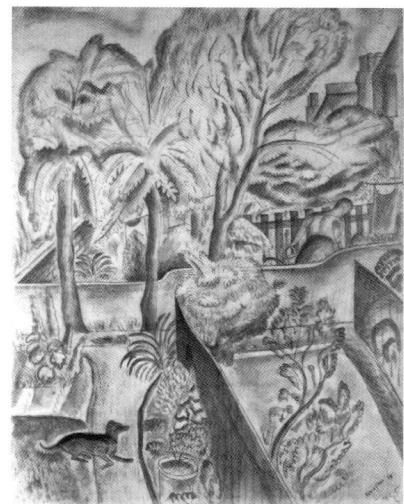

19. Brockley Gardens, Summer, 1925

Later in the autumn, Howell showed the portfolio privately to 'our best known art critic of that time', an action he repeated three times over the next few months. The third time the critic admitted that he had been too hasty and spoke of the quality of the paintings. 'By early spring, with the suggestion of using Gill live figure studies as a crowd-puller, an exhibition was mounted.'[31] *The Times* reviewer was more than sympathetic, he seemed to understand what Jones was trying to achieve: 'there are hints of Giotto, Cézanne, and - in the peculiar flexibility of the designs - Blake, but in total effect it is strongly original.'[32]

During these years, Jones's paintings of Brockley register the changes in his father's garden as well as recording the suburban world in which he had grown up and from which he was beginning to distance himself. *Brockley Gardens, Summer* of 1925 with its wide and lively range of often non-naturalistic colours, its slightly exoticized trees sweeping against a glimpse of the rigid geometry of the terraced houses, indeed suggests a desire to break into a dream or a new reality. The dog which appears to float flat across the scene augments the feeling of a dreamlike and fluid world, utterly different from *A Town Garden* of 1926 which appears to have been painted as a seasonal and emotional counterpart. It is more workaday and more abrupt, with the dog unequivocally located in a scene which, nevertheless, in the background, possesses mysterious elements. In what could appear almost to be a crucifixion metaphor, two lopped trees frame an altar-like brick wall with a rising, evanescent tree branching heavenward beyond, no more far-fetched perhaps among the suburban laundry than Spencer's *Christ Carrying The Cross* (1920) below the net curtain angel-wings of Cookham. But despite the latent mystery of the distance where the scene dissolves and everything appears about to

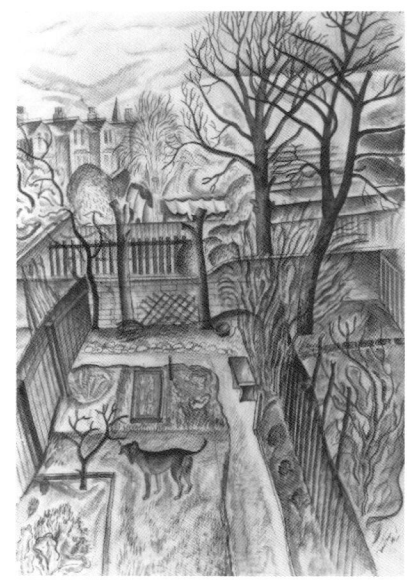

20. A Town Garden, 1926

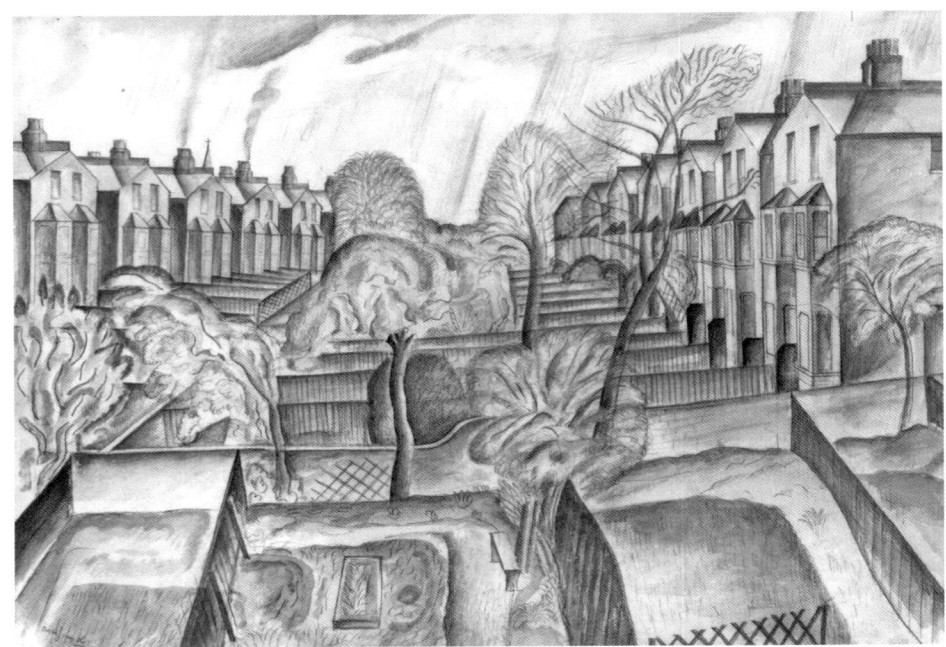

21. The Suburban Order, 1926

become something else, there is that forlorn quality later sought by the insular urban realists of the fifties such as Derrick Greaves and Carel Weight.

A more panoramic view over the same garden occurs in a painting first seen at the St. George's Gallery show where it was selling for 12 gns. More recently (1994) it appeared in a European context in the *La Ville* exhibition at the Centre Pompidou in Paris when it was included as a telling image of the grey sprawl of Victorian expansion. The deserted suburban scene under the rain is depressing; the gardens are bare, a central tree has been lopped and the distant cross atop a local church is too inconspicuous to be efficacious. There is a considerable tilt to the foreground which shows us that Jones is painting from the first floor bedroom window of his parents' house and the full, regimented banality of terraced housing is further underlined by the irony of the title, *Suburban Order*. When he zooms in on a corner of his father's garden in bloom, in *August Garden, Brockley* of 1926, he delights in its abundance, once more exoticizing the flowers and the trees.

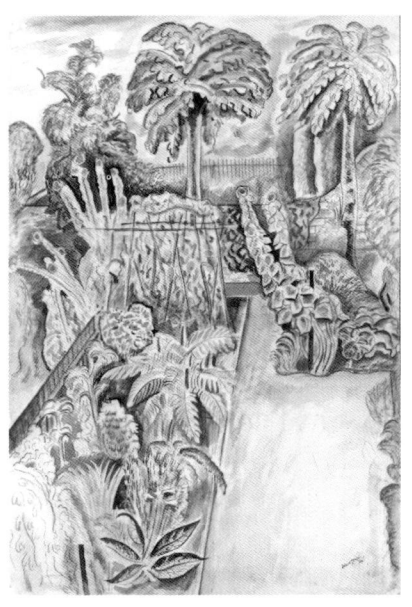

22. August Garden, Brockley, 1926

On 13 April 1928, Jones went to the Tate with the Gills. The gallery had, two years before, opened its so-called modern foreign section which included the nineteenth century French rooms. Until the Stoop bequest was put on show in 1933 there was, in Britain, scant opportunity to see important continental works of the twentieth century.[33] On the following day, the Gills and David Jones set off for France where, in Paris, Jones was content to spend the Sunday afternoon, not, surprisingly, in the Louvre, but with the Edes who were there on a visit and who had, by 1928, become dear and influential friends. Considering that artists like the Nicholsons and Christopher Wood made for the very studios of French artists, such a missed opportunity to see French painting suggests a certain parochialism. On the following day there was an excursion to Chartres when Gill and Jones had a difference of opinion about the respective merits of Chartres Cathedral and the church of St. Pierre and this engaged them in hearty discussion on their overnight train journey down to Salies-de-Béarn in the Basque country, where the Gills shared a house in a region that allowed them to experience 'a quality of goodness and quietness and even "holiness"' which seemed 'to have gone forever from England'.[34] The old town of Salies-de-Béarn is a maze of small streets and alleys, with seventeenth century houses overhanging its sluggish river. The Villa des Palmiers, a house shared with Gill's secretary and mistress, was to be found a little out of the old town, up a steep hill, and beyond it lay the rolling countryside which, to the south, became the foothills of the Pyrenees.

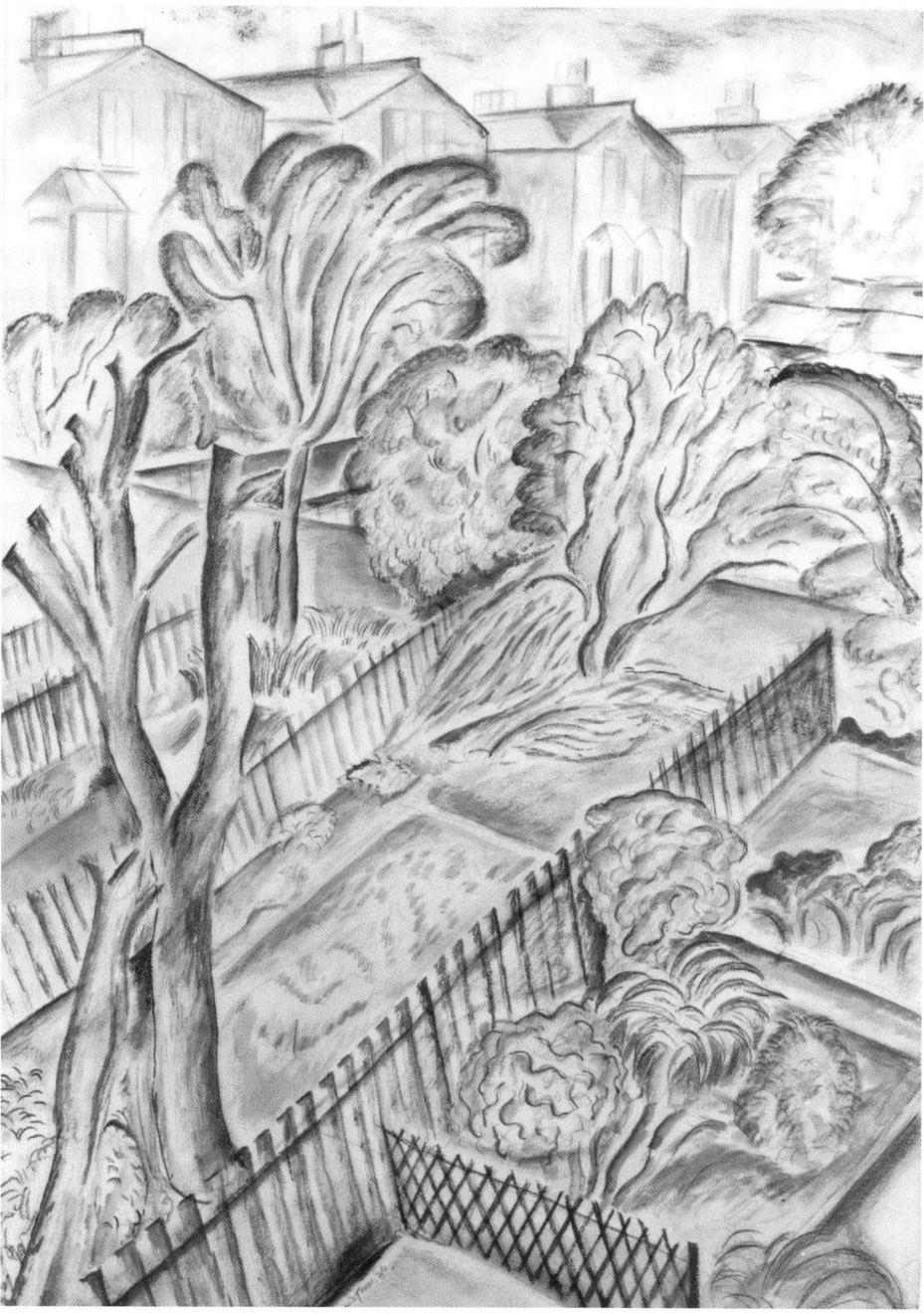

23. Foliage & Fences, 1926

107

Jones painted a number of watercolours from the first floor balcony of the Villa des Palmiers such as *Landscape, Salies de Béarn*. Here the drawing and painting come together in a way that in earlier Capel or Brockley landscapes they do not. There are delicate 'Bonnardian' blues, yellows and pinks that heighten our enjoyment of the spring landscape and yet the warmth and light of the south of France do not appear to have made a striking impact on the mood of Jones's painting even if they did enliven some of his colours. Similarly frenetic and unsettling marks, visible in watercolours made in Britain in 1927-28, can be seen; accentings are random and there is a troubling, threatening quality in the sky in this and in *Roman Land (25)*. Writing much later in life Jones wished 'there were more Bonnards in England - he's a chap I'm very fond of. I think he's the best of those marvellous French painters of that period. More magical than Degas by far. He seemed to be able to suck out 'poetry' from just anything.'[35] Yet, just how many Bonnards would Jones have had the chance to see by 1928? Fry had included Bonnard in the *Second Post-Impressionist Exhibition* but it would otherwise appear that the painter was not widely exhibited in the United Kingdom until the thirties, the decade in which Bonnard started seriously to paint watercolours.[36] So, what appears 'Bonnardian' in these Salies works is probably nothing other than that both painters, who share certain qualities, were subject to a similar southern French light. Jones would probably have seen the exhibition of Bonnard's *Drawings and Lithographs* at the Leicester and Sickert Gallery in July, 1932 and it is true that from around that date, Jones's Bonnardian habit of looking out through a window becomes more decided in its use of the divide to compromise and confound space. We may conclude, therefore, that the textured segmenting which Jones utilizes in *Landscape, Salies de Béarn* may be nothing other than a loosened version of Post-Impressionism.

Gill best expressed Jones's relation to site in an article that he published on the young painter in *Artwork* in 1930:

> Though in one place he may find more inspiration than another, it is not places that concern him. What concerns him is the universal thing showing through the particular thing, and as a painter it is this showing through that he endeavours to capture.[37]

Thus, the trees in Salies don't seem to be so very different from Brockley trees and the foothills of the Pyrenees are treated not unlike the Black Mountains around Capel. Indeed, Jones later remembered, in a letter to Giardelli, that he found the country near Lourdes 'awfully like some bits of Wales'[38] and yet Jones was, at the time of his first visit to France, beginning to allow the historic association of a site to affect him. Gill's secretary told him that from the Villa des Palmiers one could see the pass where Roland fell.[39] While Roncesvalles is actually over the border in Spain and no longer in the country of Béarn, the poetic idea was enough to allow him to append a title such as *Roland's Tree* to a simple landscape in order to mark the association. Likewise, after the Gills went back to England on 4 May, Jones went to stay with the Hagreens just outside Lourdes, for they had left Capel in 1925 as a result of Gill's intellectual and sexual insensitivity. While staying with them, Jones

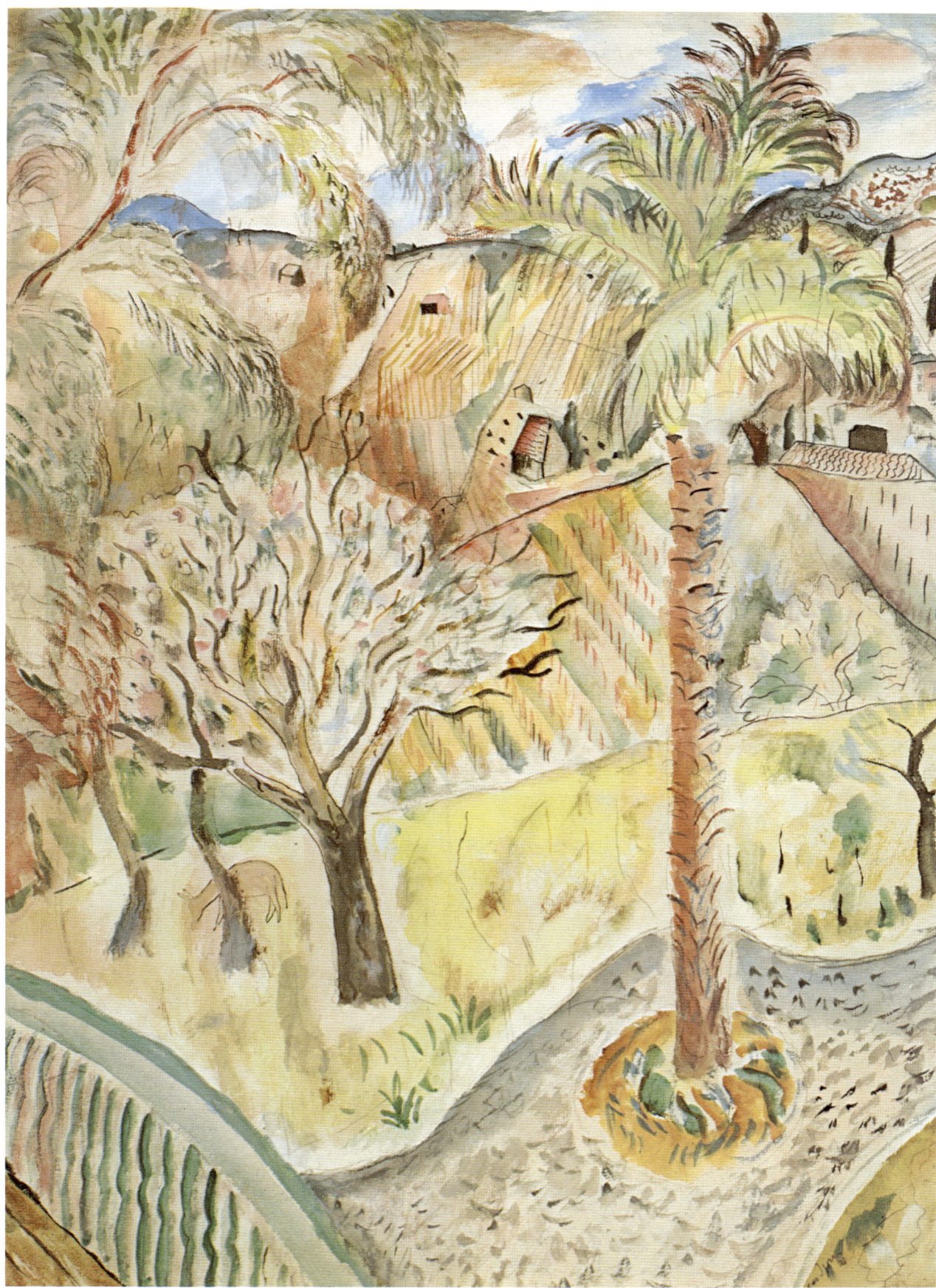

24. Landscape at Salies-de-Béarn, 1928

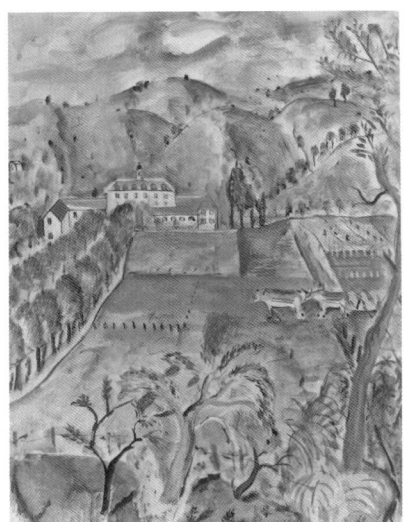

25. Roman Land, 1928

observed ox-teams ploughing which reminded him that France had once been part of the Roman Imperium, so that when he came to paint the animals at work against an old Napoleonic cavalry barracks he called the watercolour and gouache *Roman Land*. Nuances of tone and colour are subtly integrated, the shapes large, the perspective strong, and we are led back into, rather than up, the page. The warm earth reds and ochres which attract us are set on edge by the cold blue greens.

The Hagreens were living in the Chalet St. Vincent, which, on high ground opposite the Grotto, adjoined the enclosure of a convent of Dominican nuns who sang 'the office with a more marvellous beauty than I have before heard'. Jones went on to note in a letter to the Edes that 'I did a kind of picture of a nun picking roses with mountains behind and a white wall, which I don't mind in some ways'.[40] If Jones was somewhat pleased with *Dominican Lay Sister in a Rose Garden*, it is because it possesses that all over, fluid quality to which he was aspiring. The composition is so full that foreground, middle ground and distance seem to be shifting in a flux. The surprisingly dominant anchor of the dark arch acts as the only real fixed point of reference.

Lourdes itself was something of a nightmare. The 'ghastly commercialism' of the town clearly disturbed Jones: 'it's like finding a Woolworth store on the summit of The Mount of Olives'.[41] The landscape around the town was, as Jones so aptly described it in a letter to H.S. Ede, 'awfully panoramic' and as the weather was wet, the snowy mountains began to appear to Jones, not so much as rocky bulks, but 'as kind of lights hung in the sky', an effect which he had not yet learnt to paint. Perhaps his aversion to the town, coupled with his dislike of panoramic subjects, led to him sound that note of despair that later became so familiar: 'I should like to get more work done before I do return. I've done so many utter duds - it's so exhausting and depressing'.[42]

One of the great successes of the visit was *Montes et Omnes Colles* in which even the shafts of light streaming down from the sky in the centre are accommodated; these strong effects of sunlight and the proximity of the scene to the holy shrine of Lourdes doubtless account for the title which is taken from *Psalm 148*, 'Praise the lord ... mountains and all hills'.[43] Jones controls the strong meandering rhythm of the panorama by keeping the spectator's eye moving from point to point, from the clusters of different colours in different parts of the painting. The fluid hills float as in a Chinese watercolour. There is a sense of great scale but buildings are dotted about without much attention to perspective as they might be in an Italian primitive painting. The drawing is faint, offering delicate guidelines, and there is a wide variety of brushwork. The fascination for the painter is in the dancing rhythms of the foreground trees as well as the distant mountains.

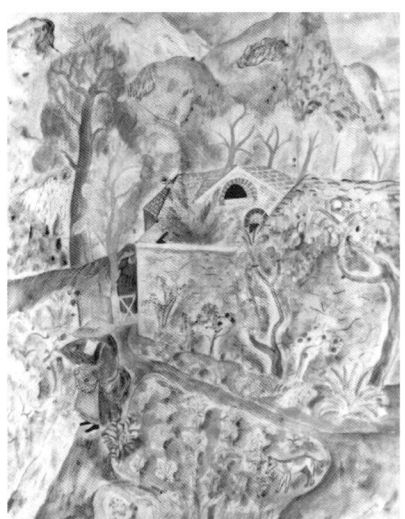

26. Dominican Lay Sister in a Rose Garden, 1928

Christopher Neve suggested that Stanley Spencer 'felt that, by drawing it, he had the power to reveal holiness in landscape ... because he could see the sanctity of quite ordinary things'; Spencer absorbed Bible stories from his father when he was a child and transposed them to his everyday surroundings.[44] Jones, free of his overt religious symbolism of earlier in the decade

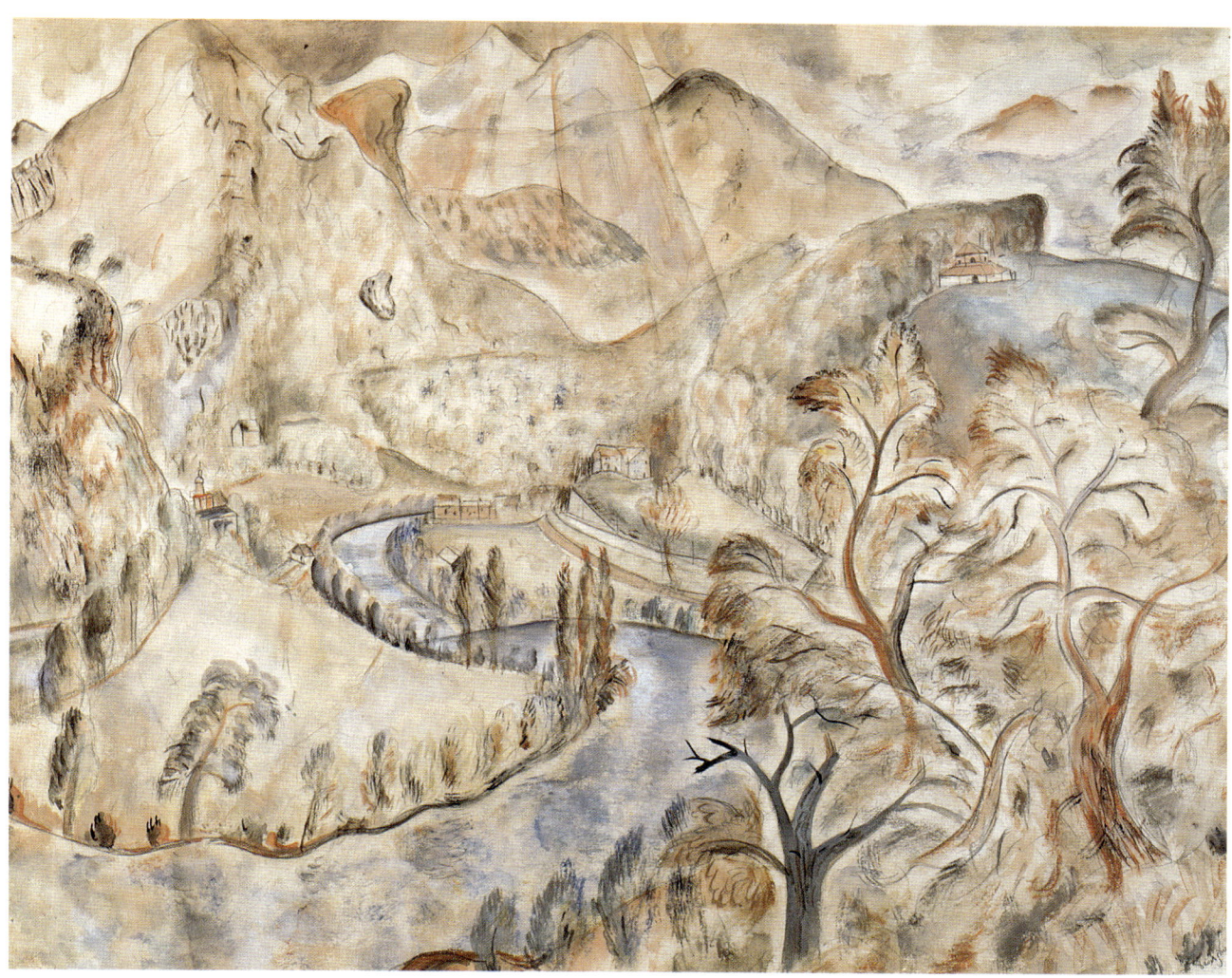

27. Montes et Omnes Colles, 1928

was beginning to seek out a similar holiness in landscape. If Lourdes had sprung up as part of that nineteenth century French Catholic revival that had nurtured the very aesthetic philosophy which Jones had found through Gill in the pages of Maritain, then it was landscapes such as this one near Lourdes that were leading him away from the conceptual stylization issuing from Primitivism, Post-Impressionism, Symbolism and the Nabis. With a loss of such stylization, Hagreen - and this is a key to his aesthetic pronouncements - thought that Jones's painting 'had begun to go to seed',[45] a judgement which falls too early and misses the glories of the following years when Jones experimented more with light and evanescence and was able, on occasion, to shed all 'fidgety'[46] mundanities in the creation of his own world.

Jones went with the Hagreens to visit the bourgeois resort of Arcachon where he painted the bay and so ended his first trip to France since the war which, despite its great success, was to be his last. Even with a financially powerful patron behind him and with the aid of many generous friends, he could not be persuaded to leave the shores of England except for therapeutic purposes and that only once and only just. In France he had encountered a landscape of heroic defeat when he found himself near the place that Roland fell. Upon his return, having re-experienced the crossing of the channel, he was inspired to make some drawings of his experiences in the trenches. These sketches provoked, to his surprise, what was, arguably, to be the most successfully integrated work of art that he ever made, a writing that became known, before it was finished four years later, as *In Parenthesis*. In the closing passage, after the great massacre on the Somme, Jones laments all those who have died in bloody conflict including

> in the country of Béarn - Oliver
> and all the rest - so many without memento
> beneath the tumuli on the high hills.[47]

SHIPS AND THE SEA

Even in an unpromising scene such as *Bristol Docks* Jones's simplifications are effective, investing the industrial scape as he had imbued the gaunt *Suburban Order* with an empty eeriness. On the left, windows of the forbidding façades are blank, on the right, a compelling perspective terminates in that ominously dark doorway; a warehouse reflects as a ghostly hull on the water but the channel offers the way to open sea.

On 3 March 1925, David Jones left Capel-y-ffin on Philip Hagreen's advice to go to Caldey Island. The monastery buildings at Capel had, in fact, been leased by Gill from Caldey monks who, in the period prior to Gill's occupancy, had used them as a place of retreat. The years during which Gill was at Capel were difficult for the Caldey monks as they had been left heavily indebted by a large building programme instituted by Dom Aelred Carlyle who, in 1913, had taken Caldey back to the Church of Rome. In fact, the monks could not extricate themselves from their financial difficulty, and early in 1929 Caldey became a Cistercian foundation. Jones considered the monastery a 'pretty hit-or-miss'[1] affair but found it a sympathetic environment in which to work and an exciting place in which to paint.

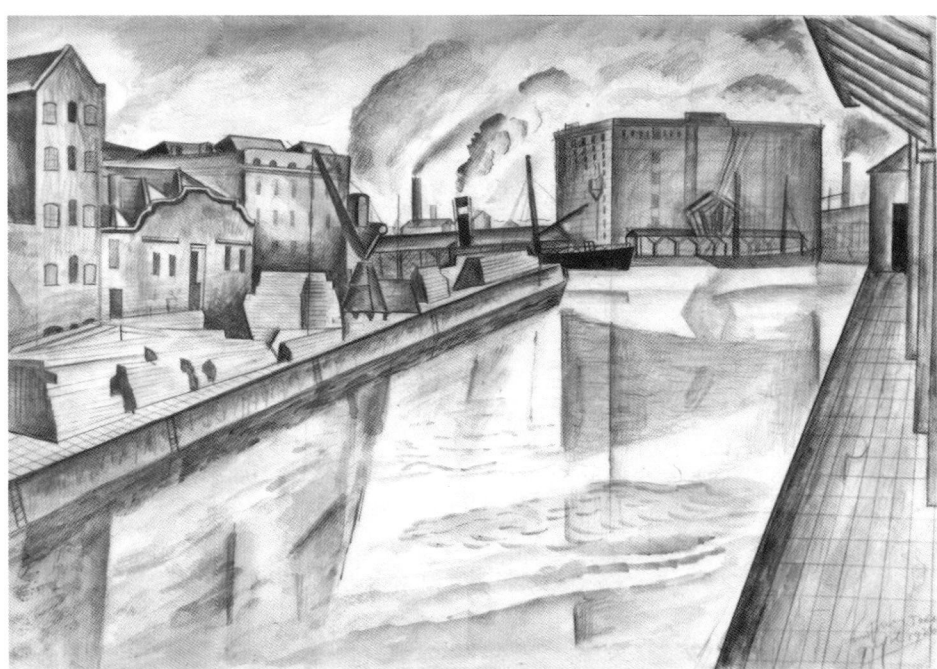

1. Bristol Docks, 1926

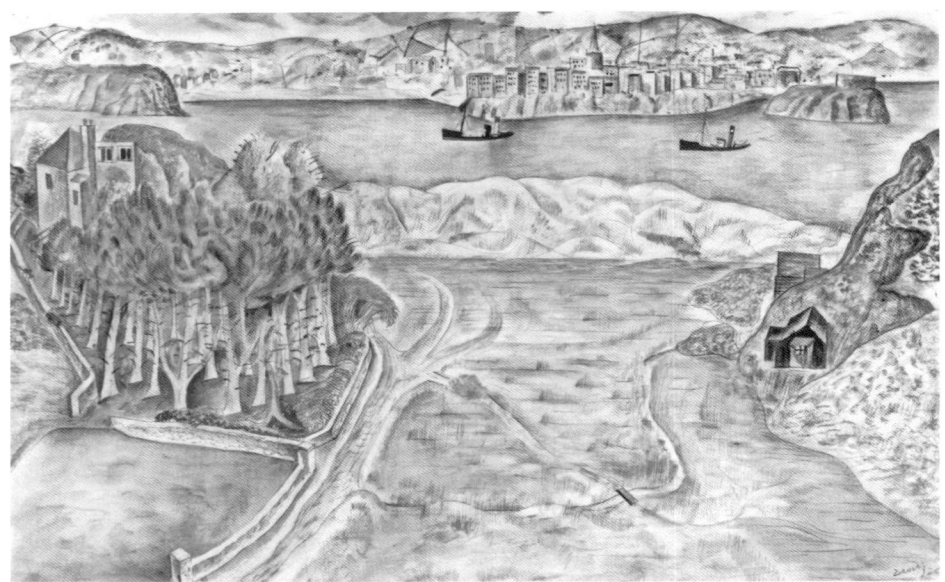

2. Tenby from Caldey Island, 1925

Caldey Island is three miles from Tenby so the closeness of the coast in *Tenby from Caldey Island* is licence on the part of the painter. The interior of the island is flat and uninspiring but the coast comprises sandy bays cupped by dangerous cliffs with many fissures, caves and blowholes. It is a smallish island some one and a half miles by three-quarters of a mile and the northern part, facing Tenby, is made of grey carboniferous limestone whereas the southern portion is of red sandstone.

During his first stay on Caldey, Jones wrote to Philip Hagreen about

> a superb plantation of new trees … which is thrilling, very thrilling - like the Garden of Gethsemane and the Garden of the Tomb and the Garden of - well - the other sort of garden, where Venus disports herself … a garden of small trees and winding paths … I have nearly been demented trying to capture its beauty even but vaguely.[2]

This is the plantation we see on the left-hand side of *Tenby From Caldey* and the toy-town vision of Tenby and the workaday boats are slight against the numinous attraction of trees that resonate with a kind of magic more telling, perhaps, because everything in the picture is kept in perfect equilibrium by an astute balance of muted hot and cool colours. At Westminster, Bayes had taught Jones to avoid the 'snare' of local colour.[3] Here Jones is at his most controlled. Even the deliberate defiance of scale secures a conceptual balance that is pictorially logical. Pencil and brush work in meticulous harmony and there is a sense of excitement even at the edges of the composition. The idea of the enchanted wood reappeared in that Capel landscape of the following year and a little later in *In Parenthesis*, when Jones wrote of the 'potency' of woods and groves where 'men come both to their joys and their undoing' and where, at the end of the book, after the wounding of John Ball at Mametz, the Queen of the Woods graces the battle dead.[4] Later still, in Jones's only truly mythopoeical landscape, *Vexilla Regis*, the wood has depth and enchantment.

Related to this painting is another view which has been mistakenly attributed as being a landscape in France;[5] the walls and red path, even the presence of a toytown so like Tenby in the previous painting, suggest that this is indeed Caldey Island. It is

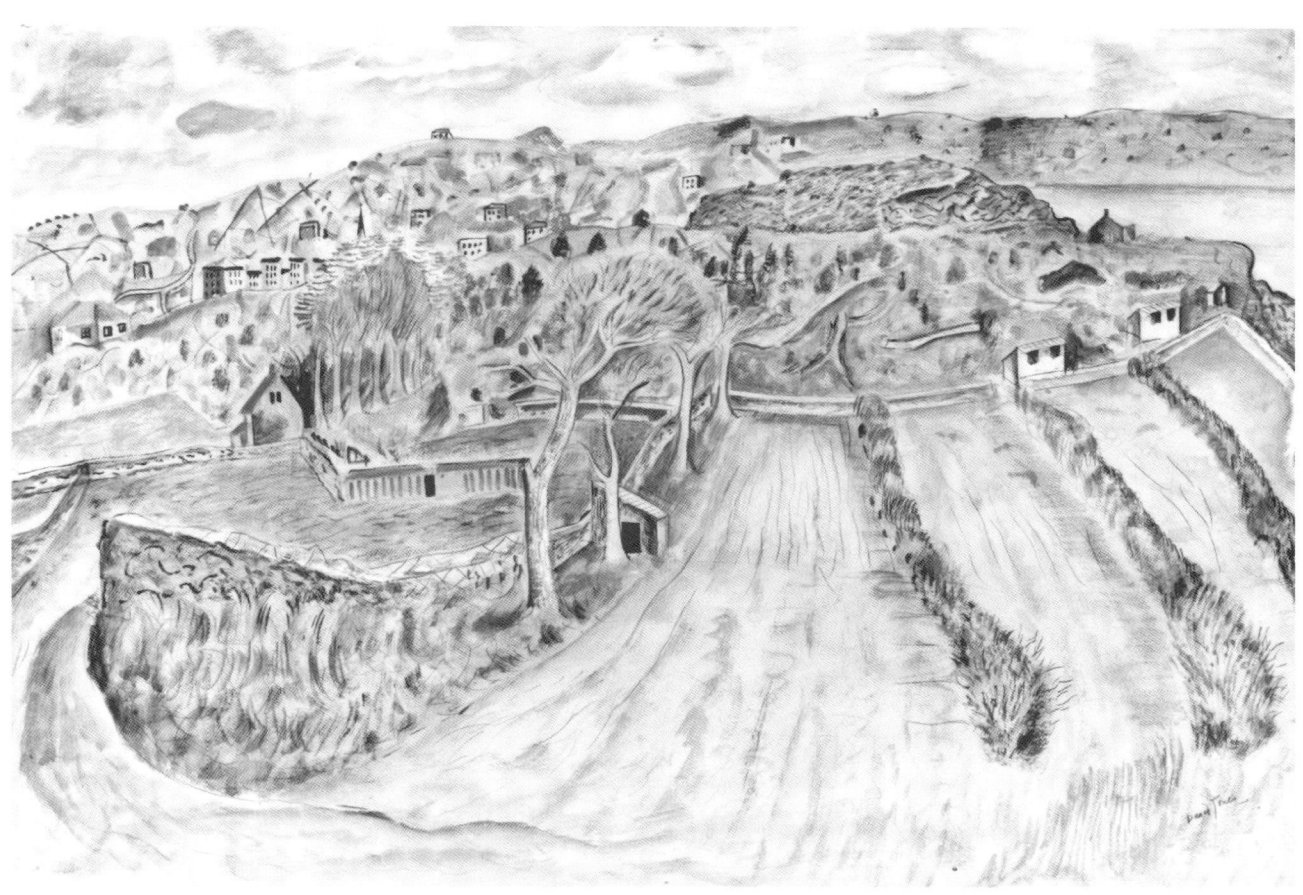

3. Landscape at the Coast, 1928

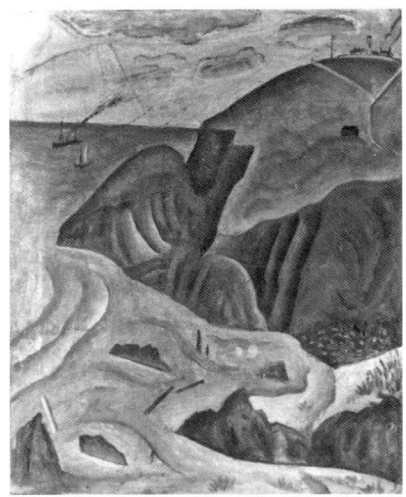

4. Coast Scene, 1925

one of Jones's most complicated landscapes with its segmenting and sophisticated lack of one point perspective taking the eye on separate journeys from differing starting points.

The coast scenes which Jones painted on Caldey in 1925 were formalistic, with the modelling respecting the dramatic changes of plane on 'the murderously sharp rocks'.[6] A similar approach is found in relevant wood-engravings; *Ship and Long Boats in a Bay* for *Gulliver's Travels* was probably engraved on Caldey and such formalism can also be seen in an oil, *Coast Scene, Wales*, a view of the red sandstone rocks of Chapel Point. Indeed, oil as a medium seems to assert form with its tendency towards opacity, whereas watercolour is more ambiguous, less substantial. Here Jones adopts a *faux-naïf* manner. The dramatic discrepancies of scale respect that convention but, as is so often the case with Jones, there is a struggle between his longing to create big, expansive forms and his apparent need to itemize tiny details which clutter and compromise his vision; the lighthouse, logs and boats interfere with the grander rhythms of the painting.

Rosenblum, writing about Friedrich's work, remarked on 'an experience familiar to the spectator in the modern world, an experience in which the individual is pitted against, or confronted by the overwhelming, incomprehensible immensity of the universe, as if the mysteries of religion had left the rituals of church and … had been relocated in the natural world.'[7] This can be seen in *Rocks and Surf, Caldey*, which, in its vastness, captures something of the sublime to be found in certain landscapes of Hodler. The looseness and generalization, the geometrical battle, punctuated by brooding washes and an enlivening calligraphy result in an epic grandeur, revealing what the poet Hopkins designated as 'instress', that tension which held the essence of an object or scene together and conveyed it to the beholder. The blissful absence of boats in this and the following painting shows Jones daring to unanchor himself from descriptive detail and accept emptiness.

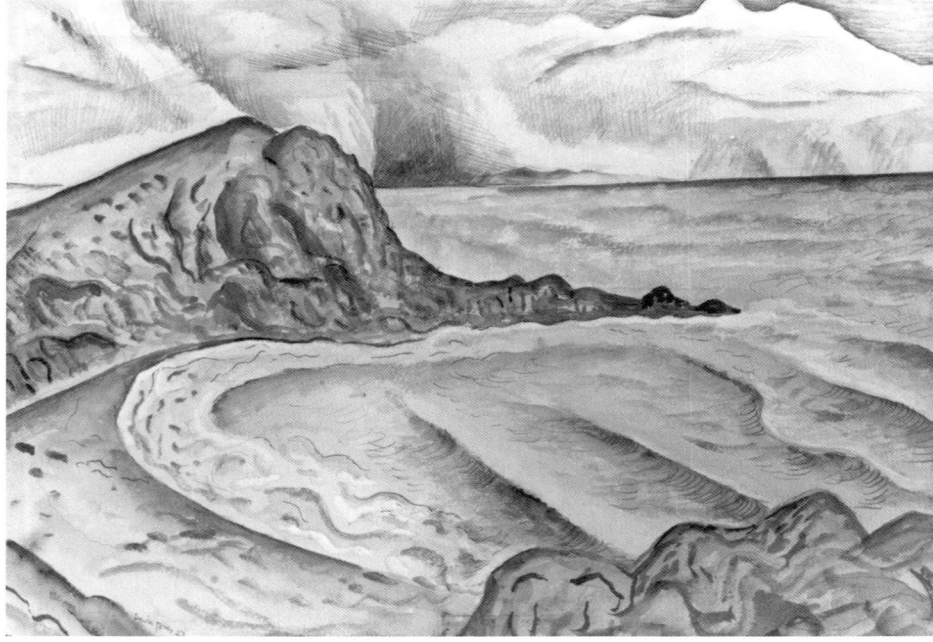

5. Rocks and Surf, 1927

116

The artist wrote to H.S. Ede from Caldey in October, 1927, about the fatigue of 'trying and failing' with his 'attempts at painting'.[8] This is an early example of what became an almost ceaseless plaint, and yet a letter written immediately after his visit declares that while some of the paintings were 'awful', and while he did 'an immense amount of tearing up at Caldey ... one or two of the remaining ones I ... think ... in a curious way the best things I have done so far'[9] - the vacillation of an artist striking out for something, not quite knowing what it is, or if the results are a success.

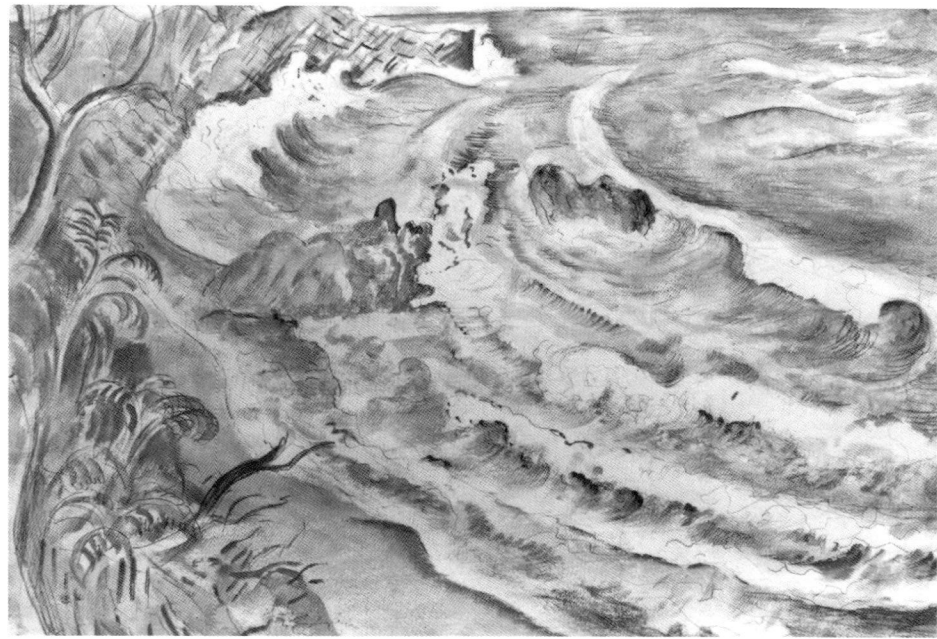

6. Surf, 1929

Jones, who was as various in his attempts at rendering water as he was in his stylistic approaches, treated the full drama of waves breaking in *Surf* of 1929. The bay is that which Jones had painted in the more formalized *Ship off Ynys Byr* of 1925 and the two paintings are virtually irreconcilable because of their different styles. Here the roaring energy of the sea is asserted, the rocking surge of the waves as they usurp the shore. Jones had written to Philip Hagreen in a letter of March, 1925, 'it is difficult not to be led up various impressionistic and realistic and otherwise dangerous paths when faced with the sea - or - even worse, to fall back upon some dead convention'.[10] In *Surf* the treatment is less stylized than hitherto, Jones is moving towards a use of watercolour which allows the qualities of the medium to manifest the subject.

As the twenties gave over into the thirties Jones was passing into the most painterly phase of his working life and water, which had always been central to his imagination, plays an increasingly important and symbolic part. Watercolour is well suited to express the mystical and poetical and transcend the blunt facts of nature as it is, in itself, fluid and insubstantial. The paper is allowed to shine through the colour so light is reflected from the white background. Whereas oil would, typically, seem to be suited to the mundane,

117

watercolour allows the dissolution of matter into something suggestive of a beyond. With a painting of the sea, water is not only the medium but also the subject - moving watercolour marks drying on the paper become a sign for water that remains ever wet and moving.

Jones's choice of watercolours is interesting. Eb Bradshaw, his maternal grandfather, had been a mast- and block-maker in the Pool of London towards the end of the nineteenth century. Although Bradshaw died before Jones was born, the boy heard much about him from his mother and grandmother whose Italian descent was visible in her features and who lived with the Joneses until David was ten.[11] Bradshaw became a figure who exemplified the good maker; re-created in the 'Redriff' section of Jones's second long poem, *The Anathemata*, Bradshaw resists doing a speedy and imperfect job. Jones confirmed in a letter that 'Redriff' was 'pretty factual reportage' and noted that his mother told him about 'the Port of London, especially the lower Pool of the river bend below ... the Tower and Greenwich'[12] which would have been at the peak of its importance during the second half of the nineteenth century, as busy as that forest of masts shown by the young Whistler in his *Wapping on Thames* of 1860-4. But while these stories of ships and the sea were exciting for the young child, it was his first actual sight of the sea at Deal that made a lasting impression on him, when after walking down a narrow street, he suddenly beheld the great expanse of water beyond.[13] After that, part of each summer during his childhood was spent on the north Welsh coast. Early on he understood that Britain was an island, accessible in those days only by boat. In the 'Middle-Sea and Lear-Sea' section of *The Anathemata* mariners experience Albion's 'screen of brume'(p 98), 'squall-mist and the rain' (p 103) before fetching up in 'Angle-Land' where such watery atmosphere not only characterizes the coasts of the 'White Island', but the interior also: naiads 'sign the whole anatomy of Britain' (p 204). Later, in *The Roman Quarry*, water, the pre-eminent element in the geography, weather, mythology and literary imagery of the insular Celts becomes an expressive image of their freedom.[14] As a Roman soldier observes, 'all is a maze of meeting damps and ebb and flow of mist and tide so that the waters are, in a manner of speaking, lord of all' (p 5). Watercolour would therefore seem to be the medium suited to re-present Britain and its coasts.

In his essay, 'The Myth of Arthur' Jones wrote:

> The folk tradition of the insular Celts seems to present to the mind a half-aquatic world - it is one of its most fascinating characteristics - it introduces a feeling of transparency and inter-penetration of one element with another, of transposition and metamorphosis.[15]

This Celtic vision of fluidity suggested itself to Jones as an image for the process of art. Poetry and painting function because of the capacity for one thing to become something else - words working metaphorically, marks on a page fusing into some form, rhythm or significance. For Jones, water becomes a governing metaphor for creativity itself. In Celtic mythology a stream or the land's edge is a place where a being can pass from the physical into the metaphysical, where, as Jones puts it in *The Roman Quarry* 'ceaseless metamorphosis is the only constant' (p35). In such places, Jones felt himself to be in a kind of creative amniotic fluid. His growing interest in atmosphere resulting from the violent changes in weather conditions in the border country and at the coast took his watercolours into a new and unanchored realm of vision. When he stopped painting the sea or the Marches there was a slow drying up of his painterly capacity.

By the time that he was painting on Caldey in 1931 Jones was using very thin washes and the scene is truly transmuted into its medium. In *Trade Ship Passes Ynys Byr,* we are not looking at rocks or waves but rocks and waves 'under the form of paint'. The drawing is done with the paint-brush, there is variety in the marking with strong contrasts of tonality and colour, and the accenting of the boat and birds helps to give volume to the bowl of the bay.

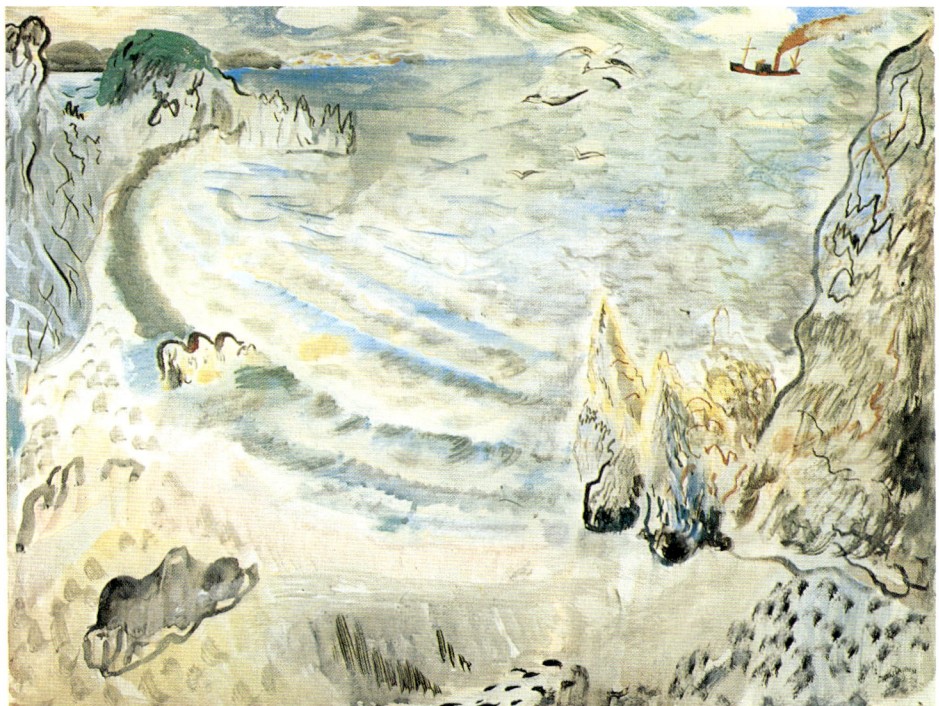

7. Trade Ship Passes Ynys Byr, 1931

While Jones was painting in this sheltered cove on Caldey an economic crisis in the late summer led to the formation of a National Government and also affected gallery sales. The market for etchings and modern fine printing subsequently collapsed and Douglas Cleverdon was one casualty of the slump; his New York agent was bankrupted by the Depression and in 1933 'the last seventy copies of the ordinary £2.2.0 edition of *The Rime of the Ancient Mariner* were remaindered by Blackwell's at seven shillings and sixpence.'[16] Culturally, this period of the early thirties was perceived as a period of crisis, accentuating, according to Paul Nash, Britain's sense of

119

'insularity'.[17] Fry's formalistic approach had been under attack since the late 1920s and studies such as Kenneth Clark's *The Gothic Revival* (1928), showed, as David Mellor points out, 'that an antiquarian, bookish, and nationalist recoil was underway',[18] something that would be of considerable importance for Jones towards the end of the decade. By 1931, the painter had moved away from his tendency towards a formalism which owed something to Fry and something to Gill, and was beginning to discover his neo-Romantic tendencies. At odds with the evolution of Ben Nicholson and Paul Nash into their modernist, Hard-edged or Surrealist phase, Jones was, in a sense, dissolving Britain in its own aquatic essence. Where 'the seas of the islands war with the ocean' (*Ana*. p 97) the British landscape and seascape become the refracted remains of that battle, its myths and histories surreptitiously impinging on a vision of nature which is in turn dissolving into a mystical order.

In 1928, Gill wrote of Jones that 'some critics have complained that, whereas his wood-engravings are overlaboured and tight, his watercolours are unfinished and loose'.[19] If that was true of 1928, how much more so of paintings done in 1931. At the Lefevre Gallery in November of that year his recent Caldey pictures were shown in the company of painters such as Frances Hodgkins and Ben and Winifred Nicholson. It was Nicholson who had 'said he liked them very much when he saw them - and wrote and asked me to send them to the Lefevre - that's how they got there.' At the time, the Lefevre was one of the most progressive and important of the London galleries, but for Jones this exhibition was somewhat of a disappointment as his pictures were hung in a dark part of the room where it was impossible to see them properly.[20]

Michael Paget Baxter, the proprietor of *The Christian Herald* had, in 1908, built bungalows along the Western Esplanade at Hove. Jones's father worked for *The Christian Herald* so the family rented No. 5 as a holiday home for several months each year in the twenties and early thirties. The publicity for Hove Bungalows Ltd. boasted of a Drawing Room

> furnished with considerable taste, and a more comfortable general living room it would be difficult to imagine ... its windows command on one side a view of Brighton Pier to the east and of Worthing Pier to the west, whilst from the verandah which opens onto it a splendid view of the sea is obtained.

> So importantly a feature of the Bungalows as this verandah is worthy of a fuller description, but it must here suffice to say that it extends 11ft. on either side of the entrance from the Drawing Room.[21]

When his brother was in the process of dying from consumption, Jones had been lodged for a time with an uncle who lived in a converted old fortress or gun emplacement right on the shore of the south coast and the spray would hit the windows.[22] Such a sensation was re-experienced at Portslade when Jones painted both from the verandah and the bedroom of the villa which 'were built literally on the sea margin so that if the weather were at all rough, surf and spray broke on the seaward balconies'.[23] To be in one of these houses is to have the feeling of being almost on the water; for a man who, to the annoyance of his mother, used to keep his Brockley bedroom floorboards bare in order to create the illusion of ship's planking,[24] the experience must have been most exciting. Certainly, the paintings that he did there towards the end of the period between 1927 and 1931 were among the works that in later years, looking back, he liked best.

The difference between the beginning and the end of the period is considerable. The 1927 Portslade paintings are either an almost anecdotal imitation of the austere style of Nash's Dymchurch paintings, or an uneasy confusion between the miniaturist, toyish style of depicting buildings, pier and boats and the more painterly Post-Impressionist style used for the sea. Although *Verandah Wall, Portslade* of 1927 is reminiscent of Nash, it also possesses a Jonesian sense of animation. The conflicting angles of the verandah roof, boat smoke, wall and horizon, and the tilting verticals which break the space, all create drama. The tops of the roof supports, which are usually seen curving over, are here squared and the three together might have evoked for the painter a submerged image for the crucifixion.

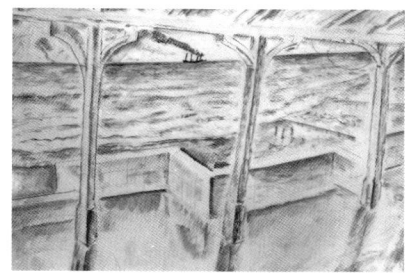
8. The Verandah Wall, 1927

While watercolour was obviously expressive of fluidity, thinned oil was used by Jones in a number of Portslade seascapes to considerable effect. *Sea View* is painted on board in viridian, prussian blue, indian red and black which combine to give a subdued, silvery greyish effect registering that Jones's lessons in tonality from Sickert had been well understood. Jones wrote that he 'did not use tone in the way' Sickert had done but learned from him how 'one colour can 'change' another by juxtaposition'.[25] The oil is thinned to give the same shifting insubstantiality as watercolour but there is an unremitting opacity which is inescapable. The boat is placed in reasonable relation to the scroll of the support and the curve of the breakwater but why does Jones not treat it in the same broad style? Its

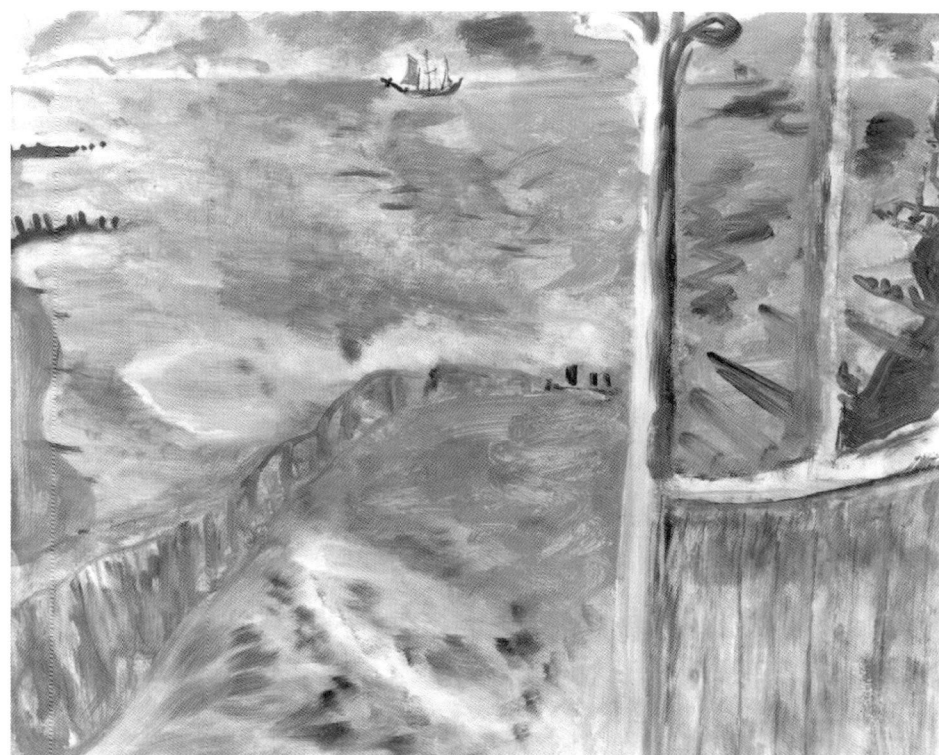
9. Sea View, 1929

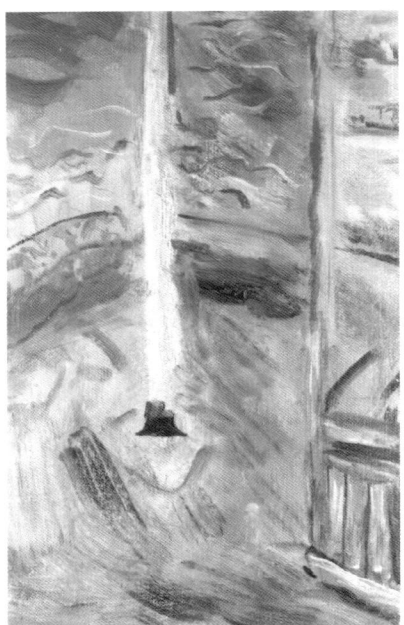

10. The Fountain (Stormy sea from
    the verandah, Portslade), 1929

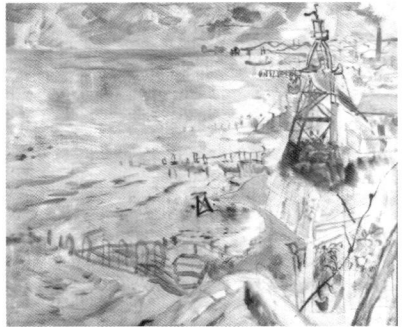

11. Factory Coast, 1931

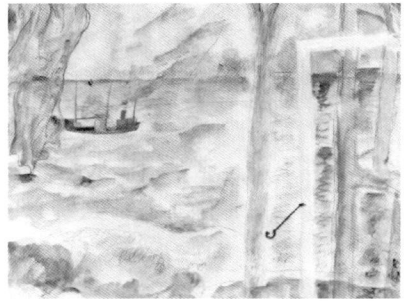

12. Portslade (detail), 1929

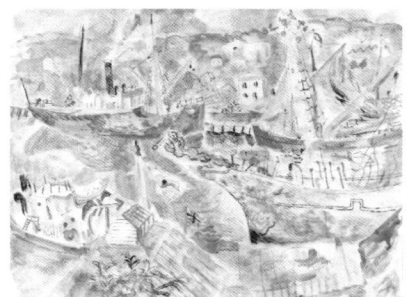

13. Place for Ships, 1931

fussiness compromises the power of an otherwise vigorous painting. *The Fountain (A stormy sea from the Verandah, Portslade)* is loose and smudgy. It is a powerful, semi-abstract oil which was obviously produced, like a watercolour, at speed. When Jones dares to let go of anecdotal details the picture grows.

Two years later, another oil, *The Factory Coast (11)*, was painted, with a kind of disgust for the ugliness of the industrial sprawl characterized by the thin mean, barbed lines and an obvious sympathy expressed by the loose, broad effects of light on the sea and in the sky. The painting evokes Jones's frustration at seeing, as he put it in the *Preface* to *In Parenthesis*, 'the petroleum … hurting the sea'. The subject is an unusual one and there is something ominous in the broad brushstrokes of the sky and something ironic in the hint of a Dufyesque frippery in the drawing with the brush.

While it is clear that he was using oil in a variety of ways, it was in water-colour that Jones's ablest south coast paintings were made. In *Portslade* of 1929 (detail - *12*) the door and verandah supports on the right set up a fascinating relation of spaces, and the curtain, ubiquitous in Jones's work, appears like some remnant, an expression of the poignancy of departure, by an itinerant who was increasingly becoming afraid of travel.

Manawydan's Glass Door (14) of 1931, is among the finest seascapes with its saturation of prussian blue merging inside and out, framed by the ochre support on the left and the blue one on the right. A transhistorical yacht begins to take on the appearance of a sailing ship with its pennant flying. We seem to be in a kind of magic realm as Jones looks through the windows towards the French coast and perhaps ponders over memories of the First World War. The 'perturbation' in the paintwork, little explosions of white on the sea and streaks of alizarin in the sky, as well as the title itself, create a wistful unease. In the passage concerning Manawydan's door in *The Mabinogion*, warriors, opening it against advice, view 'all the evils they had ever sustained … as if all had happened in that very spot … and … they could not rest.'[26] The furious activity of the late twenties and early thirties which led to Jones's first breakdown was the combined result of the great expense of artistic excitement after the break-up of his engagement and a delayed reaction to the war. And perturbation is perhaps the word that best characterizes Jones's seas - they are not the glassy, flat tracts painted by Nash at Dymchurch, nor have his treatments of waves that Whistlerian economy of Nicholson's *Porthmeor Beach, St. Ives* (1928), they are rather unsettled, troubled, restless. What is more, Jones was beginning to use mythological references in his titles and thereby float the dissolving scene in some kind of space-time continuum.

To the west of the house at Portslade, there was a small harbour but Jones does not treat the calm or shelter of the haven. In *Place for Ships (13)* spatial relationships are difficult to read and sky, landscape, boats and foreground houses almost seem to merge. Jones urges continual eye movement as his changes of focus are abrupt and his accentings odd. For Jones, by 1931 the chances for blithe calm were slight and in the paintings of the following months the voyage into the realms of watercolour took him to the edge of a dissolving world which he couldn't accept or sustain. Writing to Charles Burns in May, 1940 Jones observed that he 'would prefer an operation for appendicitis a dozen times to one bad assault on the "nervous system" - about the latter I feel more and more at sea.'[27]

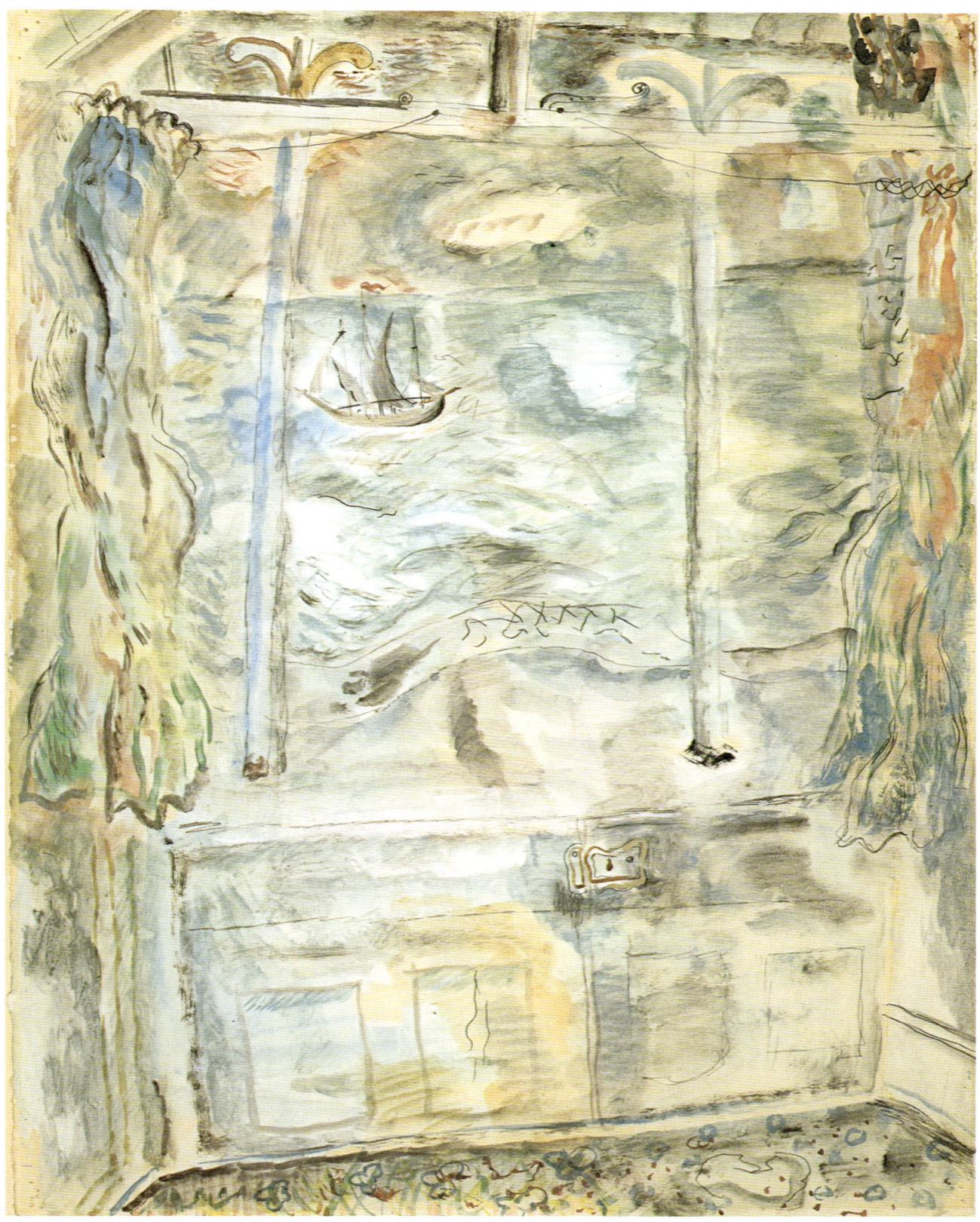

14. Manawydan's Glass Door, 1931

INTERIORS AND STILL LIFES

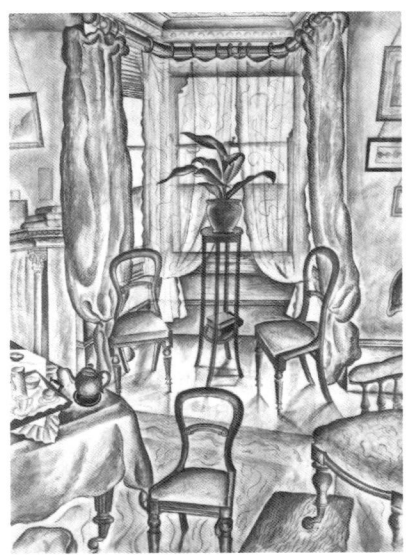

1. The Sitting Room, Howson Road, 1926

Increasingly, Jones felt the distance between the exciting environment into which his vocation led him and the sort of world in which he remembered 'a rather "racy"' older male relative responding with, '"My word! don't 'e put the butter on" when anybody became at all flowery.'[1] In the mid-twenties, by which time Brockley was little more than a base, Jones depicted the polished and ordered suburban calm of *The Sitting Room, Howson Road*, as a setting about which all has been, is and can be known. So mundane is this world that it provides a useful pretext for exploring a visual language which Jones further develops in *The Dog on the Sofa*. The tacit use of post-Cézannesque distortion to treat such a subject typifies the suburban relation of British to French Post-Impressionism. *The Sitting Room, Howson Road* is, nonetheless, well composed with two triple groupings of chair-plantstand-chair and table-chair-armchair, the former entirely visible in the mid-ground and the latter appearing from three edges of the picture, thus taking us into a scene where the planes and perspective have been cunningly distorted to give a certain rigour to the whole. The room is Edwardian and it is celebrated as something that has persisted in a changing world; elsewhere the drama of the war, the conversion to Catholicism and all the recent upheavals of Jones's life have occurred.

The Dog on the Sofa appears, by contrast, much less static. Perspectival distortion is more extreme and shadows cast by objects become a rhythmical element in the dynamic of the picture. The curves of chairs, the sinuous scroll of the back and foreground end of the *chaise-longue*, the swirls of the carpet pattern all react against the strong, straight edges in the composition, revealing that Jones is less interested by form or the relation of form for its own sake and is becoming, instead, excited by movement. The tilt of the floor is extreme, the stool and carpet-bag in the corner seem almost about to stalk across the room and the chairs on either side of the dresser are actually held in place by a strong diagonal shadow cast on the left and by the edge of the cloth on the right. Things seem to wriggle as if there is something intrinsically untenable about such domesticity. While the triple grouping around the aspidistra in *The Sitting Room* might, to spectators who know Jones well, convey a muted religious significance, in *The Dog on the Sofa* the artist has sought out a surrogate altar on the shelf of the dresser. Held by the assertive and almost parallel plane of the blue Cézannesque lappet at the foreground end of the table, this dresser is dominant.

Jones never again painted a windowless interior for its own sake. Neither the grander homes in which he lodged from time to time in the late twenties, thirties or early forties, nor the humbler rooms that he made so chaotically

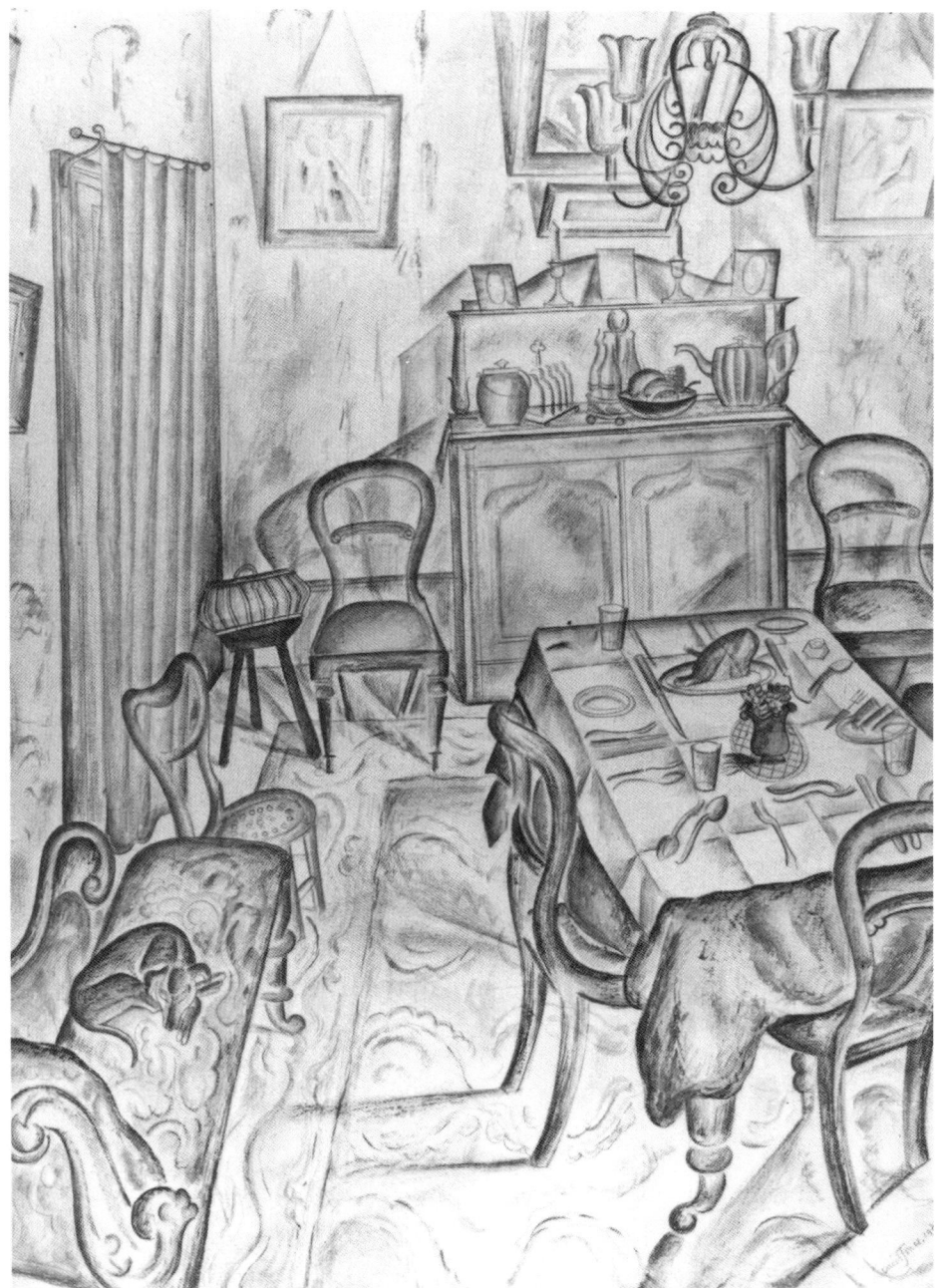

2. The Dog on the Sofa, 1926

his own in the last three decades of his life became subjects in their own right. In these two paintings of his parental home there is, as well as a gentle humour, a visible pride in what he was in the process of relinquishing, a comfortable lower-middle class suburban home in which, with so many pictures visible on the walls, there was an obvious affection for images.

There was no tradition of painting still life in English art prior to the twentieth century. For Jones's generation, to paint a still life was self-consciously to ape a continental genre. In June, 1927 Jones saw the Matisse exhibition with Eric Gill and that, along with the influence of the *École de Paris*, examples of which he might have seen in November 1924, at the Lefevre Gallery, prompted a

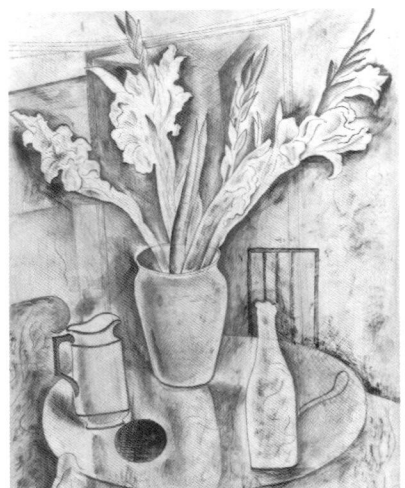

3. Still Life With Gladioli, 1927

work like *Still Life With Gladioli*. The firmly drawn outline is preserved from the Brockley interiors but here the selection of objects, as well as elements in the style, reveal an obvious debt to recent French still life: the round table or *guéridon*, the distorted wine bottle, the shadow between it and the vase carrying the hint of the form of a fluted glass, the flattened disc of the table mat, the jug, the use of a mirror to complicate the geometry of the simplified interior and the resultant sectionalizing of the image. It is imitative, and although for Jones it is an experimental picture, the relation of forms is not exciting. In a painting like this, it is clear that the artist is not adept at arranging objects and doesn't appear to know quite why he's making a still life except that it is a thing which recent artists have done. To look at a Jones still life of 1927 and then at one of 1932 is to mark the difference between a young painter playing gently with available notions about viewpoint, space and form and an adventurous artist making a response to the transcendental significance of especially chosen objects. In *Still Life with Gladioli*, the flowers interest Jones but the over-emphatic jug compromises their impact. The cross-hatching is reminiscent of his concurrent activity as an engraver and the mysterious blurring of planes and entities which was to become characteristic of his work as the twenties drew to a close had not yet been evolved. A work like this is neutral, lacking both emotion and significance. It was art for art's sake, tending in a sterile direction and utterly in sympathy with much art in a decade distinguished by uncontroversial or unremarkable subject matter.[2] It was made in the year in which Jones's engagement to Petra Gill was broken off and a retreat into art for art's sake may have provided some solace. It was, furthermore, painted in Bristol in August, in the 'arty' atmosphere of the flat and studio above Douglas Cleverdon's bookshop.

Jones had shown two Capel paintings in *Pictures, Sculpture & Pottery By Some British Artists Today* at the Lefevre Gallery in February, 1925, and it is possible that he met Ben Nicholson through his involvement in such an exhibition. In the previous year, Nicholson had been invited to join the 7&5 Society by Ivon Hitchens, one of the original members of that loose, non-partisan group which first exhibited in 1920. By 1926, when Nicholson became chairman, it was becoming the most exciting exhibiting society in Britain; at the time, it was indigenous in spirit and often romantic, less obviously indebted to the *École de Paris* than Fry's London Group. 7&5 exhibitions, according to H.S. Ede, were 'light and airy' providing a much needed lyricism in the decade following the First World War. When Jones later remarked that 'English artists are "Romantic" or nothing', he went on to note that 'even old Ben is really Romantic in spite of the appearance of French "intelligence"'.[3]

Ben Nicholson, the son of the distinguished painter and wood engraver, William Nicholson, had had the good fortune to spend several years of his youth in France and Italy and thus the opportunity to consider the latest in continental painting. Despite his avowed aim 'to bust up the sophistication all around me'[4] in an attempt to cut loose from his family, his work in the twenties was nothing if not coldly sophisticated. His still lifes owed much to recent Parisian models and he spent time in that city visiting the studios of

Mondrian and Brancusi, as well as the commercial galleries. He also exhibited in Paris, first in 1925, in the company of artists such as Gris, Miró and Moholy-Nagy, in *L'art d'aujourd'hui* and, several years later, in a joint exhibition with Christopher Wood at the Bernheim Gallery.

Nicholson was concerned with texture and form and with flattening objects. Such flattening is seen in Jones's *The Table Top* of 1928, which teases the spectator with its ambiguity between the acceptance and denial of depth. The table is used almost like a frame within a frame and each pot, seen from a different vantage point, is more or less flattened against it. A sense of Nicholson recedes after continued study, and the light and glancing shadows make it unmistakably Jones's work. The dark interior of the primitive and battered pot on the right dominates and beside it the central vase almost disappears. Jones's trick of playing with focus means that the somewhat banal diagonal arrangement of objects ceases to matter; as the eye travels to the top right hand corner, the bottom left moves out of focus. The trivial packet of cigarette papers which casts disproportionate shadows is a mere pretext for abstract accenting. Yet while the work is busy and active, there is that cool *faux-naïf* element found in contemporaneous Nicholson paintings and the thin vertical lines of room moulding towards the top right-hand corner are perhaps a distant echo of the strings of instruments so fascinating to the Cubists. Jones appears unconcerned about the forms of flowers but is interested in the arrangement merely as a pretext for a profusion of colour and texture; the tendrils of one frond on the right become almost scratches or breaks on the table, flattened as they are against its top. A testimony to the lineage from the Cubists to the cosmopolitan Nicholson to his more insular contemporaries, the painting reveals that when Jones finds neither the symbolic nor the organic, his work can remain quite empty.

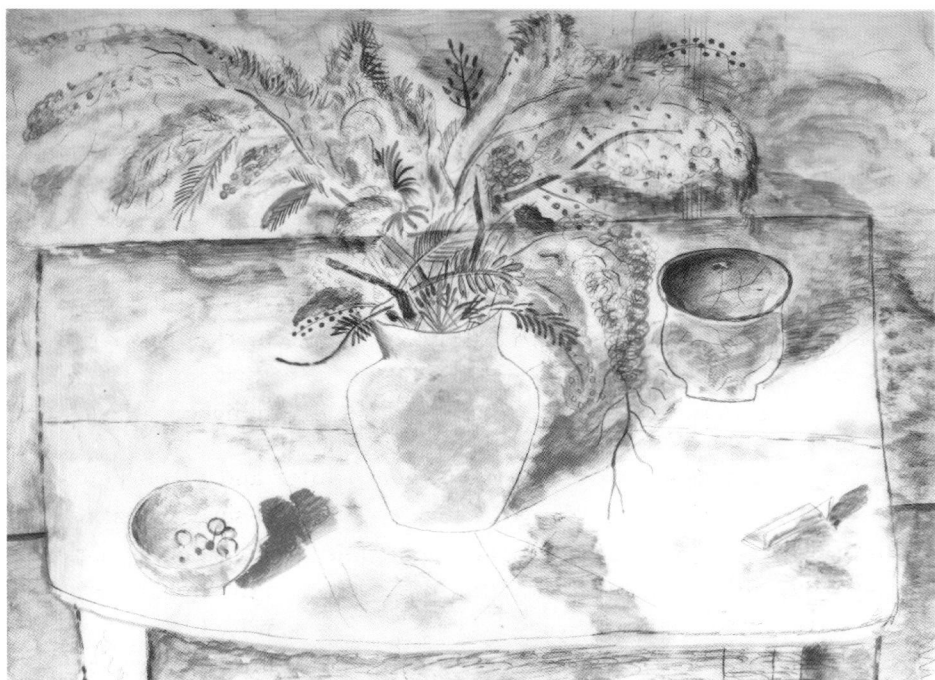

4. Still Life with Plate and Goblet, 1928

127

Writing to an old friend from Westminster Art School much later in life, Jones confessed that

> I've almost forgotten trying to paint in oils. I never did much, as you know, and always preferred doing what I wanted to do in watercolours. But I wish I'd done more oils than I have. But somehow, the other medium has seemed to suit me and then when I took to writing and also living mainly in one room watercolour ... seemed more my thing.[5]

Nonetheless, a good number of oils remain of which *Syphon and Silver* of 1930 shows Jones using a thinned oil on board to create a watercolour-like effect. Forms which only a few years earlier had been dogmatically marked by line

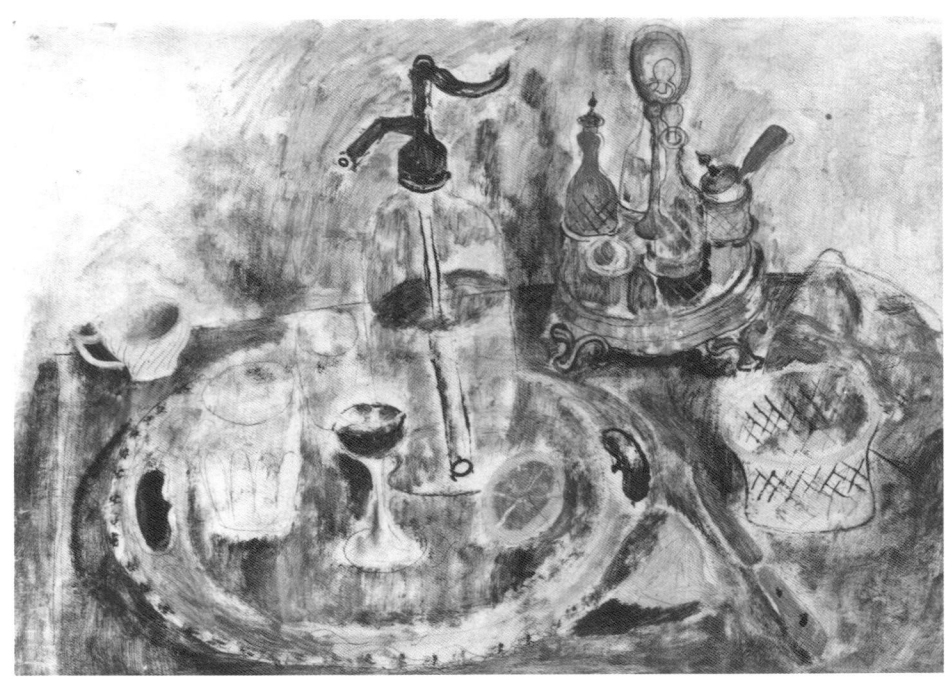

5. Syphon and Silver, 1930

are allowed to become insubstantial. Texture is not used sensually to express the surface of an object but in an abstract fashion. Despite the title, there is no attempt to show the silveriness of objects in the manner of a painter like William Nicholson, but there is an attempt to suggest the outline of flattened objects in the manner of that artist's son, Ben. Multiple vantage points are chosen and the condiment set with its lively interaction of ultramarine and red/violet is both more important and more typically Jonesian than the foreground tray with its Nicholsonian assortment of glasses and tumblers. The importance given to the circle at the bottom of the syphon's stem is typical of Jones's obsession with the point at which something is chopped off, curtailed, and is linked to his interest in nozzles.[6]

Another oil of just one year later is *The Candle and the Cup* which, with its eddies and swirls painted in broad brush strokes, is stylistically related to the

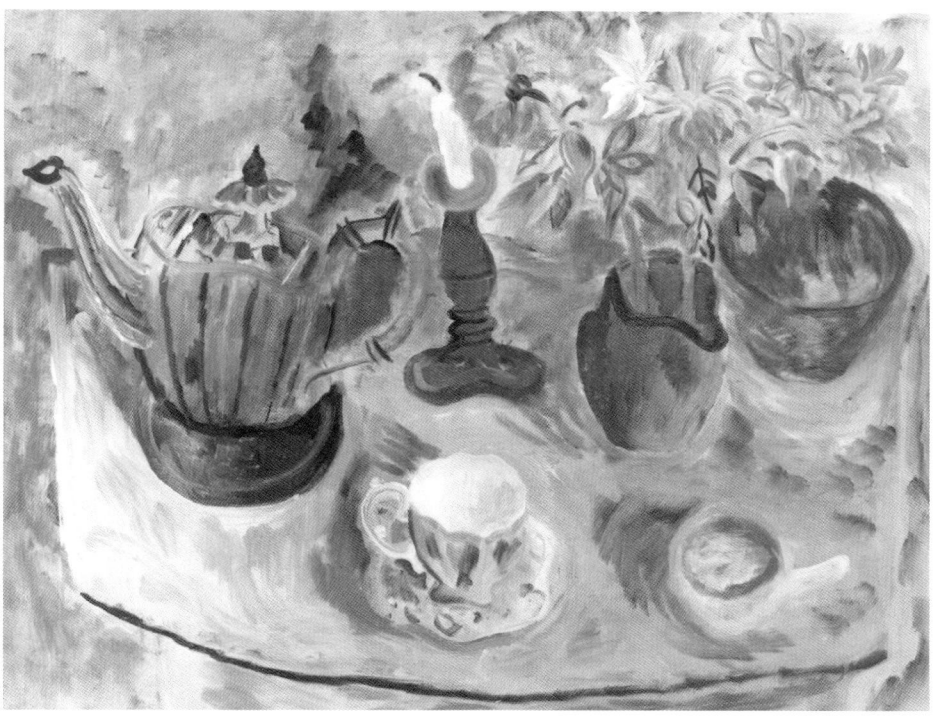

6. The Candle and the Cup, c.1931

Portslade oils. The movement in the painting is around the objects, as if a sea of uncontrollable forces is at work, and it is again clear that such movement is what absorbs Jones for he simply does not know what to do with mundane objects if they provoke no recessive intellectual significance for him. The white of the candle and the cup stabilize the eye which is, otherwise, shuttled from object to object. Distress and uncertainty, the shadow side of celebration, emerge from behind the cover of artistic emulation and begin to reveal why this artist is drawn towards the still life.

Jones spoke of *The Artist's Work Table* of 1929 as a flower painting, but it is actually an early example of his interest in the interpenetration of exterior and interior, in this case achieved not only by the vased flowers and intruding tendrils but also by an overall tonal uniformity. Painted in his bedroom in Brockley, it is no longer an evocation of a suburban world; it could be anywhere at anytime - cottage, studio, monastic cell. Perhaps because Jones has always proved unsuccessful in relating large objects on a table, he has begun to diminish them, and yet his tools appear to be itemized, not quite lovingly or sensually as a maker might, but as if they were necessary anchors in an unsettling world; the drawer on the work-table is perilously open, there is a toppling effect created by the varying diagonals, a ghosting of the table, and troubled brushwork in the rough surrounds.

A feeling of haphazardness unsettles the view painted in oils from the same window a year earlier. Jones no longer records the fixed and repetitive burden of endless terraces, as he had done in watercolours such as *The Suburban Order*. As with the items on the work-table and the lighthouse on Caldey, scale has become a problem as small and large elements come into

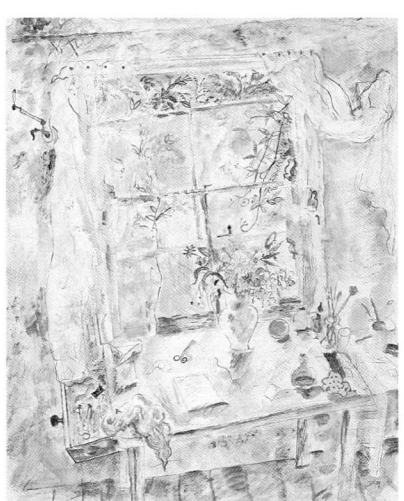

7. The Artist's Worktable, 1929

129

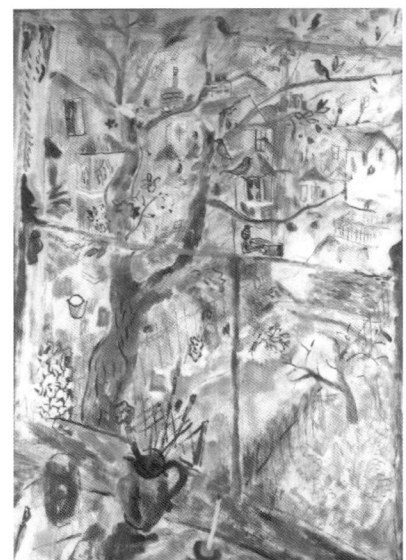

8. View From Brockley Window, 1928

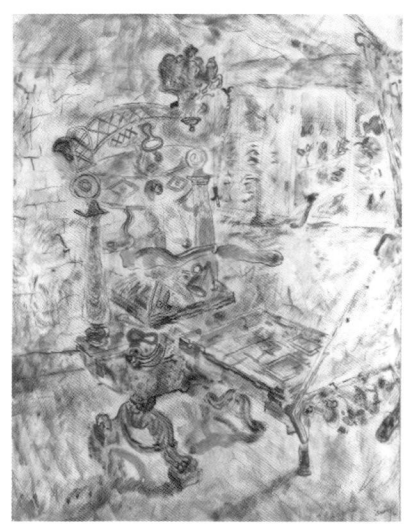

9. René Hague's Press, 1930

uneasy relation to one another. The eye flits about the canvas like a bird, unable to focus and make sense of the scene. Again, inside and outside appear to merge, helped by the form of the grip on the window latch which seems to echo that of a perching bird, despite the discrepancy of scale.

The increasing intensity of Jones's work during the packed four to five year period immediately before his first breakdown reflects the increasingly full life that he was leading. There was the constant moving from Brockley to Chelsea, to Hampstead, to Portslade, to Caldey, to Gill's new establishment at Pigotts near High Wycombe, and to Rock Hall in Northumberland, the house of his admirer and collector Helen Sutherland. In Brockley he engraved and painted and from that suburb made the great social leap to Chelsea where he met with the young Catholic bulldogs who were the motivating force behind *Order*, that short-lived *Blast* of the youthful English Catholic intelligentsia. Its editor, Tom Burns, recalled the Jones of this period as 'magnetic', 'crouched on the corner of a divan with two or three graceful girls draped round … in earnest discussion', seeming in some way 'to set the tone of the party' even though he was 'the small unkempt, unknown painter from Brockley - from outer space as far as most people in the room were concerned.'[7] At H.S. Ede's house in Hampstead, Jones mixed with artists. In Portslade he was painting and writing. On Caldey, he found himself back in a strongly religious environment and when, in May 1929, he was ill, he found it congenial to recuperate with the monks at Prinknash 'for a change and rest'.[8] At Pigotts, he re-entered Gill's eccentric world of undeliberate mock-medievalism and sexuality and lived in close proximity to his ex-fiancée who was, in 1930, married to Denis Tegetmeier. At Rock, he painted under the watchful eye of a strict and particular patron who expected guests to follow her routine with greater rigour than would have been expected from a soldier on the Western Front. It is small wonder that Jones felt himself to be in a fluid and uncertain world in which it was difficult for him to focus. The pace of life, as his writing began to expand into a full-length book and as he began to exhibit more frequently, was both exhilarating and breathtaking, if not bewildering and even frightening. In a sense, Jones couldn't quite accommodate the vigour of his own energy. In works made between 1930 and 1932 his idiosyncratic blend of mystical Expressionism began to manifest itself but he seems to have been ultimately afraid of freedom as if it would dissolve what, intellectually, he had been, during the previous twelve years, garnering. His aesthetic was tempered to the delicately lyrical and the comfortable or secured, qualities often summarized as 'Englishness', and yet the shy Expressionist emerged despite himself.

Jones made two versions of *René Hague's Press* in 1930 and of the two he preferred the less robust, considering it 'unworried' yet containing 'a lot of quite complex detail'. Of the one on the opposite page, he commented that it was 'nothing like as good - no idea where it is - may have torn it up'.[9] If Jones's favourite is tremulous, the other version is a paradoxical mix of the vital and the perilous. Imperial motifs decorate the wrought iron of the Cope's Albion Press which is shown in a tenuous condition with collapse imminent, making this Jones's earliest treatment of the theme that was to

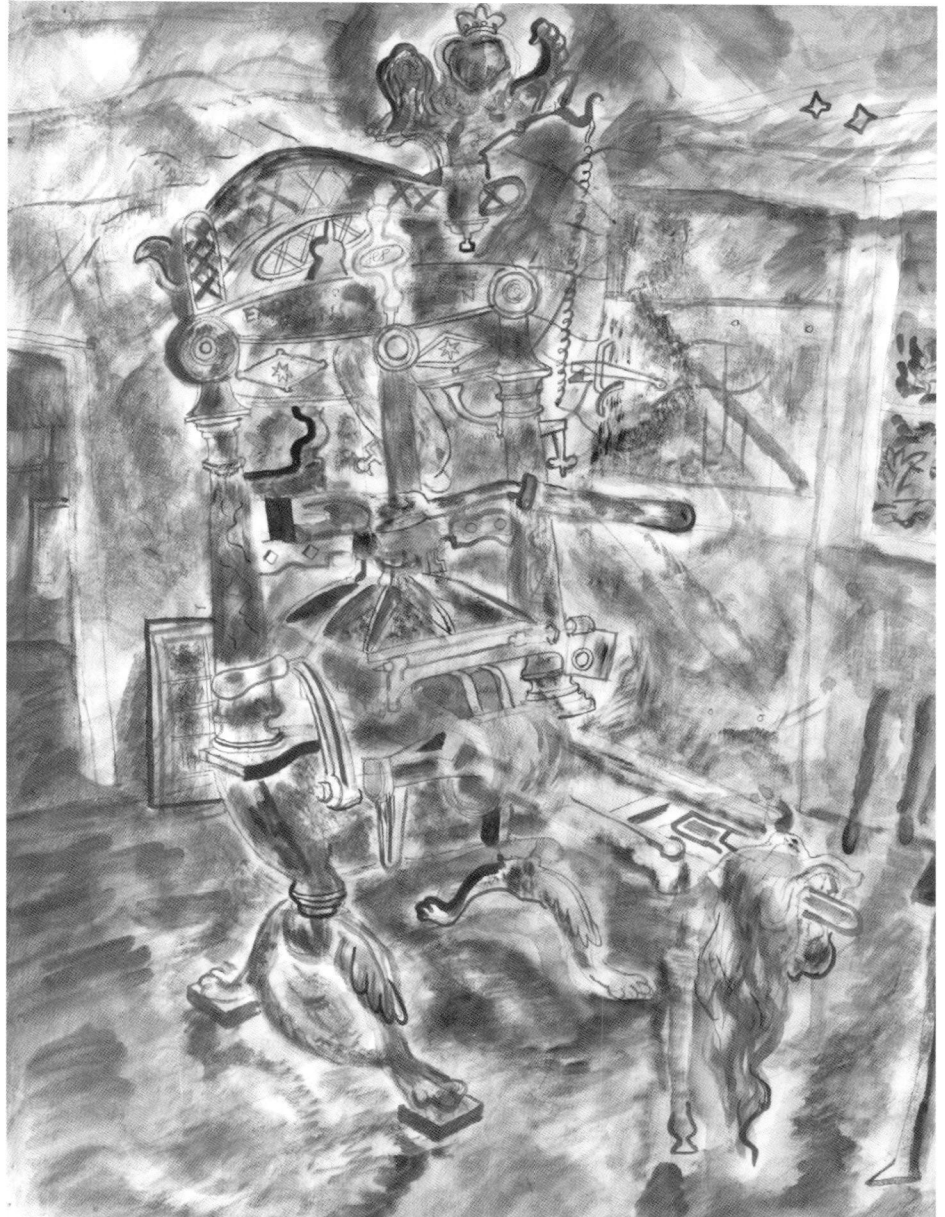

10. René Hague's Press, 1930

become so important later, imperial decline and the related decline of the West. While offering a less complex spatial vision than the version with the tympan open, it is looser and greater prominence is given to the abstract marks, elements such as the starlike shapes in the top right-hand corner which echo both the star and diamond decorations on the press in a painterly, if not altogether successful, manner. Not since his study of the army *Apparatus* (see p 25) had Jones shown so much interest in machinery, though here the press is a pretext for exploring an energy. It is not a view onto the world but rather the world re-cast by feeling. There is no emulation of an inherited language but a new freedom, and freedom for Jones is not about a formalistic fitting together but about letting go. It was made during a period when Jones was scouring his memory in order to recreate the Western Front under a form of words that would not focus, like a history of a regiment, on precise actions and statistics, but which would epiphanously or paradigmatically fuse the universal and the particular. Similarly, what the increasing agitation of many paintings that Jones made between 1928-32 shows is not still life, bowl of flowers or any external thing so much as the pressure of dislocation and destruction that, to an extent, had been caused by the war. Seven years after making this painting, after exhaustion and collapse, in a year in which the world witnessed the horror of the bombing of Guernica and another European war was looking more and more probable, Jones's *In Parenthesis* was printed by René Hague on this press.

To paint a violin on a *guéridon* is immediately to place yourself in the context of the modernist still life and indeed there had been a Picasso retrospective in June, 1931 at the Lefevre Gallery which Jones most probably visited.[10] But where Picasso would split the violin, pull it apart and reorganize it, Jones's *Violin* of 1932, is conjured from random details which are heightened and the bulk of the body is lost in the continuum of easy, loose washes. Space is equivocal: curtains appear to have no opacity and the dish with blackberries seems to float on the window-sill mediating interior and exterior. While the chin-rest is given almost as much presence as the goblet and dish, it is the symbolic resonance of those two objects, and particularly the haunting blue

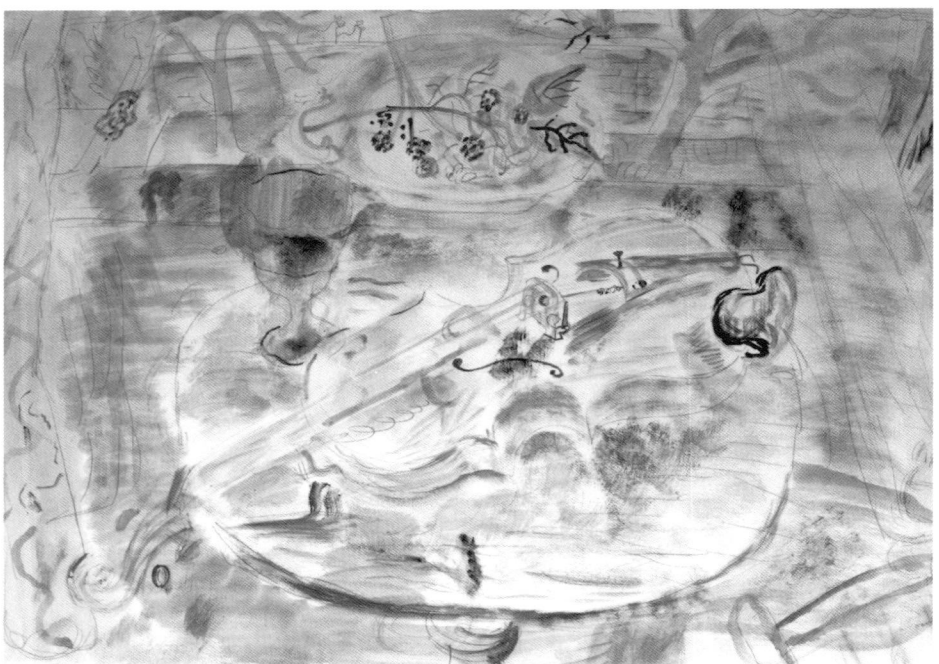

11. The Violin, 1932

of the chalice among the joyful, pale, high tones which seems to transfix the painter's imagination. *Violin and Flowers* is likewise very big and very loose, the drawing just able to anchor the free, vigorous brushwork. Flowers have been reduced to a chromatic burst of prussian blue, turquoise, lemon yellow and green. There are vertical bands of abstract colour which run down the work

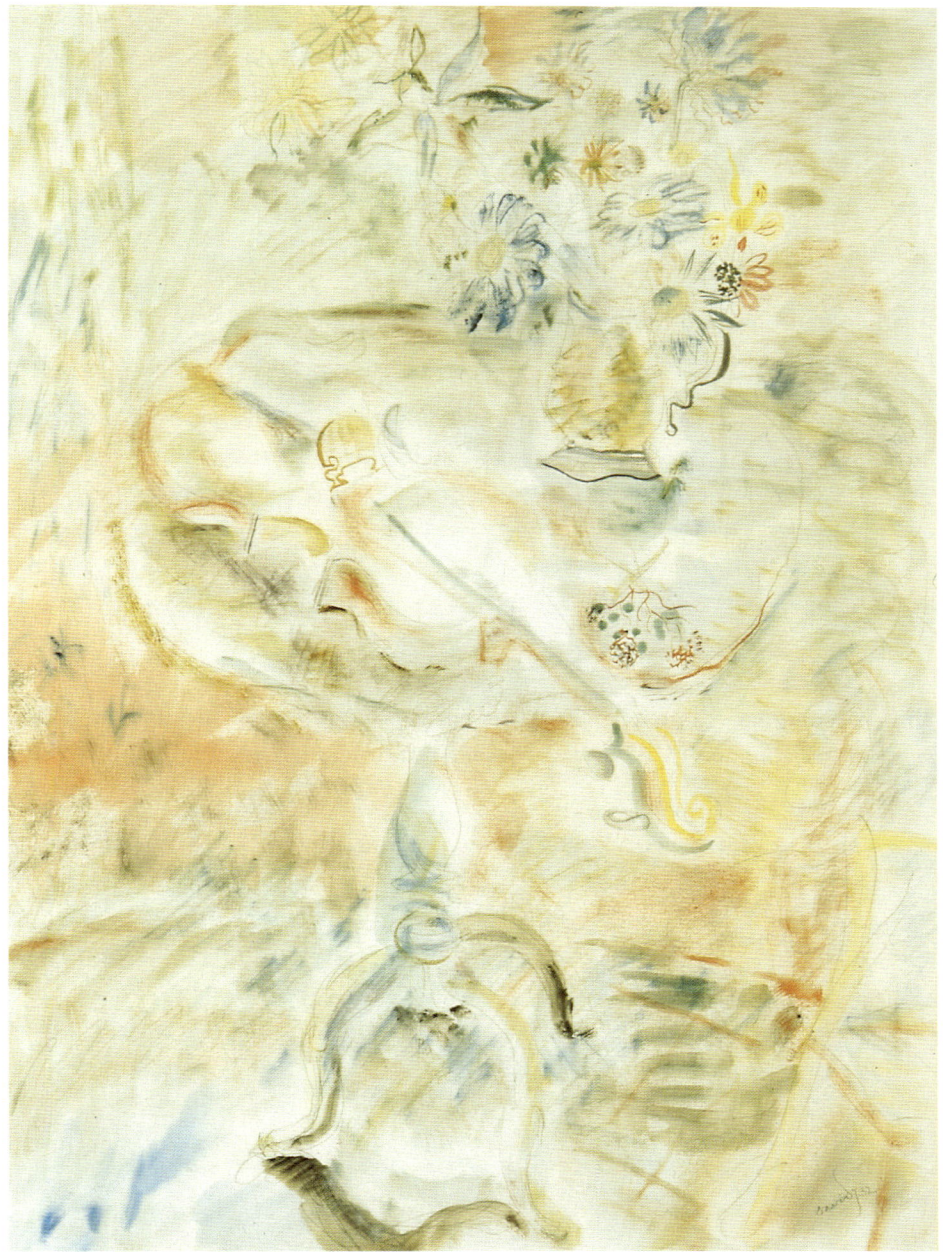

12. Violin and Flowers, 1932

without reference to object or shadow. Seen from a distance the colours harden and yet the image does not coalesce, for colour seems to float free and objects appear to be in a state of flux or dissolve.

During the late twenties and early thirties, Ben Nicholson was guiding the 7&5 Society from 'poetic naturalism' towards abstraction, and figurative tendencies were coming to be considered increasingly conservative as a second wave of interest in pure formalism rippled through the London art world. For many, abstraction meant the abrogation of the literary, parochial or numinous qualities which characterized much of the cherished insularity of British art and it was, furthermore, associated with a threatening internationalism and with the revolutionary, political left.[11] Certainly its rigour gave rise to political

133

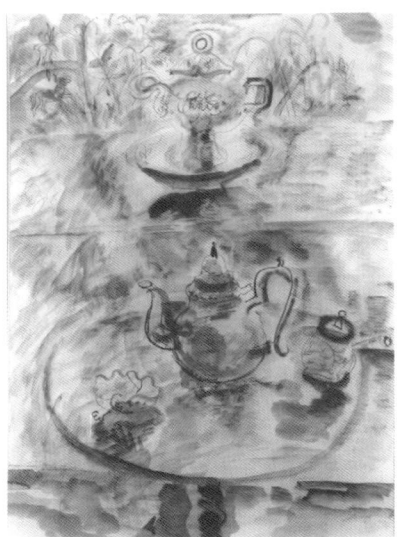

13. Hierarchy, 1932

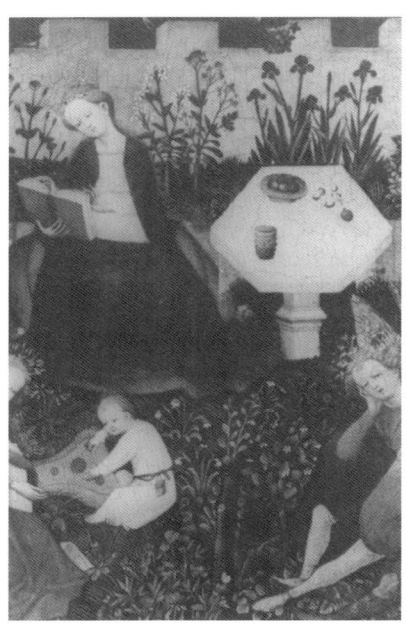

14. Oberrheinischer Meister,
Paradise Garden (detail), c.1410

anxiety; one reviewer in *The New Statesman* remarked on the 'passion for commufascist nomenclature' in some tough proclamations of Unit One,[12] a group which gathered artists who, in the words of Paul Nash, wished to express 'a truly contemporary spirit'.[13] Ironically, it had been *The New Statesman* which had castigated the 1932 7&5 Society exhibition for its 'effeminacy'.[14] David Jones's impression that the show appeared 'jolly nice' perhaps begins to suggest the gulf that was starting to open between his interests and the main thrust of experimental British art in the early 1930s.[15] If what was pleasing to Jones appeared 'effeminate' beside the disturbingly Surreal or the intellectual clarity of Hard-edged Abstraction, then it is indicative of his imminent marginalization. The fact that Jones was the biggest seller in the 1932 exhibition (he sold five works: *Curtained Outlook*, *Portrait of a Maker*, *Human Being*, *Herbaged Bay* and *In Tide*; whereas Ben Nicholson only sold three, Winifred Nicholson two, Frances Hodgkins one, and Henry Moore one) suggests that the more abstract artists in the 7&5 were not capturing the imagination of the public and that art was becoming increasingly a question of art for artists' sake.

While considerable attention was paid to the power of the abstract mark in the works that Jones was producing as the new decade began, there was also a developing interest in the significance of what he chose to include in a painting. In still life it was no longer a question of participating in an artistic exercise that was sealed off from the anxieties of the real world, but rather of selecting elements that expressed Christian associations. In *Hierarchy*, the eye travels up the paper from the domestic trivia in the foreground to a tureen whose shape has been modified and accented in such as way as to make it appear broadly cruciform. Comparison with a Celtic cross reveals an echo between the circle of the pot's lid and the circle centred on the point of intersection of the two axes of such a cross. The pot's squared right handle reflects the truncated butt end of the transverse axis and the swirling handle on the other side (seen on the right in *Briar Cup*) suggests the curvilinear abstract or sinuous animal carvings of Celtic art.

The shape of the tureen also suggests a pot or cauldron, which in turn, for Jones, suggests traditions that stand behind the Grail legend. In Celtic mythology the cup which Tadg found in the Land of the Immortals turned water into wine, and the Cauldron of Rebirth brought the dead back to life.[16] The Grail was, in its pre-Christian provenance, a dish or cup - its associations are latterly with the provision of food and formerly with life-bearing for it is shaped like a womb.[17] So, in a sense, Jones's odd accentings and strange juxtapositions, his unexpected way of presenting objects creates, as it were, a kind of intellectual Cubism. Elements distorted or allusions suggested result in a store of composite meaning that begins to accrete around the most apparently innocent domestic object such as a soup tureen. Even the idea for the rounded table or *guéridon* may not only have come to Jones through the *École de Paris* but also from the steeply tilted hexagonal table in a late medieval, pre-perspectival work such as the early fifteenth century Frankfurt *Paradise Garden*, where significant apples are seen scattered on a surface close to a crowned queen who is dressed in the blue of the Virgin Mary.

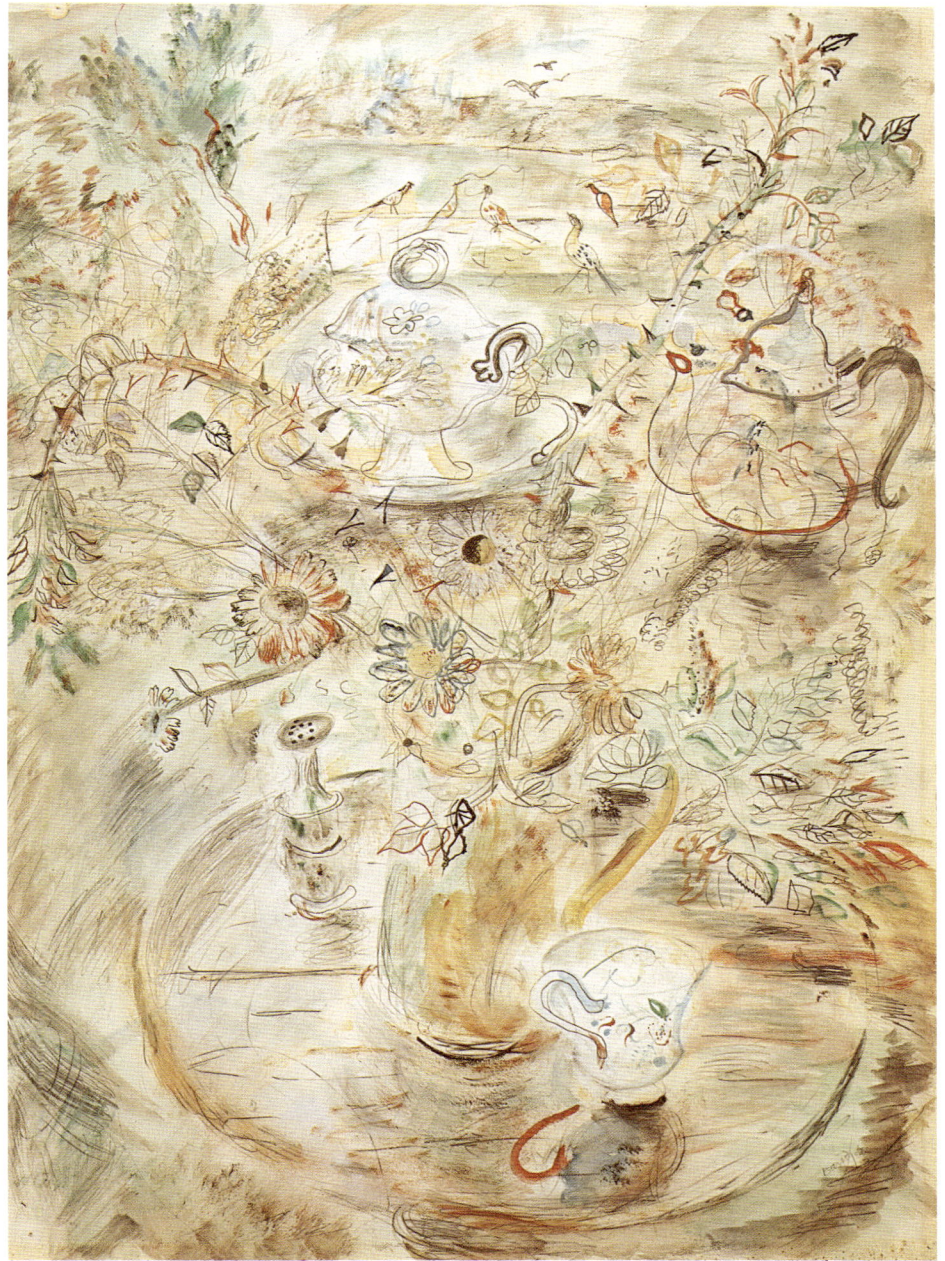

15. Briar Cup, 1932

Briar Cup is a hectic anticipation of Jones's later chalice paintings, drawn, or rather scribbled, with a wild energy that animates the liveliest of the many paintings made during the early thirties. The colour is rapidly washed in or used in a more concentrated fashion to accent odd or significant details. There is something maddened in the aggression with which the pencil marks and washes have been deposited; the world appears to be crazed and flying apart, and only a hint of compositional order is secured by the strong V of the thorny branches and by the circles echoing in the objects. The significance of these thorns would be clear to any Christian and the red accenting of the rim of the teapot spout so close appears like a drop of blood. Most importantly, the picture expresses disturbance; the distress is manifest in the act of drawing and painting. There is in it an agitation that borders on Expressionism.

135

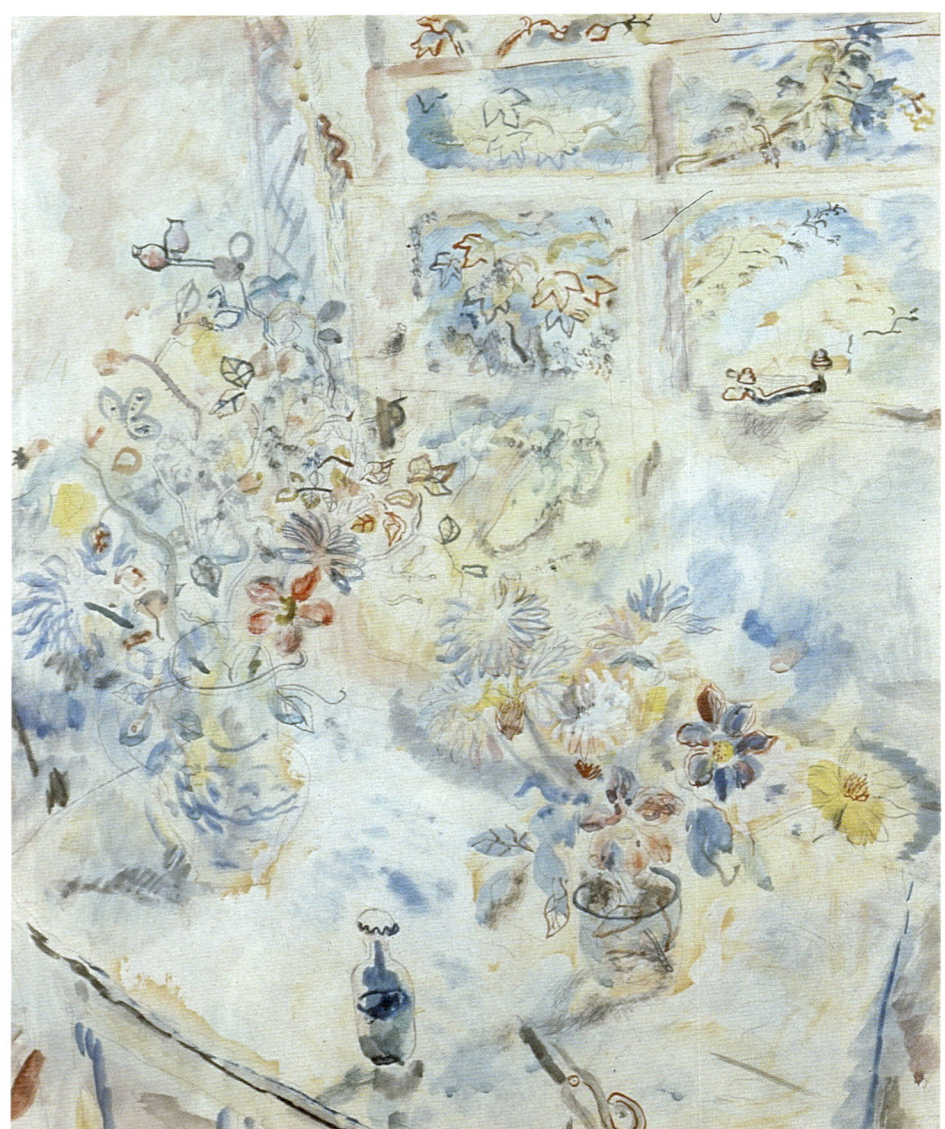

16. July Change, Flowers on a Table, 1932

There is also, during this period, the splendour of transubstantiation to be found in certain more joyous works. *July Change* is a visionary picture in which the negative spaces radiate, transforming each bouquet; some details are brought into heightened focus, others, left completely out of focus, blurring into abstract marking. The painting is about light and thus, as with certain paintings by Constable and Turner, it is about what is intangible and changing. As Hills so neatly puts it, Jones:

> is fond of painting in situations where strong light floods into his face. Where there is back-lighting academic tonal relationships may well be upset: an object in the distance silhouetted against a bright light may appear darker than anything closer to the eye … Where there is as much reflected light in a foreground, … three-dimensional objects may not have a side or facet noticeably in shadow; hence they appear to lack solidity. In so using reflected light, the modern artist runs against the tradition of European

painting. An artist of the Italian Renaissance would utilize a reflected light to retrieve the line of a jawbone from shadow; in other words, he used it to clarify form. Jones uses reflected light to create a confusion out of which a new order may be born.[18]

In his watercolours, Rouault used light 'somehow radiating out from the objects depicted ... rather than falling upon them from the outside'[19] so they could function as Christian symbols or metaphors. In Jones's work light floods in and around and through objects creating volume, denying the confines of the mundane and thus allowing a scene to dissolve into an almost mystical meditation. In his best watercolours of 1932 he aims for the moment of vision. Jones's chosen medium, dissolving as it does, is more suited to such aspiration than the oil paint so often used by the similarly intentioned Winifred Nicholson with her 'strongly developed sense of the unseen' and 'belief that the essence ... was just out of sight beyond appearances'.[20]

July Change is an intelligently constructed picture; on the angled tilt of the table-top, the scissors point the eye up into a painting in which volume and space co-exist with a sense of insubstantiality. The window denies depth by cutting perspective and also sections space. Unlike the disturbing *Curtained Outlook* of the previous year (see p 251), where all the nastiness invested in the objects appears to scatter obtusely and inescapably before the disturbed spectator, this painting achieves a serenity in which elements float away into a radiant beyond.

Ben Nicholson's still life, *Goblet and Pears* (1924), was held by H.S. Ede, perhaps not altogether too fancifully, as a metaphor for the annunciation.[21] Dissimilar to the often clinical art of its painter, the white which spills beyond the pencil line of the goblet's rim suggests effulgence. Jones would have seen this painting at Ede's Hampstead house and must have been struck by the way in which Nicholson had found a modern means of expressing light which is not used to create space but rather to express something mystical. The blur of white about the goblet's rim stands mid-way between a halo and the gentle hazes of Mark Rothko's large invitations to meditate. In the still lifes which Jones painted in 1932, those 'vast' washes,[22] he began with common domestic items for the table which, as Ede observed, were 'emblematic of the meeting together of people, the breaking of bread'.[23] The decision to paint these implements of communion would seem to be of great significance for a bachelor who was used to being looked after and yet who took the trouble to prepare simple meals for close friends and loved ones. His patron, Helen Sutherland, who offered Jones hospitality for months on end wrote, after a visit to the painter in London, that 'there is something about being given a meal, when it is prepared by the host himself, that does touch something deep in one'.[24] But while the artist can be seen in the act of loving 'God *through* created things'[25] it seems that the vibrating washes, the seas and cascades of colour are as meaningful as the objects. The white paper shining through makes the white of the table a veritable altar where something is indeed transubstantiated and made here and now present. What is immediately noticeable is the absence of drawing and while the objects are imbued

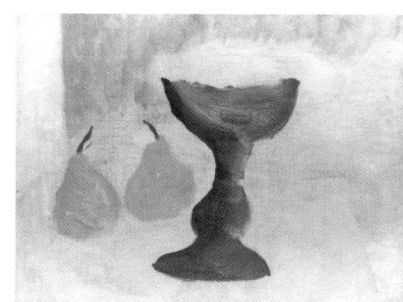

17. Ben Nicholson, Goblet and Pears, 1924

137

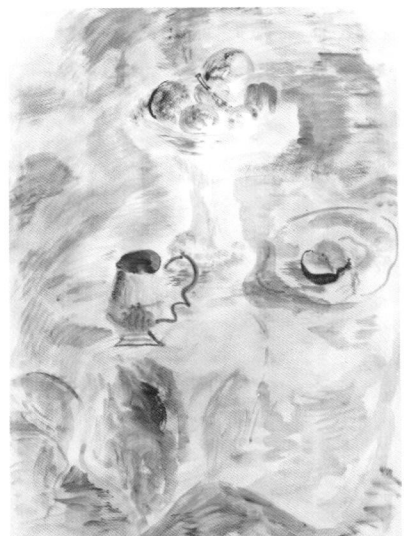

18. Still Life, 1932

with significance one senses that Jones is trying to avoid intellectual signi-fication and achieve a position like that of the Welsh Metaphysical poet, Henry Vaughan, when he

> saw Eternity the other night
> Like a great *Ring* of pure and endless light.[26]

This desire evidently unsettled Jones even though he wished to see with eyes that looked beyond; commenting on his visit to the London Group show of 1929, he observed that 'Sickert has a ... painting ... - the only thing there that seemed to have an "idea" - isn't it awful - these yards of "able" paintings of various kinds that seem only seen with the eye of the flesh.'[27] And yet, he confessed that he loathed the slippery word 'mystic' by which he meant 'that human being who is more *directly* in union with God than are most of us' and quite despaired of his distance from such a position, unable to think of 'anyone more bound up in terrestrial comforts etc. than I am - it revolts me to think of it.'[28] Nonetheless, the concept of mysticism preoccupied him throughout his life and the failure of his aspiration to approach more closely into communion with God was sublimated by his growing obsession with the forms of religious celebration.

As a painter who, ultimately, felt the need to make the 'significant' mark, he drew instinctively back from abstraction and though he clearly felt that these works were good, perhaps he felt that they didn't, despite their resonances, face up to the drama of Christianity. Reading a book on Zen Buddhism a decade later, he wrote:

> it's *all* a very different cast of 'thought' from our Western thing.
> I've got a feeling that *none* of them know about 'the dark night' of
> the Xtian mystics - and the various shades of that 'night' which are
> so inseparable from Western thought - the 'struggle' thing. Indeed
> it all seems to be directed toward pretending that there is no
> 'struggle' - the 'drama' and 'tension' etc. of our conception is
> side-tracked or something - 'resolved' I suppose they would say.[29]

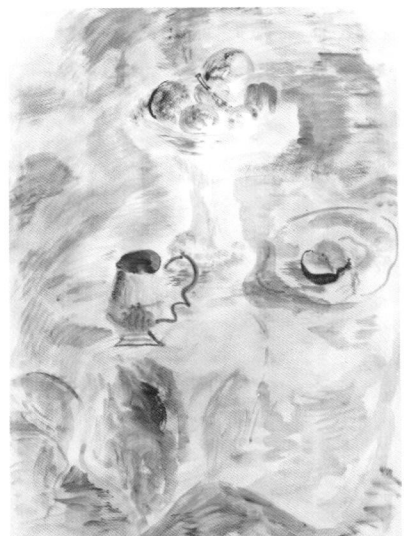

19. The Table, 1932

The objects in *Still Life with Plate and Goblet (20)* with their echo of the Last Supper and the white altar cloth are no less deliberately selected than the elements in the later Chalice paintings but the looseness of style gives the picture a welcome freedom. The painting is about different orders or vibrations in space with one actual and one ghosted goblet. It is not so much that Jones was searching, as Waldemar Januszczak and many others have suggested, 'like Moore or Nicholson or Sutherland, for something funda-mentally stable beneath all the twisted surfaces, the distractions of nature'[30] but rather for an energy which pulsates beneath creation. Jones is not, at this time, recasting the Bible in a solid, contemporary world like Stanley Spencer, nor searching for an abstract harmony like Moore or Hepworth, but trying to break into a world re-made in light and vibration. Simplicity, Brancusi observed, 'is not a thing to be aimed at. It is something one arrives at in spite of oneself, as one draws near to the meaning of things'. Jones was drawing very near. His Expressionistic watercolours of this period reveal him wrestling with internal disruption and discontent and the more meditative pictures reveal his proximity to the moment of vision. But although these large watercolours promise a moment out of time, a look beyond the mundane and gross, we do not quite catch 'heaven in a wild flower' which is the aspiration of the mystic. These watercolours hover on the frontier and refuse to echo deeply like sublime music or the conundrum of a mystical writing. They move, transfixing with their beauty, yet leave the spectator on the brink.

In some ways, it was agonizing for Jones to be practising an art by which he wished to transubstantiate creation and yet which could not, in fact, effect what he and his fellow Catholics believed took place in the Mass. He could have side-stepped the issue, abandoned representation and gone abstract, but he believed that 'our business here below is to make the universal shine out from the particular'[31] and he amassed an increasing fund of ideas and observations that he felt it important to express. He commented, however,

> that the 1932 group got nearest to what I had in mind - but *a very long way from the goal*. (I suppose that may partly explain my complete crash - I was conscious for some long time before it came that I was straining every nerve to do something more than I had power to do.)[32]

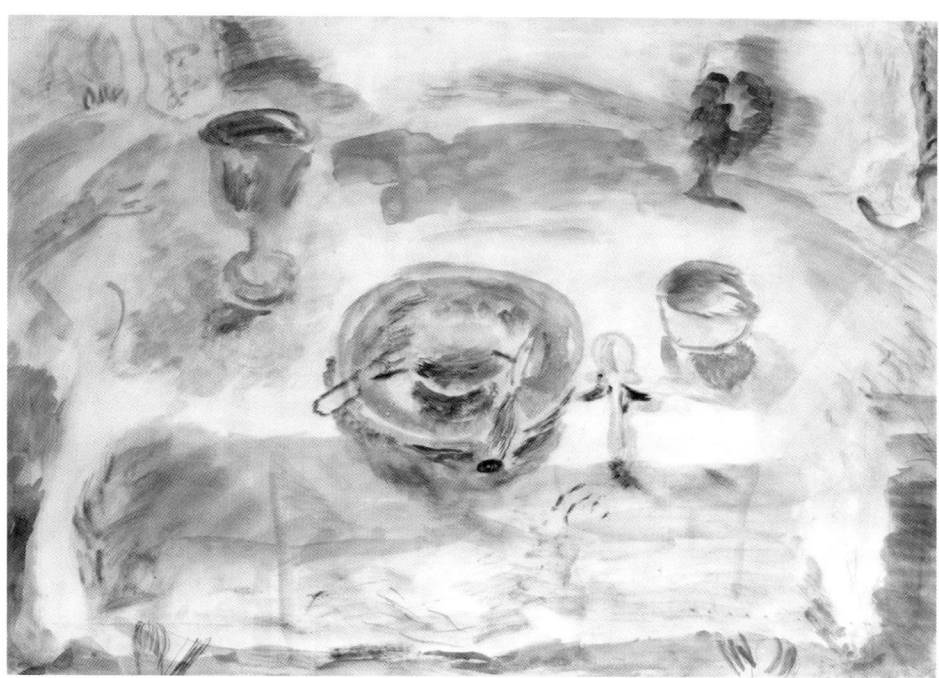

20. Still Life with Plate and Goblet, 1932

II

PROBLEMS AND POSSIBILITIES
OF THE FIGURE

The reconciliation of a sensuous artistic disposition with the strictures of a religion not only based on suffering but that also advocated the denial of any sensual urge not sanctioned by socially constraining codes, imposed a great strain on David Jones. Nietzsche ventured that 'wherever the religious neurosis has hitherto appeared on earth' it has been 'tied to three dangerous dietary prescriptions: solitude, fasting and sexual abstinence'.[1] While Jones's diet was nothing if not repetitive towards the end of his life, it was reasonably healthy and fasting did not pose a particular threat to his well-being. His desire, however, to dedicate himself to the arts and his perception that the financial uncertainties of such a life did not allow him to form any marital bond was something that proved to be a considerable strain. Yet Nietzsche's vision of religion as proscriptive must be contrasted with a belief in the efficacy of Catholicism voiced by Jones's close friend Harman Grisewood who found

> that the beauty and delight of the physical world require the transcendent not only for their explanation but so that all the human faculties may attain their full development and have their freest exercise.[2]

Tragically, the price Jones paid for the transcendent was the inhibition of the full development and free play of his sentimental and sexual nature and that, in turn, affected his artistic output.

Jones's conversion during his second period as an art student led him to the belief that all forms of sign-making were validated by Christ's offering of himself in the form of bread and wine at the Last Supper, which was the supreme artistic transubstantiative act. But what could a mere man, a mere artist do compared with such a powerful and mysterious act? Belief in such transubstantiation somehow rendered all other attempts at re-presentation a kind of failure; on one level the painter was participating in 'what has always been done', and on another he could only fall short of what could be effected by the Mass. Nonetheless, Jones retained a fundamentally unassailable belief in the power of sign-making despite the increasing difficulty of selecting valid signs in what he considered to be an unstable phase of culture. He held that mankind alone was capable of behaving gratuitously by performing some act of making that was useless in itself but which expressed emotion or signified something venerated or someone loved. He wrote, in 'Art and Sacrament', poignantly in the context of his own sensual self-deprivation, that

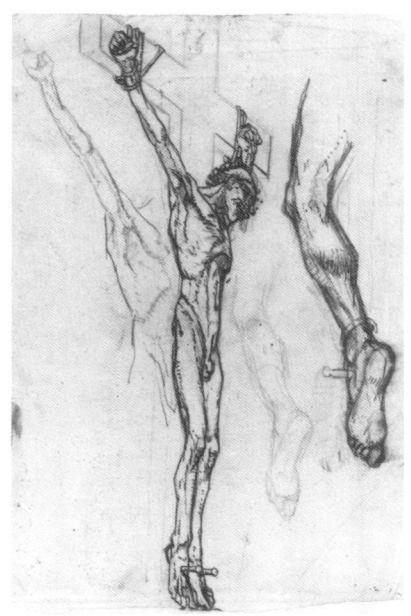

1. Crucifixion, 1920

the body is not an infirmity but a unique benefit and splendour; a thing denied to angels and unconscious in animals. We are committed to body and by the same token we are committed to Art, so to sign and sacrament.[3]

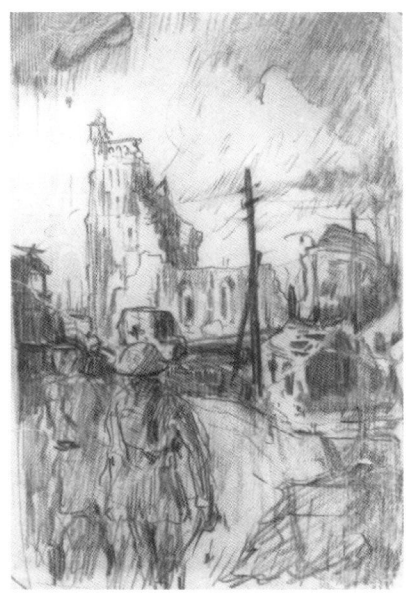

2. Ruined Church with Soldiers, 1917 (?)

Curiously, in much of his painting, that body, the human figure which is given such an important symbolic rôle in drawings such as the *Frontispiece* to *In Parenthesis* and *Aphrodite in Aulis*, hardly appears. However, a selection of sketches and hitherto unseen scribbles reveal the emotional and formal attractions and problems posed by the body. It was with the human figure in the engravings and in minor or private works that Jones most experimented with differing styles and yet he never fully developed such exploration because his increasing isolation as a painter provided him with no arena in which to do so.

The First World War was the one time during which Jones repeatedly drew the human figure. The all-over, scribbled agitation of soldiers seen against ruins unites figures and landscape in a texture of devastation. The Red Cross of the ambulance lorry placed above the helmeted officer so, as it were, to bless him, along with the ruined church and the nearby cruciform telegraph pole are ironic witnesses to the unholy condition of war.

While Jones was very aware of women, fond of women, attracted by women, his relationships with his male friends were more completely successful. Men who had been through the First World War often preferred to replicate the kinds of bonds formed under the duress of battle; in his unpublished *Epithalamion* for the marriage of his friend Harman Grisewood, Jones wrote of that 'universal attachment - the love of soldier for soldier in the union of struggle'.[4] But Jones's interest in recording his fellow men in his trench sketchbooks and the focus of *In Parenthesis* on ordinary soldiers disappears later on when his ideas become grander and less personal. Whereas *In Parenthesis* was about men, *The Anathemata*, despite its larger-than-life personalities, is about mankind and it is only in several of the later, short poems that ordinary, unmythologized people reappear. There was, in the period between, in the attempt to subsume everything symbolically or typologically, a consequent emptying out of the particular.

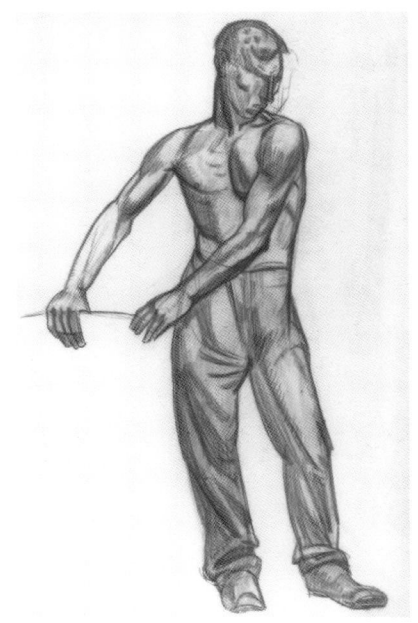

After merely recording men in the trenches, at his second art school and in the years that followed Jones turned to the formal possibilities offered by the figure. This colour drawing angularizes the model, pushes it in the direction of Constructivism or Social Realism, styles which respond to the mechanical drive of the twentieth century. We see an adult worker and not, as so often in Jones, a male trapped in adolescence. The figure is formalized in the manner of Bomberg in his *Sappers at Work* or Roberts or Lewis; Jones, as an art student, is catching up on what has happened in British art while he was away fighting on the Western Front.

Similarly, *The Roadmender* drawn for *The Town Child's Alphabet* is really an exploration of post-Cubist possibilities of spatial manipulation, seen most readily in the treatment of the pick-axe shaft which moves curiously in and

3. Male Stripped to the Waist, 1921

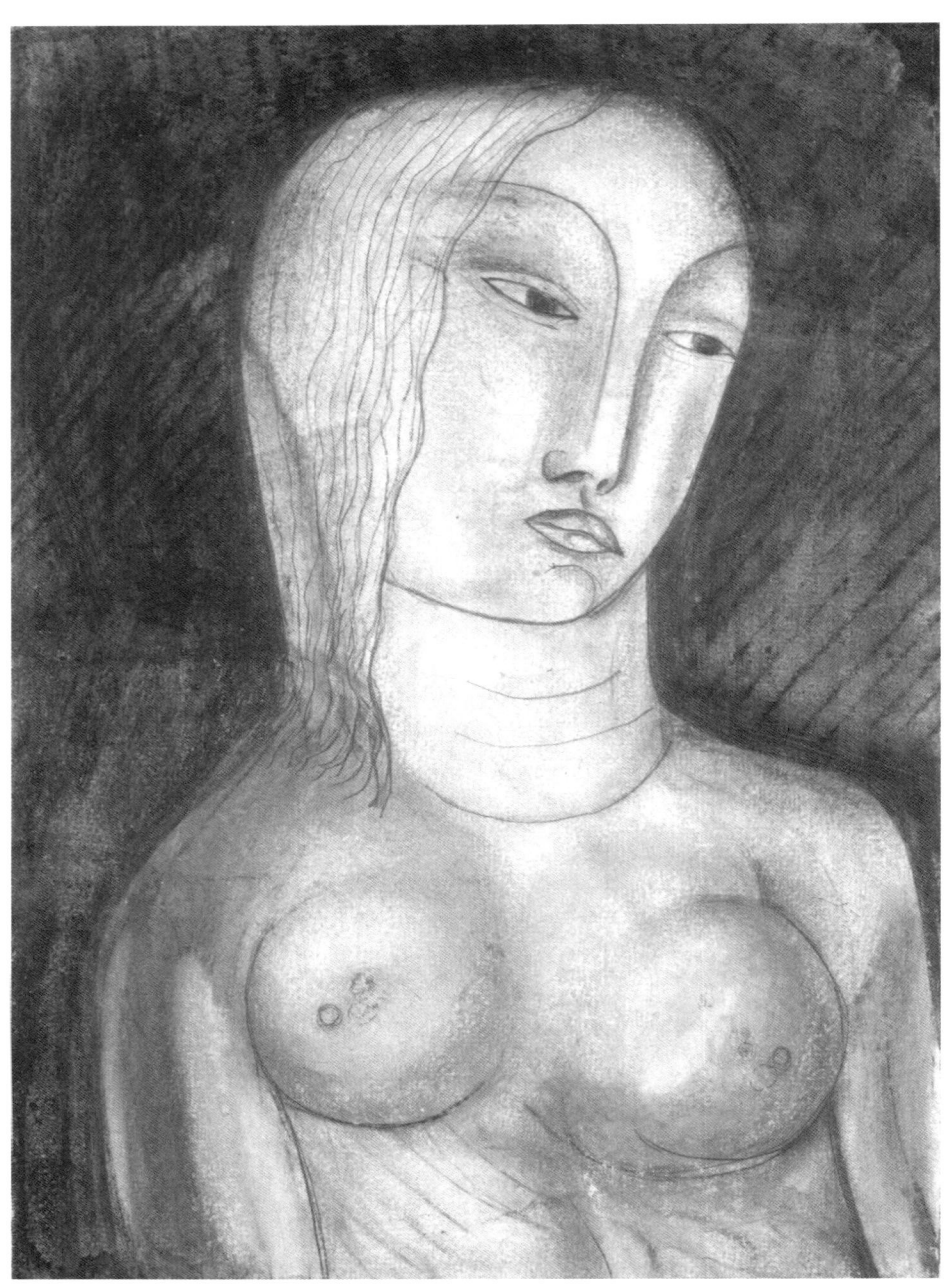
4. Nude Portrait, 1924

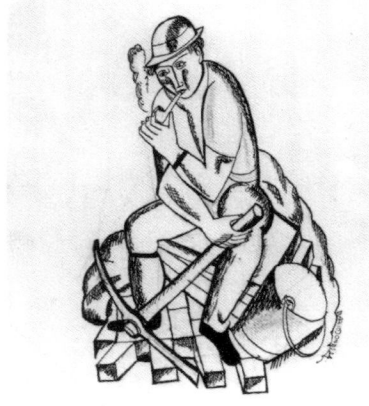
R. for Road mender.

5. R for Road mender, 1924

out of perspective. Whereas the mature Jones takes inspiration from the countryside, there is wit and charm in this urban, Léger-like, decorative Cubism.

An early pastel and pencil, *Nude* of 1924, is cool in its formalization but tantalizing. The drawing is the result of an emotionally or notionally confused image of woman, venerated but subtly malevolent, and it is realized in a style somewhere between the hieraticism of Gill and the austere, exotic and primitive sexuality of Modigliani. The breasts, which clearly gave Jones trouble (note the various placings of the nipples) remain ciphers for the sensual. All in all, there is a cold quality which suggests that the artist is comfortable at a certain distance from the sex. Much later, when René Hague showed a Carmelite mystic some of Jones's painting, the man was impressed by what he described as 'chaste sensuality'.[5]

144

Rarely in Jones's work do we see a couple embracing. In *The Garden Enclosed* (see p 247) a determined woman, casting her eclipsing shadow over a male, is, at the same time, fending off his advances. That painting is related to two other works of the same period. First, a drawing in which a zealous and passionate woman seems intent on trapping a comparatively bashful but absorbed man. This was probably a study for a small watercolour and drawing *Ego Delecto Meo*, the title of which comes from an idea which recurs throughout the *Song of Solomon* (II v. 16; VI v.3, VII v. 10), 'My Beloved is Mine'. Whereas the faces in the drawing do not quite merge as they do in Brancusi's *Kiss* with its transfixing and truly mysterious sense of union, in *Ego Delecto* two profiles create, in a familiar visual conceit, the front view of a single face, presumably suggesting some kind of harmony secured by the substitution of religion for erotic confrontation - the man has clothed himself in a monastic robe, there is a large gap between the couple, and his hand rests unequivocally outside the woman's dress. What is more, in *Ego Delecto* the man is not looking at the woman, who bears a considerable resemblance to Petra Gill, but into the distance, perhaps contemplating the spiritual road which he feels he must take. In all three works the difficulty of embrace is registered.

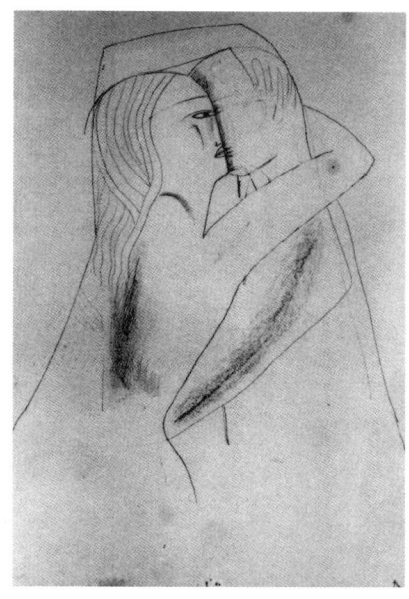

6. The Lovers, 1923

A more terrifying vision of the dangers of the opposite sex is seen in one of the most powerful and modern images which Jones produced for *Gulliver's Travels*. *Female Yahoo Embracing Gulliver* reveals a knowledge of Gauguin's wood-engravings as well as of the powerful woodcuts of the German Expressionists. The top left-hand and bottom right-hand corner with their thick black lines and thickly stylized vegetation are pure Gauguin. The vigorous black line engraving and the mask-like heads appear powerfully Expressionistic, particularly in the hand-coloured version with its complementary red and green. The breasts slapped against the buttock, the Yahoo's arm round Gulliver's genitals, and the shading between the Yahoo's legs which takes on the sexual connotation of pubic hair, make this engraving as erotic as anything that Gill produced. Jones tended to polarize women somewhat simplistically in his writing according to the tactical plottings of the patriarchal aspect of his religion, and the behaviour of this female Yahoo provided a pretext for showing woman as the devourer.

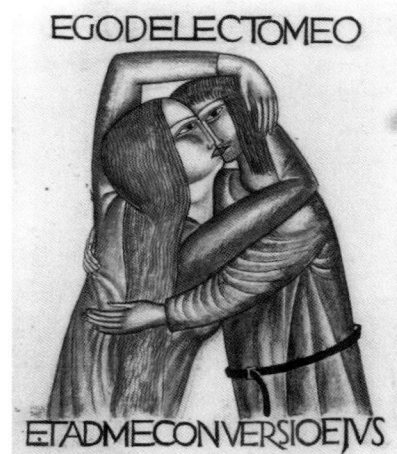

7. Ego Delecto Meo, 1924

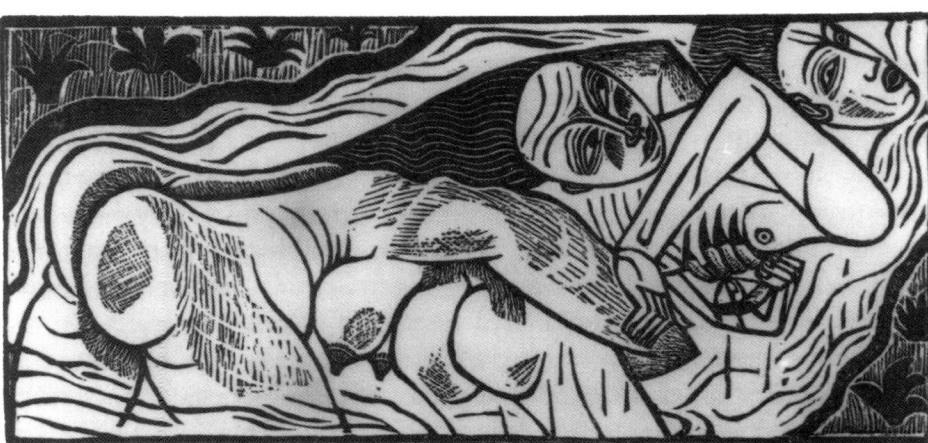

8. Female Yahoo embraces Gulliver, 1925

145

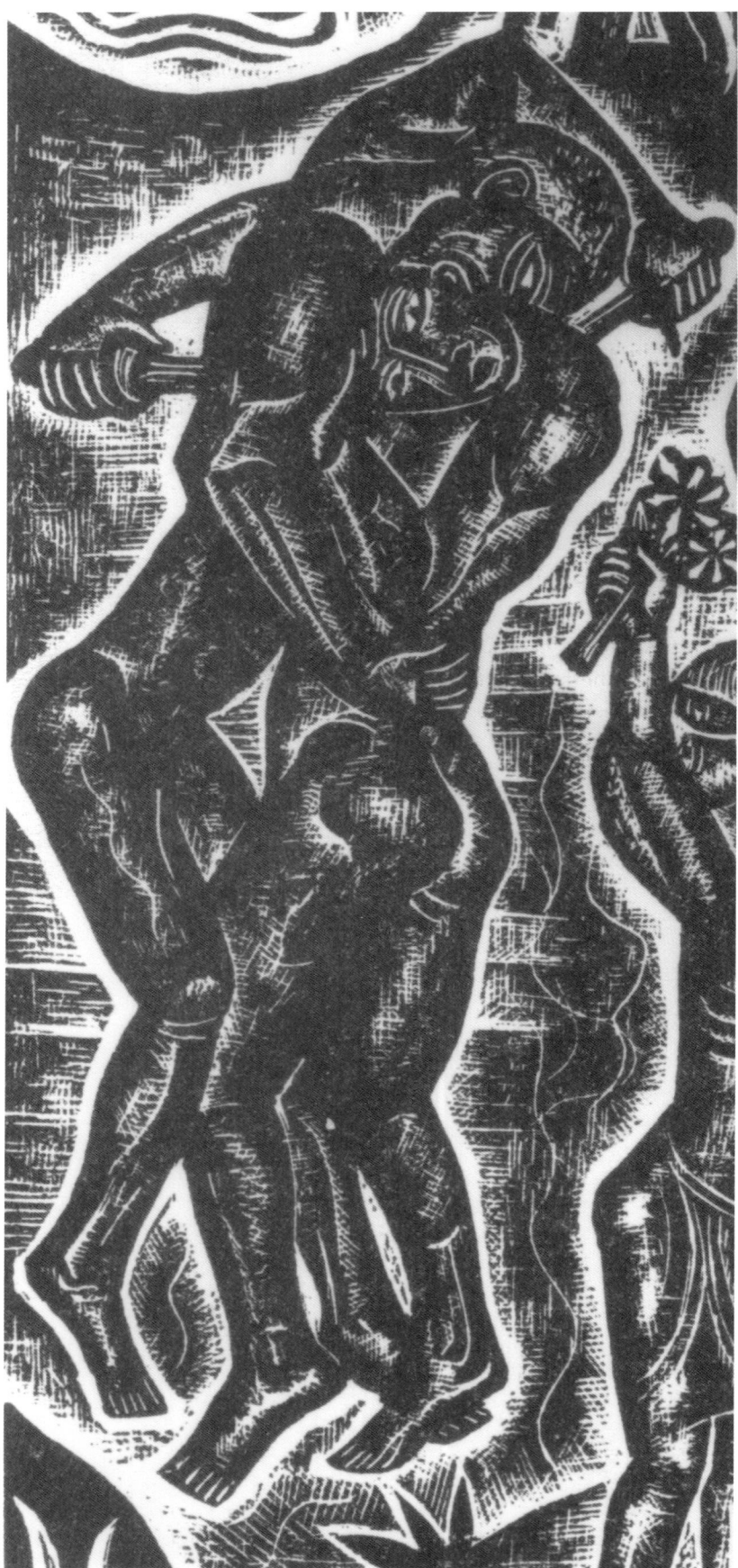

9. Frontispiece to the Book of Ecclesiastes, 1927

In a surprising illustration of the biblical story of the expulsion of the money changers *(10)*, Jones produced a design which might be characterized as a decorative Futurism; part of the *Libellus Lapidum*, Jones conveys in the one image an interesting mix of calculation and liberation.

Despite his capacity to find goodness in a 'life singularly inimical' during the war, Jones witnessed the brutality of man. In the background to an engraving for the frontispiece of the Gregynog Edition of *The Book of Ecclesiastes*, Jones created a powerful expression of violence that is singular in his work *(9)*. The absorption of the perverse and anatomically impossible embrace of the figures is a reflection of the text of Ch. IX, v. 18, 'Wisdom is better than weapons of war'.

One of the most sinister images that Jones produced was *Interchanging the Occiputs* for *Gulliver's Travels (11)*; for all his dislike of Utopias and ennui with the commission, Gulliver does seem to have stimulated a desire to experiment with continental ideas to an extent that religious projects such as *Jonah* did not. This vision of bondage and scientific machination is almost as vicious as any image produced by the contemporary German *Neue Sachlichkeit* artists. The ruthless expertise of the surgeon and the perverse, kindly cruelty of the doctor add up to a very modern vision of violation.

An extreme dislocation in Jones's life was the leap, dramatic during that period, from one class to another and it was one of the pressures which, at times, told keenly upon him. He began to move among some of the more intelligent or sensitive members of the upper and upper middle classes but he was also free to observe the brash insensitivities of other members of that society. In a drawing, not so very far removed from a satire by the

146

contemporary German artist, George Grosz, a cold, disenchanted man tickles his companion under the chin with a flower, seemingly unconcerned with his gesture or its effect upon the woman, a slightly wistful rich man's plaything *(12)*. It is a sharp criticism of the world into which Jones moved in the late twenties and early thirties, where many men appeared to have made uncaring or inappropriate marriages.

The date of the crayon drawing of flappers, 1926, suggests that this was the work entitled *Blonde* which reads so anomalously among the catalogue listings for Jones's 1927 St. George's Gallery exhibition *(13)*. This is a very different view of women from the one usually presented by Jones for these ladies seem to be preying; they crowd together expectantly to focus on the object of their interest, possibly the kind of disinterested brute of the previous image. Despite the blithe, linear style reminiscent of Matisse, they present another aspect of women's potential threat.

Jones drew the nude as an art student's exercise and then again when he was working in the company of Gill who had such an appetite for the female body. Unlike the German affinities detected in the wood-engravings, the influence here seems to be the French tradition filtered through Matthew Smith, Frank Dobson or Gill's knowledge of Maillol. The fullness of the thigh in *Nude* of 1923 (see p 148/*16*) indicates how Jones had been made aware of the astonishing size of such limbs when as an art student, he had copied classical sculpture; in such works of antiquity, as Jones noted later in the margin of his copy of Spengler's *The Decline of the West*, 'the circumference of a thigh is somehow made as extensive as a landscape'.[6] It is exactly the kind of observation that is wanting in Gill nudes of the same period; in Gill's drawing, as Jones noted, 'there is evidence of the linear, and of the lyrical - not so much of the observed'.[7] Of course, Gill had not had the same art school training and, before the mid-twenties, when he began to draw from the nude at the Académie Chaumière on a trip to Paris, had only spent about

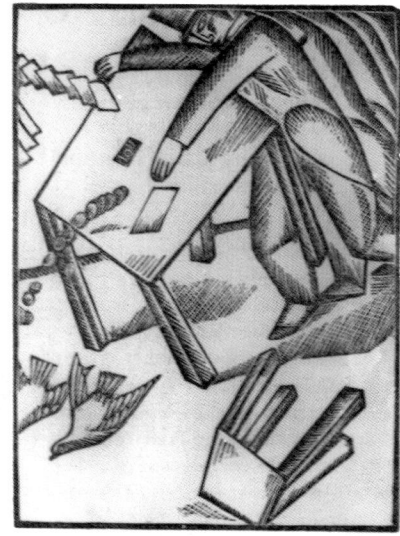

10. Expulsion of the Money Changers, 1924

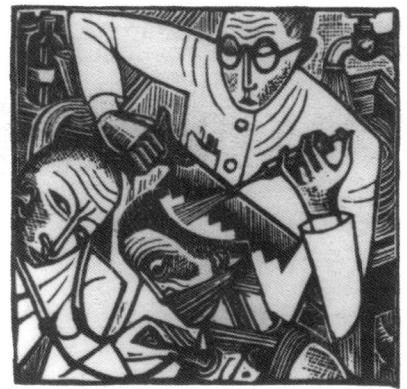

11. Interchanging the Occiputs, 1925

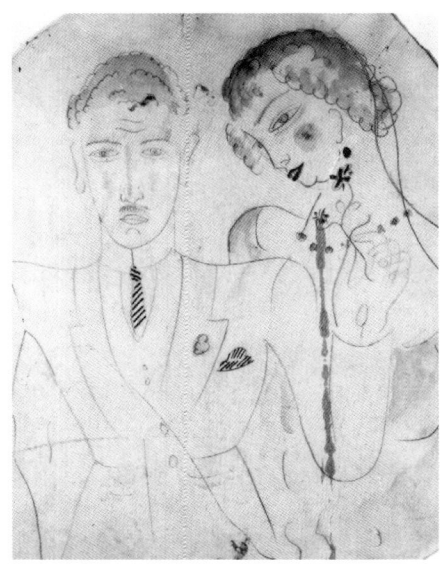

12. Man and Woman, 1930

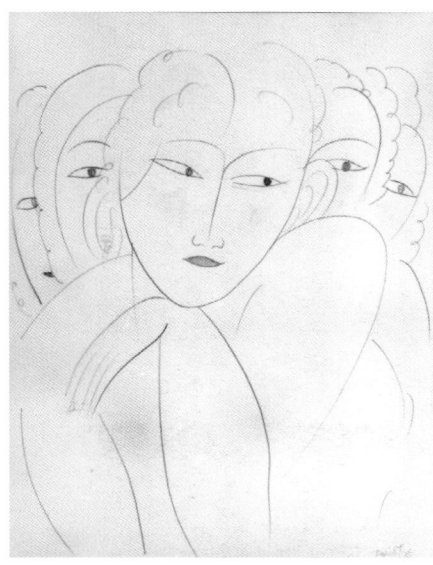

13. Girls, 1926

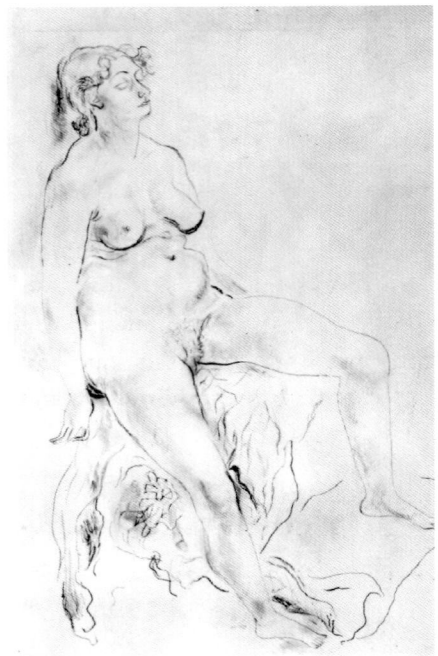

14. Nude: Miss Lilian Peterson, 1926

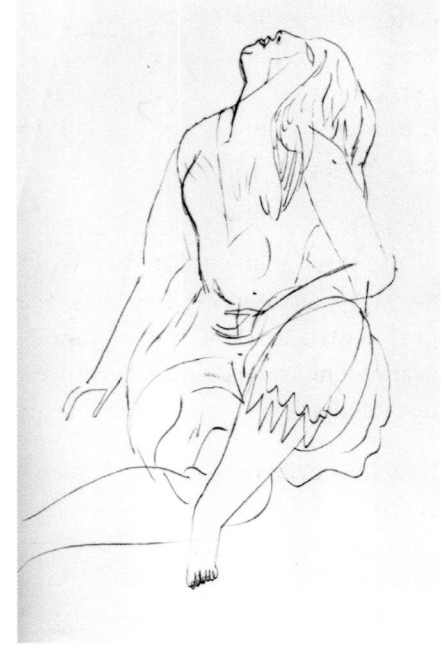

15. Woman Sunk to the Ground, 1932

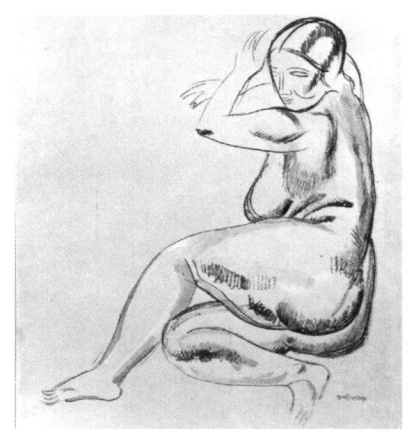

16. Nude in profile, 1923

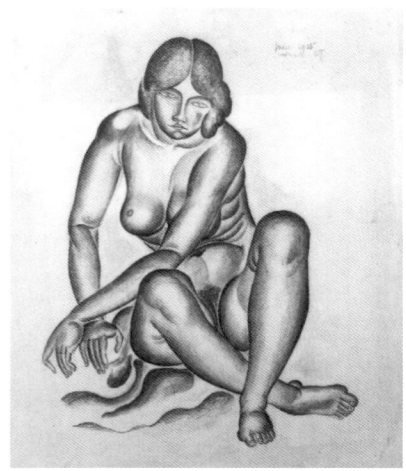

17. Seated Nude, 1925

'a fortnight in the Life Class at the … Central School'.[8] Jones's nudes generally seem more palpably human, but when his style gets too close to that of Gill the result is cold and disjointed, lacking that delicacy and sensuality of which the younger man was capable. In an awkward *Seated Nude (17)* the full-frontal pose appears unsupported and uncomfortable and those strange shackled hands reappear in Jones's later portraits.

Jones was attracted by the act of probing, veiling and unveiling both in poetry and painting.[9] *Miss Lilian Peterson (14)* of 1926 appears dreamily exhausted as if in the aftermath of some sexual encounter and the artist's sensuous enjoyment of pudenda and breasts reveals some first-hand experience of a woman's body.

With the figure in isolation treated in such exciting ways it is sad that Jones never tried to include in his paintings poses as expressive as the ink sketch of the woman sunk to the ground *(15)*, with her potential to suggest defiance, ecstasy or pain; what an expressive Magdalene she might have made.

Much later on in life, by the time that the difficulties of sexual denial and a solitary commitment to art had painfully registered themselves, Jones was advised by his psychologist to draw women as a kind of solace when depressed.[10] The resultant drawings are often slightly salacious and have little or no artistic merit. The fantasized women are usually buxom and although Petra Gill had established a norm of beauty for Jones, perhaps it was the 'fecund image' and 'abundant *ubera*'[11] of the *Venus of Willendorf* which lay behind such scribbles. Jones purged his distress in the realm of archetypes, as he had sublimated the sentimental in religious figures and situations.

It seems, however, that Jones's private drawings offered slight consolation; he once remarked that such activity was hardly a relief for the frustration of

148

being consumed by erotic desire. Such drawings of women are only interesting when they are directly related to a mythological theme. Otherwise, they are tame, touchingly coy, or inept beside the imaginative energy and extravagance of Gill's private erotica.[12] Draped and undraped at the same time, the women often reveal a glimpse of stocking or rather large drawers just visible beneath transparent skirts, but seldom anything more shocking.

These themes will be considered in further depth but even this brief survey of the stylistic possibilities of treating the figure confirms, with its focus on drawings made in the twenties, that a certain modernist excitement and experimentation went out of Jones's work after he produced his unique and evanescent watercolours. From then on, his painting changed direction and became largely a vehicle for his intellectual ideas and beliefs.

In a line drawing such as *Bathers*, a woman and a man buffeted by waves reach out to one another over the considerable distance between them. *Mr. David Jones (1895-) aetate 35* is David Jones by himself. In 1930, aged 35, he had lost the first great love of his life and he was facing up, with that single eye of dedication, to the fact that he would be alone in the pursuit of his art. The style of the drawing is curiously anticipatory of certain Pop Art cartoons, but the message is not humourous. This chapter started with Christ's arms outstretched on the cross and it ends with Jones in a domestic void, his hand outstretched and no one there to shake it.

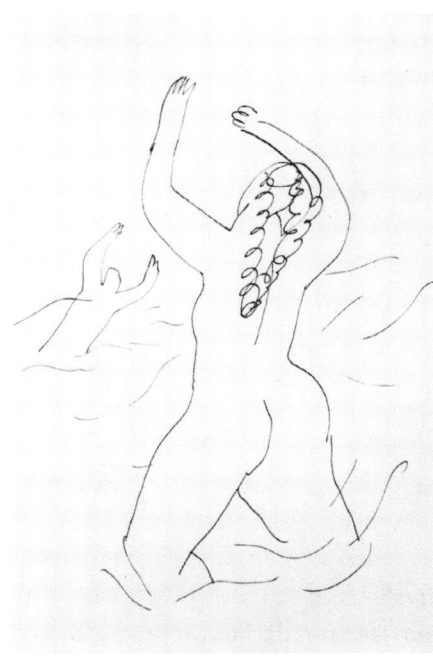

18. Two Bathers, 1928

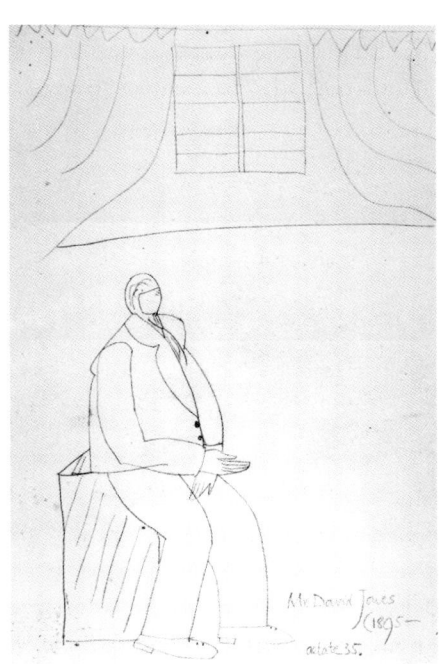

19. Mr. David Jones (1895-) aetate 35, 1930

PORTRAITS AND FRIENDS

Jones undertook next to no commissions, turning down on one occasion the offer to paint the portrait of Charles, Prince of Wales. He had sketched an earlier Prince of Wales, Edward, who became the Duke of Windsor after his abdication, as he remembered having seen him once in the trenches during the First World War. Jones's motivation for doing portraits was not unlike that of the Pre-Raphaelites who painted their friends instead of the grand subjects undertaken by their predecessors.[1] Jones's portraits were made as celebrations of friends and loved ones and portraiture in the sense of likeness was, as Jones wrote to René Hague, not something that he 'could manage very well'.[2] Male portraits were generally straightforward and swift representations of those close to him, and the women Jones painted were often tacitly mythologized in order to harness or embrace their strong emotional attraction for the painter. A review of the 1954 Tate retrospective suggested that Jones's lack of success in the genre was the result of the 'individuality of the sitter' intruding 'too greatly on the artist's private world'[3] and yet in some of the most successful portraits, those of Petra Gill, inner and outer worlds merge. Jones wrote to Ede of the '*fear* of not interpreting the personality etc. of the sitter', it was 'too much for most artists and certainly too much for me!' He went on to say, however, that Petra's was possible 'because she was always part of a whole bundle of ideas and almost part of oneself'.[4]

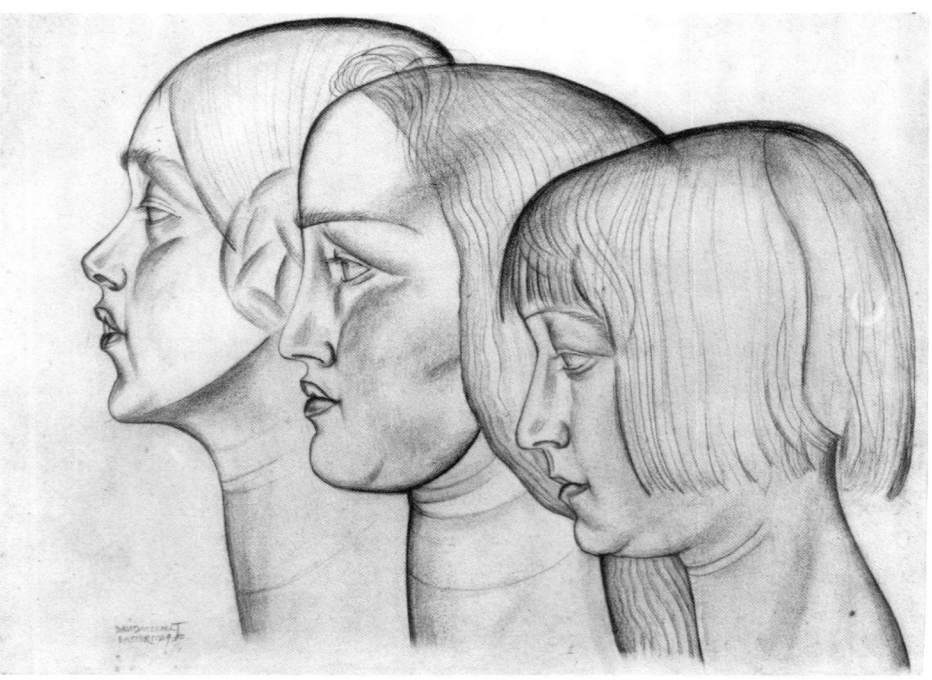

1. Elizabeth, Petra & Joanna Gill, 1924

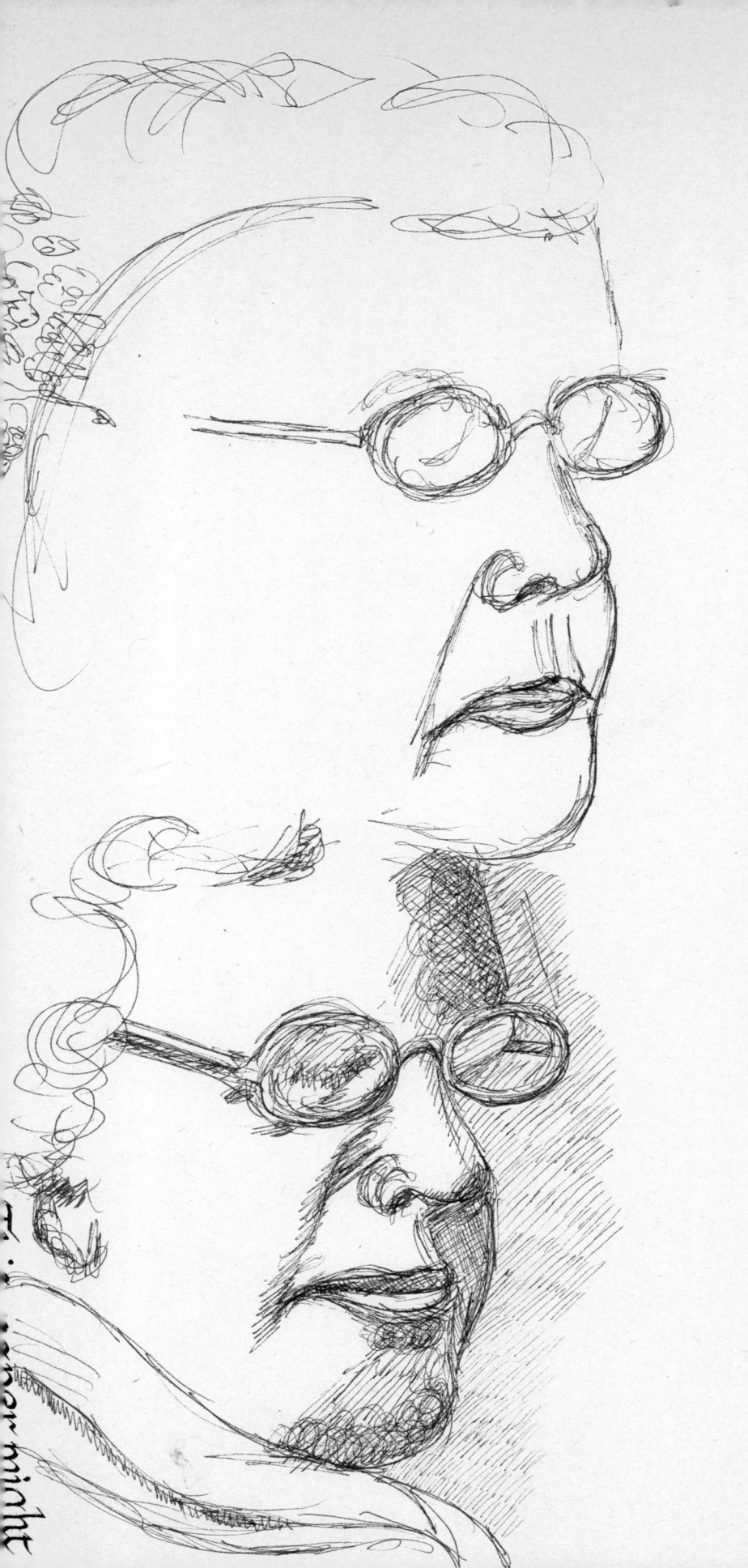

As an Easter present in 1924, Jones drew for Mary and Eric Gill a bold update of a rather insipid profile sequence which Gill had drawn of his three daughters several years earlier. It set a precedent, for the greatest proportion of the portraits which Jones made were of members of Gill's family or of their inner circle of friends. In the drawing, rhythmic accentings flatten the image so it appears like a relief such as one might find on a commemorative medallion. By virtue of her age in relation to Elizabeth and Joanna, Petra was placed centrally and happily she was also the focus of Jones's attention. She was not only the person whom Jones painted more than anybody else, but a few days after this drawing was given, she became his fiancée. She was eleven years younger than Jones which was not an exceptional age difference for people intending to get married in that period. In any case, Petra herself has suggested that as she did not have a conventional upbringing she was, at eighteen, quite grown up.[5] But her lack of education could, on occasion, pose problems; Philip Hagreen recalled that once in 1924 after their betrothal, the young couple

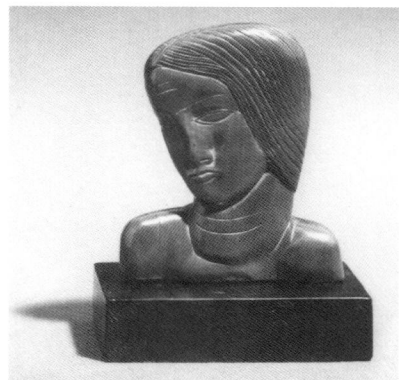

2. Head of Girl (Petra), 1923

> were sitting by our fireside. Petra said she could not understand something David had said, so he explained it. Though it was a very simple matter she still could not see it. Very patiently he went over it more fully but with no more success. Then he said - 'Tell me, Philip, is there anything in marriage to make up for having to keep one's temper with a woman?'[6]

Despite such occasional intellectual frustration, it is quite clear that Jones took great delight in his fiancée; the roundness of her breasts is echoed, in a small watercolour (3), by the hill behind and bulging cloud. Petra was to study weaving with Ethel Mairet and she is seen against a sheep fold, her hair textured like a pattern in wool. The tree on the left celebrates a burgeoning relationship and the house behind, their future together.

People close to Jones thought that he would never be able to marry. Fr. John O'Connor was all for Petra breaking the engagement off and Gill, who had been unusually easy about the liaison, agreed with him;[7] it has even been suggested that, in the end, Gill actually dissuaded his daughter from the marriage.[8] Later, others who knew the artist, such as David Kindersley, said that he 'would have made a hopeless husband'[9] and Eddie Nutgens, Gill's neighbour at Pigotts, said that Petra 'would have devoured Jones'.[10] Petra herself has remarked that the young painter could be quite prim and that living with him would have been difficult as he was not earning and she wanted children.[11]

If Jones was anxious about the economics of his vocation, surely the context in which he found himself would have reassured him; all around, families were living in a condition of 'holy poverty' and realizing their creative ambitions. Perhaps it was rather that Jones did not want to marry the fact of Petra and yet, because of a powerful attraction, he was distraught when the engagement came to an end. A gouache of Petra made about this time shows her articulated in the landscape like some earth-mother though older and harsher; the woman Jones desperately desired to mythologize was actually, on some practical and mundane level, a person.

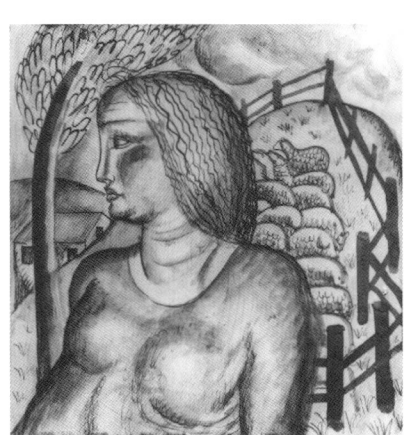

3. Petra against Sheepfold, 1924

The relationship was fraught with complex inhibitions. Petra, according to Hague, was suffering 'in repressive silence from her father's authoritarian ways'[12] and perhaps, as we now know, from his sexual liberties; Jones was fighting shy of the responsibilities of marriage. The artist much later claimed that the way to get a cat to sit on your lap is not to stroke its back; this tactic may go a long way to explain Jones's uncanny capacity to get people to do things for him but in courtship it could be a hindrance. H.S. Ede wrote to him:

> You need, I am sure, physical expression of your mental attitude. You need to *stroke* * your cat and not just think of the beauty of stroking. (* Whatever it is you want to 'stroke', stroke it and get relief - you being what you are, your stroking will hurt no-one - will only *add* to their life, whereas your denial is suicide) … You are ill for Petra and the blank it has made. If you *know* it is Petra and not the blank, can't you go for her and *insist*. It is nonsense that she knows better than you.[13]

Such physical relations as there were between them were complicated by reservations on either side.

Towards the end of 1926 there was a good deal of indecision on Petra's part between Denis Tegetmeier, who was making 'very fervent advances',[14] and David Jones who was obviously dragging his heels. Petra now saw that her fiancé was a great procrastinator who, in reality, would never take the decisive step to marriage. She broke off their engagement and decided to marry Tegetmeier who had no qualms about trying to combine the practice of his arts with the responsibilities of family life.

While Petra's decision in some sense relieved Jones from what Hague calls the 'great burden of responsibility',[15] it was also an enormous shock that confirmed his pessimistic vision. Writing to Desmond Chute, Gill, with his usual rough-shod attitude, suggested that things had worked out for the best:

> Poor old DJ was v. cut up at first but he's all right now and really much happier I think. The idea of marriage 'put the wind up' him horribly - it was an impending doom - and fond as he was of Petra it was not 'married love'. As for Petra she's a different person and so is Denis T.[16]

Philip Hagreen was more searching in his understanding of the matter. He wrote that for Jones it meant 'exile', 'David was sore wounded and alone in the wilderness.'[17] Over a year later, when Jones was staying with him in the south of France, Hagreen formed the impression that Jones

> suffered most grievously. During the six weeks at Lourdes he talked with me as perhaps he did with no one else. He had taken the solemn betrothal as a vow. A German bullet had gone through his leg but the news that came to him on Caldey went through his heart.[18]

Hagreen considers Jones's work between 1923-6 as 'a phenomenal outpouring of happy creation' terminated by the shock of 1927,[19] but it was, in fact, nothing to what Jones achieved immediately afterwards, between 1927 and 1932, during that period of artistic maturation and hectic compensation when his loss of a fiancée appears to have spurred his creativity. Kathleen Raine intriguingly suggests that Jones, who could not in her opinion have coped with marriage, had no need to wed Petra; by not marrying, he could go on celebrating her and never get over her, a state which involves the besotted in a tantalizing and endless romantic preoccupation.[20] Indeed, Petra Gill became Jones's prototype for female beauty although there were also artistic precedents; the large curving brow can be seen in Pisanello and Cranach, and the long thick neck is a Pre-Raphaelite convention.

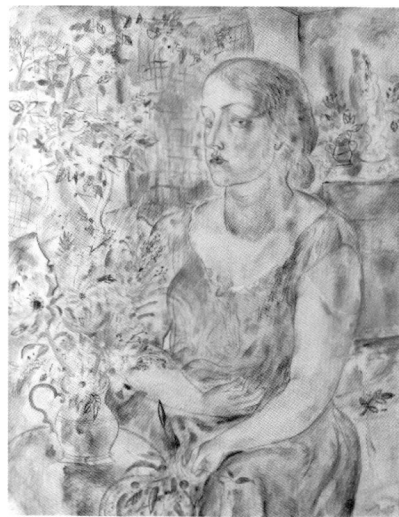

4. Petra, 1929

To celebrate Petra's birthday on 18 August, 1929, Jones was at Pigotts and it was at that time that a portrait was made with the sitter looking older than her twenty-three years. It is a well composed picture with a series of subtle and sophisticated echoing curves; curious the flimsy dress, the visible frill of underwear and slipped bra-strap in juxtaposition with the statuette of the Virgin and Child on the sideboard behind with 'MERCY' written on its base. Where the Madonna holds the infant Jesus in her arms, the cradling right arm of Petra is empty and the sprig on the floor on the right is reminiscent of the doll cast aside in *The Garden Enclosed*. The portrait was given by the Contemporary Art Society to its newly formed Welsh counterpart in 1937 to inaugurate their collection.[21]

Whereas in that 1929 portrait the sitter appeared severe and haughty, in a looser picture of 1932 she seems more youthful, more playfully sensuous and mysteriously beautiful. The portrait has the wonderful wildness which we associate with the works of that period. Grey, blue and green washes seem to grow out of the drawing and the pencil work is vigorous and spontaneous. The head of Petra manifests the one point of easy focus, an askance stillness in the midst of a hectic world. On one occasion, Kathleen Raine found Jones on the floor at Rock before a portrait of Petra which he had propped up, gazing at it. To her, it seemed that he was lost in admiration for the sitter as if, indeed, he did not wish to get over his attachment.[22]

In the 1929 portrait there were flowers crowded and flattened on the left hand side and perhaps that spurred Jones on to the idea of *Petra im Rosenhag* (7), a vision of Petra as flower goddess made in 1930-1 between the two portraits already considered. It was painted about the time that Petra had her first child, a reason, perhaps, for choosing a title which evoked the *Madonna im Rosenhag*, a northern Renaissance convention to which Jones does little more than allude. The painting is really a confluence of other traditions and allusions: the English Renaissance in its echo of a Hilliard flower-strewn miniature, the classical in its echo of the Roman Goddess *Flora* from Botticelli's *Primavera*,[23] and the Celtic with its glance at Blodeuwedd. If, as Hagreen suggests, Petra had 'destroyed' Jones, then Blodeuwedd is an apt allusion for she was guilty of killing her husband and yet she was fashioned from 'the blossoms of the oak, and the blossoms of the broom, and the blossoms of the meadowsweet' and was the 'fairest and most graceful' maiden that ever man saw.[24]

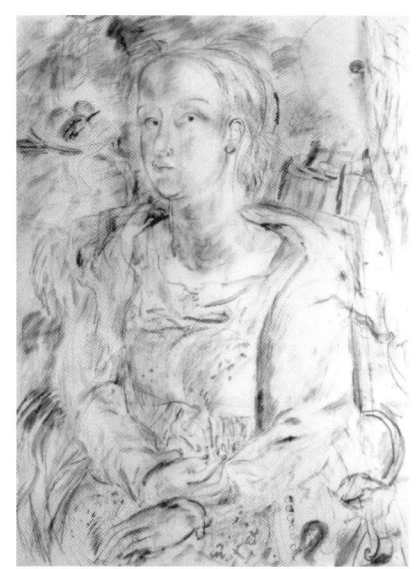

5. Petra, 1932

Unlike the majority of other portraits, *Petra im Rosenhag* was developed through several sittings; Jones tended to paint Petra whereas, for the most part, he drew others. While the desire to enlarge his expression with mythological allusion was beginning to emerge around 1930-1, it was largely contrived in a blissfully suggested and undogmatic manner. Several years later he was writing to Nicolete Gray that he would like to paint her in a 'hat with the feather and little cape like an empress, like Helen the mother of Constantine'[25] and indeed he went on to depict Petra Helen Tegetmeier in that guise. Much later in life he wanted to fetishize Valerie Price as a Romano-British woman by asking her to wear a black cape and gold torque[26] - she was to be no mere young lady come up to London from Wales but the beautiful sum of all her female Celtic antecedents. In the mid-fifties when Jones was told about the girlfriend of a young acquaintance during the course of conversation he mythologized the woman in the act of imagining her.[27] In literary or painted portraits Jones felt compelled to have a mythological model; when he attempted a portrait of Jack Hanson's wife in about 1932 he recorded that he 'could not beat up any real feeling about her, for some reason. I didn't know what she was - Athena, Diana or Persephone or whatever and if you don't know the archetype, how can you draw the type?'[28] The same proved true with his rather empty portrait of Isabella Drummond.

Petra im Rosenhag is sumptuous and large in scale. Above all, it is striking in its sensuality; this is Jones making love through his art. Petra is married and about to have a child but she appears like a buxom and tantalizing young woman who has, like Blodeuwedd, something treacherous about her. She raises her skirt in an enticing, come-on gesture, her nose is generalized to allow attention to focus on the lips, the lumpy shoulder is swollen almost like an excited penis. Yet, while she exudes a pulsating sexuality, the predominant dull blues, greys and rusty reds cool the painting and the resulting tension embodies frustration. The portrait was chosen to be included in the British Council's 1945 Paris exhibition, *Quelques Contemporains Anglais*. Jones wrote to Petra that it 'is going to Paris with some others to show the French what English painters are like!'[29]

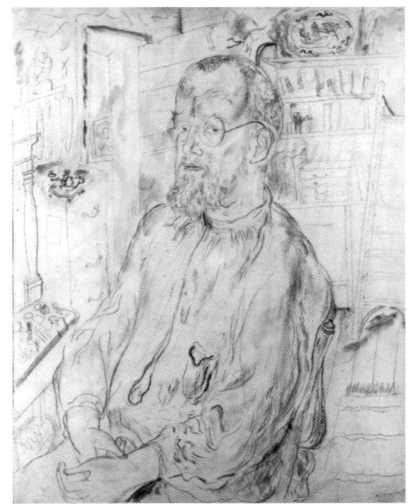

6. Eric Gill, 1930

In his portrait of Petra's father, Eric Gill, Jones presents a more reflective and even vulnerable man than Gill is generally considered to have been. He appears to feel discomfort as the object of scrutiny. He looks perturbed and the polarities of Gill's chief interests, religion and sex, are acknowledged through artefacts, the *Madonna and Child* on the left and *Girl with the Upraised Leg* in the upper right-hand corner. It is astonishing that while Gill had become a kind of father figure to the young painter and was 'very loving, very affectionate',[30] Jones sought no mythological correlative for that relationship but gave a glimpse of the rather shifty and anxious man seen in the photograph of the two men sitting together (see p 51).

Portrait of a Boy is of Gill's adopted and largely neglected son, Gordian, and it is a conventional portrait somewhat in the style of Jones's Westminster teacher, Meninsky. The date, 1928, the year in which Jones visited Salies-de-Béarn where Gordian had been sent to school, suggests that this is the

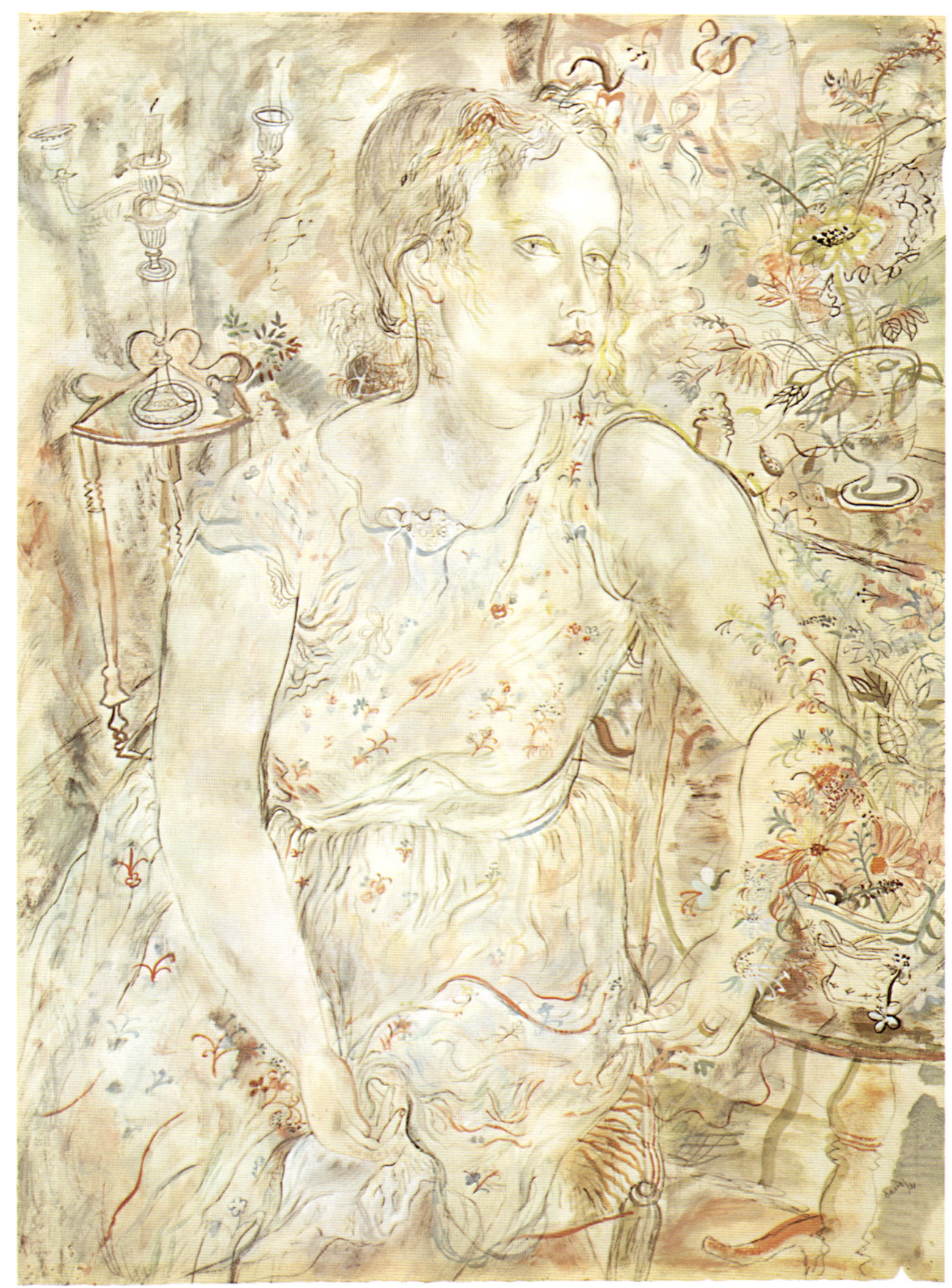

7. Petra im Rosenhag, 1931

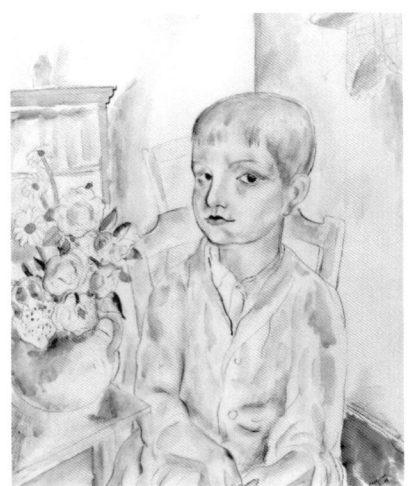

8. Portrait of a Boy, 1928

portrait once known as *The Salesian Gordian*. Because of the subtle modelling of the head we feel a psychological depth often lacking in Jones's portraits. Drawing and painting are well integrated and the eyes and lips carry the mood of the watchful and serious boy. This and *Carr's Splint*,[31] a portrait of Gordian when he broke his arm, reveal Jones's sensitivity to this child.

Desmond Chute was descended from the theatrical family of Macready who ran Bristol's two principal theatres in the nineteenth century. After studying at the Slade, he became one of the original triumvirate at Ditchling.[32] Cecil Gill considered that between his brother and Chute there existed 'a deep personal attachment … Desmond himself said that he loved Eric - and he was more than a brother, you might say. He had the sort of devotion for Eric of a lover.'[33] When Chute left Ditchling to become a priest it was Jones who, for Gill, filled the vacuum caused by Chute's departure. Cecil Gill recalled Chute as a 'Beardsley'

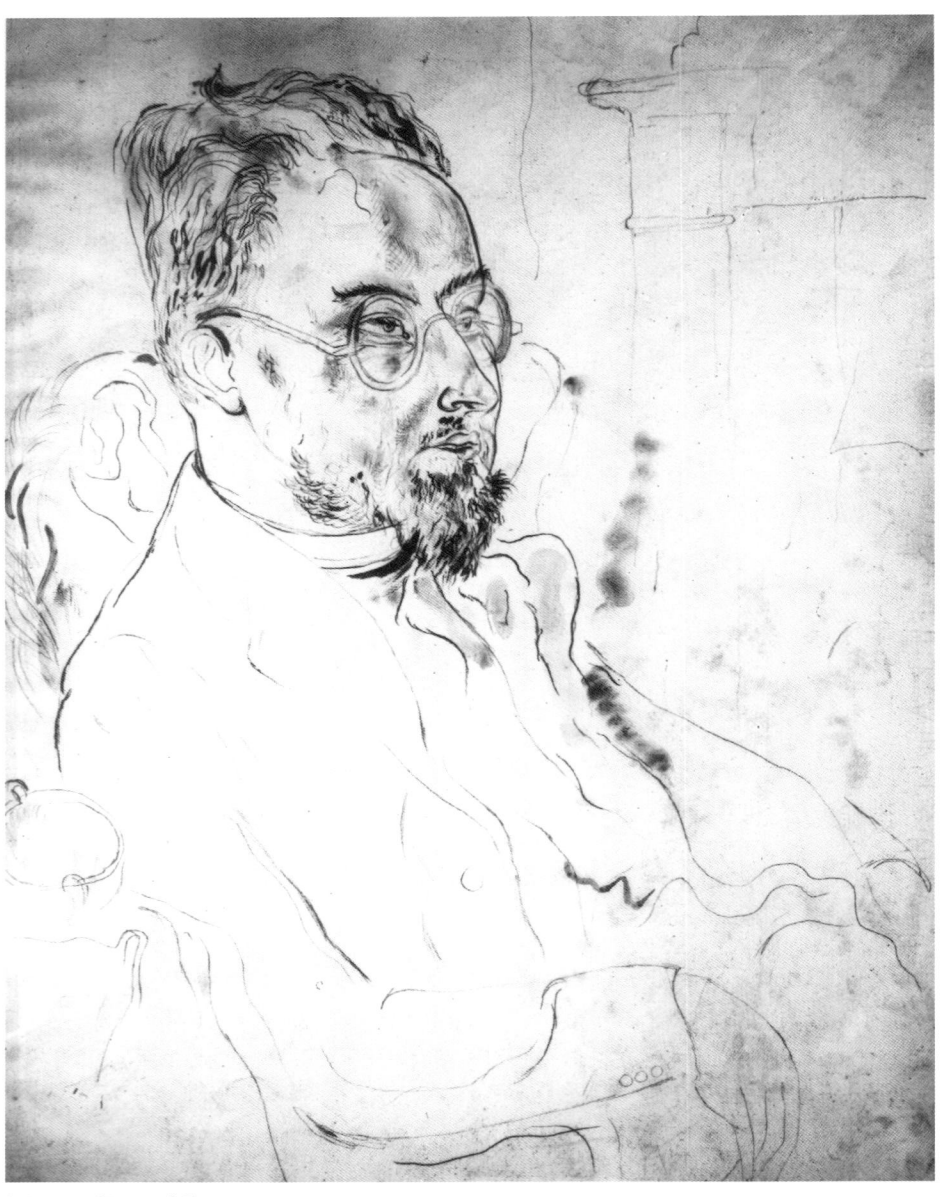

9. Portrait of Desmond Chute, (?)

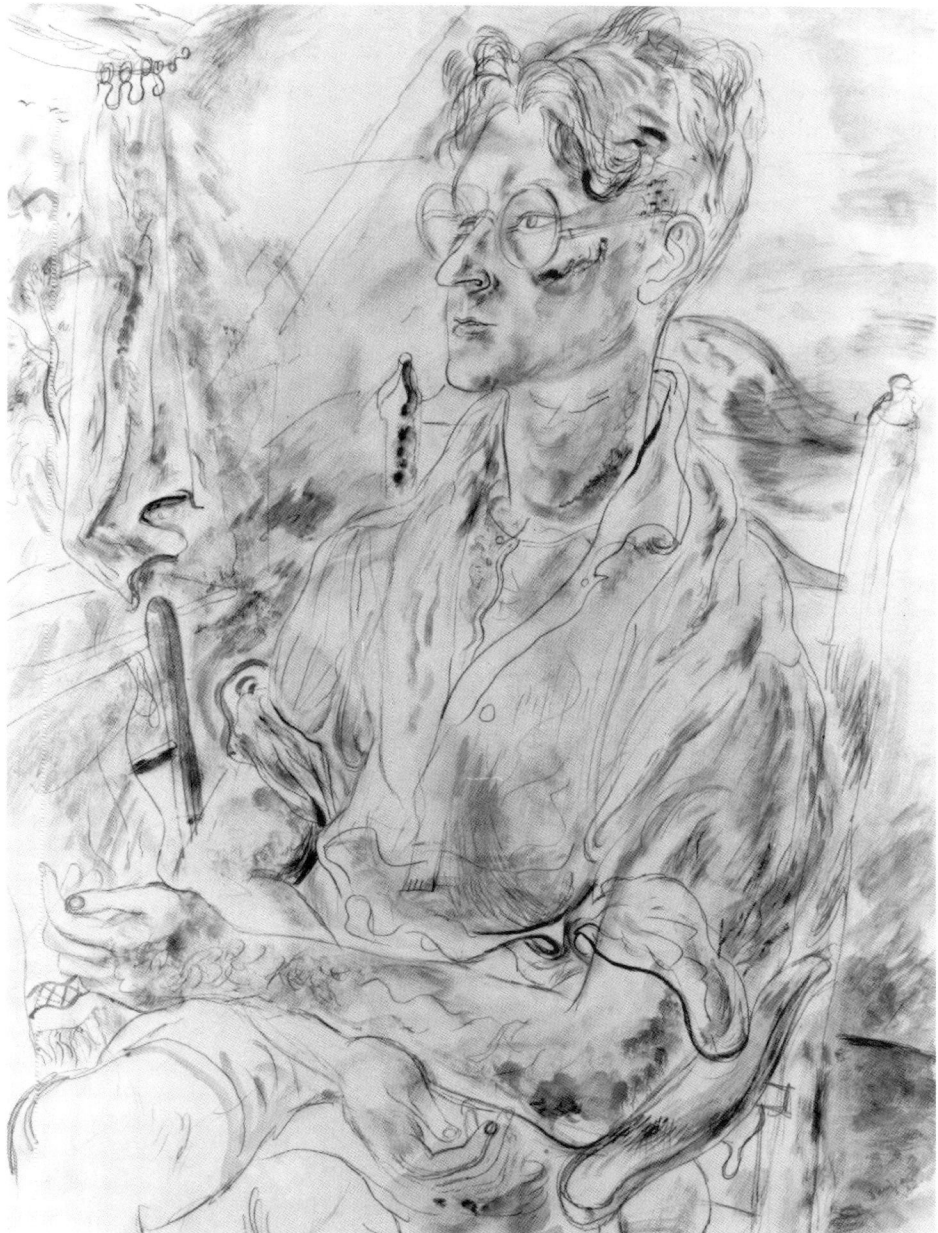

10. Portrait of René Hague, 1932

type, 'long and graceful, swathed about with shawls'.[34] There is certainly something sinister, *fin-de-siècle* and dandyish about the *Portrait of Desmond Chute*. When Jones saw a photograph years after it was made, he remarked that the little finger was 'very like Desmond';[35] Jones's fix on this tiny detail draws our attention to its discrepancy of scale and style.

A second attempt at a portrait of René Hague, Jones's close friend, was considered by the artist much later in life to be 'the best 'portrait' *qua* portrait - 'likeness' of any I've attempted.'[36] The line is rhythmic and dabs, washes and scumbles are used to enliven the pencil work. Jones met Hague and immediately befriended him when he arrived at Capel-y-ffin at the end of 1924. An *impromptu* sketch showing a bitten lip reveals something of the defiant concentration of the 'wise, witty, drunk, holy, bawdy'[37] classical scholar. Hague was an outspoken man, who had a

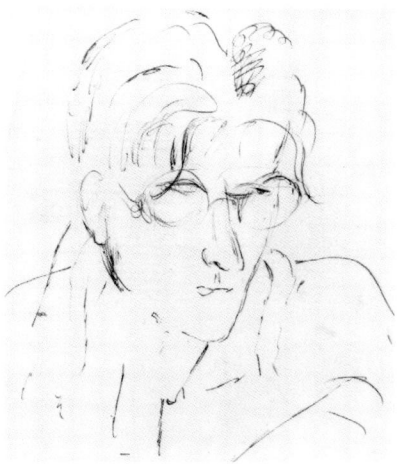

11. René Hague, 1930

157

tempestuous relationship with his eventual father-in-law, Eric Gill. The character of the relationship between Jones and Hague is captured in the numerous comical sketches which the artist made of his friend,[38] complementing the two larger formal portraits of which the second and finer was called *The Translator of the Chanson de Roland* because Hague counted among his many other accomplishments a lively translation of the *chanson de geste*. It is completely different in approach from the portrait of Jones's other close friend, Harman Grisewood, in the *Portrait of a Maker* where the sitter emerges out of the sea of paint and the artist, rather than attempting a likeness, seems to be in search of the spirit of the subject's personality.

Grisewood remembered going four or five times to Brockley to pose for Jones in his little bedroom. The painter started making a full-face portrait but after about two sittings he became infuriated with the way in which it was developing. Grisewood recalled that he had never heard such oaths before and eventually Jones took a knife to the canvas and tore it to pieces, amazing the sitter with his strength. The frail little artist had learnt from Augustus John that to paint 'you've got to be as strong as ten elephants', and so he became, when painting, vigorous and dynamic and would exhaust himself in his attempt to get away from preconceived theories and inherited modes of painting.[39]

Grisewood had quite liked the ripped-up portrait but the artist began again on a version with the sitter in a large overcoat and in a style tending towards painterly abstraction, with non-referential texturings and startlingly disparate dry brushwork. The painting was exhibited in the 1932 7&5 Society exhibition, under a title which refers to Dunbar's poem, *The Lament for the Makeris*. Anchored only by the merest details this portrait is unique though not unrelated, in style and in the cradling of the crossed hands, to *Human Being*, which was also first shown in the same exhibition.

Although Jones deleted the addition '(Self Portrait)' from the proof of the Arts Council 1954 *David Jones* catalogue,[40] he calls *Human Being*

> a quasi self-portrait in a sense, curiously enough set going by the hands from a seemingly unlikely source - that stupendous painting of Charles VII of France by Fouquet - a work I spent long in gazing at when it came to Burlington House with an exhibition of French painting in, I suppose, 1930.[41]

He also spoke of the great freedom of

> drawing in the mirror - there is no one to say, 'Oh but I've got a nose like that etc.' - one just has a 'face' hands etc. ... to do what one likes with.[42]

Compositionally, the forearms at rest form the base of a triangle which directs the spectator's gaze up to the face. Again, Jones uses thinned oil to create texture but the work is an almost monochromatic brown, enlivened only by the hanging red rag, handkerchief and tie. Although he was approaching forty, Jones chose to represent himself as a boy as if he doesn't see himself growing up.

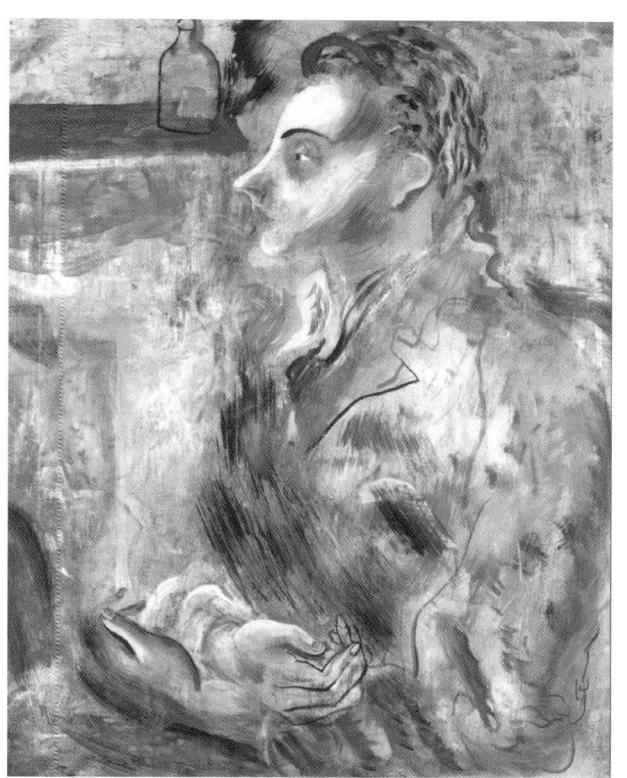

12. Portrait of a Maker, 1932

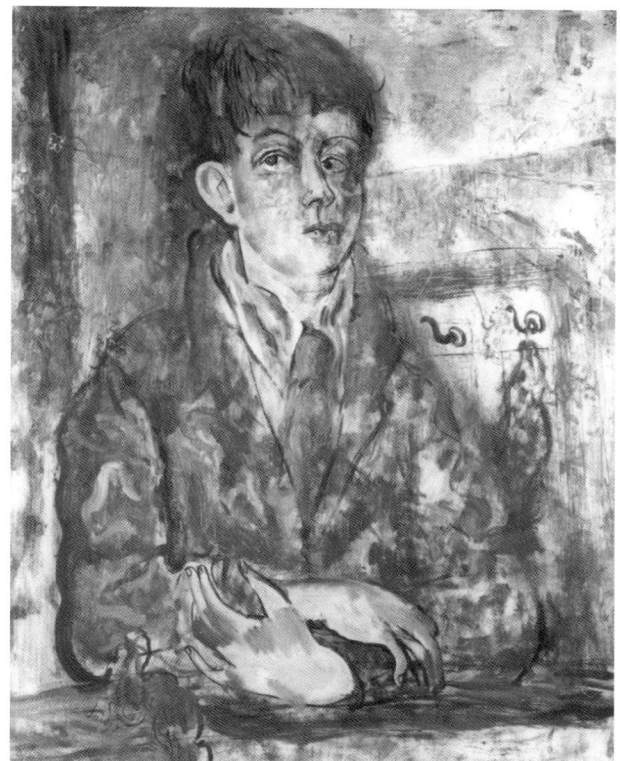

13. Human Being, 1931

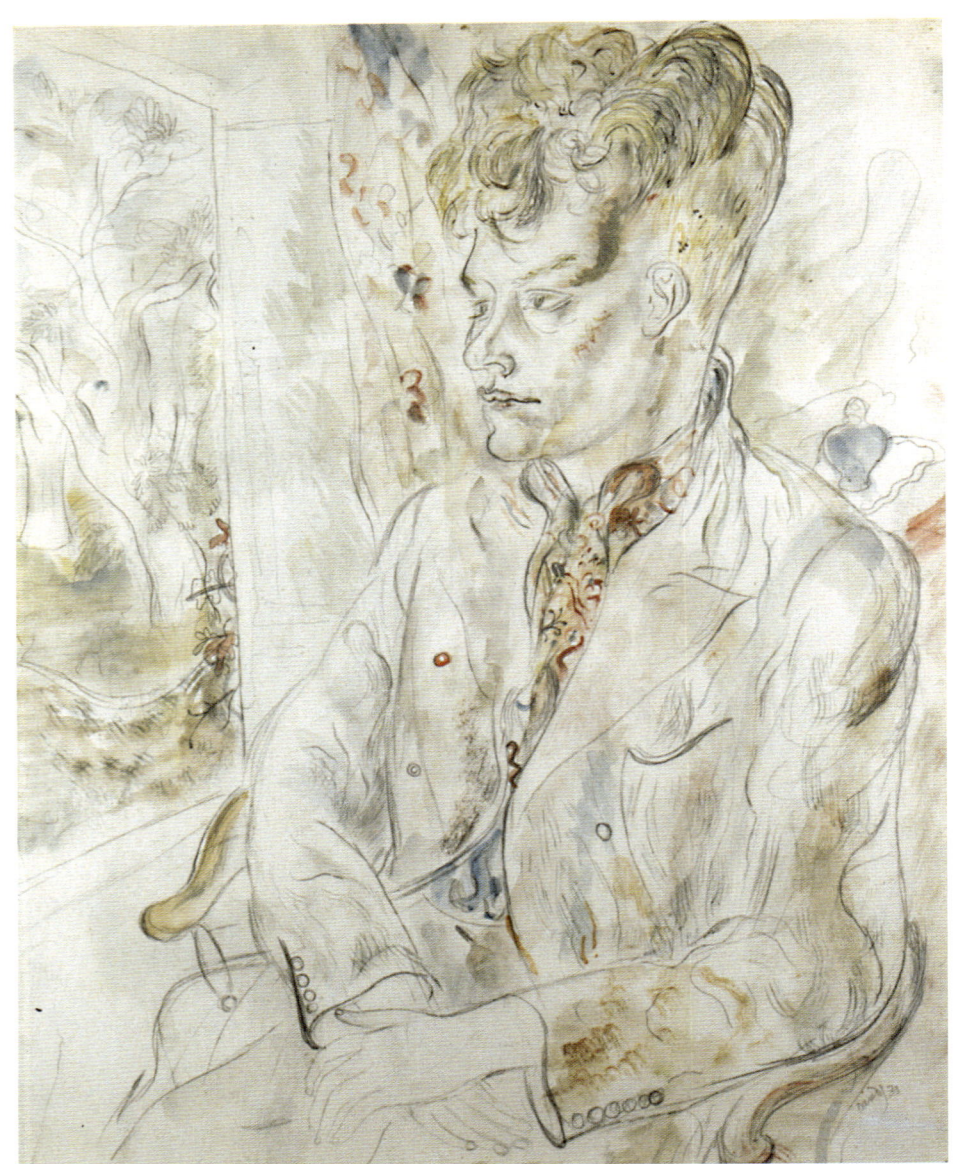

14. Portrait of Tommy Hodgkin, 1930

The *Portrait of Thomas Hodgkin* which was done at great speed is hardly painted at all, but this economy indicates one way in which Jones made a portrait and reveals the two orders of expression which he employs: literal description and abstract use of line and colour. In this instance, the delineation of the person actually lies behind the free-floating marks and the drawing and painting do not coalesce. Interest in the sitter's physiognomy gives way to reverie as we become absorbed in the world of abstract accents. Jones's tendency to choose odd points of focus is allowed to develop into an intuitive logic of colour and line independent of the descriptive prerequisite of a portrait. A series of hooked strokes, from the curved arms of the chair, the squiggle of blue at the end of the scarf, the question-mark shape on the curve at the neck, the stroke on the temple lead the eye up to the top of the head which holds the spectator's attention before allowing it to cascade down through the wavy hair and features towards the lower part of the picture where the image fades away from us.

Prudence Pelham was another important friendship which resulted from Jones's association with Eric Gill. The younger daughter of the sixth Earl of Chichester, a few years before she met Jones and Gill her family had suffered a double disaster in 1926 when her father died, followed only a week later by the death of his handsome eldest child, John.[43] Gill and Laurie Cribb cut a memorial stone and thus it was that Prudence Pelham, who had spent some time in the Paris studio of Antoine Bourdelle, came to study stone-carving under Eric Gill. Jones met her at Pigotts in March, 1929,[44] and she stayed there into the next year when the portrait was done. René Hague remembered coming into the sitting-room while the artist was at work on it and he thought there had been 'some terrible emotional storm, for Prue was sitting so quiet and upright in the corner' and Jones was 'glowering by the window'.[45] Such tension could have resulted from artistic dissatisfaction but it could also have been some emotional frustration for Jones found Pelham's mind 'heavenly',[46] her spirit exhilarating, and fell in love. She was a genuinely free, adventurous and inquisitive spirit, with a great sense of humour.[47] Three extracts from letters give a hint of her qualities. The first, about an evening at Pigotts sometime early in the Second World War reveals her rebellious energy:

> Everyone got very drunk. Joan [Hague *(15)*] gave herself a thick ear and lost her false teeth … I cooked a beautiful meal sitting on the floor, steak onions sausages and things. David was gentle and sober. After that I thought I am beautifully drunk and very happy. My name is Prudence and fuck them they can wash up. I will go for a private walk. So I went into the wood. It was lovely, quite warm and a huge improbable looking moon, broken trees, tree stumps. I fell over often, in the end I stayed down and was a little sick and sung myself to sleep.[48]

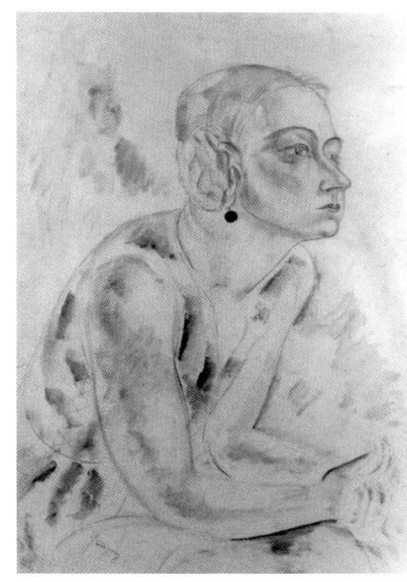

15. Portrait of Joanna Gill, (?)

> No, sorry Dai, have to go to Glyndebourne next week-end. It's wonderful you know but it's not your sort of thing exactly - seeing that you rule out anything after 14th Cent. except of course Negro Spirituals and *Frankie and Johnny were Lovers* and *Casey Jones Mounted on his Engine* and *Six Dukes Went a Fishing* - must rush now.[49]

> By the way talking of underwear please tell Ann to send me my drawers quick as a fish. She's had them quite long enough and I haven't had a clean pair since I've been here it's intolerable.[50]

Pelham was a powerful personality, poetic, original, intelligent, in conversation the intellectual equal of the generally more educated men,[51] beautiful and deeply fascinating.[52]

But while there were differences between Pelham and Jones such as her assertively anti-religious attitude and her confessed difficulty with looking at pictures - ('I've had a gruelling day with David at picture galleries, lord I'm bad at looking at pictures. I don't like those modern types.'[53]) - there were many points in common. Evidence from her letters abroad reveals that she possessed a degree of xenophobia and elsewhere she professed a dislike of Socialism. What is more, a deep bond between them was illness, Jones with his depression and increasing propensity to be susceptible to small but continual maladies and Pelham with her steadily developing disseminated sclerosis. Illness hampered her as it hampered Jones for she was 'almost never well',[54] and that prevented her from sculpting as Jones's neurasthenia made it difficult for him to paint. She suffered a depressing and often degrading cycle of hospitalizations beside which some of Jones's petty physical complaints appear as mere hypochondria:

> I knew it would be shit in a test tube, pee in a test tube let your nise [*sic*] blood drip out of your veins in a test tube … I knew it would be thumbscrews and yank off her toe-nails … I knew it would be five cigarettes a day and wash behind the ears at dawn … *Christ*, how I despise medicine I do despise it I will quarrel with it and contradict everything it says emphatically. I won't listen to it I will ignore it… .[55]

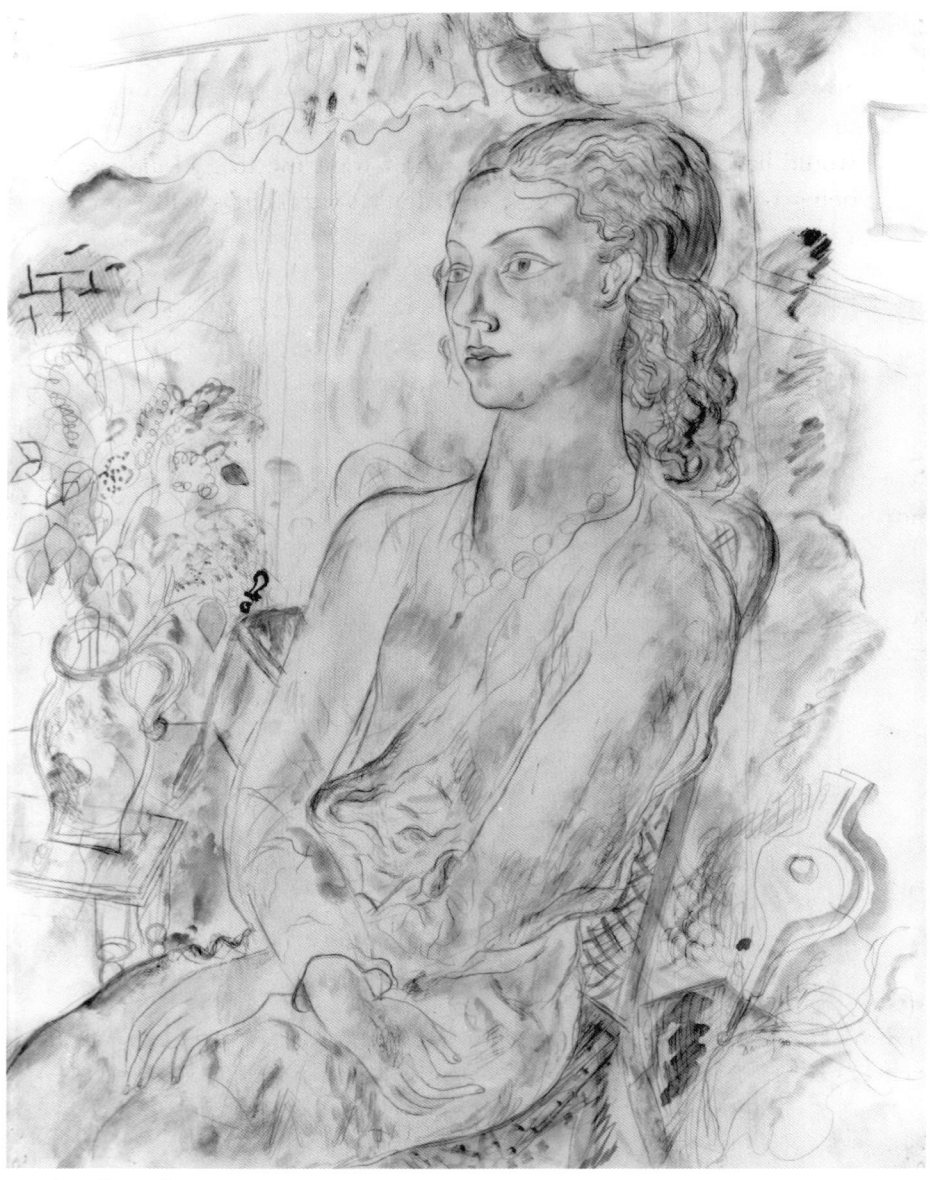

16. Lady Prudence Pelham, 1930

Unlike the Hodgkin portrait, in *Prudence Pelham* the dabs of colour lie behind the drawing of the figure and help the eye to flit across the paper. Certain abstract marks like the diagonals above the head, the chair back, or the curving bands of colour behind the sitter's hair and shoulders evoke wings and something seraphic and radiant emerges in contemplation of her face. So dominated is the picture by the angelic head that the eye has to attempt continually to reassemble the diminished body which, by contrast, seems collapsed like a marionette at rest. Instead of breasts we find folds of empty fabric. The curve of the hip is astonishingly small, the thighs clamped together and the hands almost shackled across the lap suggesting physical impediment or restriction.

Jones would send Pelham flowers, hopelessly she would invite him on a trip to Burgundy,[56] she would turn up with a Wallis purchased as a gift for him and he would send her a gold necklace, no mean Christmas present from a poor, unproductive artist.[57] She would visit him at Sidmouth where the emotional atmosphere obviously became intense:

> So very dearest David most darling David - how short it was - I did hate leaving you - I did not say it a lot because I knew I would have to go and knew you didn't want me to ... I *did love* being with you you do know that don't you? Things will come better I do believe. There are a lot of things I would write but it is not much good to write complicated personal things in a letter I think - it leaves the other person helpless under a barrage of words. Be very safe my darling Dai ... Good night my sweet David please please be happy I can't bear it when you are miserable and I have made it worse.[58]

When she left after one visit, Jones wrote 'Prudence went away yesterday morning ... my Lord, what a morning.'[59]

The almost unsupportable surprise for Jones came when Pelham got married very suddenly to a childhood friend of her brother's early in 1939. As Jones's emotional commitment had been so intense the news was a great shock:

> I love her very much and our friendship has meant everything to me. So naturally, however much this may be a 'good thing', I've naturally had a twisting, trying to get all the tangled delicate emotional bits and pieces tied up and sorted out ... She is such a marvellous and unique, truly intelligent, and beautiful person ... we were so very alike in lots of ways ... So naturally a change in her life of so fundamental a character requires in me a readjustment... .[60]

In *Human Being*, David Jones's right eye seemed to be looking inwards whereas in *Self Portrait* of 1928 his regard is direct and confrontational. He is in the act of taking stock and asking where he is going. He paints himself looking in the mirror surrounded by his work which is both evidence of his achievement and the source of his emotional and material sacrifices. He includes a Caldey painting, an elephant curiously unframed on the left, and a boxwood sculpture in the foreground.[61] Although somewhat haggard it is still a boyish face that the artist portrays in a mask-like style which, paradoxically, allows him to drop his mask.

There are no portraits *per se* painted after the mid-thirties but during the short period of working in the genre Jones had produced an original body of work. Interestingly, he later went on to paint historical or mythological figures such as *The Lord of Venedotia* or a series of Roman matrons as if he were doing their portrait; where girlfriends had been of enormous emotional importance to him in his youth, as he moved into middle age, once bitten twice shy, the inhabitants of historical and mythological worlds took on a safer reality.

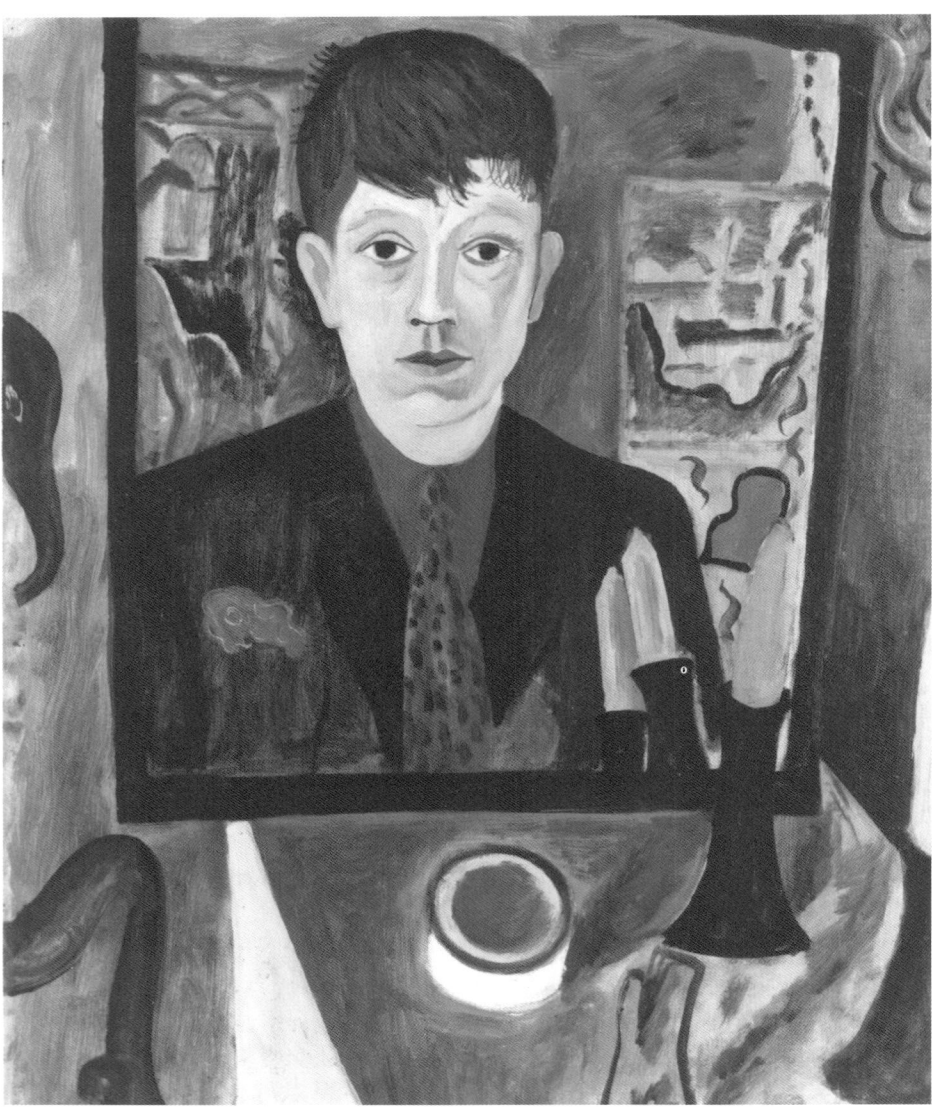

17. Self Portrait, 1928

LANDSCAPES IN A LIFE

Lopped trees reappear in a deceptively childish yet cunningly child-like view from an upper room of H.S. Ede's house in Elm Row, Hampstead. While the line persuades us, with its tentative and uneven quality, that it is indeed the work of a child, the composition and sense of space is sophisticated. It is no less controlled and contrived than the simplified planes and consequent sectionalizing of the painted version of the same scene which, despite its swiftness of execution, is considered in its attention to structure and texture. The garden seat, drawn in the first version with such seeming ineptitude, yet cleverly placed to punctuate the flower bed behind, is, in the painted version, reduced to four parallel brush strokes which participate in a series of tilted horizontals of grass border, trellis, gate, wall and house to create depth. The painted version is free and bold and the drawing is cunning in its use of the child's tendency to reduce the stability and solidity of things.

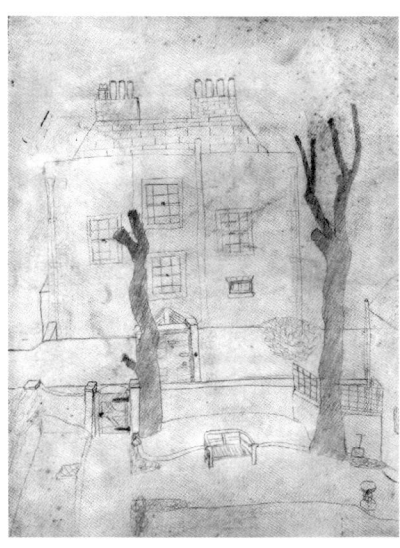

1. View from No.1 Elm Row, Hampstead, 1928

The late twenties and early thirties were the only time in his life when Jones mixed much with other painters and became genuinely part of the London art world. The vivacity and variety of his work reveal the obvious stimulation that he took from absorbing what was in the air. The man responsible for forging these artistic connections was H.S. Ede, who was such an avant-garde Assistant at the Tate that his taste for what might be acquired frequently astounded his more conservative superiors. Jones was a frequent visitor to the Edes and painted not only from the house but made at least one painting of nearby Hampstead Heath. The church-like silence within the high garden walls and the 'inward quiet' of the house itself would certainly have been fractured as gatherings at the Edes' grew to include

> quite a large section of London's artistic world. We even had the top members of the Russian Ballet, and Arnold Bennett with them; he wrote an article in one of the evening papers 'How the poor live in Hampstead'. There were 25 to supper that day, and little did they know that it had cost only ten pence per head. It was a lovely evening with Vera Moore playing the piano and two of the best 'English Singers', ... many evenings we would sit with just a few painters discussing life, or a pianist would arrive and want to play his next day's concert, or David Jones would be staying and evening after evening would read what he had written of *In Parenthesis*.[1]

By the end of the twenties and the beginning of the thirties the art scene in London was becoming more exciting and more international with a Modigliani

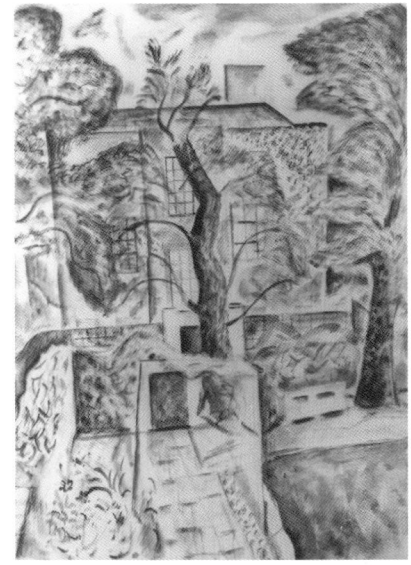

2. Elm Row, Hampstead, 1927

165

show in 1929, Léger, Metzinger and Severini in 1930, the Picasso retrospective in 1931, the *L'École de Paris* exhibition at the Lefevre in January 1932, and with Max Ernst and Miró exhibited in 1933. In December of that year, the Tate Gallery displayed its recently acquired Stoop bequest including works by Degas, Van Gogh, Cézanne, Matisse, Picasso, Braque and Modigliani; the gradual emergence of London from the cultural backwaters of modernism was beginning. The period was also one in which, along with the 7&5 Society exhibitions, the work of artists like Nicholson, Nash, Moore and Hepworth was much seen in the London galleries. After the post-war recoil from the extremes of modernism which had been felt on both sides of the channel, progressive artists in the early thirties were coming into their own; art and commerce, abstraction and architecture were working together to build a brave, if threatened, new world.

Jones was, during this period, exhibiting in several galleries, receiving interesting notices and allowing his work to become larger and more painterly. If Ditchling and Capel had provided him with an antidote to art school, then this period in London, with its exposure to the latest trends in the fine art world, provided a welcome alternative to Gill. Of course, a painter without such an uncompromising belief would have been more free to participate in the increasingly mandarin activities of the twentieth century world of the fine artist where extra-aesthetic beliefs tended to be political or implicitly spiritual rather than explicitly religious. The intellectual baggage with which Jones's chosen religion loaded him was to prove difficult to articulate in the context of modern art. Even in watercolour, 'which readily serves for the expression of a view of the natural world as the source of poetical experience',[2] Jones ultimately felt incapable of evoking the unseen without the aid of an intellectual superstructure. But, during this free and productive period, Jones attempted, as Neve observed, 'to make the visible world both itself and simultaneously something else without recourse to any sacramental sign language or code.'[3] Jones's watercolours of the early thirties increasingly dissolved his world and yet he seemed unwilling to relinquish little details and his ultimate reluctance to abandon the outward and visible signs for the inward journey kept him from fully realizing what he had begun to achieve in the loosest of his 1932 watercolours. When he made his boldest attempts to let go he found that he had to let go of painting itself. According to Kathleen Raine he had 'a fragile hold on life and needed love and beauty';[4] the British landscape and flowers provided such beauty and his friends the love.

In a drawing started at Pigotts, Jones shows the Gill girls at work tending a medieval garden enclosed of ladies and gentle beasts. The drawing was abandoned, just as that walled garden, for Jones, had been destroyed. How painful it must have been for him to receive the following description of his ex-fiancée written by her husband on the occasion of the birth of their first baby: 'Petra's serenity seems almost above this world, despising nothing and loving everything. She has a sort of spiritual radiance, which is her peculiar and worshipful character'.[5] In the wake of a broken engagement Jones had plunged into an exhausting and unsustainable bout of activity. In a letter of 1928 to Helen Ede he wrote, 'I have become an idolator and seek

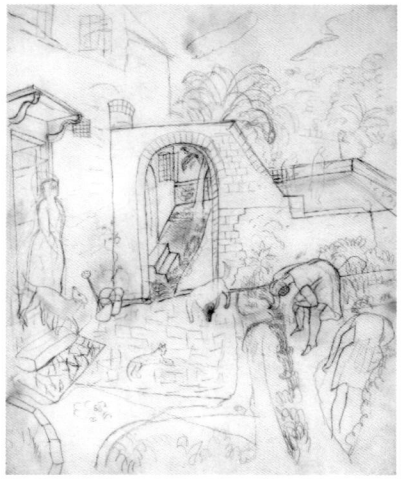

3. Sketch for Pigotts Pathway, 1930

that satisfaction in painting and engraving etc. that can only be found in God'.[6] Not only is this an indication of how seriously he took his religion, but it also suggests that he knew relief would be temporary; when the activity stopped he would collapse.

The phenomenal task of writing *In Parenthesis* was, to all intents and purposes, completed at Pigotts on 18 August, 1932,[7] and towards the end of the four-year period in which he had been writing it, he had also produced more than fifty watercolours a year. The writing had brought back the most testing period of his life. Positive reaction to his watercolours took him to the edge of having to deal with celebrity and success. Realizing that his poetry might be important and discovering that he could be a much bolder painter than he had imagined, he found himself in the position of having to discover how and where he could cope with the consequences. Money might be made after a decade of living off his parents and the Gills, and occasionally earning modest sums from engraving; in 1931, under Schedule D, Jones paid tax, albeit only £1-3-3d.

In 1932, Jones sold at that year's 7&5 exhibition as well as at Tooth's Gallery,[8] and he was represented in two exhibitions which ran concurrently at the Art Institute of Chicago. At the *First International Exhibition of Etching and Engraving* from 24 March-15 May, engravings from *The Ancient Mariner* were selling at $3.00 each, and between 31 March and 30 May, in the company of artists such as Moore, Wood, Hodgkins, Dufy, Guys and Kokoschka, Jones exhibited *Briar Casement*, *Doors By the Sea*, *Shepherdess*, and *Windy Casement* in *The Twelfth International Exhibition of Water Colors, Pastels, Drawings and Monotypes*. But despite growing success there was deepening self-dissatisfaction. He wrote to the young Nicolete Gray on 9 June, 1932, 'I've done no painting - it's awful - struggling with this beastly book and I really now think it's awful rubbish'.[9] He wrote that he 'ventured alone and unprotected into the *Royal Academy* [*Summer Exhibition*] one day last week - its horror is beyond expression - I always fondly think that perhaps a good picture will filter in by accident - but no.'[10] So Jones found himself between the backwash of mediocre Academicism and Impressionism and the growing tendencies toward Abstraction and Surrealism in the work of those contemporaries whom he admired. He was becoming isolated. One month later he was lamenting that he'd 'done no good paintings. Just can't see anything freshly.'[11] In several years of furious activity he had painted himself out. As 1932 gave way to 1933 the strain was apparent; Jones, of no fixed abode, and sensing a growing disjunction between his vision and that of his contemporaries, broke down. Months later, writing of the 1933 7&5 exhibition, he observed that 'my things look very dull and dead to me.'[12]

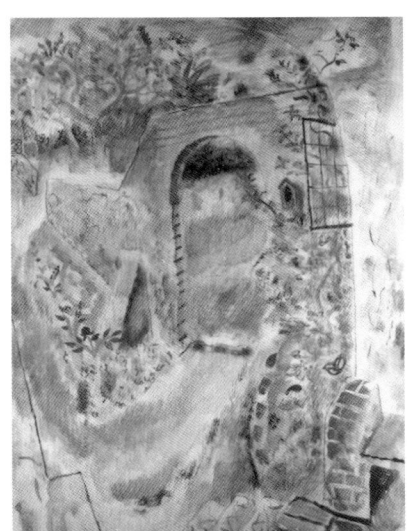

Perhaps the idea of painting *The Archway at Pigotts* came from the arch in Nicholson's *Porthmeor Beach, St. Ives* (1928) just as the white area around the dog in the distance of *Pigotts Garden* may have been inspired by Nicholson's *Birch Craig, Winter* (1930). In both of Jones's works, there is an intensification of perspective, an unhappy amount of irritating detail mixed with the more exciting general sense of unease. In *The Archway at Pigotts* (a subject which Jones tackled several times) there is the idea of passage and many of the elements in the painting seem to be surrounded by light. In *Pigotts Garden (5)*

4. Archway at Pigotts, 1930

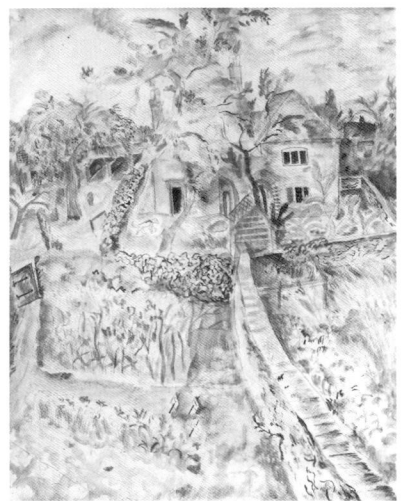

5. Pigotts Garden, 1931

the archway is included but difficult to see through the trees which grow across the house. There are two focal points split by the wall which sweeps into the picture and terminates at the shed; to the left is another of Jones's dark doorways. From a distance there appears to be a concentrated sense of depth, whereas closer to the painting, there is an intriguing separation of different areas.

The artist often stayed at Pigotts between Gill's move there in September 1928 and the autumn of 1933 and occasionally in the years that followed. Five miles from High Wycombe and therefore conveniently close to London, it was isolated from the surrounding villages by a steep wooded hill covered in beech trees. The regimen at Pigotts was less overtly religious than at Ditchling or Capel and the various dwellings and workshops were placed so as to form Gill's beloved quadrangle.[13] At first, Jones shared a bedroom with René Hague over Gill's engraving studio but, after Hague married, he joined the couple in their tiny cottage which was so small that when Jones stood to paint at the window, he would completely block the passage between kitchen and living room, much to the annoyance of Joan Hague.[14] Worse was that in order to get to their own bedroom, the Hagues were obliged to pass through the small bedroom occupied by Jones. If, by 1931, he was writing that his paintings were a 'ghastly mess … you know - gone',[15] by May 1933, he was suffering a severe depressive psychosis. René Hague records that it took the form of 'an increasing quietness, a brooding, outward signs (in language and behaviour) of an exasperated bafflement: "I can't work … the whole thing's a monumental bollux, a first-class buggeration."'[16]

Enclosure, with its conflict of dry broad brush strokes recalling a Portslade sea-scape, is one of the few oils done at Pigotts. The bold and rapid brushwork,

6. Enclosure, 1931

168

the line which zigzags its way towards the bottom right hand corner, the shaking houses, all conjure a perturbed world which is nonetheless quieter than the work of a painter who readily expresses his inner conflict such as Soutine. Yet to recast what is seen through a stressed or idiosyncratic vision is to work Expressionistically and it is necessary to assert Jones's Expressionistic energy because his watercolours - and particularly watercolours faded by over lighting - do not, at first sight, declare their full drama; delicate, lyrical and 'fey'[17] are responses most often heard instead of frail, turbulent or manic which would often be more apt. Quite simply, watercolour hasn't the bombast of oil, but like chamber music it can be tense or turbulent despite its restricted resources.

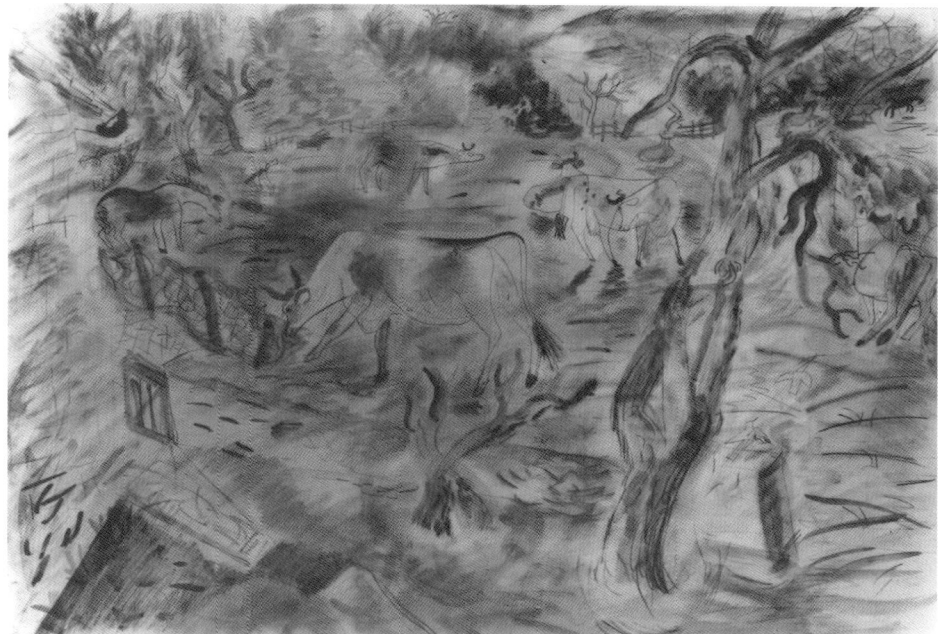

7. Gunman's Field, 1932

In 1932, *Gunman's Field* shows a world in greater turmoil. The figure with the gun is Mary Gill's gardener yet he might as well be a soldier with the nearby tangle of barbed wire;[18] indeed, Jones has written *Enfilade* on the back of the picture. This more turbulent work was considered successful; Jones wrote to H.S. Ede that the painting was 'one of the few I've done that I really like a good bit.'[19] It was also one of the four paintings (along with *Violin and Flowers* (see p 133), *Portrait of Prudence* (see p 162), and *King's Cup* which he personally selected for the 1934 Eisteddfod.[20] Certainly, the watercolour is marked by hectic drawing, angry scribbling, manic scratching and a barrage of washes.

Jones's breakdown came after months of insomnia. Unwisely staying with his parents in Brockley, he remembers hearing the clock strike the quarter-hour all through every night:[21] his nerves became as frayed as the ends of the blankets he had gnawed at Pigotts. Jones and his friends had met in an upstairs room in the house of Tom Burns in St. Leonard's Terrace, Chelsea, during the late twenties in order 'to reform the wounds in the Catholic religion',[22] and it was Tom Burns

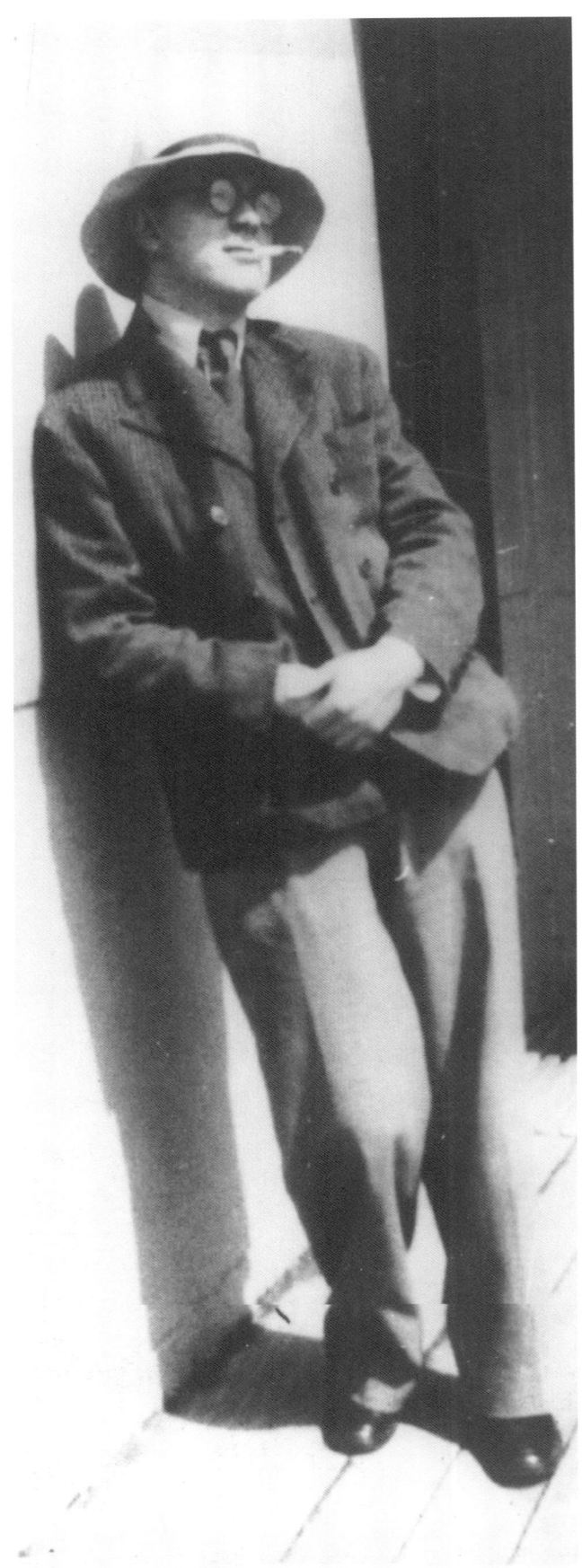

who now took charge of Jones's own psychological wounds. His brother, Dr. Charles Burns, sent Jones to a neurologist who specialized in neurasthenia which resulted from active military service. Charles Burns had himself suffered from shell-shock during the war and his elder brother, David, had been killed two weeks before the Armistice. Tom Burns, the youngest, was the motivating force behind the idea of Jones's recuperatory trip to the Middle East. He was responsible for all the arrangements and the cost, but to get Jones 'equipped and actually aboard the P&O boat in London dock was a long haul', for the artist was 'in the depth of a nervous depression and everything was frightening'.[23] They went first to Cairo and stayed with the 'tremendously kind' Ralph and Manya Harari.[24] From Cairo, Jones flew to Lydda in Palestine, reading Thomas Malory in the plane, and from there proceeded to Jerusalem by car. He went to stay at the Austrian Hospice where he met Eric Gill who was in Jerusalem to carve panels for the New Archaeological Museum and who appeared as a 'great bearded man like Tolstoy dressed in ... an Arab skirt with Arab head-dress'.[25] Thomas Hodgkin, on the staff of the Governor of Palestine, was also staying in the Hospice and would dine with Gill and Jones and they would talk in Hodgkin's room till about eleven. While Jones spoke 'as much and as gaily as he ever did' when Hodgkin had met him in England, the young man also noticed that he couldn't resist showing how miserable he was and that this got on Gill's 'nerves, who for all his gentleness has such robustness himself that he looks on all spiritual malady as sin and shows it.'[26] Jones found Bethlehem 'convincing' but expressed a growing disenchantment when he witnessed the infringement of technological advance. A café below his Hospice window played either Arab music or Mozart, neither much to his taste, and he observed that when 'you see an electric light wired to a venerable fig tree in the valley of Hinnon, your misery is complete'.[27]

Hodgkin wrote that the painter hated Jerusalem; he

> came ... against his will under the pressure of friends who thought that they knew what was good for him, and is wretched and grows wretcheder as the heat grows intense.[28]

> Egypt has given him mosquito bites as big as billiard balls and perpetual stomach ache –

170

he can eat little - loathes the hospice food … He is a stone lighter and naturally troubled by his lightness. He does look ill, but then he always did.[29]

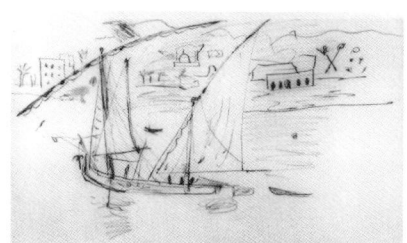

9. The Nile, Egypt, 1934

Of Jones's unfavourable attitude to the place, Hodgkin appositely asked, how could anyone feel 'anything else when one's stomach is out of order, let alone one's soul?'[30]

The trip resulted in very little visual work and no more than a few sketches remain. The artist wrote, 'if only one were *alive* one could paint a bit here'.[31] However, the impact of seeing British soldiers on duty in Palestine, looking not only like figures from the First World War but also like soldiers from the Roman occupation of Judea, prompted a good deal of Jones's later poetry; the image of modern soldiers seeming like 'a section from the Antonia, up for duties in Hierosolyma'[32] was a powerful spur to Jones's transhistorical vision. But, while the trip made a considerable impression on Jones's literary imagination, it appears to have done little or nothing for his mental health; Jones wrote from Port Said, 'I don't think it's done much good. It's all too exhausting.'[33] The whole venture was dismissed by the artist as somewhat of a bother and his depression and inability to work continued. A decade later he was still seeing the neurologist, Dr. Woods, and depression plagued him intermittently for the rest of his life.

Yet, if we compare *Gunman's Field* painted in 1932, in the period leading up to Jones's breakdown, with *The Farm Door*, a rare work of 1937, we can see that Jones has been able to reconcile his inner fury and despair with his obvious delight in a scene. The animation has been harnessed and a random mark, like that complex, free-floating shape in the bottom right-hand corner which is actually the shadow around the end of a curtain, takes on the form of an antlered animal as seen by a Lascaux cave-painter. Even its ochrous colour is somewhat reminiscent of the brown haematite.

Eliot's viewing of prehistoric cave paintings led him to understand that 'art never improves' and that all art enters a simultaneous order.[34] Jones was, likewise, keen to assert the ubiquity and perennity of the act of gratuitous but significant making, first witnessed all those millenia ago:

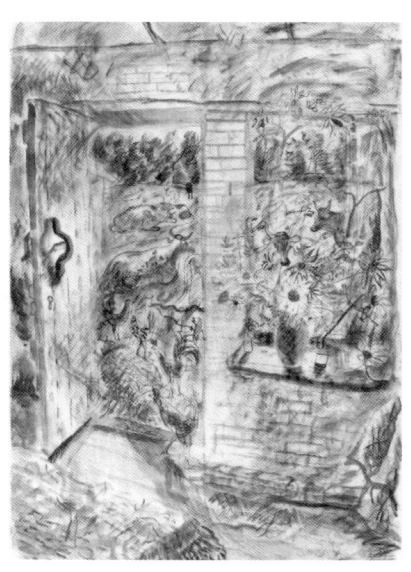

10. Farm Door, 1937

> And see how they run, the juxtaposed forms,
> brighting the vaults of Lascaux; how the linear is wedded
> to volume, how they do, within, in an unbloody manner,
> under the forms of brown haematite and black manganese on
> the graved lime-face.

Celebrating the freedom of such sign-making, Jones goes on to lament the latter-day decline in artistic standards resulting from the institutionalizing of art:

> O God!
> O the Academies![35]

But despite his growing attempt to understand the rôle of the artist in prehistory and history, Jones was finding it difficult to make art for the

171

present. His first breakdown occurred exactly at the moment when he lost his place in the context of modern British art. While recent success could have led to the taking of a studio, during this period Jones became more exclusively surrounded by a circle of friends who were intellectual rather than artistic. Unlike Gill, Jones believed that 'Rich people ought to give to artists'[36] and so cast himself on the generosity of his more affluent patrons and friends. Illness left him unable to work and the support of his most important patron was crucial; writing in 1935, Jones stated that had Helen Sutherland 'not helped me during this time of being ill *I can't imagine* what I should have done. - It's been really wonderful - I've sold nearly all my saleable pictures - alas - now there are no more'.[37]

Sutherland was the daughter of a self-made Scottish millionaire who had worked himself from the position of clerk to that of Chairman of P&O Shipping but her own fortune had been left to her by her mother. After her nine-year, loveless marriage to the Liberal M.P. Richard Denman was annulled, art and friendship became her solace. This autocratic, elegantly dressed woman was attracted by the *avant-garde* and in the twenties read Joyce and Woolf, attended the Russian ballet and started buying paintings. She was interested in André Derain, seeking out his dealer, Paul Guillaume, on a visit to Paris and marvelling over an 'exquisite still life' which held 'the heart of beauty'.[38] Interestingly, a singular Derain *Still Life* of 1911[39] reveals a remarkable stylistic affinity with another Sutherland favourite, Ben Nicholson, and the religious overtones of the objects chosen, goblet and bread, would have appealed to Jones. Writing much later in life to Saunders Lewis, Jones noted that he was also attracted by Derain's still lifes:

> ... as you say they seem 'monumental and ageless'. He ... was not, compared with some others ... regarded as quite so important by my artist acquaintances ... But for some reason or other, I especially liked his work, ... or, at least, the 'still-lifes'.[40]

Despite a private life that became as colourful later as his painting had been early on, the conservatism of Derain's painting in the 1920s appealed to an English painter who was a little shy of the more extreme experiments of modernism. Furthermore, one senses that Derain never lived up to the early triumph of Fauvism; even that self-assured body of work which he produced in the 1920s, so eminently a part of Guillaume's own collection in the Orangerie, cannot match his earlier vision. From the vantage point of 1967, when that letter to Lewis was written, perhaps Jones discerned some affinity with a painter who had done his most effective work early in his career. In the catalogue of *British Contemporary Painters*, an exhibition presented at the Albright Gallery in Buffalo in 1946 and at selected museums in the U.S.A. and Canada in the first half of 1947, A.C. Ritchie noted that, 'Jones, Hodgkins and Pitchforth, whatever their differences, have something in common with what might be called the decorative wing of the School of Paris whose leaders are Matisse, Derain and Dufy.' Ritchie pertinently went on to remark that 'Jones combines ... his curious combination of French sophistication with religious romanticism'.[41]

In 1925 Helen Sutherland met the Nicholsons and, at the *7&5 Society Exhibition* of 1926, had already bought two paintings by Winifred and one by Ben.[42] She bought Courbet and Seurat and later, Wood, Hepworth, Gabo and Mondrian. As E.C. Hodgkin notes, 'It required courage as well as taste for Helen to go on with these purchases from young painters who were known to a few and admired by even fewer. "This shows the folly of letting an unmarried woman loose with a lot of money" was the general reaction.'[43] She was a collector of insight and independent will; she ultimately kept her Picasso in a cupboard because she decided she did not like it.[44] She collected painters as well as paintings; Nicolete Gray observed that Ben Nicholson and David Jones were the artists whom Sutherland liked best[45] and Kathleen Raine suggested that, above all, Sutherland loved Jones.[46]

In 1928, Sutherland leased Rock Hall, a gaunt, fortress-like building at the core of which is a tower built in the fifteenth century. The present structure is Regency, but the façade is possessed of an austerity every bit as severe as its sometime mistress whose favourite house it was. The interior was painted rather than hung with paper and always kept in mint condition; on one occasion Jones spilt ink down one of these walls and spent all day painting out the stain.[47]

Edward Hodgkin's impression of Jones's appearance at Rock is vivid:

> He wore strongly coloured clothes. I remember particularly a peacock blue tweed suit and another tweed of rich brown, both with rather short and tight double-breasted jackets, somewhat naval in cut. He usually wore gay flannel shirts and thick monochrome ties which produced huge fat knots. His hair was short and almost black, but left in a slightly casual disarray which he would sometimes scrape with his fingers into a new arrangement as he caught sight of his face in a looking-glass … His clothes, his quick movements - he had a particular way of making small vertical chopping movements with his hands, his elbows kept close to his sides, or smoothing the air with one hand held horizontally, as if he were stroking a cat - gave the impression that he might be … an aesthete. His smooth grey (puttee-coloured, he called it) innocent face made him look younger than he was.[48]

Helen Sutherland was a dry and severe women who terrorized many, including David Jones. At her house there was no smoking and no drinking before meals.[49] Edward Hodgkin, who met Jones while staying at Rock, remembered how at the end of the morning they would decamp to the nearest pub, a good twenty minutes walk away, down a beer and return briskly for fear of being late for lunch.[50] Every visitor to Rock appears to have found it demanding to the point of ordeal; Hodgkin records that

> visitors were expected to join in all activities arranged for their benefit, whether this was a long walk in the hills, reading Wordsworth aloud after dinner, going to church, or listening to

a recital of music. At all times you were expected to pull your weight with intelligent conversation. You were not expected to bring muddy shoes into the house, to make loud noises, to ask for special favours in the way of food and drink, to read *The Times* before she did, to sleep with your bedroom window shut, or to stay up after your hostess had decided it was time to go to bed.[51]

At Rock, the gong would 'crash' for lunch,[52] and at her subsequent establishment in the Lake District, Jones remembered that the same house rules applied, writing that 'the gongs go off for breakfast rather positively'.[53] Such was the rigour of her domestic routine that when Helen Sutherland died in 1966, Jones observed that 'she'll push them around in Heaven quite a bit'.[54]

While Sutherland could be harsh (Hepworth's triplets were a moral judgement on Ben Nicholson for having left Winifred),

> she always felt that artists were, in morals as in everything else, different from the rest of mankind, and that non-artists must be cautious in judging them. They were the givers; we were the takers. They enriched the world; it was for us to enjoy the fruits of their genius and be thankful.[55]

What interested David Jones at Rock was the outlook. The high viewpoints in the paintings which the artist made while staying there each August, and occasionally at other times of the year,[56] are taken from his bedroom at the top of the house or from the small sitting-room set aside for visitors just above the front door.[57] These overlook the church, lake and stone cottages comprising the village of Rock which we see in *Chapel in the Park* and related

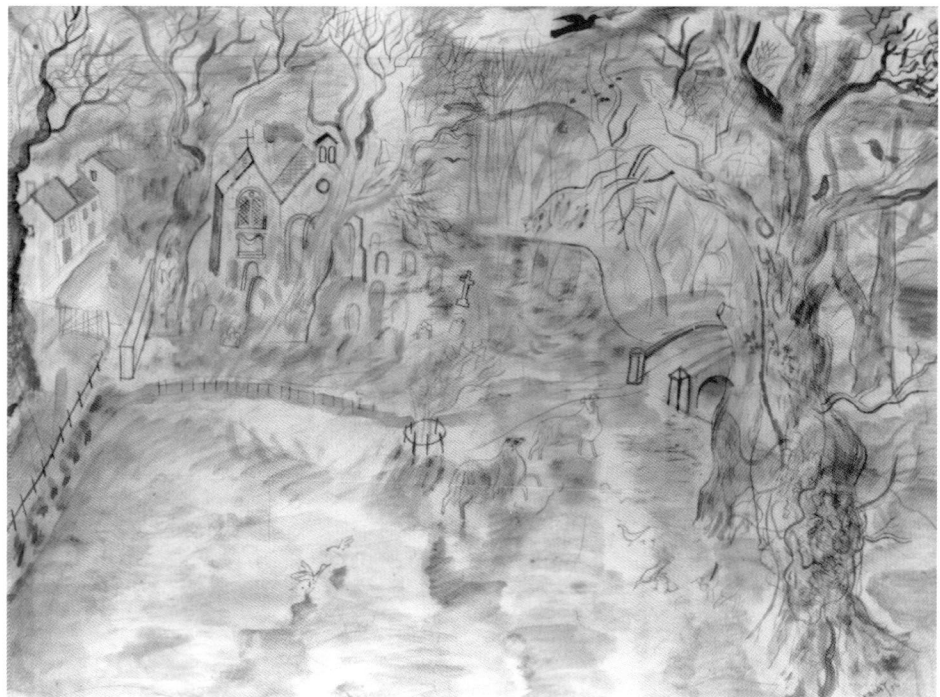

11. The Chapel Perilous, 1932

paintings made during the early thirties. Some of these are wild sketches with a minimal amount of watercolour washed on, and in others, blobs and bands of intense colour fracture the scene in a strange manner. Foregrounds are often empty for there was a lawn in front of the house flanked by trees though Jones plays with the view: he brings the church closer, enlarges the tiny bridge, almost loses the tranquil pond in the energy of his application of colour and paints the trees leafless and buffeted; the top part of *Chapel in the Park* has something of that bleak fright running through the winter landscape that Breughel expresses.[58] The church and gravestones are subject to strange emphases and in *The Chapel Perilous (11)* the curved headstones are like transparent doorways to a beyond. The bold cruciform gravestone is placed, strangely, almost exactly where Helen Sutherland would be buried over three decades after the painting was made.

Jones had begun to use literary titles for his paintings. Malory was part of Jones's mental landscape, woven into the warp and weft of *In Parenthesis* and the cycle of stories had been considered for a series of engravings. Jones knew that the countryside around Rock was supposed to have Arthurian associations; he wrote to Sutherland in 1929 that 'Alnwick is probably 'Joyous Gard' where Sir Launcelot had his castle and was buried'.[59] And there were other historical features which made Northumberland an attractive place for Jones to stay and to work; Hadrian's Wall was close by and while he later recalled that he would 'curse inwardly' having to make what was 'a really early start to some place in the car and then walk for miles up to the Wall and along it', he was glad that he had participated:

> it is the most evocative of 'remains'… though so little is left, one feels the presence of the Legions in a most extraordinary way, perhaps because one can see its alignment for miles going over rises in the hills and dipping out of sight.[60]

Indeed, such an experience gave the artist 'the feeling of the past still living in the present'.[61]

Jones worked on *In Parenthesis* during his first visits and it seems that the bulk of the painting at Rock was done later, either just pre-breakdown or soon after the worst of it was over. The *Chapel Perelus* from Bk. VI Ch. 15 of Malory enters the text of Jones's poem at two important points. In Part 3, during the night march, Ball and his companions are shepherded by Lieutenant Jenkins into a place where the upturning of defences has created a burial yard; Malory's description of the environs of the dreadful chapel aptly evokes the macabre. The passage is used again in Part 7, where it serves well to mark the battle's carnage.[62]

Why did this pleasant Northumberland park with its gentle church and the 'silverness'[63] of its northern light become associated in Jones's imagination with Launcelot's difficult task in the Chapel Perelus? Why was Jones so taken with this episode? In Malory, in order to enter the chapel and obtain the piece of cloth (material with a similar power as the Shroud of Turin or as restorative as communion bread itself) Launcelot has to face a battle:

he sawe by hym there stonde a thirty grete knyghtes, more by a yerde than any man that ever he had sene, and all they grenned and gnasted at sir Launcelot. And when he sawe their countenance he dredde hym sore, and so put his shylde before hym and toke his swerde in his honde redy unto batayle.[64]

Passing through them unmolested, Launcelot enters the chapel where he sees 'a dymme lampe brennyng' and so departs with the healing piece of cloth. Is not the essence of the story like Jones's first sight of the Mass in a ruined building on the Western Front? And is the figure of Launcelot who had 'rode a grete whyle in a depe foreste'[65] not unlike Jones himself? Part of the difficulty in obtaining the redeeming piece of 'sylke' was the threat made by a sorceress near the Chapel, that if he proceeded in his quest Launcelot would never see Gwenyvere again.[66] The relation of Jones's acquired religion to his difficulty in getting physically close to the women he fell in love with perhaps provoked his interest in the figure of Launcelot. Launcelot is drawn to Guinevere, the unobtainable and proscribed, and she represents that impossible choice between allegiance to something hallowed (King Arthur/religion) and amorous attraction. Launcelot in his moral dilemma is a figure to whom Jones would return; a religion which made love without marriage impossible and a career that promised insufficient financial rewards to support a family meant that a 'chapel' was indeed, for Jones, perilous.

Window at Rock was made in 1936, after the worst of the first breakdown, in years that were generally unpropitious for Jones's painting. Hills claims that it was Jones's 'first successful drawing after four years of nervous illness'[67] and, indeed, Jones thought it was one of his better watercolours.[68] Drawing and painting are well integrated and the interpenetration of inside by outside gives the work a truly transubstantiational quality. The living wood of the great trees in the park is traversed by the dead wood of the window frame providing an implicit religious sign that looks forward to the later tree and chalice paintings. Nicolete Gray notes that the foreground is no longer 'empty', and the 'whole painting is more balanced'.[69] In this respect it resembles *The Farm Door* of the following year, and if Jones had lost a little of his hectic intensity, the increasingly sporadic successes of these years are marked by a quality of balance in their composition.

After 1931 the members of the 7&5 Society had to be re-elected annually and in 1934, as if by some pre-emptive Freudian slip, Jones was left off the list of re-elected members in the minutes made at the Annual General Meeting. A notice was sent out with the error followed by a corrected list. In the same year, Frances Hodgkins resigned from the Society although the hanging committee wrote to her saying that it would 'be glad to consider any work of a non-representational kind by her for inclusion in the next exhibition'. The increasing commitment to abstraction was indicated by the move to rename the Society 'The 7&5 Abstract Group', with exhibitions becoming totally non-representational. Sidney Hunt, one of the more innovative members of the 7&5 and editor of the short-lived *Ray - Art Miscellany* had written in his Editorial to *Ray II*, in a tone reminiscent of *Blast*,

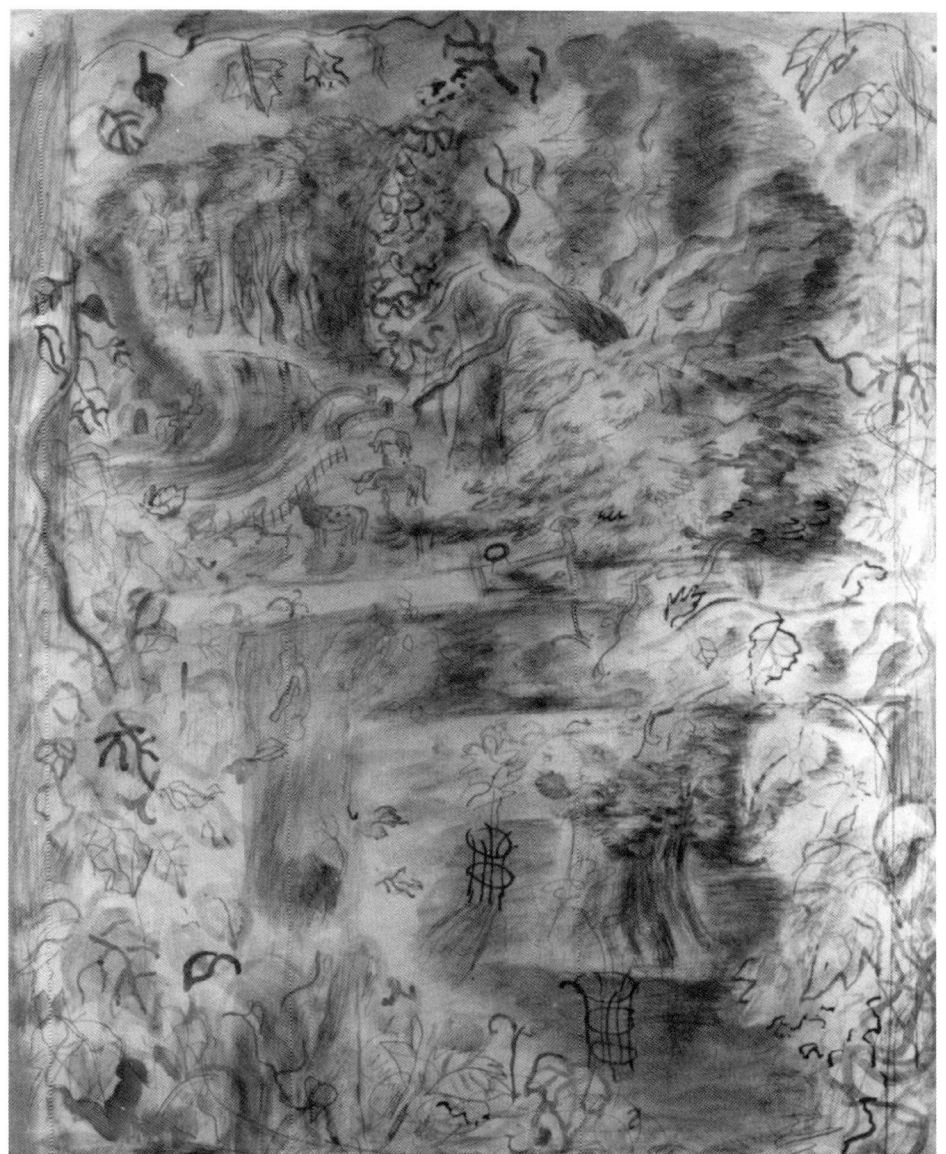

12. Window at Rock, 1936

'We are bored stiff with our feeble fauves and the maidenly good taste that passes for art appreciation in many English circles'.[70] In such a climate, Jones got the least number of votes among all the re-elected members and, as the voting papers survive, we can see that among those who voted against him were Ben Nicholson, Barbara Hepworth and John Piper.[71] For the March show at the Leicester Gallery Jones was a non-exhibiting member. Again in 1935, he was a non-exhibiting member; it was partly that he had done little or no painting and partly that his work was now decidedly at odds with the 7&5 ethos as well as with much that was provoking interest in the London art world. The following year, Jones wrote to Ede: 'I have just received a communication from the Worshipful Company of 7&5 to the effect that I am not a member - having only registered two votes at the last election. What a pity I did not send in my dignified letter of resignation a year ago - but in a way it's much nicer to be hoofed out'.[72] While Jones's reaction appears typically offhand, one must ask how it might have hurt him to be voted out of

177

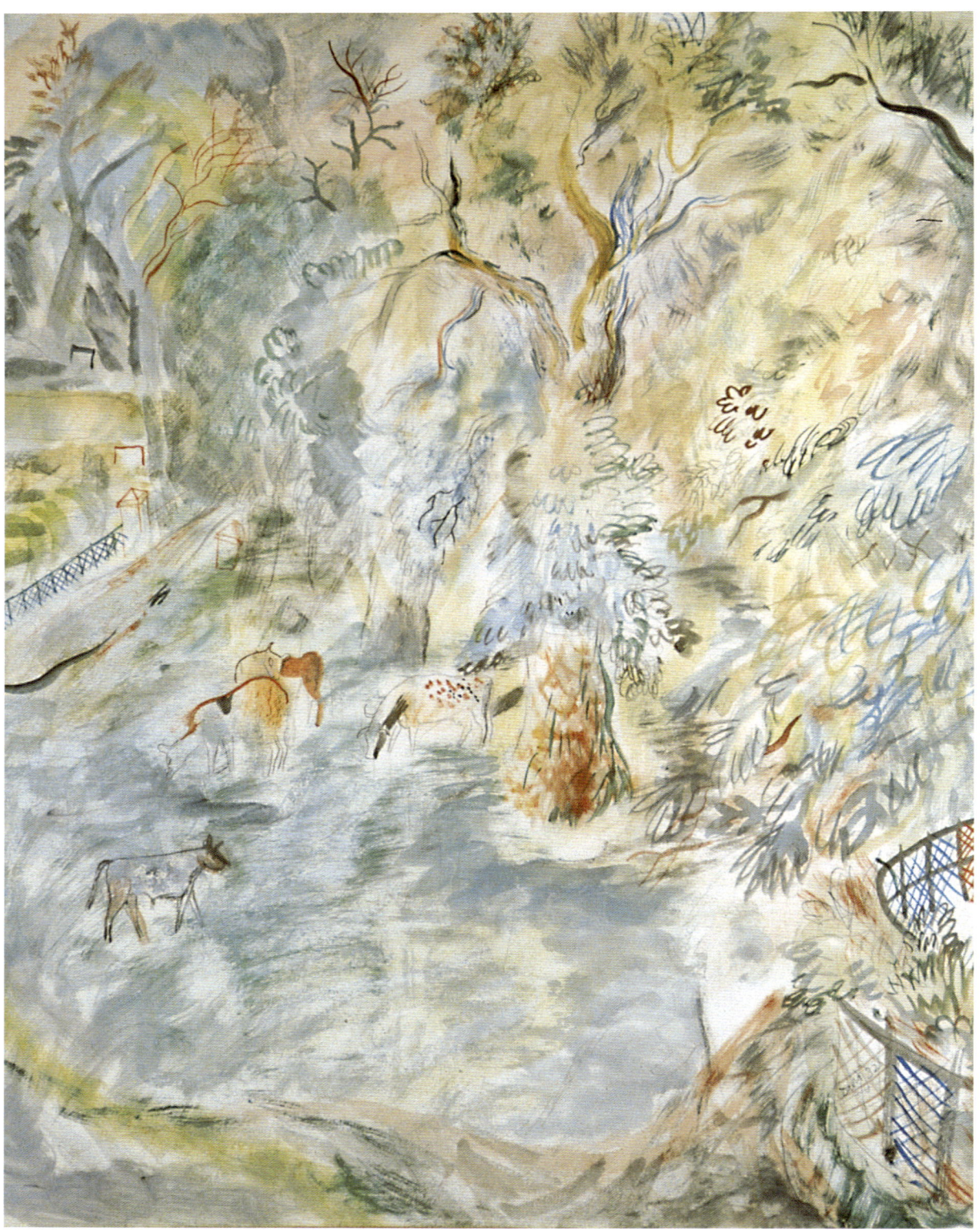

13. Cattle in the Park, 1932

such a group. If he rationalized it by saying his work would no longer go with theirs, nonetheless, he must have been aware of how he had been stimulated by his association with other innovative artists, by their range of styles and their preference for oils. He must have felt it as a rejection of his work as a painter at a time when he was finding it almost impossible to paint.

In 1935, Jones wrote to Ede showing a just perception of his rôle in the changing art world of the thirties: 'It is all very well for *you* to say 'D.J. is the best!' the whole point is am I?? - Everything is so deceiving - I don't imagine there is any solid achievement in any of my stuff'.[73] But Ede remained steadfast in his commitment to Jones; early in 1938 he wrote from Chicago during an American lecture tour, 'I've shown slides of your work and talked of you exclusively to about 20,000 people!!!'[74] If Gill, at Ditchling, had provided a refuge for shell-shocked ex-soldiers, then later in the twenties, Ede's house had, Jones wrote, been a 'harbour for battered men'.[75] Jones remembered that 'I do so often look back on the days I used to come so frequently to Hampstead and laugh with you round the fire. I do not think I could have stood those years without coming'.[76]

The period before Jones's breakdown was a difficult time for artists in Britain; the economic and attendant political crisis seems to have given birth to an ideological combat in the art world between nationalism and internationalism. *The Studio* appeared to be advocating nationalism, contending that 'Britain is looking for British pictures, of British people, of British landscape'.[77] John Betjeman was on the side of the nationalists contending that the word 'modern' was becoming 'old-fashioned'.[78] Against all this, the formation of Unit One in 1933 with architects like Wells Coates and Colin Lucas and artists such as Moore, Hepworth, Burra, Nash, Wadsworth, and Nicholson, was successful in publicizing their new achievements in modern art and in introducing to a wider public styles such as Biomorphism, Abstraction and Surrealism.[79] Unit One was a counterblast for modernism and with Gropius, Gabo, Moholy-Nagy and Mondrian coming to Britain during the thirties, Barbara Hepworth observed that 'suddenly England seemed alive and rich - the centre of an international movement'.[80] In 1934 Nicholson declared that 'painting and religious experience are the same thing, and what we are all searching for is the understanding and realization of infinity - an idea which is complete, with no beginning, no end, and therefore giving all things for all time.'[81] In the following year he gave his visual version of this statement by exhibiting his white reliefs at the Lefevre Gallery, works which Harrison suggests, 'may be seen as the major contribution by an English artist to the European Modern Movement in the first half of the twentieth century.'[82] In 1936, Nicolete Gray, whom Jones had met at Rock in the late twenties as a schoolgirl in long plaits,[83] organized an ambitious show called *Abstract and Concrete* in which English and Continental artists exhibited together. It toured the provinces with works by Calder, Giacometti, Léger, Miró, Nicholson, Calder, Hepworth, Kandinsky and Moore before coming to the Lefevre Gallery where it received the serious attention of the critics. Nonetheless, the British would be slow to relinquish a love of the landscape and this reluctance was one of the motivating forces of

Neo-Romanticism which began to emerge in the mid-thirties and with which David Jones would have some relation.

Jones's neurologist, Dr. Woods, had suggested that the painter 'must cultivate a masterly inactivity'[84] which, in a sense, he was compelled to do by his sheer inability to paint during the middle years of the thirties; as he wrote to Ede, 'there *is* something I'm dying to get out but somehow it's pretty buggered up in some way'.[85] He was also 'more or less under doctor's orders to keep out of London all I can'.[86] Not being able to face Christmas, 1934, in the capital, Jones and his friend Tom Burns went to spend the holiday at the Quay Hotel, Hartland Point, about seventeen miles from Bideford in Devon. Jones stayed for a few weeks at the '*horribly* expensive' hotel 'right on the cliffs' where, despite the Atlantic breakers, he does not seem to have been moved to paint.[87] In fact, Jones obviously felt no better; 'I wish I were really alive'[88] he wrote to Nicolete Gray, expressing the impossibility of realizing his desire to mythologize her in paint. In London he left behind a small stock of saleable paintings at several galleries including the Leicester, Tooth's, the Lefevre, Zwemmer's and the French Gallery.[89] Early in the new year, Tooth's and Zwemmer's requested him to collect old, unsold paintings and, as he was producing no new work, his financial instability continued to be a source of considerable anxiety.

From Hartland Point he went to take refuge on the unlikely Victorian esplanade at Sidmouth where he stayed in a hotel which Harman Grisewood described as being 'of remarkable ugliness'.[90] The town was small and un-promising but the ugly Fort Hotel was '*very* comfortable'.[91] The pattern of life over the next few years was that he spent most of his time in Sidmouth, with intermittent and longish excursions to Rock, Pigotts, Chelsea and to Brockley. His doctor's advice to steer clear of London suggests that Jones found the competitive art world too exacting; as he was not producing in the way that he had intended, he experienced it as an arena of defeat. There was also a sense of ostracization from recent trends; writing to Nicolete Gray in June 1936, he asked, 'Do you like the Surrealist Exhibition? - I do think they talk such irritating stuff about it'.[92] The response is almost blimpish, so perhaps David Jones might be seen to have fitted in with life in what he called this 'colonel-ridden little town'.[93]

Friends came to visit him but must have been somewhat amazed by the fact that one of the most promising British painters and engravers of the twenties was living in such a stuffy backwater. Prudence Pelham, who first visited early in 1935, wrote in various letters about 'that bugger of a salon by the lobster fire place' in the hotel, 'those loathly red cliffs', 'the lioness-coloured sea' and urged Jones to return to Hartland.[94] In a typically absurd comparison, Pelham described her experience of Jerusalem as 'a kind of Sidmouth to me disliked a good deal but comparatively pleasant and safe and known.'[95]

While Pelham delighted the artist with her visits and Eric Gill came for a few days in early 1936, Jones was generally surrounded by less high-spirited individuals and was also beginning to feel the 'isolation of the middle-aged'.[96]

The historian Christopher Dawson, with his gloomy prognosis for the survival of the West, turned up in Sidmouth. Jones found him 'frail and ill', discovered that he 'never sleeps without a drug and then not much',[97] and that he was 'pretty sunk with the complications of mind and body like all of us'.[98] Of his own state, he described how difficult it was 'to see any way through this maze of conflicting pressures'.[99] He found an apt reflection of the conundrums twisting him in the statement of a Welsh poet which he sent, circled in red, in a letter to René Hague:

> I am not sick - I will not be - and by God above I am not well - By Peter I am not dead, and God knows I am not alive.[100]

Surrounded by Catholic intellectuals who, as Grisewood remembers, were so far to the right as to be off the political map, Jones did not share in the developing rise of social consciousness and Socialist sympathy that excited many artists during the decade. He wrote to Nicolete Gray that he had 'a soft spot in my heart for Hitler ... but it's a complicated kind of softness'.[101] He went so far as to draft an essay on the international situation, 'The Pursuit of Peace', but his admiration for the German dictator must be placed in the context of his disappointment with the apparent flaccidity of England's politicians. He admired Hitler's stand against the 'sticky tyranny of commercialism' and spoke out against 'the instruments or creators of capitalist exploitation'.[102] Yet, he was clearly perplexed politically; his reading in modern history led him to confess that 'it would be so simple to be a Communist', noting 'what howling unspeakable shits the early industrialists were'.[103] But in reaction to the God-denying, revolutionary left, many Catholics sought refuge in the right wing's professed acceptance of religion and its avowed dedication to the preservation of venerable European traditions. As Harman Grisewood put it,

> Mere opposition to Fascism or Nazism seemed to me sterile. The dictators seemed to have some positive ideas for a European culture. Their ideas might be false, and even detestable, but England and England's politicians seemed to have none.[104]

When Jones read, as many others did, *Mein Kampf* in the thirties, it was the 'hate'[105] thing that he found so disturbing and any anti-Semitism in Jones would have been tempered by Grisewood's experience of what was really happening in Germany when he visited Berlin in 1939; Grisewood was 'sickened' by what he saw and castigated himself for not having understood sooner what was going on.[106] Upon his return he urged the BBC to allow him to broadcast the horror of the situation but the official line was one of appeasement and so cello music, deemed to be pleasant to the German public able to receive the BBC, was played instead.

The Abdication crisis of 1936 deeply affected Jones as it seemed to be a blow against the monarchy and this in turn led to a perception of Fascism versus Democracy 'as largely an affair of the *sword* against *money*'.[107] Harman Grisewood speaks for the circle to which Jones belonged:

> it was firstly the King's authority and the issue for us was one of loyalty to him ... In that brief period when he was King, Edward

181

VIII, as a leader, lit an enthusiasm which I have not seen since among young people in Britain ... I felt that something was at stake far beyond the King's happiness or the moral issues involved in his marriage. It was the possibility of a new enlightened and positive society which was threatened ... When it was over I knew that a certain set of values had been defeated. The defeat has been permanent ... the turn things took was for the worse ... We would be, culturally, in opposition.[108]

It would also be fair to place Jones, in respect of politics, along with 'early modernists' such as Pound whose thinking about the arts, Kermode noted, 'implied, in other spheres, opinions of a sort not normally associated with the word radical'.[109] This is confirmed by Grisewood who again clarifies and con-textualizes the position:

Our interest in political theory and in social questions arose as an inference from aesthetic and philosophical beliefs ... Art, religion, history were our themes. If this or that appreciation or proposition is true aesthetically, does it weaken or support, we would ask, this other proposition in terms of the Christian religion?[110]

Further consideration will be given to Jones's position in relation to the political right, but for the moment, it must be noted that the deepening gloom of the late thirties did nothing to alleviate his creative difficulties. The many dangers of the international situation 'paralysed' his 'creative' spirit in April 1939, for he found the English attitude and its '*moralizing*' sickening, 'all the old 1914 nonsense over again only much worse'.[111]

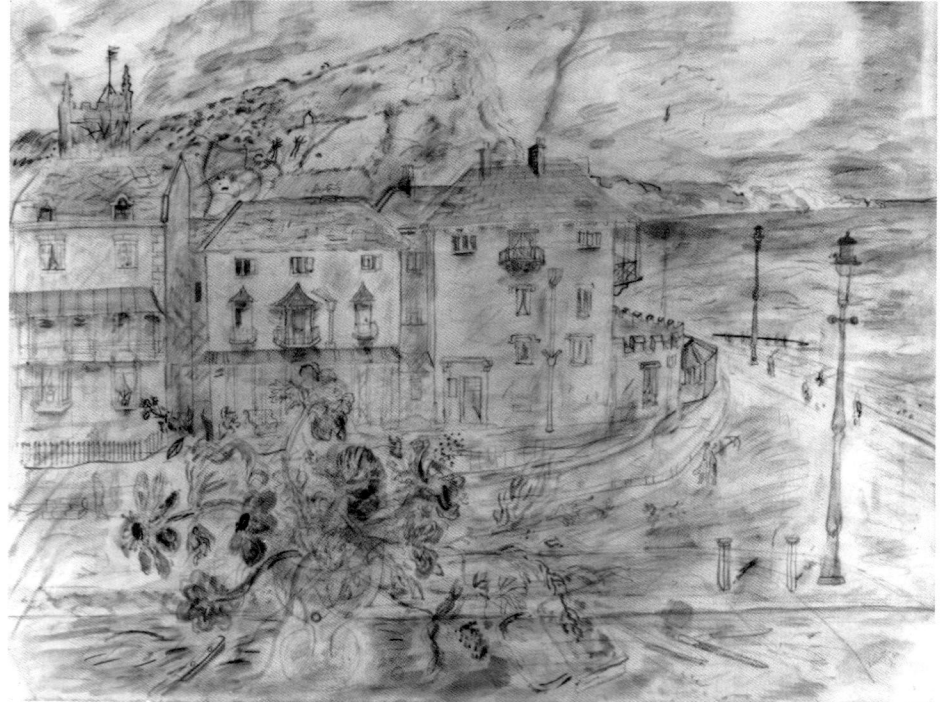

14. Victorian Corner, Sidmouth, 1940

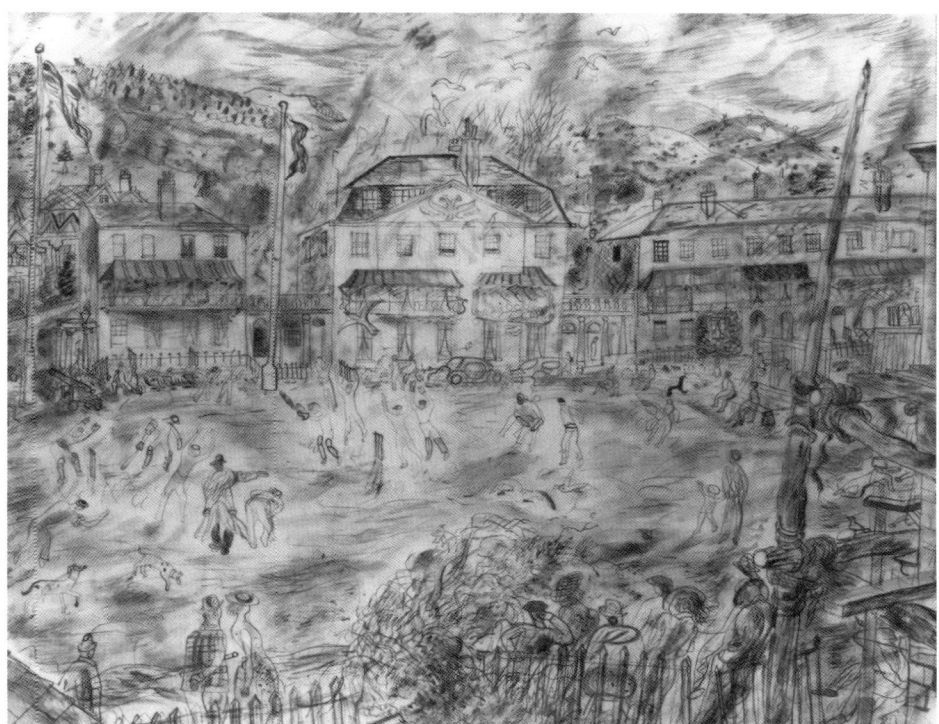

15. Cricket Match, Sidmouth, 1937

What little painting Jones did in Sidmouth is curious; he turned his back on the 'cocoa' coloured ocean, which, with its occasional 'great gales and vast seas',[112] would have fired his imagination only a few years earlier. He chose, instead, to paint the Victorian buildings in a rather fussy manner with comic ciphers or caricatures for people. *Victorian Corner, Sidmouth* is one of the better examples and includes one of Jones's first chalices of flowers on a window-sill which opens out onto the sweep of the street beyond. The interest in the picture seems to be located in the flowers or in the threatening sky and, indeed, it was painted in wartime in 1940 during Jones's last trip and remains, like most of the Sidmouth paintings, an illustrational record of the scene from a room at the front of the hotel. For economic reasons, Jones often took a 'box of a room' at the back which he got 'cheap' and which was 'warmer' to write in.[113] That room overlooked the cricket pitch and so Jones tackled the apparently banal scene of *The Cricket Match*. As is often the case, he reduces distance and brings the houses across the green closer. While the subject seems unpromising and the cricketers themselves are simple but expressive, there is a deft control of colour and a striking sense of atmosphere which make the spectator wonder what the picture is really about. The token cannon of a seaside town is included and a piece of upright wooden scaffolding menaces the scene like an ancient spear. Jones had disparaged his work in a letter to Ede two years earlier as only being a 'tentative reminder of the kind of 'world' some of us friends happen to like'.[114] *The Cricket Match* presents what was considered to be a national pastime, but, in 1937, with somebody 'caught out', it offers a view of that England threatened.

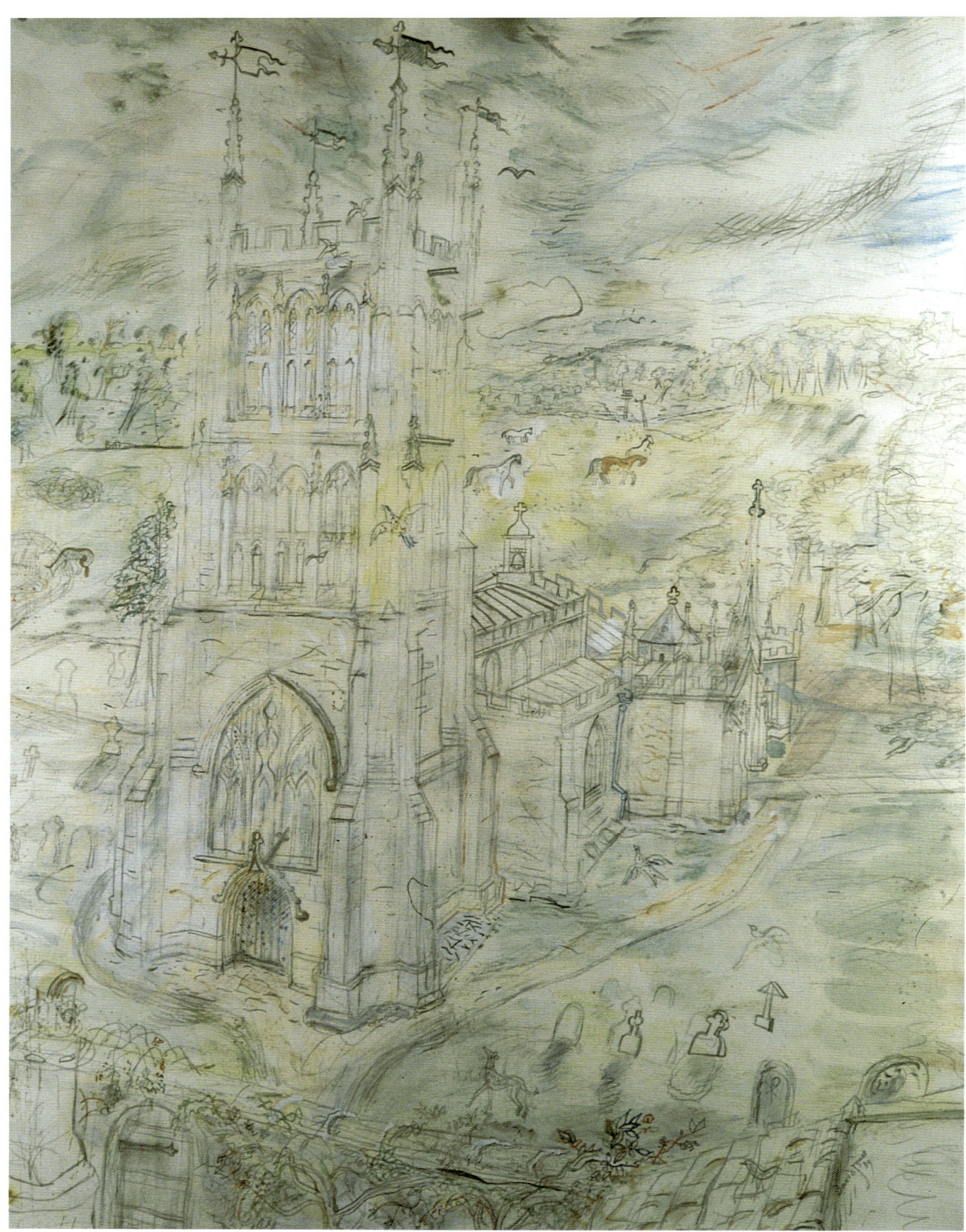

16. Church Tower at Mells, 1939

Although at Sidmouth the surrounding landscape was of little interest to Jones, there was a neolithic standing stone overlooking the sea where, a-typically, with his detestation of being out of doors, the artist would go and sit sometimes and ponder[115] and enjoy the 'type of solitude' which 'brings you to your own private senses in some way'.[116] He knew that while he stayed 'in hiding' at Sidmouth his nerves 'were not so bad' but that they deteriorated as soon as he ventured 'into the great world! … the hermit-armour of that … little town … does seem to suit me - but you can't go on forever leading that type of life'.[117] Exceptions to this occurred when Jones felt comfortably cosseted and coddled elsewhere by close friends; during certain prolonged visits to such people he was able to produce a few successful paintings. It happened while staying with Christopher Dawson in Yorkshire,[118] at Mells with the Asquiths and with the Grisewoods at Gatwick Park.

When Turner painted Sidmouth, he had 'knocked some life into it'[119] but for Jones, it seemed that the place could merely sustain him in a state of creative limbo. The day that France fell he was operated on for acute appendicitis, with a priest in attendance.[120] But by then, Jones had begun working on *Guenever*, a sudden, unexpected and dramatic change of subject from the wet promenades of the sweet Devon seaside town.

LAST LANDSCAPES AND STILL LIFES

The end of the thirties 'was a lonely time for David ... our group was breaking up. The unmarried members were getting married and taking their careers seriously. Our youth was over. The war clouds were gathering.'[1] Harman Grisewood, who made that assessment, paradoxically found himself harbouring Jones immediately after his own marriage in 1940. Somehow, the painter and writer who could not cope with London during peacetime was more happy to spend long periods there during the war. London during the black-out held a certain aesthetic fascination for Jones who took a childlike delight in the red and green flares that soared into the sky at the start of an air-raid; writing to Petra Tegetmeier in January 1940, he observed that the city had 'the feeling of a besieged town and a very *real* feeling and it's nice that all the advertisement signs and all the commercial electric displays have vanished'.[2] It was 'an odd experience being here ... with all the familiar civilian things - and yet ... living in circumstances not much removed at some moments from the Front Line.'[3] Jones 'smiled with contentment at the growl and mutter of guns' but in keeping with his experience on the Western Front slept with his boots on.[4] At times, he would be disturbed by the explosions, maintaining that houses were unsafe, whereas in the trenches he had felt more protected.[5] In October, 1941, he took lodgings in a boarding house in Sheffield Terrace off Church Street, Kensington, and saw much of his friends the Grisewoods, Bernard Wall, Louis Bussell, the Grays, the architect and sculptor Arthur Pollen and his wife Daphne who was a painter. He also had the opportunity to meet old acquaintances such as the painters Edward Woolf or Ben Nicholson, whom Jones found 'a bit more 'human' ... somehow more tolerant or friendly'.[6] Jones still suffered from sleeplessness and the inability to work, but it was, compared with the long periods spent in Sidmouth in the late thirties, a pleasantly sociable time and, above all, a time during which he received many invitations to exhibit. The reasons for this are hardly surprising. Jones's art with its tendency towards the lyrical and its increasingly literary overtones celebrated 'Britishness' and its inherent humanism answered a need in a population which felt its heritage and territory threatened. Cultural nationalism was the completely understandable response of a country imperilled by foreign invasion; Pevsner began his series of lectures at Birkbeck entitled *The Englishness of English Art* and Collins began its *Britain in Pictures* series. Even A.S. Hartrick, Jones's old Camberwell teacher, chaired the Hanging Committee for a 1943 exhibition at Fulham Public Libraries entitled *Recording Britain* and asked his ex-pupil to enter a 'For Sale' painting to go with those of his already included and not for sale. Just as John Piper's work depicted the secular and ecclesiastical architecture threatened by Nazi bombing, so Jones's less precisely situated scenes hinted at something inexorably British. The past was felt as present, worthy of celebration and preservation.[7] Venerable Wales had begun to reassert its appeal for painters and particularly for Neo-Romantic artists such as Sutherland, Craxton, Minton and Vaughan. As with certain works of these painters, Jones's art, at least superficially, appeared somehow reassuring.

With the *Luftwaffe* pounding London came practical anxieties; Jones wrote to his patron expressing concern about the chance of a bomb destroying the work which he had stored in the house of his friend, Tom Burns, who was away in Spain: 'Anyway there are the pictures at your place and those at Michael Sadler's and a few bits and pieces at Pigotts, some very early ones at Brockley so some will survive I've no doubt'.[8] Fear of destruction proved to be not totally unfounded; after *The Luxuriant Branch* of 1932, which was offered for sale by the Redfern Gallery, had been destroyed by a bomb, Rex Nan Kivell the director of the gallery wrote to Jones that

> I have taken most of your watercolours away for safety into the country, but there are still about seven or eight away on different Exhibitions. You can rest assured I will take the greatest care possible with your work as I like it too much to allow it to take risks.[9]

The success of Jones's show in January 1940 suggests the commercial sagacity of such care. *The Times* called the painter 'one of the most original of contemporary English artists' and observed that 'Constable's remark about J.R. Cozens, that he was "all poetry" might fairly be applied to this artist'.[10] An article in the *Nairobi Standard* reported that Jones had 'stimulated the hitherto stagnant war-time art market by selling £400 worth of pictures during the first few days'.[11] The exhibition of twenty watercolours had been a sudden inspiration on the part of the gallery and, as Jones wrote to a friend, was 'surprisingly successful considering the war and everything - nearly all old pictures but ... it was nice seeing them assembled and well hung for once. I mean by 'old' pictures mostly done between 1927-33 and a few done since I got ill.'[12]

Jones was shown regularly throughout the war years at the Redfern, his work priced at between 25 and 30gns. Non-commercially, he was shown at the National Gallery, from which the masterpieces had been removed for safe storage in a Welsh mine and the walls re-hung with contemporary artists chosen by the War Artists' Advisory Committee or by the Council for the Encouragement of Music and the Arts, which in 1944, mounted a *David Jones* touring exhibition. At the National, Jones was shown in *British Art Since Whistler* in 1940 and he was among the *Six Water Colour Painters of Today*, mounted in 1941. When the gallery put rooms at the disposal of the Tate, Jones was shown there in the *Tate War-Time Acquisitions*, of 1942.

Part of Jones's success was doubtless that he enjoyed the support of Kenneth Clark, who by the early 1940s was a powerful figure in the art world, socially well connected and a man who, at only twenty-nine, had been appointed Director of the National Gallery. Jones was friendly enough with Clark to ask him to keep the newly cleaned *Christ and the Money-changers* by El Greco hanging in the National for an extra week, a request with which Clark complied.[13] Over two decades later Jones asked Clark to write a short article on his painting for an edition of *Agenda* which was being brought out to honour the poet and painter; Clark was approached, Jones wrote, because he was someone 'whose critical perceptions I trust'.[14]

As the war drew to a close, Jones's reputation appeared secure. His flamboyant dealer at the Redfern, pleased with recent sales, wrote to the artist saying 'when you do find some more under the bed, … let me have them.'[15] A review by Michael Ayrton in *The Spectator* was extreme in its praise:

> This month sees the re-opening of the St. George's Gallery at No. 81 Grosvenor Street, with a pleasant mixed show. A number of 'the names' are represented from Renoir to Paul Nash, and the *École de Paris* predominates. The most exciting exhibit is 'Fuchsia Hedges', a superb David Jones.[16]

Yet in the very same month, Francis Bacon's *Three Studies of Figures at the Base of a Crucifixion* (1944) went on show at Lefevre Gallery and announced a new and more visceral art. Nonetheless, Jones's work was toured around Europe and across North America in what he called the 'Kultur Putsch' and what the British Council honestly labelled 'cultural propaganda'.[17] He was among the *Nine British Contemporaries* to be shown in the British Council Galleries in the Champs Elysées before it went on to Marseilles. Herbert Read and Henry Moore were present at the opening on 2 November which was attended by Brancusi, Lhote and Braque but despite the Council's hope that it would 'meet with sincere appreciation from the Paris public and not merely receive the usual polite uninterested official acknowledgement',[18] it had a rather tepid reception from a Paris wary of relinquishing its leadership of modern art.

Jones's work was used as part of the post-war drive to promote British art abroad in an attempt by the authorities to assume cultural leadership of a devastated Europe; *Fifty Years of British Art* was toured around the many capitals during 1946-47 in an attempt to assert the attraction and value of that elusive and allegedly gentle quality, 'Englishness'. *Modern Paintings from the Tate,* including Jones's *Guenever* (illustrated in the catalogue), *Chapel in the Park*, *The Terrace*, and *The Four Queens,* was shown in cities including Vienna, Amsterdam, Brussels and at the Jeu de Paume in Paris. In 1946-7, six of Jones's pictures were toured with work by Piper, Spencer, Burra, Sutherland, Moore and others in *British Contemporary Painters* starting at the Albright Art Gallery, Buffalo, and going on to Cleveland, Worcester, Toronto, St. Louis and San Francisco. Jones was discussed and reproduced in H.J. Pairs's *English Water Colours* published in 1945; celebrated in Michael Ayrton's *British Drawings* published in 1946; and, although it was not published until 1949, Robin Ironside's *David Jones* in the *Penguin Modern Painters* series had been under preparation since the early forties.[19]

While Jones complained about the cut taken by the gallery and its charge for mounts, he profited from the substantial price rises after the end of the war;

Sea From the Verandah which had been offered for sale in October 1941 for 30 gns. suffered from a slight depression in prices in 1943, when it was put on sale in the Redfern's *Summer Exhibition* at 25 gns. but re-appeared in the *Summer Exhibition* of 1946 priced 75 gns., three times its mid-war cost. As an index, not only of the fluctuations of the art market but also of the Redfern's estimation of Jones's reputation, it is interesting to observe the shifts in price of the apparently unsellable *Dark Sea* of 1935. In the *Summer Exhibition* of 1946, it was offered for 125gns. After the successful exhibition which Jones shared with Derek Hill and Bryan Wynter in the late spring of 1948, the gallery raised the price to 175 gns. in its *Summer Exhibition*. Despite the deepening dollar crisis of the summer of 1949, the gallery increased *Dark Sea* to 225 gns. in that year's *Summer Exhibition*, but in 1950 and 1951 the price dropped to 125 gns. and, still unsold, dipped again to 95 gns. in 1952, well below its post-war figure. Other paintings such as *Portrait of a Maker*, the price of which had been increased after the 1948 exhibition to between 150 and 175 gns., went down to 75gns. over the same period.

So Jones was selling but not producing enough new work to sustain an income from sales sufficient to meet his needs. His nervous trouble returned.[20] In 1944, he suffered 'the worst winter I've ever had'[21] with five attacks of flu and two months in bed. He was far from well or happy and his patron and friends were paying for his inactivity, for his inability to paint, as well as for the psychological treatment that was supposed to resolve his creative blocks and alleviate his depression. His output was sporadic but there were fresh achievements such as *The View From Gatwick Park*, with its delicate drawing, and clarifying selectivity. The high viewpoint, which on the right gives the feeling of being up in the trees, opens out to a traditional landscape panorama. There was also a last series of landscapes made from Helen Sutherland's Cumbrian house at Cockley Moor to which she had moved after her lease on Rock Hall ran out in 1939.

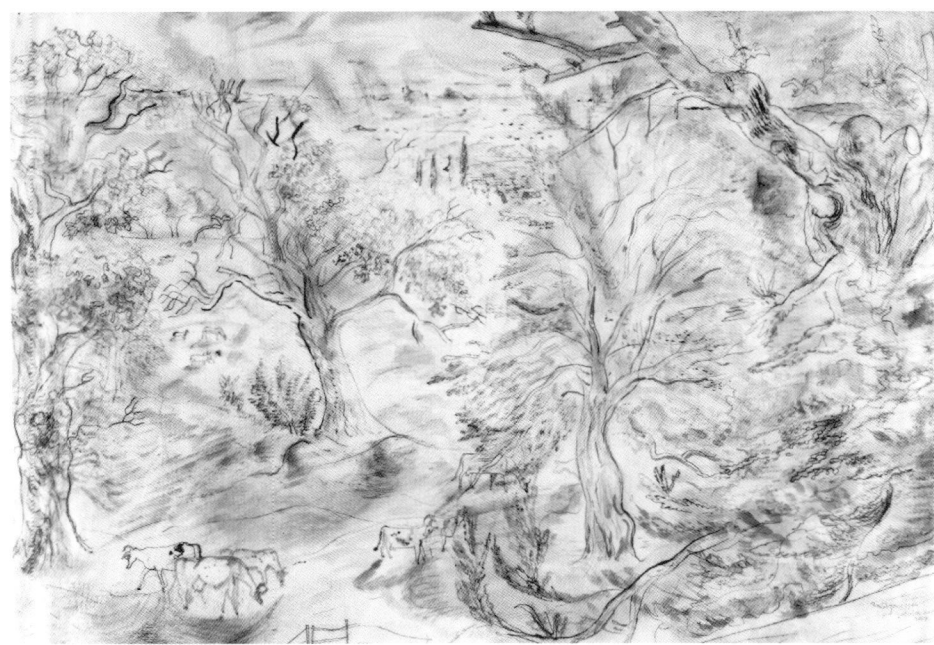

1. View From Gatwick House, 1946

189

Close to Ullswater in the Lake District, Cockley Moor was an estate of 196 acres, 1340 feet above sea level near the tiny village of Dockray. Its old farmhouse, which had already been enlarged, was extended and remodelled at Helen Sutherland's request by Sir Leslie Martin, the architect who refashioned the interior of Kettle's Yard, Cambridge, and there is some similarity between the two with their large, light interior spaces.[22] Altogether humbler yet more modern than Rock, Martin responded to the situation of the house by placing large picture windows overlooking the Aira Beck to Common Fell and Round How and to the higher peaks of Place Fell and High Dod on the far side of Ullswater. Jones, who visited in the late summer of 1946, wrote that

> The view from my bedroom window … is very remarkable … Very high up and faces a line, or rather successive lines, of hills - very bare hills. The foreground is sparsely cultivated here and there but mostly pasturage with trees … I've been trying to paint with conspicuous un-success. As a matter of fact it's a very difficult kind of thing to paint and also I expect I'm rusty … Royal Academy pictures in all directions but also of course it's incredibly beautiful and a new Turner sky each hour.[23]

Jones seeks an almost oceanic movement in the bumpy first landscape on the opposite page. In the second, the forms in the landscape are being shaped to significance; Jones had become much preoccupied with what he called 'the inward continuities of the site', with revealing that the Celtic 'Modron' and the Roman 'Matrona are one',[24] and so he was slightly disappointed to find himself in what he considered to be a landscape unmarked by history. There was, however, a Roman fort to the north of Cockley at Troutbeck, sites of temporary camps, and to the south and visible at its highest points from Sutherland's house was the High Street, the track of an old Roman road over on the other side of Ullswater. This provided the firm horizon line in the watercolour which Jones called *The Legion's Ridge*. Not only does this title, with its explicit historical reference, charge Jones's landscape but his enlarging of the hills in the middle distance suggests anthropomorphism, as if a sleeper is laid out beneath a sheet. The idea of a sleeping lord, a *rex quondam rexque futurus*, who would come as a saviour in troubled times, was a potent one for Jones. In *The Sleeping Lord*, a short poem written in the 1960s, Jones asks:

does a gritstone outcrop
incommode him?

does a deep syncline
sag beneath him?
or does his dinted thorax rest
where the contorted heights
themselves rest
on a lateral pressured anticline?
…
Does the land wait the sleeping lord
or is the wasted land
that very lord who sleeps?[25]

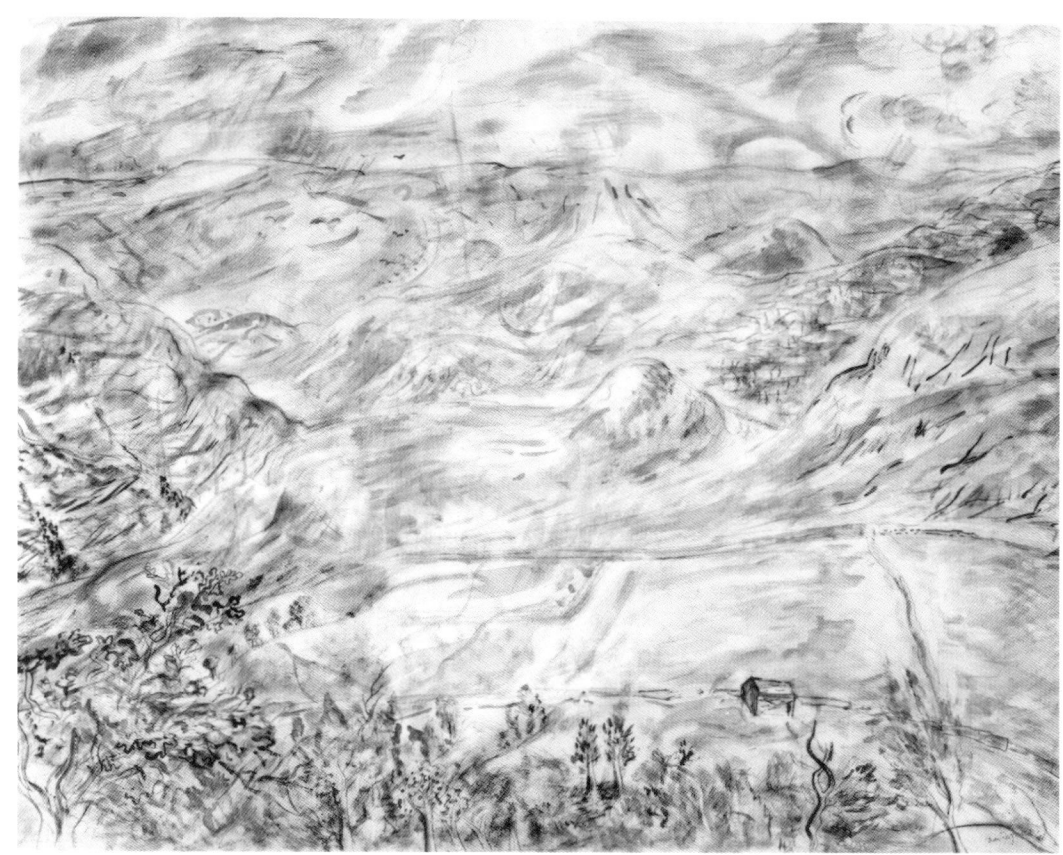

2. Cockley Moor, 1946

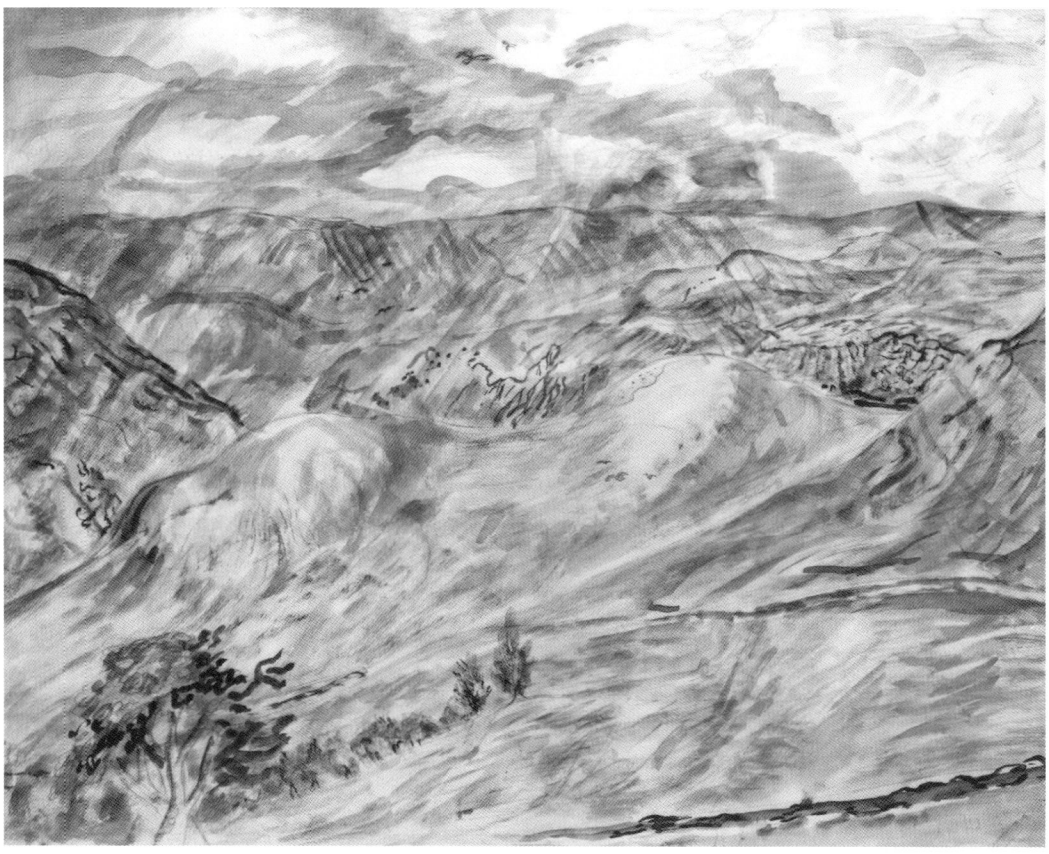

3. The Legion's Ridge, 1946

In some of the paintings made at Cockley Moor, Jones goes for a loose, all-over effect; a release from the far tighter and more allusive manner in which he had been working in the late thirties and early forties in the mythological drawings. He found it 'a hellish difficult landscape to paint', attributing part of the difficulty to his being out of practice.[26] Writing to Helen Sutherland on All Saint's Day, 1946, about his recent work at Cockley Moor, Jones commented, 'don't know what I think about them - you can see *something* in some of them and then it goes again - rather boring.'[27] Jones's reaction suggests that his historical and polemical method had in some way altered his vision and that he had moved away from the desire to make images which communicated through the effects of light on form. Yet a painting like *The Legion's Ridge* with its colour washes, blobs, scumbling and sketchy lines does successfully and pictorially embody a mythological idea and Jones seemed truly to be painting, as Paul Nash had professed, not 'for the landscape's sake' but for the 'things behind'.[28] As with many contemporary Neo-Romantic artists, history is embodied in landscape and 'mythologized into nature'.[29]

Suspicion of a certain limitation in his range was a contributory factor in the return of depression during the late summer of 1946. While at Cockley Moor, depression overtook the artist in the form of unsupportable fright. Dr. Charles Burns arranged for Jones to stay at Bowden House, Harrow-on-the-Hill, for psychological treatment. Unlike the neurologist Jones met in the early thirties and whom he had continued to consult until well into the war, Dr. Crichton Miller and, more particularly, Dr. Stevenson realized that because his main conflict displayed itself 'in relation to painting' their patient must paint.[30] Accordingly, Jones started to draw the varied trees in the densely planted garden of the nursing home. During the six months that he spent at Bowden House, he made many studies from his window.

While Jones's estimation of his own capacity to paint was a cause of distress, there was clearly a larger and growing anxiety about the rôle and efficacy of the artist in the modern world, and so it is interesting to observe that the series of trees painted at Bowden House moves from simple studies through a sequence of increasingly loaded drawings with titles taken from the *Anna Livia Plurabelle* section of Joyce's *Finnegans Wake* and on into the mythopoeic *Vexilla Regis*, in which Jones uses the trees to re-present ideas about the crucifixion stimulated by his knowledge of two early Christian hymns.

Trees at Bowden House is one of the first in the sequence and the treatment of the foliage at the top has a lively, Gainsborough-like effect, and all over the paper the artist reveals a scribbling delight in using his materials once again. Although the scene is summer there is a decidedly autumnal feel which related to, and perhaps provoked, the development of the association with Joyce's text.

Joyce had been stimulated by Giambattista Vico's cyclical vision of history, which, like Jones's use of Spengler's patterning, allowed the underlying resemblance of corresponding periods of different cultures to emerge from below superficial difference. Joyce used Vico as a 'trellis' for *Finnegan*;[31]

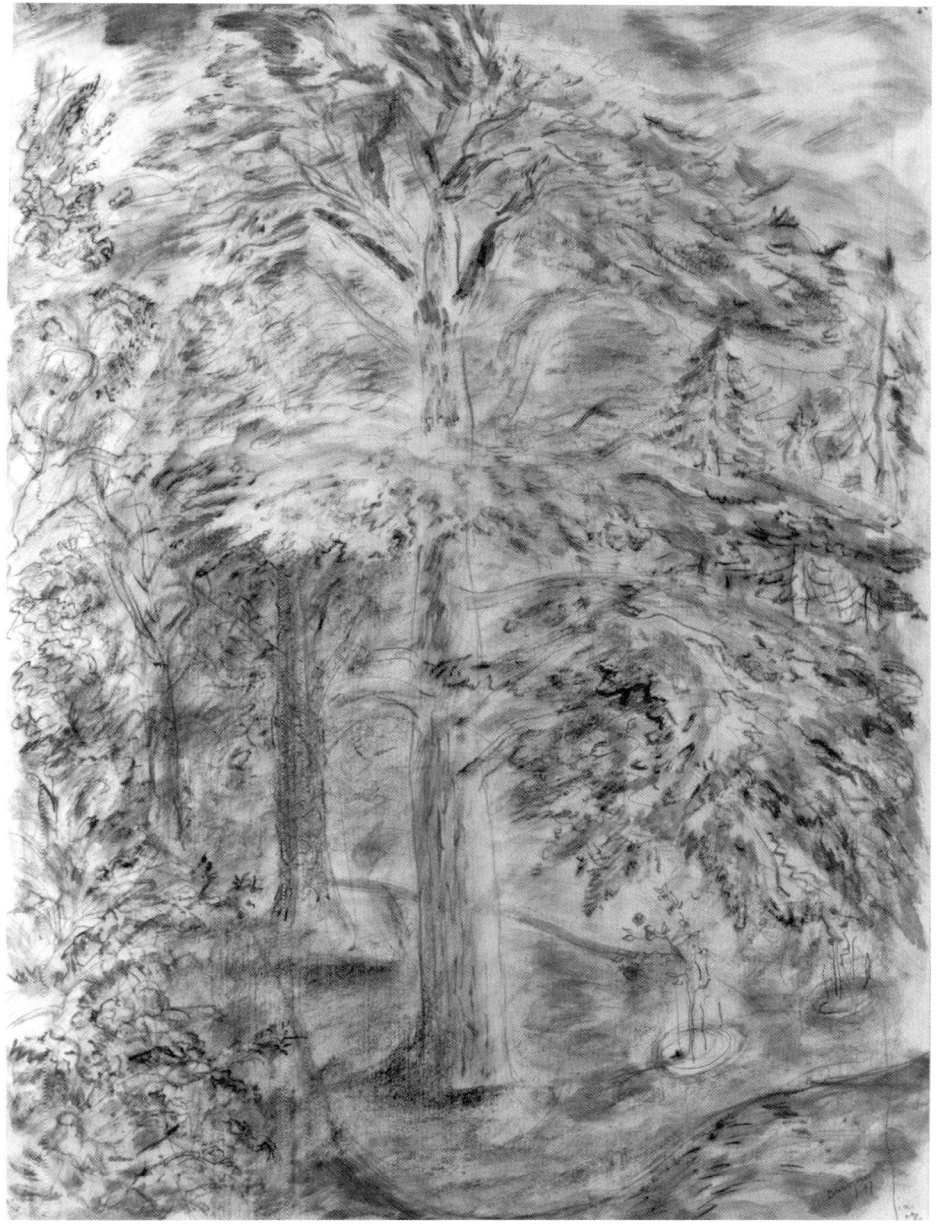

4. Trees at Bowden House, 1947

similarly, Jones was inspired by Spengler's seasonal analogy for the repeating pattern of all cultures. Jones marked in his copy of the *Skeleton Key to Finnegans Wake*, the footnote suggesting that 'The Spenglerian and Joycean analyses of modern times essentially agree'.[32]

Joyce's *Anna Livia Plurabelle* had deeply impressed Jones when René Hague read it to him in the early thirties, and sometime in the late forties or early fifties Jones was working on a poem called 'Caillech', which seems to have been closely inspired by Joyce's piece.[33] Anna Livia is, among other things, the river Liffey which, by virtue of its nearly circular form is used as a geographical image for Vico's cyclical theory (Joyce starts the section with 'O'). The fragment also occurs at the end of one phase of Joyce's version of Vico's cycle so that many of the images are of darkening and hardening, even the washerwomen who chatter out the text become, at the end, stone and elm. Jones's titles, *My Branches Lofty*, *The Dusk is Growing*, and *Tys Elvenland* are all taken from the end of the *Anna Livia* fragment and relate, both visually and notionally, to *Vexilla Regis*. Joyce's thinking seems to have become a part of Jones's mindscape, resulting in written imagery, an inscription expressing the important idea of cultural peregrination and continuity, as well as adding a philosophical resonance to his paintings and drawings:

> Look, look, the dusk is growing! My branches lofty are taking root ... It's churning chill. Derwent is rising ... Tys Elvenland! Teems of times and happy returns. The seim anew. Ordovico or viricordo ... Northmen's thing made southfolk's place ....[34]

The words 'Tys Elvenland' are particularly interesting; not only do they provide two of the over 500 river puns in the 19 page section ('Tys Elv' & 'Elfenland') but include the Danish for 'small river', *elve*, and the Danish for 'hush', *tys*, as well as the Dutch for 'fairyland', *elvenland*. Both 'hush' and 'fairyland' are concepts associated with growing dark. Images of chill which Jones found in Spengler were also to be found in Joyce, as was the cyclic vision of history itself ('seim anew' and 'Ordovico or viricordo' = The order of Vico and 'I remember you' [*Italian*]) as well as the idea that the Norse (northmen's) parliament or 'thing' was built on what is now Suffolk (southfolk's) Place, Dublin.[35]

So Jones's Bowden House tree paintings are carrying an intellectual charge which develops in each successive version. In the catalogue of the Redfern exhibition of 1948 it is interesting to mark the progress from *First Tree*, *Second Tree*, into *Merlin's Tree*, when the mythopoeic imagination starts to work, on into the Joycean references with their Viconian ideas complementing those of Spengler, the sequence culminating in *Vexilla Regis*.

Spengler in his *Decline of the West* speaks of late Western or 'Faustian culture' in the following terms:

> ... tender to the point of fragility, fragrant with the sweetness of late October days ... come the Zwinger of Dresden, Watteau, Mozart. At last, in the grey dawn of Civilization [that 'inevitable *destiny* of the Culture ... a conclusion ... death following life'[36]], the fire in the Soul dies down ... The soul thinks once again, and in Romanticism looks back piteously to its childhood; then finally, weary, reluctant, cold, it loses its desire to be, and, as in Imperial Rome, wishes itself out of the overlong daylight and back ... in the womb of the mother, in the grave.[37]

Jones saw the period in which he lived as analogous to the Imperial giving over into post-Roman times and considered Western culture to have hardened into a civilizational phase.[38] Seasonally appropriate images evoke this in his poetry and prose: 'a new chilliness is in the air', the 'December of our culture', 'the strengthening chill of the utile shrivels roots in us all'.[39] Roots which, Jones considered, grew the '*Arbor decora et fulgida*', the 'beauteous and shining tree' of the *Vexilla Regis*, the paradoxically rootless, yet fruitful, tree of the Christian cross.

So Jones responded pleasurably to the act of drawing under doctor's orders, choosing trees, those symbols of strong growth, power and aspiration, but as exhilaration quickly withered he reverted to subjects related to 'darkening' and 'ending'. The depth of his depression which had taken on the full drama of the decline of a culture ossifying into a civilization revealed itself in the series of drawings which had been initiated to resolve his personal dilemma.

Spengler's conception of 'Faustian' culture was that it was dedicated to '*extension*' and the 'architectural actualizing of' Faustian 'world-feeling' was the Gothic cathedral with its 'pillars and clustered-pillars that grow up out of the earth and spread on high into an infinite sub-division and interlacing of lines and branches';[40] 'the Faustian soul in the springtime necessarily arrived at an architectural problem which had its centre of gravity in the spatial vaulting-over of vast, and from porch to choir dynamically deep, cathedrals'.[41] In *The Anathemata*, Jones uses these ideas to express our culture's springtime when Christianity was at its most vital:

> ... in the young-time, in the sap years:
> between the living floriations
> under the leaping arches
>
> ...
>
> ... on west-portals
> in Gallia Lugdunensis
> when the Faustian lent is come
> and West-wood springs new
> (and Christ the thrust of it!)
>
> ...
>
> when, under West-light
> the Word is made stone.[42]

The word 'thrust' suggests that Christ, the inspiration behind the culture, was also the crucified victim of 'West-wood' (cross). All these associations are related to the prime architectural symbol of Spengler's Faustian culture, the cathedral ('west portals'/ 'stone') which was itself inspired by the 'West-wood' (forest).

Painters of the Danube School such as the Cranachs and Altdorfer produced some of the first real European landscapes in which thick forests lure the spectator into their dark interiors while the trees thrust vertically up to heaven. At times in Altdorfer's work, landscape is allowed to carry and express the emotion with little or no human intervention. Jones's water-colour, chalk and gouache, *Tŷs Elvenland*, appears to be descended from sixteenth century German painting and relates such landscapes to the ideas of Spengler. It presages the end of a culture by depicting a source of its early aesthetic inspiration. The use of white creates an airiness, an exaltation, and yet there is, at times, a muddled impression conveyed by the interrelations of the branches. When rhythm and space are controlled, the work succeeds but the feeling of looking into the depths brings confusion. Curiously, the fore-ground trunk which is seen near the bottom of the picture as a fully rounded

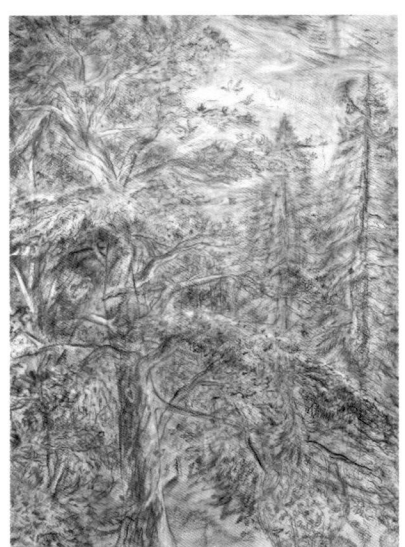

5. Tys Elvenland, 1947

form is flattened as it rises and narrows. Similarly, the other trees appear less decisively drawn towards their top as if they shy away from achievement. In *Tys Elvenland,* a tree which in purely plastic terms is charged with transcendental intensity also works as a concealed, yet direct, reference to the cross with its highlighted horizontal branches suggesting the transom. It is, indeed, only one step away from the explicit mythopoesis of *Vexilla Regis*.

There is an ancient legend that, by virtue of the blood of Christ, the rootless tree of the cross became living[43] and Jones celebrates this in *Vexilla Regis*, the title of which refers to an early hymn celebrating the phenomenon. Jones wrote to H.S. Ede's mother who purchased the painting that

> the *main* jumping-off ground was, I think, a Latin hymn we sing as part of the Good Friday liturgy in the Roman rite. Two hymns, in fact, one starting *Vexilla Regis prodeunt*. ... and the other starting: *Crux fidelis* ... a rather long hymn

dealing with 'the Cross as a Tree in concise and very noble and moving language'.[44] Jones added to these celebrations of the cross as a tree, the vision of it stretching 'from earth to heaven' in the Anglo-Saxon poem, *The Dream of the Rood*.[45] Jones went on, in the letter to Mrs. Ede, to explain that the general idea of the picture was

> associated, in my mind, with the collapse of the Roman world. The three trees as it were left standing on Calvary ... The leopard's pelt and trumpet in the left-hand bottom corner are supposed to be the instrument and insignia of a Roman bucinator or trumpeter, as though the owner of them had been part of the guard on Calvary ... The tree on the left ... is, as it were, the tree of the 'good thief', it grows firmly in the ground and the pelican has made her nest and feeds her young in its branches - Our Lord is likened to a pelican in her piety in one of the Latin hymns of Thomas Aquinas. The tree on the right is that of the other thief, it is partly tree and partly triumphal column and partly imperial standard - a power symbol, it is not rooted to the ground but it is part supported by wedges. St. Augustine's remark that 'empire is a great robbery' influenced me here. It is *not* meant to be *bad* in itself but in some senses proud and self-sufficient ... I should like to make plain that none of this symbolism is meant to be at all rigid, but very fluid ...[46]

Jones wrote, in notes drafted for his doctors at Bowden House, that the horses in the picture 'fitted well with my conception' about the collapse of the Roman world: 'strayed and riderless horses - horses in the wild ... Welsh ponies - an outpost landscape. Welsh hills. Cromlech - remains of classical buildings - shrine of the *Deae Matres*'.[47] But in his attempt to evoke such cultural deposits, Jones creates a kind of landscaped garden of sham classical monuments; prospects and focal points in forest and beyond terminate with fountains and follies in the way that these were incorporated into the vistas of the English landscape garden by Bridgeman or Kent, their inspiration taken

196

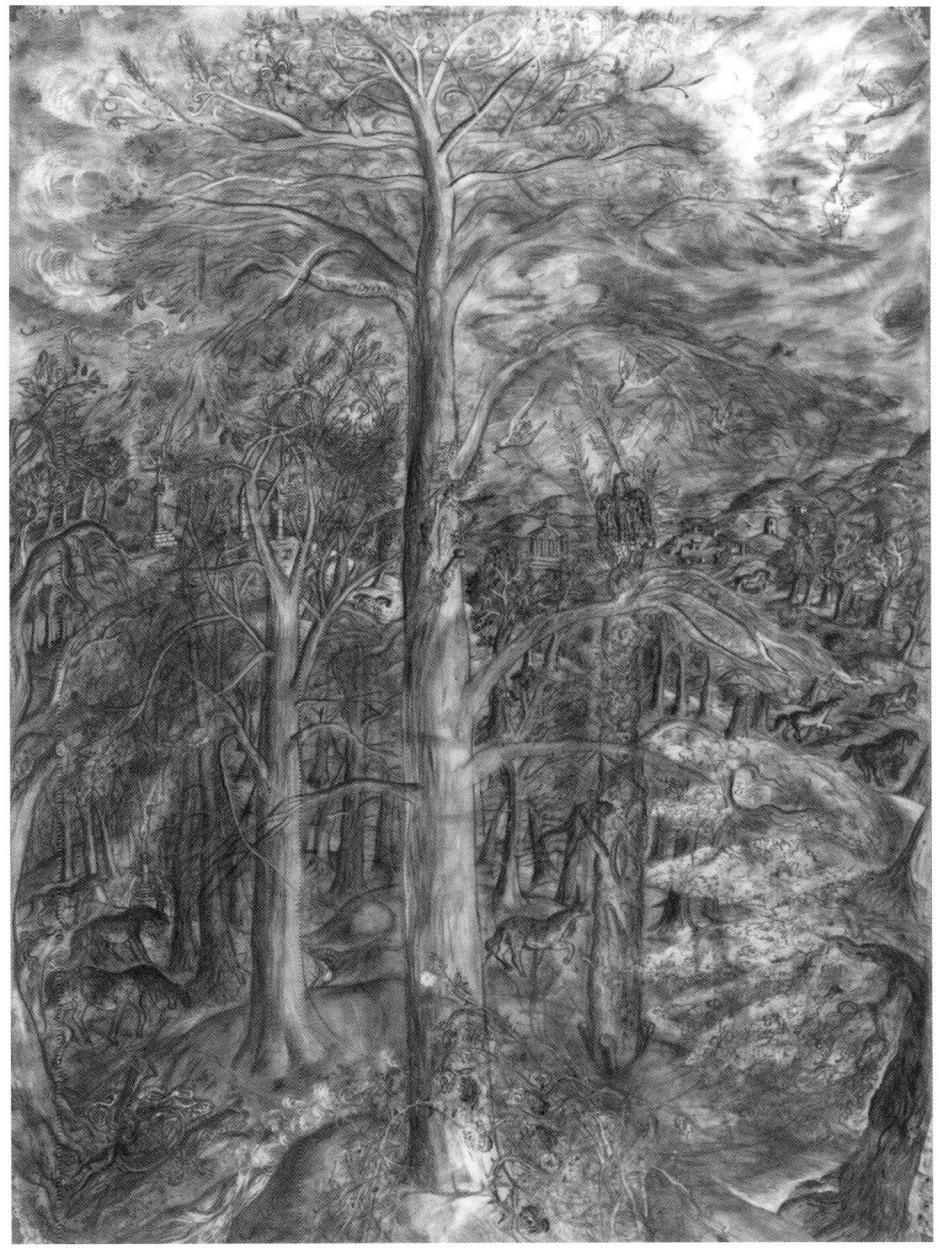

6. Vexilla Regis, 1947

from Claude Lorraine's vision of the idealized or poetic landscape. Jones's garden is transhistorical and the classical temples and triumphs do give way to wilder hillsides on which a Celtic hill circle and a post-Roman tower can be seen but there is a confusion of style and Jones admitted that *Vexilla Regis* 'is after all somewhat of an "illustration" as well as a picture'.[48] During the period in which it was made, he wrote some notes for his doctors which give us a valuable insight into how the mythopoeical imagination begins to dominate:

> I was still exploring the possibility of using the view outside with
> slight adjustment and without other aids as eagles, doves, lilies
> etc. - The roses and thorns were there in the flower bed and
> only had to be 'moved into position' so to say. But gradually the

picture assumed a 'view of trees *at sunset*' feeling - *exactly* what I did not want - a 'realism' of a somewhat academic sort and a dreariness of technique became more and more offensive - each attempt to suggest the conceptual nature of the picture only resulted in further falsity and betrayed the inherent dilemma ... Is the picture a 'view' from a fixed point, a visually observed tract of country - or is it a number of conceptions so juxtaposed as to form what is called 'a design' ... each concept put down in plastic terms and plastically and formally related to each of the other concepts - as 'realistic' and 'visual' even as 'photographic' as you like, but always seen *sub specie aeternitatis* - that's my idea of a picture.

Now when great difficulties arise in a painting when it is falling between many stools one tends to grab at any relatively satisfactory bit (where the forms and their juxtaposition are suggestive in some way) and exploit that direction in the hope that perhaps even if the original conception is thereby weakened or changed, nevertheless the picture will be of some formal significance.[49]

An increasingly complex clutch of literary and historical allusions is attempted in a single visual image. While structured in a cunning manner with varying perspective and a compartmentalizing of minute details in the spaces created by trees and branches it indeed falls 'between stools', the conceptualization has not been pushed far enough from realism and this results in stylistic solecism. There is an uncomfortable blend of heightened realism, even Surrealism, full-blown romantic light effects co-exist with illustrational naturalism and with the curiously stylized scrolling atop the central tree; there is an emblematic *fleur-de-lys*, a glory, and a pervasive strain of sentimentality which inheres in Neo-Romanticism. A kind of tastelessness compromises Jones's conception and yet the artist has uncovered a powerful natural image for the crucifixion and in this, the last of his landscapes, has conceived an approach which was original.

His comment that the drawing was illustrational must be probed; in its tendency towards realism it could, indeed, be so considered, but also, and more importantly, it could be said to illustrate Jones's psychological dilemma. Jones can be seen to be 'thief' in his complicity with Empire and 'sacrificial victim' in his marginal rôle in relation to society. At the turning point in his therapy the rootless tree is seen to be earthed once again and this expresses his renewed capacity to work; in the ensuing years Jones not only painted and lettered, he also extracted the material for *The Anathemata* from the heap of poetic fragments on which he had been working. The vision of the tree stretching heavenward reveals, once again, the aspiration of the mystic, but because the treatment at Bowden House was ultimately imperfect or incomplete Jones relapsed to rootlessness: his vision of civilization withered, emphasized in the cut-off stems of flowers in the Calix paintings. He moved in 1964, down the hill from his lodgings in Harrow to a residential hotel in the pebble-dash banality of Metroland.

Yet before that, in the period after coming out of Bowden House nursing home in a more positive frame of mind, Jones took a room at Northwick Park Lodge on the other side of Harrow Hill. That he did not immediately give up his room in Sheffield Terrace because he couldn't face moving all his stuff,[50] suggests that the pressure of poverty was not quite as extreme as he made out. Helen Sutherland had largely footed the 16 gns. a week bill at Bowden House, and in the period immediately after leaving, and he received £130 of assistance from The Artists' Benevolent Fund.[51] Various friends were also giving money or persuading official bodies that they might aid the artist, who, nonetheless, complained incessantly about his perilous financial situation.

Northwick Park Lodge was a porticoed, grey brick, Victorian house run by Christopher Carlisle, an ex-Harrow master. The house provided Jones with another community. The evening meal was taken with other lodgers and there was an *Encyclopaedia Britannica* in the dining-room which would be consulted during the course of the long and lively meals. The residents were an odd mixture including a retired diamond merchant and a sad lady from Leicestershire who was down on her luck. The proximity of Harrow School meant that some masters lodged at Northwick and through these Jones developed contacts with historians and classicists. One history master remembers how Jones would ask endless questions about post-Roman Britain, Bede, Wales, and speculate about what it would have been like to be a legionary.[52]

When Jones arrived at Northwick, he found Carlisle to be an 'awfully nice and remarkable man',[53] but the proprietor began to drink heavily and a few years later could be found wandering drunk about the house in his dressing-gown with a bottle in his hand. Mrs. Carroll, the housekeeper who lived in the basement, cooked basic and greasy food, which meant that the endemic odour of dry rot was enriched by the smell of frying.

Jones's room was on the third floor, a large, light rectangular space with big sash windows from which he looked down on the overgrown garden, an orchard, playing-fields and out towards London where, on a clear day, it was possible to see St. Paul's. Jones spent a good deal of time at this window and drew from it, delighting in his 'high-perched room in that rambling, ill-kept, but "creaturely" house'.[54]

He continued to paint and draw trees as he had done at Bowden House. Because of the high vantage point, *Storm Tree* of 1948 gives us the feeling of actually being up among the branches. It is one of the best of the series that Jones drew from this window and in it the simple reportage, which weakens so many of the other drawings done at this time, is transformed into vitality and movement. The fir tree has taken on a fuzzy presence, harmonizing with the abstract crayon markings of a picture much concerned with focus, vibration and mood. As his therapy appears, at least temporarily, to have calmed Jones, he moves away from heavy symbolism and back into a sensual delight in the physical world. *Tree at Northwick Park (8)* is even further removed from the illustrational, radiating the spreading splendour of the tree and suggesting the autumnal without describing or insisting upon it. A

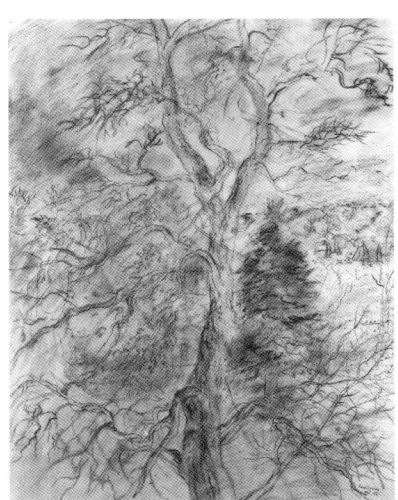

7. Storm Tree, 1948

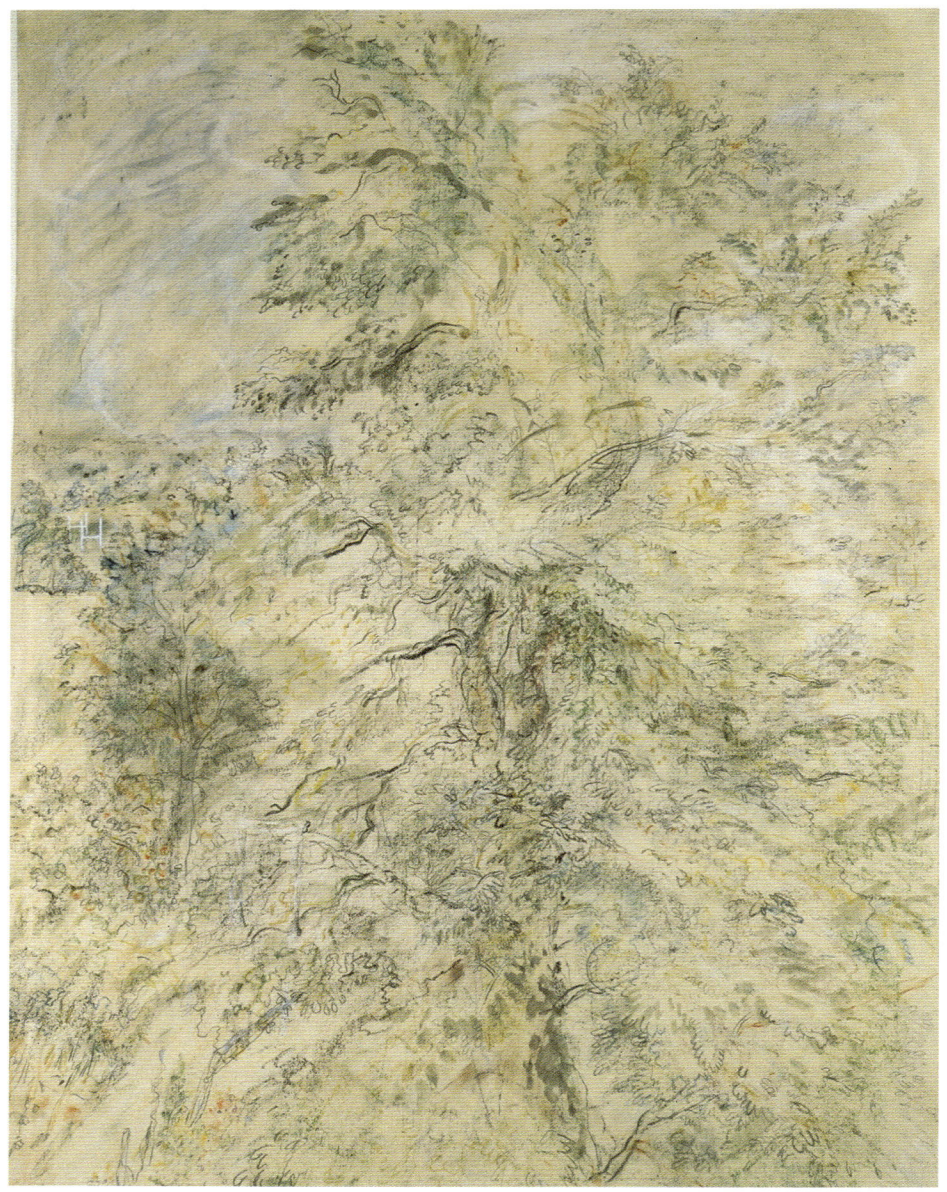

8. Tree at Northwick Park, 1948

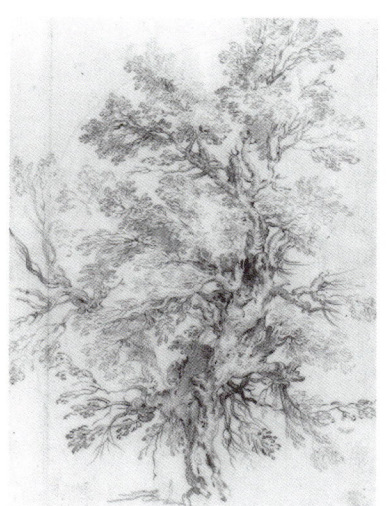

9. Nicolas Lancret, A Tree, 1730

delightfully sensual blend of crayon, chalk, watercolour and pencil, it owes something to the French tradition exemplified in the red chalk tree of Nicholas Lancret *(9)*, follower of Watteau, or to later British artists such as Gainsborough with his generalized impressions of foliage. Jones regains his old capacity with his all-over effects, shifts of focus and the feeling of coming close to the essence of the thing observed.

In January, 1948, there was a small exhibition of Welsh painters at the Heal's Gallery and Jones was included.[55] In March and April *The English Window* and *Wildcat* were shown in Vienna at the Albertina in *Austellung Moderner Englischer Graphik und Aquarelle Kunst*. In the catalogue, the creator appeared as 'David Joines' an inadvertent reminder that the artist was someone who fits something together, deriving from the latin root *ar*, 'to fit'.[56] Later in the year, four works went to Canada in a show entitled *Contemporary British*

Drawing which included *The Storm Tree* and two other items which had been exhibited at the important Redfern Gallery exhibition in the late spring. Of the thirty-two Joneses then on show, twenty-six had been painted or drawn either at Bowden House or immediately afterwards at Northwick and Jones wrote to Dr. Charles Burns thanking him

> for all you did toward getting me to Bowden and all that - without which none of these pictures would have been done. I still feel I've got quite a lot to learn and get through with regard to my psychology and the treatment of it - but what has already been done with regard to painting is very great and I am truly most grateful for your part in it.[57]

The notice in *The Spectator* was tepid:

> I do not know how long it is since David Jones last held an exhibition of his work, but his pictures are rare enough for a new show of recent chalk and watercolour drawings at the Redfern to be something of an event. I found that event, considered as a whole, a little disappointing … Many of his new pictures … seemed a little thin; the means were there but the ends were not sufficient … There is a group … of trees, some of which, though slight, are pleasant enough. The general effect, however, is somewhat repetitious.[58]

Indeed, Jones wrote to Helen Sutherland that

> The press have been most disappointing - with nothing at all or somewhat feeble snippets, the *New Statesman* not even deigning to mention my show in their current review of Redfern and other galleries. Wyndham Lewis in *The Listener* dismisses the show as 'characteristic water-colours representing a fairy-book world'. I confess I was sorry to read that from him - for he has - or had once upon a time [a fairytale jibe?] - a good brain and he might, one would have supposed, have understood at a deeper level than that remark suggests. I don't mind much about the press on the whole but I do find a total misapprehension and lack of perception on the part of people who ought to see deeper very depressing.[59]

While this feeling of being misunderstood was one that would persist until the end of his life, Jones also noted that 'art criticism is in a bad state at the moment partly because no proper space is given it in newspapers … all linked up with the paper shortage and the general pressure of other news etc.' so that a painter could not expect '*proper* criticism or *proper* understanding'.[60]

During the exhibition Jones had to go to London almost every day and he saw many old friends; Winifred Nicholson, having just come over from France, turned up unwittingly at the opening. Cecil Collins saw the show and left an appreciative note.[61] Kenneth Clark wrote a letter expressing the opinion that the exhibition contained work that was superior to Jones's earlier achievements and stated his particular liking for *The Lord of Venedotia*. The Gill family came,[62] but Helen Sutherland, oddly and insensitively, felt it impossible to leave her garden at Cockley Moor.

According to Gallery receipts, the sales, after commission, amounted to £1,840-4-0 including items such as *Mr. Carlisle's Acacia* going to Australia for £125; *The Lord of Venedotia* and *Tys Elvenland* for £125 and *Sunday Mass* for £150. In various letters however, Jones, interestingly, records a much smaller sum of about £1,000 worth of sales out of which the gallery took a third, the taxman half and speaks of related 'general expenses' which left him with very little indeed.[63]

Jones was, in the late forties and early fifties, showing a continuing interest in the exhibitions of his contemporaries Ben Nicholson, Matthew Smith, Ivon Hitchens and Cecil Collins, as well as in large exhibitions devoted to works from the past: Ravenna Mosaics; Rubens; *Art Treasures From Vienna*, at which, judging by his annotations in the catalogue, he was interested by Breughel the Elder, Dosso Dossi, Rembrandt, Rubens and Tintoretto; *Landscape in French Art 1550-1900*; and *Masters of British Watercolours from the Seventeenth To Nineteenth Centuries*, at which he seems to have been attracted by a wide range of exhibits. Between 1949-51 Jones himself was often selected for national and international exhibitions. Three of his works which had been purchased by the Arts Council went on exhibition as part of *Contemporary British Art* at the New Burlington Gallery in November and December 1949. He was represented in *The Private Collector* exhibition at the Tate in 1950, as well as in Germany, at the Venice *Biennale*, and in the USA in 1951.

His capacity to produce was, however, once again affected when his already shaky health began to deteriorate. Several months before the big Redfern show, Jones had fallen on some frost and broken his ribs.[64] His letters of the period invariably began with a litany of physical complaint:

> Tomorrow I go to the hospital to let them photograph my insides all day ... (for what is somewhat pathetically called 'a complete Barium meal', it sounds like an initiation rite. Perhaps it is!).[65]

> I have a vile throat, pharyngitis - it gets better and then not so good again and then to make matters more pleasant 'pink eye', conjunctivitis, which is beastly because one can't see to write or anything much ... sore throats lasting weeks and weeks are very exhausting and this eye thing is most annoying.[66]

> I've got fibrositis in the back ... which is a bore.[67]

Jones's body was now showing almost uninterrupted signs of pressure and stress.

His attitude towards his painting remained unresolved and one manifestation of this was a souring of his relations with the Redfern Gallery. As late as 7 May, 1952, Jones was writing to Rex Nan Kivell asking for payment for what was still owed from sales of the 1948 exhibition. The total sum, 'about £670',[68] tends to confirm that the sales were indeed higher than Jones had suggested in letters to his friends. Despite a payment in 1951 and despite the fact that there was an obvious tax advantage in staggered payment, such a delay was cause for complaint. Jones's demand was made in response to a gallery request for more paintings; as the artist had been working on preparing *The Anathemata* for publication, he had had no time to paint. Clearly, writing poetry, essays and letters was absorbing Jones's increasingly diminishing energy.

The Redfern included old works in its 1953 *Coronation Exhibition* but by the mid-fifties it seems that Jones wished to terminate his association with the gallery. A letter drafted in obvious choler reveals some of the points of contention:

> It is true I have been working on one or two things which are in no sense, as yet, intended for public exhibition. I am extremely occupied with a number of matters and not at all well and am not able to receive visitors. [crossed out: As you have written to me, I think it only just to say that I have no intention of exhibiting at some future date with the Redfern Gallery.] I should appreciate a detailed statement of what, in the view of your Accountants, is owing to me .... I had hoped that you would have perceived my not inconsiderable distress some years back, when I came into the Gallery to find a number of works on exhibition which I had not, myself, released for exhibition, some not mine at all. I am prepared to forget about that, but I must state positively that I did not and do not approve of the manner in which they were exhibited or sold without being referred to myself. Their diffusion has caused me considerable embarrassment.[69]

The letter suggests perhaps that the gallery was selling pictures already offered to other people. It possibly refers to some signed forgeries executed as a joke by René Hague, and alludes to paintings in portfolios stolen by relations of friends who were too close to the painter to make litigation comfortable.[70] The forgeries have also turned up at Christie's[71] and in 1993 one of them was offered for sale by another West End gallery in the mistaken belief that it was a Jones and not a Hague.

Such errors, along with the gallery's autonomous attitude towards exhibition and sale, led to Jones's decision to 'keep clear of dealers as far as possible' and not to 'deal with them at all if I can help it',[72] a financially arrogant attitude for an artist whose earned income was neither steady, nor, as the fifties progressed, significant. It recalled the position towards the art market and dealers adopted by Gill, who, according to Hagreen, 'thrust down to hell all Art Dealers, Bankers, users of custard powder and those who like a pleasant view from a window'.[73]

If Jones had at times produced 'pleasant' views in which the window itself became a mere mediator of interior and exterior, the windows in his last work take on a greater significance with their frames becoming symbolic of the cross.

Furthermore, the window was, according to Spengler, an important expression of the soul of western culture: 'The *window as architecture* ... is peculiar to the Faustian soul and the most significant symbol of its depth-experience. In it can be felt the will to emerge from the interior into the boundless'; cathedral windows are '*translucent*' and '*bodiless*' and therefore, close in spirit to Jones's more fluid dissolution of interior spaces.[74]

Even in *The Outward Walls* and in *Flora in Calix Light,* the window is seen to access a kind of transfigured beyond. *The Outward Walls* is implicitly religious and the cross created by the transom and mullion of the window is pointed by the emphatic black line at its base and the translucent whitening on either side of the upright; the flagpole outside recalls the spear that pierced Christ. While large and joyful in scale, and with prettily patterned floral curtains reminiscent of Botticelli drapery, that sense of the hectic and maddened is not far away.

In the early 1950s, Jones produced his last series of still lifes. These, along with the paintings of the early thirties, he liked best of all his works.[75] The *guéridon*, or that echo of the marble table from the medieval courtly garden, returns in certain works such as *Gwyl Dewi Sant*. In others such as *Table Top (12)* that flattened, uptilted surface reminiscent of Nicholson re-appears. On these surfaces, Jones places a chalice with flowers, delicately yet energetically depicted and among which, more often than not, can be found the thorns that evoke the crucifixion. So, in a brilliantly chosen visual metaphor, Jones expresses one of his most profound concerns. Sometimes the chalice is placed on a white cloth reminiscent of the altar, flanked by a necklace or rosary and sometimes a missal is included in the arrangement. Sometimes, as in *The Flowering Chalice* which Jones thought was probably the best of the series, a real tree beyond appears to grow out of the chalice uniting the idea of tree and communion cup, an idea reinforced by the window mullion which calls to mind the rootless tree of the cross. The cup shape, one of the oldest significant markings of neolithic man, burgeons with the splendour of natural beauty. Jones's interest in the chalice was linked to his preoccupation with the central contribution made to cultural continuity by the Mass. When changes to the rite were introduced, Jones considered them to be another instance of the decline of the West. Even the Chalice itself was modified in order to follow changes in the rubric and Jones despaired that 'the underlying implications ... are plain enough - all in the *direction* of eroding the *signa* of the *Mysterium Fidei*.'[76]

Gwyl Dewi Sant: St. David's Day (11) is a hectic, all-over composition. The chalice is placed off-centre, with a ghosting of the rim that is characteristic of Jones's desire to get an element right as well as being a device by which he dissolves substantiality. The daffodils celebrate St. David's Day with such craggy vigour and excitement that they seem to take wing. In *Table Top*, the reflections on the large surface are evocative of a softer, almost watery spirit world. The triple grouping suggests the crucifixion and the support on the china deer forms a cross. In another, *Chalice with a Necklace*, there are few blooms, the odd anemone and many thorns. The composition flies outwards and Jones's odd accentings show us that in a transfigured state certain details

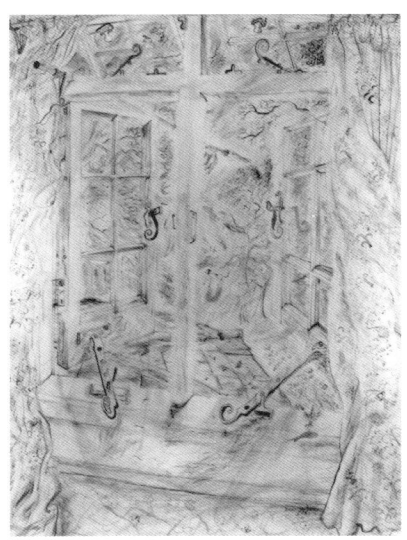

10. The Outward Walls, 1953

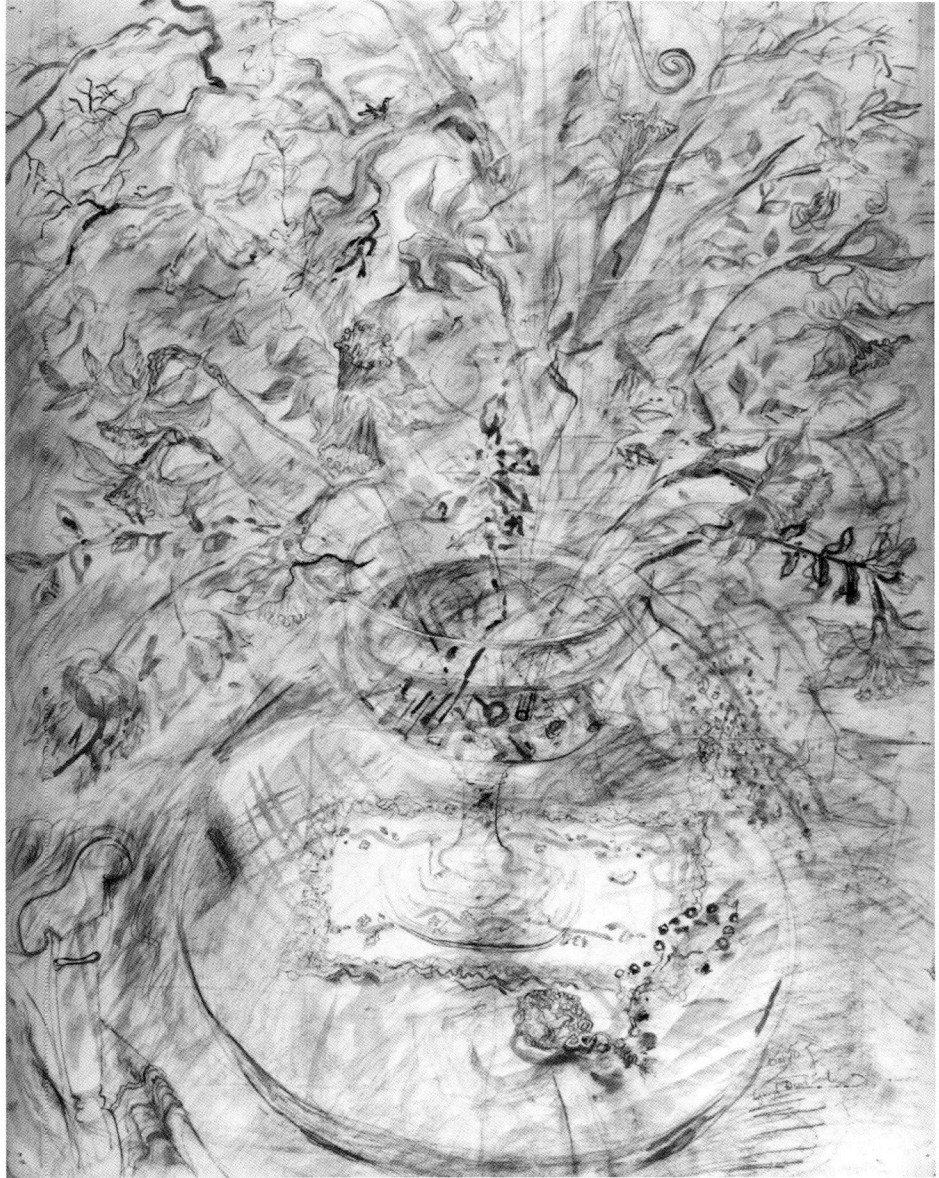

11. Gwyl Dewi Sant, 1954

rush at the painter and possess him. Sadly, the missal and the necklace, which appears as a surrogate rosary, have something slightly obsessional as if Jones is trying to anchor himself with religious paraphernalia. He is pulled between the hell of a religion suffering from cultural decline and the heaven of meditating on earthly beauty which occasions a kind of ecstasy.

Suggesting a loss of judgement or of control, Jones wrote:

> … the central bowl with the water and the stalks … comes out all right whereas the table and other things on it so often just won't cohere, try as I may. One … gets, in a sort of way, bored with them - so they won't play. Something of that sort I've often found to happen. It's a very tricky business indeed - finding out what one is *really* trying to do in any given picture.[77]

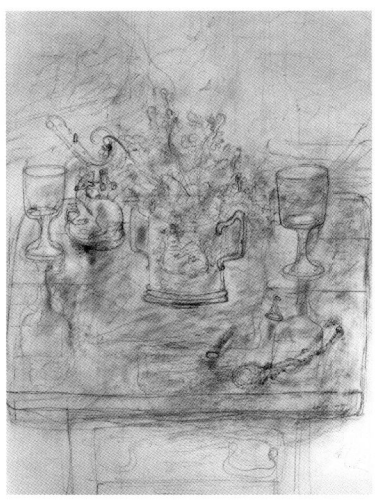

12. The Table Top, 1950

205

These paintings came nowhere near so easily as his earlier still lifes. Jones worked much more slowly and wrote of how it could take 'ten days, to do a watercolour of some flowers in the window'.[78] The most formal of the late flower paintings is one which Jones painted early in the series, *Flora in Calix Light*. It is more intellectually developed and is a more stressed version of the similar *Mehefin*. The table top provides a large expanse against which colour is strewn. The formal organization is masterly, providing an anchor for the scattered delight of 'sweet heaven ... astrew'.[79] The triple grouping of the vessels is a metaphor for the triple grouping of the crucifixion. Out of the central chalice pours abundance and beauty, the flowers representative of Christ's blessing. The other two goblets, like the thieves, are empty. The window in the background at the left is drawn meticulously and the inter-section of mullion and transom is significantly accentuated. The window latches thrust towards the central chalice, suggestive of the spear that pierced Christ's side, but are turned back, as it were, by the power radiating from the goblet. On the right hand side, to balance the prominent drawing of the window, is a solidly coloured hieroglyphic tree, standing for all trees and calling to mind, in this context, the wood of the cross and the tree of life. The shape created by its foliage is none other than an inversion of the chalice shape and this posits further links between the celebration at the last supper and the death of Christ upon the wood of the cross. Light permeates every-thing and even the aura which surrounds the central chalice is so consistent with the sense of effulgence elsewhere in the painting that it does not descend into an over-emphatic religious symbolism as in certain of the late religious paintings; Jones has found a new manner of evoking the crucifixion which is brimful of physical and intellectual splendour. Although there is such evidence of celebration in Jones's late work, he was inclined to see in everything evidence of a decline. While the tradition of placing a tin or pewter chalice 'on the breast of every priest at his burial'[80] moved Jones, the flowers which he placed in his glass chalices were increasingly dissatisfying reminders of contemporary decline:

> I do thank Joan for the flowers - they look heavenly now I've put them into a thing on the table by the window. There don't seem to be any real flowers any longer. The sods one buys at the florists are bloody useless - God! what a civilization.[81]

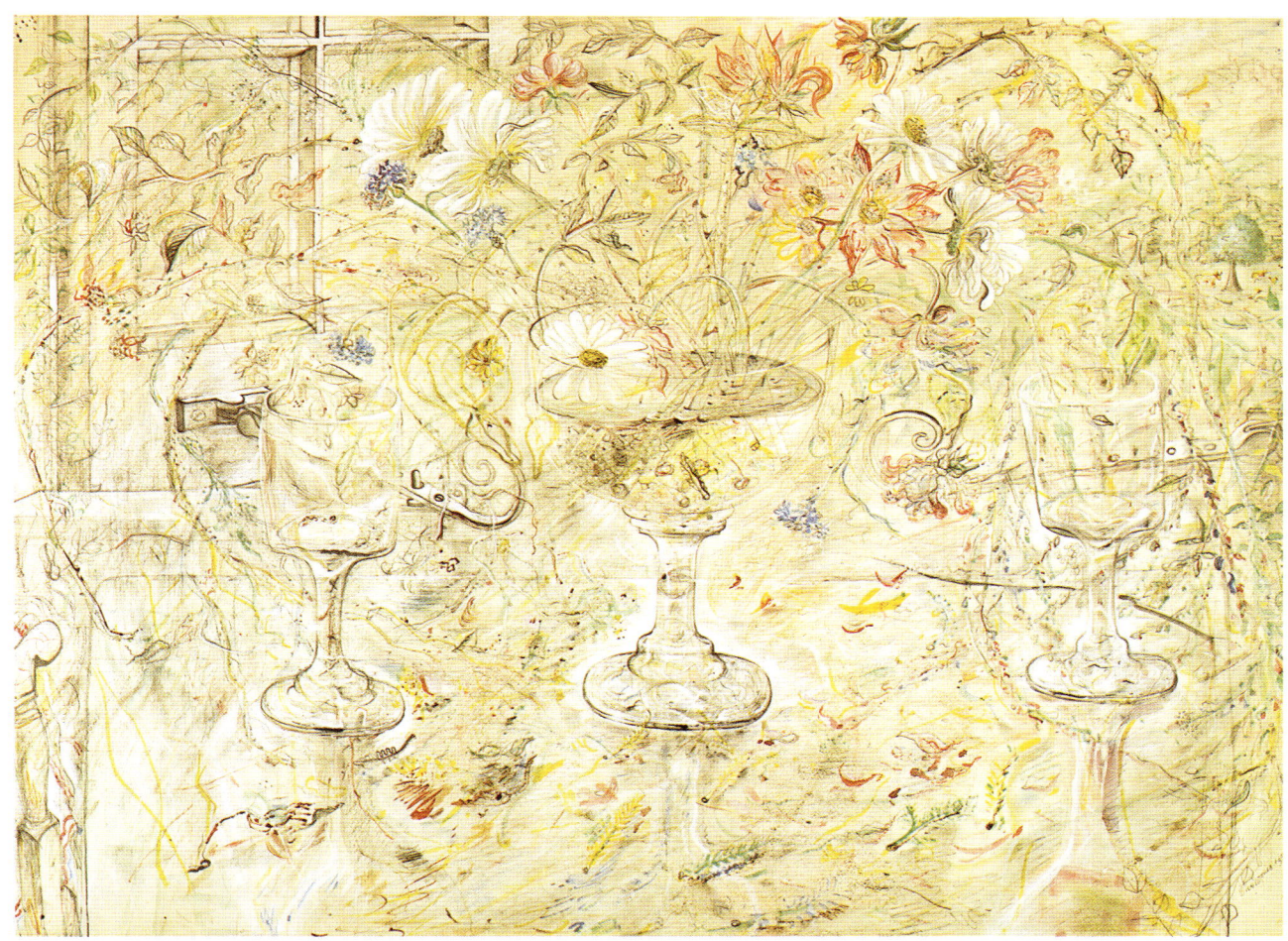

13. Flora in Calix Light, 1950

THE RICOCHET OF WAR

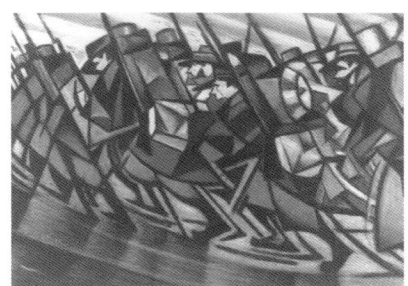

1. C.R.W. Nevinson, *Marching Men*, 1916

Without appreciating as much at the time, Jones fought in a war that was waged against the avant-gardism of Germany.[1] His own art school training and the general absence of an avant-garde in England meant that his early experience of modernism had been limited. Sickert noted in 1911 that English painting was 'kept alive, a dim flickering flame by tiny groups of devoted fanatics mostly under the age of thirty' and that the 'national taste' broke 'these fanatics'.[2] Indeed, champions of modernism had to turn their attentions elsewhere; in the introduction to his catalogue for the *Second Post-Impressionist Exhibition* in 1912, Roger Fry noted that the style was 'flourishing, one might almost say raging, in Switzerland, Austro-Hungary, and most of all in Germany'.[3] While a good number of British artists reflected the superficial calm of the Edwardian world, continental painters such as Meidner, Kandinsky, Le Fresnaye and the Futurists were anticipating apocalypse. And yet, in England, by 1914, there were one or two stirrings among groups who responded to the increasing exposure to continental developments.[4] The Bloomsbury painters were approaching their most abstract phase, Wyndham Lewis's *Rebel Art Centre* opened in the Spring of 1914, challenging Fry's *Omega Workshop*, and, at the same time, the Italian Futurist leader, Marinetti, returned to London for a well publicized visit supported by Lewis. The first *Blast*, the publication of the Vorticists, appeared in the summer, condemning native lethargy: Britain, as one of the first countries to have industrialized, should face up to the reflection of mechanization in its art.[5] As the country moved into an increasingly mechanized conflict against Germany, that plea seemed to take on a new urgency. The contemporary critic, P.G. Konody, in his book on C.R.W. Nevinson, suggested that 'The artistic language of the past had no idiom that could adequately express the grim, hard, mechanical character of a war in which the decisive element is the efficiency of laboratories and engineering works.'[6] Nevinson, who had been much influenced by the Italian Futurist leader,[7] imagined in the autumn of 1914 that the war would act as 'a violent incentive to Futurism'.[8] In fact, the war had a demoralizing effect on the Vorticist group which broke up as the euphoria surrounding the outbreak of hostilities gave way to almost universal despair; a detached artistic position such as Marinetti's callous and offensive idea that war was 'the sole hygiene of the world'[9] was one of the casualties of the grim realities of combat.

The Front was described by Konody as 'a Futurist atmosphere of speed and noise and concentrated energy'[10] which reduced men to sub-human conditions, but it was the innocence and humanity of the victims and the humour with

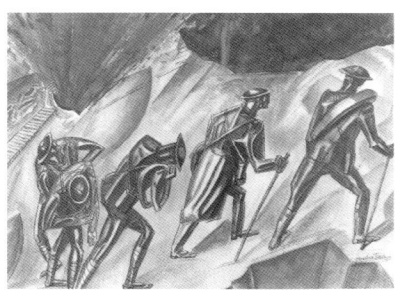

2. Wyndham Lewis, *Officers and Signallers*, 1918

which they sustained themselves that Jones chose to express in his long prose poem, *In Parenthesis*. In sketches made in the years during which he was writing or in which he was awaiting publication, Jones did not stress the modernity of the war but rather the fragility of the victims. He did not employ Nevinson's Futurist technique *(1)* and neither was there a mechanization in the treatment of his soldiers in the manner of Wyndham Lewis's automatons *(2)*. However, Jones and William Roberts *(4)*, at different times, chose a compositional implosion to convey the explosive nature of trench combat. Roberts's formalized distortions expressed the brutalizing effect on the soldiers, whereas Jones's simple sketch *(3)* shows the men awkwardly negotiating their threatened trench.

An eerie, surreal view of the western front was achieved in Nash's first oil, *The Mule Track (5)* of 1918. The vision was somewhat stylized yet the scale absurd and nightmarish, presenting the universal destruction of the landscape. Despite Nash's desire to awaken the consciousness of those at home,[11] the explosions appear almost elegant, registering the kind of aesthetic effect that Jones felt was made by bombs exploding over London during the Second World War. The painting does not create so powerful an impact as Nash's own verbal record: 'black rain out of the bruised and swollen clouds … the stinking mud … evilly yellow, the shell-holes … with green-white water, the roads and tracks … covered in inches of slime'.[12] Jones realized his supreme treatment of the war in words, yet words chosen and assembled with a painter's habit of visual searching.[13]

If the First World War had been emotionally interpreted by the British as a struggle to preserve their social values then it is ironical to note that it acted as a great instrument of social change and cultural transformation. However, in respect of twentieth century art, for some time after the war, the conservatives were victorious; there was a reversion towards conservatism in the art of the post-war world and some of the more adventurous pre-war British artists who survived the conflict felt that their destruction of artistic traditions had been somehow too swift and too violent.

That Jones fought so readily on the side of conservatism is understandable, not only in light of the patriotism that engulfed Britain, but also in light of his later beliefs and attitudes. But it was a conservatism more far-reaching than is usually understood by the word, and in his poetry Jones gave expression to a belief in tradition, paradoxically in a form which responded to the very pressures which were breaking down the traditions being celebrated. When, a decade after the war had ended, he came to explore the conflict in a searching manner, it was not only the humanity of the behaviour of the men in the trenches but the sense of 're-participating in history'[14] that he wished to celebrate. What was most important to Jones was not the preservation of the Edwardian vision of 'Old England' but an attempt to place the war in the context of related conflicts. By the early 1930s, he had absorbed Eliot's and Pound's lesson about the 'presence' of the past[15] and had come to feel that the 'texture' of any 'historic present' was 'linked, necessarily, with a whole historic past'.[16]

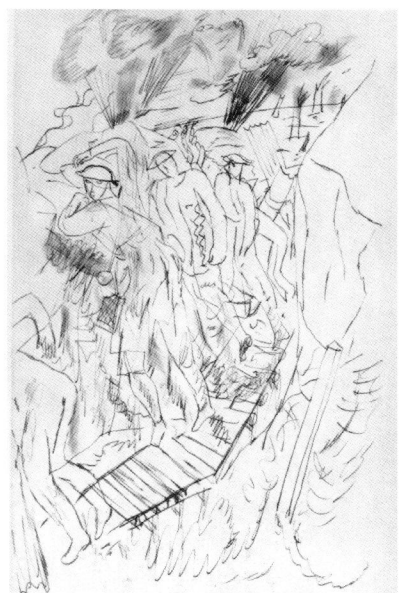

3. Trench Sketch, 1937

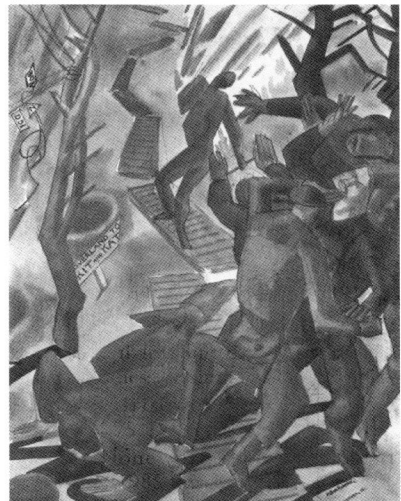

4. William Roberts, The Ypres Sector, 1918

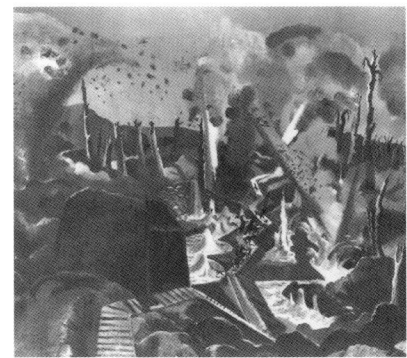

5. Paul Nash, The Mule Track, 1918

The chapter concerning his time at Westminster School of Art revealed how the war became an important theme for Jones during his second spell as an art student. With the passage of time, he was able to place his experience of the war in a larger context, the events of 1914-18 became reactivated through his mythopoeic imagination which began to emerge in painting as a result of his first and highly innovative prose poem. Certainly, the perturbation of war stayed with him; a remark like 'he never got out of the trenches'[17] registers more than a *penchant* for army slang and military metaphors. Imagine month upon month of incessant noise, sporadic flashing and explosion, life lived in a narrow gully often flooded and usually stinking, the worst nightmare imaginable, and then you might be able to begin to understand the indelible horror of the trenches and why David Jones suffered from recurring bouts of terror throughout his life.

As a young soldier serving in France, Jones had written short articles for the parish magazine at home such as *Is it worth it?* and *Somewhere on the Western Front*, committed and patriotic, discussing the un-Britishness of giving up and using a crude mythology to characterize the enemy as 'the war-lords of Odin'. By the time Jones came to make a mature and personal work of art about the war it was 1928 and the need for tactical propaganda or, indeed, the possibility of painting any kind of direct response to the subject had been exhausted. An engagement with the war would have to propose some new creative vitality. In visual terms this would be a work like Stanley Spencer's chapel at Burghclere (1923-32), but for David Jones it was to be a literary masterpiece which contextualized an experience of the war in a highly original manner.

Jones actually began what became *In Parenthesis* with the idea of doing 'a lot of illustrations with long "captions" of a sort'[18] and it seems that when the text

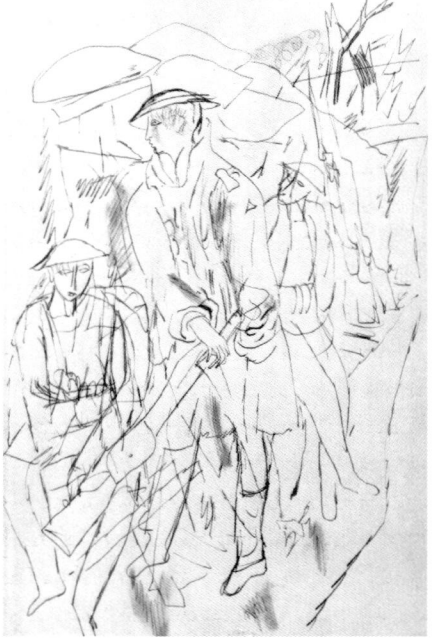

6. Three Soldiers in Trench with Rifle, 1932

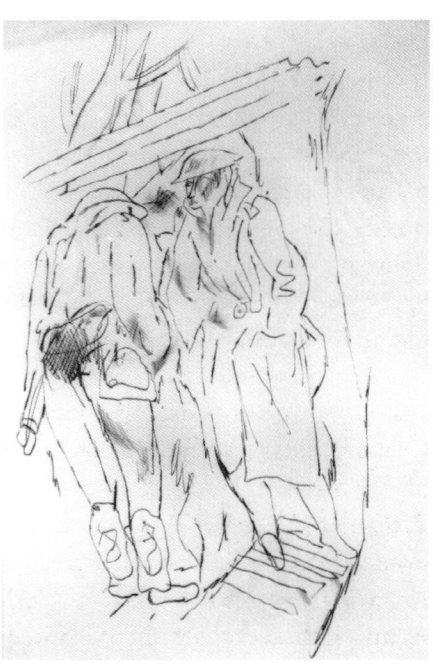

7. Two Soldiers Chatting in a Trench, 1932

was finished Jones half-lamented that the visual dimension was minimal (only a frontispiece, endpiece and a map were included): 'It would have been good to have been able to do engravings but then that would mean waiting until I am able and *going through it all again in another medium* - another matter of years.'[19]

The impromptu sketches which decorate the manuscript do, indeed, suggest that Jones had a visual dimension very much in mind and yet one aspect of the motivation or challenge to write had been to see how 'form' and 'content' would work 'in *a writing* as compared with the same problems in ... the visual arts',[20] and this, combined with his fatigue and the fact that he certainly did not 'want to use photographic reproduction of things', meant that Jones allowed the book to be, in the end, 'a simply printed document without embellishments or additions of any kind'.[21] Although the ambition to go through *In Parenthesis* 'in another medium' was unrealized, he did begin to explore the possibility; some ink sketches made in 1932 *(6,7)*, the year that the manuscript was finished, are quite possibly attempts to provide the beginnings of visual material for the book; the emphasis on the linear may suggest that the drawings were prefatory sketches for possible copper engravings.

In 1931, Jones made a watercolour and drawing that was used as a frontispiece for R.H.J. Steuart's reminiscences *March Kind Comrade*. As with the drawing made for *In Parenthesis* several years later, its contention is obviously that soldiers are innocent victims and that war is 'a monumental bollocks'.[22] The figures have an uncomfortable relation to the strange landscape that has been thrown up round about them. Jones keeps the eye flitting from area to area, securing that moving, all-over quality that he continually sought, expressing what he described as the 'meandering comfortless and untidy'[23] terrain of the line around Givenchy. And yet, in the top left-hand corner barbed wire tendrils take on something of the young branches of plants and this reminds the spectator that the landscape would, in time, replenish itself.

Llys Ceimiad: La Bassée Front 1916 (9), a pencil, ink and watercolour drawing was made in 1937, the year in which *In Parenthesis* was published. It works many familiar elements into an assured composition. The conflicting angles of the duckboards, figures, rifles, picket irons and blasted trees give the whole picture a sense of confusion and imminent explosion. The soldiers wait, ill-fitted victims, almost floating in this nightmare world; the twisted, boyish figure at the top evokes the unsuitability of the bulk of the army to its task. Speaking of this picture for a British Council slide programme of his work, Jones commented that '*Ceimiad*' means 'champion' or 'hero', and that '*Llys*' means 'a court or place of importance';[24] the trenches are seen as a place of heroes although there is nothing conventionally heroic about the figures included. Certainly, it is not the kind of heroism suggested by the propagandistic bravura of Christopher Williams in his oil, *Charge of the Welsh Division at Mametz, July 11th, 1916*.[25] C. R.W. Nevinson, in response to official displeasure at one of his ironically more conventional treatments of the war, *Group of Soldiers*, retaliated by saying that he refused to paint 'castrated Launcelots and insult the British Army with such sentimental bilge';[26] Jones's soldiers are kinds of castrated Launcelots, but wounded heroes rather than the idealized, super-human visions

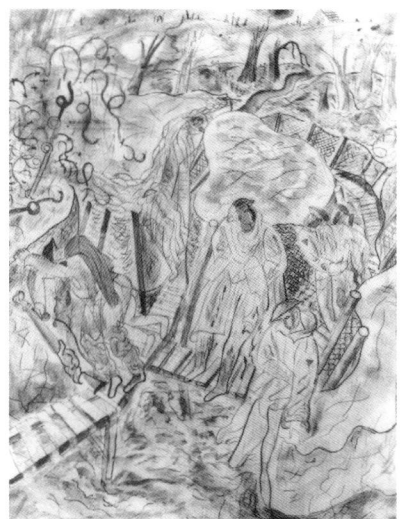

8. March Kind Comrade, 1931

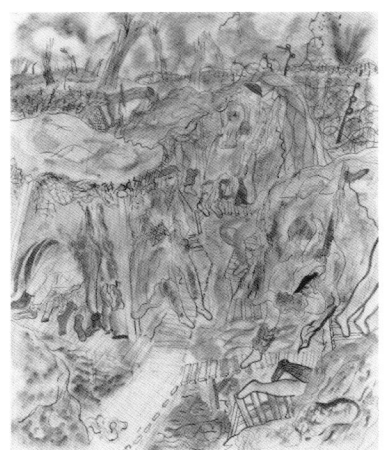

which disgusted Nevinson. In *Llys Ceimiad* all the colours are pale and some are unrealistic like the blue helmets of the two foreground soldiers. The vivid orange triangle on the shoulder of the man at the back holds the gaze as does the similarly strong black outlined eye of the central map reader who casts a cynical, questioning stare back at the spectator. The scene is fluid, flattened at the right and yet with a sense of depth in the centre. The scoop of pencil which hooks the map reader admits anger and accident into Jones's picture. Not only its obfuscatory title, the socks and leggings suggestive of chain-mail, but also the triple grouping of the three main figures recalling a crucifixion and the inverted cross of the duckboards, suggest that the transhistorical, mythologizing imagination has begun to work.

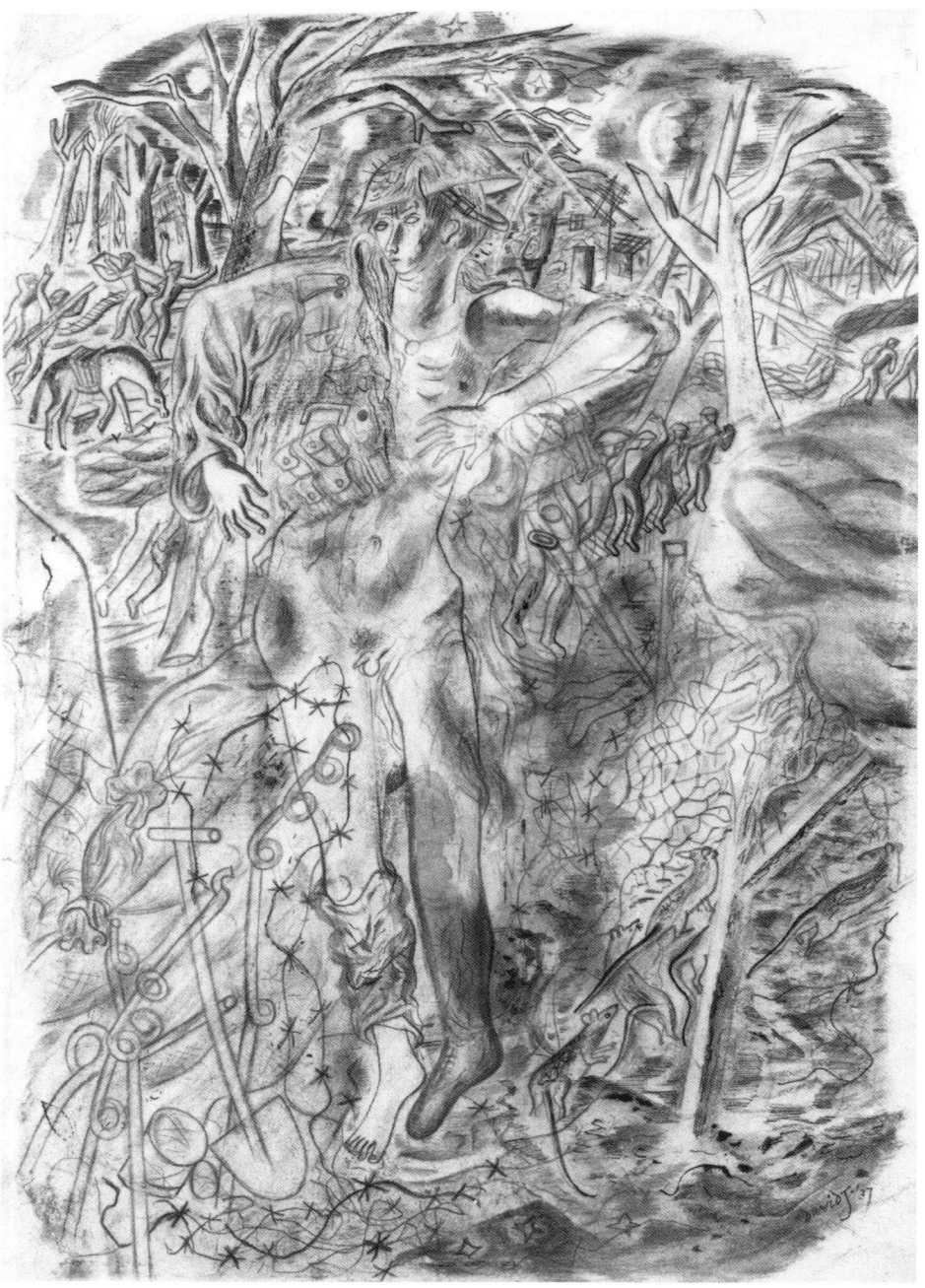

10. In Parenthesis – Frontispiece, 1937

After writing his war book, Jones found a means of visually exploring some of the cultural dimensions that he had discovered in the process of writing. Thus, he was led towards a new kind of transhistorical picture-making which gave over into a related mythological world. The *Frontispiece* to *In Parenthesis (10)* is in pencil, ink and watercolour. The figure, placed centrally, roughly cruciform in pose, his helmet strap a kind of halo, is obviously emblematic. Arms askance, awkward like the broken trees, he fights with a remnant of his uniform. Is he struggling to equip his natural innocence for his task or is he making the humane plea that all this martial panoply must be discarded? Like Dai Greatcoat, the universal soldier in Part 4 of *In Parenthesis*, the figure in the frontispiece 'adjusts' his clothing; like Dai, he takes on a transhistorical dimension. Dai Greatcoat served 'By Agned mountain / On Badon Hill', and in the drawing the awkward left leg of this soldier fades from nakedness into something reminiscent of chain mail. Barbed wire curls perilously close to his tiny genitals,[27] the shape of his diminished fertility mocking that of the misplaced power of cannon. Limbs are dislocated and a wound is visible; the figure balloons before the carrying party like some apotheosis of their cares and capabilities. The body is re-ordered in the way that a Cubist figure might be, each part presented differently. The strong contours of the limbs are defied by painted shadows which take the body out into the landscape. The large, billowing painted area devoid of drawing on the right sets the whole painting in motion and while clusters of over-detailed drawing do distract from the adventurous effects in paint, Jones has successfully contrived the transitions of scale. The world is a waste land but Jones asserts the fragility and humanity of the participants. It is a place where men's dreams are fractured, as stars seem to lie strewn among the barbed wire on the ground.

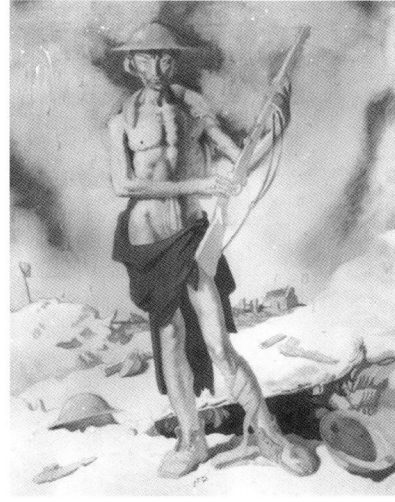

11. William Orpen, Blown Up, 1917

It is possible that Jones may have seen William Orpen's *Blown Up (11)* in the Imperial War Museum when he went to consult a trench map for the writing of *In Parenthesis*.[28] Orpen's painting could have suggested to Jones, with its areas of bold white, a way of giving largeness of scale to a relatively small image, for Jones uses such whiteness to good effect in his drawing. The archetype of the universal soldier has been taken up more recently by the German artist, George Baselitz, in his *Vorwärts Wind (12),* but Jones's treatment reigns supreme, chosen as the final image in the Barbican's comprehensive 1994 exhibition, *The Bitter Truth*.

In some way, Jones's desire to make sense of everything, to invest everything with significance, results from his participation in the senseless destruction of the war:

> You ought to ask: Why,
> what is this,
> what's the meaning of this.[29]

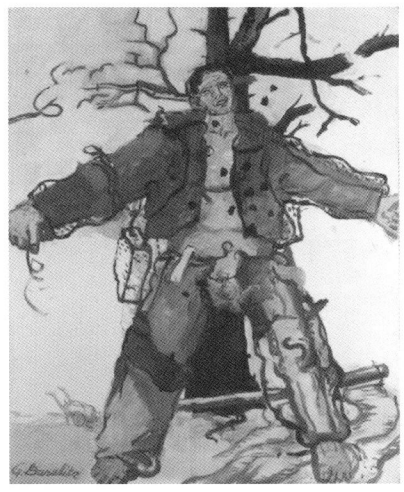

12. George Baselitz, Vorwärts Wind, 1966

The mythographical approach attempted to garner meaning and make the past co-terminous with the present. The success of this attempt at salvage could only be partial. The strained vision, the discrepancy between venerated contents and available forms, register the impossibility of making a whole, a shape which could withstand cultural fracture. If Jones's work from the late twenties until his death was an attempt to make cultural sense out of a bleak civilizational situation, then the war in its recurring manifestations, fear, breakdown and disillusionment, gave Jones a piercing understanding of the modern capacity for destruction.

THE HIATUS AND THE WHOLE

THE MYTHOLOGICAL WORKS

At Dalrymple Hall a concert included 'Griffith's Answer to Harold' and passages from 'Henry V' recited by Master Walter Jones. During the concert, 'A Grand Torchlight Procession' featured his sister as Britannia and Master Walter as Cadwal, a Briton. This entertainment, with its echoes of the Elizabethan Court Masque, took place in a suburban front room in Brockley and Master Walter, who also designed the front cover of the programme, later dropped his first name and became known as David Jones.

The boy grew up delighting in myth and history, surrounded by a family who encouraged his enthusiasm. At an early age, he spat on the tomb of Edward I in Westminster Abbey in protest against that king's conquest of Wales. An uncle, with whom he was lodged while his brother was dying of tuberculosis, urged him to memorize Macaulay's *Lays of Ancient Rome* and even made wooden armour, which he covered with silver, so that the child could recite extracts in costume.[1] Some kind of surprising link may have been created between Wales and Catholicism at an impressionable age when he was taken to Holywell with its many shrines and monuments celebrating the miraculous restoration to life of the martyred St. Winefride; to stumble on such a glut of Catholic 'repository art' in the context of Non-Conformist Wales was, to some extent, as absurd as finding the commercial vulgarity of Lourdes in the mountainous scenery of the Pyrenees. The child's interest in the visible aspects of history is evident from the long walks he took to Greenwich to see 'Nelson's relics'[2] and is confirmed by a fellow pupil who sat next to him in Class Six at Brockley Road School and who remembered at least one occasion, when they 'went to the tower of London to look at armour'.[3] Such interest was continued into adulthood; Hilary Pepler gave *Heraldry for Craftsman and Designers* to Jones as a birthday present on All Saint's Day, 1921.

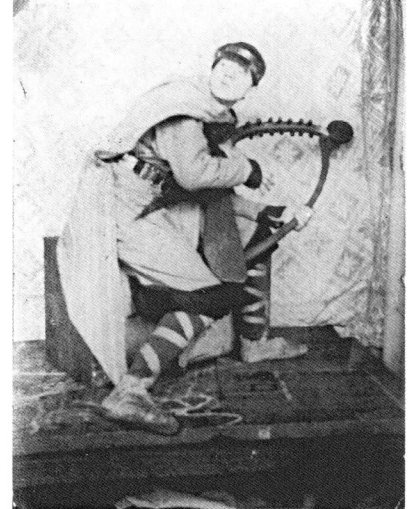

1. David Jones as a Welsh Bard, c. 1910

Jones's early enthusiasm for story gave way to interest in history and mythology. As a very young child when his mother sang *Johnny's So Long at the Fair*, the boy cried because he wanted to know what happened to Johnny.[4] By the age of fifteen he was reading Lady Charlotte Guest's translation of *The Mabinogion*, a translation of *Giraldus Cambrensis*, and for his sixteenth birthday his father gave him a history of the Welsh people.

Jones intended to dedicate his precocious drawing talents to historical illustration and, at Camberwell, Savage and Hartrick encouraged him by example. Despite Hartrick's contacts with Impressionism, both he and Savage worked under the lingering influence of Pre-Raphaelitism.[5] Hartrick's illustrations to Maurice Hewlett's *The Forest Lovers (2)*, a copy of which he

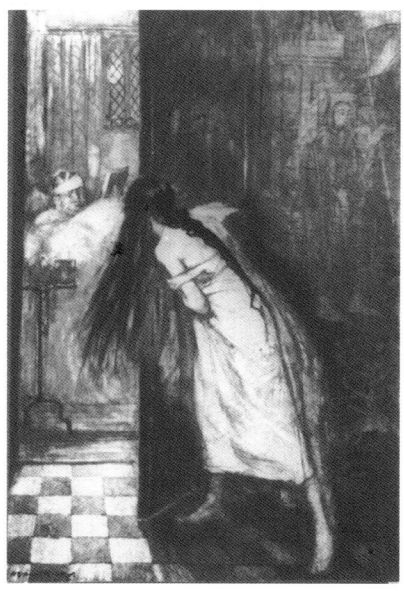

2. A.S. Hartrick,
   Illustration for 'The Forest Lovers', 1909

214

gave to his student, David Jones, as a gift in March, 1914, clearly reveal the imaginative and fanciful world of the painters, identified by a recent exhibition as 'The Last Romantics'. The continuing effect of such an aesthetic can be seen, not only in images that Jones produced during the First World War, but also much later in life. The key to Jones's eventual incompatibility with the dominant tendencies of twentieth century art is to be found not only in his attraction to an encyclopaedic Medievalism, but also in his artistic roots which go back through Hartrick, Savage and his contemporaries, Walter Crane, Sturge Moore, Ricketts and Shannon, into that newer and dreamy kind of encyclopaedism, Symbolism. Indeed Jones has been perceived as 'a late Victorian'[6] and even as the 'last of the Symbolists'.[7]

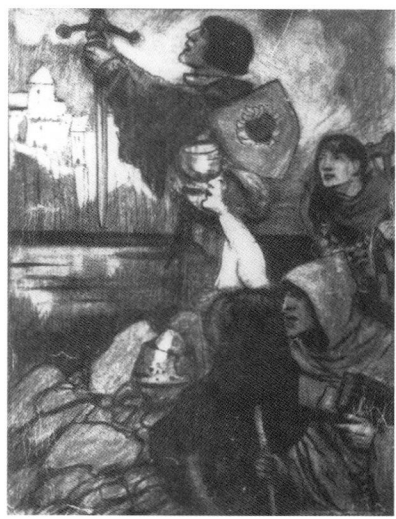

3. The Quest, New Year, 1918

In a preparatory drawing made in his trench sketch book for a Christmas greeting card we can see the historical preoccupations of childhood filtered through that aesthetic. A print made by Jones's father (3) from the soldier's final illustration was sent out as a New Year greeting for 1918 with Jones's chivalric text, *The Quest*, inside. In this short story there is a Lady, 'most desirous fair', a Minstrel 'exceeding well skilled' and the moral is, that 'when thou liftest high thy battle-blade, strike not but to make men free'. The pastiche reveals a full diet of Dalrymple Hall and a conspicuous inconsistency of style which is at least absent from the accompanying image.[8] Surprisingly, even at that late stage, the war was being celebrated by a participant in the heroic images which had been used to create the emotional preconditions for the struggle. Jones saw his involvement in the war as part of a tradition; he was doing what had always been done by young men.

A similar archaizing tendency was also used by Jones during this period to sublimate sentimental expression. *Knight and Girl (4)*, made when he was back from the Front in 1916 is, in fact, a self-portrait with a one-time girlfriend, Elsie Levitt. The image is a mistily Symbolist vision echoing a painting such as Rossetti's *The Wedding of St. George and Princess Sabra (5)*. Scenes set in archaic or exotic situations are a persistent tactic of disguised confession by Symbolist painters. Such paintings were encoded; the literary situation has to be read and then, if the full power of submerged expression is to be appreciated, the personal significance deduced.

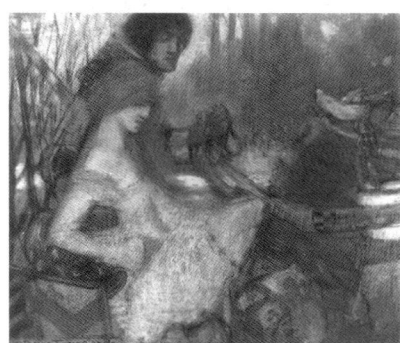

4. Knight and Girl, 1916

Pre-Raphaelitism with its literary preoccupations fascinated Jones from the first. A similar predilection for the exactly delineated historical element, a passion for archeological detail became an obsession in his mature mythographical drawings which are as full of historical detritus as the background of Rossetti's vision of St. Cecilia in the *The Palace of Art*. The Pre-Raphaelites reactivated the theory that poetry and painting are related arts with similar functions and that image and text can augment one another.[9] Jones's creative activities likewise converged; in his mythographical drawings he expressed in visual terms what had begun to preoccupy him in his poetry.

As Jones came to maturity there was a strain in British art that reacted against the superficiality of Impressionism. However, the search for Significant Form also implied a certain impoverishment; the theory was intellectually

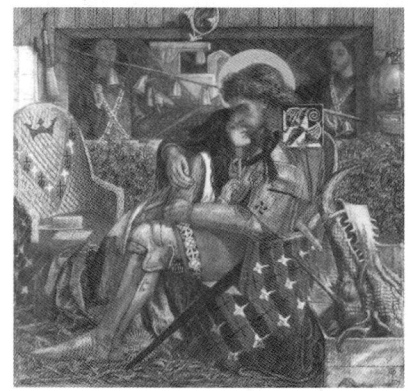

5. Dante Gabriel Rossetti, The Wedding of
St. George and Princess Sabra, 1857

215

demanding but there was an emptying out of content or meaning. Laurence Binyon noted that an artist like Botticelli cared 'nothing for the representation' of mass and relief 'for their own sake' but as devices capable of expressing 'the emotion of the spirit within the form'.[10] The Symbolists alone, in their 'rearguard action on behalf of an older ... hopelessly doomed culture',[11] looked back over recent post-Romantic aesthetic preoccupations to artists like Botticelli, Mantegna and Rubens. For all the painterly splendour of the larger forms, details in paintings by Rubens carry an important allegorical message. The Celtic stone circle, barely visible in the landscape beyond the chubby *Bacchus* (1638-40)[12] links northern and southern mythology. The mediterranean Bacchus, renowned for his inspirational influence on poets, is juxtaposed with Druidic mysticism and poetry. The cross-cultural link is just the kind in which Jones would become interested. *Vexilla Regis* blends a northern landscape tradition and the idea of the *Yggdrasil* from nordic mythology with elements of Trajan's Column, showing 'standard bearers who carried the *signa* of the cohorts'.[13]

Jones significantly used a military metaphor to describe 'Post-Impressionist theory and practice infiltrating the English front';[14] it was apt because it seemed that the knights and fairytales of the 'Last Romantics' could not be assimilated into a modern idiom as they were elsewhere. Kandinsky is the artist *par excellence* who takes a Medieval chivalric world and re-makes it according to the painterly abstraction of the twentieth century. His good fortune was to be sustained by a vital and colourful Russian Folk Art which in some sense paved the way for the bold formal experiments in his paintings up to about 1920. No such Folk Art existed in England and France and the cerebral nature of much Symbolism made it self-conscious, referential and élitist. The literary artistic tradition which had captivated Jones as a child ran to ground and re-emerged at the end of the 1930s as Neo-Romanticism.

One major source of literary inspiration which dominated Victorian and Pre-Raphaelite painting with its rich potential for political and personal allegory was the Arthurian cycle.[15] By the late 1920s, Jones was reading Malory and considering Cleverdon's request to do a series of engravings for an edition. One drypoint, *The Wounded Knight*, remains from this unrealized project and the fact that Jones chose such an image as his first response to the *Morte D'Arthur* indicates that even in his early thirties, Jones, by showing the wounded warrior at sunset and the riderless horses scattering, focused on the cycle's concern with decline. Jon Silkin notes that Malory, 'although speaking of heroism and the chivalric code, also speaks of a society ... provoked into war by treachery, and its disintegration finalised by war'.[16] So the Arthurian cycle dealt with a period which could be seen as contemporaneous with Jones's time according to a Spenglerian analysis of history. As with his own writing, Jones suggested, using Spenglerian metaphors, that Malory's 'artistry was of the late autumn, whereas his sources were of the springtime'.[17]

While Jones felt his separation from art movements in the 1930s[18] it is necessary to observe how patriotic and proto-Neo-Romantic tendencies helped to contribute to Jones's sudden turn towards mythological illustration at the end

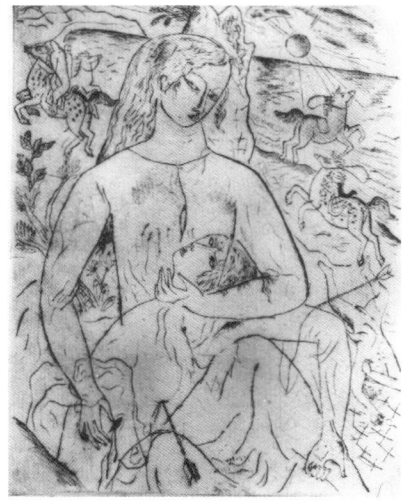

6. The Wounded Knight, 1930

of that decade. There had been, during the late twenties and early thirties, a great number of books published celebrating the British landscape, and rural preservation and exploration societies were started, all suggesting that there was a sense of threat from industrialization and, as the decade drew to a close, from foreign invasion.[19] David Mellor has observed that Nash and Sutherland resolved 'the cultural tension between "going modern" and "being British"' by making the British landscape part of the contemporary artist's range of interest, by creating a '"heroic" national pastoral'. A seamless and unified vision of Britain, actually strained by serious unemployment and unresolved industrial relations, was thereby constructed. There was, in certain quarters, a turning away from impersonal and international abstract art and a resurgence of British themes and indigenous traditions. Paul Nash, in speaking of his relation to the English countryside at Silbury Hill and Avebury, noted that he painted '*after* Nature, rather than *from* Nature'. For Nash, 'place' was 'not merely a picturesque scene; it was a congeries of interacting associations, fantasies and memories'.[20] Jones became caught up in that *zeitgeist*.

Much of the thirties was for Jones a time of distress, impoverishment and estrangement. Despite abstraction, despite the rise of the more socially aware documentary approach of painters like Coldstream, intimations of a loss of 'England' and threat from abroad led certain artists to 'seek consolation in the homely, familiar British pastoral and a new humanitarianism.'[21] The Neo-Picturesque which burgeoned in the work of painters like John Piper and writers like John Betjeman was a prelude to a Neo-Romanticism in which an often fragile or assailed calligraphy tempers a robust reassertion of the chthonic energies of nature. Neo-Romanticism which reinvested the land with emotional or spiritual significance also looked to the literariness of Pre-Raphaelitism and their heirs, the 'Last Romantics', for a range of imagery and elements of style. As Mellor observed:

> Under pressure from the writings of Herbert Read, Pevsner, Robin Ironside, Piper and Michael Ayrton ... by the 1940s an alternative history was in construction, one which disregarded Renaissance monumentality and volumetrics as being central to art. Instead a perceived set of continuities between Celtic, Gothic, Romantic and the Modern were given precedence. A disembodying linear style was the constant thread ... An 'Expressionist', 'visionary' genealogy was being constructed for a British visual culture in troubled times, a genealogy independent of Continental forces, drawn from seemingly indigenous criteria. By the time of Read's *British Contemporary Art* (1951) this cultural nationalism is assumed and self-supporting. In his landmark essay of 1936, 'England's Early Sculptors', Piper reversed the Renaissance paradigm and placed the apogee of British art during a period of Celtic supremacy, linear and rhythmical.[22]

Jones, who combined a Romantic susceptibility to nature with a medieval capacity to see things as religious signs of something else occupied an important, if independent and eccentric, position in relation to this resurgence of indigenous expression.

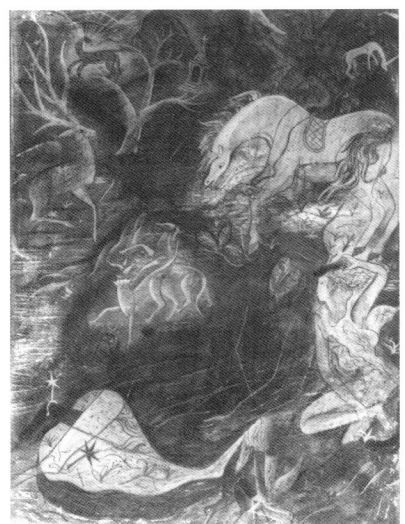

7. Merlin Land, 1931

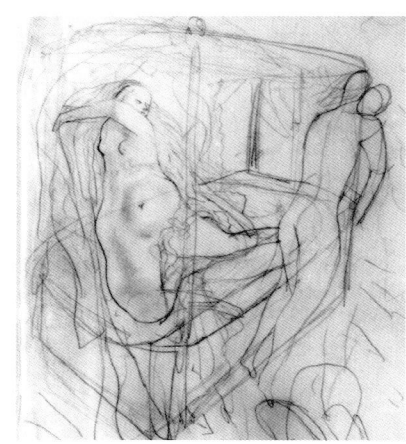

8. Sir Gareth and Dame Lyones '2', 1940

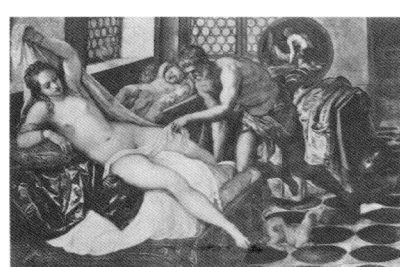

9. Jacopo Tintoretto, Vulcan, Venus and Mars, 1555

Summarising Jones's visual work for a French radio audience, René Laplat observed that '*David Jones est un arrière-petit-cousin de Merlin l'enchanteur.*'[23] *Merlin Appears in the Form of a Young Child to Arthur Sleeping (7)* of 1931, and later used as the illustration *Merlin Land* in *The Anathemata*, is an early example of the fragmenting fluidity of Jones's later paintings. In its blend of dreamy austerity, its sentimental and Surreal fragility it looks forward to the paintings of the wartime and post-war Neo-Romantics. The idea obviously grew out of Jones's considerations for Cleverdon's *Morte D'Arthur* project and its style is a blend of twenties Neo-Classicism such as can be seen in works by Picasso and the saccharine style of some of Jones's animal copper engravings.

Ten years after considering an edition of Malory, Jones wrote to H.S. Ede: 'have done an illustration to the *Morte D'Arthur* - a large watercolour … it took me about seven weeks on and off to do - but I like it'.[24] Only a couple of weeks later, he wrote again saying,

> I wish I had not said anything about the *Morte D'Arthur* because now it seems not much of a work - and I don't think you'll like it. Only one thing it's got a lot of things in it - packed tight and rather confused and takes you an hour to see it. It will cost a lot of money anyway.[25]

The Trustees of the Tate Gallery eventually proved willing to pay; as John Rothenstein wrote in a letter to Jones two years later,

> When the Board saw your two Arthurian drawings they were keenly interested and are most anxious to have the first option to purchase the whole series when complete. Certain of the Trustees thought them the finest things you had done. In the event of the series not being extended, I feel sure that the Board would like to acquire the two which they have already seen.[26]

Which in due course they did.

Jones's treatment of Arthurian material both in painting and poetry is compelling because the artist re-experienced its themes of cultural anxiety or of sexual disquiet. As this second element appears to dominate works such as *Guenever* and *The Four Queens,* discussion will be postponed until the next chapter and, for the present, an interesting sequence of drawings which show Jones's approach to a subject which never resulted in a fully finished watercolour and drawing will be discussed. The motivation to illustrate Malory Bk. VII ch. 22 appears to have been the vision of Dame Lyones naked on her bed, in a dynamic and sensual pose. Proportionally, she starts as a *Venus of Willendorf* recast through the eyes of Tintoretto or Rubens *(8)*, but as Jones moves from drawing to drawing she loses both her expressive posture and that continent of flesh between her hips. Powerful lines descend along the sides of Lyones's body, curve down and around into the line of her legs, and, in the later versions, carry on, diagonally upward, through Gareth's torso, along his arm and into his sword. Jones admired the sensual and expressive linearity of Tintoretto's nudes and marvelled at *Susanna and the Elders* when it

218

came to the Tate in 1949; certainly the pose of the first sketch shown here has some affinity with Tintoretto's *Vulcan, Venus and Mars (9)*. Throughout all the seven extant stages Lyones remains the focus of the artist's attention and in several sketches even the body of the man turning to defend her seems a variation on a feminine theme rather than a creditable knight. The most developed drawing in the series is set, Neo-Romantically, in a ruined building with the moon and stars appearing through a break in the ceiling. The conception of the figures has lost grandeur but there is a welcome lack of finish. The symbols of the four evangelists and the crucifix which decorate the tops of the bed are merely suggested in a way which contributes to, rather than detracts from, the movement of the drawing.

The story behind the image is of Gareth of Orkney who came to Arthur's court and worked for a year as Beaumaynes, the spit-turner, before being knighted by Launcelot. He later fell in love with Lyones and in the castle of

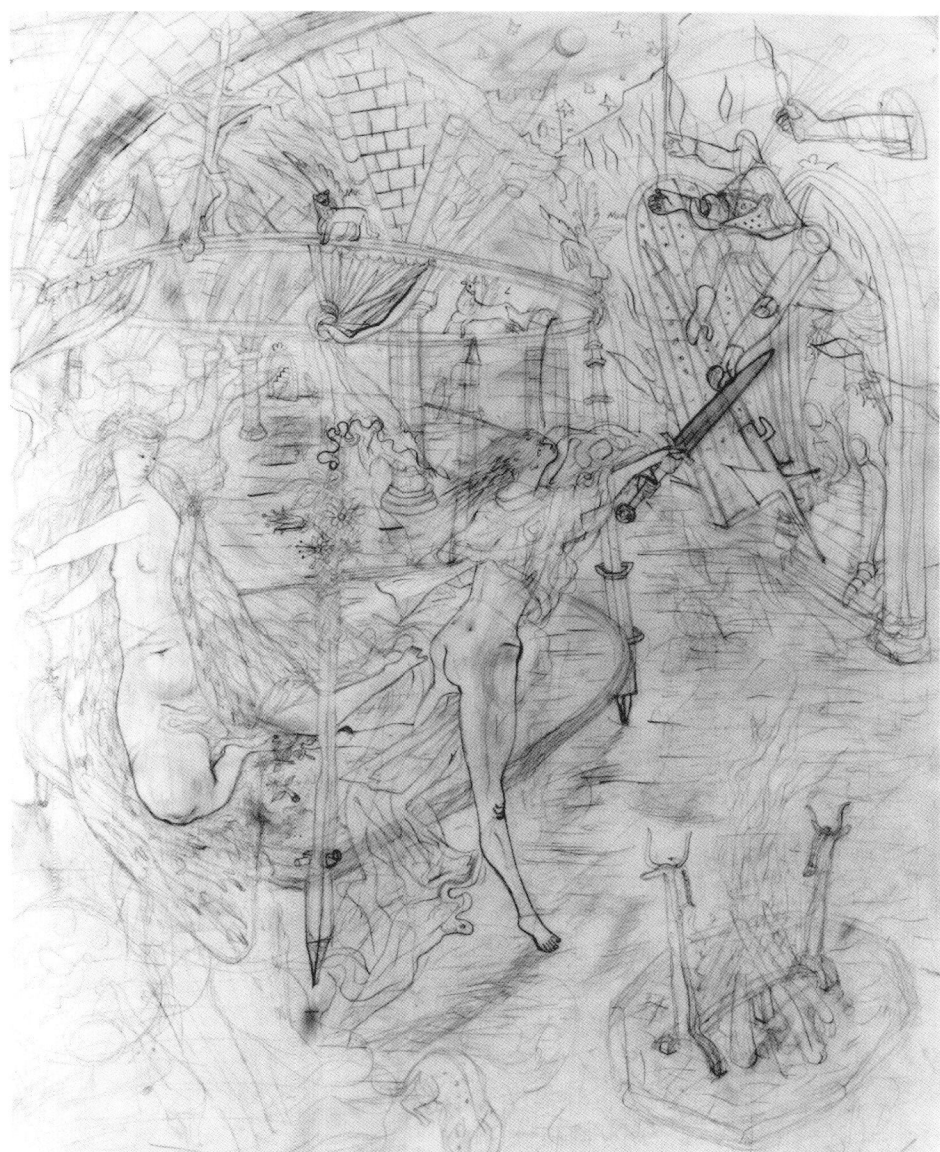

10. Sir Gareth and Dame Lyones, 1940

Sir Gryngamour, Gareth and Lyones 'brente bothe in hoote love' until her sister, Lyonett, considering that she was behaving immodestly, tried to destroy their love by 'hir subtyle craufftes'. Great 'couchis and thereon fethir beddis' were set in the hall but just as the lovers started to kiss, Gareth 'sawe an armed knyght with many lyghtes aboute him, and this knight had a longe gysarne [battle-axe] in his honde'.[27] To punish him for his supposed sexual misdemeanour, this knight wounds Gareth, somewhat euphemistically in the thigh; the event, Jones wrote, 'struck me as being of great psychological interest'[28] and, in the picture, he draws attention to the sexual element of the tale: the candle placed before the genitals of the armed knight and the spiked but garlanded bed posts are expressive of the joy and pain of love. But the idea of the sexual wound that is healed, for Gareth recovers and ultimately marries Lyones, could not hold Jones's interest and so he abandoned the idea. A sketch of another scene which was never developed was *Arthur Mortally Wounded* and again the story did not concern a sexual theme, which appears to have been the source of attraction for Jones in these Arthurian stories. Stories which treated ultimate failure such as the tales of Guenever and Launcelot, and Trystan and Essyllt, were more compelling and, therefore, explored more fully. In such tales when sexual difficulty is related to cultural difficulty or where sexual maiming is responsible for cultural desiccation these tales grew in Jones's imagination.

Cultural imperilment is expressed through the texture of a distressed surface in the final version of *The Lord of Venedotia (13)*. Clearly, this lord is of the land; the torrent of his cloak is more expansive than the hills beyond and the texture of agitated markings is uniform across the paper. Again a series of drawings exists in which Jones can be been seen to work towards this effect while, at the same time, weakening his expression by overworking background details which detract from the face's and the picture surface's poignant expression of plight. An almost sinister figure in the first drawing shown here *(11)*, the Lord becomes ambiguous *(12)*, and then, in the final version, a telling image of noble vulnerability.

The Lord of Venedotia is one of those half-historical, half-mythological figures like Cunedda Wledig or Macsen Wledig, interesting to Jones because they offer the possibility of historical continuity: 'alone among the peoples of this island the leaders of the Bret-Wealas arose from within the Western Xstn imperium'.[29] Part of Jones's personal distress was his awareness of the fact that, as Patrick Reyntiens put it, 'England had lost a historical and mythical probity'; Jones rather felt that 'Welsh culture, to which he felt he belonged, might not yet have done so.'[30] And while much of Jones's work is set in a time of cultural disintegration it is also about cultural fortitude, it presents a kind of imperilled optimism. The British Council bought *The Lord of Venedotia*, but Jones himself was less satisfied, writing to Saunders Lewis that 'I don't feel it's much good - I've gone "academic" in some way'.[31]

In *The Princess with the Long-Boats* (1948-9), there is a distinct echo of Henry Moore's graphic style with its weathered texturing and, certainly, Jones had a great liking for Moore's drawings, preferring them to the carvings.[32] Wax

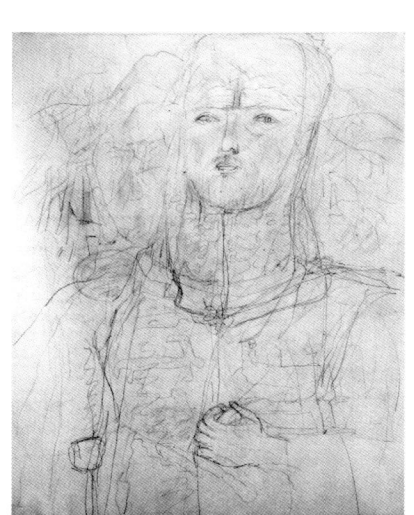

11. Sketch for the Lord of Venedotia, 1948

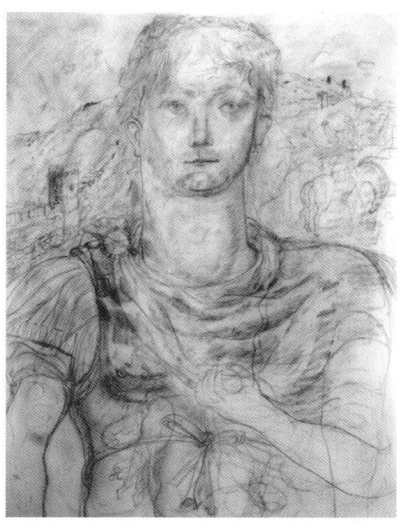

12. Cunedda Wledig, 1948

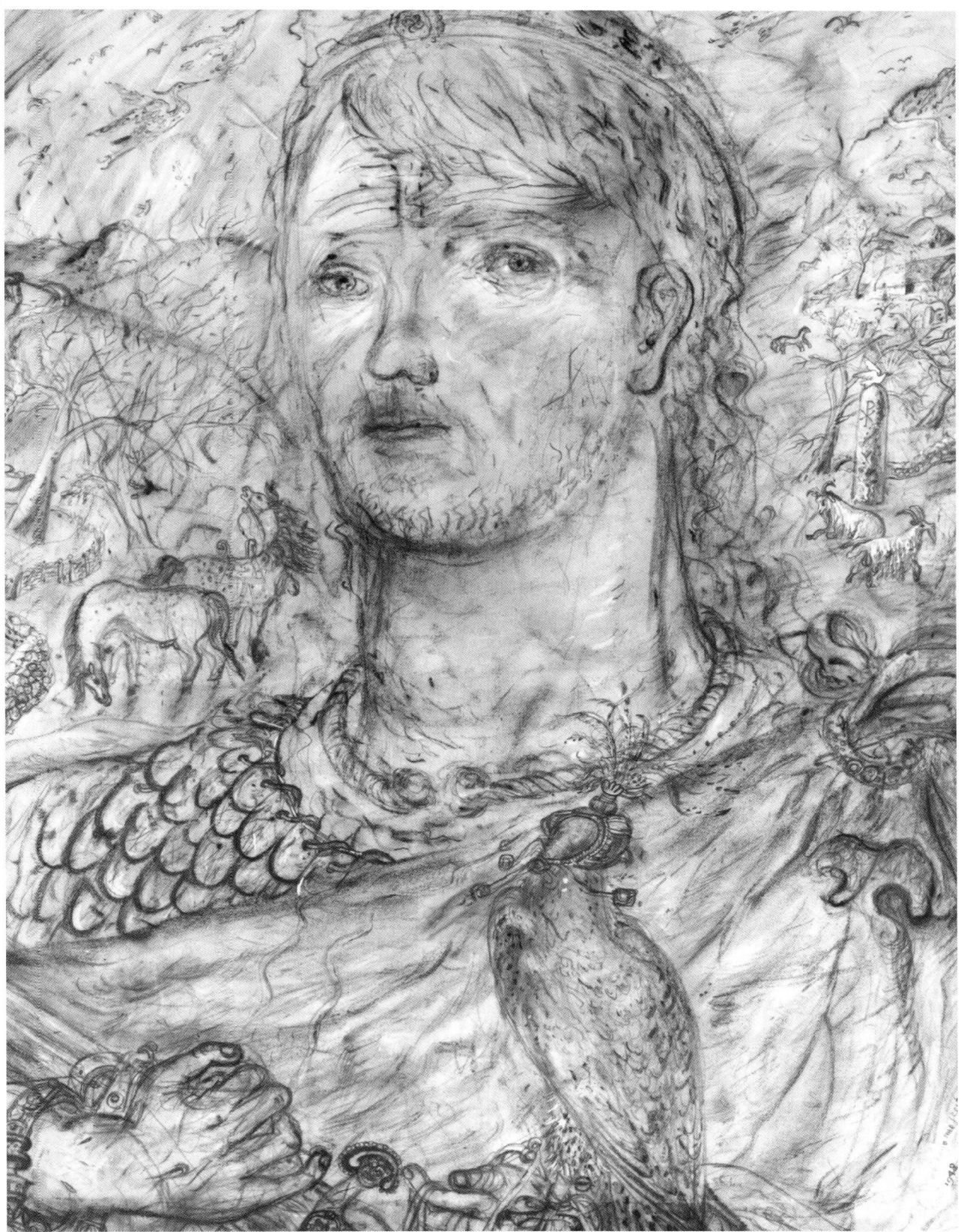

13. Lord of Venedotia, 1948

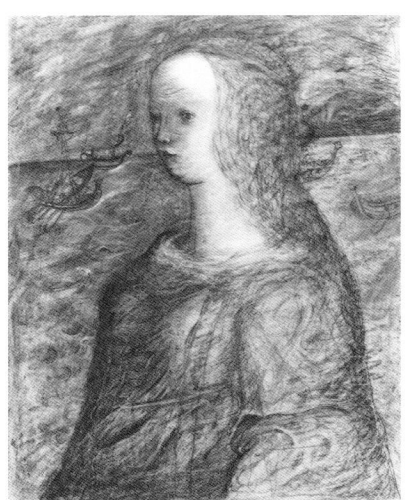

14. A Girl, Sea and Boats
(Princess with Long-Boats), 1949

crayon creates a penumbral, dreamy effect and the stars are not so diagrammatic as they often are in Jones's work. Another source of inspiration would appear to be High Renaissance portraiture for the work is unusually tonal, tending towards *chiaroscuro* and the treatment of the sea is, furthermore, reminiscent of Leonardo's *Deluge*. Just as *The Lord of Venedotia* was osmosed into the landscape, so the breast of the Princess affronts the sea like a great promontory. She has the high forehead familiar from Petra Gill but the flesh has that bone-like whiteness which Jones would use again for the face of Essyllt. Bone and stone reflect the Neo-Romantic association of the body and the land seen in Moore's figures which emerge out of and merge with the rocks and the soil. Jones made two attempts at illustrating the tragic tale of the love of Trystan and Essyllt. Of the two the first, which Jones tore up and had reconstituted, is in an illustrational style reminiscent of Arthur Rackham. The second version, on which Jones worked and worked, has that obsessive finish of the Medieval miniature. While the plunge of the boat deck is infinitely more exciting in the first version, Jones would never have been able to include what he considered to be the necessary detail; in March, 1960, he wrote to Grisewood about this picture:

> I've transferred it now on to another piece of paper - which is a ghastly operation - but I could not do what I wanted with it on the original paper, and I did not want to lose the feeling of it by making endless alterations and adjustments which I wish to make. So there was no alternative but to transfer it … The first one now becomes rather like the *natural scene* and the one I'm working on the actual 'art-work'.[33]

These last words are interesting for they reveal that Jones was searching for an artificiality, an obviously 'made' work; perhaps the best analogy would be something akin to an illuminated manuscript illustration - precise, informative, replete with meaning - a world away from the evanescence of the 1930s watercolours or indeed the earlier version of the painting. In that version, the ship has the roughness of a weathered and buffeted craft. The mast and rigging dramatically constrict the lovers and the second, smaller mast sets up a rhythm within the painting as well as increasing the length of the ship - powerful features lost in the second version. Where the earlier version has a kind of post-Romantic vitality which immediately appeals to the twentieth century eye, the finished picture must be understood not only as being about a mythological subject but as possessing a historical manner of working so that we are left with doubts about the pertinence, the 'nowness' of the painting. Details are researched, not only from a nautical viewpoint but from the art historical; the ship's boat is 'copied' from a 'little vessel in a painting reproduced in a book I have on Fouquet'. As this part of the drawing was considered 'unfinished' by Jones,[34] we can see how far he is from the modern artist's feeling for the incomplete.

Trystan ac Essyllt reworks one of the crucial moments in the love literature of the European tradition in a manner that makes of it an historical curiosity, lacking the sense of urgency we perceive in the best of Jones's writing. Jones himself

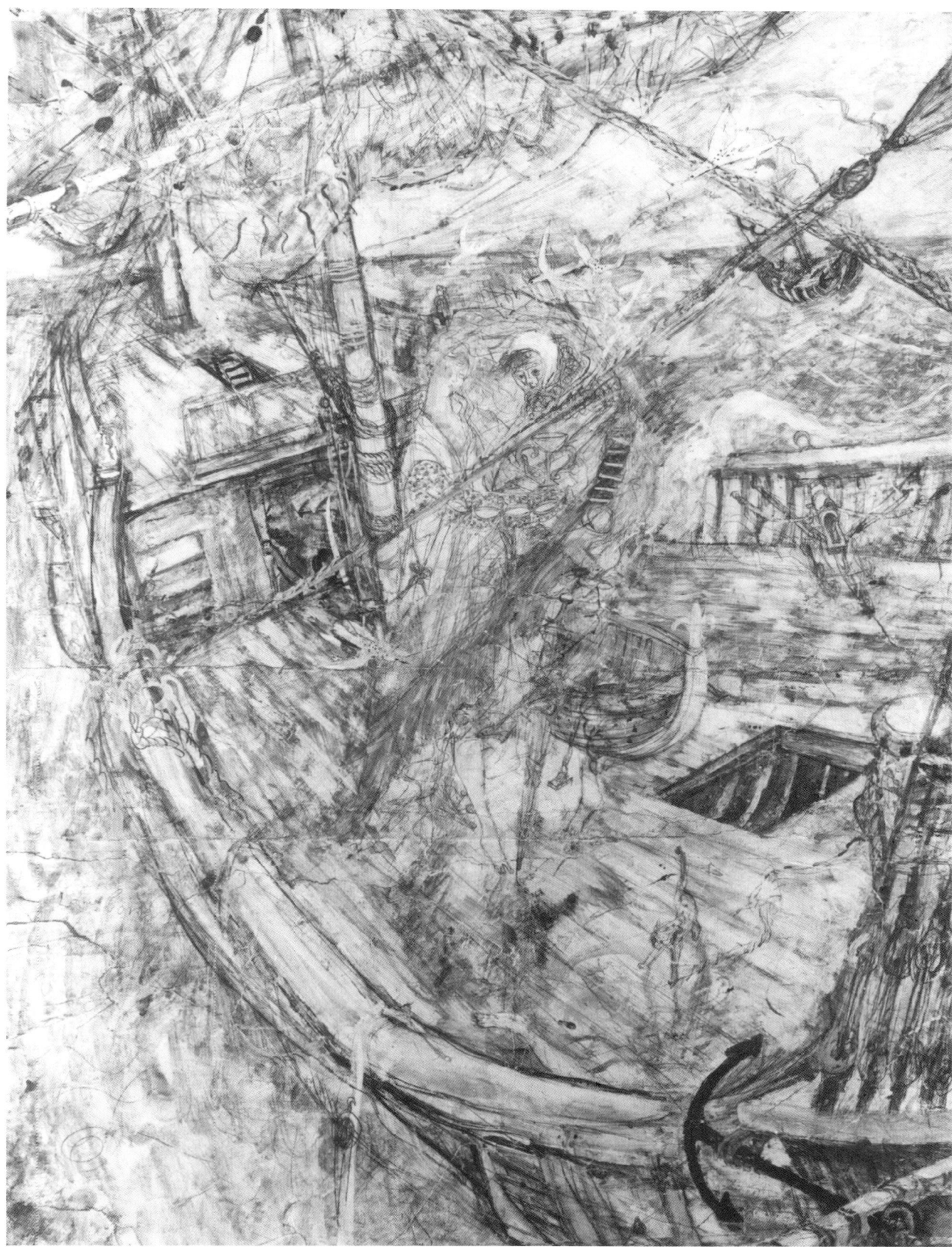

15. Trystan ac Essyllt, 1962

realized that he became overwhelmed by detail and lost the feeling of wholeness achieved in the earlier version: 'it's the hardest thing I've tried to do ... I think it is because I have tried to find out so many things in some detail about the ship and its tackle.'[35] He confessed to René Hague that he couldn't get on with his picture, feeling 'quite exhausted by the complications';[36] writing to Janet Stone he said,

> I can't see how to ... It's a real dilemma of, I suppose, a sort of aesthetic nature - baffled and uncertain. True I am 'depressed' but I don't think it's that, for I'm used to that. It's something more complicated ... But the arts are strange things, *up to a point* one can get things done by sheer application and determination - but only up to a point and I seem to have come onto a patch (a rather prolonged patch) when just trying hard does not seem to work.[37]

Trystan ac Essyllt is, in fact, an achievement that turns deliberately away from contemporary modes both in its searching out of authentic details and in its assiduous itemizing of significant elements. Trystan and Essyllt both have one shoe off, suggestive of their intimacy; even the explicit spurs on the deck were, as Jones wrote to Arthur Giardelli, 'meant merely to indicate somewhat ineffectively that he was but half dressed owing to larking about in the cabin with Essyllt'.[38] The sword between them is both the symbol of their hitherto pure relationship and a phallic proposal close to her raised shift. But while this sword is given almost undue prominence how disappointing is the obfuscation of the fateful chalice lost against the breastplate of Trystan's armour.

Other effects are apt. Because the scale of the lovers is too large for the ship on which they stand, strangely upright against the rake of the deck, it is as if they inhabit another world; the circle created by Essyllt's extended arm, horn-like neck and head is completed by her swirling hair which envelops Trystan in a golden shower of her desire. Trystan has the dismayed and bewildered expression of a victim as he crumbles within the orbit of the fatal attraction. An early sketch with its wild, scribbled drawing, when placed beside the residual work, leaves us in no doubt about the desiccating effect of Jones's late-Faustian antiquarianism. Jones has submerged his desire to render a charged moment beneath a stifling amount of recorded information:

> It is St. Bridget's Day, in the evening. Part of the constellation of the Bear, Arcturus, is seen in juxtaposition to the bear on the pennant flown from the foremast. I didn't put in the stars just because I thought they would look nice: I attempted to place them with the aid of one of those diagrams from a newspaper, showing the position of the stars that month. This might sound rather absurd, but I must have something concrete to go by ... The ship is sailing from Ireland to Cornwall, into a head wind, which is blowing from the south-east ... In the small boat on the left are a couple of Irish wolf-hounds, intended as a present for King Mark - and that was about all he got out of the transaction.[39]

Jones's search for verisimilitude, his painstaking research to include the details of 'something concrete', stands in complete contrast to artists who take purely formal inspiration from observed or researched data. Picasso spoke of his interest

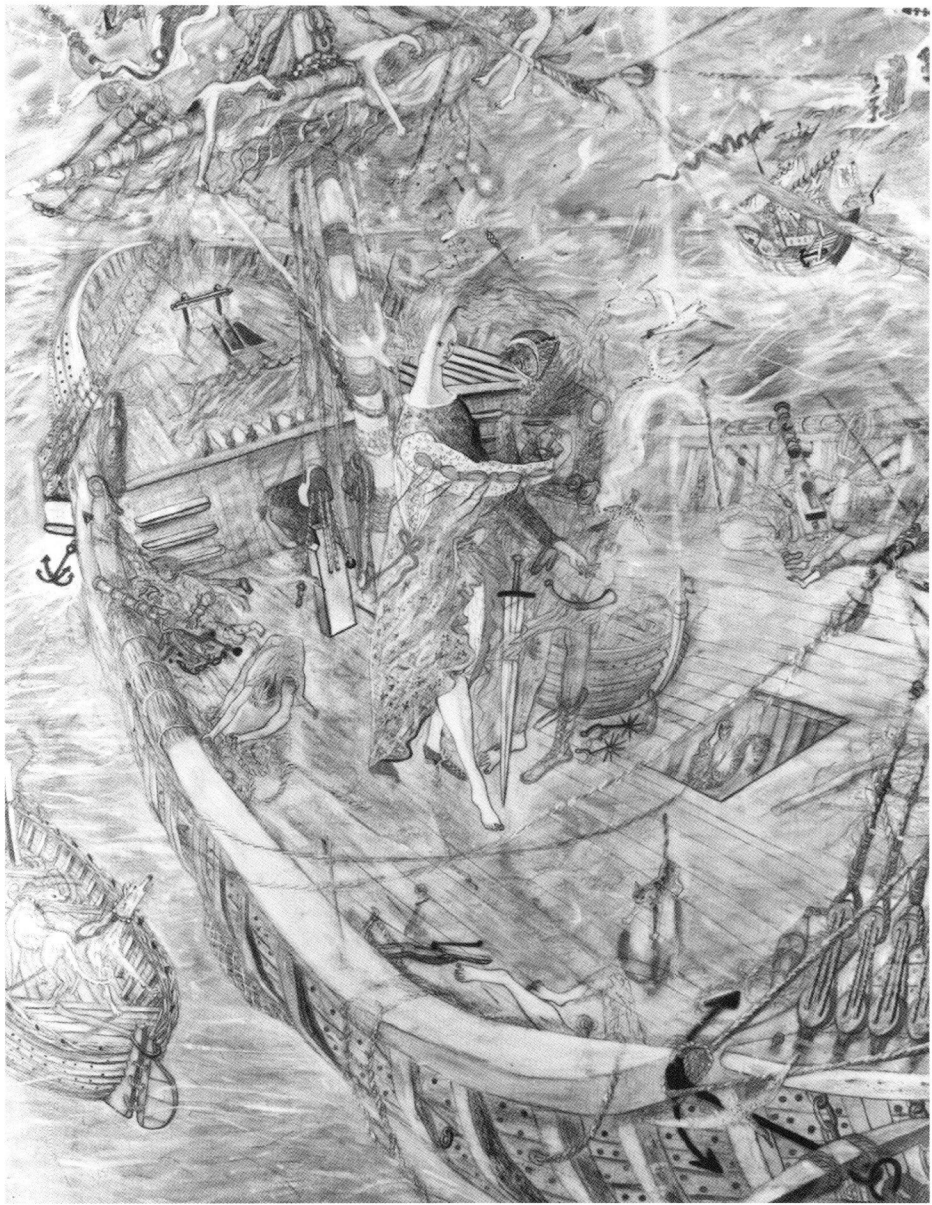

16. Trystan Ac Essyllt, 1962

in astronomical charts, describing how he used them as a point of departure for a new way of drawing by connecting 'a number of points … by lines'.[40] Jones's use of the stars, naming them on a rough sketch, reveals a pedanticism that allows the essence of his picture, as well as formal considerations, to escape; the significant moment of the drama will be lost beneath this 'heap of all that I could find'.[41]

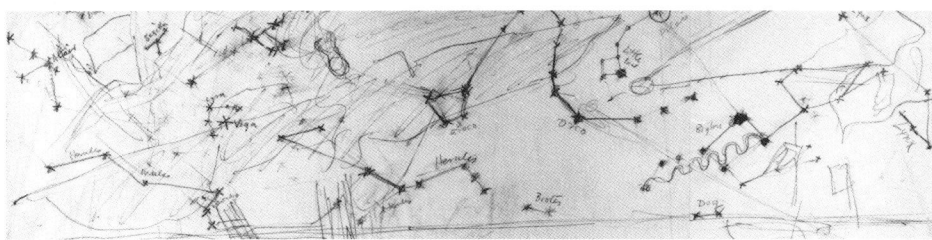

17. Study of Constellations, 1960

225

Jones wrote to Janet Stone, while working on *Trystan ac Essyllt*, contending that

> before I can deal with Tristan and his girl on the main deck of my windswept ship I've got to find out all manner of stuff in some detail - not for accuracy's sake at all - for that doesn't matter a damn - but in order to get the feel of the thing … .[42]

Accordingly, Jones would allow himself to take great liberties, such as drawing the ribs of the vessel outside the horizontal strakes, which he knew very well was absurd but he '*did* want to have them showing'.[43]

The painter, Sarah Balme, watched as Jones worked on *Trystan ac Essyllt* with his tray of pencils in front of him, spiralling into himself, wrapping a curved arm round the hand that was drawing, moving his mouth frantically with concentration. There was a lot of rubbing out, wetting and smudging.[44]

In 1943, Jones had gone to a lantern slide lecture on Blake with his old teacher Hartrick and seeing Blake's watercolours projected meant that a certain 'tightness' which he found disagreeable in the work disappeared when the images were magnified.[45] Such a reaction relates to one of the problems of *Trystan*; it is either too big or too small. It is a *tour de force* that doesn't fit into a twentieth century idea of picture-making but takes us back to the Medieval or Renaissance miniature, to book illustration. To the modern eye the painting is full of the most distractingly relentless detail: the green-hatted 'Tommy' manning the gun, the dancing bear on the pennon in the top right-hand corner, surely a self-quotation from his childhood *Dancing Bear*, the light from above descending and terminating in a *fleur de lys* on the front of the ship's boat - a symbol of the Trinity and a reminder of the rôle of the French Iseult Blanc Manys in the tragic unfolding of the tale - all these obscure the delicacy of some looser drawing and blind the spectator to those elements which point to the drama of the situation such as the wave sweeping over the gunwale, curling in a potent manner like Essyllt's hair. Although the painting appears to be constructed so that the eye roams on a voyage of constant discovery it does not coalesce into the drama of that overwhelming and fateful predicament.

This manner of working over the whole image was not only like the medieval manuscript page but also like the Pre-Raphaelites who gave equal weight to all parts of the picture and all the details of the subject. A continental Symbolist like Moreau, prone to the same obsessive concern with accurate detailing, could often redeem the power of his idea by his theatrical ability to accentuate and dramatize the important elements of his vision. An inability to modulate an image is something that in the past had eluded a good number of English artists; Delacroix observed in their work a tendency towards overemphasis.[46]

Jones marked in his copy of Raymond Lister's *Edward Calvert* the response made by John Giles to Calvert, when the latter observed that an oil sketch was unfinished. 'Yes, sir,' said Giles, 'and I am glad it is not finished - no room to get a thought in edgewise. It's wretched work, sir; they never know when to stop!'[47] Oswald Spengler wrote of the nineteenth century German realist painter, Wilhelm Leibl, that he

> could not bring himself to let his pictures go, and worked over them again and again to such an extent that they became cold and hard. Cézanne and Renoir left work of the best quality unfinished because, strive as they would, they could do no more.[48]

In his copy of Spengler's *The Decline of the West,* Jones marked this passage and wrote 'good' beside it, noting below that 'the "unfinished" Cézanne has a "completion" that is only found in the greatest painting.'

In an unidentified draft, Jones wrote on the subject of Pre-Raphaelitism,

> At bottom I'm pretty sure it has little to do with painting *qua* painting. I mean in the sense that, say, the French Impressionists or Turner or Constable have to do with painting, or for that matter Blake whose drawings however 'literary' ... always compel attention merely as powerful linear forms. The Pre-Raphaelites, very seldom, if ever, give one the feeling that the work is a living contribution to painting or drawing as such ... The truth is that it was so largely a sociological, 'moral', literary, religious or pseudo-religious urge and they never really (as it were) 'transubstantiated' their 'content' under the form of paint ... Anyway I think that in one way or another almost all Pre-Raphaelite painting, for all its great qualities and intense feeling and observation of the appearance of nature lacks vitality in design and lacks a feeling for *Painting* as such. It's never absolutely convincing and free and inevitable as really great painting is ... They are a constant fascination to me for a number of reasons - and the analysis of their goodnesses and badnesses is a most intriguing subject ... .[49]

Jones must have been distressed indeed to perceive a similar effect in his late mythological work. Considering *Gwener* which he painted just before *Trystan ac Essyllt* Jones remarked that 'It is a *bit* pre-Raphaelite and that won't do, for me, in 1959. I have got a bit of pre-Raphaelite lurking in me, and, it ain't no bloody good vis-à-vis painting'.[50]

There was, of course, another important source for Jones's desire that his paintings should contain recessive symbols. It would be apt to recall that in *Art et Scholastique*, Jacques Maritain suggested that the stature of a work of art is in proportion to its powers of signification:

> The more there is of knowledge, or of things presented to the understanding, the vaster will be the possibility of joy; this is why Art, in so far as it is ordered to Beauty, does not, at least when its object permits, stop at forms or at colours ... but it takes them also as making known other things than themselves, that is to say *as signs*. And the thing signified may itself be a sign

in turn, and the more the work of art is laden with significance
… the vaster and the richer and the higher will be the possibility
of joy and beauty.[51]

Jones subscribed wholeheartedly to this Medieval Scholastic idea and yet he entertained a very real intellectual perception of the problems this posed for the twentieth century artist. The kinds of assurance which underpinned the iconographical procedures of Classical, Medieval or International Gothic artists were at odds with post-Romantic subjectivism. Eclecticism was a compelling and individual device, but controlling an array of styles and ideas posed problems for artists. Jones wrote to Cecil Collins:

> We chaps are in a curiously torn-this-way-and-that state with regard to painting - too much divergent stuff impinges on our consciousness - in fact all the art of the world from Classical Greece back to cave-painting and forward to all the hotch-potch of theories of 'now' … I think these eclectic influences are the cause of much trouble to us - but such is the situation and it cannot be avoided - but it does make greater difficulties than the layman realizes … It is difficult to narrow down the problems or outflank them - or discover exactly how to transmute the multifarious influences so that they become an integral part of one's own 'thing'.[52]

What Jones does - and this is what makes much of his work valid - is to upset signification by casting it adrift on a sea of chaos. When he allows his symbols to be modulated by this chaos, when they become unfixed by it, Jones is often at his most successful. When too dogmatic, he is at odds with his age. Jones's later paintings function within the tension between a desire for cultural order and vitality and an acknowledgement of cultural plight and private chaos.

In the mythographical drawings we find a passion for precise denomination, eclecticism and temporal rhyme, yet that important structural characteristic of literary modernism, the hiatus, is largely ignored. What is broken and discontinuous on the printed page seems to become a kind of encyclopaedic continuum in Jones's mythographical drawings and watercolours. This is not altogether disadvantageous as it is a useful way of asserting that the activities of different ages have a contemporaneity which is part of Jones's purpose; the difference embedded in different languages, for example - *onager* (Latin)/ field artillery (English) - is dissolved when the eye perceives the visual and functional similarity between two such engines. Such connections can often be more easily established by showing objects than by naming them although Jones, in his poetry, is ardent in his search for linguistic echoes.

In writing, the search for the exact word is legitimate; there is an implicit precision in words which, when utilized to the full, distinguishes the best poetry and releases meaning and suggestion of more meaning. But to render elements in a painting with a draughtsmanlike verisimilitude is to behave in a contrary manner to the particular expressive potentialities of twentieth-century art. Ezra Pound stated in a broadcast that 'if you are writing a poem which contains history, the history of the poem has to be just as good as the history in a prose work. You can't put in as many details, but the basis has got to be as solid'.[53] Now Jones, and it is a problem with certain passages of his writing as well as certain of the mythological paintings, put in too many details. A comparison between the first attempt at *Trystan ac Essyllt* and the second attempt demonstrates the vitality of the former, its way of letting, as Jackson Knight said of Virgil, 'historical fact "shimmer through"',[54] and the insistent, pedantic nature of the latter.

In the mythological paintings, a sense of the contemporary escapes because that concomitant of the hiatus, the multiple viewpoint, where one voice or vision is interrupted because it cannot sustain its intention, has been ignored. Cubism created a new aesthetic language out of the wish to escape from the single point of view. The multiple viewpoint grew from a desire for a more complete understanding of an object and from an insecurity about the rightness or appropriateness of a single proprietorial viewpoint. Painters saw round and through objects and hiatuses interrupted the forms. While in David Jones's early work there is evidence of some assimilation of the Cubist aesthetic, of the need for hiatus in his thirties watercolours, the spatial ordering of his later mythographical works owes more to a Medieval visual realm; their dominated, fully drawn manner is akin to the confident product of a more coherent or stable phase of culture. There is little doubt in the drawing. Ambiguity is not permitted because the intellect is over-determined by the message that it wishes to propound. When any single element carries a multiple significance it usually does so within the confines of an accepted tradition. Only occasionally, in the best works, do the symbols strain against iconographic norms and register something immediate, disturbing and personal.

The idea behind many of these works is that their venerated system of signs and stories is under threat. This is the intellectual proposition that supports the paintings but no adequate visual language has been found that is able to embrace the magnitude of the idea. The setting is usually stressed and stricken yet the iconographic elements bleat out their old messages. There is hardly ever, as in, say, the first few pages of *The Anathemata*, a formal realization of the 'precarious' nature of the 'civilizational' situation. Only when the cataloguing of the significant elements is embraced by a grandly metaphoric visual conception such as in *Vexilla Regis* or *Aphrodite in Aulis* does a compelling image overpower the intellectualism of the dominating idea. *Vexilla Regis* is primarily a landscape and one with a depth of mood that is rare in later Jones; it also creates a metaphor for the crucifixion and is not a litter of symbols merely illustrating and embroidering the story. This is, as we have seen, even more true of a work such as *Flora in Calix Light*.

By comparison, pictures such as *The Mother of the West* and particularly *The Paschal Lamb*, are hideously overdrawn catalogues of classical and Christian deposits. *The Paschal Lamb* was admittedly envisaged as an illustration for *The Anathemata* but it resembles, in its method, other works of the same period conceived purely as independent visual entities. Considering an earlier painting such as *Curtained Outlook* of 1932 (see p 251), the sense of fragility and latent terror is so much more expressive of 'the ship-wreck of the world in general'[55] than the explicit, and in some ways trivial, foreground of *The Paschal Lamb* (see p 238). On the table in one of Jones's vast, washy, early 1930s still lifes the significance of the chosen elements of cup, dish and fruit are apparent but not intrusive. In the cluttered mythographical works the exhausting itemization of cultural signifiers sinks the intention that stands behind the procedure beneath the weight of research and scholarship. Unlike much of Jones's poetry these paintings seem curiously prosaic, they appear to have little *rapport* with our time. They are presented to us as being important - but why? The obsession for meticulous detail is perhaps being used to try to hide rather than to reveal: the spectator is only allowed to know what the painter feels in the most general terms such as wonder at the Annunciation in *Y Cyfarchiad I Fair* or regret in *The Mother of the West* and Edward Hopper has wisely stated that any digression in painting from the revelation of emotion 'leads … to boredom'.

In the twentieth century, narrative became more problematic in painting and artists tended to move away from the telling of stories. David Jones's particular manner of presenting his narrative, often the elaboration of a single idea through many incidental units, falls short of success because it is out of step with the language of twentieth century art. In their over-elaborated explicitness the later works seem to lack the mysterious incompleteness that is the hallmark of much of the best of twentieth century painting. They are so at odds with the contemporary language of visual art that they appear a little quaint where they should, by virtue of their subject matter, devastate. If Jones had criticized the Arthurian poetry of Charles Williams because, 'Somehow, somewhere, between content and form, concept and image, sign and what is signified, a sense of the contemporary escapes'[56] then he himself must stand, in respect of his mythographical drawings, so accused.

Twentieth century music, literature and painting have all accepted the hiatus because a too complete and monocular rendering of anything could only be an act of authorial arrogance in an age of relativity and continued self-questioning. Osip Mandelstam wrote in *The Noise of Time* that 'Where for happy generations the epic speaks in hexameters and chronicles I have merely the sign of the hiatus'.[57] Now in Jones's poetry not only the broken lines, the abrupt changes of time and locality but even the larger form itself, 'fragments of an attempted writing', acknowledge the hiatus. Jones's honest inability to make things cohere - the experience also of Ezra Pound - meant that there is breakage, the formal expression of the civilizational predicament. The continuity of the systems with which the West had constructed itself, validated itself and explained itself was found to be breaking up so that there was a necessary embedding of difficulty and discontinuity in modernist works. Readers were asked to persevere. They learnt to negotiate the hiatuses, fill in the ellipses, so that in a broken and discontinuous text the reader pieced together, out of a sequence of glimpses, a new, allusive, but ultimately incoherent whole.

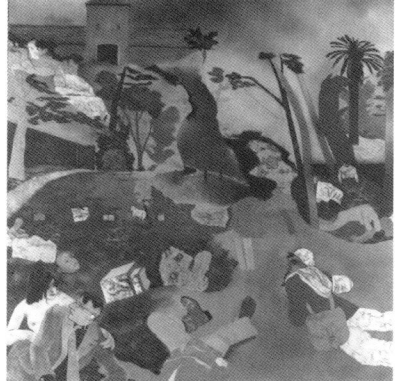

18. R.B. Kitaj, If Not, Not, 1975-6

A narrative painting, because it usually shows a moment lifted from a story, asks the spectator to add meaning to the moment chosen by filling in a before and after. During this century, spectators have been exposed to painting that has no before or after, to an artefact that is, in itself, the sum total of its expressive capacities. No external symbolic or literary significance stands behind the marks on many twentieth century canvases so that works with too much narrative, too much meaning, seem immediately odd. The transportation of Jones's poetic vision into the realm of painting led to problems and anachronisms. His style was at odds with the situation in which the abstract mark had become potent and paradoxically significant in our sign-littered world. Yet there have been artists in the second half of the century such as Rauschenberg, Rivers and Kitaj *(18)* who have reconciled modernist conceptions of narrative with contemporary modes of picture making. Painterliness decomposes the specific within their images, but tangible strands of recognizable elements carrying the story or message remain visible.

Jones's work is packed with cultural debris and, according to the Spenglerian prognosis of the decline of the West, is therefore very much about the contemporary situation. The pressure of this idea even breaks into an apparently trite watercolour and drawing of a somewhat ephemeral subject, English people about their business and pleasure on a windy day at the seaside. The edge of a building seen at the extreme right of *Promenading at Sidmouth* with its many fissures and its gull at the top, significantly spread-eagled, at once puts us in mind, in the context of Jones's *oeuvre*, of a ruined classical column and the Roman eagle. Jones insists on the presence of the past. Christopher Dawson who was 'one of the people,' Jones wrote, 'to whom I am very greatly indebted'[58] reflected the Spenglerian perception of the period in his book, *The Modern Dilemma*:

> Modern Europe stands today very much in the same position as
> that of the Roman Empire in the first century B.C. Like Rome it
> has conquered and organized the world ... But its work, like that
> of Rome, has been vitiated by its lack of spiritual purpose and by
> a selfishness and economic exploitation.[59]

In *Epoch and Artist,* Jones noted that 'Spengler had very special insight into the cyclic character of the periods of decline, and certainly the trend, as far as we can see, of the contemporary world, verifies a number of his conclusions'.[60] 'Culture' was a process of becoming but 'civilization' has become; Spengler notes that '*Pure* Civilization as a historical process' consists of 'a progressive *taking-down* of forms that have become inorganic or dead'.[61] So Jones uses imagery from Roman times to express aspects of the hard, modern, factual world and turns to the decline of Rome or to the post-Roman period to mirror the decline of Britain's empire. By contrast he associates the Celtic world with a society of creative potential and sees, in the peripheral aspect (from a Roman point of view) of that society, an apt imaginative setting for the great event that happened at the other extremity of the then known world, the birth of the Christian God (*Y Cyfarchiad I Fair*). The relation of Roman agencies of communication to the dissemination of

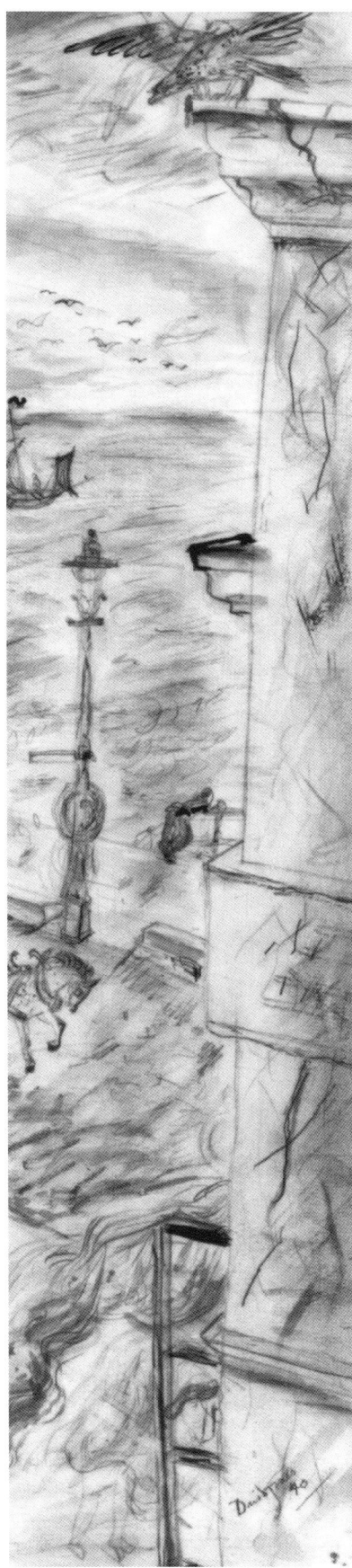

19. Promenading at Sidmouth (detail), 1940

231

that obscure, peripheral cult is one of Jones's most frequent preoccupations (*Vexilla Regis*, *The Paschal Lamb*).

Such a notion of contemporaneity entertains a vision of history that is shared by literary modernism's tendency to de-historicize time by juxtaposing elements from different epochs. If events are contemporaneous, if a pattern of culture is inevitable, then a person escapes, through the idea of simultaneity, from the burden of history, from causal responsibility. The ritualistic cadences and hieratic modes of poets like Eliot, Pound and Jones suggest that the transhistorical habit has affinities with ritual which takes place both inside and outside of time.

While Jones feels forced to admit the veracity of Spengler's contentions, he tries in his poetry, by eclectic juxtaposition and formal innovation, to give a new vitality to ideas, symbols and stories and contradict Spengler's contention that for late Western, or 'Faustian' man, 'nothing remains but the mere pressure, the passionate yearning to create, the form without the content'. Jones laments but attempts to salvage and celebrate. Jones's task is difficult; he stands, as the Priest he describes at the beginning of *The Anathemata*, alone in the waste land where

> dead symbols
> litter to the base of the cult-stone.[62]

A passionate inclination to make works of art and a vision of cultural desiccation gave rise to neurosis and Jones had an acute sense of how he fitted into the Spenglerian analysis:

> Perhaps, *in a sort of way*, I'm more in the position of a Gaul after some centuries of Romano-Hellenistic 'naturalism' had largely obscured the native Celtic thing ... And aside from the 'academic' training I tend to a sort of 'naturalism' - I mean not 'Abstract' with a cap. 'A'. Whereas that 'Celtic' art is fundamentally, utterly ... an 'abstract' art in the most pronounced sense.[63]

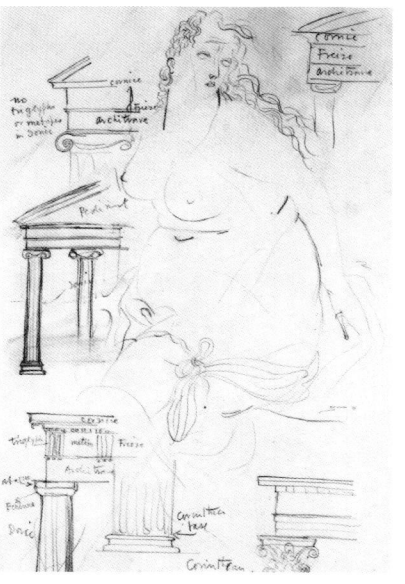

20. Sketches for Aphrodite, 1938-40

Both *Aphrodite in Aulis* and *The Mother of the West* were made in the early years of the Second World War at a time when Jones was deep in his reading of Spengler, so it is hardly surprising that both combat and ideas about contemporaneity were very much on his mind. *Aphrodite* has a largeness which derives from its symmetrical composition around a strong central axis. The distance is helpfully sectioned by the columns which mark different orders of architecture and by Aphrodite herself. So full of organizational felicities is the drawing that although Jones has included a plethora of elements, it does not seem overcrowded. So strong is the composition that the weaknesses, instances of slight or mannered drawing, do not seriously compromise its overall effect. The figure with his helmet outstretched, for all his strength as part of the composition, is, in himself, flimsy, and, like the horses or the birds and the god's eyes or even Aphrodite's face, seems to belong to a more lightweight and fanciful strain of English Neo-Romanticism. The plume of the helmet of the horseman bidding farewell and its relation to the twisted

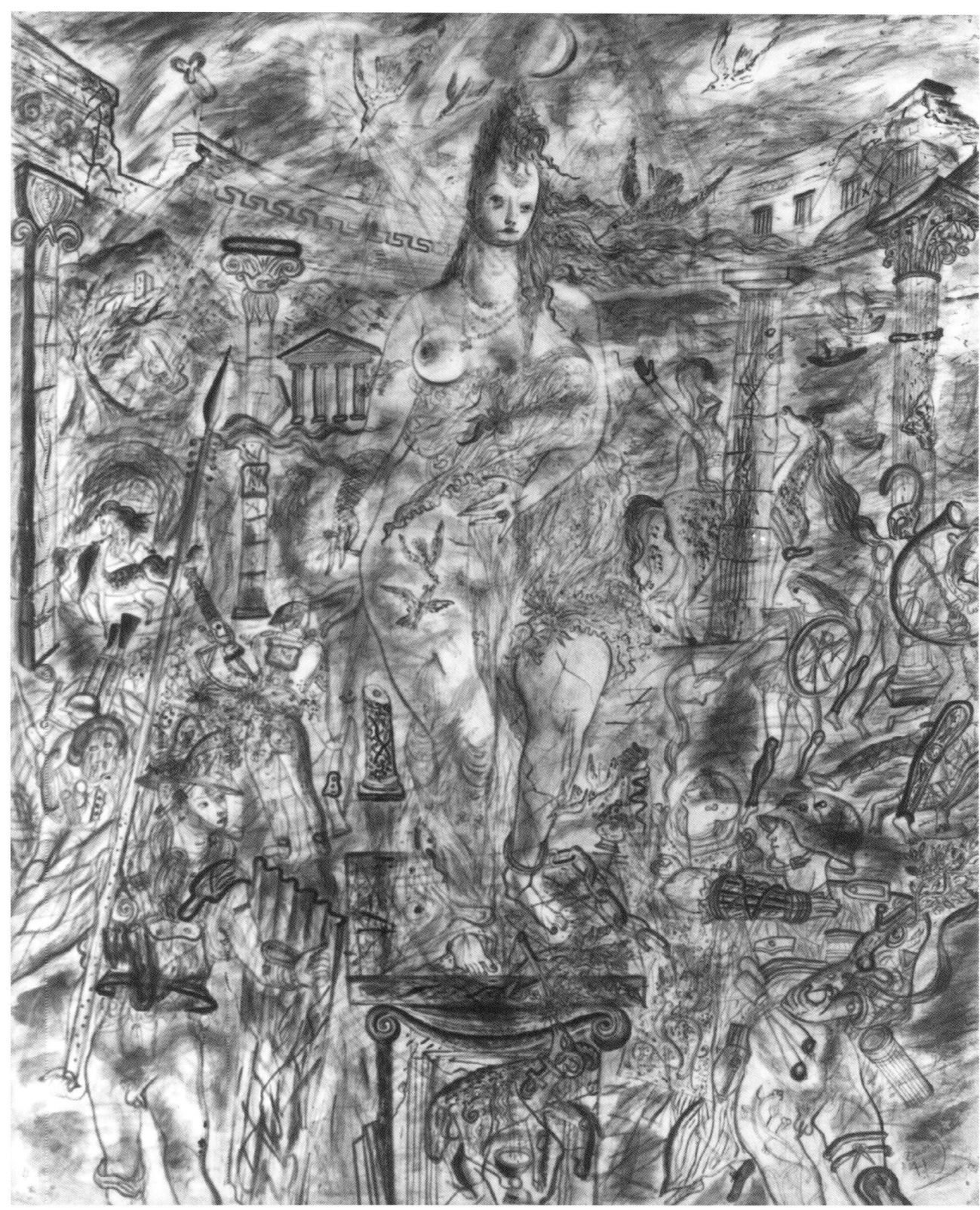

21. Aphrodite in Aulis, 1941

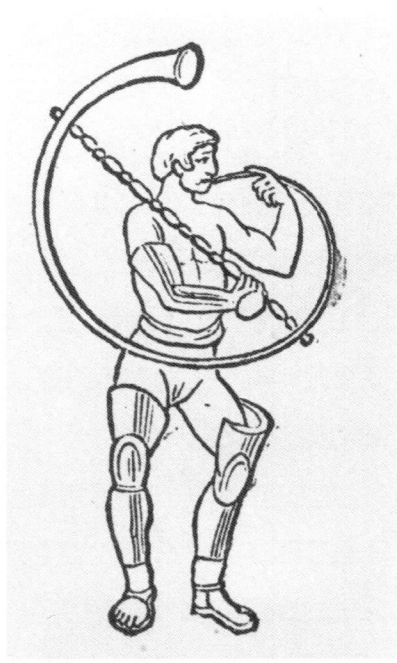

22. Anon., Bucinator from Seyffert's Classical Dictionary, 1894

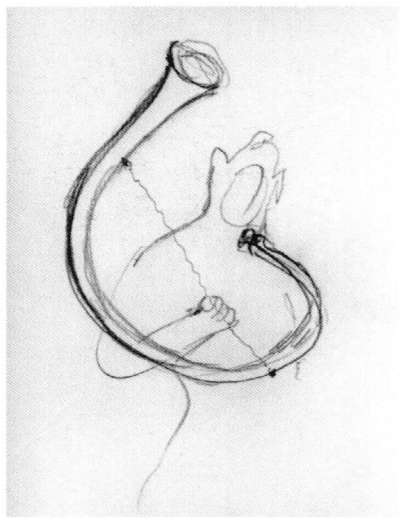

23. Sketch of a Bucinator, 1941

horse's head, the two split by the Doric column, are expressive of the dislocation of farewell. The eye is led down this horse's mane to the helmet of the soldier in front of the Corinthian column and that helmet is strongly mirrored by the *bucina*, the shape of which Jones found in Seyffert's *Dictionary of Classical Antiquities*.[64]

Clearly, the figure of Aphrodite, part statue, part woman, on a plinth yet chained, wicked yet innocent, voluptuous yet coy is a mother of the West. She is venerated by these men but she has also given birth to them, had sex with them and has been wounded by them. Jones wrote to René Hague that

> My intention in changing Iphigeneia to Aphrodite in the title was to include *all* female cult-figures, as I have written somewhere the figure is all goddesses rolled into one - wounded of necessity as are all things worthy of our worship - she's mother-figure and *virgo inter virgines* - the pierced woman and mother and all her foretypes.[65]

In other words, she is the summation of the male view of woman in Western tradition and she is circumscribed by the fears and fantasies that have determined woman as conceived by and for men. By placing a reductive conception that subsists on archetypes or clichés on a plinth, Jones reveals the goddess as a repository for anxieties and desires.

The triple grouping with the soldier carrying a spear like that of Longinus puts us in mind of the crucifixion and the lamb that bleeds into the chalice on the plinth on which Aphrodite stands suggests that this is intentional. Iphigeneia was sacrificed to Artemis by her father Agamemnon in order that the becalmed Greek ships might, when the goddess was propitiated, sail for Troy. The fact that the mounted horseman, perhaps Agamemnon himself, bids farewell suggests that the sacrifice has already taken place. The fact that a priest censes the plinth brings to mind the passage in de la Taille which Jones believed shed 'a sort of reflected radiance upon the sign-world in general',[66] the passage that demonstrated the relationship between offering (Mass) and sacrifice (crucifixion): 'Christ having put himself SYMBOLICALLY in the state of Victim, pledges to God for us that Death with whose sacramental signs he clothes himself … behold, already here at the Supper, the sacrifice of Calvary.'[67] In *Aphrodite in Aulis*, Jones brings together symbolical and actual immolation and it is interesting that he considered using it as an illustration for *The Anathemata*,[68] the poem which grew from 'thoughts in the time of the Mass'.

Aphrodite is a statue that the painter wants to bring to life - her cracked stone limbs grow into voluptuous real flesh. In Ovid, it is Aphrodite to whom Pygmalion prays, asking for a wife like the statue that he himself has created:

> When Pygmalion saw these women [the Propoetides, the first to prostitute themselves in public], living such wicked lives, he was revolted by the many faults which nature has implanted in the female sex, and long lived a bachelor existence, without any wife to share his home. But meanwhile, with marvellous artistry,

234

he skillfully carved a snowy ivory statue … Pygmalion gazed in
wonder, and in his heart there rose a passionate love for this
image of a human form … Sometimes he addressed it in flattering
speeches …

As Jones often does in his poetry and prose.

He dressed the limbs of his statue in women's robes and put
rings on its fingers, long necklaces round its neck.

The kind of adornments gracing countless women that Jones drew, apparently as a kind of therapy, from the late 1940s to the 1960s.

Pygmalion, having made his offering, stood by the altar and
timidly prayed saying, 'If you gods can give all things, may I have
as my wife, I pray' - he did not dare to say: 'the ivory maiden'
but finished 'one like the ivory maid'.[69]

Aphrodite in Aulis, with its vision of woman as both maimed and venerated
suggests the source of the poet and painter's sexual distress. Women so
defined, so symbolized could only be adored, abhorred or forgiven, they
could hardly be lived with as a partner.

Jones adapts the story of Ilia giving suck to Romulus and Remus, showing his
she-wolf, *The Mother of the West (25)*, nourishing a wounded *Agnus Dei*. Rome
is presented as responsible for the crucifixion of Christ (hence the Paschal
candle in the right forepaw) and the agency which facilitated Christianity's
growth (giving suck to). Around this relationship between Rome and Christianity lies the machinery of war and the wreckage of religion. To the left of
the wolf's head, a priest falls stricken by an arrow and behind him stands a
ruined chapel recalling, perhaps, the ruin in which Jones as an infantryman
on the Western Front, first witnessed the Mass. The scene appears to be an
outpost of an assailed Roman Empire, hence, according to the Spenglerian
scheme, contemporaneous with Jones's own time, and the landscape also is
suggestive of the Western Front. But the potent contemporaneous link,
positing the similarity of wooden siege engines and field artillery, is contrived
explicitly, in a diagrammatic manner; the drawing demonstrates a knowledge
of how such engines work but does not express what such machines can do;
they appear like *maquettes* or accurate toys. In *The Mother of the West* the
elements surrounding the animals are too many and too small, compromising
the largeness and grandeur demanded by the theme. It is original in its
concept but unsuccessful in its form. There is repetition and stubborn
insistence. There is a veritable military museum of siege engines and there
are more stigmata than in the most overdecorated church's collection of
'repository art'. The idea, to celebrate the darker side of Western tradition,
a complicated history of conquest that made possible the spread of
Christianity, is somehow lost. Indeed, is that the idea of the painting? For
with such a clutter of detail we are not allowed to discover the painter's
feelings about the complexity of this relationship. Does war make a mockery
of religion? Does religion redeem war? Are both elements merely facts in the

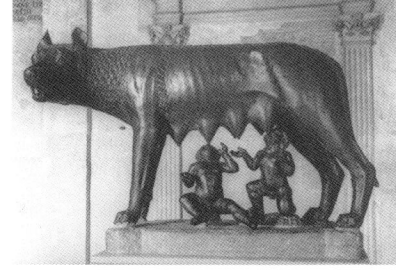

24. Anon., Bronze She-Wolf, (?)

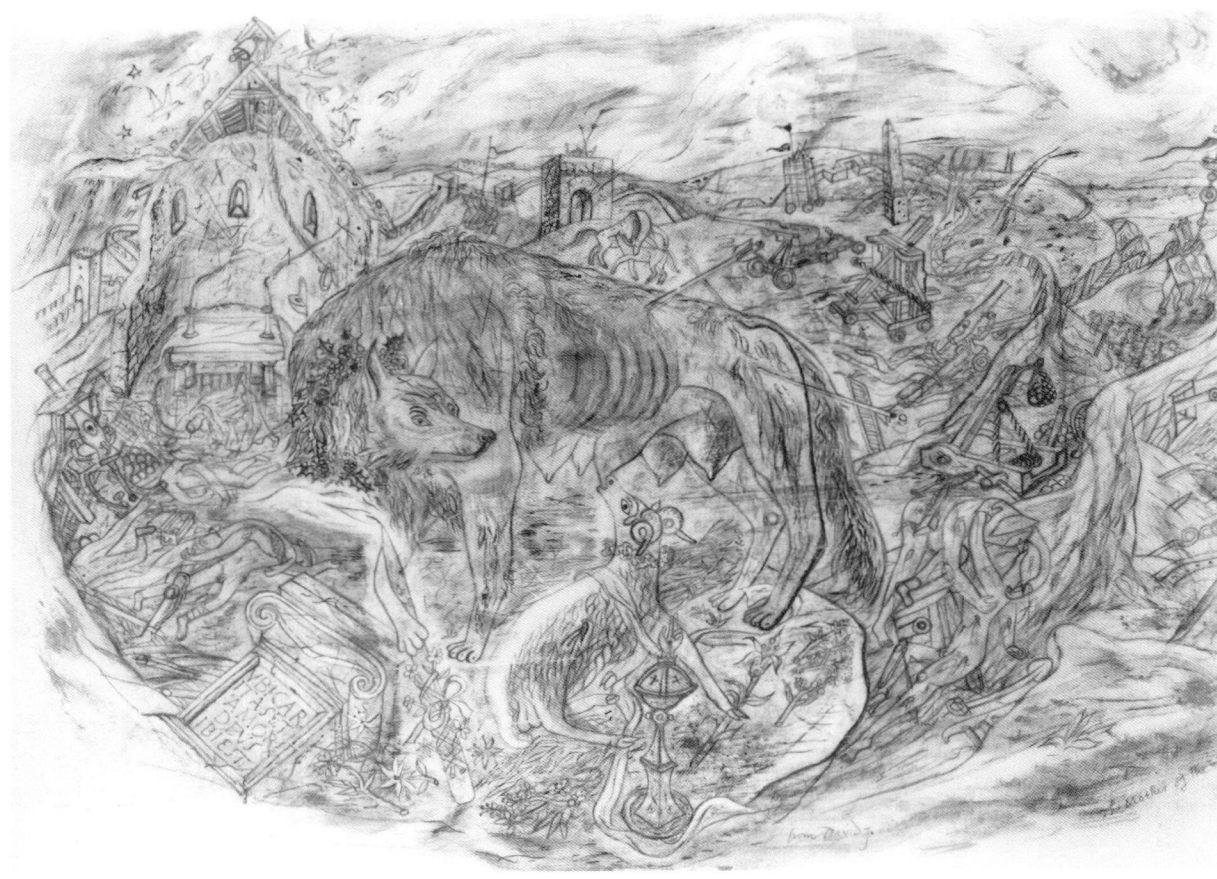

25. The Mother of the West, 1942

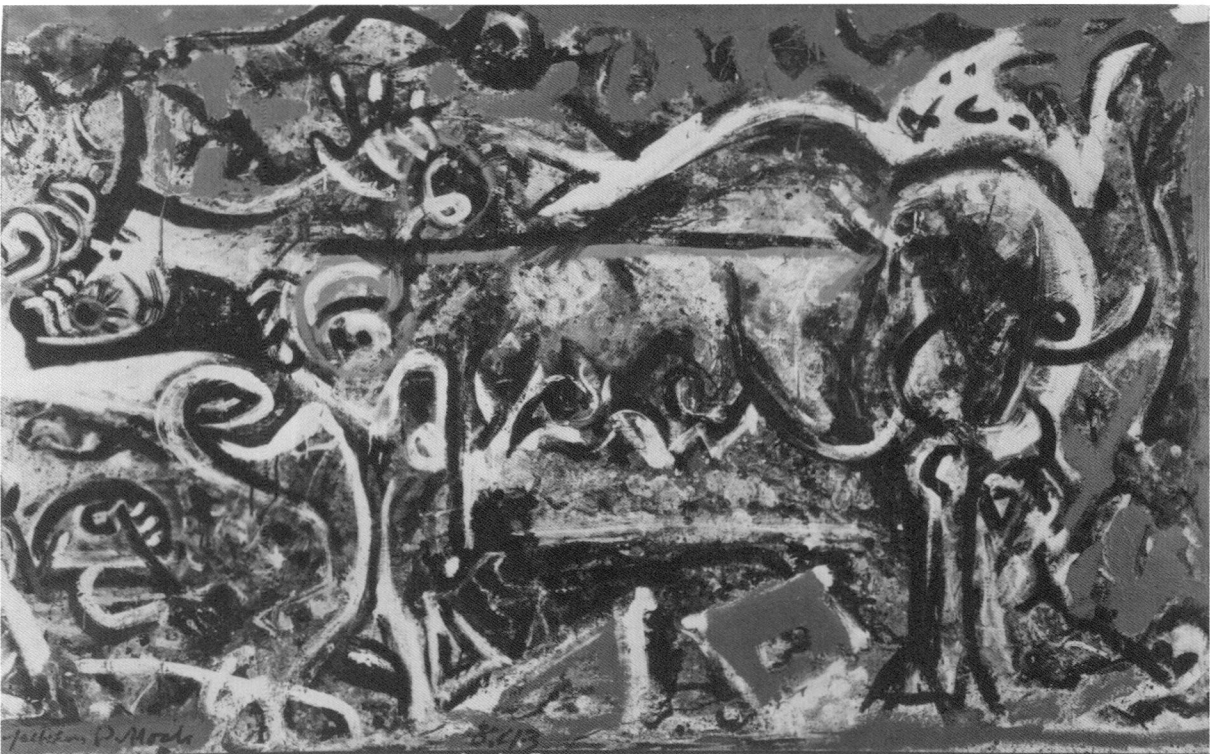

26. Jackson Pollock, The She-Wolf, 1943

chaos of an incomprehensible world? And if that is true, why do the wolf and the ram, not among Jones's best animal drawings, pictorially compromise, with their size and iconographic stolidity, the sense of turmoil in the panorama beyond? *The Mother of the West*, like many works of this period, asserts the burden of the past, but is it not an earlier version of the theme *(27)* in which we see a wolf, suddenly distracted in mid-step, against a wild, fraught landscape more suggestive of civilizational break-up? The wolf is prowling in an 'after-time' in which scattered civilizational remains are neglected in an unpopulated wilderness. It is a time of change, suggested pictorially by the fact that it is, equivocally, dawn or dusk (and hence a Viconian or Spenglerian phase of transition between one stage of culture and another). This earlier version is a looser, more poignant work because of the absence of explicit and overworked Christian iconography and because of a lack of distracting detail. A related sketch (see p 93) is likewise a powerful and chilling expression that no more than hints at the idea. Jones wrote to Mary Gill about the final version of the work with the frequently expressed opinion that 'it did not really come off'.[70]

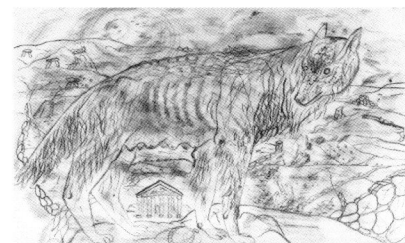

27. Sketch for Mother of the West, 1941

By coincidence, a more painterly, more ambiguous, more potent and semi-abstract treatment of a mythopoeic wolf was made in 1943, about the same time as Jones's watercolour and drawing, by Jackson Pollock. Lacking overt information, Pollock's work suggestively recreates through its medium some of the emotions evoked by the title, *The She-Wolf (26)*. It is an ambiguous, dangerous and yet venerated beast which pictorially embraces both Lascaux and the present day. It is a subject 'under the form of paint' whereas Jones's work is an intellectual itemization of a complex idea, instructional rather than emotive. There is the feeling that the research involved in making Jones's drawing has been used to distract the artist from posing difficult questions. The many elements function like doodles which alleviate distress but which are never scrutinized for their hidden and deeper meaning.

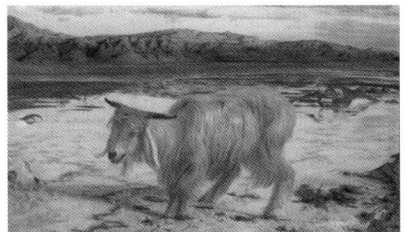

28. William Holman Hunt, The Scapegoat, 1854

In *The Victim,* which was the tailpiece to *In Parenthesis,* a poem in which the soldiers are viewed, in part, as scape-beasts whose function was to carry the sins of the community beyond its limits, Jones presents the *Agnus Dei* pierced by the spear which pierced Christ's side.[71] On a rather more productive visit to the Holy Land than Jones's, Holman Hunt painted his *Scapegoat (28)* in the salt marsh at the appropriately named Oosdoom, on the banks of the Dead Sea. There were two models for the painting as the first goat which Hunt purchased died, doubtlessly carrying off the sins of the tribe.[72] Hunt's painting presents a haunting image by heightened realism. Jones's image falls mid way between the symbolic and the real. The less gainly animal in a preparatory sketch is more expressive than the finished drawing, but it lacks the potency of a related modern vision of the misadventure of western civilization, Robert Rauschenberg's *Monogram (30)*, an absurd ecological victim, a natural being encircled and constricted by the man-made. The blatant contrast of the textures of tyre and animal hair and the arresting juxtaposition of two unassociated realms make of an idea a strong visual statement.

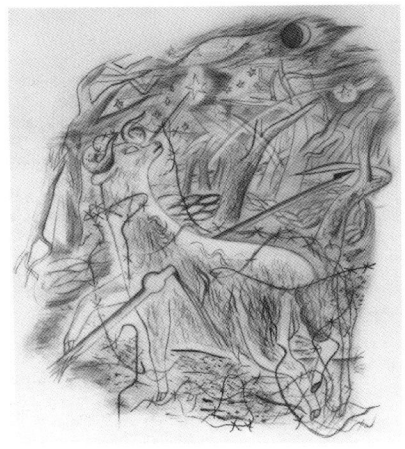

29. Sketch for The Victim, 1937

Even in the aspect of Pop Art which is celebration rather than satire the idea of decline is implicit; the principles that stand behind the cult-objects or

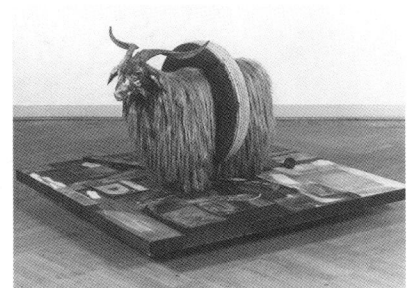

30. Robert Rauschenberg, Monogram, 1959

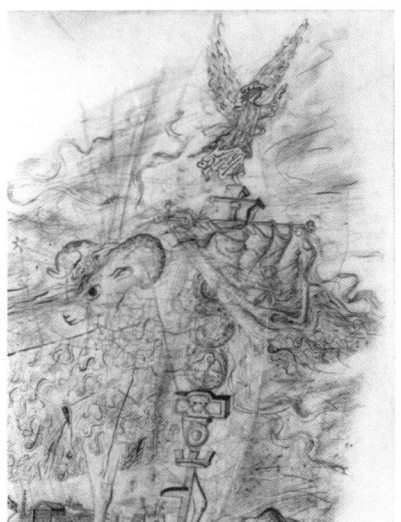

31. The Paschal Lamb (detail), 1951

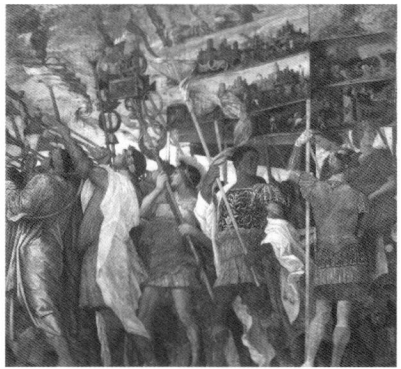

32. Andrea Mantegna, Triumphs of Caesar (detail), 1490

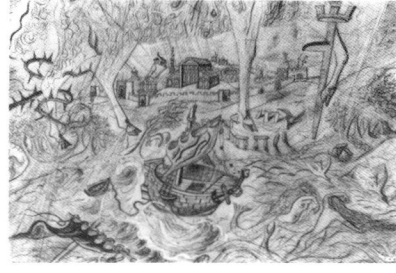

33. The Paschal Lamb (detail), 1951

personages selected for celebration in earlier phases of Western culture are more recessive than the bland and superficial icons of Pop. While Pop artists inhabited a wasteland of Coke bottles and Lucky Strike, and the Abstract Expressionists jettisoned subjects in order to return to a primitive vitality, Jones clung desperately to what he believed was the important residue of his culture. Over and above his perception of civilizational break-up, Jones continued to express his belief in Christianity. But as we have observed, the tension between a sense of civilizational failure and the persistence of Christian belief appears insupportable and we are frequently left with a somewhat mawkish celebration of the procedures or iconography of religion.

The Paschal Lamb is intended to be a celebration but its overall effect is that of stress and ruin. Jones writes about the painting, with its potential title of *Agnus Triumphalis*, in a way that reveals the full obsession of his historical, encyclopaedic mind:

> The standard the Lamb carries is that of the Legio of the XX Victrix ... The Urbs is seen from the North-West. The big building is meant to stand for the Lateran and the Gates along the wall from left to right are Porta Appia, P. Latina, P. Metrovia, Porta Asimaria, P. Praenestina, P. Tiburtina and then at the extreme right the Castra Praetoria. And the hills from left to right are Aventine, then high up, Capitoline, then Palatine, then (to the right of the roof of the Lateran), Quirinal, Viminal and Esquiline ... I know I consulted various maps and things, but may have got it wrong ... the Lamb has his right fore-foot in the centre of a megalithic circle and is meant to appear to be step-ping with care so as not to trample down the older cults and pieties. The storm tossed barque - well - that's suggestive of all sorts of things - the argosy of man the barque of the church (looks a bit empty I admit!) - the mermaids - sirens etc. the wild hills (no doubt with Wales in mind!) - anyway representing the orbis outside the urbs... .[73]

In the drawing, there is a crazed itemizing of each detail to fulfil the obsessive conception. The detailing of the *vexilla* recalls the attention paid to historical detail in Mantegna's *The Triumphs of Caesar (32)* of the 1490s which reflected the delight in the rediscovery of the splendours of the classical world; Jones's distressed visions rather express panic and pedantic antiquarianism.

A good example of how such an over-determined interest in historical veri-similitude can vitiate a painter's work would be to make a comparison bet-ween an early and late painting by Jacques-Louis David. *The Oath of the Horatii* with its restrained and apt interest in archeology provides a telling expression of Republican virtues. A later painting like *Leonidas at Thermopylae*, a litter of classical allusion without any big or deeply felt idea, is merely kitsch. A work by David's contemporary, Anne-Louis Girodet de Roucy-Trioson, the apocalyptic *Les ombres des héros français reçues par Ossian dans l'Elysée aérien (34)*, a satiric replica of a painting commissioned for the *Salon Doré* at Malmaison, in which the soldiers of Bonaparte are welcomed not to heaven any more but to hell, resembles Jones's eclectic cultural panic. In its swirl of myth and military it looks back to Rubens and anticipates David Jones.

Reginald Savage, Jones's Camberwell teacher, was stylistically indebted to early pen drawings by Rossetti and Burne-Jones but his ultimate source of inspiration was Dürer.[74] This example was passed on to Jones and it manifests itself in *Y Cyfarchiad I Fair* or *The Annunciation in a Welsh Hill-Setting* which was the last large drawing that Jones made and one which Stravinsky wanted to buy when he visited Jones in Harrow. It clearly lacks modernity and a sympathetic response is more likely if we consider it in an earlier historical context; indeed, it shares much in common with the world of Dürer. For all its detail, this large, delicate drawing on cream paper does not appear cluttered but rather seems to expand.

The distorted scale of *Y Cyfarchiad I Fair (36)* gives to the figure of Mary a monumentality; the smallness of her hands and feet throw her head into greater prominence. The thoughtful repose of her face contrasts with the animation of the surrounding landscape. In the fleet, slender figure of Gabriel there is an echo of Botticelli. Both figures stand within what has been called a '*hortus conclusus*'[75] and what Jones would more probably have thought of as a *bangor*, a wattled enclosure which for the medieval Welsh marked out an area of religious significance. Kenneth Clark notes that this particular *bangor* was seen and drawn by Jones when he was with Gill at Capel-y-ffin about thirty-five years before he made this painting. Gabriel and Mary are situated beneath the constellations of Jupiter (the Roman equivalent of the Godhead), Libra (Justice) and Virgo (the Virgin). From Jupiter descends a light beam which terminates on the sword blade in a white disc of light reminiscent of the wafer of communion and thereby suggesting transubstantiation in the moment of Annunciation. Another god's eye descends from Jupiter to the Roman wolf which seems part wolf, part domestic dog.

The imagery surrounding the Virgin is drawn from the world of *The Mabinogion* and that co-exists with classical elements as Arthur Giardelli has shown; Mary

> is a Welsh girl … She is also Eve, the mother of all living, for she still holds the apple whose eating brought us to the knowledge of good and evil. Beside her on the fence sits the owl, for she is also Minerva … Rhiannon may originally have meant Great Queen. We are told that the singing birds of Rhiannon, who here surround her on the wing or sit perched on the wattled fence, would bring sleep to the living and awaken the dead.[76]

There is also in the figure, something of Olwen in whose wake white flowers spring up[77] for there are white flowers on the ground whose naïve conception takes us back to Jones's childhood. The owl is also suggestive of Blodeuwedd who was changed into an owl for an amorous misdemeanour, as Mary's pregnancy gave rise to suppositions about impropriety.

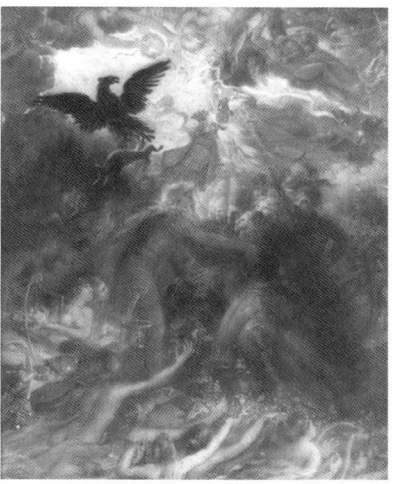

34. Anne-Louis Girodet de Roucy-Trioson, Ossian Receiving Napoleonic Heroes, c.1802

239

The assembly of birds is impressive, including a swallow, a falcon, an eagle, a kingfisher and a heron - Clark picks out the goldfinch, 'the long-accepted symbol of Christian sacrifice'[78] - and this again is an example of the Medieval tendency of Jones's mind towards inclusiveness. Jones makes some practical modifications to established iconography such as substituting the wild fox-glove for the convention of the cultivated lily, for this is an *Annunciation in a Welsh Hill-Setting*. He introduces obscurity by using unfamiliar mythologies but the painting remains perfectly clear: all creation attends to the good news of the coming of the Saviour.

Y Cyfarchiad I Fair represents a certain kind of triumph but it appears to be an impossible triumph for the mid-twentieth century. Jones had begun auspiciously with an early visual aptitude and coming to maturity he showed sensitivity to the increased possibilities of picture-making in an eclectic age. How did this harden into generally stiff and over-laboured allegorical drawings? Part of the problem was that Jones, by 1940, had few close friends who were painters so that he had very little vital contact with other artists. In a draft of a response to Augustus John's obituary in *The Times*, Jones remembers how a friend of his had seen John 'shed tears on seeing one of his earlier paintings, being aware that he could never again recapture the particular quality of that work'.[79]

If mythology is intended as a short circuit to an emotion, then the last thing that mythography should entail is clutter. Jones's pedantry seeks to pin down the facts of his case while concealing the very emotions which prompted his interest in the subject. Metaphor alone circumvents the need for too much matter as an idea is metamorphosed into a charged visual image. Certain of Jones's works come perilously close to the drawings of Alan Sorrell, that unashamedly illustrational artist with a fascination for Roman, post-Roman, and Medieval times. At the worst, elements in Jones's late mythological paintings are left cold and there is no assimilation of the glut of matter which is left blatant and undigested. Clive Bell observed that the Pre-Raphaelite painters were 'not artists, but archaeologists who tried to make intelligent curiosity do the work of impassioned contemplation',[80] later noting that detail had become 'the fatty degeneration of art'.[81]

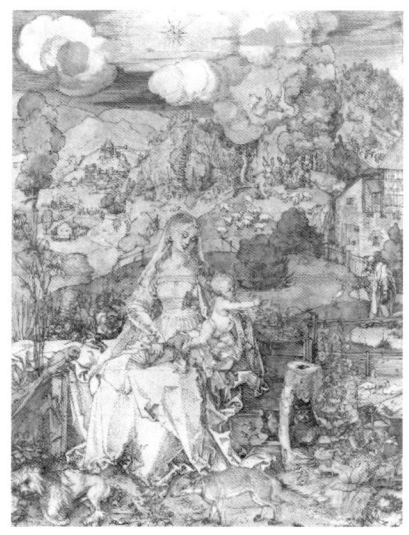

35. Albrecht Dürer, The Virgin with the Multitude of Animals, c.1503

Yet Jones somewhere thought that this literary way of making painting was a necessary result of the age in which he lived; writing to Helen Sutherland about the need for allusion he stated:

> I believe Eliot's 'Waste Land' is his best poem and the best poem of all this period. But it is *not* because of Eliot that many writers have concerned themselves with mythological and somewhat obscure 'allusion-writing' - it is because this groping age, with its specialist preoccupation into this and that and the other branches of science and history and idea, have filled the air with these things and the poets inevitably (along with other people) assimilate and become part of these investigations ... and not only the *content* but the *form* of their writing must needs take on 'new' aspects. It is not a 'fashion' it is an inevitable trend.[82]

240

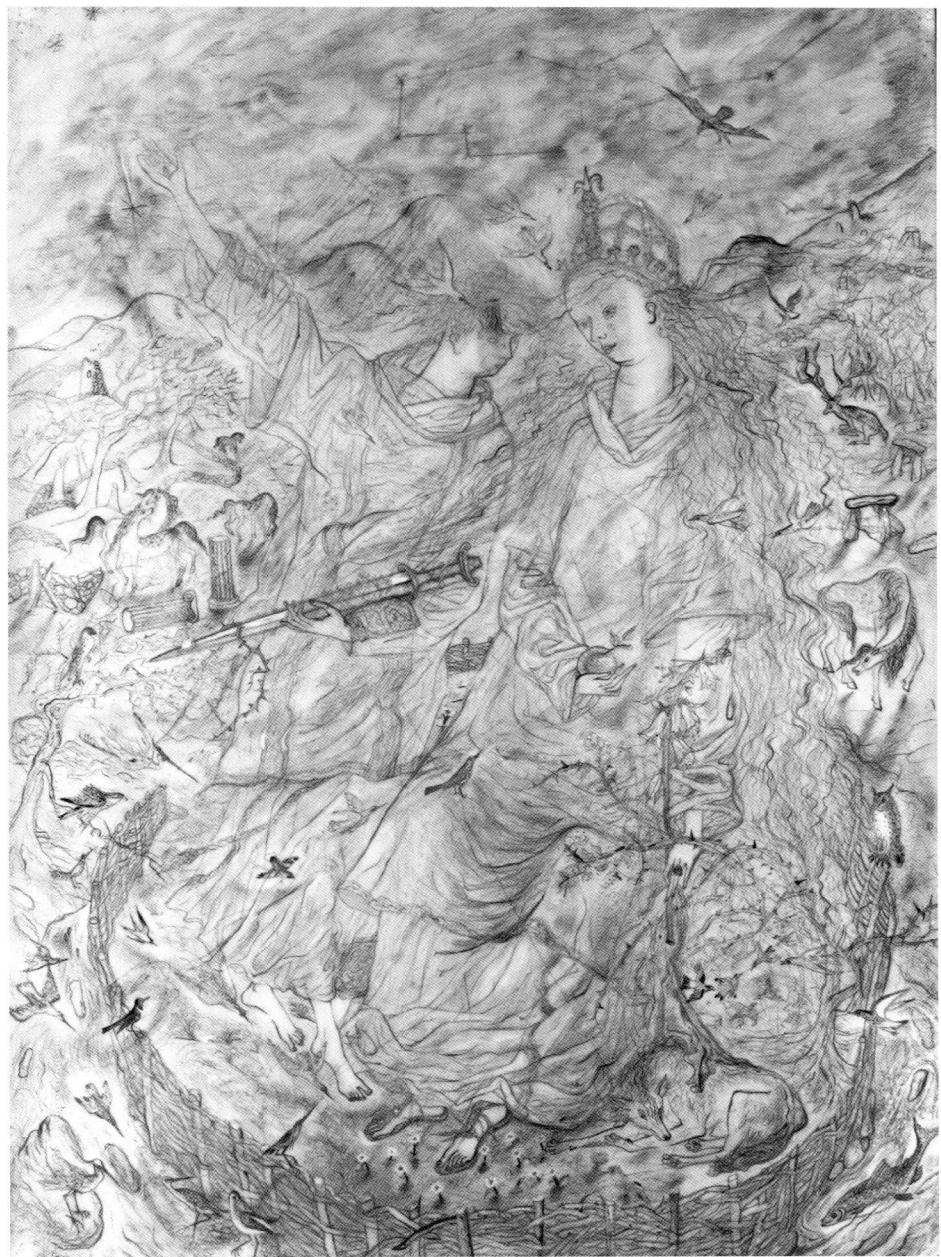

36. Y Cyfarchiad I Fair (The Annunciation in a Welsh Hill-Setting), 1963

The many stories or visions brought together in Jones's modernist poems give them a size or scope as images played upon the imagination can be fluid and infinite. By contrast, his mythographical drawings and watercolours, while they present allusive scenes and fragments of stories, do so in such an unpainterly manner that the subject becomes clogged with information. In a work where everything is given uniform importance as a sign, the total significance collapses under the strain. Jones wrote in a letter of April, 1960, 'What I *want* to do is one full of all the complications and allusions but executed with the directness that used to be in my still-life and landscapes - that's what I want to do before I die.'[83]

INTERNAL PRESSURES

Jones observed, 'I often feel terribly old and outmoded nowadays',[1] so an offer, in 1951, of nomination to what he once called that 'loathsome institution', the Royal Academy, was hardly pleasing and was firmly resisted.[2] Nine of his works had been hung in *British Painting 1925-50*, an Arts Council exhibition which formed part of the 1951 Festival of Britain. 'The Skylon ... I thought pathetic - neither amusing, nor elegant, nor impressive', Jones wrote after visiting the Festival, 'The "abstract" "art works" all ... looked bad ... a kind of meaninglessness pervaded them - at least in that particular setting.'[3] And progressively, Jones found the sparkle of the abstract shimmering in and around the ostensible subjects of his own pictures to be an elusive quality and he was, as the years passed, painting less and less.

The Anathemata was published in 1952 to the acclaim of fellow poets, but its inherent difficulty precluded a wide response. The devotion of a considerable proportion of his time to writing did not cease with publication as the material for the poem was extracted from a mound of poetry which, ideally, was intended to form a much longer composition. Jones continued to work on his 'fragments of an attempted writing'; an immense task, largely hidden from his acquaintances.

When not reduced to inactivity by illness he was continually hard at work yet baffled by the lack of understanding which often greeted his efforts, demoralized by his own perception of his imperfections and failure and bemused by the fact that 'Whatever I do I can scarcely make ends meet and I work till 2 a.m. always.'[4] After a visit to a Matthew Smith exhibition, he wrote to Kenneth Clark, 'I've *often* wished I could have been a *real painter* such as he was.'[5]

In 1954 a major retrospective exhibition toured Aberystwyth, Cardiff, Swansea, Edinburgh, and went to the Tate Gallery between 17 December and 30 January, 1955. It included seventy-four paintings, fifteen drawings, sixteen engravings and five inscriptions. It added up to a prodigious show and, after seeing the exhibition in Edinburgh, Helen Sutherland wrote to the artist:

> I found it intensely moving to see these works of so many devoted years. They did seem to me like an offering, a sacrifice - a broken spirit and a contrite heart (and a sweet savour) but broken like the bread is broken, to make a new wholeness - a holy communion after their kind.[6]

Sutherland, whose responses to art tended to accentuate the sweet and positive, here offers a telling suggestion of the emotional and human cost of this making and this chapter explores, not only Jones's last years, but previous areas and aspects of his entire life and career to observe how this breaking enabled and prohibited the making or completing of works of art.

Among the pressures experienced by Jones were those all-important and tricky relationships with parents, the pressures of a belief system which ignored the physical facts of humanity, the uncertainty of income for the practitioner of an art, and, with a move into a society vastly different from that in which he had been brought up, anxieties about class. None of these pressures are extraordinary but brought to bear on an extremely sensitive being who had suffered prolonged exposure to a corrosive existence on the Western Front they took on a larger aspect. Jones's considerable ability to tuck what was disagreeable out of sight sustained him through his early manhood and resulted in some fine works of art, but as delayed reaction to his early emotional life, the war and the forbidding nature of his adopted religion began to manifest themselves, the man collapsed under the weight of all his internalized pressures. His emotional life was compromised and what he had suppressed during and after the war came to terrorize him in the form of extreme and often unrelenting fright. He broke down and spent the second half of his life on an emotional precipice, capable of tumbling into profound depression at any time. His impossible sentimental life, his intellectual and creative suffering and sheer illness took their toll on his artistic output.

David Jones was the darling of his mother, the youngest and most precocious child whose privileged position was secured during his adolescence when, in 1910, his older brother Harold died of tuberculosis. A feeling of power and omnipotence, nurtured by the forceful personality of his mother, would also have been offset by a gnawing guilt at 'usurping', even 'killing off' his brother. Jones was empowered by his mother's love and devotion as well as constricted both by her determination and her need. A certain ambivalence in the child/parent relationship is visible in an ink sketch made probably in the late twenties or early thirties. The naughty cherub, naked before the authority figure suggests an expulsion from paradise, an event which in *Genesis* resulted from sexual or intellectual curiosity and which led to a severance from authority. The torn book in the form of wings suggests rebellion of a religious/angelic nature as well as the fact that the child likes to read, enjoys stories and perhaps that his own relation to the word is secret and cut off from his parents. It could reflect his father's unusually strong antipathy to Jones's conversion and also the fact that he started writing *In Parenthesis*, quite possibly at about the time this drawing was made, 'in terrible secrecy. My father kept saying, "What on earth are you doing?" People are frightful, they won't let you alone to get on with anything.'[7] Amongst the usual scatter of child's clothing and toys is to be seen an open tube spilling its fluid. As it is one of the many cylinders among the child's mess, obvious phallic or sexual connotations could be read out; more interesting, however, is the relation of paint and therefore painting to

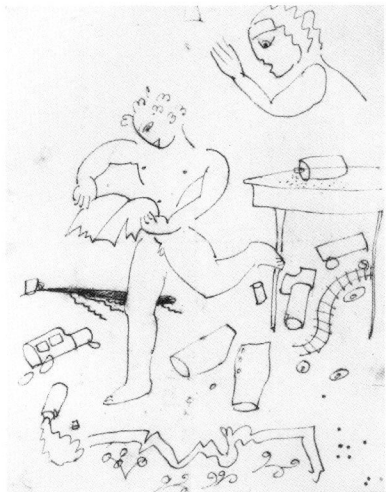

1. The Destructive Child, 1930

243

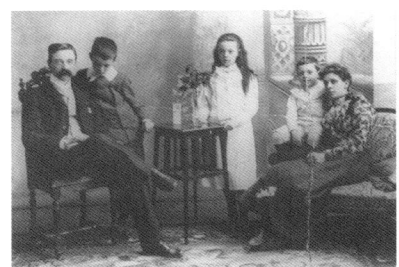

2. Jones Family Group (David Jones on right with his mother), c.1898

the authority figure. Jones picked up several signals from his mother, not least of which was her fright about his economic security should he take to painting professionally. Another signal which Jones picked up from her was that marriage and picture-making were incompatible activities. Is the implicit signal of the spillage not the idea of wasting the potential to procreate through the recreation of life in art? In the drawing, the echo between the position of mother and child suggests that there is some persistence in the pressure of the relationship; the break has not been cleanly made. While there is a kind of perverse joy about the image, suggesting that the child has not obeyed the cautions of the authority figure, instruction given in too severe a manner or misremembered becomes a scold.

A more unequivocal image of maternal constriction was manifest in that mid-twenties carving *Mother and Child* (see p 82) where the infant appears trapped. That Mrs. Jones was a forceful and egotistical character is revealed by a letter which she wrote to her son when he was in the trenches. The petty preoccupation with her world and her family vanity is marked and insensitive in relation to the actual situation in which her offspring finds himself 'in Flanders … in what happened to be a bad bit of the line, drenched with rain and wet mud': 'really David, the spelling in your last letter was a disgrace to the family - a child of four could do better'. Here is an almost tyrannical desire not to let go, exacerbated, doubtless, by the loss of her elder son.

During his years in the trenches, Jones witnessed the camaraderie of men under fire but we must also remember that it was part of his purpose as a soldier to bayonet and to kill. In the trenches Jones experienced violence and carnage as well as tenderness. The fact that he once asked not to go on leave as he did not want to become involved in his family's moving house gives some indication of his feeling of intense belonging to his battalion as well as to the possible tensions at home. Some unidentified notes drafted while in Bowden House, possibly for an application to the Artists' Benevolent Fund, speak of his 'long-standing chronic neurosis' as being not only 'related to experiences in being wounded in the 1914-18 war' but also 'to early domestic worries',[8] worries perhaps centred on the death of his older brother, Harold. Later, during his first sustained period of nervous breakdown in the early thirties, Jones preferred the haven of H.S. Ede's house in Hampstead and thought it less 'struggle than going back to Brockley'.[9] To be caught up in domestic trivia during or after Armageddon was something that many First World War fighters eschewed and which, after the war, led to incomprehension and isolation.

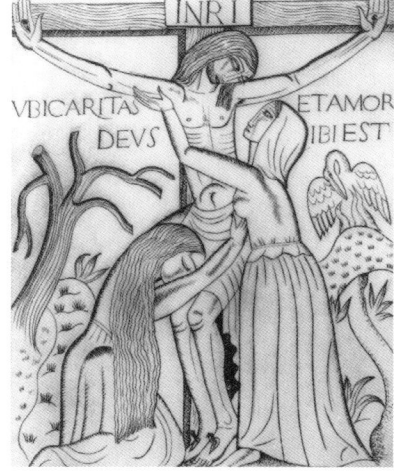

3. The Crucifixion, 1926

In the engraving, *The Crucifixion* of 1929, Mary, Christ's mother, openly embraces her Son. The other Mary, head bowed down in front of the lap of Christ, in mirror image of the self-sacrificing Pelican, deflects her gaze in the direction of his wounds. This penitent Mary has given up a licentious life for Christ and it is significant that she is depicted regarding wounds that in their piercing nature bear some affinity to the act of coition; the person choosing to fix his or her vision on the Cross embraces pain and often sacrifices the physical pleasures of the flesh. Most importantly, by keeping his eyes firmly fixed on the mother, the son avoids the sexual pressure of the other woman whose head is in his lap. Wilhelm Reich has suggested that

The cult of the Virgin Mary is drawn upon very successfully as a means of inculcating chastity … in the emotional life of Christian youths, the Mother of God assumes the role of one's own mother, and the Christian youth showers upon her all the love that he had for his own mother at one time, that very ardent love of his first genital desires. But the *incest prohibition* cleaves his genital desires into an intense longing for orgasm on the one hand and asexual tenderness on the other… .[10]

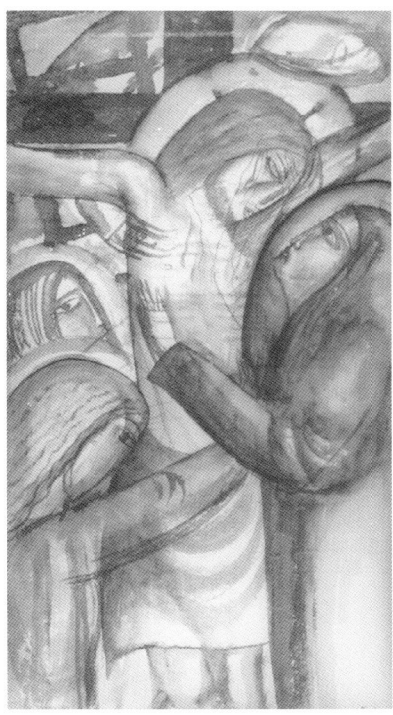

4. The Crucifixion, c.1924

Now the conversion of repressed eroticism into religious motivation, Reich suggests, pertains 'not only to the incestuous desire, but to *every* natural genital relationship with a woman'.[11] Reich is mistrustful of extremes of religious devotion, feeling that such thinking is prompted by 'the *unconscious* struggle against one's own sexual needs'.[12] Jones, in his notes for his doctors at Bowden House, noted that masturbation

> dealt with leniently in the confessional, as a constantly recurring and persistent weakness and frailty … is *never* regarded as anything other than, to use theological language, 'a sin' - an offence against human dignity because it is regarded as an irrational act.[13]

Reich goes on to draw a sorrowful image of a person dominated by patriarchal religion which, he feels, is based on 'the negation of sexual need'[14] and indeed draws its power from the suppression of genital sexuality:[15]

> The emotional structure of the genuinely religious man can be briefly described as follows: biologically, he is subject to sexual tensions just as all other human beings and creatures. Owing, however, to his assimilation of sex-negating religious conceptions, and especially to the fear of punishment that he has acquired, he has completely lost his ability to experience natural sexual tension and release. Consequently, he suffers from a chronic state of physical excitation, which he is continually compelled to master … As a result of the suppression of his sexual energy, he has lost his capacity for happiness as well as the aggressiveness necessary to deal with life's difficulties.[16]

From the testimony of a close friend at Ditchling, Jones, like Desmond Chute whose ordination was delayed while his incontinence was discussed by the Church authorities, suffered from abnormally swift excitation and premature ejaculation.[17]

Freud provides a vision of the Christian story in relation to a male child's Oedipal desire to kill his father:

> In the Christian doctrine … men were acknowledging in the most undisguised manner the guilty primaeval deed, since they found the fullest atonement for it in the sacrifice of this one son. Atonement with the father was all the more complete since the

245

sacrifice was accompanied by a total renunciation of the women on whose account the rebellion against the father was started. But at that point the inexorable psychological law of ambivalence stepped in. The very deed in which the son offered the greatest possible atonement to the father brought him at the same time to the attainment of his wishes *against* the father. He himself became God, beside, or, more correctly, in place of, the father ... The Christian communion ... is essentially a fresh elimination of the father, a repetition of the guilty deed.[18]

When his own father showed his displeasure at his son's decision to join the Catholic Church, David Jones took refuge with a strong-willed surrogate father, Eric Gill. Gill gave Jones a vivid experience of the polarization between a religious framework to life (through the Dominican Offices which they shared) and an easygoing attitude towards the pleasures of the flesh. There was a tension in the Gill establishments between religion and the erotic. With one hand Gill gave Jones the opportunity of connubial bliss through an engagement to his daughter, Petra, and with the other, through his religious example, he denied Jones any such thing. Gill had a strongly proprietorial relationship to his daughters which in two cases had been sexualized and of three potential sons-in-law, only Jones was openly favoured. Gill was sexually astute and alert; if he had become a surrogate father then he had manoeuvred Petra into being more acceptable to Jones as a kind of sister than as a wife. Furthermore, because of her father's incest with her, Petra had been placed in a similar relation to Jones as Jones's own mother; by making his daughter a 'wife', Gill had created an implicit taboo for his surrogate son. Jones could no more 'kill' Gill than his own father. Consciously, it is improbable that Jones knew anything of Gill's sexual experiments with his daughters but it is interesting to note that Jones was drawn to a woman who, for obvious reasons, might experience some difficulty in expressing her own sexuality. The psoriasis on Petra Gill's arm was probably exacerbated by the stress resulting from her relations with her father from which she 'suffered in repressive silence'.[19] It is true that Petra Gill's eventual family life seems to have redeemed what could have left painful emotional scars but it is also true that in her late teens and early twenties, having had recent relations with her father, she does seem to have shown a degree of reticence; Ede wrote to Jones, 'You are ill for Petra ... can't you go for her and *insist*. It is nonsense that she knows better than you'.[20]

If we look closely at the wonderful early oil, *The Garden Enclosed*, we can see how far Jones was perhaps aware of the sexual undercurrents of the situation. First of all, the strong rhythms of the canvas suggest that it is an extremely sensual and dramatic work. Even the title is fraught with incestuous subtexts. A quotation from *The Song of Solomon*, the title is taken from a passage in which the graces of the church are extolled in terms of personal physical beauty. The text in Ch.IV v.12 is 'A garden enclosed *is* my sister, *my* spouse; a spring shut up, a fountain sealed.' Prohibition is further suggested by the strict translation from the Hebrew of what is rendered in the *Authorized Version* as 'enclosed': 'barred'. 'Sister' and 'spouse' suggest a similar

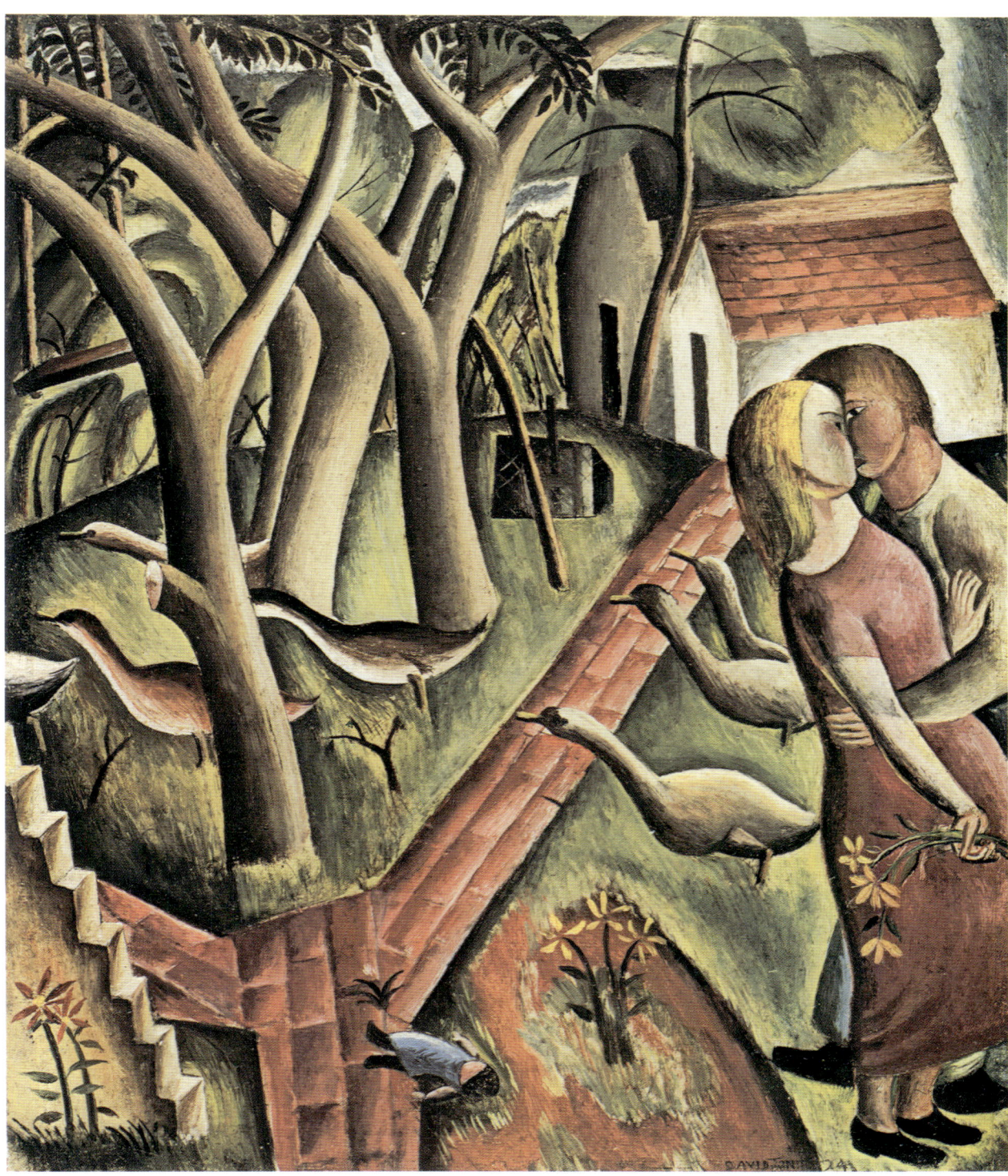

5. The Garden Enclosed, 1924

incestuous confusion to that provoked by Gill's sexual relationship with the daughter who became engaged to the man he had taken into his extended family almost as a son. When we add that the garden enclosed in fifteenth century painting was where the Virgin sat on the ground[21] and that it became a symbol of her virginity itself, we are led into the arena where suppressed incestuous longings, converted, as Reich notes, into devotion to the Virgin Mary, were beginning to be confronted.

So intimidating was the prospect of marriage that Jones instinctively chose a figure who was in no state to accept his advances. Engagement was, of course, intended to culminate in marriage but even in the year in which they became engaged there seems to have been doubt in the artist's mind about the possibility of a successful conclusion. In *The Garden Enclosed* geese seem to be fleeing; there is the possibility that marriage will 'cook his goose' in relation to work, although 'geese' also hint at rescue: 'he'll be a man among the geese when the gander is gone' suggests getting rid of the father in order to achieve sexual maturity.

As already noted, paths terminate in several paintings made at this time, not at the front door of the house offering an invitation to domestic bliss, but obtusely at the corner of the building. Likewise, the door to Gill's domain on the cover of this book is disturbingly dark, as are many doorways in Jones's paintings of the late twenties and early thirties. The tiny doll in blue, carved for her by her father, and cast on the path may indeed suggest the baby that won't be made. As Philip Hagreen recalled, 'David had given his love and it had been thrown away'.[22] The discarding of the doll could also be seen as an intuitive vision of Petra's loss of innocence. The swing hints at Petra's swings of attitude towards the projected marriage as well as Jones's own indecision. The male figure in the painting comes in from the edge of the canvas like an intruder and the girl seems to be warding him off; after such a recent involvement with her father, at the age of eighteen, she was quite possibly incapable of considering coitus with another man but she was capable of physical intimacy.[23] Evidence from Ede's correspondence suggests that it was Jones who urged such caresses and the length of Petra's subsequent engagement to the shell-shocked, ex-Trappist, Denis Tegetmeier, suggests that it took her some time to come to terms with her adult sexuality. The image of Jones on Caldey immediately after the break-up of his engagement, stroking the red-haired girl and banging his head against the wall, must be seen as an expression of his anguish at failure. Sadly, years later, some kind of unresolved relationship continued in Jones's mind. It was a teasing and almost provocative woman seen in two of the portraits of Petra and as late as 1933, Jones wrote in a letter to Hague, 'Please give ... lots of, nay all of my love to Petra'.[24]

After the termination of his engagement, Jones threw himself into work, but as the twenties drew to a close he was assailed by three unresolved problems. The trials of the war were once again brought home to him by his writing *In Parenthesis*, his sexuality was perplexing, and he was still using his parents home in Brockley as his work base, bewildered by the gulf between his origins and the new circles in which he was moving. Two interiors, one of

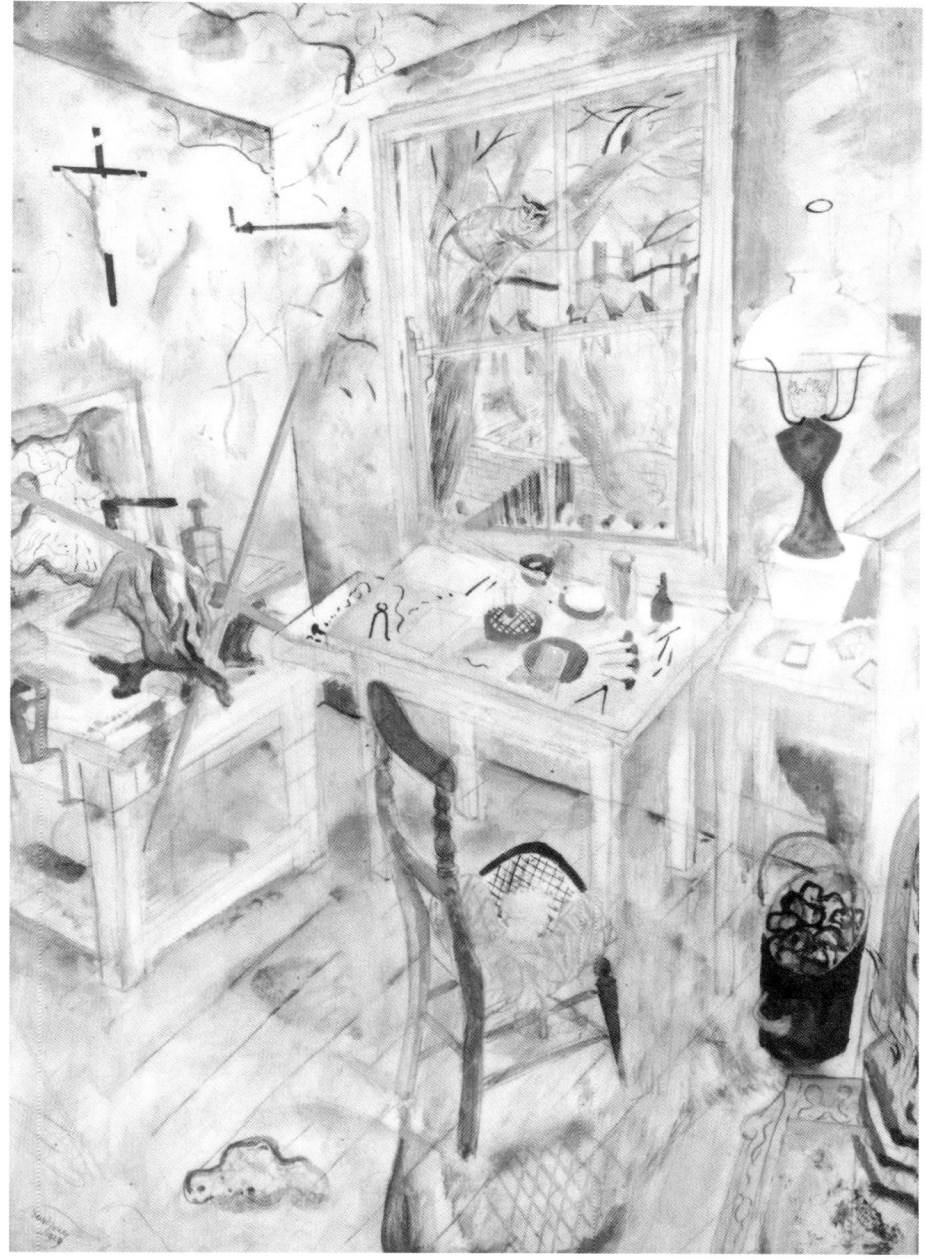

6. The Engraver's Workshop, 1929

the late twenties and the other of the early thirties reflect the kinds of pressure which Jones was feeling. In *The Engraver's Workshop* of 1929, all the straight lines have been ruled in a definite attempt to impose some order in a workspace well known for its untidiness. The room is presented cracking up and only limited by a defining frame not unlike the rectilineal demarcations that Bacon later used. Eric Gill had encouraged Jones to create in an orderly manner by asking him to think of the artist's work-table as an altar. Gill would have been pleased to observe the careful way in which the tools were laid out on the table from which rises a window presenting a scene as if it has been transubstantiated into a picture hanging on the wall. The scene focuses, unfocuses, and refocuses as so often in the best of Jones and there is a quality of ease or even enchantment. Fire and light flank the 'altar' in the form of hearth fire, oil lamp and gas jet. The light of the oil lamp emerges from a base, the form of which resembles the shape of the chalice. On the left, the gas jet appears almost like an arrow which has pierced the old ruined walls and which points menacingly to the crucifix. The map of Wales adds to the sense of a distant temporal dimension and the escape from the suburban banality of the present is suggested by crucifix, arrow, wood, fissure, fire and manual implements. The scumbling around the coal-scuttle suggests agitation, hinting at the experience Jones described to Nicolete Gray, that 'when looking at some quite ordinary object like a coal-scuttle' he could be seized with terror. In *The Engraver's Workshop* it pulls the eye and demands attention.

In the early thirties, the submerged Expressionism which palpitates beneath Jones's attempt at surface calm becomes more visible. The tendency is towards a kind of automatic writing, more often than not registering anger or frustration; the artist feels compelled to violate space with aggressive and otherwise meaningless marks. It is as if he is somehow furious but just manages to harness anger by hinting at an elusive radiance. Shifts of style are perhaps tactical; changing medium or manner prohibits prolonged exploration of his deepest recesses. Yet, as we move close to the first breakdown, we see the ructions breaking the surface. In *Curtained Outlook* of 1932, one of Jones's greatest achievements, the world appears to dissolve, one plane merged into or engulfed by another; walls crack, curtains transform almost into flames consuming the gable opposite. Jones tolerates that urgency which can be a factor in good or great art. The cracks in the wall reflect internal stress. The flowers on the window-sill are mere ghosts of flowers and the foreground detritus is in some way insignificant and yet it is an itemization of the necessary incidentals which sustain the sick or neurotic. The title is indicative of a person ill or disturbed who has a 'curtained outlook'. The frightened artist who can't keep hold of things retreats into his room to draw and sees nothing but evidence of his inner chaos. Interior pressures find no sympathy, explanation or respite in the world at large so he makes a meaningful painting about the approaching state of meaninglessness. In intention it is not unlike Van Gogh's gouache *Window of Vincent's Studio at St. Paul's Hospital (7)* of late spring 1889.

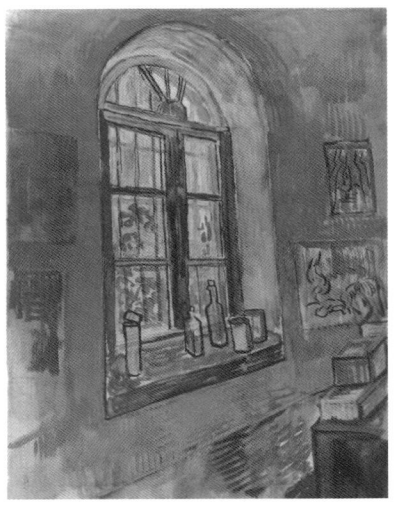

7. Vincent van Gogh, Window of Vincent's Studio at St. Paul's Hospital, 1889

Denied marriage to one of Gill's daughters by a nexus of internal pressures, is it surprising that he paints one of the buildings of Gill's settlement at Pigotts veiled behind a curtain which appears almost to ignite into flame, 'set on fire' in an attempt to consume the pain of sexual deprivation? The house has a balcony suggestive of that prototype for difficult and forbidden love, *Romeo and Juliet* Act II sc. ii. Windows appear ambiguously like prison bars but they are flung wide as if the painter wishes to look in and see what is really going on in other people's marital lives. This is not Jones the evanescent, pretty English watercolourist, this is Jones the inhibited and crushed, painting out his interior world of distress and strain. It is Jones the Expressionist trying to hold on to the 'actually loved and known'. But as the activity of painting got livelier and angrier, the artist himself became quiet, brooding, baffled and unable to paint.[25] Jones's painting was admitting too much so he refused to continue.

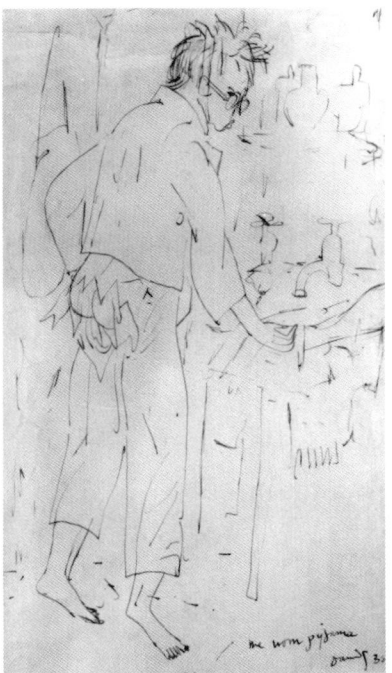

8. Torn Pyjamas, (?)

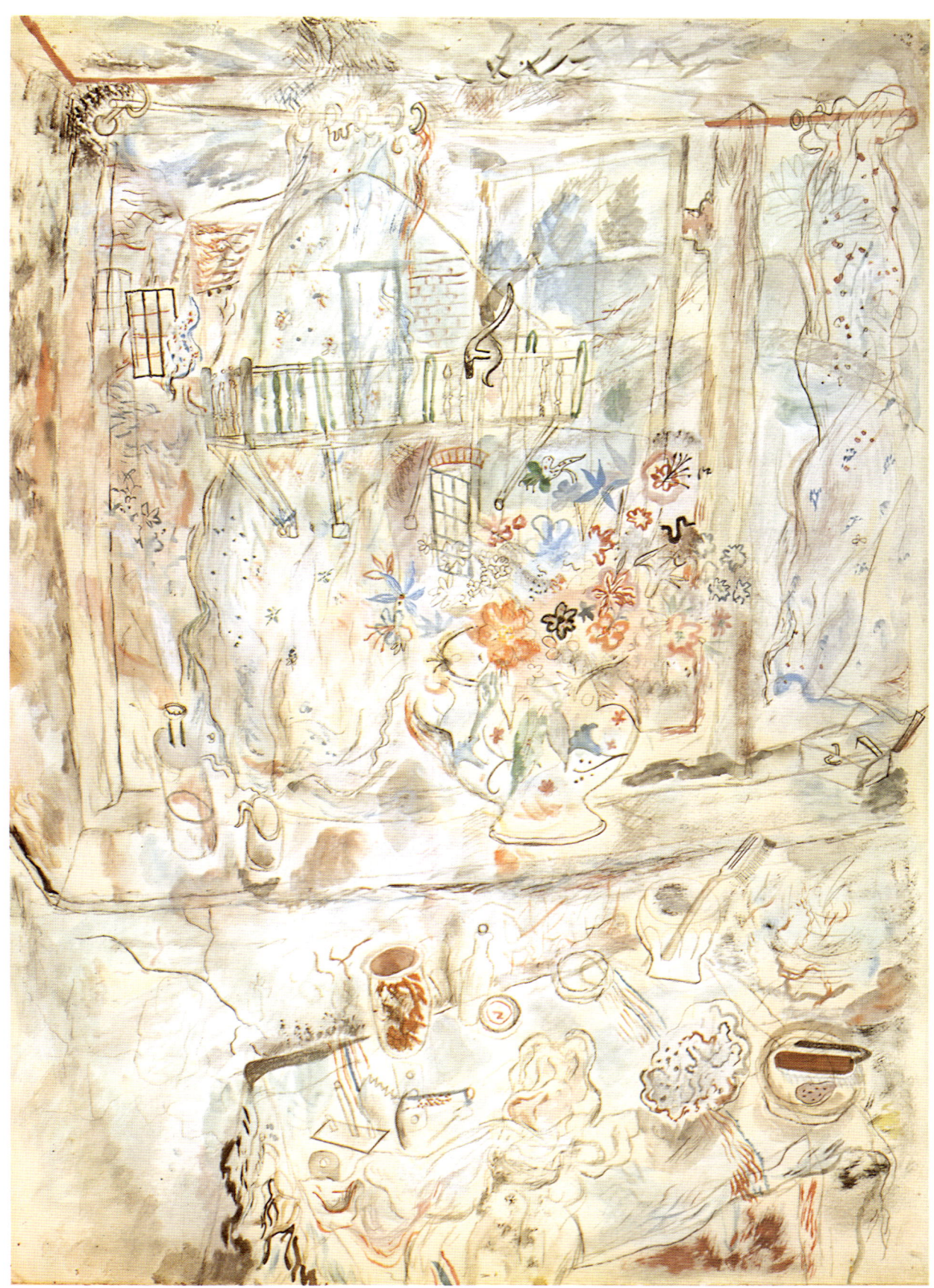

9. Curtained Outlook, 1932

Approaching forty and at the height of his artistic powers, Jones suffered his first breakdown. While Hague is right to attribute it to many causes, he appears starkly insensitive in his denial of the rôle played by the war.[26] Grisewood seems more realistic when he writes:

> No one who survived 1916 was the same as before. For some - my father for example - life itself came to an end. He was 36. But it was worse for the youngsters like David who at 21 were beginning their adult life - and yet were maimed for ever after … every impressionable person who fought in the front line trenches did suffer some permanent damage which went under the generic name of shell-shock.[27]

The simplistic diagnosis of Jones's condition was indeed a delayed reaction to the war, 'shell-shock' or neurasthenia, and he was prescribed rest and a break from painting. Tellingly, in a book published in the year of Jones's first breakdown, Hugh Crichton-Miller, who later treated Jones after his second big breakdown in 1946-47, noted that 'Cases of traumatic neurosis (popularly described as 'shell-shock') were found under psycho-analysis to be due to a desire for erotic gratification, the symptoms being subjected to great distortion'.[28] Jones was clearly disappointed by the inefficiency of professional help and remained in a state of pretty near continuous psychic disorder throughout the rest of the thirties, forties and, despite the better treatment in 1947, intermittently until he died. It must be realized that for the greater part of his working life Jones was in a state of psychological shock against which his achievement must be measured.

After the trip to Cairo and the first trip to Sidmouth, Jones appeared to have got through the worst of his collapse but he was, in February 1936, writing to Ede about his 'partly invalidish type of existence'.[29] It was during that period that he was developing a deep affection for Prudence Pelham and while aspects of her character considered already would obviously make her attractive to a man like Jones, there are others which may have been even a bigger spur to his affection. Although she was a member of those upper classes which made a strong appeal to Jones, she had an ease and bearing that cut across class. Jones could enjoy her *mien* and fortitude, her intellect, her humour and yet feel utterly comfortable, at least until the security of a sexless relationship began to give rise to discontent.

The class question was a persistent problem; Petra Tegetmeier remembered Jones's parents as humble and ordinary with a pinch of Cockney in their speech. In the late twenties Jones found himself in the world of debutantes and Lords, for among that class and among the Catholic intelligentsia he found people who were aware of the mighty drama of culture and civilization and yet who were not 'of the left', an impossible political position because of its denial of 'the supernatural order'.[30] Yet negotiating the demands of the social situation was a source of constant anxiety; he recalled being '*terrified* of Lady Chichester and chaps coming and me all in rags'.[31] Jones revealed his discomfort in a letter to Tom Burns, describing himself as

'supernumerary, attached, pending allocation to unit' (as the
military jargon goes) to the upper classes - yet with my roots
among the lower orders (of whom I have *great fear* and whose
reactions I *hate*, but for whom I feel a deep *understanding* at the
same time).[32]

He went on to praise the apparent anonymity of the army and, indeed, one
might add to that the asocial context of communities like Ditchling, and
Capel-y-ffin. A dream which Jones described reveals preoccupation with
class, romance and conflicting attitudes towards sex:

> she came into the scullery at Brockley in black velvet and spoke
> in her dear full voice 'in another moment they found themselves
> in each others' arms' and oddly enough the *Hawks daughter* was
> frying some meat on the gas stove and stood by with an air of
> disapproval and then came up and shook hands - all very odd.[33]

Hague goes so far as to say that, in his adopted circles, Jones claimed that he
felt himself at times to be an 'imposter' and yet so admired the 'assured
standing' of the upper classes 'based on an aristocracy of birth and tradition'.[34]

Prudence Pelham was not only someone with the right social credentials who
nonetheless easily transgressed the impositions of social codes, she was also
ill and seemingly suffered from unresolved psychological pressures. Jones had
been drawn to Petra Gill with her strange past and in the thirties he curiously
found himself falling in love with someone whose relation to sex was far from
happy; in the period before her marriage Pelham was racked by a vision
suggestive of repression:

> Prudence began to think she was being haunted. There was a
> 'Mister Black' she said, who was obsessing her night and day - an
> almost physical presence, whom she could not get out of her
> mind. She said he had some of the features of a former butler at
> Stanmer, though she couldn't think why this person should wish
> to harm her.[35]

The fact that Pelham was in such a highly wrought mental state and the fact
that misfortune, depression and chronic ill-health dogged her may indeed
suggest some psychological sickness, a malady which Jones called, thinking
perhaps of the many casualties - Meninsky, Chute, Dawson and Pelham - the
'Black Death' of their generation.[36] In Pelham, Jones had once again chosen
an impossible relationship; again he could avoid facing the deepest and most
emotionally crippling issue, his unresolved attachment to his mother and how
it was inhibiting him.

That bond was in some ways broken by her death in 1937 and Hills has
observed that Jones begins to treat sexual themes in his major works after she
dies. Subjects chosen from the *Morte D'Arthur* with its vision of cultural
catastrophe linked to amorous complication resulted in his anger, visible in
the more violent abstract marks of earlier works, becoming more defined

and localized. In the imperial twilight of the Arthurian world Jones found not only a correlative for a new dark age, but in Malory's episodes concerned with the difficulty of love, a remote context in which to explore aspects of his own problematic attitude towards sex; where this occurs, the vision gives way to a treatment of a theme that goes beyond the mere illustration of an idea or episode.

In Book XIX Ch.6 of Malory, Launcelot wishes to prove his love for Guenever, so he 'sette hys hondis uppon the barrys of iron, and pulled at them with suche myght that he braste hem cleane oute of the stone wallys ... And than he lepe into the chambir to the queene.' It has been suggested that Jones in his painting posits a relationship between the love of Launcelot for Guenever and Christ for his bride, the Church. Certainly the stigmata on Launcelot's feet, the crucifix and crown above Guenever suggest that this may be so. But surely the real narrative of *Guenever* emerges from behind this intellectual manipulation of symbols. The tension, the drama, the *raison* of the work resides in its expression of a man's sexual torment because of his devotion to the Church.

Launcelot has entered this confused space through a window far too small for his body, clearly suggesting a constricted approach. He comes into an area where a light region of central calm focuses the spectator's attention on Guenever's naked body and on the uncluttered passage beyond her leading to the altar on which stands the tabernacle which is shaped like her bedhead and which has a vulval slit. Around this central relationship, the eye is disturbed by a frantic, fluid intensity. Everything has been thrown up into the air; objects seem to fly through space and one is reminded of the erotic significance of flying objects in Surrealism. This turmoil, the phallic bed-supports,[37] fire irons, spikes and candles on either side of Guenever's head, the oddly penile aspect of the ribbed vaulting above the Crucifix at the left hanging down towards the head of the bed, all attest to the pressure of erotic desire. The work has a vitality because the essence of the story, the difficulty of erotic love, is re-experienced urgently and in an unexpected manner. The vitality derives from the intensification of an existing complex. It is not just a graphic retelling, an illustration, but a re-presenting of the material within the emotional orbit of the painter's experience or feeling. Its main agency of communication is its disturbed fluidity which is a particularly a-literary device.

The Four Queens (11), made in the following year, exhibits a similar expression of sexual distress. The ostensible subject is from Malory Book VI Ch. 3 where four Queens contend for the love of Launcelot. The Knight appears stricken at the feet of four seductresses. His helpless eyes stare in the direction of a swan in a sexually available position, and fix on its neck around which a bow, always associated with sauciness in Jones's work, is tied. All about Launcelot are symbols of sexual promise or threat: bare feet, bowed feet, a gartered leg, exposed breasts. Even the knight himself and his accoutrements attest to sexual drama. What is that strange vulval shape that rests between his legs and why do the spikes of his spurs point towards it? Most significant is the frenzy of the bewildered horse twisting round the lance. As Paul Hills notes,

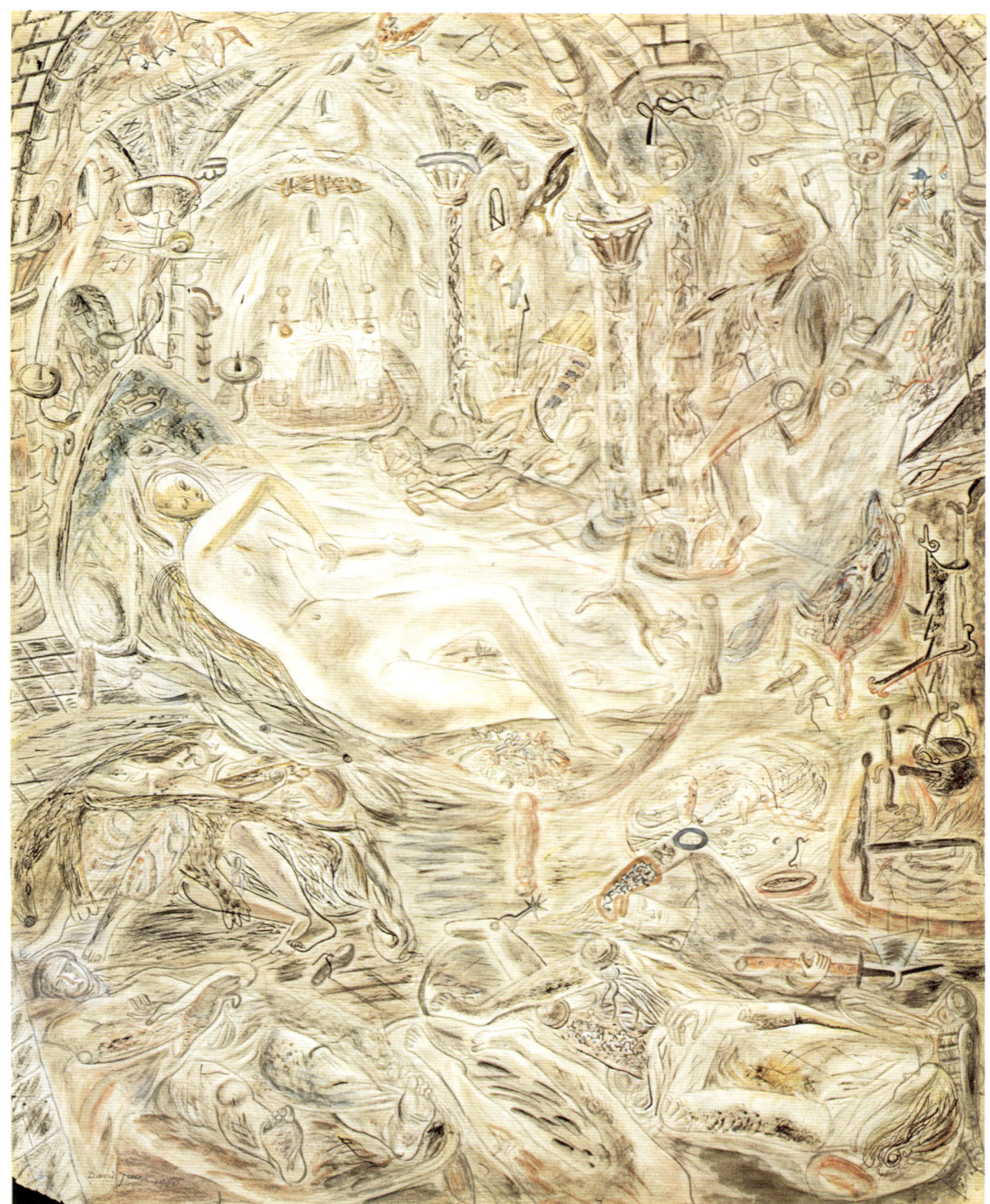

10. Guenever, 1940

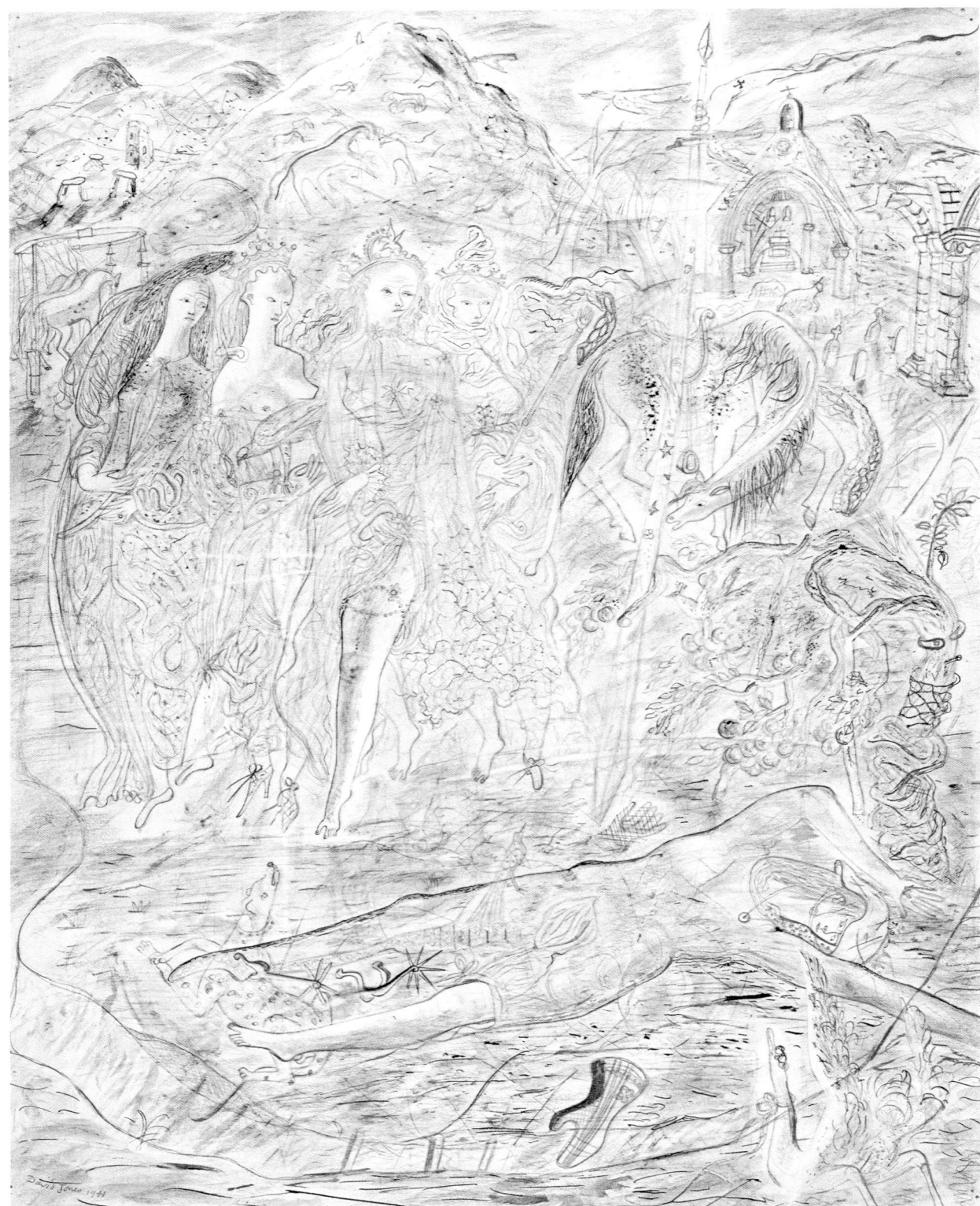

11. The Four Queens, 1941

for 'Freud the horse is a pre-eminent symbol of male sexuality'[38] and this horse and lance mark and problematize the striking pictorial division between the four lascivious queens and the womb-like chapel. Furthermore, lances in the Grail strand of Arthurian romance suggest a complex of religious anguish and sexual maiming. The subtext is again about the relationship between sexual life and devotion to the church, a dramatic analogue to the vision of Launcelot's fidelity in the face of temptation.

Launcelot, who represents extreme moral confusion in Malory, a man torn between duty and love, was obviously an apt image for Jones's own confusion about his duty to art and the church and his great drive and inclination to fall in love. Writing to Grisewood about his inability to face up to difficulties with Prudence Pelham he observed

> I do see why Launcelot ran 'wood mad' in the trackless forest for four years so that no man might know him is easily under-standable, but all one does is to smoke cigarettes and drink an extra whisky or something.[39]

When the Blitz started Jones was 'stirred … by beautiful girls wearing steel helmets at jaunty angles'[40] and he began to explore, more overtly, his sexual reactions through incidental drawings. The panic-stricken face of the boyish young corporal seen in close proximity to the sexy, buxom woman seems to register a strongly felt anxiety. More detached and voyeuristic is Jones's transsexual erotic fantasy in which an idealized breast emerges from the dishevelled uniform of a female air-raid warden. Her hand around the cylinder of the torch suggests that the intention behind the drawing may have been an onanistic spur.

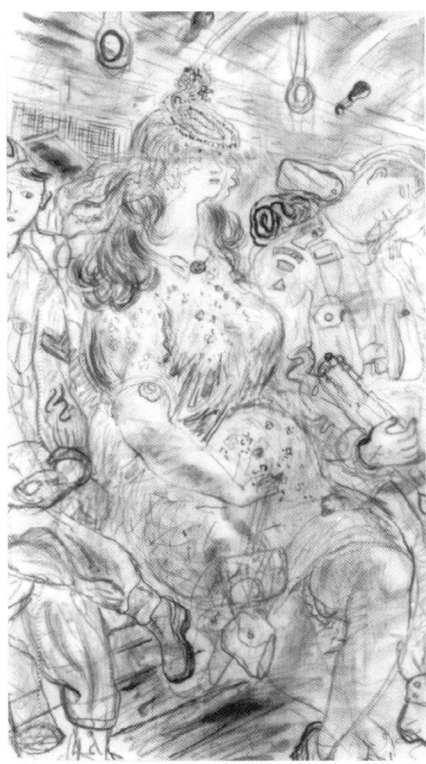

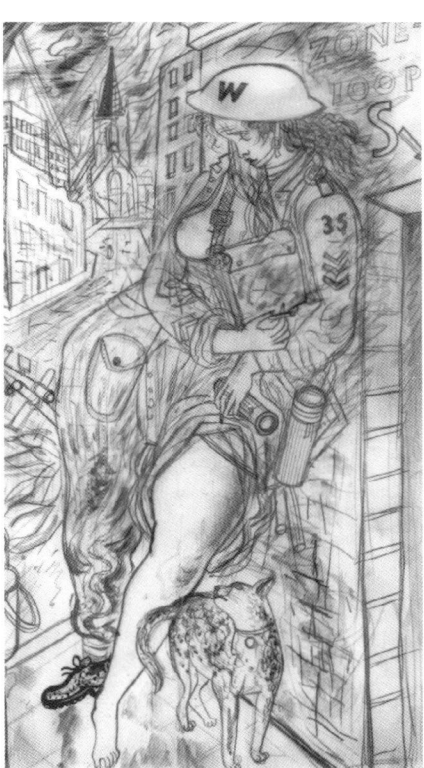

12. Woman, Soldier & Schoolboy on Tube, 1940

13. Woman Warden During the Blitz, 1941

257

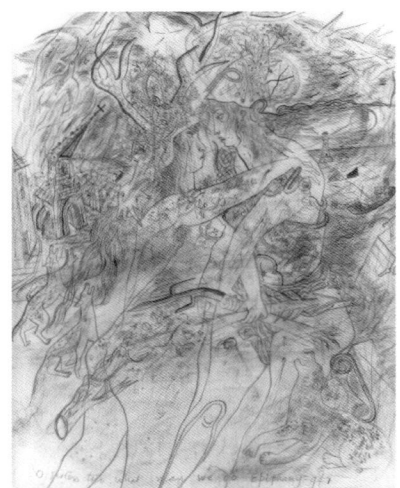

14. Epiphany 1941 – Britannia & Germania Embracing, 1942

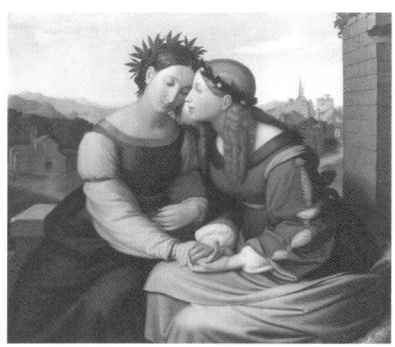

15. Friedrich Overbeck, Italia and Germania, 1828

Some of the larger works of the war years are riddled with a sexuality that has obviously got out of control. Despite its ostensible subject, (the embracing of nations who are engaged in what Jones calls in *The Anathemata*, 'fratricidal wars') *Britannia and Germania Embracing* of 1941 represents the two countries as sisters, one of whom is actually seen abusing the other in a quasi-sexual manner with the shaft of her spear.

There is a painting by the Nazarene, J.F. Overbeck, called *Italia and Germania* (1828) in which two women, holding hands and leaning together, express the love and understanding of the two countries. In Overbeck's serene painting the German has braids and sits before a German hill town, the Italian wears laurel leaves and behind her there is an Italian lake and church. Jones's picture likewise includes cultural traditions such as a Gothic church and an Ionic capital but they have been ruined. The women appear depraved, and desperate sexual longing seems to have replaced Overbeck's sentimental vision of cultural harmony. Hills has noted that 'time and again in Jones's art, instruments of procreation and instruments of wounding - guns, stick bombs, knives, lances, nails and fluked spears - appear interchangeable in a kind of visual naming of parts'.[41]

Jones's conscious motivation for producing such an image of appeasement was born of his admiration, as the thirties had developed, for the German leadership. He responded to Hitler's appeal to a lower-middle-class interest in roots and a 'folkish' world view and to his appeal to the upper class desire for the preservation of tradition. Fascism also made a strong appeal to ex-servicemen, the trench fighters of the First World War, in its attempt to recreate 'the atmosphere of youthful comradeship, heroism and idealism'.[42] As late as 1938, after reading a speech of Hitler's from the *Telegraph* on the lawn at Pigotts, Brocard Sewell recalls Jones rounding off his recitation with the exclamation, 'Great stuff!';[43] Jones even perceived a resemblance between his face and that of the Führer[44] and he wrote in 'The Pursuit of Peace'

> … there is much in both the Fascist and Nazi revolutions that demand our understanding and sympathy. They represent, for all their alarming characteristics, an heroic attempt to cope with certain admitted corruptions in our civilization.[45]

It must be stressed that Nazi ideology was reported, Nazi atrocities were not. In the early thirties, some surprising figures such as the left-wing Auden, and Shaw and Wells had shown some enthusiasm for the movement. Nazism cultivated a religious fanaticism during its performances and Hitler was likened to Christ. As more evidence of the Nazis' criminal attitude towards the Jews was received, Jones began to oppose the régime. Certainly, during the war and after the war Jones was forced to admit that his support for the Nazis had been quite wrong.[46]

Wilhelm Reich is again useful in his considerations upon the sexual and psychological preconditions of Fascist thought. Just as the capacity to work can be impaired by sexual frustration so can sexual suppression, in Reich's view, give rise to 'conservatism, fear of freedom, in a word, reactionary thinking'.[47] On a national scale, Fascism can be seen as 'the resistance of a sexually as well as economically deadly sick society to the painful but resolute revolutionary tendencies towards sexual as well as economic freedom, a freedom the very thought of which instills the reactionary man with mortal terror.'[48] Anxiety about cultural loss and collapse became embroiled in Jones's wrestling with his suppressed sexuality. The mythological paintings are so often cries of sexual as well as civilizational *angst*.

There was no question of Jones having been in any way cured after his first breakdown. He merely existed, treading water until another wave of mental illness would all but drown him. After finishing *The Four Queens* in 1941 such an attack occurred:

> This damned sleeplessness has returned. It seems so *maddening* that all I want to do and care about is to paint and that is the *one* thing that makes me really *ill*. What a fate ... It is *absurd*. I don't much fancy going to see old Woods again - this is no time for *another ten* years of 'masterly inactivity'.[49]

However, as late as 1944, he was still, after several more severe attacks, visiting the inefficacious Woods.[50] When he had to register for Industrial Service early in the war, a doctor gave this review of Jones's state of health:

> In 1932 he had a nervous breakdown and developed symptoms of mental depression - a depressive psychosis. The condition was severe. The course has been marked by improvement with relapses. He has been unfit for consecutive work in his own profession for nearly ten years. He is unstable, and under stress of duty would relapse. He is, in my opinion, quite unfit for routine service... .[51]

Many of Jones's friends considered him as an 'honorary celibate priest'[52] and indeed it is obvious that the residue of sentiments nurtured at Ditchling including thoughts about becoming a monk lingered on over the decades. Yet there is much evidence that the religion which at one time sustained him, had, in some respects, become a burden;[53] writing in 1940, Jones maintained

> I feel personally, ... that *intellectually* one's position is unmoved and unmoveable - but *emotionally* (or whatever the word should be) one is completely cut off - dried up, unperceptive - and all the efforts and words of 'religious' leaders seem to be just almost without meaning. I, too, have been terribly distressed about all this ... this inability to even *begin* to what is called 'pray' - in any strength-giving or straightforward way ... intellectually, I don't personally find it more difficult - I mean one can, as much as ever, see through all sceptical argument - the religious state remains the only *rational* one - but for myself it gets harder to *implement* or something: this nervous collapse of mine over these many years, has, *I think*, taught me that not many of the popular and accepted and believed-in theories, or convictions about

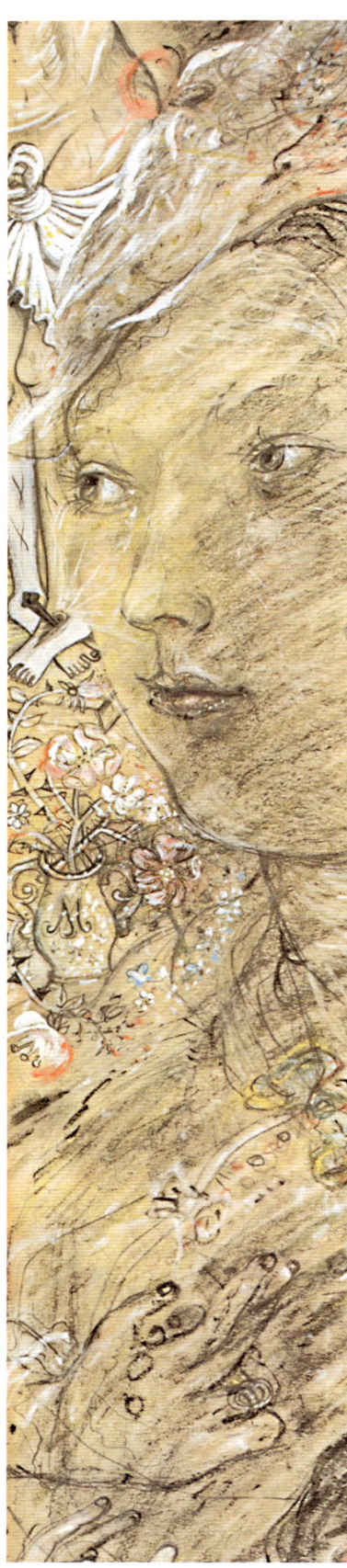

16. Sunday Mass: In Homage To G.M. Hopkins S.J. 1948 (detail), 1948

'heavenly consolation' etc. hold much water - I have become accustomed to living in a state of continuous fear … that buggered up all one's intentions and made ineffectual most of one's possible abilities. In many respects this was seeming to have lifted a good bit and I was *beginning* to take stock of the wreckage so to say … well, my beginning to emerge from my *subjective* barrage seems to have coincided with an *objective* barrage on 'all flesh'. Like waking up from a hideous and very private night-mare to find the house on fire … I think that perhaps, in a vast and seemingly lunatic catastrophe people come to learn as nerve-cases come to learn, that all such clichés as, say, 'God will help you' … 'There is nothing really the matter with you' etc. etc. (all those imbecile but well-meant suggestions that people make constantly to anyone with 'neurasthenia') - The thing is, I suppose, one has somehow got to hold on to the fact that 'God is helping one' in the most hideous and catastrophic exterior circumstances as he is when one is in the very pit of some psychological-pathological state. *This seems to reduce the matter to a pure intellectual concept.* *

[left hand margin:] *It has always been my main difficulty - How to make *effective* what is, perhaps, quite clear to the intelligence. Few people seem to be able to make any useful suggestion on this point. That's why I wonder if one is up the wrong street in some way, but I can't see where.[54]

When Jones drew from memory[55] a series of drawings of girls at Mass, he brought his delight in women and his unresolved sexual longings into the orbit of religious practice. Close to the sensitive and sensual eyes and lips of the girl on the left of *Sunday Mass: In Homage to G.M. Hopkins S.J.* we are only allowed a glimpse of two parts of the figure of Christ on the cross: his loincloth knotted across his genitals and that phallic nail probing the stylized, almost vulval wound which we first encountered in the copper engraving, *The Crucifixion.* In the worst manner of *ersatz* religious expression, rays of light shine out from the wound, illuminating the right side of the woman's face. In another of these visions of girls at Mass *(17)*, the whole stress under which Jones was suffering is revealed. The high forehead deriving from Petra Gill and Cranach has bulged madly, against all proportion; the head has assumed undue importance and yet the intellect, as Jones suggested in the letter above, has offered no solution.

Jones was well aware of the difficulties of making religious art in the twentieth century but early in his creative life he had made simple and direct expressions of his faith in the mystery of the Mass such as in the wood engraving *Candlemass* of 1923. By 1930, in the same medium, religion has been brought into the orbit of the artist's personal conflict. In *The Bride*, there is a stressed, over-fluid intensity about the buxom figure spiking her votive candles beneath the spiked feet of her Lord. Images of sacrifice, sexuality and penetration come together in a stressed vision of a ceremony in

260

which Jones could play no principal part. On a print sent to René Hague, the artist acknowledged, 'it's a very Pre-Raphaelite piece I fear ... Pray for me.'[56] Indeed, the right side of the engraving foreshadows the unbalanced intensity of an obsessively overworked drawing and watercolour, *A Latere Dextro* of 1943-9.

Jones drafted a letter to *The Tablet* in response to an article which John Rothenstein had written on religious art:

> The best works of the average modern artist tend to be idiosyncratic, personal in expression and experimental in technique, of a sensitivity more intimate and private than public and corporate, mostly small, just managed, with the artist 'all out' - for the tentative and searching requires peculiar effort ... One of your correspondents rightly said that the 'best' of any period should be at the service of the sanctuary - yes - but the best in painting can only be at the service of public and corporate acts and institutions when the best artists stand, so to speak, on the scaffold of a corporate tradition. We have no such tradition.[57]

Ironically, powerful reworkings of scenes from religious history could be made by artists who stood apart from Christianity such as Picasso with his *Crucifixion* of February, 1930. The ambiguity of forms, the eclecticism of myth and story add up to a fresh and striking evocation of a worn theme. In Jones's *A Latere Dextro*, the view was a composite vision of two churches Jones attended, the Carmelite Church in Kensington and Our Lady and St. Thomas of Canterbury in Harrow. Jones applies his manner of making mythological paintings to an actual scene that takes place both in and out of time, the moment of transubstantiation when wine becomes blood. The difficulty about this work is that it is glutted with dramatic incident allowing no room for that Post-Impressionist sense of transubstantiation. It is an intricately organized picture; the eye is led through the work by a series of echoing circles. It is Pre-Raphaelite in its obsession with detail, and yet it fades in and out of focus as our eye moves across the surface giving a range of textures and suggesting different orders of existence. The cope of the Priest seems to melt into thin air just as the Censer seems to appear from nowhere. The kitsch repository art which litters the church is matched by over-literal paranormal effects such as the treatment of the stigmata on the priest's hands, or the disconcertingly lifelike Mary of the statue on the left, or the *Agnus Dei* of the *bas-relief* in the lower right-hand corner.

Jones added a couple of centimetres on either side of the paper when the original proved to be too small to include all that he wished. It is a technically over-accomplished but mawkish and neurotic picture, a picture too insistent, too literal in its assertion of religious mystery. All the technical effort is squandered; as Jones has found no metaphor, the painting cannot transubstantiate. It is as if the artist is trying, too dogmatically, to assert the possibility of religious efficacy and it remains a frenzied testimony to Jones's religious and sexual dilemma. With a particularly animated Virgin seen cradling the wounded Jesus, the sub-text to this painting is the confession of a man who has put his

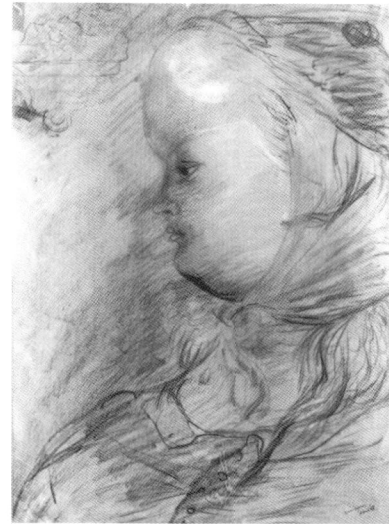

17. Girl at Mass, 1948

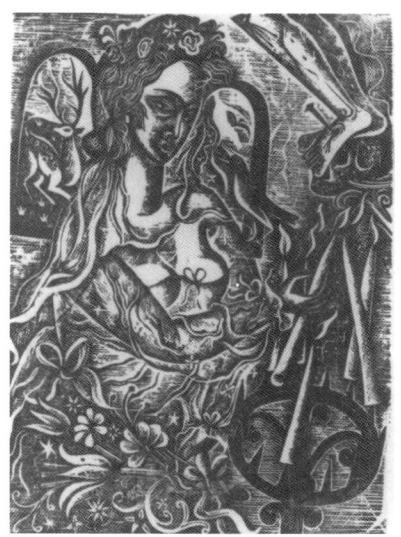

18. The Bride, 1929

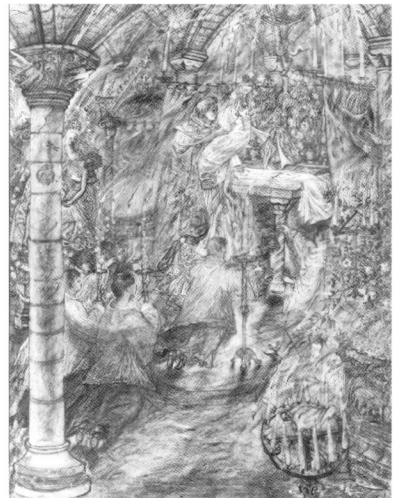

19. A Latere Dextro, 1949

faith in the Mass and is left wounded by his lack of emotional and sexual expression. Indeed, the 'inward wound' of which he speaks in relation to Nennius at the beginning of *The Preface* to *The Anathemata* meant for Jones something that was civilizational, sexual and religious. Jesus's wounds proved not to be redeeming but at least cognizable.

With the return of extreme fright and nervous collapse in 1946-7 Jones went to Bowden House from where he wrote to his patron, Helen Sutherland:

> I've been drawing a good deal lately - the trees from my window - All part of the treatment to get one back to one's proper avocation, especially so in my case as the conflict which set up this nervous illness is especially bound up* [rhm: * I don't mean painting is the 'cause' - *far from it* - but that the symptoms display themselves most clearly in relation to painting in my case] and chiefly manifested in painting (... the findings of the psychologists tally completely with what one had supposed *but* the reasons for which one did not and *could not* know without their aid) - on their theory it must be fought out therefore in painting (to a large extent) - and they consider I have reached the stage in the treatment when this must be faced - so consequently an attempt to paint again has been inaugurated under supervision as it were.[58]

What is perhaps significant about this letter is its lack of significance, its evasion. Time and time again Jones half tells what is going on and, in a way, that is as much as many of his friends and associates would have wanted to hear. The relation of 'symptoms' to painting is explained in part by Jones's vision of the incompatibility of painting and the civilizational situation:

> It is difficult to see how the peculiar qualities that characterize the art of painting can continue to co-exist with a civilization such as our own is or is becoming. A painting is a *sign* in the sense that a sacrament is a sign, an effective sign. In a civilization as fundamentally alien to sign and symbol (that is valid symbol, i.e. symbol which corresponds under its own forms, with some existing reality) as our own the task of the painter is made correspondingly more difficult ... both layman and artists are puzzled by the naturalness, directness and validity which characterize the art of this or that past period as compared with the extreme stress, oblique approach, acute experimentation, eclecticism, comparative rareness of complete integration, specialness of effort, extreme contradiction of direction which characterize it today.[59]

He noted in the margin of those notes prepared for his doctors that the 'invalidity' pervading a painter's symbols 'sets up a strain ... produces a neurosis'.[60]

Jones found the dredging and delving 'Inevitably a strain in many ways - for one has to *think quite hard* in order to collaborate with what the doctor is attempting to achieve'.[61] He was anxious as many artists would be about the 'possible effect of analysis on the peculiar balance of ingredients in my painting'.[62] Of the tree drawings done at Bowden House, Jones wrote, 'I like some of them quite genuinely - but *must* admit that I can't see it as authentic* [*i.e. not yet as much me as my pre-breakdown work ...]'.[63] Jones's resistance to combating his problem resulted in the use of narcosis[64] and the now discredited electric shock treatment.[65]

The doctors were attempting to unravel that complex of neuroses the origins of which we have been observing. Towards the end of his life, Freud

> arrived at the point of regarding a child's relation to his parents, dominated as it is by incestuous longings, as the nuclear complex of neurosis. This revelation of the importance of incest in neurosis is naturally received with universal scepticism, by adults and normal people ... principally a product of the distaste which human beings feel for their early incestuous wishes, now over-taken by repression.[66]

The natural aversion to the question of incest had been observed by Sir James Frazer, and Freud was convinced that the 'earliest sexual excitations of youthful human beings are invariably of an incestuous character and that such impulses when repressed play a part that can scarcely be over-estimated as motive forces of neuroses in later life'.[67]

When Jones watched Philip Hagreen's four-year-old daughter wanting to take a cumbersome new toy up to bed, Hagreen recalled that the artist remarked 'It's strange how early in life one wants to take what one loves to bed with one'.[68] In relation to that remark it might be of interest to note that up to about the age of five Jones slept in a cot next to his mother's bed.[69]

When in Bowden House Jones began to admit 'that *everything* one does is conditioned by one's psychopathology' and when he came to understand 'far better the ramifications of the sexual impulse and how the fear of assuming the 'father figure' position works in the most unexpected conjunctions and see how all my life I've avoided such a position in innumerable and subtle ways'[70] he was beginning to admit the strength of the taboo he had experienced against ousting his father. The possible tangle of confused emotions set up by the death of a brother who had teased Jones as a young child and who could have been seen, as an older brother, in the act of challenging the father, provoked emotions such as fright, awe, and guilt which would have further complicated the situation. The strength of the taboo against ousting his father, occasioned by the strength of his oedipal longing, rendered Jones's sexual life impossible and, by extension, his creative life difficult. Freud noted that 'obsessional prohibitions ... are forcibly maintained by an irresistible fear. ... an internal certainty, a moral conviction, that any violation will lead to intolerable disaster.'[71] In Jones's case we must stress that if the oedipal intention was strong, so was his struggle against it, giving rise to the tension out of which he realised his undoubted achievement as a creator.

How Jones's taboo extends from his fear of his own sexuality to an incapacity for work is suggested by Freud's explanation of the transmutation of neurosis:

263

> in the case of taboo, the principal prohibition, the nucleus of the neurosis, is against touching … The prohibition does not merely apply to immediate physical contact but has an extent as wide as the metaphorical use of the phrase, 'to come in contact with'. Anything that directs the patient's thoughts to the forbidden object, anything that brings him into intellectual contact with it, is just as prohibited as direct physical contact … Obsessional prohibitions are liable to displacement. They extend from one object to another along whatever paths the context may provide, and this new object then becomes … 'impossible' - till at last the whole world lies under the embargo of 'impossibility'.[72]

Here we find the personal complement to the civilizational dimension. Jones's mother, as we have noticed, was strongly associated in his mind with the act of drawing and painting; she had given him his first example by her own work, she encouraged him but she was anxious about his neglect of more scholarly activities and she was anxious about his future. The mother voice within him must have been goading him to become learned, to throw in his lot with the respectable world or at least word, and so Jones became, at the expense of the purely plastic, the essayist, the broadcaster, the poet. As Jones remarked in 1973, 'Freud really had it right, this father/mother relationship'.[73] And what is more, painting itself is a physical and sensual act; its spontaneity admits disorder, panic, and excitement. Painting, not surprisingly, allowed problems to percolate into the conscious.

Another aspect of his dilemma was that, with no income of his own, Jones was obliged to seek the indulgence of friends to enable him to get away from home. He needed to break away and make a breakthrough, but with the mystical vision after which he appears to have been straining apparently beyond his grasp, he broke down. In the years that followed, the church and the intellectual establishment which had been part of his making now compounded his unmaking. If his first breakdown had much to do with a glimpse of success and the problems that posed for someone avoiding the position of the father figure, the second serious breakdown was to do with failure. Failure of painting, of his culture, failure in love. He chose impossible relationships, never asked the girls who could have said 'yes' and had a neurotic dislike of physical closeness; late in life he would rub and rub drinking glasses long after they were clean,[74] he couldn't bear to use a bath that someone else would have used but would rather wash at a sink.[75] According to Grisewood he was resigned to not having physical enjoyment saying, 'I never wanted to wake up next to a woman - that would be disgusting to me'.[76] From Jones's declaration to his doctors at Bowden House, it appears that physical intimacies were only experienced with Petra 'and nothing approximating to them was experienced in the other love affairs, these were confined to less intimate embraces.'[77] The teaching of his religion meant, of course, that an intimate relationship would imply commitment which explains why intimacy occurred in the context of his engagement. As Jones put it:

I do not question the findings [of the doctors] at all about my fear etc. with regard to sex - but I do emphatically say that over and beyond those symptoms of imbalance in my own make-up, there is the concept of 'not marriage' as a perfectly rational desire in order to pursue what appears to this or that person to be a greater good ... A Catholic at all events cannot marry except with the primary intention of building up a family. Rightly or wrongly, I have *always* known or felt this not to be my job - from my teens I have had this in mind. This *may* be a 'rationalization' of my inhibitions and fears of sex, but, discounting those, the attitude seems to be completely defensible and reasonable.[78]

In a pamphlet written by Crichton-Miller a decade before he received Jones at Bowden House, the psychologist noted that

in all these unending problems of the adolescent who is reluctant to grow up, we see one common failing. The adolescent is missing the opportunity of orientating his life to the future. The repressions and maladjustments of this phase can generally be classed under this broad formulation. But this forces us to ask ourselves how far our adult patients have achieved an orientation to the future. In this respect the problems of adolescence ... and old age all partake of a common nature. This consists in the repression of considerations of the future and a refusal to prepare for the new adaptations that will be called for. The adolescent is therefore always prone to cling to the prerogatives of childhood and avoid the responsibility consistent with his real age. The filial basis must give way to the mutual giving and taking of marriage, and that in turn must yield to the parental basis of giving without expecting a return.[79]

Jones obviously never progressed through these important stages and as he grew older his dislike of change became so pronounced that it gave rise, at times, to acute agoraphobia. He remembered that even in the First World War 'I so detested "changes" once I'd got used to a situation, and the people involved, that I *positively disliked* coming out of the trenches ... even though I was pretty scared in them!'[80] After his second breakdown any kind of change or decision became an appalling prospect so when Northwick Park Lodge was closed Jones stayed on there refusing to move until an alternative was eventually found for him. The omnipotent child likes to disavow, resign responsibility and yet by a cunning sleight of hand, call the tune. Freud noted 'in obsessional neuroses that the survival of the omnipotence of thoughts is most clearly visible'[81] and Jones's capacity to act in an omnipotent fashion is clear from his incredible ability to make people want to do things for him. Jones, observed one close friend, 'was used to being totally spoilt';[82] five years after his stay in Bowden House he was still using the laundry service of the Nursing Home occasioning a gently caustic remonstrance from Crichton-Miller:

My dear D.J., I like to have my linen well-laundered. Of course, I do not like paying the bill but I like the feel of the receipted invoice! So what do you say to making the payments for your laundry direct without going through our intermediate hands?[83]

One important area in which Jones refused to accept responsibility was the question of money and that was compounded with the discomfort or ill-adjustment of the 'poor artist' in social relations with the rich. Although programmed to modest living he was almost forced by the expectations and tastes of those around him to grander notions. Helen Sutherland would send Jones his third-class fare to Rock, but he would pay a supplement, travel first and change to a third class compartment just before arriving at Alnmouth and being met by the morose chauffeur, Mills.

His occupation forced him into a canny attitude towards money; living at home or with the Gills in the twenties and early thirties and thereafter often staying with friends, his financial needs were slight. From the mid-thirties he did need more money but by then he had developed a network of friends who were willing to help which was useful during a period in which the pattern of artistic patronage changed and corporations began taking over from the individual; Shell-Mex, for example, gave Graham Sutherland his livelihood during the thirties. As that decade progressed, many painters were being forced into the media in order to earn a living[84] and Kenneth Clark took steps to create funds for artists such as Coldstream or Pasmore that would enable them to keep painting. In the forties, he answered a request from H.S. Ede to help David Jones.

Despite making £332 from the sale of paintings by the Redfern, Goupil and Leicester galleries in the period from November 1939 to March 1940 (£115 of which had been advanced and £41-12-0 of which would be returned to the dealers to cover the costs of mounts), and despite netting £22 from the private sale of a picture in August 1940, Jones wrote to Tom Burns that he was not getting any money at all 'and have only a tiny bit that I'm living on, which will soon exhaust itself'.[85] It seems a somewhat surprising plaint when Jones was living rent free at Burns's house in Glebe Place, had recently made substantial gallery sales, and received regular support from Helen Sutherland. Indeed the successful Redfern show of January 1940, the occasional private sale and the extremely modest royalties from *In Parenthesis* would not have put his earned income for 1940 much below that of an artist like Graham Sutherland who in 1941-2 earned £435;[86] the difference was that Sutherland's income was on the up and Jones was clearly anxious that if he was not painting he would have nothing to sell. In March, 1941, he wrote to Grisewood, 'Please give my love to everyone - I hope they don't run after you in the street … saying - Friends of Jones, the debtor'.[87]

During the war some of the prices obtained for recent works were not inconsiderable, and, as indicated, there was an increase in the price of Joneses immediately after the war. Nonetheless, the artist claimed absolute poverty and, during the forties, H.S. Ede decided to set up a fund to compensate the fact that a friend of Jones 'who has contributed largely to his upkeep all these years cannot continue to do so'. Ede was attempting to 'get a few people who together might produce £6 a week or £300 a year to be given to him anonymously.'[88] When the proposition was put to Clark he replied, 'You know how greatly I admire his work and like him personally. I will gladly contribute £50 a year and could increase this sum if you cannot find enough other admirers … to bring the total up to the £300 required.'[89] The fund was accordingly set up and Clark wrote over two years later that it was his 'intention to go on paying David Jones £25 a quarter until further notice'[90] which appears, in fact, to have been March, 1953. The fund, however, was still in existence in the 1970s.

A typical beginning of letters to Helen Sutherland from the end of the war until well into the fifties is 'Thankyou very very much for your letter and for your cheque'.[91] Sutherland was tireless and generous in her aid, but she was clever enough to protect her interests:

> what I think I've been wondering is whether I might now revert to buying a picture - instead of an allowance - or if it seems better to keep up a regular allowance then perhaps it could be earmarked for me to get a painting - it seems a little hard *not* to be able to get one now and then? but, *as it were*, to help *other* people to acquire them!?[92]

By the beginning of the 1950s money matters seemed to have eased, although Jones's perception of the situation was little better. His professional income for the year ending March 1951 was £587 including personal gifts totalling £185 and he was obviously not in desperate straits as cheques would often remain uncashed.[93] By the middle to late fifties things had, however, taken a turn for the worse and in 1959 he wrote to his patron asking for a loan of £180; his income from his activities as a painter and writer were between £35-42 per year between 1956 and 1959,[94] a situation modified by the successful application for a Bollingen Foundation Grant in 1959.

Yet during that time of particularly low earnings, Jones, who lived frugally, continued to behave in some ways quite like the English gent; a letter from Walters & Co. (Oxford) Ltd. of May 1958 is revealing:

> Referring to the Five Pairs of Half Hose recently returned to us with your letter of April 30th, we have made enquiries in an effort to obtain a similar hose in softer wool and now submit on approval for your examination Two pairs of Two Steeples Half Hose i.e. Fernia 83 @ 11/6 per pair and Fernia H. Heavy at 15/6 per pair… .[95]

From L.G. Wilkinson, Tailor of Hanover Square: 'I note that the Trousers are a little tight in the fork and should be pleased to rectify this when you are able to spare them.'[96] and from Ward & Co, Tailors of 35 Savile Row (and Harrow) Jones received sample shirt patterns.[97] The apparently impecunious artist appears to the manor born. It would, of course, have been necessary for Jones to maintain a certain standard among associates and he would have taken the habits of his often affluent friends but Grisewood suggests that there was also a feeling of 'coming home to a world he belonged to'.[98] So here again we have ill-adjustment and discrepancy; an apparent liking for the finer things of life and a certain style (taking taxis, going to expensive outfitters) and a perception of poverty derived from childhood, and exacerbated in early manhood by his precarious professional existence.

In the sixties Jones added to his awards: £100 from the Welsh Arts Council for *Epoch and Artist* in 1960; £200 in 1962 from The Society of Authors Travelling Fund (bizarre for a man who would hardly budge from Harrow-on-the-Hill); his Civil List Pension, granted for £150 in 1954 went up to £350 in 1967. The biggest change to his financial situation occurred in 1964 when Helen Sutherland died and left him £6000; yet Peter Orr, who met him in that very year, recalls that Jones was 'obsessed with poverty'. Certainly Jones had never made an effort to alleviate his financial situation even by accepting random offers of employment; in August, 1950 he was unable or unwilling to accept an offer from William Coldstream to spend a day instructing Slade students individually. His early refusal to take certain exams at Camberwell which would have qualified him to teach permanently in an art school is interpreted quite credibly by Gray as an early example of 'the man who was always to find certain quite ordinary requirements impossible';[99] it could be considered shrewd. Towards the end of his life he somewhat luxuriously felt less and less inclined to sell his works. Money was a source or symptom of neurosis but the situation was something Jones controlled with consummate skill and omnipotence.

According to Stanley Honeyman, Jones thought it 'perfectly right and proper that people with more cash than artists should give their patronage by giving money.'[100] In the sixties and seventies, Honeyman was tireless in helping with and advising the artist about his financial matters; in 1971, he managed to arrange an annuity for Jones that yielded over £400 a quarter. Nonetheless, in the last decade of his life Jones showed a loss for income tax purposes from his professional activities as an artist, because, as his accountant put it, he did not sell paintings, saying that he needed them around him for inspiration. He 'hadn't painted for years and had no wish to put a commercial value on his work as an author as he felt too deeply about it to do so.'[101]

Ironically, in 1964, the very year in which Jones became well and truly financially secure, he made a move which psychologically must have confirmed his notions about poverty. After the lofty perch in Northwick Park Lodge, close to the cultural life of Harrow School, he moved down the hill to the Metroland bleakness of the streets around Monksdene Residential Hotel. The corridors of this establishment with its aquariums and curly wrought iron brought 'a Moroccan brothel' to one visitor's mind.[102] When he moved in, the French windows of Jones's 'oblong, rather dark'[103] room on the ground floor looked out onto a garden. But, as if to make Jones's vision of the waste land more complete, that garden was soon dug up and converted into a car-park. The very fact that Jones could tolerate such circumstances leads one to suppose that he was, to a certain extent, blind to his environment or too ill really to care. In a sense Monksdene was the most humble and inappropriate place in which he had ever lived. A friend's assessment was that 'Monksdene may not be heaven but, like hell, it is of a permanent nature and removes the insecurity of tenure which you have known for years'.[104]

In 1962 Jones had a renewed attack of the nerve trouble that had taken him to Bowden House; in the intervening years his body had registered a catalogue of illness, suggesting continued internal stress.[105] This time it was decided to treat the condition with 'a complicated system of capsules, pills, tablets, drugs of about six different kinds' as if the doctors had given up with analysis or therapy.[106] The regimen was complicated and Jones had to make a coloured chart 'to remember which particular drug ... to take in what quantity at what hour';[107] as he put it in another letter, 'there are *so many of them* that I can't remember when to take them.'[108] He continued to see Dr. Stevenson regularly but wrote, in April of the following year,

> I can't say I'm in 'good shape'. I've been on this regimen of capsules, pills etc. since last summer and don't feel really any better than when I started. My doctor [in margin: 'The psy-chiatrist...'] tells me I am better even if I don't feel so!'[109]

The side-effects of the large numbers of drugs were considerable: lethargy and loss of focus, so that Jones would omit words from letters and other writings, 'making nonsense'.[110] Nardil, a drug often prescribed for agoraphobia and generalized anxiety, can result in memory deficiency, general confusion, muscle cramps, tremors and insomnia as well as visual and auditory hallucinations.[111] Nembutal, which is no longer used in such an indication, is so depressive that it can be employed as an anaesthetic; it affects the breathing and the motor commands of the body. Certainly a cocktail of anti-depressants and tranquilizers such as Nembutal, phenobarbitone, Drinaryl, Trofanil and Librium was not an innocent combination, but was one that would not have been considered an abnormal prescription in the early 1960s for a depressive with sleeping difficulties. Jones was told by Dr. Bell, who prescribed the drugs, that he 'should accept incapacity ... and count himself lucky if it were painless'.[112] Jones, having been frightened as a child when his aunt became senile, and having witnessed senility overtake his own mother, could only accept this advice.

The drugs took their toll on his capacity to work and affected his general behaviour. T.S. Eliot, who had witnessed the harrowing effects of drugs on his first wife, spoke to Jones about the lethargy-inducing effect of large doses of Nembutal and enlisted the help of Harman Grisewood in trying to dissuade Jones from using the drug. But there was habituation if not dependence and Jones was convinced he needed Nembutal in order to sleep.[113] The resultant drowsiness probably contributed to a perception of ageing; in 1965 he wrote that 'I feel about *twice as old* as I did a couple of years ago.'[114] The general loss of muscle control and fogginess may have been a contributory factor in the weakening of bodily control which eventually led to a fall in which Jones broke his pelvis, resulting

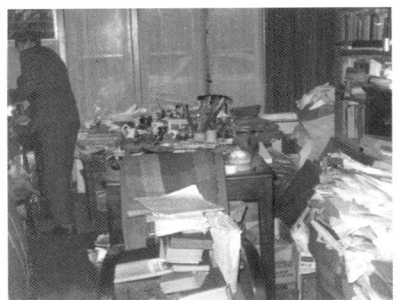

20. Janet Stone, David Jones at Monksdene, 1967

in his move to the Bethanie Nursing Home and thence to the Calvary Nursing Home for the duration of his life. The pills seemed to be a last desperate attempt on the part of his doctors to deal with the apparently incurable complex of psychological disturbances but they resulted in, or at least did not eradicate, disorders such as an eight or nine day bout of almost non-stop hiccups.[115]

The agoraphobia of a man who had always detested change and who felt ill whenever he had to move, became more pronounced in later life. If his visit to the private view of his Tate retrospective in 1954 had been the first time that he had gone out for three weeks,[116] then a decade later at Monksdene he hardly ever left the building; 'I never go much beyond the hallway out there' he said to a reporter who had come to interview him.[117] Jones even wanted to 'build a barrier of sandbags halfway up' his French windows.[118] He became anxious sitting out in a friend's garden, constantly turning and looking longingly at the house. When this friend managed to organize a trip to the *Bonnard Exhibition* at the Royal Academy in 1966 and she had to leave him in the Academy forecourt while she parked her car, he went into a state of complete panic. Once she returned and they went into the exhibition, Jones relaxed, marvelling at the paintings, particularly enjoying the ones of Marthe in the bath such as *Nu à la Baignoire* (c.1938-41).[119]

Not going out, Jones had no fresh air, no exercise. The pills meant that he was unable to drink whisky, a privation he found deplorable. He experienced rages 'of impotence', hurling books across the room when he was looking for things[120] and there was a constant fear of a return of the extreme forms of his neurosis. He had never been cured. In the mid-fifties he struck a young Harrow schoolmaster as fragile, lonely and 'painfully inarticulate', somebody with a longing to talk but who found it difficult; he would grope in the air with hands, use the word 'thing' as an endless substitute for the more precise term and became lost for words when talking about the First World War.[121] He would telephone friends late at night with a doom-laden voice and talk for ages, slowly being coaxed from depression till he would start to giggle. Giggling, that manic form of laughter, that tension not so far removed from a symptom like hiccups, was just another sign that things were being bottled up, that the 'horrors were being kept underground'.[122] One friend summed up his understanding of Jones as 'depressed, distracted, inhibited, paralysed'.[123]

That his therapy had not entirely overcome the complex tangle of neuroses is revealed by the fact that in the late 1950s, he fell desperately and impossibly in love. He became intoxicated by the vivacity of a young Welsh woman and it seems to have hit him with the force of an ageing man realizing that he had never enjoyed his youth. Never having enjoyed the full pleasure of romantic love, mis-timed, it hit him with a velocity that would have shaken a younger, fitter man.

Valerie Price, nonetheless, was a tonic for Jones. There had been an immediate *rapport* between them when they met in 1958 as a result of an exchange of letters about Wales in *The Times*. They talked politics and giggled a lot. He described her as

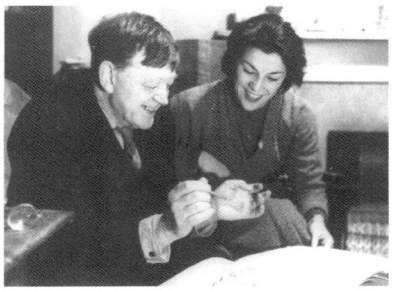

21. David Jones & Valerie Wynne-Williams, (?)

very, *very* reserved by nature, and though, on the surface, extrovert and gay and 'practical', and 'matter of fact', underneath all this ... is deep feeling and, as is not uncommon among truly and wholly Welsh people, a whole flood of curbed and dammed-up emotion.[124]

She managed to get Jones to stop smoking. She got him out to meet a House of Commons Committee on the future of Welsh Broadcasting. She met Dr. Stevenson and discovered that the psychiatrist was being used as a scapegoat for Jones's refusing to do things.[125] He fell more and more desperately in love and she found, at times, the relationship draining; there would be phone calls at home, sometimes at work, and she felt that she could not keep pace with his demands.

Some knew the full extent of his lovesickness; a short meeting after months of not seeing her gave him enormous pleasure, lunch at the Paddington Hotel ('We'd never before had a meal in a restaurant, so that was fun and peaceful and unstrained and it was nice taking her to the London Library afterwards.'[126]) gave rise to the kind of delight found in a young lover:

> Not that we talked about anything at all really. Just that she was terribly sweet to me ... I know it all sounds so stupid and in everyway absurd, but somehow, (in a way I don't pretend to understand at all) we seem to meet on some point, *or on some plane*, and from this last meeting I feel that it's just as real to her ... but I don't think it is ... It all seems so *totally* [double under-line] other from what chaps talk about when they speak of a 'passion' or of 'being in love' with someone ... As far as I can see (of course one can deceive oneself) there is no feeling of wanting to possess anything, or of jealousy, or even desire (although, I know, of course, it's partly physical) - it seems more like a kind of dumb *compassion* - and a *mutual* compassion between two people *wholly remote* from each other in most respects. Anyway the experience of loving her so much has helped me, in part, to understand the extraordinary and un-accountable 'attachments' that one has only before heard of second-hand or read about in the histories. It makes all the stuff about 'love' just *bloody silly*. For one thing although it's ob-viously, *in part*, physical, in another way it's as remote from the physical as anything could be, and seems to have no connection with ordinary physical desire whatever. It is just something that 'is'... I wish I could convey how 'un-romantic', 'passionless', and 'ordinary' the situation is between V. and myself, and yet, underneath, the wholly unaccountable feeling that makes me weep so often.[127]

In his tendency to deny his physical attraction he seems again unable to confront his sexuality, particularly when we consider that he told Saunders Lewis of his desire to marry Valerie Price, she in her mid-twenties and he almost a teenager in love at over sixty. Lewis counselled:

it would seem to me that you'll have to accept that burden and keep it *your* burden, just love her, the lovely girl, and accept the hopeless ache of it. I dare not say more. Except that I am very very concerned for your peace and for hers.[128]

When friends advised him to give up the friendship, Jones tried to rationalize the situation:

> After all how *could* she understand the sophisticated tangle that goes on in my mind. She has a very kind heart and after all, lives in a different world from mine in *most* ways and is, after all, only beginning her life in one sense. I must get it more in just proportion and I hope I shall.[129]

By the time of their meeting at the Paddington Hotel, Valerie Price had herself become Mrs. Wynne-Williams but that does not seem to have stopped Jones from pining for her, or from sending her roses for her birthday. For her part, she was not a good letter-writer but when she wrote she noted that despite her busy life she thought of him[130] and even offered practical aid such as doing his laundry although by that time she was in North Wales and he was in Harrow. As late as 1971, a telephone call from her at Christmas thrilled him: 'it was heavenly hearing her voice again - those Welsh vowels alone are inimitable'.[131]

His father's death in 1943 had resulted in the loss of Jones's 'only blood affinity'[132] with the Welsh and Price was cherished as 'through and through of the Welsh'.[133] Astoundingly, he confessed that 'She's the only Welsh woman I've ever met really'[134] and wrote, 'she represents 'Wales' to me and I'm as much cut off from 'Wales' as I am from her - I *really believe* that that accounts for quite a bit of my intense feeling about her.'[135] As already noted, he wished to imagine her in flowing black cloak and it is clear that, despite the obvious directness of Jones's feelings, the need to place women in some historical or mythological context remained.

Throughout the fifties and sixties Jones scribbled out biro or pencil fantasies of buxom women which seemed to offer some kind of immediate relief to his frustration. But when he developed female subjects into more complete and serious works they exhibited extreme stress, if not a kind of madness. A woman painted in a way and in a situation which seems not unrelated to the painting *Gwener* sits, blessed by a god's eye, crowned by doves carrying a circlet of flowers with her dress clasped together by a series of telltale bows, used in the evocation of the most intense erotic desire *(24)*. Such an image is the sad testimony to a maker, once vigorous and innovative, truly unmade by psychological distress.

The original title for *Gwener (23)* was 'The Lee-Shore', a dangerous place for voyagers. Its overall effect is Surrealist with odd conjunctions such as the out of place and utterly modern window and a blocking stone wall on which 'Elri' (Valerie) is scribbled in Greek graffiti. In the foreground, a cross-bow crawls like a insect, bed-linen hangs like ladies' underwear, bows abound,

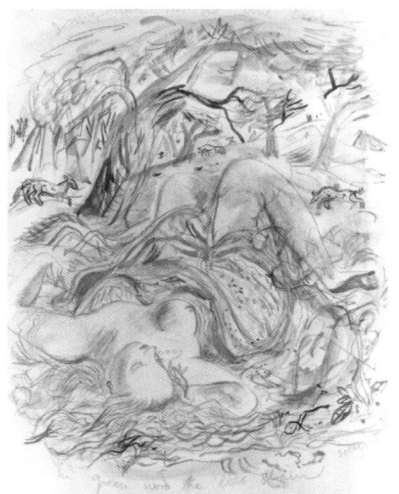

22. Girl in Landscape 'In the Green Wood She Lies Slain', 1938

the sea is in tempest. The Mass, represented by the Chalice, stands guard on the opened window. Flesh tones are heightened and frilly knickers are pulled half-way down Gwener's legs and the shoes, which Jones explained away with scholarly references to Lady Llanover's studies on Welsh costume, are clearly, in this context, erotic symbols. A particularly painful stigma has pierced the thigh (like the old Grail metaphor for sexual impairment) close to the artist's sensuous evocation of the female bottom. Around the figure of Gwener there is a storm of distress, a frenzy such as we have seen disturbing many of the paintings; arrows, which Jones calls 'stray arrows from the battle', fly into the room. These are rather arrows of desire but wide of the mark. And with Gwener, as with Guenever, the woman's body with expanse of flesh promises an island of calm, a refuge for the eye from the melodrama that grips the rest of the painting. But Gwener is facing away from the artist; woman is the haven of relief, a promise of calm but denied and hence desperately desired. The painting trembles around the very source of Jones's torment: the forbidden female.

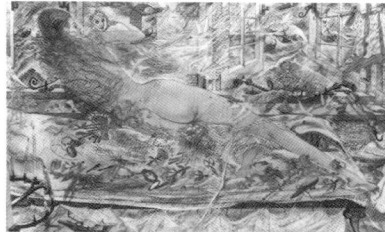

23. Gwener, 1959

So disturbed was Jones's sexuality that it provoked such obsessively over-worked pictures. It was as if he were channelling his frustration into the end of his pencil or paint brush. An artist's work is involved with the fulfilling of the self, an attempt to overcome fantasy and escape the mere projection of personal obsessions; where David Jones does not overcome the projection of his sexual self-deprivation his work is compromised.

During his last decades, Jones was living among 'the heap of all that he could find' and feeling desperately misunderstood. Yet, from the ashes of a career as a visual creator, he managed, while being assailed by depression and drugs, to produce a series of highly original and modern works full of great beauty. Through the fitting together of words resonating with meaning, the repositories of thousands of years of culture, and with a sure abstract sense Jones redeemed himself and, with the inscriptions and in his late poems, became a maker remade.

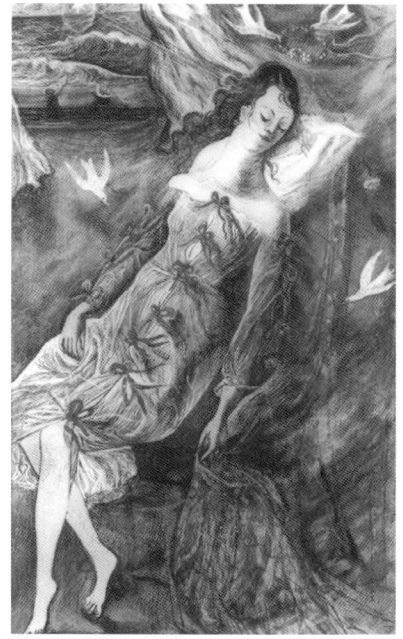

24. Woman with Bows, 1959

RESONANT ABSTRACTIONS

Despite the emotional and psychological problems there was a great flowering towards the end of Jones's life, a convergence of many of his most cherished ideas about form and content; the sentimental difficulties, pressures of religion, his vision of history and civilizational dis-ease did not impair Jones's capacity to realize his magnificent inscriptions. He was a bard, a 'carpenter of song' and a celebrant. He was a maker of shapes and forms and the inscriptions were often useful artefacts as well as pure art, devotional aids used like 'Mass cards on the altar ... to help him through his daily office'.[1] Jones had bridged the gap between the Ditchling ethos and the more abstract art of his contemporaries and he did it without losing sight of his civilizational predicament, for the letters which make up the inscriptions often appear embattled, a purely formal expression of struggle and loss.

Arbor Decora (1956) provides a good example. What first strikes the spectator is the tumbling movement across the surface and the idiosyncratic forms based on three different styles of lettering: Greek, Roman and Anglo-Saxon. 'PVRPVRA', painted in imperial and penitential purple which for Catholics would recall Lent and Advent, immediately catches the eye. The uneven intensity of the background gives the inscription not only a two-dimensional movement but also a sense of three-dimensional space. The irregular letters with seriphs that lead the eye off at varying angles, push and pull the spaces in between, making the white surface vibrant. Certain words immediately impinge - 'PVRPVRA', 'FVLGIDA', 'SANCTA' and 'REGIS'; attention is drawn by their different colours, which at first sight appear to have been chosen arbitrarily. The eye slithers down these egregious words to the bottom line, painted in a tone that seems to embrace the royal purple of 'PVRPVRA' and the greeny yellow of 'FVLGIDA', 'REGIS' and 'SANCTA'. It provides a precarious plinth for the other and later cultural deposits. The most recent of these is the Anglo-Saxon of the surround, whose fluid letter forms embrace the Latin text. Implicit in the relation of these various letter forms is Jones's whole message about the formation of his culture.

So far, in the act of apprehension, there has been no attempt to read the text, the primary experience is visual, perhaps followed by the feeling of linguistic disorientation and cultural multiplicity.

A second example: *Nam Sibyllam*, which Jones considered to be 'one of the best'[2] inscriptions, engages the eye like a page of writing, starting at the top left-hand corner. The viewer begins to read but is perhaps again deterred by the mixture of unfamiliar languages: Latin, Greek, Middle French, Welsh and

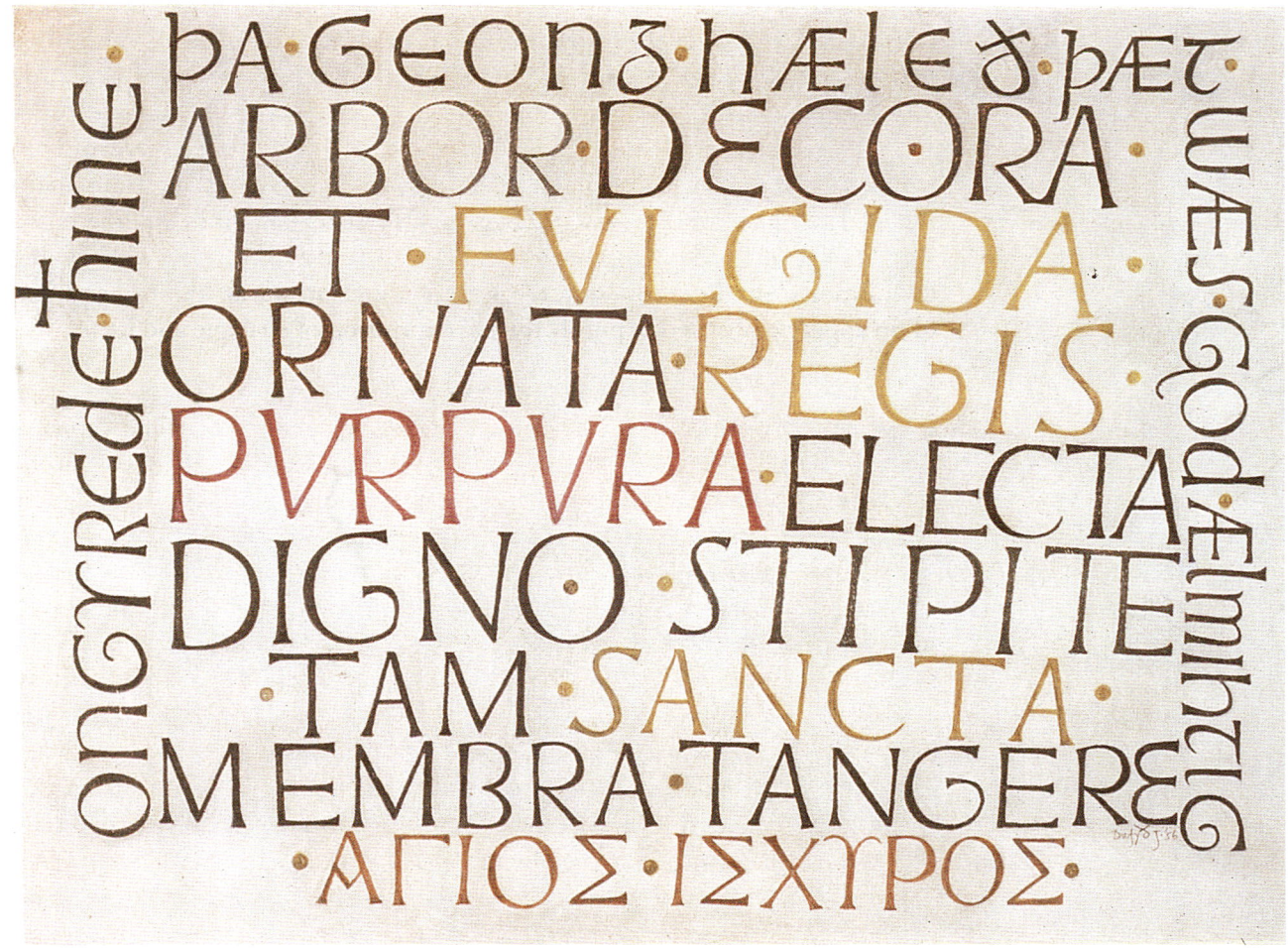

1. Arbor Decora, 1956

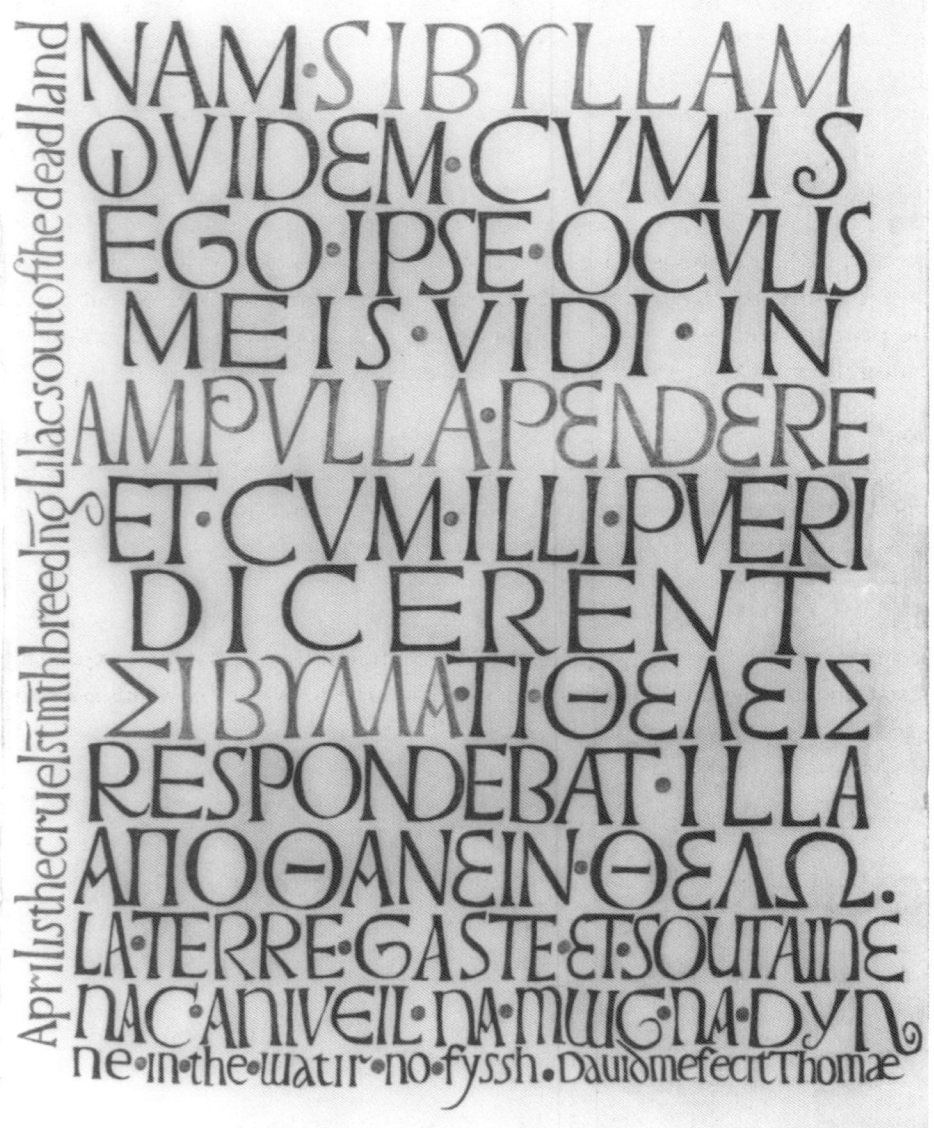

2. Nam Sibyllam, 1958

Middle English. The most linguistically accessible text is the quotation from T.S. Eliot's *The Waste Land* ('April is the cruellest month, breeding Lilacs out of the dead land') which is crushed vertically and, at first sight, illegibly up the side of the page. Despite the desire to read the whole inscription, the spectator retreats into visual appreciation and postpones the intellectual challenge of understanding, at least for a while.

Leaving any cultural intention aside, Jones deliberately chose Latin as the predominant language for his inscriptions because few small words are used, and because there was a 'magic' about a language not fully understood.[3] As he put it in a letter to Helen Sutherland, 'Latin has the … advantage of presenting one with a sort of pattern first and then only slowly (if at all!) the meaning of all (or some!) of the words.'[4] In the work of many modern calligraphers the

276

sheer fact of isolating a fragment of text and thereby giving it undue importance can result in the heightening of a sentiment which, wrenched from the complex interrelations of its matrix, appears simplistically embarrassing; Jones's macaronics avoid this. Indeed, Jones went so far as to say that he found the making of an inscription in English boring because the '"meaning" is too obvious' and it 'lacks mystery'.[5] He also claimed that English words '*interfere*' because their 'meanings are too close to me'.[6] Abstract visual patterning is the artist's primary intention and literary communication is secondary, although clearly, the inscriptions represent a coming together of Jones the learned poet and Jones the painter; for the painter, questions of form and movement would be primary concerns while the poet chose texts because of their immense cultural significance, their emotional power.

Jones claimed that the inscriptions, like his carvings, were 'amateur' and 'personal'. Lettering is principally a public and functional art and although a good number of Jones's inscriptions were occasional and function as celebrations of specific events or festivals they do so in a 'private'[7] capacity. They are not tablets, gravestones, advertisements or even letters to be placed publicly in a landscape as with the lettering of an artist like Ian Hamilton Finlay. The inscriptions are, however, objects, artefacts, physical fragments often expressing a sentiment celebrated in Jones's poetry. The urge to write *The Anathemata* and the Mass poems in *The Roman Quarry*, all part of the same complex making, spilled over, towards the end of Jones's life, into the desire for a visual shape in words more reified than even the carefully positioned text on the pages of the poems. Certain inscriptions act as a kind of score that directs the sound and gesture of the Mass through which the word becomes incarnate; the priests in *The Anathemata* and in *The Kensington Mass*, in their acts of celebration, give some indication of the function of certain of the inscriptions.

> should you be elbow-close him
>   you may catch his
> soft-breathed-out
>   PER CHRISTVM DOMINVM NOSTRVM
>
> …
>
>   He has no
> need of the rubric's nudge: *osculatur altare in medio*.
> for what bodily act other
>   would serve here?
> Creaturely of necessity
>   for we are creatures.[8]

Indeed, it would have been most interesting if Jones had conceived the relatively short 'Kensington Mass' as a lettered series, thereby breaking into a new form of sequential inscriptions. Jones's feeling about paintings being 'things'[9] is manifest in inscriptions. To the modern spectator they might be obscure to the point of abstract triumph, for the artist they were private mantras replete with meaning.

Letter forms trail a series of connotations. A style of lettering speaks volumes. The Gothic letter form carries with it a sense of the intellectual density of

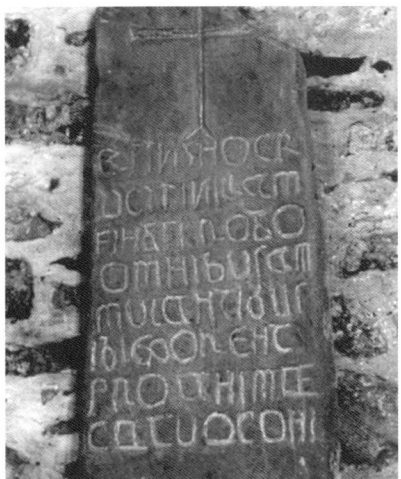

3. Ewan Clayton, Caldey Stone, (?)

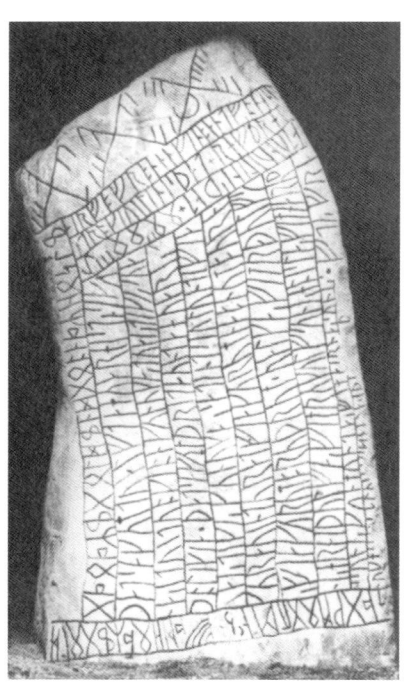

4 Anon., Runic Stone, (?)

German culture. Jasper Johns's colourful map of the United States[10] shows each state named in letters stencilled from sheets that were widely available at 5¢ and 10¢ Stores or Woolworths throughout the U.S.A. in the 1950s and 60s - with homely patriotism Johns asserts the Main St. aspect of his painted States. So what about David Jones's stylistic subtext; what is the semiology of his letter forms? From where do they derive and to what purpose did he put them?

Believing, as an art student, that Roman lettering was 'a lost art that no one could emulate'[11] he was surprised to find, on meeting Eric Gill, that there could be a 'living lettering' based on Roman forms and that 'inscription-making was very much a part of a living inheritance'.[12] Later in the 1920s, on Caldey Island, Jones saw a relic which would have provoked his imagination. In the Old Priory there was a stone with an incised cross, a Latin inscription in debased Roman lettering below and an Ogham inscription around the edge.[13] After he began to perceive the affinity between his own and the post-Imperial Roman times, Jones realized that forms derived from the Roman alphabet, but in a broken and embattled state, might be culturally expressive of a decline and aftermath in which failing tradition is struggling to survive. He observed that Gill's whole endeavour was undertaken as if 'a culture of some sort existed',[14] but knew himself that this was not the case. The critic John Dreyfus perceived, in looking at the inscriptions, 'a feeling of tenseness, anxiety and depression',[15] so they reflect the emotional states as well as the intellectual position of the artist. Like the poems, the inscriptions intercut dispersed and often macaronic fragments of text in a way that is truly modernist. The sides of Jones's letters waver as if worn by age or assailed by doubt and many of the inscriptions carry the poignancy of a worn cypher from a lost civilization. In the studied struggle involved in their making, Jones's inscriptions have something of a cry in the wilderness and something of the quality of runes about them. Runes were often of religious significance and were possessed of magic powers. They appear to have been carved on surfaces that were difficult to incise, surfaces that were durable - as if the survival of the text was vital. Like much of twentieth century art, the demonstration of technical dexterity does not appear to have been of great importance and yet there are rhythms and tensions in the disposition of the forms which are not dissimilar to those in Jones's work. Furthermore, the earliest runic alphabet of the second or third centuries was formed, like Jones's own letters, by modifying the Greek or Roman alphabet. Not only are Jones's modified Roman forms expressive of cultural plight, they are also apt, as the texts which he chose to letter are usually classical or pre-Renaissance Christian. He wrote that:

> I try always to find a precedent for all the shapes I use. When uncial or Gothicised etc. letters appear in a word in juxtaposition with Roman caps, it is always for some reason of evocation, of recalling, the historic provenance of that word. The word *haubergeon* in that long inscription [*Cloelia Cornelia*] is a good example - you simply *can't* inscribe that word - so utterly of the North-European middle ages, in Roman capitals; it looks absurd and evokes nothing.[16]

To earlier European inspirations for Jones's inscriptions we can add the Victorian sampler, the presence of which would have been common in a semi-detached, suburban household like that of Jones's parents in Brockley or, as Saunders Lewis suggested, on Welsh cottage walls.[17] The sampler's qualities of benediction, remembrance, celebration and sage counsel all can be found in aspects of Jones's often liturgical inscriptions. Samplers were aesthetic objects. Jones, in his inscriptions, reconciled picture-making with Gill's idea of art as artefacture. They were things *per se* as well as signs.

As his texts have a seemingly uncomfortable relation to the twentieth century, the inscriptions are appropriately composed of fragments and the letter forms often have an embattled appearance. Indeed, compare any weathered example of Roman lettering - a tablet which the years have worn down and deprived of its confident, square-cut authority - with an example of expert modern letter-cutting by someone like Eric Gill or Laurie Cribb and you will at once perceive Jones's affinity with the former. Jones's altered forms suggest the historical processes that have been working upon the beliefs and dictums of earlier epochs. His letters or texts are redolent of a past, or several pasts. As Gray notes, Jones's sources are hard to trace; the Romans themselves 'used a variety of styles'[18] and she has counted no less than twelve forms of 'G' and sixteen forms of 'R' in Jones's work. Inasmuch as different forms conjure different associations the inscriptions can mark, by juxtaposition, patterns of cultural peregrination or echo.

The decades in which Jones produced a large number of his inscriptions witnessed the rise of another art form which explored how words which carry a message can be used to achieve an aural and visual impact - Concrete Poetry. This was an international art form, just as many of Jones's texts can be seen as European, and the preoccupations of certain concrete poets reflect some of Jones's obsessions. Lexical fragmentation is used to make a cultural comment in a work by the English poet, John Furnival, *The Fall of the Tower of Babel*. A close-up of part of this work reveals a 'confusion of noises'[19] made up out of, *inter alia*, 'Peace for the World' and its Russian equivalent, '*Meer za Meeram*'. A runic quality can be found in a work like Edgard Braga's *Vocábulo* of 1966. Braga, a Brazilian concrete poet, uses, like Jones with his cultural deposits, hints of medieval Portuguese lyrics in his works.

Cultural criticism similar to Jones's own:

> ... discarded contraceptives to drape the fern roots on the heath
> ... and the Odeon counterfoil ...[20]

can be found in the work of Décio Pignatori, the Brazilian concrete poet and translator of Pound's *Cantos*. The elements of 'Coca Cola' are reformed into '*cloaca*', latin for sewer. And in a 1965 manifesto in the preface to *Concrete Poetry International*, Professor Max Bense made some observations about the movement which have much to do with Jones's inscriptions:

> concrete poetry is not involved with grammatical or consecutive linear relationships of words ... it is not constructed in the sort of sequence in which words follow each other in our consciousness

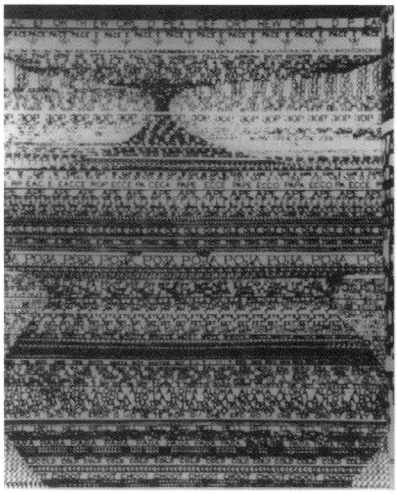

5. John Furnival, Tower of Babel, 1964

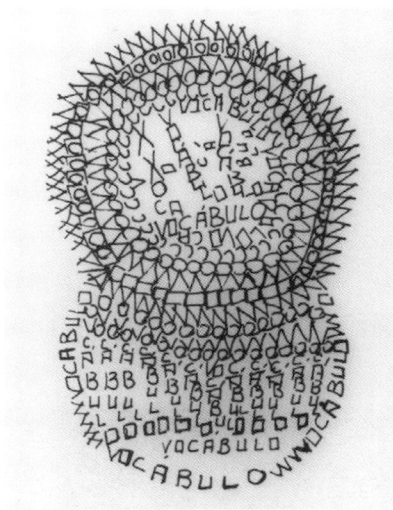

6. Edgard Braga, Vocábulo, 1966

beba coca cola
babe   cola
beba coca
babe cola caco
caco
cola
        cloaca

7. Décio Pignatori, Beba coca, 1967

... concrete poetry is based on the visual relationships of various elements and their relationship to the ... space within which they are contained.[21]

The origin of the formal innovations of the Concrete poets are commonly attributed to Mallarmé with his interest in the placing of words on the page. But long before the nineteenth century, scribes were interested in formal experimentation: large capitals, contractions, words in different colours and varied page layouts. In the sixteenth and seventeenth centuries the emblem poem such as George Herbert's *Wings* exploited layout for expression. But certainly, in the modern period, Mallarmé's influence on Eliot and Pound and on the Futurist and Surrealist interest in typography has affected many aspects of literature, art, graphic art and advertising. Marinetti, Kandinsky, Klee, David Smith, and Jasper Johns have all used letter forms or abstract 'alphabets' to make cultural statements or to create rhythms.

The idea of making the word flesh was dear to Eric Gill and, at Ditchling, Jones found the apprentice pieces of lettering cut on tablets disposed around the community, set into walls inside and out, placed in niches, proclamational but part of everyday life.[22] Jones's earliest attempts at lettering in engravings, such as the *Welfare Speaker* for *The Game* of February, 1922 are merely functional and appear of little formal interest to the young artist. In *Our Lady Was a Milkmaid* (1923?), the lettering grows to fill the halo and letters are placed in a more imaginative relationship to one another but the letter forms are, more or less, pure Roman and we get little impression of how Jones was going to deviate from the example of a traditional letter-cutter like Gill. But, in the 1924 woodcut *By the Mystery of thy Holy Incarnation*, Jones's first Christmas engraving after coming to Capel, we can see how clumsiness or inexperience suggested some potential avenues of exploration. The jagged, jolting relation of the letters is heightened by the changes of size, punctuated by the use of square dots and softened by the preponderance of the letter O. Jones placed dots so as 'to divide words and not to punctuate' in the manner that they were sometimes employed 'by the letter-cutters in Antiquity'.[23] In *By the Mystery* words appear crushed as if they have been badly organized on the page and arbitrary divisions such as 'wh/ole' add excitement and an element of surprise to the text. Oddity is exacerbated by the joining together of certain letters making new and often ungainly forms and by the inversion of an N. Philip Hagreen remembered that at Ditchling,

> One thing that Hilary [Pepler] could not drive into David's head was the obvious fact that printing must reverse the image. When there was lettering he was liable to put some of it wrong. I remember one block that had an inscription of which he got four or five letters facing the wrong way. George [Maxwell] came to the rescue and very skillfully laid a piece into the block - and then David got two of the letters wrong.[24]

A yet more radical indication of the abstract potential of letter forms is found on the back of the small boxwood carving *Mother and Child*, made at

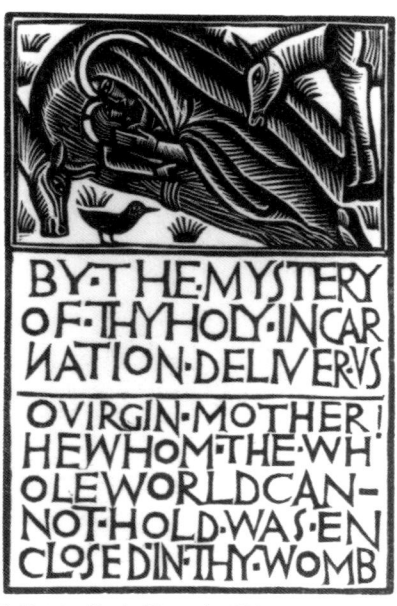

8. Nativity ('By the Mystery'), 1924

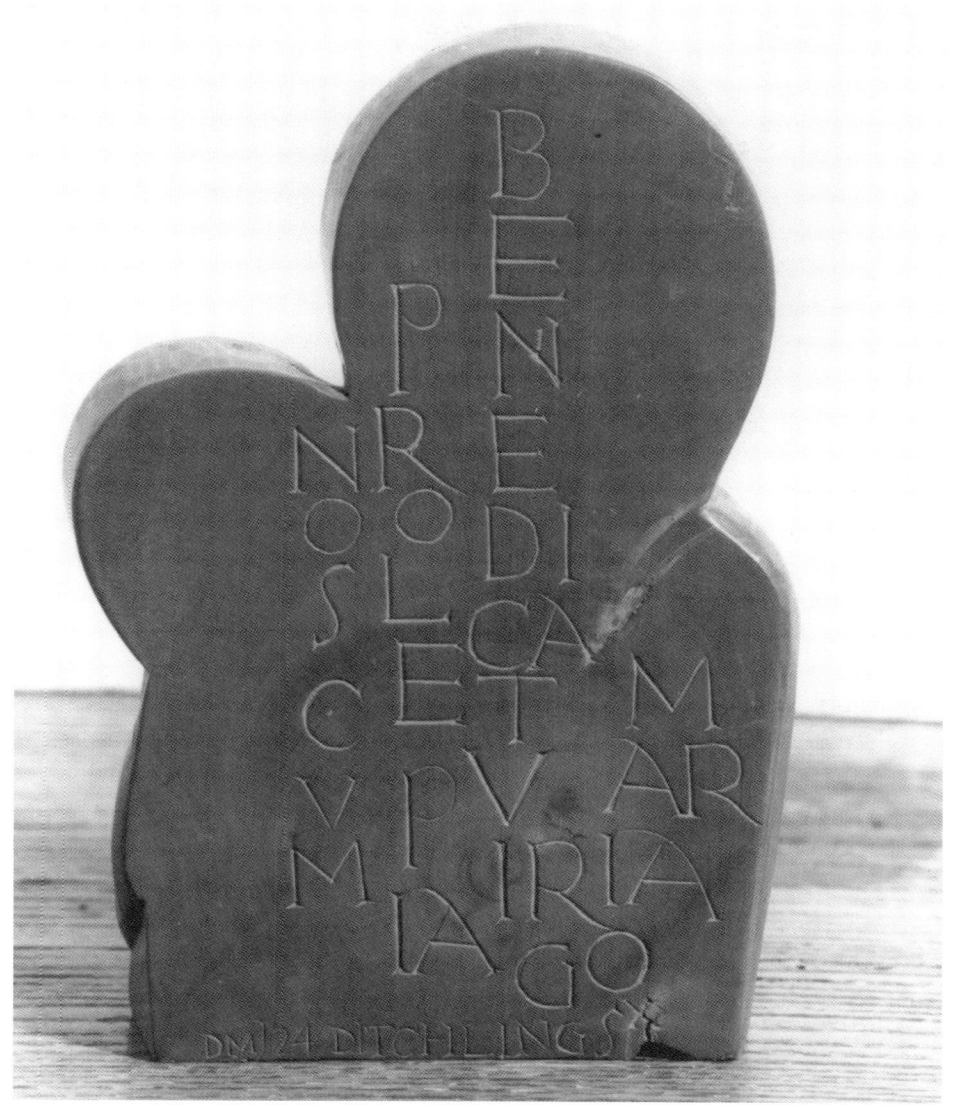

9. Madonna and Child (reverse), 1924

Ditchling in 1924. The logic of the disposition of the letters is determined by the way that they relate visually to one another and to the shape of the block rather than by the normal function of merely making sense.

Jones's earliest inscriptions were far from self-conscious and, more often than not, occasional - a greeting card, for example. They could 'add grace to utility' such as *Joan's Saucepan Board* painted at Pigotts, or a decorative shoe-box lid done for Petra. During the Second World War, Jones masked the institutional and functional ugliness of his ration book with his own lettering. Again, later in life, Jones turned to intimate and occasional inscriptions, picking up the burin once more in 1959 to carve some words on the back of a cameo he gave to Valerie Wynne-Williams or to cut words on a couple of stones which she had found on Welsh beaches.

It was not really until the 1940s that the inscriptions became serious, self-conscious works. In the earliest of them, the letters are large and placed simply

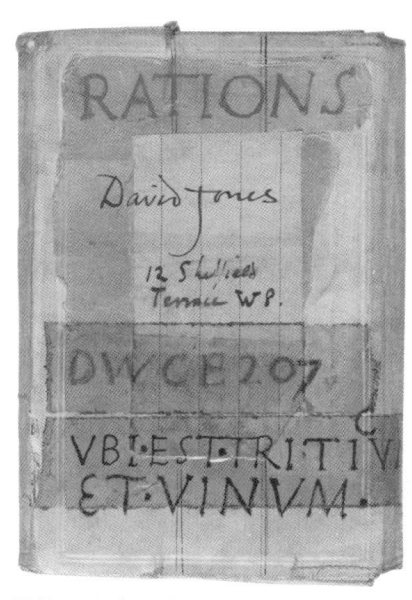

10. Ration Book, c. 1942

281

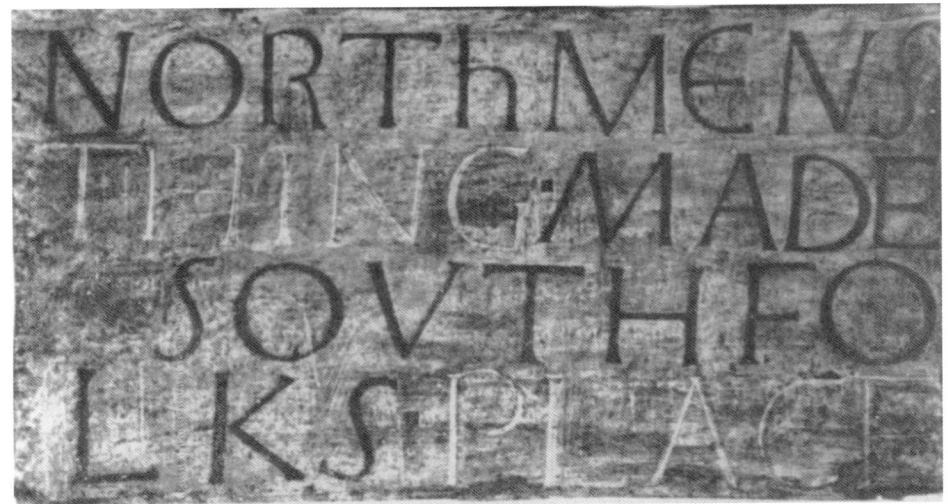

11. Northmens Thing Made Southfolks Place, 1945

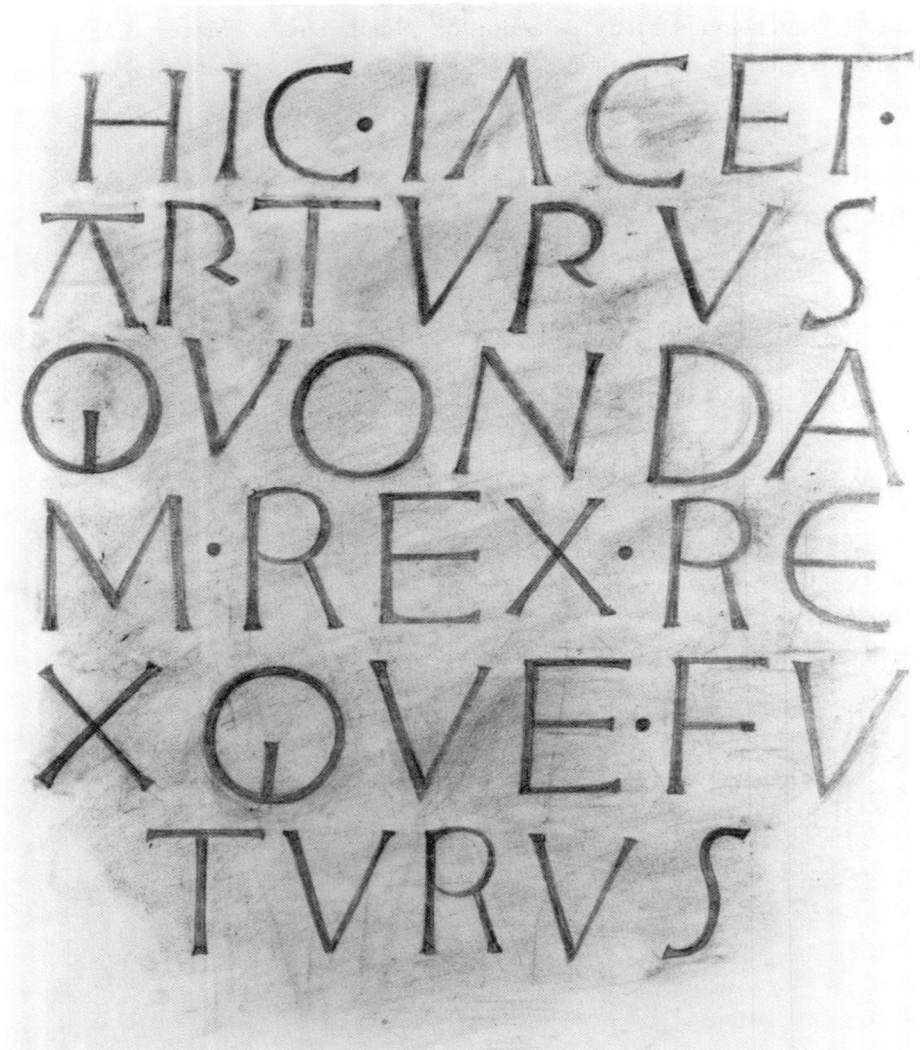

12. Hic Iacet Artvrvs, 1949

on the page. By 1950, in a second phase, the letters diminish in size and a sense of edge becomes important and one senses that Jones is building an enclosure; about 1956 an increased clarity of space is manifest. Such a general overview is not, by any means, watertight and is merely offered as a rough guide through an imposing bulk of work made over several decades.

Between the end of the war and before his second breakdown, Jones's first important inscriptions were pieces that registered a kind of cultural rear-guard action. Both *Northmens Thing* (used in *The Anathemata* as an illustration) and *Hic Iacet Artvrvs* belong to a group (which includes *Optima Goreu*; *Roma Capvt Orbis*; and *Senatvs Popvlvsqve*) that were made with watercolour and wax crayon - rubbed on over a textured surface to mimic the effect of a weathered or lichenous stone. Of all the inscriptions these look most like relics from a lost age or the survivors of some catastrophe.

The text of *Northmens Thing* which comes, as already noted, from the *Anna Livia Plurabelle* section of Joyce's *Finnegans Wake*, expressed for Jones 'how then became now'. It celebrates 'the change of people on the unchanged site'. The words communicate this even independently of their original context and in the inscription the idea is underpinned by the selection of 'Northmens … Made Southfolks' in a darker colour; the other elements, 'Thing' and 'Place' appear in a less durable, lighter tone and the final CE almost disappears. Formally, the work is peculiar; as in that early wood engraving, a word, 'FO/LKS', is broken in a bizarre manner and the L at the beginning of the last line is in strange isolation. The left side is spacious but the right side crushed. The lettering slopes slightly, giving the whole a movement and sense of urgency. The tilted S of 'Mens' and 'Folks' posit a formal as well as notional link. A lower case h splits the top line and letter forms mutate. The total effect of texturing is like the smudged X-Ray of some palimpsest and the splintering of words suggests how cultural inheritance is not always unproblematic, certainly sporadic and not necessarily durable.

There are two versions of *Hic Iacet Artvrvs* which date from the late forties, of which the one reproduced here is by far the more exciting - indeed it is one of the most mobile of Jones's inscriptions. While the letters are so spaced apart as to appear almost in abstract configuration on the paper, it is formally well organized and 'ARTVRVS', 'REX' and 'TVRVS' are centered.

The letter forms themselves are surprising - an A without a cross-bar in exciting relation to a V in the line below $\overset{I\Lambda}{V}$; an A with a top bar $\overline{\Lambda}$ is likewise singular and works in interesting vertical relation to the letters below it:

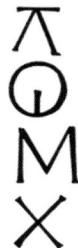

The short-legged Rs and the ⊙ are, in the opinion of Nicolete Gray, 'almost certainly derived from Dark-Age' Italian inscriptions.[25] These truncated Rs give a staccato rhythm to the word:

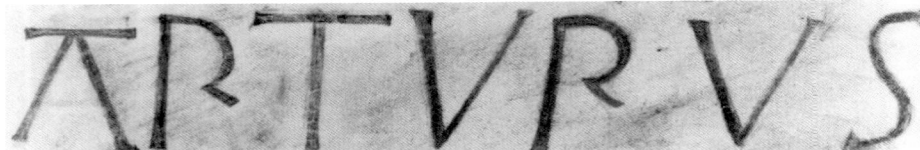

It has a certain dash, appropriate to the name of an 'organizer and leader of a mobile field-force'.[26] The whole inscription possesses the impetuosity of handwriting and yet, at the same time, it is a considered structure. The text is legible and yet the eye delights in travelling up and down and horizontally to enjoy the exciting formal relationships between the quirky letters.

When Jones started painting inscriptions without a wax crayon background the impact became less immediately evocative of past time. He proceeded, very much in the manner of a painter, making instinctive modifications as he went along. There was, as he notes, 'endless … adjusting and modifying … as for an O well, something in the nature of a miracle would be required to get it even remotely what one wanted first go.'[27] David Kindersley gave an interesting account of how Jones made his inscriptions:

> He would draw out his letters first of all without thinking about the spacing at all, they would be all crammed up on one side of the paper. It didn't seem to bother him that they looked like this. Then, if he was working in pencil he would paint in white over the letters and readjust their position on the page thinking about each letter in relation to the ones next to them and the whole piece began to work - it was quite magical really. He just knew how to get the letters all working together on the paper. I don't think he had an idea of what it would all look like before he started. It wasn't as if his eyes could project onto the paper what he wanted … When the letters first hit the paper they were so unbalanced rather like those terrible signs that you see about saying 'SCHOOL FÊTE' where the letters were falling off the sign post, not a thought for the spacing, yet he could transform all that. It was tremendous … [28]

Another eyewitness recalls that Jones claimed that the inscriptions took even more concentration than the paintings.[29]

Texts were added in the margin rather as when Jones amplified an idea in one of his letters to his friends. Indeed, the arrangement of these communications, with their marginalia often curving right round the main text and with insertions into insertions, gives some indication of how the reflex of Jones's thinking may have contributed to the form of the inscriptions (21). A

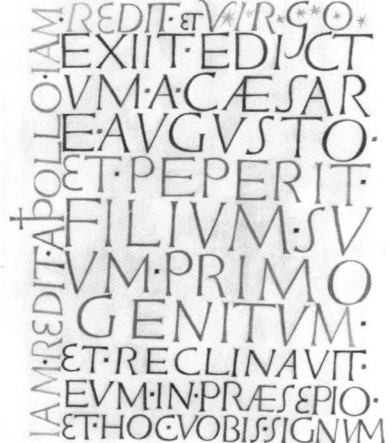

13. Iam Redit et Virgo, (?)

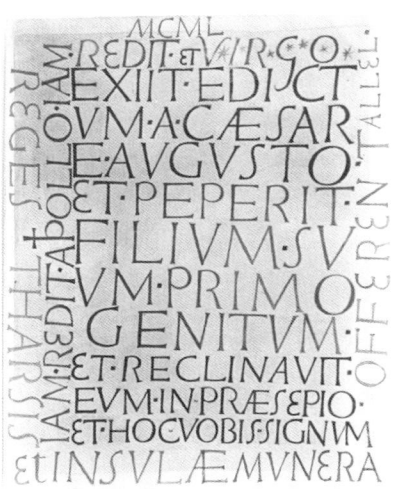

14. Iam Redit et Virgo plus hand-painted additions, (?)

photograph of the inscription *Iam Redit et Virgo (13)* was embellished by a hand-painted text when sent to a friend *(14)*.

Despite its charm, *Dvm Medivm Silentivm*, an inscription made for Christmas 1952, is full of vitality, fragility and a self-conscious awkwardness that is the hallmark of much twentieth century art. This tilting and irregular inscription is held in check by the comparative regularity of the bottom line which is like a keel on which the rest rides,[30] and by the carol that delicately embraces and embellishes the portentous Latin of the Introit for the Sunday within the Octave of Christmas.[31] Even the affected cross on the ℏ helps to pull the eye in order to stabilize the composition.

In complete contrast is the lucid, cool modernity of *Pwy Yw* made in 1956 as a design for a large painting on the wall of a chapel in a Carmelite Convent in Wales but rejected by the nuns as being too esoteric. Technically, it was far from easy; Jones remarked in a letter to Vernon Watkins that there are only 19 letters in the first line whereas there are 32 in the fourth.[32] The tracks of text, Latin and Welsh, are translations of one another. Not only does the inscription appear large with its wide *viae* of painted Chinese White background and the relatively regular bands of lettering but it actually was Jones's largest inscription. The approximate regularity of the whole is broken both by the staggered margin and by the occasional use of a different colour for the initial letters of certain words. The use of the curved G, which is graceful here, can, along with an affected R (for example, in *Yn Y Gaeaf Oer* of 1960), become at times unwittingly expressive of the kind of 'bogus "Celticity"'[33] which Jones himself detested. It is a trait, like the embellishment of certain inscriptions with flowers or the whimsy in certain paintings, that Jones apparently felt unable to suppress.

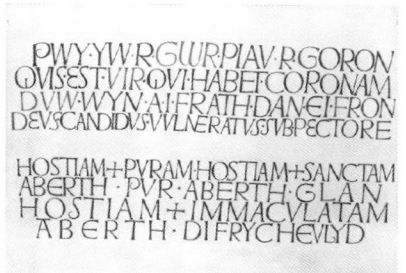

15. Pwy yw r gwr, 1956

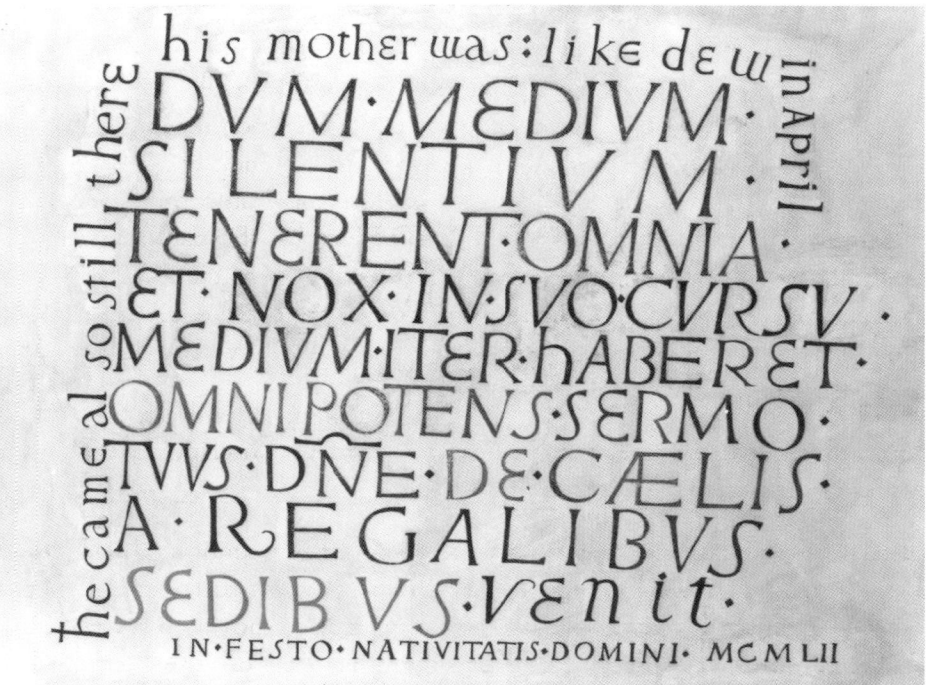

16. Dvm Medivm Silentivm, 1952

285

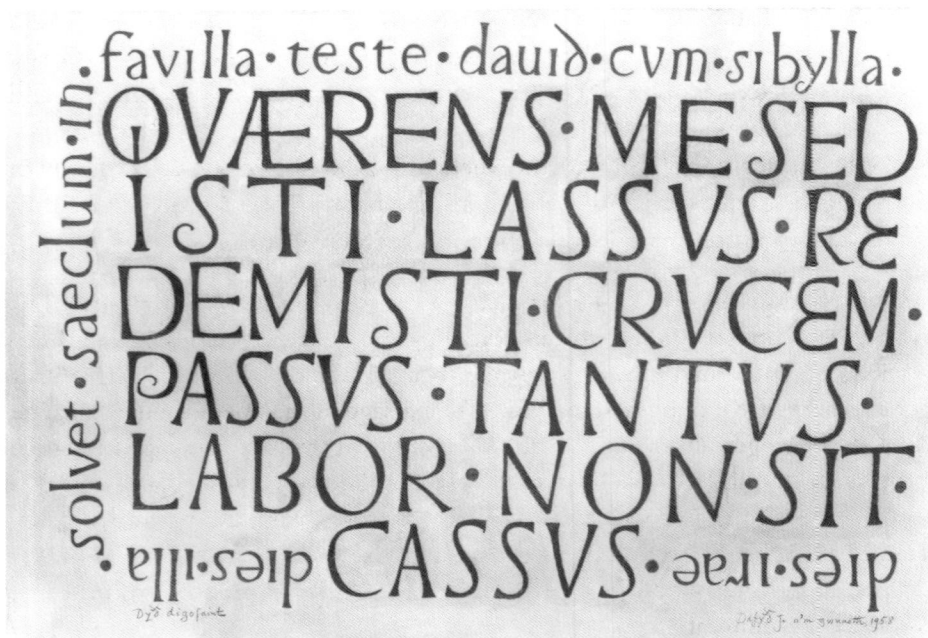

17. Qvaerens Me, 1958

The artist commented that his

> usual process is to cover the surface of smooth, hot-pressed watercolour paper with Chinese white, because I make innumerable re-adjustments as I go along. That gives one a chance to make these variations by using white and as it were, painting into the existing background. I know people think that it is a fairly straightforward job, and one just draws the thing out carefully and then applies the paint, but I have found that in that method there is a lack of freedom. Most of the corrections and changes are in order to get the unity that is essential in any art work of any sort; also a feeling of movement.[34]

As Jones marked in a book he had from his student days, 'Chinese White being more dense, and the particles more compact than the Flake White employed in oil-colour, it is capable of reflecting more light.'[35]

There is in *Pwy Yw* a tantalising movement towards and away from the spectator which interacts with the pointing and counterpointing of diagonals and the clear, uniform tracks of white which run between the lines of text. All told, it is one of Jones's most modern masterpieces.

While lower case letters seem inappropriate for the heavy *Dies Irae, Dies Illa*, in the inscription which begins *Qvaerens Me (17)*, the CASSVS breaks this borderline dramatically. If the gravity of the text is not communicated by the cases of the letters, there is, on the other hand, a great feeling of space and size about the work and an optical dazzle which works the eye in a not dissimilar fashion to the gentler effects of Op-artists such as Vasarely. The angling and weighting of the seriphs animate the page; the *viae*, which is what Jones designated the spaces between the lines, are large and exciting.

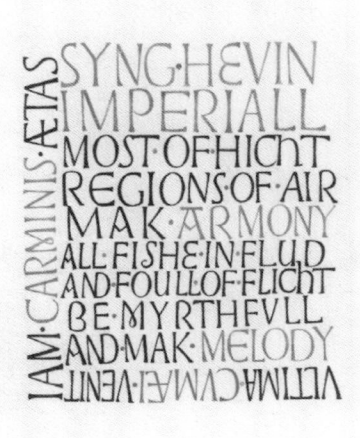

18. Syng Hevin Imperial, 1961

Produced for Faber and Faber's Christmas card for 1961, *Syng Hevin Imperiall* is a block of lettering with a huge border giving the space necessary to create the effect of exultant exclamation. With its complementary purple and yellow it balances in 'armony'. There is a simplicity, a lack of affectation. The M in the border helps to bond the vertical to the horizontal text. The M of MYRTHFVLL, apart from presenting a somewhat jocular form of the letter, avoids the repetition with another M immediately beneath.

The affectations in *What Says his Mabinogi* are, at first sight, irritating but perhaps necessary to break up this relentless mass of text which is a lettered version, executed in 1958, of a passage from 'Mabinog's Liturgy' in *The Ana-themata* (pp 207-8), published in 1952. The passage in the poem is unfortunately split on two pages although it is laid out generously with a great deal of space surrounding the lines. In the inscription the text becomes crushed and crowded between confining borders and the word 'world' from the poem has been changed to 'orbis' which, with its fatter letter forms, is visually more effective; aurally, however, 'whole', 'world' and 'hold' offer a pleasing mixture of assonance and alliteration.

This use of a text from one of his own poems throws up interesting questions about the relation of the inscriptions to the poems. Apart from the pure abstract delight of many of Jones's inscriptions, we have observed that the texts themselves are important; they compress meaning like a short poem, mantra or prayer. They are allied to Jones's own poetry and seven inscriptions are included among the pages of *The Anathemata*; sometimes these have been placed to screen text from notes so their content does not always relate directly to the text on the facing page.

A changing pattern of words across a page is an expressive device that Jones, like other modernists, used in his poetry. René Hague, the printer who set *In Parenthesis*, not in two column crown folio as Jones wished but on the more typical Faber and Faber demy octavo page, considered that 'typography' hadn't 'the flexibility' Jones desired.[36] This suggests that the artist was intuitively aiming for a text with a much more experimental form, indeed a new, or very old, art form which would truly unite shape and meaning. The importance of '*Idem in Me*' in the lettered title page to 'The Tribune's Visitation' is explained by Jones in a long note. The binding idea of the poem, *Idem in Me* and various ideas such as the contemporaneity of the situation are brought together, co-present in the inscription which thus becomes part of the total work of art.

Like the Concrete poets, Jones took considerable pains in his own poems to determine a satisfactory visual form on the page. Successive drafts of most passages reveal the difficult search for a satisfactory layout. The explicit instructions to the printers attempted to secure the exact form he wished.[37] Part of the intention was to control the vocal scoring of a poem; in his *Preface* to *The Anathemata* he wrote

> I intend what I have written to be said. While marks of punctuation, breaks of line, lengths of line, grouping of words or sentences and variations of spacing are visual contrivances they have here an aural

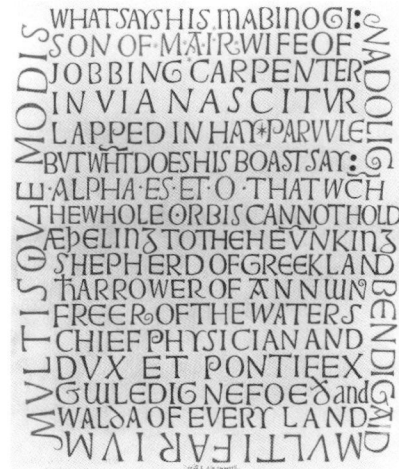

But what does his Boast say?
Alpha es et O
        that which
the whole world cannot hold.
Atheling to the heaven-king.
Shepherd of Greekland.
Harrower of Annwn.
Freer of the Waters.
Chief Physician and
dux et pontifex.

19. The Anathemata p 207, 1952

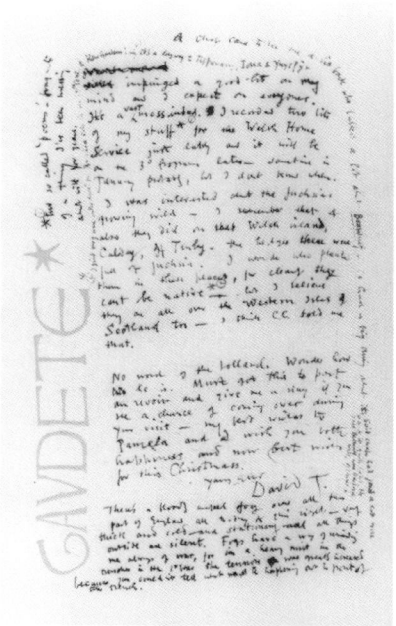

20. What Says His Mabinogi, 1958

21. Gavdete Letter, December, 1956

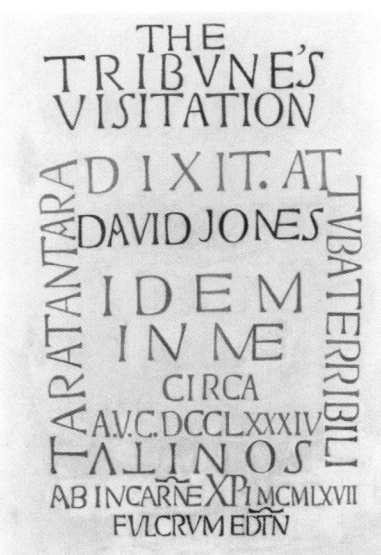

THE
TRIBVNE'S
VISITATION
ARATANTARA DIXIT. AT TVBATERRIBILI
DAVID JONES
IDEM
IN ME
CIRCA
A.V.C.DCCLXXXIV
TALINOS
AB INCARÑE XPI MCMLXVII
FVLCRVM EDTN

22. The Tribvne's Visitation, 1967

and oral intention. You can't get the intended meaning unless you hear the sound and you can't get the sound unless you observe the score … it is meant to be said with deliberation - slowly as opposed to quickly … .[38]

Good advice for most poetry, and certain kinds of prose, it clearly reveals Jones as a mixed-media artist who could have created an extended art work in which written and spoken word and visual form would come together. The chief characteristic of modernist writing is its opacity. The reader is made aware of the words as possessing the physical characteristics of shape and sound, good in themselves and not only clumsily functioning as a system of enclosing meaning. They are visible and sensual pleasures rather than codes to be only used but not appreciated.

If Jones's first writing, *In Parenthesis*, had been ventured to see how questions of 'form' and 'content' worked in a writing 'as compared with the same problems in the visual arts'[39] then the inscriptions were ventured to create a shape from texts which, as they were replete with meaning, freed the artist to concentrate on purely formal problems. Jones's obsessive etymological preoccupations were clear from the letters he wrote towards the end of his life but the word itself in the inscriptions, considered visually on the page, was purged of that scholarship and became formally self-sufficient. The fact that the sum of meaning is etymologically embedded in a word and there for all to discover meant that the search for more meaning was vested in the spectator. As the making of paintings and drawings became increasingly difficult, Jones, with the word, was back on course, back on the track of his belief that art was not representational but essential. As he wrote to Helen Sutherland, 'it has a kind of satisfaction this lettering. It has an abstract quality which is a "good thing"'.[40]

As with the poems, while the content of the inscriptions looks back to the past, their formal exploitation is of the present. What had been, in Jones's late drawings, a pessimistic view of cultural impoverishment in a hardened and illustrational style became, in the inscriptions, a refreshingly vital and innovative celebration of cultural components. Jones brings cultural deposits into the orbit of the present using a mode that speaks to the twentieth century's fascination with bold abstract patterning and cultural variety. Jones concerned himself, untroubled by questions about content, with the very basics of visual art, and late twentieth century calligraphers have learnt much from his innovative example. Notwithstanding Dreyfus's perceptions of 'anxiety and depression', for as we have seen such qualities run through Jones's life no less than through his making, among the many and various arts which Jones practised with remarkable success and some understandable failure, the inscriptions as a whole are marvellously strong, and frequently bright and joyful. If the Word was difficult to incarnate literally or metaphorically in the context of twentieth century art then the word, that palimpsest of cultural continuity, peregrination and change could be used economically yet with intellectual delicacy and largesse in the poetry and with abstract power and grace in the inscriptions; many of these come off the page like a song that has been heard for millenia yet has been excitingly re-scored to hold our attention today.

INTEGRATION AND A CHANGING WORLD

In 1961, looking back over thirty years of sporadic activity as a painter, Jones remarked, 'I sometimes think that I stopped being a good artist in the 1930s and since then it's been a kind of aftermath'.[1] The title *The Maker Unmade* contains no implicit criticism but rather a deep recognition of the pressures that disturbed Jones, some of which were palpable and some of which issued from the tenacious yet pampered spirit of the artist, though, certainly, phantoms are no less real than bayonets to those who see or feel them.

Jones was an extraordinary sensibility and intelligence, in some ways more subtle and curious than the intellectual strictures which he humbly accepted, but in terms of physical and psychical energy he was unable to sustain the sheer volatility of his creative vigour. After the auspicious revelation of a re-markable talent as a child, he suffered the Western Front, that explosion of the unimaginable into the delicate orbit of a susceptible imagination. Small and weak, other soldiers would take pity on Pte. Jones and, from time to time, carry the heavy rifle of 'the poor little sod'.[2] Throughout the rest of his life the war remained a permanent wound. Anniversaries of key events that Jones experienced during the conflict were remarked in letters to friends. He turned his sharp pencil on a peaceful picture-postcard view of the Spekes-worth Valley sent years later, and traced the empty shell of a landscape pounded by artillery. Nearly half a century after his military service he spoke of the memory of war as being 'like a disease'.[3]

Strategically, the withdrawal to Ditchling, the finding of an enclave in which to function and develop that opened onto an arena in which he could shine like a star was ideal. Eric Gill was so well connected and the English Catholic world so small that Jones enjoyed a ready audience and immediate acclaim. With the body of work that he produced, freed from economic pressures by living either at home or with the Gills, and through connections easily forged, he was able, with his talent and industry, to become a presence in the London art world. During this period he proved to be the most exciting of the English artist-engravers, producing strong and original work which also acknowledged and at times embraced the experiments of continental prac-titioners, and he swiftly became one of the finest British watercolourists of the modern period, in the company of Paul Nash and Edward Burra.

Between 1925-32 Jones's work had been constantly exploratory. A strong formalism had given way to a freedom and Expressionism that defied the solidity of objects in search of an intuited underlying energy. He threw off the impersonality of the Neo-Thomist aesthetic, painted many vigorous oils and evanescent watercolours, often denying the spectator the ease of immediate clarity in order to provoke a deeper understanding. His perception that 'all art…is *abstract* and that all art *re-presents*, whereby form and content are one'[4] placed him in a strong middle ground between the conservatives who advocated that the 'painter's proper business is with the warm breathing world'[5] and the progressive Nicholson striving for the pure, non-referential yet spiritual expression of a white-out. During the twenties and early thirties the positive influence of France and Germany was manifest in Jones's work. The importance of French culture in particular must not be underestimated: through Hartrick (and, therefore, indirectly Legros), Sickert, the influence of Post-Impressionism, Symbolism, and the Nabis, through Denis and Neo-Traditionalism via Dom Theodore Bailey and Jacques Maritain, the latter also transmitting the riches of French neo-Thomist aesthetic philosophy.

Jones was, in certain ways, more artistically ambitious than contemporaries such as Nicholson, less chic, less icy, but eventually less painterly as his visual intuition gave way to intellectual pedantry in many of his later pictures. Jones subsequently moved away from an approach to painting which was crucial to twentieth century picture-making and about which Kandinsky so perceptively observed:

> Form is often the most impressive when least coherent. It is often most expressive when outwardly most imperfect, perhaps only a stroke, a mere hint of meaning.[6]

Form was also, according to the Scholastic philosophy which had influenced Jones, a reflection of what was in the artist's mind, so when he aspired towards a mystical dissolution of a burdensome or trivial existence, Jones's forms were on the point of liberation.

As he strove towards artistic integration and amplification, Jones faced that dilemma for Christian artists of reconciling attachment to the physical world of making with the renunciation held to be necessary in following a spiritual path. Artists in the church have two vocations, a situation that taxes their energy and sets up obvious conflicts; while Jones's artistic acts were consecratory in nature, his moral and theological attitude became one of renunciation. In facing this profound quandary Jones encountered three areas of opacity, resistance and confusion: his friends' understandable inclination to avoid the depths of introspection, the insufficiency of Christian teaching on the subject of common emotional problems, and the amorous and sexual experimentation that went on around and about him either in Catholic or in artistic circles. In his first contacts with psychiatry his doctors were also inadequately prepared to deal with a sensibility preoccupied by a search for artistic integration and spiritual quest. Under the strain of his dilemma, Jones crumpled. He was unable to articulate the dimension of his despair and although friends made well-meant attempts to relieve his suffering there was no-one with sufficient insight to help him overcome the crisis. *In Parenthesis*, finished in 1932 could, like a rite of passage, have exorcized the war; instead the effort led him into deepening depression. His pictures, after an energetic

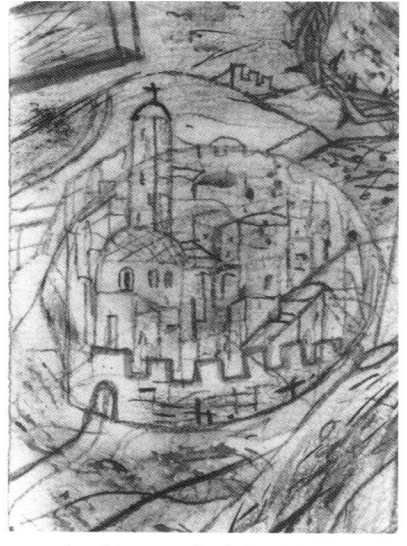

1. St Helen of the Cross (detail of Walled City), 1944

output, were on the brink of bigness and abstraction, but, following medical advice, he stopped painting for several years. In his groping towards mysticism he had been torn between self and selflessness, wanting, on the one hand, to express himself physically and bodily, as in his approaches to women, and on the other, in his imaginative vision of the world to let go of the embodied and the tactile, which is observable in his 1932 still lifes. Such dilemmas have presented problems for many painters in the twentieth century: how embodied, how fragmented, how sublime, how abstract should a painting be? Klee, Picasso and Kandinsky have tackled such issues; Jones, while he was a lesser painter, also addressed these important considerations.

His spirit exhausted, his youthful optimism worn, Jones was cosseted and contained by a small circle of highly refined, highly conservative Catholic intelligentsia, some of uncertain health and pessimistic outlook. Christopher Dawson, wrote Jones to Hague, 'seems to think that *all* modern efforts at creative work, by being cut off from "our culture tradition" are necessarily in the void' - hardly an opinion conducive to inspiring creativity. It was not long before Jones's attitude towards picture-making had capitulated to such malaise; writing to Grisewood about his art in 1942 he confessed, 'I walk round it … think about it, have a peep at it - rather like a patient'.[7]

The overwhelming weight of cultural *angst* made for a loss of humour in Jones's work. There are human jokes in *In Parenthesis*, there is a playfulness in his incidental comic drawings during the 1920s and 1930s which have a truly European flavour. There is a deftness of touch which meant that even in apparently modest pictures Jones experimented ambitiously. However, the light, the airy, the childlike took their toll on several painters of the period - Ben and Winifred Nicholson separated, Christopher Wood took his life and Jones suffered a nervous breakdown. Jones had delighted in the liberation learned from continental modernism but was eventually reclaimed by the indigenous Symbolism of a latter-day Pre-Raphaelitism which had been his preconditioning and which became, in its Neo-Romantic guise, his destiny.

George Orwell described the thirties as 'a scenic railway ending in a torture chamber';[8] Jones tumbled on the torture early in the decade and his personal distress coupled with the deteriorating international situation gave him the opportunity to contextualize and typify himself as a microcosmic decline of the West. If the civilizational prognosis was correct, then he could honestly be nothing other than ill. His gloom, his endless malady, like that of certain friends, was symptomatic of their vision of the sinking of the West. Of course, in post-Romantic terms isolation and illness are often held to be the prerequisite of powerful expression - artists are almost expected to be sick, aberrant, and they become, like Jones's soldiers on the Western Front, scapegoats for a civilization gone awry. His acceptance of poverty, chastity and obedience, given modern materialism, added a testing blend of Medieval Christianity to an inauspicious post-Romantic vision. Romantic artists, in their infirm isolation, tend to idealize a past. Treading among the wastes of 'spilt religion',[9] Jones, that late Romantic, attempted, with a chalice shaped to an already obsolete form of the liturgy, to scoop the spillage back into some kind of venerable vessel. But the arts are not only about gathering everything in but also about knowing what to leave out. Paul Klee noted in his *Diary*, 'Nature can afford to be prodigal in everything, the artist must be frugal down to the smallest detail.'[10] Surely it is not, as Jones would have it, that the 'arts abhor any loppings off of meanings'[11] but rather that in perturbed periods they require a continual redressing of meaning, or squads of questionable connotations will run wild through a work like those unfortunate horses in *Vexilla Regis*, leftover traces of states and systems no longer tenable.

By the late thirties, there was a tendency for Jones's painting to be either an expression of his repressed sexuality or a vehicle for his ideas and philosophy. The latter was an attempt to retrieve and garner what he felt had been lost. When Degas tried his hand at poetry and spoke with Mallarmé about finding a suitable idea with which to end a sonnet, it was the poet who reminded Degas that sonnets are made with words and not ideas. Jones was both painter and poet and creatively it seems that he was, in some of his later painting, compromised by taking inappropriate instruction from the wrong voice. When his images are governed by the urge to conserve, a cogent, powerful and painterly visual logic is often sacrificed. Evidence from his correspondence and his choice of acquaintances reveal an obsession with history, ideas and etymology and a declining visual curiosity. Writing proved to be a more suitable medium for expressing what he urgently felt and he faced painting with a certain degree of bewilderment. Desiring to 'make significant for the present what the past holds' he was, in fact, attuned to a very select vision of the present. For all his eclecticism, he was not adventurous enough to embrace his aim in a way likely to catch the disinherited imagination. Donald Davie has appositely pointed out that Jones might have grown as an artist 'if his self-denying patrons had not exerted themselves so consistently to cushion him from the economic and ideological realities of the world he was living in.'[12] His friends were certainly of great intellectual influence and financial aid to the artist but they formed a highly circumscribed subset within the larger ideological conflicts of the twentieth century. Jones, of course, chose his friends as much as they chose him and it is unlikely that he would have been disposed to listen to widely differing viewpoints. He came as a religious and social refugee to his adopted world and he embraced its traditions wholeheartedly. His search for meaning and pattern were sincere but the adjectives in the following extract from the poem, 'A, a, a, Domine Deus' suggest that his cultural perspective is a foregone conclusion:

> I have run a hand over the trivial intersections.
> I have journeyed among the dead forms
> causation projects from pillar to pylon.[13]

The adjectives 'trivial' and 'dead' (as indeed 'inane' below) indicate that it is not quite true that Jones has

> tested the inane patterns
> without prejudice;[14]

he has begun his quest from an entrenched position from which he looks out over what to him appears as a sprawling wasteland.

A grand vision of civilizational doom allowed him to overlook some of the insupportable details of the reality of the west. While Jones was musing analogously on his post-Roman vision of *Wallia* as a receptacle for the creative spirit, Robert Medley was in Wales drawing the miners, and the GPO Film Unit was recording some of the bitter truths about Britain's inheritance. Living at the frontier of an intellectual and technological revolution, Jones could only look beyond into darkness and see no new light. Qualities embedded in his religion which appear pertinent to the well-being of many kinds of people could only be apprehended decked in ancient lineaments. The system was desiccating the springs of ancient wisdom yet the catalogue of cultural misadventure proved more absorbing than those ancient springs themselves; in this respect Jones is at a far remove from the full-blooded and spirited William Blake. The changing world order meant a changing order of signs and Jones did not sufficiently recognize that the increasingly slippery discontinuum of twentieth century intellectual history called for new evocations.

As he became increasingly anguished by cultural loss so his mind took on the nature of an encyclopedia though, interestingly, one not organized in the linear, logical manner of a written treatise but in the fashion of a more modern organization of material. Indeed, Jones could have embraced the 'automatic devices';[15] he zaps from *onagers* to field artillery in the way that the information organization of CD-Rom proliferates associatively. However, despite his lifeline of reference books, grammars, maps and missals it became increasingly obvious to Jones that 'not only one's terminology but the whole of one's ideas behind that terminology have less and less meaning and this has happened with alarming speed.'[16] During his lifetime people had moved from seeking support from the past to questioning the social and political complex which created that past, from seeing art as an eternal expression of the nobility of the human spirit to observing its changing parameters as resulting from differing political realities. Somewhere Jones actually understood this, stating in his essay 'The Pursuit of Peace', that you 'have to have a fairly large police force, I imagine, before it is possible for a neurotic aesthete like myself to exist at all.'[17]

It was stimulating to juxtapose transhistorically yet somewhat dangerous to place things 'out of time' in the 'time of the Mass';[18] the danger of ritual is, as Berger reminds us, that it 'bestows on events a significance gathered from the past and precludes innovation or the thought of it.'[19] Jones believed in 'metamorphosis and mutability'[20] but always within the confines of immutable sign systems so that his work must be seen, indeed, in parenthesis. The Mass could no longer make sense of everything and this led to the considerable anguish of Jones's maturity. The danger in constant memorial of the death of Christ on the cross is to dwell on the sacrifice and not to move on either to the resurrection of the body or the spirit. This religious or ritual fixation on the Mass, with which Jones all too eagerly complied, hampered his spiritual development and was eventually a toxic ingredient in his own bodily, emotional

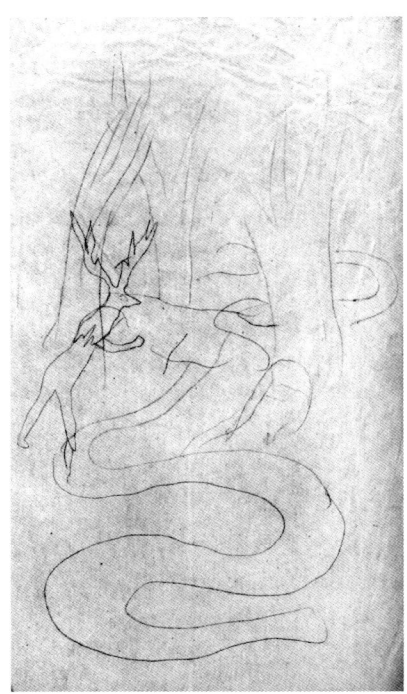

2. Horned Man, (?)

and spiritual suffering, his own deprivation, which perhaps, in ordering a taxi or buying himself a fine pair of half hose he was taking steps to remedy.

With his second bout of psychological treatment at Bowden House, he began to make progress; the image of *Vexilla Regis* promised some kind of spiritual step forward despite the 'manifold lurking places'[21] of obvious neuroses. The cross of Christ, the focus of suffering, became a well-rooted, growing tree, aspiring from earth to heaven. But promise gave way, once again, to despair. After the second Vatican Council held between 1962-5, Jones happened upon a reason for protesting against the ignorance of the Church to which he had committed himself wholeheartedly, and was roused enough to protest vociferously. His protest was misdirected; he railed against the change in religious observance rather than the far more serious fact that when he had most needed guidance and companionship in his profoundest periods of despairing he had found no one within the Church capable of comprehending him.

Jones aspired to integration but his times and his intellectual relationship to them refused him. Yet his triumphs were legion. As a maker of inscriptions he deserves an important place in the history of the art. The poems are powerful and speak, even with their formal debt to his modernist forbears, with a unique voice. In his essays and letters his consideration of the nature of art and the rôle of the artist provides an important contribution to that eternal debate. His painting styles were a continual quest for individual expression and, as art with less overt ideological freight or constraint appeals more directly and more widely, it is significant that Jones's less obviously polemical images of the late twenties and early thirties held his own interest throughout his life as they can, in their freedom, hold ours today.

The artist, like the priest, should be effective along that boundary between the world and the spirit. But whether or not transcendence is accepted, it is a function of art to carry the mind into a deepening and more supple understanding of life, either by probing a difficult reality or by extending the aspirations of the mind into a new appreciation of capacity or complexity. Art excoriates and castigates, selects and celebrates, and David Jones was, in several media and against all sorts of adversity, an original and prodigious artist.

LIST OF ILLUSTRATIONS

15 David Jones,
Ruined Church, Flanders 1917 1917.
Pencil on paper, 15 x 22.5.
The Trustees of David Jones's Estate.

16 David Jones,
Soldier Carrying Duckboard 1916.
Pencil on paper, 12 x 17.5.
Imperial War Museum, London.

17 C.R.W. Nevinson,
Reliefs at Dawn 1917.
Oil on canvas, 71.1 x 91.4.
Imperial War Museum, London.

18 David Jones,
A Dug Out 1917.
Pencil on paper, 12.5 x 17.5.
Imperial War Museum, London.

WESTMINSTER SCHOOL OF ART

1 David Jones,
Crucifixion - Squared Up Drawing 1919 (?).
Pen, ink & colour wash on paper, 76.9 x 46.
Tate Gallery Archive.

2 David Jones,
Front Line Festubert 'The Islands' 1916.
Charcoal on paper, 10 x 17.
The Trustees of David Jones's Estate.

3 David Jones,
Trench Drawing - Squared Up Detail of Standing Figure Playing Harmonica 1920 (?).
Pen, ink & wash on paper, 55.7 x 38.4.
Tate Gallery Archive.

4 David Jones,
Squared Up Trench Drawing 1920 (?).
Black ink, pen & brush on paper, 69.5 x 110.
Tate Gallery Archive.

5 David Jones,
The Betrayal 1920 (?).
Black ink & wash on paper, 42.5 x 66.6.
Tate Gallery Archive.

6 David Jones,
The Betrayal 1920 (?).
Oil on paper, 36.1 x 61.5.
Tate Gallery Archive.

7 David Jones,
Gardening 1920.
Oil on canvas, 75 x 106.
Art Gallery of South Australia.

8 David Jones,
Seated Woman 1921 (?).
Pencil on paper, 29 x 19.5.
The Trustees of David Jones's Estate.

9 David Jones,
Dorothy Price 1920 (?).
Chalk and watercolour on paper, 44.5 x 26.5.
Private collection.

10 David Jones,
Torso 1921.
Ink and pencil on paper, 31 x 26.
The Trustees of David Jones's Estate.

11 David Jones,
An Afternoon in the Park - Greenwich (London) 1921.
Ink and crayon on paper, 25.5 x 35.5.
Wolseley Fine Arts.

12 David Jones,
Landscape in the Downs 1920.
Ink, pencil and crayon on paper, 25.5 x 36.5.
Wolseley Fine Arts.

THE YEARS WITH ERIC GILL

1 Jan Verkade,
Saint Sébastien 1892.
Tempera on cardboard, 46.5 x 23.
Saint-Germain-en-Laye, musée départemental du Prieuré.

2 David Jones,
The Game, No. 29 August 1922 including *Husband Leaving Wife & Crucifixion* 1922.
Wood-engraving, 21 x 14.
Wolseley Fine Arts

3 David Jones,
Church for Toy Village 1922 (?)
Wood.
Private collection

4 David Jones,
Four Puppet Heads 1922 (?).
Wood, between 22-28 x 6.2-7.8 x 3-3.4.
Bethnal Green Museum of Childhood.

5 David Jones,
Door locks 1921 (?).
Wood.
Ditchling Museum.

6 David Jones,
Wooden Salad Spoon and Fork 1924 (?).
Wood.
Private collection.

7 David Jones,
St. Dominic's Press Bench Books including *Christ Sending Forth His Disciples* (E46) 1925.
Wood-engraving, 30 x 9.5.
Private collection.

8 David Jones,
Mr. Gill's Hay Harvest 1926.
Watercolour and pencil on paper, 56 x 37.
Private collection.

9 Anon.,
Photograph of David Jones and Eric Gill 1927 (?).
Photograph.
The Trustees of David Jones's Estate.

HIERATIC EVASION: CHRIST AND THE SAINTS

1 Eric Gill,
Christ Before Pilate - Westminster Cathedral, Stations of the Cross 1918.
Hoptonwood stone carving, 170 x 170.
Westminster Cathedral.

2 David Jones,
Christ Before Pilate 1922.
Pencil on paper, 20.5 x 20.
National Museum of Wales.

3 Bernard Meninsky,
Soldiers on a Platform 1918.
Oil on canvas, 91.4 x 71.1.
Imperial War Museum, London.

4 David Jones,
Crucifixion 1922-3.
Oil on wooden boards, 71 x 43.
National Museum of Wales.

5 David Jones,
Jesus Mocked 1922.
Oil on wooden boards, 112.1 x 105.4.
National Museum of Wales.

6 David Jones,
St. Dominic 1923.
Oil on wooden boards, 110.5 x 43.
National Museum of Wales.

7 David Jones,
The Entry into Jerusalem on Palm Sunday 1923.
Watercolour and pencil preparatory drawing for Ditchling mural.
Private collection.

8 David Jones,
Mural of Christ's Entry (detail) 1923.
Oil on wall, 117 x 178 & 117 x 27.
Ditchling.

9 Anon.,
Apostles at the Last Supper c.1180.
Fresco.
Abbazia San Pietro in Valle.

10 David Jones,
Mural of Christ's Entry (Cum Floribus et Palmis) 1923.
Oil on wall, 117 x 178 & 117 x 27.
Ditchling.

11 David Jones,
St. Ignatius. Bishop of Antioch, Martyr 1922.
Watercolour & pencil on paper, 11.8 x 14.
Austin Desmond Fine Arts.

12 David Jones,
St. Hilary Raising a Man from the Dead 1922.
Watercolour on paper, 19 x 19.
National Museum of Wales.

13 David Jones,
St. Gregory who sent St. Augustine to England 1922.
Watercolour and pencil on paper, 17 x 21.5.
Spink & Son Ltd.

14 David Jones,
St. Gregory 1924.
Watercolour & pencil on paper, 16.7 x 13.9.
Wolseley Fine Arts.

ENGRAVINGS AND ILLUSTRATIONS

1 David Jones and Eric Gill,
Westward Ho (E1) 1921.
Wood-engraving, 12.5 x 8.7.
Private collection.

2 David Jones,
The Most Holy Rosary (E4) 1921.
Wood-engraving, 8 x 9.5.
Private collection.

3 David Jones,
Judas, with Caiaphas and the Devil (E45) 1924.
Wood-engraving, 7.8 x 6.
Austin Desmond Fine Arts.

4 David Jones,
Nativity with Ox and Ass - 2nd State with hatching added (E42) 1923.
Wood-engraving, 11.5 x 10.
Private collection.

5 David Jones,
Dominican Friar (E48) 1924.
Wood-engraving, 6 x 4.8.
Private collection.

6 David Jones,
Family at the Hearth (E27) 1922.
Wood-engraving, 7.5 x 9.
Private collection.

7 David Jones,
The Scourging at the Pillar (E55) 1924.
Wood-engraving, 5 x 10.
Wolseley Fine Arts.

8 David Jones,
Crucifixion (E58) 1924.
Wood-engraving, 5 x 10.
Private collection.

9 David Jones,
Child's Rosary Book - Cover (including *The Visitation* E50 & *Finding in the Temple* E53) 1924.
Wood-engraving, 20 x 13.
Private collection.

10 David Jones,
The Natural Law (E78) 1924.
Wood-engraving, 5.7 x 8.4.
Private collection.

11 David Jones,
Libellus Lapidum - Cover (Including *David Jones and Hilary Pepler Mounted on Pegasus*, E64) 1924.
Wood-engraving, 11.5 x 8.5.
Private collection.

12 David Jones,
J for Jazz-man - Original drawing for illustration to *Town Child's Alphabet* 1924.
Pencil, ink & watercolour on paper, 19.5 x 14.5.
National Museum of Wales.

13 David Jones,
D for Dustman - original drawing for illustration to *Town Child's Alphabet* 1924.
Pencil, ink & watercolour on paper, 19.5 x 14.
National Museum of Wales.

14 David Jones,
Gulliver is Knocked Down by the Apple - Preparatory drawing for *Gulliver's Travels* Vol I p 107 (E101) 1925.
Pencil on paper, 25 x 20.
Wolseley Fine Arts

15 David Jones
Gulliver Creeps through the Gate in Lilliput (E87) For *Gulliver's Travels* Vol I p 25, 1925.
Wood-engraving, 26.50 x 20.
Private collection.

16 David Jones,
Ship and Long-Boat in Bay (E95) For *Gulliver's Travels* Vol I p 79, 1925.
Wood-engraving, 26.5 x 20.
Private collection.

17 David Jones,
Gulliver is Seized by a Monkey (E102) For *Gulliver's Travels* Vol I p 112, 1925.
Wood-engraving, 12.5 x 5.5.
Private collection.

18 David Jones,
Archangel Gabriel Appears to Jonah (E137) *The Book of Jonah* p 3, 1926.
Wood-engraving, 32 x 26.
Private collection.

19 David Jones,
The Repentant People of Nineveh Praying (E146) *The Book of Jonah* p 12, 1926.
Wood-engraving, 32 x 26.
Private collection.

20 David Jones,
Jonah is Seized by the Sailors (E140) *Book of Jonah* p 10, 1926.
Wood-engraving, 8.5 x 13.
Private collection.

21 David Jones,
The Artist (E161) for Eric Gill's *Christianity and Art* 1927.
Wood-engraving, 11.5 x 7.
Private collection.

22 David Jones,
Noah offers a Sacrifice (E171)- Artist's Proof for *The Chester Play of the Deluge*, 1927.
Wood-engraving, 16.5 x 14.
Private collection.

23 David Jones,
The Flood (E168) for *The Chester Play of the Deluge*, 1927.
Wood-engraving, 16.2 x 14.
Private collection.

24 David Jones,
The Lion and the Farmer (E173) for *The Seven Fables of Aesop*, 1928.
Copper-engraving, 10 x 8.
Private collection.

25 David Jones,
The Lion and the Farmer - Preparatory drawing for E173 - *The Fables of Aesop* 1928.
Pencil on paper, 6.5 x 8.3.
Austin Desmond Fine Arts

26 David Jones,
The Mariners - Preparatory Drawing for E188 - *The Rime of the Ancient Mariner*, 1928.
Pencil on paper, 13 x 17.
Bloomsbury Gallery.

27 David Jones,
The Mariners (E188) in *The Rime of the Ancient Mariner*, 1928.
Copper-engraving, 18 x 13.5.
Private collection.

CARVINGS

1 David Jones,
The Bear (E2) 1921.
Wood-engraving, 6 x 9.
Private collection.

2 David Jones,
The Bear 1922.
Boxwood carving, 6 x 9 x 2.5.
Private collection.

3 David Jones,
Crucifix Pendant 1923 (?).
Boxwood carving, 8 x 5 x 2.
Private collection.

4 David Jones and Eric Gill,
Crucifix on Gill's Base, 1926 (?).
Boxwood carving on stone base. Base: 9.5 x 25.5 x 6. Carving: 14 x 8 x 2.
R.A. Gekoski.

5 David Jones,
The Crucifixion,
Boxwood carving, 12.6 x 10 x 2.5.
Private collection.

6 David Jones
Crucifixion 1925 (?).
Boxwood carving, 11.4 x 7.6. x 2.
National Museum of Wales.

7 David Jones,
Madonna and Child 1924 (?).
Boxwood carving, 10 x 7.5. x 2
Private collection.

8 David Jones,
Mother and Child 1924 (?).
Boxwood carving, 10 x 7.5. x 2
Private collection.

9 David Jones,
Sancta Helena O.P.N - Pendant 1926 (?).
Boxwood carving, 5.7 x 2.5. x 2
Private collection.

10 David Jones,
Torso, 1925 (?)
Sycamore carving, 6.5 x 4. x 2
Private collection.

11 David Jones,
Carving of standing figure (St. Dominic) 1923 (?)
Wood carving, 73 x 16 x 11.
The Trustees of David Jones's Estate.

ANIMALS

1 David Jones,
Cat and Hare 1904 (?).
Pencil on card, 20.2 x 12.6.
Tate Gallery Archive.

2 David Jones,
Animal Drawn in Trench 1917.
Pencil on paper, 15 x 18.5.
Imperial War Museum, London.

3 David Jones,
Three Calves 1921.
Pencil on paper, 25.5 x 20.2.
Tate Gallery Archive.

4 David Jones,
Goat 1925.
Pencil on paper, 17 x 19.5.
Austin Desmond Fine Arts.

5 David Jones,
Pigs at Capel-y-ffin 1926.
Pencil on paper, 25 x 42.5.
The Trustees of David Jones's Estate.

6 David Jones,
Pasture by Water 1926.
Watercolour & pencil on paper, 57 x 39.
Austin Desmond Fine Arts.

7 David Jones,
Wild Boar 1927.
Watercolour & pencil on paper, 24.4 x 33.
Private collection.

8 David Jones,
Animals Approaching the Ark (E166) from *The Chester Play of the Deluge* 1927.
Wood-engraving, 16.2 x 14.
Private collection.

9 David Jones,
The Albatross (E184) from *The Rime of the Ancient Mariner* 1928.
Copper-engraving, 18 x 13.5.
Private collection.

10 David Jones,
'Wear Sox' - Dog sitting, Dog biting and woman (?)
Pencil on paper, 32 x 25.
Austin Desmond Fine Arts.

11 David Jones,
Dog Biting Branch on Prospectus for Engravings by Eric Gill 1933 (?).
Ink and pencil on paper, 32 x 25.
Austin Desmond Fine Arts.

12 David Jones,
Dog sleeping 1927.
Pencil on paper, 14 x 15.5.
The Trustees of David Jones's Estate.

13 David Jones,
Cath Gartref - (detail) 1930.
Watercolour & pencil on paper, 61 x 48.2.
Private collection.

14 David Jones,
Elephant - trunk raised 1927.
Pencil on paper, 24 x 32.
The Trustees of David Jones's Estate.

15 David Jones,
Elephant 1927.
Watercolour & pencil on paper, 31 x 44.
Private collection.

16 David Jones,
Agag 1930.
Watercolour & pencil on paper, 32 x 47.
Private collection.

17 David Jones,
Leopard 1930.
Watercolour & pencil on paper, 18 x 44.5.
Pallant House, Chichester.

18 David Jones,
Lynx 1929.
Watercolour & pencil on paper, 33 x 34.5.
Newport Art Gallery.

19 David Jones,
The Old Animal from Tibet 1930.
Watercolour & pencil on paper, 40 x 47.6.
National Museum of Wales.

20 David Jones,
Chapel in the Park - (detail) 1932.
Watercolour and pencil on paper, 60 x 52.5.
The Tate Gallery, London.

21 David Jones,
Sketch of Wolves 1942 (?).
Pencil on paper, 20.5 x 32.8.
Tate Gallery Archive.

APPROACHES TO LANDSCAPE

1 David Jones,
Tregaron 1913.
Oil on canvas, 36.7 x 49.5.
National Library of Wales.

2 David Jones,
Richebourg St. Vaast 'Jan 24th 1916' 1916.
Pencil on paper, 10 x 17.5.
The Trustees of David Jones's Estate.

3 David Jones,
Ploegsteert 1916.
Charcoal on paper, 12 x 17.2.
Imperial War Museum, London.

4 David Jones,
Kent Landscape 1920.
Coloured pencil on paper, 27.5 x 21.
The Trustees of David Jones's Estate.

5 David Jones,
Landscape in Kent 1921.
Oil on canvas, 69.5 x 89.5.
Private collection.

6 David Jones,
Landscape (South Downs) 1921.
Oil on canvas board, 52 x 42.1.
Tate Gallery Archive.

7 David Jones,
Ditchling Landscape 1924.
Pencil & crayon on paper, 25 x 35.
Austin Desmond Fine Arts.

8 David Jones,
The Garden Path, Ditchling 1924.
Pencil, ink, watercolour & gouache, 35 x 25.
Private collection.

9 Pablo Picasso,
Landscape, Autumn 1908.
Oil on canvas, 101 x 81.
Museum of Modern Art, New York.

10 David Jones,
Capel Landscape 1925.
Watercolour & gouache, 38.5 x 28.
Private collection.

11 David Jones,
Capel-y-ffin 1926-7.
Watercolour & gouache on paper, 55 x 37.
National Museum of Wales.

12 David Jones,
Y Twmpa with Conifers 1925.
Watercolour on paper, 35 x 51.
The Trustees of David Jones's Estate.

13 André Derain,
The Church at Vers 1912.
Oil on canvas, 65 x 91.
National Museum of Wales.

14 David Jones,
Nant Honddu (also known as *Y Twmpa*)
(E 127) 1925.
Copper-engraving, 8 x 5.5.
Private collection.

15 David Jones,
Autumn Landscape, Capel 1925.
Watercolour & gouache on paper, 39 x 57.
The Trustees of David Jones's Estate.

16 David Jones,
Y Twmpa - Capel 1926.
Watercolour & pencil on paper, 35 x 51.
The Trustees of David Jones's Estate.

17 David Jones
Landscape at Capel 1926.
Watercolour & pencil on paper, 56 x 38.2
Private collection.

18 David Jones,
Honddu River Fach - 'Afon Honddu Fach' 1926.
Watercolour & pencil on paper, 38 x 56.
Private collection.

19 David Jones,
Brockley Gardens, Summer 1925.
Crayon, pencil and watercolour on paper, 51 x 39.
Austin Desmond Fine Arts.

20 David Jones,
A Town Garden 1926.
Watercolour & pencil on paper 53 x 35.
Private collection.

21 David Jones,
The Suburban Order 1926.
Watercolour & pencil, 37 x 58.
Portsmouth City Museum & Art Gallery.

22 David Jones,
August Garden, Brockley 1926.
Watercolour & pencil on paper, 58 x 38.5.
Private collection.

23 David Jones,
Foliage & Fences 1926.

Ink and watercolour on paper, 55 x 38.
Private collection.

24 David Jones,
Landscape at Salies-de-Béarn 1928.
Watercolour & pencil on paper, 60 x 43.5.
Private collection.

25 David Jones,
Roman Land 1928.
Pencil, watercolour & gouache on paper,
65.4 x 50.8.
National Museum of Wales.

26 David Jones,
Dominican Lay Sister in a Rose Garden 1928.
Pencil, watercolour & gouache on paper,
62 x 48.
Private collection.

27 David Jones,
Montes et Omnes Colles 1928.
Pencil, watercolour & gouache on paper,
48.5 x 60.5.
Whitworth Art Gallery, Manchester.

SHIPS AND THE SEA

1 David Jones,
Bristol Docks 1926.
Watercolour & pencil on paper, 26.5 x 35.5.
Private collection.

2 David Jones,
Tenby from Caldey Island 1925.
Watercolour & gouache on paper, 34.3 x 52.
National Museum of Wales.

3 David Jones,
Landscape at the Coast (Landscape in France, title
given by The National Museum of Wales*)* 1928.
Watercolour, gouache & pencil on paper,
39.5 x 57.
National Museum of Wales.

4 David Jones,
Coast Scene 1925.
Oil on canvas, 53 x 30.
Private collection.

5 David Jones,
Rocks and Surf 1927.
Watercolour & pencil on paper, 34 x 41.
Private collection.

6 David Jones,
Surf 1929.
Watercolour & pencil on paper, 38 x 56.
Whitworth Gallery, Manchester.

7 David Jones,
Trade Ship Passes Ynys Byr 1931.
Watercolour & gouache on paper, 46.5 x 59.5.
Private collection.

8 David Jones,
The Verandah Wall, 1927.
Pencil, watercolour & gouache on paper,
38 x 54.5.
Private collection.

9 David Jones,
Sea View 1929.
Oil on canvas, 40 x 60.
Towner Art Gallery, Eastbourne.

10 David Jones,
The Fountain (Stormy sea from the verandah,
Portslade) 1929.
Oil on canvas.
Austin Desmond Fine Arts.

11 David Jones,
Factory Coast 1931.
Oil on canvas, 50.8 x 61.
Private collection.

12 David Jones,
Portslade (detail) 1929.
Pencil, watercolour & gouache on paper, 61 x 49.
Private collection.

13 David Jones,
Place for Ships 1931.
Watercolour & pencil on paper, 49 x 64.1.
Private collection.

14 David Jones,
Manawydan's Glass Door 1931.
Watercolour, gouache & pencil on paper,
63.5 x 49.
Private collection.

INTERIORS AND STILL LIFES

1 David Jones,
The Sitting Room, Howson Rd. 1926.
Watercolour & pencil on paper, 52 x 37.5.
Leeds City Art Gallery.

2 David Jones,
The Dog on the Sofa 1926.
Watercolour, gouache & pencil on paper,
53 x 38.
National Museum of Wales.

3 David Jones,
Still Life With Gladioli 1927.
Watercolour, ink, crayon & pencil on paper,
42.5 x 34.5.
Private collection.

4 David Jones,
Still Life with Plate and Goblet 1928.
Watercolour & pencil on paper, 45.4 x 57.8.
Victoria & Albert Museum, London.

5 David Jones,
Syphon and Silver 1930.
Oil on board, 50 x 69.
National Museum of Wales.

6 David Jones,
The Candle and the Cup c.1931.
Oil on canvas, 59 x 75.
The Trustees of David Jones's Estate.

7 David Jones,
The Artist's Worktable 1929.
Watercolour & pencil on paper, 62 x 40.
Private collection.

8 David Jones,
View From Brockley Window 1928.
Oil on canvas, 68 x 50.
Private collection.

9 David Jones,
René Hague's Press 1930.
Watercolour on paper, 62 x 48.
Private collection.

10 David Jones,
René Hague's Press 1930.
Watercolour & pencil on paper, 60 x 44.5.
Private collection.

11 David Jones,
The Violin 1932.
Watercolour & pencil on paper, 57.1 x 78.7.
Victoria & Albert Museum, London.

12 David Jones,
Violin and Flowers 1932.
Watercolour & pencil on paper, 74 x 54.
The University College of North Wales,
Bangor.

13 David Jones,
Hierarchy 1932.
Watercolour & pencil on paper, 75 x 55.
Private Collection.

14 Oberrheinischer Meister,
Paradise Garden (detail) c.1410
Städelschen Kunstinstitut, Frankfurt am Main.

15 David Jones,
Briar Cup 1932.
Watercolour & pencil on paper, 76.5 x 55.2.
Private collection.

16 David Jones,
July Change, Flowers on a Table 1932.
Watercolour & pencil on paper, 59.5 x 46.7.
Pallant House, Chichester.

17 Ben Nicholson,
Goblet and Pears 1924.
Oil on canvas, 37 x 44.5.
Kettle's Yard, University of Cambridge.

18 David Jones,
Still Life 1932.
Watercolour on card, 78.7 x 58.4
The Arts Council of Great Britain.

19 David Jones,
The Table 1932.
Watercolour on paper, 76 x 54.5.
Austin Desmond Fine Arts.

20 David Jones,
Still Life with Plate and Goblet 1932.
Watercolour on paper, 55.5 x 75.
Private collection.

PROBLEMS AND POSSIBILITIES
OF THE FIGURE

1 David Jones
Crucifixion 1920.
Pencil, blue-black ink on paper, 42.5 x 31.2.
Tate Gallery Archive.

2 David Jones,
Ruined Church with Soldiers 1917 (?).
Pencil on paper, 22.5 x 14.5.
The Trustees of David Jones's Estate.

3 David Jones,
Male Stripped to the Waist 1921.
Pencil and crayon on paper, 47 x 28.
The Trustees of David Jones's Estate.

4 David Jones,
Nude Portrait 1924.
Pencil, ink & watercolour on paper, 28 x 19.5.
Private collection.

5 David Jones,
R for Road mender 1924.
Pencil, ink & watercolour on paper, 17.8 x 12.8.
National Museum of Wales.

6 David Jones,
The Lovers 1923.
Pencil on paper, 42.5 x 32.3.
Ditchling Museum, Sussex.

7 David Jones,
Ego Delecto Meo 1924.
Watercolour, pen & pencil on paper, 18.5 x 15.
Private collection.

8 David Jones,
Female Yahoo embraces Gulliver (E121) p 109 of
Gulliver's Travels Vol. II 1925.
Wood-engraving, 26.5 x 20.
Private collection.

9 David Jones,
Frontispiece to the Book of Ecclesiastes (detail of
stabbing figures) 1927.
Wood-engraving, 17 x 11.
Private collection.

10 David Jones,
Expulsion of the Money Changers (E77) - *Libellus
Lapidum* 1924 p 20.
Wood-engraving, 17.8 x 12.4.
Private collection.

11 David Jones,
Interchanging the Occiputs (E113) 1925.
Wood-engraving, 5.7 x 5.7.
Private collection.

12 David Jones,
Man and Woman 1930.
Pencil, ink & watercolour, 26 x 24.5.
Austin Desmond Fine Arts.

13 David Jones,
Girls 1926.
Watercolour & pencil on paper.
Private collection.

14 David Jones,
Nude: Miss Lilian Peterson 1926.
Watercolour & pencil on paper, 55 x 38.
The Arts Council of Great Britain.

15 David Jones,
Woman Sunk to the Ground 1932.
Ink on paper, 32 x 20.
The Trustees of David Jones's Estate.

16 David Jones,
Nude in profile 1923.
Watercolour on paper.
Private collection.

17 David Jones,
Seated Nude 1925.
Pencil & crayon on paper, 31 x 24.5.
Private collection.

18 David Jones,
Two Bathers 1928.
Ink on paper, 16 x 13.
Austin Desmond Fine Arts.

19 David Jones,
*Mr. David Jones (1895-) aetate 35 - Self-Portrait,
Aged 35* 1930.
Pencil on paper, 37 x 27.
Austin Desmond Fine Arts.

PORTRAITS AND FRIENDS

1 David Jones,
Elizabeth, Petra & Joanna Gill 1924.
Watercolour & pencil on paper, 28.5 x 39.7.
Private collection.

2 David Jones,
Head of Girl (Petra) 1923.
Boxwood on ebony base, 9 x 7.
Private collection.

3. David Jones,
Petra against Sheepfold 1924.
Watercolour, ink & gouache on paper.
Private collection.

4 David Jones,
Petra 1929.
Pencil, watercolour & gouache, 71.3 x 59.3.
Glynn Vivian Art Gallery and Museum, Swansea.

5 David Jones,
Petra 1932.
Watercolour & pencil on paper, 75 x 55.
Private collection.

6 David Jones,
Eric Gill 1930.
Watercolour & pencil on paper, 61.5 x 49.
National Museum of Wales.

7 David Jones,
Petra im Rosenhag 1931.
Watercolour, pencil & gouache on paper,
76.2 x 56.
Private collection.

8 David Jones,
Portrait of a Boy 1928.
Watercolour & pencil on paper, 62 x 48.3.
Whitworth Art Gallery, Manchester.

9 David Jones,
Portrait of Desmond Chute (?).
Watercolour & pencil on paper.
Huddersfield Art Gallery.

10 David Jones,
Portrait of René Hague (*The Translator of the
Chanson de Roland*) 1932.

Watercolour & pencil on paper, 76.5 x 56.
National Museum of Wales.

11 David Jones,
René Hague 1930.
Ink on paper, 24 x 31.
Private collection.

12 David Jones,
Portrait of a Maker 1932.
Oil on canvas, 76 x 61.
Agnews.

13 David Jones,
Human Being 1931.
Oil on canvas, 74 x 60.
Private collection.

14 David Jones,
Portrait of Tommy Hodgkin 1930.
Watercolour & pencil on paper, 60 x 48.
Private collection.

15 David Jones,
Portrait of Joanna Gill (?).
Watercolour & pencil on paper, 54 x 38.
Private collection.

16 David Jones,
Lady Prudence Pelham 1930.
Watercolour & pencil on paper, 58 x 45.
Stoke on Trent City Museum & Art Gallery.

17 David Jones,
Self Portrait 1928.
Oil on canvas, 60.9 x 50.8.
Art Gallery of New South Wales.

LANDSCAPES IN A LIFE

1 David Jones,
View from No.1 Elm Row, Hampstead 1928.
Pencil on paper, 30.9 x 23.3.
The National Gallery of Scotland, Edinburgh.

2 David Jones,
Elm Row, Hampstead 1927.
Watercolour, gouache & pencil on paper.
Austin Desmond Fine Arts.

3 David Jones,
Sketch for Pigotts Pathway 1930.
Pencil on paper, 60.5 x 48.
Wolseley Fine Arts.

4 David Jones,
Archway at Pigotts 1930.
Watercolour, gouache & pencil on paper, 65 x 49.
Private collection.

5 David Jones,
Pigotts Garden 1931.
Watercolour & pencil on paper, 83.5 x 49.2.
Cecil Higgins Museum, Bedford.

6 David Jones,
Enclosure 1931.
Oil on canvas, 60 x 75.
Private collection.

7 David Jones,
Gunman's Field 1932.
Watercolour & pencil on paper, 57 x 78.
Private collection.

8 Anon.,
Photograph of David Jones on board ship going to Cairo 1934.
Photograph.
Private collection.

9 David Jones,
The Nile, Egypt 1934.
Ink on paper, 32.5 x 20.
Wolseley Fine Arts.

10 David Jones,
Farm Door 1937.
Watercolour & pencil on paper, 62.5 x 61.
National Library of Wales.

11 David Jones,
The Chapel Perilous 1932.
Watercolour & pencil on paper, 48.2 x 61.
Private collection.

12 David Jones,
Window at Rock 1936.
Watercolour & pencil on paper, 60 x 50.
Private collection.

13 David Jones,
Cattle in the Park 1932.
Watercolour and pencil on paper, 60 x 48.
Private collection.

14 David Jones,
Victorian Corner, Sidmouth 1940.
Watercolour & pencil on paper, 48.5 x 61.
The Trustees of David Jones's Estate.

15 David Jones,
Cricket Match, Sidmouth 1937.
Watercolour & pencil on paper, 48 x 61.
Private collection.

16 David Jones
Church Tower at Mells 1939
Watercolour and pencil on paper, 62 x 49
Private collection.

LAST LANDSCAPES AND STILL LIFES

1 David Jones,
View From Gatwick House 1946.
Pencil, chalk & watercolour on paper,
47 x 68.6.
The Tate Gallery, London.

2 David Jones,
Cockley Moor 1946.
Watercolour & pencil on paper, 50 x 60.
Austin Desmond Fine Arts

3 David Jones,
The Legion's Ridge 1946.
Watercolour on paper, 50 x 60.
Private collection.

4 David Jones,
Trees at Bowden House 1947.
Watercolour, crayon & pencil on paper,
76 x 56.5.
Private collection.

5 David Jones,
Tys Elvenland 1947.
Watercolour, chalk & gouache on paper,
75 x 55.9.
Queen's College, Oxford University.

6 David Jones,
Vexilla Regis 1947.
Watercolour & pencil on paper, 76 x 55.9.
Kettle's Yard, University of Cambridge.

7 David Jones,
Storm Tree 1948.
Watercolour, pencil & pastel on paper, 61 x 48.
The British Council.

8 David Jones,
Tree at Northwick Park 1948.
Watercolour, crayon, chalk & pencil on paper, 78 x 56.
Private collection.

9 Nicolas Lancret,
A Tree 1730.
Chalk on paper, 35 x 25.
The British Museum, London.

10 David Jones,
The Outward Walls 1953.
Watercolour on paper, 77.5 x 58.
H.M. The Queen Mother.

11 David Jones,
Gwyl Dewi Sant 1954.
Watercolour, crayon & pencil on paper,
77.5 x 58.
Private collection.

12 David Jones,
The Table Top 1950.
Pencil & crayon on paper, 74 x 55.
Private collection.

13 David Jones,
Flora in Calix Light 1950.
Watercolour & pencil on paper, 56.5 x 76.5.
Kettle's Yard, University of Cambridge

THE RICOCHET OF WAR

1 C.R.W. Nevinson,
Marching Men 1916.
Gouache on paper, 13.9 x 20.3.
Imperial War Museum, London.

2 Wyndham Lewis,
Officers and Signallers 1918.
Ink and watercolour on paper, 25.4 x 35.6.
Imperial War Museum, London.

3 David Jones,
Trench Sketch 1937.
Ink on paper, 33 x 20.
Imperial War Museum, London.

4 William Roberts,
The Ypres Sector 1918.
Ink and watercolour on paper, 36.8 x 29.8.
Imperial War Museum, London.

5 Paul Nash,
The Mule Track 1918.

Oil on canvas, 60 x 90.
Imperial War Museum, London.

6 David Jones,
Three Soldiers in Trench with Rifle 1932.
Ink on paper, 33 x 20.
Imperial War Museum, London.

7 David Jones,
Two Soldiers Chatting in a Trench 1932.
Ink on paper, 33 x 20.
The Trustees of David Jones's Estate.

8 David Jones,
March Kind Comrade 1931.
Watercolour & pencil on paper, 30 x 20.3.
Private collection.

9 David Jones,
Llys Ceimiad: La Bassée Front 1916 1937.
Ink & pencil on paper, 38.1 x 31.7.
National Library of Wales.

10 David Jones,
In Parenthesis - Frontispiece 1937.
Ink, watercolour & pencil on paper, 38 x 28.
National Museum of Wales

11 William Orpen,
Blown Up 1917.
Pencil and watercolour on paper, 58.4 x 43.2.
The Imperial war Museum, London.

12 George Baselitz,
Vorwärts Wind 1966.
Oil on canvas, 162 x 130.
Galerie Michael Werner, Cologne

THE HIATUS AND THE WHOLE

1 Anon.,
Photograph of David Jones as a Welsh Bard
c. 1910.
Photograph.
The Trustees of David Jones's Estate.

2 A.S. Hartrick,
Illustration for 'The Forest Lovers' 1909.

3 David Jones,
The Quest New Year, 1918.
Printed by Jones's father from an illustration done by Jones, 18.5 x 13.5.
The Trustees of David Jones's Estate.

4 David Jones,
Knight and Girl 1916.
Pastel on paper, 15 x 17.
The Trustees of David Jones's Estate.

5 Dante Gabriel Rossetti,
The Wedding of St. George and Princess Sabra 1857.
Watercolour on paper, 36.2 x 36.2.
The Tate Gallery, London.

6 David Jones,
The Wounded Knight (for projected *Morte D'Arthur*) Trial proof 1st State - (E 204) 1930.
Drypoint on paper, 20 x 16.
Private collection.

7 David Jones,
Merlin Land (Merlin Appears in the Form of a Young Child to Arthur Sleeping) 1931.
Gouache and pencil on paper, 26.7 x 20.3.
Private collection.

8 David Jones,
Sir Gareth and Dame Lyones - '2' 1940.
Pencil on paper, 38 x 25.
The Trustees of David Jones's Estate.

9 Jacopo Tintoretto,
Vulcan, Venus and Mars 1555.
Oil on canvas, 134 x 198.
Alte Pinakotek, Munich.

10 David Jones,
Sir Gareth & Dame Lyones 1940.
Pencil on paper, 61.5 x 48.
Austin Desmond Fine Arts.

11 David Jones,
Sketch for the Lord of Venedotia 1948.
Pencil on paper, 57 x 44.
Austin Desmond Fine Arts.

12 David Jones,
Cunedda Wledig 1948.
Pencil & coloured chalk on paper, 50.8 x 40.4.
Private collection.

13 David Jones,
Lord of Venedotia 1948.
Pencil & black chalk on paper, 74.5 x 62.
The British Council.

14 David Jones,
A Girl, Sea and Boats (Princess with Long-Boats) 1949.
Pencil, crayon & chalk on paper, 40.6 x 33.
The Scottish National Gallery, Edinburgh.

15 David Jones,
Trystan ac Essyllt 1962.
Pencil, watercolour & gouache on paper, 77.5 x 57.1.
National Museum of Wales.

16 David Jones,
Trystan Ac Essyllt 1962.
Pencil, watercolour & gouache on paper, 75.6 x 55.9.
National Museum of Wales.

17 David Jones,
Study of Constellations 1960.
Pencil on paper, 32 x 56.
National Museum of Wales.

18 R.B. Kitaj,
If Not, Not 1975-6.
Oil on canvas, 152.4 x 152.4.
The National Gallery of Scotland, Edinburgh.

19 David Jones,
Promenading at Sidmouth (detail) 1940.
Watercolour & pencil on paper, 50 x 62.
Private collection.

20 David Jones,
Sketches for Aphrodite 1938-40.
Pencil on paper, 32.7 x 21.
The Tate Gallery, London.

21 David Jones,
Aphrodite in Aulis 1941.
Pencil, ink & watercolour, 63 x 49.5.
The Tate Gallery, London.

22 Anon.,
Bucinator from Seyffert's Classical Dictionary, 1894.
National Library of Wales.

23 David Jones,
Sketch of a Bucinator 1941.
Pencil on paper.
The Trustees of David Jones's Estate.

24 Anon.,
Bronze She-Wolf.
Bronze statue.
Capitoline Museum, Rome.

25 David Jones,
The Mother of the West, 1942.
Pencil, ink & watercolour on paper, 26 x 36.
Laing Art Gallery, Newcastle upon Tyne.

26 Jackson Pollock,
The She-Wolf 1943.
Oil, gouache & plaster on canvas, 104.5 x 167.5.
Museum of Modern Art, New York.

27 David Jones,
Sketch for Mother of the West 1941.
Pencil & watercolour on paper, 20 x 32.
Private collection.

28 William Holman Hunt,
The Scapegoat 1854.
Oil on canvas, 87 x 139.8.
Lady Lever Gallery, Port Sunlight.

29 David Jones,
Sketch for The Victim, (*Tailpiece* to *In Parenthesis*) 1937.
Pencil, ink & watercolour on paper, 38.1 x 28.
National Museum of Wales.

30 Robert Rauschenberg,
Monogram 1959.
Mixed media, 122 x 183 x 183.
Moderna Museet, Stockholm.

31 David Jones,
The Paschal Lamb (detail) 1951.
Watercolour & pencil on paper, 47.6 x 35.5.
Private collection.

32 Andrea Mantegna,
Triumphs of Caesar - The Trumpeters, Bearers of Standards and Banners (detail) 1490.
Hampton Court Palace; H.M. Queen Elizabeth II

33 David Jones,
The Paschal Lamb (detail).1951
Watercolour and pencil on paper, 47.6 x 35.5.
Private collection.

34 Anne-Louis Girodet de Roucy-Trioson,
Ossian Receiving Napoleonic Heroes c.1802.
Oil on canvas, 34 x 28.
The Louvre, Paris.

35 Albrecht Dürer,
The Virgin with the Multitude of Animals c.1503.
Pen, ink and watercolour, 32.1 x 24.3.
The Albertina, Vienna

36 David Jones,
Y Cyfarchiad I Fair (The Annunciation in a Welsh Hill-Setting) 1963.
Crayon, pencil and watercolour on paper, 77.5 x 57.8.
National Museum of Wales.

INTERNAL PRESSURES

1 David Jones,
The Destructive Child 1930.
Ink on paper, 16 x 12.
Austin Desmond Fine Arts.

2 Anon.,
Jones Family Group (David Jones on right with his mother) c.1898.
Photograph.
The Trustees of David Jones's Estate.

3 David Jones,
The Crucifixion, (E135) 1926.
Copper-engraving, 14.5 x 12.
Private collection.

4 David Jones,
The Crucifixion c.1924.
Watercolour on paper, 12 x 21.5.
Private collection.

5 David Jones,
The Garden Enclosed 1924.
Oil on canvas, 35.6 x 29.8.
The Tate Gallery, London.

6 David Jones,
The Engraver's Workshop 1929.
Watercolour & pencil on paper, 58 x 42.
Private collection.

7 Vincent van Gogh,
Window of Vincent's Studio at St. Paul's Hospital 1889.
Gouache & black chalk on paper, 61 x 47.
Rijksmuseum Vincent Van Gogh, Amsterdam.

8 David Jones,
Torn Pyjamas (?).
Pencil on paper, 22 x 15.
Private collection.

9 David Jones,
Curtained Outlook 1932.
Watercolour & pencil on paper 78.5 x 55.
The British Council.

10 David Jones,
Guenever 1940.
Pencil, ink & watercolour on paper, 62.2 x 49.5.
The Tate Gallery, London.

11 David Jones,
The Four Queens 1941.
Watercolour, ink & pencil on paper 62 x 49.
The Tate Gallery, London.

12 David Jones,
Woman, Soldier & Schoolboy on Tube 1940.
Watercolour & pencil on paper, 31.5 x 19.5.
The Trustees of David Jones's Estate.

13 David Jones,
Woman Warden During the Blitz 1941.
Watercolour & pencil on paper, 32 x 20.
Private collection.

14 David Jones,
Epiphany 1941 - Britannia & Germania Embracing 1942.
Watercolour, ink, crayon & pencil on paper, 29.9 x 23.5.
Imperial War Museum, London.

15 Friedrich Overbeck,
Italia and Germania 1828.
Oil on canvas, 91.7 x 102.
Neue Pinakotek, Munich.

16 David Jones,
Sunday Mass: In Homage To G.M. Hopkins S.J. 1948 (detail)1948.
Watercolour, chalk & bodycolour on paper, 56 x 38.
Private collection.

17 David Jones,
Girl at Mass 1948.
Chalk and crayon on paper, 47 x 34.
Private collection.

18 David Jones,
The Bride, (E200) 1929.
Wood-engraving, 13 x 11.
Private collection.

19 David Jones,
A Latere Dextro 1949.
Pencil,chalk, watercolour & gouache on paper, 61 x 47.
The Trustees of David Jones's Estate.

20 Janet Stone,
Photograph of David Jones at Monksdene 1967.
Photograph.
Private collection.

21 Anon.,
Photograph of David Jones & Valerie Wynne-Williams.
Photograph.
Private collection.

22 David Jones,
Girl in Landscape 'In the Green Wood She Lies Slain.' 1938.
Watercolour & pencil on paper, 25.5 x 19.5.
Private collection.

23 David Jones,
Gwener 1959.
Watercolour, gouache & pencil on paper, 38 x 57.2.
Private collection.

24 David Jones,
Woman with Bows 1959.
Watercolour, gouache & pencil on paper, 32 x 19.
Private collection.

RESONANT ABSTRACTIONS

1 David Jones,
Arbor Decora 1956.
Watercolour on paper, 38 x 51.5.
Private collection.

2 David Jones,
Nam Sibyllam 1958.
Watercolour on paper, 60 x 40.5.
Private collection.

3 Ewan Clayton,
Caldey Stone
Photograph.

4 Anon.,
Runic Stone.
Photograph.

5 John Furnival,
Tower of Babel 1964.
From *Anthology of Concrete Poetry* 1967.

6 Edgard Braga,
Vocábulo 1966.
From *Anthology of Concrete Poetry* 1967.

7 Décio Pignatori,
Beba coca.
From *Anthology of Concrete Poetry* 1967.

8 David Jones,
Nativity ('By the Mystery') (E80) 1924.
Wood-engraving, 11.5x7.5.
Private collection.

9 David Jones,
Madonna and Child (Reverse side with carved inscription) 1924.
Boxwood carving.
Private collection.

10 David Jones,
Ration Book c. 1942.
National Library of Wales.

11 David Jones,
Northmens Thing Made Southfolks Place 1945.
Crayon, pencil and watercolour on paper, 20 x 37.
Private collection.

12 David Jones,
Hic Iacet Artvrvs 1949.
Pencil & crayon on paper, 56.5 x 44.5.
Private collection.

13 David Jones,
Iam Redit et Virgo.
Watercolour & chinese white on paper, 40.5 x 33.
Private collection.

14 David Jones,
Iam Redit et Virgo plus hand-painted additions on a photograph to send as a letter.
Private collection.

15 David Jones,
Pwy yw r gwr 1956.
Watercolour, gouache & Chinese white on paper, 59 x 77.
National Library of Wales.

16 David Jones,
Dvm Medivm Silentivm 1952.
Watercolour, gouache & Chinese white on paper, 49.5 x 61.5.
Private collection.

17 David Jones,
Qvaerens Me 1958.
Watercolour and Chinese white on paper, 32.5 x 54.8.
Private collection.

18 David Jones,
Syng Hevin Imperial 1961.
Gouache on paper, 47 x 38.
Private collection.

19 David Jones,
The Anathemata p 207 of text 1952.

20 David Jones,
What Says His Mabinogi 1958.
Watercolour & Chinese white on paper, 76 x 67.
Private collection.

21 David Jones,
Gavdete Letter, December 1956.
Watercolour and ink on paper, 32 x 20.
Private collection

22 David Jones,
The Tribvne's Visitation 1967.
Watercolour & Chinese white on paper, 39.5 x 27.
National Library of Wales.

INTEGRATION AND A CHANGING WORLD

1 David Jones
St Helen of the Cross (detail of Walled City) 1944
Pencil, ink & watercolour on paper, 24 x 19.
Private collection.

2 David Jones
Horned Man (?)
Pencil on paper, 27 x 16
The Trustees of David Jones Estate.

NOTE: ALL DIMENSIONS GIVEN IN CENTIMETRES.

SHIFTS OF FOCUS

1 Jones, notes drafted for Mid-Century Authors in the John J. Burns Library, Boston College, Chesnut Hill, Mass. Among Jones's papers was found a drawing of Brockley made by H.B. Willis R.W.S. (1810-1884) showing it as a woodland. This is now in the Jones Collection, Tate Gallery Archive.

2 Jones, letter to Dr. Charles Burns, 29 June 1948, in the possession of Paul Burns.

3 Jones, letter to Janet Stone, 22 January 1972, in Bodleian Library, Oxford.

4 Harman Grisewood, letter to Peter du Sautoy, 28 January 1979, in The Harman Grisewood Papers, Georgetown University Library, Washington D.C.

5 *The Sunday Times,* 8 June 1975.

THE EARLY YEARS

1 Jones, *David Jones: Artist and Writer* A tape-recorded commentary on his paintings, ed. Peter Orr (London: British Council, 1973).

2 Jones, 'In illo tempore' in *The Dying Gaul and Other Writings*, ed. Harman Grisewood (London: Faber and Faber, 1978) p 23.

3 *Idem.*

4 Jones, Notes for the Tate Gallery made at the request of H.S. Ede in 1935. Quoted in *David Jones - a Memorial Exhibition*, Kettle's Yard, Cambridge, February 1975. Jones always spoke 'with admiration of her delicate paintings and drawings' - Aneirin Talfan Davies, Introduction to *David Jones - Letters to a Friend.* (Swansea: Triskele, 1980) p 7.

5 Jones, unidentified autobiographical fragment in National Library of Wales, 1985 Purchase, Group C Box 11.

6 Jones, *The Dying Gaul* p 24.

7 Unidentified newsclipping among the Harman Grisewood Papers at Georgetown University Library. Illustrated were two drawings by Jones, *A Lioness* and *A Rhinoceros*.

8 Jones, unidentified autobiographical fragment in NLW 1985 Purchase, Group C Box 11.

9 Jones, in *The Dying Gaul* p 23.

10 Note in Jones's childhood sketchbook in the Tate Gallery Archive.

11 Jones, Notes for the Tate Gallery made at the request of H.S. Ede in 1935.

12 Philip Hagreen, letter to René Hague, 16 May 1978. Photocopy in NLW. By permission of the heirs of Philip Hagreen.

13 Jones, unidentified autobiographical fragment probably written in the 1960s. NLW 1985 Purchase, Group C V/6.

14 Sir John Rothenstein, *Modern English Painters - Innes to Moore.* (London: Eyre & Spottiswoode, 1956; Arrow Books, 1962) p 289.

15 *Ibid.* p 293. cf. Jones's own opinion expressed in the 1935 Notes for the Tate and quoted in Robin Ironside, *David Jones* in Penguin Modern Painters series (Harmondsworth, 1949) p 4. Only a photo of this painting now exists; see letter to H.S. Ede, 27 March 1943, in Kettle's Yard, Cambridge.

16 Jones, unidentified autobiographical fragment probably written in the 1960s. NLW 1985 Purchase, Group C V/6.

17 Mollie Elkin, in conversation, 27 March, 1992.

18 Jones, Notes for the Tate Gallery made at the request of H.S. Ede in 1935.

19 Jones, letter to René Hague, 9 April 1960 in *Dai Greatcoat - A Self-Portrait of David Jones in His Letters*, ed. René Hague (London: Faber and Faber, 1980) p 180.

20 Jones, *The Dying Gaul* p 26.

21 Jones, unidentified autobiographical fragment probably written in the 1960s. NLW 1985 Purchase, Group C V/6.

22 *Camberwell School of Art: Prospectus for the 14th Session 1910-11* p 7.

23 Jones, letter to René Hague, 27 December 1933, in David Jones Papers in the Thomas Fisher Rare Book Library, University of Toronto.

24 London County Council meeting of the Joint Advisory Sub-Committee of 27 January 1911, p 4. In Vol. 6 of *Minutes*, Camberwell School of Art.

25 Jones's handwritten note on the bottom of p 233 of A.S. Hartrick, *A Painter's Pilgrimage Through Fifty Years* (Cambridge, 1939). Copy now in the possession of the Trustees of David Jones's Estate.

26 See *Dai Greatcoat* p 201. Eliot, the establishment figure, took the Underground whereas Jones, on the fringe and living in apparent poverty, took taxis.

27 A.S. Hartrick, *A Painter's Pilgrimage* p 7.

28 David Jones, letter to Helen Sutherland of 9 September 1951, in Tate Gallery Archive. Hartrick did a watercolour portrait of Gauguin which was shown in the 1966 Pont Aven exhibition at the Tate.

29 Jones, *The Dying Gaul* p 26.

30 A.S. Hartrick, *A Painter's Pilgrimage* p 7.

31 A.S. Hartrick, *Drawing* (London: Pitman and Sons, 1928) p 23.

32 A.S. Hartrick, *A Painter's Pilgrimage* p 209.

33 Jones, letter to H.S. Ede of 15 April 1943 in Kettle's Yard, Cambridge. As late as 1943, Jones was seeing Hartrick, 'a heavenly chap, and near eighty and still all alive' - letter to H.S. Ede of 3 May 1943.

34 Jones, rough draft of a letter to *The Times* in NLW 1978 Dep. Box II/29.

35 Jones, notes drafted for a biography for *Mid-Century Authors* in The Burns Library, Boston College.

36 Jones, Notes for the Tate Gallery made at the request of H.S. Ede in 1935. Quoted in *David Jones - a Memorial Exhibition*, Kettle's Yard, Cambridge.

37 *Camberwell School of Art Prospectus* p 11.

38 *Ibid.*

39 See *The Last Romantics - The Romantic Tradition in British Art* ed. John Christian (London: Lund Humphries/Barbican, 1989) pp 39 & 167.

40 Jones, letter to H.S. Ede, 15 April 1943 in Kettle's Yard, Cambridge.

41 Jones, letter to René Hague, 9-15 July 1973, *Dai Greatcoat* p 246.

42 In conversation with A.J. Hyne, June, 1992. This painting was smoke-damaged by an incendiary bomb in the Second World War.

43 Eric Gill, *Letters* ed. Walter Shewring (London: Jonathan Cape, 1947) p 149.

44 Jones in *Dai Greatcoat* p 26.

45 William Blissett, *The Long Conversation* (Oxford: Oxford University Press, 1981) p 116.

46 Jones, Notes for the Tate Gallery made at the request of H.S. Ede in 1935. Quoted in *Dai Greatcoat* p 20.

TRAINING IN THE TRENCHES

1 A letter from The Artists' Rifles of 12 November 1914, in NLW 1985 Purchase, Group C.

2 See William Gaunt, *The Pre-Raphaelite Tragedy* (London: Jonathan Cape, 1942) p 91.

3 *Dai Greatcoat* p 26.

4 Jones, letter to Grisewood of 1 January 1964, quoted in *Dai Greatcoat* p 195.

5 Blissett, pp 117 & 120.

6 According to experts at the Imperial War Museum the regulation would depend on whether or not the sector was, at the time, sensitive. While the work of official war artists did have to be vetted, sketching may well have been permitted as a way of allowing men to

pass time calmly.

7 Blissett, p 23.

8 In the sketchbook Jones identifies himself as '22579 6 Platoon B Company' (Imperial War Museum No. 5927), whereas in his handwritten notes in *A History of the 38th Welsh Division* by Hugh Rees (London: 1928) Jones records that after October 1916 he was in 'D Company'. Jones's copy in the NLW.

9 Jones, Sketchbook, Imperial War Museum Archive No. 5927.

10 Yet another would be the drawing of the periscope in the Royal Welch Fusiliers Museum at Caernarfon.

11 Jones, letter to René Hague 24 September 1974, in Fisher Rare Book Library, Toronto.

12 Jones, letter to Helen Sutherland of 9 February 1948, in Tate Gallery Archive.

13 Jones, letter to Grisewood of 14 November 1970, in Georgetown University Library.

14 Jones, letter to René Hague of 4 March 1974, in Fisher Rare Book Library, Toronto.

15 Ernst Jünger, *In Stahlgewittern* (Berlin: 1931) p 100 quoted in Modris Eksteins, *Rites of Spring* (Bantam: London, 1989; Black Swan 1990) p 201.

16 There are a few exceptions such as when official war artists like Orpen seem to have been allowed to break the rule, if painting German corpses.

17 Unidentified ms. re war - written possibly during the 1940s or 1950s in NLW 1985 Purchase, Group B Box 7 V/4.

18 Jones, letter to Petra Tegetmeier of 9 March 1930. Quoted in Jonathan Miles, *Backgrounds to David Jones* (Cardiff: University of Wales Press, 1990) p 94.

19 Unidentified ms. re war - written possibly during the 1940s or 1950s in NLW 1985 Purchase, Group B Box 7 V/4.

20 While the staff of The Imperial War Museum are unable to state specifically, from the scant evidence of the uniform, whether or not the drawing is of a German, they do suggest that the treatment is typical of the manner in which Germans were depicted in contemporary drawings.

WESTMINSTER SCHOOL OF ART

1 Jones, Preface to *In Parenthesis*, p xv.

2 Jones, Notes made in 1935 for the Tate.

3 Now in the Tate Gallery Archive. See Paul Hills, '"The Pierced Hermaphrodite" David Jones's Imagery of the Crucifixion' in *David Jones: Man and Poet* ed. Matthias (Orono, Maine: National Poetry Foundation, 1989) p 426. See also Blissett pp 19 & 143: Jones 'acknowledged the specific influence of *The Rescue of Arsinoë* on his own composition' and Jones talked 'about his early enthusiasm for Tintoretto's *Susanna and the Elders*.

4 Douglas Cleverdon, *The Engravings of David Jones* (London, Clover Hill Editions, 1981) p 10.

5 See *Dai Greatcoat* p 218.

6 Jones, letter to René Hague of 9-15 July 1973, in *Dai Greatcoat* p 249.

7 Jones, 'The Fatigue' in *The Sleeping Lord and Other Fragments* (London: Faber and Faber,

1974) pp 31-2.

8 Wilfred Owen, 'At a Calvary near the Ancre' in *The Collected Poems of Wilfred Owen* ed. C.Day Lewis (London: Chatto & Windus, 1963) p 82.

9 Jones, letter to Aneirin Talfan Davies of 27 November 1962 in Davies, *David Jones - Letters to a Friend* p 80.

10 Richard Shone, *Bloomsbury Portraits* (Oxford: Phaidon, 1976) p 36.

11 Clive Bell, *Art* (1914) (Oxford: Oxford University Press pbk., 1987) p 44.

12 *Ibid.* p 195.

13 Malcolm Yorke, *The Spirit of Place* (London: Constable, 1988) p 107.

14 A draft of 'Notes on the 1930s' published in *The London Magazine*, Vol. 5, no. 1 (April, 1965) and reprinted in *The Dying Gaul* p 42, in NLW 1985 Purchase, Group C V/6.

15 Georges Aurier in *Mercure de France*, March 1891, quoted in Bernard Denvir, *Post-Impressionism* (London: Thames and Hudson, 1992) p 144.

16 In a review he 'pointed out that form alone is unlikely to be the source of aesthetic emotion: something had to be fused with it to give it significance ... '. Quoted in Spalding, *British Art Since 1900* p 62.

17 Eric Gill ms. notes on David Jones in NLW 1978 Dep Box III/27 p 1. Quoted in Jonathan Miles, *Eric Gill and David Jones at Capel-y-ffin* (Bridgend: Seren, 1992) p 147.

18 Jones, letter to Grisewood of 4 September 1971 in *Dai Greatcoat* p 232.

19 Cleverdon, *The Engravings of David Jones* p 2.

20 Jones, unidentified autobiography perhaps drafted in the 1960s NLW 1985 Purchase, Group C Box 11.

21 See Philip Hagreen, letter to 'Tom' of 23 November 1985.

22 Dorothea de Halpert, unpublished memoir (1986) in the possession of Beatrix Dufort.

23 *Ibid.*

24 From 'Arts and Crafts' in a special number of *The Studio*, 1916.

25 Henry Tonks, 'Wanderyears' in *Artwork* 1929, quoted in Ysanne Holt, *Philip Wilson Steer* (Bridgend: Seren, 1993) p 59.

26 Holt, *Philip Wilson Steer* p 59.

27 Walter Bayes, in 'The Grammar of Drawing' Pt. 1 in *The Architectural Review* (London, January 1924) 12.

28 *Westminster School of Art Prospectus 1918-19* p 5. Also, letter from the Record Keeper of the Director General's Dept., GLC Record Office, County Hall of 8 May 1989.

29 Jones, unidentified autobiography probably drafted in the 1960s, NLW 1985 Purchase, Group C V/6 .

30 Jones quoted in Davies, Introduction to *David Jones - Letters to a Friend* p 15.

31 Jones, unpublished letter to Dorothea de Halpert of 9 January 1936, in the possession of Beatrix Dufort.

32 'Meticulous' as Jones described Lawrence, with his 'long, serious face' and his 'mind the details, Miss Weston' - unpublished letters to Dorothea de Halpert of 15 August 1942 when

Jones had, by accident, bumped into his old teacher at the Tate and of 20 February 1943, both in the possession of Beatrix Dufort.

33 Bayes, 'The Grammar of Drawing' Pt. 1, 12.

34 *Westminster School of Art Prospectus 1920-1.*

35 Yorke, *The Spirit of Place*, p 32.

36 Stella Bowen, *Laughing Torso* (London, 1924) p 45. Quoted in Holt p 61.

37 See John Milner, *The Studios of Paris* (New Haven & London: Yale University Press, 1988) p 13.

38 Wendy Baron, *The Painters of Camden Town 1905-1920* (London: Christie's, 1988) p 19.

39 H.S. Ede, 'David Jones' in *Horizon* (London: August 1943) p 127.

40 John Hoole, *Bernard Meninsky - Catalogue of Exhibition July-Sept 1981* pp 3 & 10.

41 Jones quoted in *Dai Greatcoat* p 21.

42 Gabriel White, in *Bernard Meninsky* p 21.

43 Jones, notes drafted on painting while at Bowden House in 1947.

44 Nora Meninsky, the painter's widow, in conversation 19 December 1988.

45 Hans Feibusch, in *Bernard Meninsky* p 26.

46 Mary Audsley in conversation, Spring 1994. Also Jones, unidentified autobiography probably drafted in the 1960s, NLW 1985 Purchase, Group C V/6.

47 Jones, notes drafted on painting while at Bowden House in 1947.

48 Jones, quoted in Blisset p 129. See also Paul Hills 'The Romantic Tradition in David Jones' in *The Malahat Review* (Victoria, British Columbia, No. 27, July 1973) p 43: 'Jones admired him both for his hatred of aesthetes (he wore stable-boy leggings) and his knowledge of the craft of painting' particularly his 'tonal discipline'.

49 Blissett, p 13.

50 Jones, letter to Grisewood of 24 August 1956, in *Dai Greatcoat* p 170.

51 Jones, *In Parenthesis* p 49.

52 Bayes, 'The Grammar of Drawing' pt. 1, 16.

53 *Ibid.* p 13.

54 Jones, unidentified autobiography probably drafted in the 1960s, NLW 1985 Purchase, Group C V/6.

55 Perhaps called *The Reclaimers* as a painting of that title was offered for sale by Jones at the 1920 *Goupil Gallery Salon*.

56 Jones, letter to A.J. Hyne of 25 May 1971, in the possession of the addressee.

57 Peter Orr, in conversation, September, 1993.

THE YEARS WITH ERIC GILL

1 James Jones, letter to his son of 24 August 1921, NLW 1985 Purchase, Group C Box 8.

2 Eric Gill, letter to David Jones of 5 March 1921. In a private collection

3 See Gerald B. Phelan, *Jacques Maritain* (London: Sheed & Ward, 1937) pp 31-2. See Miles, *Backgrounds to David Jones* Ch. 1 & 2 for a discussion of Neo-Thomism in relation to Jones and Gill.

4 Jones, letter to Grisewood of 14 November 1970 in Georgetown University Library. Dr.

Pusey was a mid-nineteenth century High Anglican and author of 'The Doctrine of the Real Presence' (1856).

5 See NLW 1985 Purchase, Group C V/6 - Unidentified autobiography probably drafted in the 1960s; René Hague quoted in Peter Orr, 'Mr. Jones Your Legs are Crossed - A Memoir' in *Agenda - Special Issue on Myth* Vol 15 Nos. 2-3 (London, Summer-Autumn 1977) 112; Blissett, p 126; *Dai Greatcoat* p 247.

6 Jones, *The Dying Gaul* p 20.

7 See Denvir, *Post-Impressionism* p 110.

8 Jones's celebration of how the particular expresses the universal in 'The Tutelar of the Place' in *The Sleeping Lord* p 60.

9 See 'Post-Impressionist theorists, however bad their paintings, were always loudly asserting that their aim was to make a 'thing' - let's say a mountain ... *under the form of paint*' - Jones, letter to Grisewood of 4 September 1971 in *Dai Greatcoat* p 232.

10 Malcolm Yorke, *Eric Gill* (London: Constable, 1981) p 208.

11 Jones, transcript of an interview for the BBC with Guy Brenton and Douglas Cleverdon, May 1961.

12 See Jones to Hague of 19 January 1973: 'Eric ... used to ask 'significant of what'? I never thought that quite fair because ... a work ... was a 'thing' in itself with its life deriving from a juxtaposition of forms' - in Thomas Fisher Rare Book Library, University of Toronto.

13 See Gill *Diaries* in the Williams Andrew Clark Memorial Library, University of Southern California at Los Angeles: 19 July 1921, 'David Jones came at noon and stayed the night' / 20 July, 'Letters and acc.[ounts] all day long and talk with D. Jones etc.' / Jones at Ditchling in August 3, 7, 15 and went away on the 30th. Jones made frequent visits throughout the autumn before he took up residence: 20 September, 'David Jones came back from Bradford' / 5 November, 'David Jones ... came for the weekend' / 16 November, 'To Brockley in Eve with David J. for the night' / 13 December, 'Grinding and mixing colours with D.J. in n.'/ 18 December, 'Drew portrait of David J. in n.'.

14 Jones, Ms. draft in NLW 1978 Dep. Box V/7.

15 Eric Gill, letter to Jones of 5 March 1921. In a private collection.

16 Jones, transcript of an interview for the BBC with Guy Brenton and Douglas Cleverdon, May 1961. See also 'they are rotten places, art schools ... ' - David Jones, letter to Helen Sutherland of 9 October, 1950 in Tate Gallery Archive.

17 Jones, unidentified autobiography, probably drafted in the 1960s in NLW 1985 Purchase, Group C V/6.

18 Philip Hagreen, letter to René Hague of 30 April 1978 - photocopy in NLW.

19 Harold Rosenberg, 'The Aesthetics of Crisis', *The New Yorker* (New York: 22 August 1964) p 114.

20 Eric Gill, Afterword to 'Liturgical Art' in *Orate Fratres* 14 February, 1927 (St. Paul, Minnesota, USA).

21 Petra Tegetmeier is the married name of Eric Gill's second daughter, Petra; in conversation, April 1989.

22 Hagreen to Hague, 15 February 1978. Photocopy in NLW.

23 See Jones, letter to Saunders Lewis in *Agenda - David Jones Special Issue* Vol. 11 No. 4 - Vol. 12 No. 1 Autumn-Winter 1973-4 24, where Jones himself remarks on this phenomena: 'so things I've chanced to experience or gaze upon don't usually move me at the time, but sometimes afterwards ... '.

24 T.S. Eliot, 'Tradition and the Individual Talent' (1919) in *Selected Prose of T.S. Eliot* ed. Kermode (London: Faber and Faber, 1975) p 43.

25 See Cleverdon, *Engravings* p 6.

26 Jones, handwritten note on pp 72-3 of Donald Attwater, *A Cell of Good Living* (London: Geoffrey Chapman, 1969). Copy in NLW.

27 Jones, letter to Evan Gill of 6 August 1961.

28 See Peter William Cribb, unpublished account of the Ditchling Community, 'Joseph Cribb and the Guild of St. Joseph and St. Dominic Founded in 1920 at Ditchling in the County of Sussex' p 43.

29 Philip Hagreen, letter to René Hague, quoted in *Dai Greatcoat* p 29.

30 See particularly, John Ruskin, 'The Relation of Art to Use' - a lecture given before Oxford University, Hilary Term 1870 in *Lectures on Art* (London: George Allen, 1904) and *Unto the Last* (London: George Allen, 1906).

31 William Morris, 'The Aims of Art' in *Collected Works* (London: Longmans Green & Co., 1915) Vol. XXIII p 94.

32 Jones, 'A Note on Mr. Berenson's Views' (1950) in *Epoch and Artist* ed. Harman Grisewood (London: Faber and Faber, 1959; pbk. 1973) p 274.

33 Philip Hagreen, letter to René Hague of 4 October 1978. Photocopy in NLW.

34 They lived in the spirit of the Rule of the First Order (Friars, Priests and Lay Brothers).

35 Philip Hagreen, letter to Hague 5 March 1978 in NLW. In an unidentified letter in NLW of October 1962, a correspondent from Ampleforth wrote to Jones about the 'violent sanctity' of McNabb.

36 Ferdinand Valentine O.P., *Father Vincent McNabb* O.P. (London: Burns and Oates, 1955) p 289.

37 It was also translated with John O'Connor while Gill and Jones were in Bradford between 8 - 15 August 1922 working on the Stations in St. Cuthbert's. By contrast, a few days later Gill was beginning a 'drawing of fucking for Fr. O'Connor' - Gill *Diaries* August 1922.

38 René Hague, letter to Barbara Wall of 31 December 1977 quoted in Barbara Wall, *René Hague: A Personal Memoir* (Wirral: Aylesford Press, 1989) p 52.

39 Jacques Maritain, *Art and Scholasticism* trans. J.F. Scanlan (London: Sheed & Ward, 1930) p 9.

40 Jones, *Epoch and Artist* pp 12 & 183.

41 Maritain, *Art and Scholasticism*, p 9. See also, St. Thomas Aquinas, *Summa Theologica* trans.

The Fathers of the Dominican Province (N.Y.: Benzinger Bros., 1947) I-II Q 53 3rd Art, Vol. I p 813.

42 Maritain, *The Philosophy of Art* pp 83-4.

43 David Jones, unpublished letter to Desmond Chute of 6 February 1956. In a private collection.

44 Eric Gill, *Diaries*, 29 June 1924 in William Andrews Clark Library in Los Angeles.

45 Eric Gill, *Autobiography* (London: Jonathan Cape,1940) p 228. For a more complete account of Gill at Capel-y-ffin see Miles, *Eric Gill and David Jones at Capel-y-ffin*.

46 Petra Tegetmeier remembered that Jones was unhelpful with the chores - in conversation, April 1989. There are several sketches and studies for the painting.

47 See Miles, *Eric Gill and David Jones at Capel-y-ffin* p 48.

48 Jones, transcript of an interview for the BBC with Guy Brenton and Douglas Cleverdon, May 1961.

49 Robert Speaight, *The Life of Eric Gill* (London: Methuen, 1966) p 228.

50 Jones, quoted by H.S. Ede in 'David Jones' in *Horizon* August, 1943, 133.

51 Attwater, *A Cell of Good Living* p 72.

52 Jones, transcript of an interview for the BBC with Guy Brenton and Douglas Cleverdon, May 1961.

53 Hague in *Dai Greatcoat* p 32.

54 Jones in typescripts of 1961 BBC 3rd Programme Broadcast on Eric Gill produced by Douglas Cleverdon in the Harry Ransom Humanities Research Centre, University of Texas, Austin.

55 Hagreen, letter to Hague 27 February 1978. Photocopy in NLW.

56 Eddie Nutgens in conversation at Pigotts, October 1981. Quoted in Miles, *Backgrounds* p 33.

HIERATIC EVASIONS: CHRIST AND THE SAINTS

1 Charles Harrison, *English Art and Modernism 1900-1939* p 171. Bomberg was poultry farming. Nash was, after the war, an artist without a subject - see Harrison, p 147.

2 Bell, *Art* p 261 & see also p 82.

3 Though, as Charles Harrison perceptively notes, 'his style came increasingly to reflect a habit of formalization rather than a process of critical transformation' - Harrison, p 158.

4 Quoted by Andrew Causey, 'The Everyday and the Visionary' in *British Art in the 20th Century - the Modern Movement* ed. Susan Compton. (London and Munich: Royal Academy of Arts Prestel-Verlag, 1986) p 196.

5 For example, see Gauguin's portrait *Aita tamari vahine Judith te parari* (1893-4) reproduced in *Gauguin* - Exhibition Catalogue from the Grand Palais, Paris, 1989 (Paris: Réunion des musées nationaux, 1989) p 307.

6 Bayes, 'The Grammar of Drawing' Pt 2 in *The Architectural Review* p 57.

7 See also Cork, *The Bitter Truth*, pp 308-9.

8 See David Jones, transcript of interview by Guy Brenton and Douglas Cleverdon for the

BBC, May 1961.

9 In theological terms they include: the Agony in the Garden, the Flagellation at the Pillar, the Crowning with Thorns, Jesus Carrying his Cross, and the Crucifixion.

10 Philip Hagreen, letter to René Hague, quoted in *Dai Greatcoat* p 30.

11 Philip Hagreen, letter to René Hague of 22 February 1978. Photocopy in NLW.

12 Paul Cézanne in conversation with Joachim Gasquet in *Cézanne, A Memoir with Conversations* (London: Thames & Hudson, 1991) p 176.

13 Quoted in Peter Fuller *Images of God* (London: Chatto & Windus, 1985; The Hogarth Press, 1990) p 46.

ENGRAVINGS AND ILLUSTRATIONS

1 Eric Gill, *Diaries*, 1 November 1921, in William Andrews Clark Library, Los Angeles. The engraving was done on Jones's birthday.

2 Jones: 'It looked absolutely heavenly before the letters were painted' - letter to Nicolete Gray, 1963 (a.d. IX Id. IAN. MCMLXIII) in Tate Gallery Archive.

3 Cleverdon, *Engravings* p 3.

4 Saunders Lewis, 'Epoch and Artist' *Agenda David Jones Special Issue* (London: Agenda, Spring and Summer 1967) Vol. 5 Nos. 1-3, 112.

5 See Sir James Frazer, *The Golden Bough* (London: Macmillan, Abridged Ed. pbk. 1957) p 754.

6 Wilfred Owen, letter to Osbert Sitwell of 4 July 1918, quoted in *The Collected Poems of Wilfred Owen* p 23.

7 See Cleverdon, *Engravings* p 4.

8 See Blissett, p 72.

9 See Albert Garret, *A History of Wood Engraving* (London: Bloomsbury Books, 1986) pp 100, 135.

10 Wyndham Lewis, 'Notes on Some German Woodcuts at the Twenty One Gallery' in *Blast* No. 1 - quoted in *Wyndham Lewis on Art* ed. Michel and Fox (London: Thames and Hudson, 1969) p 39.

11 Hilary Pepler in his 1934 essay, 'The Hand Press' quoted in Cleverdon, *Engravings* p 4.

12 *Idem*. The fifth volume of *The Game* (1922) used the theme of the Ten Commandments in the cover engravings.

13 See Cleverdon, *Engravings* p 8 where he remarks on the 'comparative flaccidity of the last five' images.

14 See Cleverdon, *Engravings* p 9.

15 Philip Hagreen to Hague, 10 April 1978. Photocopy in NLW.

16 Philip Hagreen to Hague, 22 February 1978. Photocopy in NLW.

17 *Ibid*.

18 Timothy Wilcox, ed. *Eric Gill and the Guild of St. Joseph and St. Dominic* Exhibition Catalogue, (Hove Museum and Art Gallery), 1990 p 55.

19 Eric Gill, Unlisted Writings, 1924 in William Andrews Clark Library, Los Angeles.

20 Eric Gill, postcard to R.A. Walker, 30 January 1928 in the William Andrews Clark Library, Los Angeles.

21 See Robert Gibbings, 'The Golden Cockerel Press' in *The Woodcut - An Annual* No. 1 (London, 1927).

22 Gibbings, 'The Golden Cockerel Press' p 14.

23 See Miles, *Eric Gill & David Jones at Capel-y-ffin*, pp 33, 59, 126-7.

24 There are some of these in the Burns Library, Boston College.

25 Gill, *Diaries* 30 November 1925 & 1 December 1925 in the William Andrews Clark Library, Los Angeles.

26 Jones, 1935 Notes for the Tate in Kettle's Yard, Cambridge.

27 Desmond Chute, letter to Eric Gill of 22 February 1926 in the William Andrews Clark Library, Los Angeles.

28 Cleverdon, *Engravings* p 11.

29 Quoted by Blissett p 10.

30 *The Times*, 20 October 1927.

31 Robert Gibbings, 'Biography of the Golden Cockerel Press' - Supplement to *The London Mercury* November 1931 Vol. XXV No. 145.

32 *Ibid*.

33 Eric Gill, letter to Enid Clay of 1 March 1924 in the William Andrews Clark Library, Los Angeles.

34 There is some controversy about whether or not Jones agreed to this. Cleverdon maintains that 'there exist a couple of coloured artist's proofs on india-paper, which must have been coloured by David himself; and the prospectus (of which a coloured proof was found among his papers) definitely states that many of the blocks will be hand-coloured under his care. So he may have forgotten that he had originally agreed to the colouring' - *Engravings* p 11. Some evidence suggesting that at this time Jones may not have been adverse to the idea of hand-colouring is the existence of a hand-coloured, signed copy in a private collection in Glasgow of what is perhaps his first copper engraving: *Nant Honddu* dated 'dmj 25'. It has been painted in watercolour and adorned with an early example of lettering: '*benedicite montes et colles domino benedicite vniversia germinantia in terra domino*'. The result of colouring is, however, that it compromises the bigness and the emptiness of the design.

35 Philip Hagreen to Hague, 19 February 1978. Photocopy in NLW.

36 Paul Hills, *David Jones* - 1981 Exhibition Catalogue (London: the Tate Gallery, 1981) p 73.

37 Eric Gill, *Christianity and Art* (Capel-y-ffin: Walterson [pseud. Attwater], 1927) p 8.

38 David Jones, letter to Juliet and Richard Shirley Smith of 11 February 1961 - in the possession of the addressees.

39 Jones, letter to Reynolds Stone of 23 September 1958 in the Bodleian Library, Oxford. The artist's admiration for Bewick was clearly considerable; he possessed *Thomas Bewick and his Pupils* by Austin Dobson, and Prudence Pelham gave him *Engravings on Wood by Thomas Bewick* when it came out in 1947.

40 Jones, draft of letter to Roger Billcliffe, Assistant Keeper, British Art, Walker Gallery, Liverpool of 21 May 1968, in NLW 1978 Dep. Box II/3.

41 'Biography of the Golden Cockerel Press',

The London Mercury Vol XXV No 145.

42 See Cleverdon, *Engravings* p 13.

43 David Jones, letter to Cleverdon of 22 June 1977, quoted in Cleverdon, *Engravings* p 14.

44 Cleverdon, *Engravings* p 12.

45 Jones, letter to Cleverdon of 22 June 1927, quoted in *ibid*. p 14.

46 Jones, letter to Cleverdon of 5 August 1927, quoted in *ibid*. p 15.

47 Jones, 'An Introduction to *The Rime of the Ancient Mariner*' in *The Dying Gaul* p 187.

48 *Ibid*. p 189.

49 *Ibid*. p 186.

50 Gill, letter to Jones of 10 June 1928 - in a private collection.

51 Jones, letter to Cleverdon of 17 June 1928, quoted in *Engravings* p 16.

52 Jones, 'An Introduction to *The Rime of the Ancient Mariner*' in *The Dying Gaul* p 187.

53 *Ibid*. p 188.

54 Jones, letter to Cleverdon of 30 August 1928 in the Tate Gallery Archive.

55 The sketch is in NLW 1978 Dep. Box V/12.

56 Michael Ayrton in *The Spectator* (London, 3 November 1944).

57 These appeared in *The Pageant* (London: Henry & Co.). *The Albatross* had appeared in the 1896 volume, p 161 and *He Stoppeth One of Three* on p 29 of the 1897 volume.

58 Jones, letter to Cleverdon of 16 May 1929, quoted in *Engravings* p 20.

59 Jones, letter to Janet Stone of 27 April 1965, in Bodleian Library, Oxford.

60 Jones, letters to Helen Ede of 13 August 1928 and to H.S. Ede of 29 August 1928, both in Kettle's Yard, Cambridge.

61 Jones, letter to H.S. Ede of 24 October 1929, in Kettle's Yard, Cambridge.

62 Jones, letter to Cleverdon of 14 February 1929, quoted in Cleverdon, *Engravings* p 20.

63 H.S. Ede in *Horizon*, August, 1943, p 125.

64 Jones, letter to Gill from Sidmouth 21 May 1938, in the William Andrews Clark Library, Los Angeles.

SMALL CARVINGS

1 See Philip Hagreen, letter to René Hague of 10 April 1978, in NLW. Jones did design larger wooden figures such as the Sts. Dominic and Francis which were placed on either side of the door on the outside of the west wall of the Chapel at Ditchling. See Wilcox, p 31 for a photo.

2 See Cleverdon, *The Engravings* pp 7 and 23 and Gill, *Diaries* e.g. 6 April 1922, in William Andrews Clark Library, Los Angeles.

3 R.L. Charles, 'David Jones - Some Recently Acquired Works' in *Amgueddfa: Bulletin of the National Museum of Wales*, 22 (Cardiff: National Museum of Wales, 1976) p 4.

4 *Idem*.

5 Maurice de la Taille, *The Mystery of Faith and Human Opinion Contrasted and Defined* trans. by J.B. Schimpf (London: Sheed & Ward, 1930) p 212.

6 David Jones, *The Anathemata* (London: Faber

and Faber, 1952, pbk. 1972) p 188.

7 David Jones 'The Fatigue' in *The Sleeping Lord* p 36

8 *Idem*.

9 Jones 'Art and Sacrament' in *Epoch and Artist* p 163.

10 See Donald Attwater, *The Penguin Dictionary of Saints* (Harmondsworth: Penguin, 1965) p 165: 'the earliest writers do not mention St. Helena ... she may have been dead before' the alleged finding of the cross.

11 A.J. Hyne, in conversation 1992.

12 Jones, autobiographical notes: 'he has sculpted in wood but not professionally' - in NLW 1985 Purchase, Group C Box 11/2.

13 Philip Hagreen letter to René Hague of 10 April 1978. Photocopy in NLW.

14 The Madonna Lily symbolizes the Virgin's purity.

ANIMALS

1 Jones quoted in *Dai Greatcoat* p 27.

2 Jones, *In Parenthesis* p 54.

3 Now in the Vancouver Art Gallery, Canada.

4 Jones, letter to Reynolds Stone of 23 September 1958, in the Bodleian Library, Oxford.

5 *The Times*, 23 April 1927.

6 Nest Cleverdon, in conversation 30 March 1989.

7 See Garrett, *A History of Wood Engraving* pp 132-3.

8 This sketch by Gill, 'Man is Matter and Spirit, both real and both good' is reproduced in Miles, *Eric Gill and David Jones at Capel-y-ffin* p 66.

9 Jones, Preface to *In Parenthesis* p xiv.

10 Jones, 'The Sleeping Lord' in *The Sleeping Lord* p 93.

11 Kathleen Raine in conversation with Naim Attallah *The Guardian*, 23 March 1993. Laika was put into orbit at the beginning of November, 1957.

12 Hills, *David Jones*, p 92.

13 Jones, letter to Helen Sutherland of 6 September 1940, in Tate Gallery Archive. It was after Harman Grisewood's wedding.

14 Jones, draft of letter to Roger Billcliffe, Assistant Keeper, British Art, Walker Gallery, Liverpool of 21 May 1968 in NLW 1978 Dep. Box II/3. re. *Panthers* (Walker Art Gallery).

15 The Minute Book of the 7&5 Society, 26 January 1928, in the Tate Gallery Archive.

16 Douglas Cleverdon, *Word & Image IV* Catalogue of National Book League Exhibition (London: 1972) Jones's copy in the possession of the Trustees.

17 *The Times*, 13 May 1930.

18 Jones in *David Jones: Artist and Writer*, a tape-recorded commentary on his paintings.

19 Jones, draft of letter to Roger Billcliffe, Assistant Keeper, British Art, Walker Gallery, Liverpool of 21 May 1968 in NLW 1978 Dep. Box II/3. re. *Panthers* (Walker Art Gallery).

20 Jones told this story to Stanley Honeyman. In conversation, 1992.

21 Jones, letter to Vernon Watkins of 14

March 1956 in *David Jones: Letters to Vernon Watkins* ed. Pryor (Cardiff: University of Wales Press, 1976) p 30.

22 In the collection of The British Council.

23 Owned by Vancouver Art Gallery.

24 Jones, letter to Jonathan Scott of 15 November 1961, in the possession of the addressee.

APPROACHES TO LANDSCAPE

1 See Paul Sandby's *XII Views in North Wales being a part of a Tour through that Fertile and Romantick Country under the Patronange of the Honorable Sir Watkin Williams Wynn Bart.*, published in 1776. See also Graham Reynolds, *Watercolours - A Concise History* (London: Thames & Hudson, 1971) p 56.

2 Hills, *Malahat Review* p 45.

3 Jones, letter to Arthur Giardelli of 4 September 1964, in the possession of the addressee.

4 See Eric Rowan, *Art in Wales* (Cardiff: University of Wales Press, 1985) p 11.

5 See Blissett, p 118.

6 Jones, 'Autobiographical Talk' in *Epoch and Artist* p 29.

7 See Harrison, *English Art and Modernism* p 168.

8 Paul Nash, letter to Martin Armstrong quoted in A. Bertram *Paul Nash* (London: Faber and Faber, 1955) p 149.

9 Jones, letter of 20 February 1943, to Dorothea de Halpert in the possession of Beatrix Dufort.

10 *Ibid*.

11 See Spalding, *British Art Since 1900* p 69.

12 Unpublished Memoir (1986) of Dorothea De Halpert in the possession of Beatrix Dufort.

13 Jones, typed biographical data of '20.10.53' in NLW1985 Purchase, Group C Box 15/24, and also unidentified autobiography probably drafted in the 1960s in Box 11. Jones suggests that it was in 1920 but Goupil Gallery records in the Tate Gallery Archive reveal that paintings were accepted from 1919.

14 Jones, 'Autobiographical Talk' in *Epoch and Artist* p 30.

15 Philip Hagreen, notes after a conversation with René Hague, 14 July 1978. Photocopy in NLW.

16 Hagreen, letter to René Hague of 18 July 1980 p 1. Photocopy in NLW.

17 Tom Cross, *Painting the Warmth of the Sun* (Penzance and Guildford: Alison Hodge and the Lutterworth Press, 1984) p 19.

18 See Blissett p 19, when Jones nominates Spencer and Nicholson.

19 Paul Hills, *The Malahat Review* p 43.

20 See Cleverdon, *Engravings* p 11.

21 Tom Stagles, Laboratory Technician, Rowney Ltd. provided this information.

22 John Rothenstein, *Summer's Lease* (London, 1965) p 127.

23 Hague in *Dai Greatcoat* p 32.

24 Philip Hagreen, letter to Stella Wright of

28 January 1978. Photocopy in NLW.

25 John Rothenstein, *Modern English Painters - Innes to Moore* p 288.

26 Eric Gill, *Letters* p 150.

27 Eric Gill, *Diaries* 9 October 1924 in William Andrews Clark Library, Los Angeles.

28 Eric Gill, letter to David Jones of 11 April 1927 in a private collection.

29 Eric Gill, letter to Desmond Chute of 29 May 1927 in the Gleeson Library, San Francisco.

30 *GK's Weekly* (London, 7 May 1927).

31 Arthur Howell in *Frances Hodgkins - 4 Vital Years* (London: Rockliff, 1951) pp 4-9.

32 *The Times*, 23 April 1927.

33 In 1924, the Lefevre Gallery exhibited *Works of some of the Most Eminent French Painters of Today* including Derain, Matisse and Picasso and in 1926 there was Douanier Rousseau at the Lefevre Gallery and Gris, Léger, Picasso and Severini at the Mayor Gallery.

34 Gill, *Autobiography* p 230.

35 Jones, letter to Dorothea de Halpert of 29 December 1960 in the possession of Beatrix Dufort. See also *Dai Greatcoat* pp 225-6: 'I think old Bonnard makes Degas (by comparison and in general terms) much less great - enormously skilful and a superb draughtsman and painter - but somehow "worldly" and lacking in the quiet, indefinable poetry of Bonnard.'

36 Reynolds, *Watercolours* p 181.

37 Eric Gill, *Artwork No. 23* (London, 1930) p 17.

38 Jones, letter to Arthur Giardelli of 4 September 1964, in the possession of the addressee.

39 See *In Parenthesis* n. 15 pp 221-2.

40 Jones, letter to the Edes of 21 May 1928. Quoted in *Dai Greatcoat* pp 45-6.

41 Jones, letter to the Edes of 21 May 1928. In Kettle's Yard, Cambridge.

42 *Ibid*.

43 See also *Isaiah* Ch. LV v. 12: 'the mountains and the hills shall break forth ... into singing'.

44 Christopher Neve, *Unquiet Landscape* (London: Faber and Faber, 1990) pp 31-2.

45 Philip Hagreen, letter to René Hague of 1 April 1978. Photocopy in NLW.

46 Hagreen cautioned that it is 'rash to come too near to Turner. In the light of his glory David's things are thin, mannered, and fidgety.' - Hagreen, letter to Hague of 27 March, 1978. Photocopy in NLW.

47 Jones, *In Parenthesis* p 163.

SHIPS AND THE SEA

1 Blissett, p 21.

2 Jones, letter to Philip Hagreen of 26 March 1925 in Dai Greatcoat p 34.

3 Jones, notes on painting drafted at Bowden House, and Bayes, *The Architectural Review* Pt 2 p 56: '... local colour, by virtue of which grass is green and my hair alas no longer black ... is very largely adjectival ... Our interest in colour we use consists not in what it is but in what it does to the other colours of the scheme...'.

4 Jones, *In Parenthesis*, pp 66 & 185-6.

5 Mark L. Evans, *The Derek Williams Collection* (Cardiff: National Museum of Wales, 1989) p 31.

6 Jones, letter to Philip Hagreen of 26 March 1925 in *Dai Greatcoat* p 34.

7 Robert Rosenblum, *Modern Painting and the Northern Romantic Tradition* (London: Thames and Hudson, 1975 pbk. 1978) p 14.

8 Jones, letter to H.S. Ede of 27 October 1927, in Kettle's Yard, Cambridge.

9 Jones, letter to H.S. Ede of 4 November 1927, in Kettle's Yard, Cambridge.

10 Jones, letter to Philip Hagreen of 26 March, 1925. Quoted in *Dai Greatcoat* p 34.

11 Jones, letter to Saunders Lewis of 17 April 1970, in NLW.

12 Jones, letter to Saunders Lewis of 17 April 1970 in NLW. Quoted in Miles, *Backgrounds to David Jones* p 139.

13 Blissett, p 51.

14 See Jones, *The Roman Quarry and Other Sequences* ed. Grisewood and Hague (London: Agenda Editions, 1981) p 13: 'All the bounding naiad ways...'.

15 Jones, *Epoch and Artist* p 238-9.

16 Cleverdon, *Engravings* pp 17-18.

17 Nash quoted in David Mellor 'British Art in the 1930s: Some Economic, Political and Cultural Structures' in *Class, Culture & Social Change - A New View of the 1930s* ed. Gloversmith (Sussex: Harvester Press, 1980) p 186.

18 David Mellor, 'The Body and The Land' in *A Paradise Lost* ed. Mellor (London: Lund Humphries/Barbican, 1987) pp 37-8.

19 Eric Gill, Notes on David Jones dated 7 August 1928, in NLW - 1978 Dep. Box III/27.

20 Jones, letter to Helen Sutherland of 18 November 1931, in the Tate Gallery Archive.

21 The Hove Bungalows Ltd., advertising pamphlet.

22 Blissett, pp 101-2.

23 Jones, *David Jones: Artist and Writer* a tape-recorded commentary on his paintings.

24 Hills, *David Jones* p 89.

25 Jones quoted in Davies, *David Jones Letters to a Friend* p 15.

26 See *The Mabinogion* trans. Lady Charlotte Guest (London: J.M. Dent, 1906) pp 46-7 and the epigraph to *In Parenthesis* which is taken from it.

27 Jones, letter to Dr. Charles Burns of 29 May 1940 in the possession of Paul Burns.

INTERIORS AND STILL LIFES

1 Jones, letter to Janet Stone of 30 March 1965 in the Bodleian Library, Oxford.

2 See Harrison, *English Art and Modernism* pp 167-8.

3 Jones, letter to H.S. Ede of 29-30 August 1942, in Kettle's Yard, Cambridge.

4 Ben Nicholson, quoted in Cross, *Painting the Warmth of the Sun* p 22.

5 Jones, letter of 29 December 1960, to Dorothea de Halpert. In the possession of Beatrix Dufort.

6 See Hills, 'The Pierced Hermaphrodite' p 440.

7 Tom Burns, *The Use of Memory* (London: Sheed & Ward, 1993) p 164.

8 Jones, letter to Cleverdon of 13 May 1929, quoted in *Engravings* p 20.

9 Jones, letter to Janet Stone of 27 April 1965, in the Bodleian Library, Oxford.

10 See 'Did you get to the Picasso show?' - letter to Nicolete Gray of 8 July 1931 from Pigotts where he was enjoying the beech-woods and continuing his 'attempts to paint in oil', in Tate Gallery Archive.

11 See Harrison pp 252ff.

12 Quoted in David Mellor 'British Art in the 1930s: Some Economic, Political and Cultural Structures' in *Class, Culture & Social Change - A New View of the 1930s* ed. Gloversmith (Sussex: Harvester Press 1980) p 189.

13 Paul Nash, letter to *The Times*, 2nd June 1933.

14 *The New Statesman* 27 February 1932, 263.

15 Jones, letter to Nicolete Gray of Ash Wednesday 1932, in the Tate Gallery Archive.

16 See Alwyn and Brinley Rees, *Celtic Heritage* (London: Thames & Hudson, 1961) p 313.

17 *Ibid.* See also Jessie L. Weston, *From Ritual to Romance* (Cambridge: Cambridge Press, 1920).

18 Paul Hills, *The Malahat Review* p 47.

19 Fuller, *Images of God* p 46.

20 Neve, *Unquiet Landscape* p 98.

21 See Jeremy Lewison, *Ben Nicholson* (London: Tate Gallery, 1993) p 27.

22 Prudence Pelham described one of them as 'simply vast. I can't remember ever, since leaving Stanmer, inhabiting premises huge enough to hang it in.' - undated letter to David Jones in the possession of E.C. Hodgkin.

23 H.S. Ede, *Horizon*, 134.

24 Helen Sutherland, letter to David Jones of 1 March 1945, in NLW 1985 Purchase.

25 David Jones, letter to H.S. Ede of 4 November 1927, quoted in *Dai Greatcoat* p 45.

26 Henry Vaughan, 'The World' in *Collected Poems* ed. Rudrum (Harmondsworth: Penguin, 1976) p 227.

27 Jones, letter to H.S. Ede of 24 October 1929, quoted in *Dai Greatcoat* p 46.

28 Jones, letter to H.S. Ede of 4 November 1927, quoted in *Dai Greatcoat* p 45.

29 Jones, letter to Dr. Charles Burns 25 May 1942, in the possession of Paul Burns.

30 Waldemar Januszczak, review of David Jones 1981 Tate Gallery exhibition in *The Guardian* 22 July 1981.

31 Jones, 'James Joyce's Dublin' in *Epoch and Artist* p 304.

32 Jones, letter to H.S. Ede of 19 August 1943, quoted in *Dai Greatcoat* p 124.

PROBLEMS AND POSSIBILITIES OF THE FIGURE

1 Friedrich Nietzsche, *Beyond Good and Evil* trans. Hollingdale (Harmondsworth: Penguin Books, 1973) p 58.

2 Harman Grisewood, *Why Am I Still a Catholic?* ed. Hoare (Oxford: Oxford Polytechnic, 1980) pp 4-5.

3 Jones, 'Art and Sacrament' in *Epoch and Artist* p 165.

4 Jones, note 2 p 6 of the unpublished *Epithalamion for H & M from DJ* - 'the larger part ... made during the night of 18 September 1940, at 61 King's Road Chelsea'.

5 René Hague, letter to David Jones of 7 May 1966, in a private collection.

6 Jones, annotation to pp 250-1 of Volume One of Oswald Spengler, *The Decline of the West* trans. Atkinson (London: Allen and Unwin, 1932).

7 Jones, *Epoch and Artist* p 294.

8 Eric Gill, *Introduction to The Engravings of Eric Gill* (Bristol: Douglas Cleverdon, 1929).

9 See also, Hills, 'The Pierced Hermaphrodite' pp 437-8.

10 Nest Cleverdon, in conversation 30 March 1989.

11 Jones, *The Anathemata* pp 59-60.

12 See Miles, *Eric Gill and David Jones at Capel-y-ffin* pp 63-8.

PORTRAITS OF FRIENDS

1 See Timothy Hilton, *The Pre-Raphaelites* (London: Thames and Hudson, 1970) p 59.

2 Jones, letter to René Hague of 1 January 1973, quoted in *Dai Greatcoat* p 238.

3 Review in the *Times Weekly* 23 December 1954.

4 Jones, letter to H.S. Ede of 15 April 1943, in Kettle's Yard, Cambridge.

5 Petra Tegetmeier, in conversation April, 1989.

6 Philip Hagreen, notes made after a conversation with René Hague 14 July 1978. Photocopy in NLW.

7 Eric Gill, letter of 11 March 1927 to Desmond Chute in the Gleeson Library, San Francisco: 'John O'Connor was all for Petra's breaking it off years ago'.

8 Kate Campbell, in conversation, summer 1993.

9 David Kindersley, interview with Vernon Gill 20 April 1967, at the William Andrews Clark Library, Los Angeles.

10 Eddie Nutgens, in conversation at Pigotts, October 1981.

11 Petra Tegetmeier, in conversation, April, 1989. Philip Hagreen remembered Jones's 'serious' tease about Petra paying for her own engagement ring which Hagreen made for ten shillings. In a letter to 'Tom' of 23 November 1985.

12 René Hague, letter to Harman Grisewood of 25 January 1980, in Georgetown University Library.

13 H.S. Ede, fragment of an undated letter to Jones in NLW 1985 Purchase, Group B I/11.

14 David Kindersley, interview with Cecil Gill, 20 April 1967 at the William Andrews Clark Library, Los Angeles.

15 See *Dai Greatcoat* p 42.

16 See Eric Gill, letter to Desmond Chute of

11 March 1927 in the Gleeson Library, San Francisco.

17 Philip Hagreen, notes made after a conversation with René Hague 14 July 1978. Photocopy in NLW.

18 Philip Hagreen, letter to René Hague of 18 July 1980. Photocopy in NLW.

19 Philip Hagreen, letter to René Hague of 12 June 1978. Photocopy in NLW. Hagreen's aesthetic judgements must be qualified. He wrote 'Of David's work I would say that a great deal is enormously good but some of it is very bad.' - Philip Hagreen letter to Stella Wright of 28 January 1978. Photocopy in NLW. But, as René Hague wrote to Nicolete Gray in the late 1970s, 'Philip himself hardly progressed beyond what we called the flat-faced Christs of Ditchling, and as soon as D. began to put more into his work, it became unintelligible to P.' - undated letter in Tate Gallery Archive.

20 Kathleen Raine, in conversation, 6 August 1993.

21 Rowan, *Art in Wales* p 14.

22 Kathleen Raine, in conversation, 6 August 1993.

23 A painting which Jones enjoyed seeing 'tremendously' later in his life, when it came to Burlington House just before the Second World War. Jones, letter to H.S. Ede of 15 January 1951 in Kettle's Yard, Cambridge.

24 See Guest, *The Mabinogion* p 74.

25 Jones, letter to Nicolete Gray of 10-11 January 1935, in the Tate Gallery Archive.

26 Valerie Wynne-Williams, in conversation, October 1994.

27 Geoffrey Treasure, the historian and Harrow schoolmaster who knew Jones at Northwick Park Lodge in 1955, in conversation 20 June 1994.

28 Jones, letter to Harman Grisewood of 5 August 1952, quoted in Thomas Dilworth, *The Shape of Meaning in the Poetry of David Jones*, Toronto: University of Toronto Press, 1988 p 23.

29 Jones, letter to Petra Tegetmeier of Palm Sunday, 1945 in the possession of the addressee. See also, 'to show the inhabitants of Newcastle what coal is really like' - Jones, letter to Grisewood of 4 July 1945, quoted in *Dai Greatcoat* p 130.

30 Jones, transcript of an interview for the BBC with Guy Brenton and Douglas Cleverdon, May 1961.

31 *Carr's Splint* is now in the National Gallery of Canada in Ottawa.

32 Wilcox, *Eric Gill and the Guild of St. Joseph and St. Dominic* p 47.

33 Cecil Gill, interview with David Kindersley at the William Andrews Clark Library on 20 April 1967.

34 *Ibid.*

35 Walter Shewring, in a letter to Paul Hills.

36 Jones, letter to René Hague of 1 January 1973, quoted in *Dai Greatcoat* p 238.

37 Barbara Wall, René Hague - A Personal Memoir p 26.

38 There is *Dvo Homines Per Aqvam Nobis Resti-tvervnt Rem* (Reproduced in Miles, *Eric Gill and*

David Jones at Capel-y-ffin p 139), which recorded the incident when Hague and Jones climbed the hill above the monastery on Christmas Eve 1924 to dislodge a stone which had blocked the stream which was the Gills' water supply; there are also ink drawings of Hague on manuscripts in the National Library of Wales, a comic drawing in Jones's letter to Gill of 21 May 1935 now in the William Andrews Clark Library in Los Angeles. There is also a sketch of Hague as a Victorian Army Officer in Jones's letter to Prudence Pelham of 29 April 1935 now in The Fisher Rare Book Library, University of Toronto.

39 Harman Grisewood, in conversation 31 October 1992.

40 Proof in NLW 1978 Deposit, Box 10.

41 Jones, 'David Jones: Artist and Writer', a tape-recorded commentary on his paintings.

42 Jones, letter to H.S. Ede of 15 April 1945 in Kettle's Yard, Cambridge.

43 See E.C. Hodgkin, unpublished memoir, 'Prudence Pelham' in the possession of the author. Also Dr. Miriam Rothschild, in conversation 26 August 1994.

44 Eric Gill, *Diaries*: 14 March 1929: 'Prudence P. came in eve.' & 15 March - 'DJ arrived at Pigotts' - William Andrews Clark Library, Los Angeles.

45 René Hague, letter to David Jones, 21 May in a private collection.

46 David Jones, letter to René Hague of 29 April 1935, quoted in *Dai Greatcoat* p 70.

47 See Hodgkin, 'Prudence Pelham' pp 1 & 18.

48 Prudence Pelham, undated letter to E.C. Hodgkin of 1940 or 1941. In the possession of the addressee.

49 Prudence Pelham quoted by David Jones in a letter to Stanley Honeyman of 30 August 1973. In a private collection.

50 Prudence Pelham, letter to David Jones of 7 January 1936, concerning people to do his mending. In the posession of E.C. Hodgkin.

51 Margaret Grisewood, in conversation June, 1993.

52 Harman Grisewood, in conversation 31 October 1992.

53 Prudence Pelham, undated letter to E.C. Hodgkin in the possession of the addressee.

54 Hodgkin, 'Prudence Pelham' p 13.

55 Prudence Pelham, quoted in *Ibid.* p 14.

56 Prudence Pelham, letter to David Jones of 13 July 1938. In the possession of E.C. Hodgkin.

57 There is a letter of 29 December 1936, from Pelham thanking Jones for the gift which 'does not strangle me'. In the possession of E.C. Hodgkin.

58 Prudence Pelham, letter to David Jones of March, 1937. In the possession of E.C. Hodgkin.

59 Jones, letter to René Hague of Shrove Tuesday, 1935 in the Fisher Rare Book Library, University of Toronto.

60 Jones, letter to the Edes of 11 April 1939 in Kettle's Yard, Cambridge, quoted in *Dai Greatcoat* p 91.

61 Jones remarked that the oil technique used

here was similar to that of Christopher Wood, quoted in Renée Foree, *Art Gallery of New South Wales Catalogue of British Paintings*, 1987.

LANDSCAPES IN A LIFE

1 H.S. Ede, *A Way of Life* (Cambridge: Cambridge University Press, 1984).

2 Harrison, p 169.

3 Neve, *Unquiet Landscape* pp 94-5.

4 Kathleen Raine, in conversation 6 August 1993.

5 Denis Tegetmeier, letter to David Jones of 4 November 1930, in NLW 1985 Purchase, Group C.

6 Jones, letter to Helen Ede cf 13 August 1928, in Kettle's Yard, Cambridge. The word 'idolator' had been used by Jones's father at the time of Jones's conversion to Roman Catholicism.

7 There was, of course, some rewriting and additions were made after this in the five year gap before publication but the text had been substantially fixed by this date. The Preface was written in Sidmouth in 1935.

8 'I did sell my other picture at the 7&5 and two at *Tooth's*' - Jones, letter to Nicolete Gray of 10 March 1932 in the Tate Gallery Archive.

9 Jones, letter to Nicolete Gray of 9 June 1932 in the Tate Gallery Archive. The book is, of course, *In Parenthesis*.

10 Jones, letter to Nicolete Gray of 10 June 1932 in the Tate Gallery Archive.

11 Jones, letter to Nicolete Gray of 11 July 1932 in the Tate Gallery Archive.

12 Jones, letter to Petra Tegetmeier of 8 February 1933, in NLW 1985 Purchase, Group C.

13 See Fiona MacCarthy, *Eric Gill* (London: Faber and Faber, 1989) pp 225 & 265-6.

14 See *Dai Greatcoat* pp 46 & 49.

15 Jones, letter of 28 July, 1931, quoted in *Dai Greatcoat* p 50.

16 *Dai Greatcoat* p 55.

17 Even so intelligent a critic as Malcolm Yorke dismisses Jones's romanticism as 'fey' in *The Spirit of Place* p 24.

18 Jones, letter to H.S. Ede of 25 June 1936, in Kettle's Yard, Cambridge.

19 Jones, letter to H.S. Ede of 12 July 1938, in Kettle's Yard, Cambridge.

20 See Jones, letter to H.S. Ede of 22 June 1934, in Kettle's Yard, Cambridge.

21 See Blissett, p 67.

22 Harman Grisewood, in conversation 31 October 1992.

23 Tom Burns, *The Use of Memory* p 165.

24 Jones, letter of 3 May 1934 to Victoria Ingrams in the possession of the addressee.

25 Thomas Hodgkin, letter to his mother of 30 May, 1934 in *Thomas Hodgkin - Letters From Palestine 1932-6* (London: Quartet Books, 1986) p 60.

26 *Ibid.* Letters of 30 May, 25 June and 1 July, 1934 pp 60, 67 and 70.

27 Jones, letter of Corpus Christi, 1934 to Victoria Ingrams. In the possession of the addressee.

28 Thomas Hodgkin, letter to his mother of 14 June 1934, in *Thomas Hodgkin - Letters From Palestine* p 64.

29 *Ibid*. Letter of 30 May 1934, p 60.

30 *Ibid*. Letter of 3 June 1934, pp 62-3.

31 Jones, letter of 3 May 1934 to Victoria Ingrams. In the possession of the addressee.

32 Jones, letter of April 1971, to Saunders Lewis, quoted in *Dai Greatcoat* p 57.

33 Jones, letter to Dorothea de Halpert from Bodell's Hotel '(Facing the Sea)', Rue Kitchener, Port Said 10 July 1934, in the possession of Beatrix Dufort.

34 See Hugh Kenner, *The Pound Era* (London: Faber and Faber, 1975; pbk. 1972) p 30.

35 See *The Anathemata* p 60 and for a discussion of the passage see Miles, *Backgrounds* pp 113-14.

36 Harman Grisewood, in conversation 31 October 1992.

37 Jones, letter to Dorothea de Halpert of 14 January 1935, in possession of Beatrix Dufort.

38 See Nicolete Gray, Introduction to *Helen Sutherland Collection - a pioneer collection of the 1930s* (London: Arts Council, 1970-1) p 14.

39 Now in the Statens Museum for Art in Copenhagen.

40 Jones, letter to Saunders Lewis of 3 December 1967, NLW.

41 A.C. Ritchie, *British Contemporary Painters*, 1946 (Albright Art Gallery, Buffalo, N.Y.) p 20.

42 See Gray, Introduction to *Helen Sutherland Collection* pp 13 & 15, and also Kathleen Raine in conversation 6 August 1993.

43 E.C. Hodgkin, 'Helen Sutherland' unpublished memoir in the possession of the author p 19.

44 Kathleen Raine in conversation 6 August 1993.

45 Nicolete Gray, *Helen Sutherland Collection* p 22.

46 Kathleen Raine in conversation 6 August 1993.

47 *Ibid*.

48 E.C. Hodgkin, 'A Note about David Jones', in *London Magazine* (London: August - September 1994) p 64.

49 See Gray, *Helen Sutherland Collection* p 18 and also Kathleen Raine in conversation 6 August 1993.

50 Hodgkin, 'A Note about David Jones' p 68.

51 Hodgkin, 'Helen Sutherland' p 13.

52 Jones, letter to Harman Grisewood of 5 August 1931 in Georgetown University Library.

53 Jones, letter to Beatrix Dufort of 23 August 1946 in the possession of the addressee.

54 Jones, letter to René Hague of 7 May 1966 in NLW.

55 Hodgkin, 'Helen Sutherland' pp 40-1.

56 See Jones, letter to Janet Stone of 15 March 1965 in the Bodleian Library, Oxford.

57 Hodgkin, 'Helen Sutherland' p 8.

58 In *In Parenthesis*, Jones wrote of a night march through the trenches: 'the close dark; the stumbling dark of the blind, that Breughel knew about - ditch circumscribed; this all depriving darkness split now by crazy flashing' - p 31.

59 Jones, letter to Helen Sutherland of 7 October 1929, in the Tate Gallery Archive.

60 Jones, letter to Janet Stone of 15 March 1965, in the Bodleian Library, Oxford.

61 Jones, letter to A.J. Hyne of 19 June 1974, in the possession of the recipient.

62 See Miles, *Backgrounds* pp 83-4.

63 See *Dai Greatcoat* p 39.

64 Sir Thomas Malory, *The Works of Sir Thomas Malory* ed Vinaver (London: Oxford University Press, 1954) p 203.

65 *Ibid*. p 201.

66 *Ibid*. p 203.

67 Hills, *David Jones* p 103.

68 Jones, 'David Jones: Artist and Writer' a tape-recorded commentary on his paintings.

69 Nicolete Gray, *The Paintings of David Jones*, (Hatfield & London: John Taylor, Lund Humphries Tate Gallery Publications, 1989) p 39.

70 Sidney Hunt, Editorial to *Ray II - Art Miscellany* (London, 1927).

71 Minute Book, voting papers and letter in the Tate Gallery Archive.

72 Jones, letter to H.S. Ede of 3 April 1936, in Kettle's Yard, Cambridge, quoted in *Dai Greatcoat* p 82.

73 Jones letter to H.S. Ede of 22 August 1935, in Kettle's Yard, Cambridge.

74 H.S. Ede, letter to Jones of 13 February 1938, in NLW 1985 Purchase, Group C.

75 Jones, letter to H.S. Ede of 8 February 1936 in Kettle's Yard, Cambridge.

76 Jones, letter to H.S. Ede of 25 November 1936 in Kettle's Yard, Cambridge.

77 *The Studio* Vol CIII No 467, February 1932, Editorial, 'What is wrong with Modern Art?', 64.

78 John Betjeman, 'The Death of Modernism' in *The Architectural Review*. December 1931 172-4, quoted by Mellor in 'British Art in the 1930s: Some Economic, Political and Cultural Structures' in *Class, Culture & Social Change* p 203.

79 See Harrison, pp 240 & 250.

80 Barbara Hepworth, *A Pictorial Autobiography* (Bradford on Avon: Moonraker Press, 1970) quoted in Cross, *Painting the Warmth of the Sun* p 48.

81 Ben Nicholson in *Unit One* (to accompany a touring exhibition) ed. Herbert Read, (Cassell: 1934) - quoted Cross, *Painting the Warmth of the Sun* p 47.

82 Harrison, p 264.

83 Jones, letter to Janet Stone of 4 April 1963 in the Bodleian Library, Oxford.

84 Jones, letter to Stanley Honeyman of 30 August 1973.

85 Jones, letter to H.S. Ede of 3 April 1936, in Kettle's Yard, Cambridge.

86 Jones, letter to Dorothea de Halpert of 14 January 1935, in the possession of Beatrix Dufort.

87 *Ibid*.

88 Jones, letter to Nicolete Gray of 10-11 January 1935, in the Tate Gallery Archive.

89 *Ibid*.

90 Harman Grisewood, in a talk at the David Jones Conference, Pembroke College, 30 June 1978, published as 'Remembering David Jones' in *Journal of Modern Literature XIV*: 4 Spring, 1988, p 571.

91 Jones, letter to H.S. Ede of 7 March 1935 - quoted in *Dai Greatcoat* p 65.

92 Jones, letter to Nicolete Gray 24 June 1936, in the Tate Gallery Archive.

93 Jones, letter to Dorothea de Halpert of 22 July 1937, in the possession of Beatrix Dufort.

94 Prudence Pelham, letters to David Jones of 19 October and 22 November 1935, and 2 February 1936, in the possession of E.C. Hodgkin.

95 Prudence Pelham, letter to David Jones of 2 February 1935, in the possession of E.C. Hodgkin.

96 Jones, letter to René Hague of January 1936, in the Fisher Rare Book Library, University of Toronto.

97 Jones, letters to René Hague of Easter and 2 July 1935, in the Fisher Rare Book Library, University of Toronto.

98 Jones, letter to Harman Grisewood of 10 July 193, in Georgetown University Library.

99 *Ibid*. and this passage is quoted in *Dai Greatcoat* p 75.

100 Jones, letter to René Hague of Shrove Tuesday, 1935 in the Fisher Rare Book Library, University of Toronto.

101 Jones, letter to Nicolete Gray of 24 June 1936, in the Tate Gallery Archive.

102 Jones, 'The Pursuit of Peace', unpublished essay, copy in Georgetown University Library.

103 Jones, letter to Harman Grisewood of 20 July 1935, in Georgetown University Library.

104 Harman Grisewood, *One Thing at a Time* (London: Hutchinson, 1968) p 118.

105 Jones, letter to Harman Grisewood of 24 April 1939, quoted in *Dai Greatcoat* pp 92-3.

106 Grisewood, *One Thing at A Time* pp 127 and 137.

107 Jones, letter to H.S. Ede, 11 April 1939, quoted in *Dai Greatcoat* p 90.

108 Grisewood, *One Thing at a Time* pp 101-05.

109 Frank Kermode, *The Sense of an Ending* (New York, Oxford University Press 1966-67) p 110.

110 Harman Grisewood, *One Thing At a Time* p 83.

111 Jones, letter to H.S. Ede, 11 April, 1939, quoted in *Dai Greatcoat* p 90.

112 Jones, letter to Dorothea de Halpert of 9 January 1936, in possession of Beatrix Dufort and letter to H.S. Ede of 7 March 1935, quoted in *Dai Greatcoat* p 65.

113 Jones, letter to H.S. Ede of 25 November 1936, in Kettle's Yard, Cambridge.

114 Jones, letter to H.S. Ede of 22 August 1935. Kettle's Yard, Cambridge.

115 See Jones, letter to Nicolete Gray of 24 June 1936, in the Tate Gallery Archive.

116 Jones, letter to Harman Grisewod of 14 February1938, from the Fort Hotel, quoted in

Dai Greatcoat, p 84.

117 Jones, letter to Dorothea de Halpert of 22 July 1937, in possession of Beatrix Dufort.

118 See Jones, letter to Eric Gill of 8 July 1935: 'What a marvellous place Kit Dawson has - I have enjoyed being there - It's certainly Capelish ... ', letter in the William Andrews Clark Library, Los Angeles.

119 Jones, letter to Nicolete Gray of 24 June 1936, in the Tate Gallery Archive.

120 See Jones, autobiographical notes in NLW 1978 Dep.Box II/49.

LAST LANDSCAPES AND STILL LIFES

1 Harman Grisewood, talk at the David Jones Conference on 30 June 1978 - published in *Journal of Modern Literature XIV*: 4 Spring 1988, 565-576.

2 Jones, letter to Petra Tegetmeier of 27 January 1940, in NLW 1985 Purchase, Group C.

3 Jones, letter to Helen Sutherland of 6 September 1940, in the Tate Gallery Archive.

4 Grisewood, - talk at the David Jones Conference on 30 June 1978 - published in *Journal of Modern Literature XIV*: 4 Spring, 1988, 572.

5 See Bernard Wall, Headlong Into Change (London: Harvill Press, 1969) p 120.

6 Jones, letter to H.S. Ede of 29-30 August 1942, in Kettle's Yard, Cambridge.

7 See 'Prehistory from the Air' in Axis (London: Winter, 1937).

8 Jones, letter to Helen Sutherland of 6 September 1940, in the Tate Gallery Archive.

9 Rex Nan Kivell, letter to David Jones of 4 November 1940, in NLW 1985 Deposit Group C Box 15.

10 *The Times*, 10 January 1940.

11 *Nairobi Standard*, 23 February 1940.

12 Jones, letter to Dorothea de Halpert of 7 February 1940, in the possession of Beatrix Dufort.

13 Jones, letter to Tom Burns of 16 May 1942, quoted in *Dai Greatcoat* p 118.

14 Jones, draft letter to Kenneth Clark of 9 October 1966, in NLW 1985 Purchase, Group B II 5.

15 Rex Nan Kivell, letter to David Jones of 2 February 1945, in NLW 1985 Purchase, Group C.

16 Michael Ayrton, in The Spectator 16 April 1945.

17 Jones, letter to Harman Grisewood of 4 July 1945, quoted in *Dai Greatcoat* p 130 and Alfred Longden, Director of Fine Arts, The British Council, letter to David Jones of 8 June 1945, 'the Council's cultural propaganda' in NLW 1985 Purchase, Group C.

18 Alfred Longden, Director of Fine Arts, The British Council, letter to David Jones of 8 June 1945, in NLW 1985 Purchase, Group C.

19 Robin Ironside's Introduction is dated 1943.

20 Jones, letter to H.S. Ede 29-30 August 1942, in Kettle's Yard, Cambridge.

21 Jones, letter to H.S. Ede 13 March 1944, in Kettle's Yard, Cambridge.

22 The drawing room was 46 x 17 ft. with a sitting room on the first floor. See estate agent's brochure for the sale of the property when Helen Sutherland left it.

23 Jones, letter to Beatrix Dufort of 23 August 1946, in the possession of the addressee.

24 See Jones, *The Sleeping Lord* p 21.

25 Jones, *The Sleeping Lord* pp 71-2, 96.

26 Jones, letter to Louis Bussell of 20 August 20 1946, in the Burns Library, Boston College, Mass.

27 Jones, letter to Helen Sutherland of All Saints Day 1946, in the Tate Gallery Archive.

28 Paul Nash, letter to Gordon Bottomley of 1 August 1912, in *Poet and Painter: Being the Correspondence between Gordon Bottomley and Paul Nash 1910-1946* eds. Abbott and Bertram (London: Oxford University Press, 1955) p 42.

29 See Nanette Aldred, 'A Canterbury Tale' in *A Paradise Lost* ed. Mellor (London: Lund Humphries/Barbican, 1987) p 118.

30 Jones, letter to Harman Grisewood of 24 August 1947, quoted in *Dai Greatcoat* p 134.

31 James Joyce to Padraic Colum quoted in Richard Ellman, *James Joyce* (London: Oxford University Press, 1976) p 565.

32 Jones's annotation to Joseph Campbell and Henry Morton Robinson, *A Skeleton Key to Finnegans Wake* (London: Faber and Faber, 1947) p 15 n. 1, copy in NLW.

33 See Miles, *Backgrounds* pp 160-3.

34 James Joyce, *Finnegans Wake* (New York: The Viking Press, 1959) pp 213-15.

35 See Roland McHugh, *Annotations to Finnegans Wake* (London: Routledge and Kegan Paul, 1980) pp 213-15.

36 Spengler, *The Decline of the West* Vol. I p 31.

37 *Ibid*. Vol. I p 108.

38 See *In Parenthesis*, p 176; *The Anathemata* pp 50, 231; *The Roman Quarry* pp 7, 42, 172.

39 Respectively from *The Dying Gaul*, p 157, *The Sleeping Lord* p 64, and *The Dying Gaul*, p 178.

40 Spengler, Vol. I p 396. Jones marked this passage in his copy. Copy in NLW.

41 *Ibid*. Vol. I p 184.

42 Jones, *The Anathemata* pp 49 & 92-3.

43 'Par la vertu vivifiante du Précieux Sang, l'arbre mort auquel le Christ avait été attaché redevient vivant. Une antienne très populaire commençait par: O crux, viride lignum. Cette idée mystique, popularisée par saint Bonaventure dans son Lignum Vitae, a inspiré un certain nombre d'oeuvres d'art.' - Réau, *Iconographie de L'Art Chrétien* p 483.

44 Jones, letter to the mother of H.S. Ede of 28 August 1949, quoted in *Dai Greatcoat* pp 149-50. The *vexilla* was originally 'a small, square piece of cloth attached to a cross-bar carried on a pole' - Grahame Webster, *The Roman Imperial Army* (London: A.C. Black, 1969) p 139. Jones noted that the *vexillae* which would have inspired Fortunatus, the author of the hymn, 'were standards, imitative of a past imperium, but in fact now carried before petty Merovingian dynasts at fratricidal wars of loot. Such was the sordid violence from

which the poet gave the liturgy this enduring image of banners. It is the sort of thing that poets are for; to redeem is part of their job,' Jones in *The Tablet* 26 April 1958 reprinted in *Epoch and Artist* pp 260-1 as 'The Eclipse of a Hymn'.

45 J.A.W. Bennet, *Poetry of the Passion* (Oxford: Oxford University Press, 1982).

46 Jones, letter to Mrs. Ede of 28 August 1949, quoted in *Dai Greatcoat* p 150.

47 Jones, notes drafted for his doctors at Bowden House, 1947, in Georgetown University Library.

48 Jones, letter to Mrs. Ede of 28 August 1949, quoted in *Dai Greatcoat* p 151.

49 Jones, notes drafted for his doctors at Bowden House, 1947, in Georgetown University Library.

50 See Jones, letter to Beatrix Dufort of 26 April 1948, in the possession of the addressee.

51 See letter to Jones from *The Artists' Benevolent Fund*, of 10 October 1947, in NLW: 'to tide you over a difficult period ... when you leave the Home in which you are living at present'.

52 For this and some general observations about Northwick Park Lodge, Geoffrey Treasure the Harrow master and historian who lodged there for a while, in conversation 20 June 1994, and with Maurice and Sarah Balme, October 1994.

53 Jones, letter to Kenneth Clark of 20 May 1948, in the Tate Gallery Archive.

54 Jones, quoted in Hodgkin, 'A Note about David Jones', 70.

55 The review in *The Spectator*, 23 January 1948, spoke of 'a lovely David Jones'.

56 See O.E.D. and *Epoch and Artist* p 150.

57 See David Jones, letter to Dr. Charles Burns of 29 June 1948. In the possession of Paul Burns.

58 M.H. Middleton, The Spectator 4 June 1948, 674.

59 Jones, letter to Helen Sutherland 12 June 1948 in the Tate Gallery Archive. See also, Jones letter to Dr. Charles Burns 29 June 1948: 'Yes, I was sad to read that thing of Wyndham Lewis - that was bad - I always had a great respect for his mind - but he seems to have no longer his old vigour or understanding. I don't say this because of his superficial remark on my own work but from other bits of evidence.', in the possession of Paul Burns.

60 Jones, letter to Dr. Charles Burns of 29 June 1948, in the possession of Paul Burns.

61 See Cecil Collins, letter to David Jones in the Tate Gallery Archive.

62 Jones, letter to Helen Sutherland of 15 July 1948 in the Tate Gallery Archive.

63 *Idem*.

64 'so I'm bound up with adhesive bandage - the irritation of which is beastly ... I've been doing some drawing from the window - trees,' David Jones, letter to Helen Sutherland of 4 February 1948, in the Tate Gallery Archive.

65 Jones, letter to Helen Sutherland of 14 August 1950, in the Tate Gallery Archive.

66 Jones, letter to Helen Sutherland of May Day 1951.

67 Jones, letter to Helen Sutherland of Friday 24 August 1951, in the Tate Gallery Archive.

68 Jones, draft of letter to Rex Nan Kivell of 7 May 1962, in NLW, 1985 Purchase, Group C Box 15.

69 Jones, undated draft of a letter to Rex Nan Kivell in NLW 1985 Purchase, Group B II/8.

70 'I lost various portfolios containing some of my works of all sorts & some in the same portfolios not mine at all. These got into the hands of various dealers and have been sold. I believe I told you that the circumstances of their disappearance were such that it was impossible for me to do anything about it. It's an awful nuisance and embarrassment, to say the least, but it's no use groaning over spilt milk. I expect I ought to have taken some sort of legal, or anyway, some sort of action at the time, but I didn't as it was all too complicated.', Jones, letter to Dorothea de Halpert of 3 August 1962, in the possession of Beatrix Dufort. Jones states that the incident took place about 8 years before that letter was written, i.e. c. 1954.

71 Stanley Honeyman, letter to the Victoria and Albert Museum of 14 May 1984, in the Tate Gallery Archive.

72 Jones, letter to Dorothea de Halpert of 3 August 1962, in the possession of Beatrix Dufort.

73 Philip Hagreen, letter to René Hague of 27 February 1978. Photocopy in NLW.

74 Spengler, Vol I p 199.

75 Jones, 'David Jones: Artist and Writer', tape-recorded commentary on his paintings.

76 Jones, letter to Bernard Wall of 2 July 1967. In this letter Jones also explains how a silversmith had told him that modification to the Chalice would have to be made in order to reflect the change in the rubric which no longer required the Celebrant to keep his thumb and forefinger closed until the ablutions.

77 Jones, letter to Juliet & Richard Shirley Smith of 11 February 1961, in the possession of the addressees.

78 Jones, letter to Janet Stone of 6-7 September 1960 in the Bodleian Library, Oxford.

79 Gerard Manley Hopkins, The Wreck of the Deutschland in The Poems of Gerard Manley Hopkins eds. Gardner and MacKenzie (London: Oxford University Press, 1970) p 58.

80 Jones marked this passage with a double line in the margin of his copy of Thomas Atkinson, A Glossary of English Architecture (London; 7th edit., 1948).

81 Jones, letter to René Hague of 9 April 1960, quoted in Dai Greatcoat p 181.

THE RICOCHET OF WAR

1 See Eksteins, Rites of Spring pp 18, 122, 168.

2 Walter Sickert, 'Post-Impressionists' in Fortnightly Review, January 1911, quoted in Eksteins, Rites of Spring p 170.

3 Roger Fry, quoted in Samuel Hynes, The Edwardian Turn of Mind (Princeton: Princeton University Press) 1968 p 334.

4 Even before Roger Fry's First Post-Impressionist Exhibition there had been numerous opportunities to see the work of the Post-Impressionists in London.

5 See Spalding, p 51.

6 P.G. Konody, Modern War - Paintings by C.R.W. Nevinson (London: Grant Richards, 1917) p 8.

7 Spalding, p 49.

8 Ibid. pp 55-6.

9 Filippo Marinetti, 'Founding Manifesto' of Futurism (1909) quoted in C. Tisdall and A. Bozzolla, Futurism (London: Thames and Hudson, 1977) p 177. As Blast noted, 'The War has exhausted interest for the moment in booming and banging ... Marinetti ... will have to abandon war-noise more or less definitely.' War Number ed. Wyndham Lewis (London: John Lane, July 1915).

10 Konody, p 19.

11 Richard Cork, 'The Vorticist Circle, Bomberg and the First World War' in British Art in the Twentieth Century p 140.

12 Letter of 16 November 1917, to his wife in Outline: An Autobiography and Other Writings (London, 1949) pp 210-11 quoted in Eksteins, Rites of Spring, p 204.

13 Evelyn Waugh stated that it was 'a painter's realism which lifts' Jones's work 'above any of Mr. Eliot's followers and, in many places, above Mr. Eliot himself' - review of In Parenthesis in Night and Day (London: 1 July 1937) 32.

14 Jones, draft of a letter to Bernard Bergonzi in NLW 1978 Dep Box II/6. quoted more fully in Miles, Backgrounds p 85.

15 T.S. Eliot, in Selected Prose of T.S. Eliot p 38.

16 Jones, Draft for Preface for the BBC recording of In Parenthesis, Tate Gallery Archive.

17 Stanley Honeyman and Peter Orr, recorded conversation in NLW 1985 Purchase, Group B I/8.

18 Jones, draft of letter of 27 April 1962, in NLW, 1978 Deposit Box 11/4.

19 Jones, letter to H.S. Ede of 8 February 1936 in Kettle's Yard, Cambridge.

20 Jones, draft of a letter to 'Miss Jones', 20 August 1968, in NLW, 1978 Dep. Box 11/4.

21 Jones, letter to H.S. Ede of 8 February 1936 in Kettle's Yard, Cambridge.

22 Jones, In Parenthesis p 180.

23 Jones, in Cleverdon, Word and Image p 50. Also quoted by Paul Hills in David Jones p 104.

24 Idem.

25 In the National Museum of Wales.

26 Robert Cumming Artists at War, 1914-18, Catalogue of exhibition at Kettle's Yard, Cambridge, October-November 1974 p 11.

27 When A.S. Hartrick noted that his teacher, Legros, cut 'at the smallest opportunity ... the size of the genitals' on a male nude because Michaelangelo always made them small, Jones noted, at the bottom of his copy of Hartrick's A Painter's Pilgrimage p 7: 'As a matter of fact that is very good advice though I did not know Legros had observed it. But certainly the proportion in a male figure is enhanced by so doing. - D.J.'.

28 See Jones, draft of a letter to 'Miss Jones' of 20 August 1968. NLW, 1978 Dep. Box 11/4 where he speaks of his sources used in writing. The Orpen was in the Imperial War Museum at that date and the museum was considered one of the best places in London to look at modern art.

29 Jones, In Parenthesis p 84.

HIATUS AND THE WHOLE

1 See Blissett, pp 101-02 and also David Jones, letter to Harman Grisewood of 9 October 1971, in Georgetown University Library and quoted by Thomas Dilworth in The Shape of Meaning in the Poetry of David Jones p 78.

2 Jones, letter to Arthur Giardelli of 9-11 August 1973.

3 Howard Grimmitt, who after seeing the Jones Tate Retrospective in 1955, wrote to the painter to ask him if indeed he was the David Jones who sat next to him at school. Letter in NLW 1985 Purchase, Group C.

4 Jones, letter to Lady Pamela Donner of 26 April 1962. Photocopy in the Tate Gallery Archive.

5 A Millais Retrospective at the Grosvenor Gallery in 1886, had re-kindled interest in Pre-Raphaelitism and medievalism - See Spalding, British Art Since 1900, p13.

6 In a review in The New Statesman 18 May 1979, 730.

7 R.L. Charles, 'Some Recently Acquired Works by David Jones', p 13.

8 For example of the uneven literary style: 'huge boulders, cruelly rough, encumbered all their paths, and it was hard going'. A copy of The Quest is in the possession of the Trustees of Jones's Estate.

9 See Hilton, pp 50-51.

10 Laurence Binyon, 'The Art of Botticelli, An Essay in Pictorial Criticism'.

11 Christian, Introduction to The Last Romantics p 20.

12 In the Hermitage, St. Petersburg.

13 There is an image of this among some miscellaneous papers of David Jones in the Harman Grisewood Papers in Georgetown University Library.

14 Jones, draft of a letter to The Times in NLW 1978 Dep. II/29 quoted in 'The Early Years' (p 20).

15 See Hilton, pp 177-8.

16 Jon Silkin, Out of Battle (Oxford: Oxford University Press, 1972; pbk., 1978) p 336.

17 Jones, 'The Myth of Arthur' (1940-1) in Epoch and Artist p 245.

18 See Jones, 'Notes on the 1930s' in The Dying Gaul p 41.

19 See Steve Ellis, The English Eliot p 80.

20 Harrison, p 296.

21 Mellor, in Class, Culture & Social Change - A New View of the 1930s p 185.

22 *Ibid*. pp 37-8. Herbert Read quotes Jones on abstract art (p 36) and reproduces *The Gentle Bird* of 1950 in *Contemporary British Art* (Harmondsworth: Penguin, 1951).

23 René Laplat in a broadcast of 8 July 1948 on the BBC French Service.

24 Jones, letter to H.S. Ede of 27 June 1938 in Kettle's Yard, Cambridge.

25 Jones, letter to H.S. Ede of 7 July 1938 in Kettle's Yard, Cambridge.

26 John Rothenstein, letter to David Jones of 23 June, 1941 in NLW.

27 Malory, Book VII ch. 22 p 247.

28 Jones, letter to Arthur Giardelli of 11 April, 1965, in the possession of the addressee.

29 Jones, in a letter to *Poetry Wales* Vol. 8, No 3 Winter, 1972, 7.

30 Patrick Reyntiens, in *The Tablet* 25 November1989, 1364.

31 Jones, letter to Saunders Lewis of 21 June1961, in NLW.

32 See Jones, letter to Helen Sutherland of 26 November 1948 in Tate Gallery Archive: 'But I like Henry's drawings better than his carvings' and see Blissett, p 26.

33 Jones, letter to Harman Grisewood of 12 March 1960, quoted in *Dai Greatcoat* p 179.

34 See Jones, letter to Arthur Giardelli of 9-11 August 1973.

35 Jones, letter to Harman Grisewood of 12 March 1960, quoted in *Dai Greatcoat* p 179.

36 Jones, letter to René Hague of 9 April 1960, quoted in *Dai Greatcoat* p 181.

37 Jones, letter to Janet Stone of 6-7 September 1960, in the Bodleian Library, Oxford.

38 Jones, letter to Arthur Giardelli of 9-11 August 1973.

39 Jones, 'David Jones: Artist and Writer', a tape-recorded commentary on his paintings.

40 Pablo Picasso, letter first published in the Russian review, *Ogoniok* in 1926 and reprinted in *Studio Magazine* Vol 103, 1932.

41 Jones quoting Nennius in the Preface to *The Anathemata* p 9.

42 Jones, letter to Janet Stone of 28 January 1960, in the Bodleian Library, Oxford.

43 René Hague, letter to Mike Richey of 20 February 1978, in the possession of the addressee.

44 Sarah Balme, in conversation, 17 October 1994.

45 Jones, letter to H.S. Ede of 3 July 1943, quoted in *Dai Greatcoat* p 123.

46 Eugène Delacroix, quoted in William Vaughan, *Romantic Art* (London: Thames and Hudson, 1978) p 232.

47 Underlined in Jones's copy of Raymond Lister, *Edward Calvert* (London: Bell, 1962) p 49. Copy in the NLW.

48 Spengler, Vol. I p 292.

49 Jones, unidentified fragment in NLW 1978, Dep. V/1. quoted by Anne Price-Owen.

50 Jones, letter to Janet Stone of 13-14 October 1959, in the Bodleian Library, Oxford.

51 Jacques Maritain, *The Philosophy of Art* trans. Fr. John O'Connor (Ditchling: St. Dominic's Press, 1923) p 95.

52 Jones, letter to Cecil Collins of 15 July 1948, in the Tate Gallery Archive.

53 Ezra Pound, radio broadcast from 'Round the Microphone' (Broadcast 5 May 1943) quoted in 'Fragments of an Atmosphere' by Mary de Rachewiltz in *Agenda* (London: 1979-80) Vol. 17-18, 167.

54 W.F. Jackson Knight, *Cumaean Gates* (Oxford: Basil Blackwell, 1936) p 160.

55 Jones in *Word and Image IV* No. 119.

56 Jones in 'The Arthurian Legend' in *Epoch and Artist* p 209.

57 Osip Mandelstam, *The Noise of Time* trans. Brown (London: Quartet, 1988) p 110.

58 Jones, letter to Nicolas Jacobs of 21 April 1966 in the possession of the addressee.

59 Christopher Dawson, *The Modern Dilemma*, No. 8 of *Essays in Order* (London: Sheed & Ward, 1932) p 25.

60 Jones, *Epoch and Artist* p 242.

61 Spengler, Vol. I pp 32-3.

62 Jones, *The Anathemata* p 50.

63 Jones, letter to Blissett of 11-12 June, 1967 quoted in Blissett p 47.

64 See Oskar Seyffert, *A Dictionary of Classical Antiquities* rev. & ed. Nettleship & Sandys (London: William Glaisher, 3rd ed. 1894) p 100.

65 Jones quoted in René Hague, A Commentary upon The Anathemata of David Jones (Wellingborough: Skelton, 1978) p 38.

66 Jones, Epoch and Artist p 163 n.1.

67 de la Taille, *The Mystery of Faith - An Outline* pp10-11.

68 See Jones's letter to H.S. Ede of 31 August 1949, in Kettle's Yard, Cambridge.

69 Ovid, *Metamorphosis* Bk. X trans. Innes (Harmondsworth: Penguin, 1955) pp 231-2.

70 Jones, letter to Mary Gill of 1 January 1943, in the possession of Petra Tegetmeier.

71 For more about the function of the scapegoat see, Mircea Eliade, *The Myth of Eternal Return* trans. Trask (London: Routledge and Kegan Paul, 1949) p 53.

72 See Hilton, *The Pre-Raphaelites* p 110.

73 Jones, letter to Nicolete Gray of 15 March 1964 in the Tate Gallery Archive.

74 See *The Last Romantics* p 168. See also his *The Waterway to Stettin* reproduced in The Pageant of 1896, 125.

75 Kenneth Clark in *Agenda* - David Jones Special Issue 1967, 99.

76 Arthur Giardelli, 'The Artist David Jones' in *Eight Essays* ed. Roland Mathias (Llandysul, 1976) pp 96-7.

77 See *The Anathemata* p 152; *In Parenthesis* p 155; & Guest, *The Mabinogion* p 110.

78 Kenneth Clark in *Agenda* - David Jones Special Issue 1967, 99.

79 Jones, draft of a letter to in NLW 1985 Purchase, Group B.

80 Bell, *Art* p 185.

81 *Ibid*. p 222.

82 Jones, letter to Helen Sutherland of 25 November 1941, in the Tate Gallery Archive.

83 Jones, letter to René Hague of 9 April 1960, quoted in *Dai Greatcoat* p 182.

INTERNAL PRESSURES

1 Jones, letter to Helen Sutherland of 13 December 1952, in the Tate Gallery Archive.

2 Jones, letter to Eric Gill of 21 May 1935 in the William Andrews Clark Library, Los Angeles.

3 Jones, letter to Charles Burns of September 1951, in the possession of Paul Burns.

4 Jones, letter to René Hague of 29 February 1960, in the Fisher Rare Book Library, University of Toronto.

5 Jones, letter to Kenneth Clark of 16 November 1960, in the Tate Gallery Archive.

6 Helen Sutherland, letter to David Jones of 15 November 1954, in NLW.

7 Jones, in conversation with Nesta Roberts, *The Guardian* 17 February 1964.

8 Jones, draft of notes in Georgetown University Library.

9 Jones, undated and unsent note to René Hague, dated by Hague as from the period of his first breakdown. In the Fisher Rare Book Library, University of Toronto.

10 Wilhelm Reich *The Mass Psychology of Fascism,* trans. Carfango (Harmondsworth: Pelican, 1975) p 198.

11 *Idem.*

12 *Ibid*. p 90.

13 Jones, notes for his doctors at Bowden House 1947, in Georgetown University Library.

14 Reich p 178.

15 *Ibid*. p 195.

16 *Ibid*. pp 178-9.

17 See Philip Hagreen, letter to 'Tom' of 5 September 1985: 'Eric had told me that David suffered from some abnormality which made his sex-works work too easily ' This also suggests that Jones talked about sex with Gill.

18 Sigmund Freud, *Totem and Taboo* (1913) trans. Strachey, (London: Routledge, 1950; pbk. 1960) pp 154-5.

19 René Hague, letter to Harman Grisewood of 25 January 1980, in the Fisher Rare Book Library, University of Toronto.

20 H.S. Ede, letter to Jones in NLW.

21 Kenneth Clark, *Landscape into Art* (London: John Murray, 1949, new edit. 1976) p 16.

22 Philip Hagreen, notes made after a conversation with René Hague, 14 July 1978. Photocopy in NLW. Petra Tegetmeier said, in conversation, that her father carved the doll.

23 Jones wrote, for his doctors at Bowden House, that their physical relationship stopped 'just short of' 'sexual connection ... Mutual masturbation would be the most accurate description', notes in Georgetown University Library.

24 Jones, letter to René Hague of 1 May 1933, quoted in *Dai Greatcoat* p 54.

25 See Hague in *Dai Greatcoat* p 55.

26 See Hague in *Dai Greatcoat* p 58.

27 Harman Grisewood, letter to Derek Shiel of 12 May 1994, in the possession of the

addressee.

28 Hugh Crichton-Miller, *Psycho-Analysis and its Derivatives* (London: Butterworth, 1933) p 72.

29 Jones, letter to H.S. Ede of 8 February 1936, in Kettle's Yard, Cambridge.

30 Jones, letter to René Hague of 8 May 1937 in the Fisher Rare Book Library, University of Toronto.

31 Jones, letter to René Hague of 3 June 1935 in the Fisher Rare Book Library, University of Toronto.

32 Jones, letter to Tom Burns of 14 September 1940, quoted in *Dai Greatcoat* p 107.

33 Jones, letter to René Hague, St. Luke's Day, 1934 in the Fisher Rare Book Library, University of Toronto.

34 René Hague in *Dai Greatcoat* p 136.

35 E.C. Hodgkin, unpublished memoir of Prudence Pelham pp 20-1.

36 Jones, letter to Harman Grisewood of 14 February 1938, quoted in *Dai Greatcoat* p 85.

37 Perhaps the iron bedposts serve the same end as the prominent bedpost in Rembrandt's *The Bedstead* (1646) and *Joseph & Potiphar's Wife* (1634) Both in the Rijksmuseum, Amsterdam and reproduced in Edward Lucie-Smith, *Sexuality in Western Art* (London: Thames and Hudson, rev. edit. 1991) pp 185 & 195.

38 Hills, 'The Pierced Hermaphrodite' p 428.

39 Jones, letter to Harman Grisewood 23 June 1939, quoted in *Dai Greatcoat* p 93. See also Colin Wilcockson, 'Presentation and self-presentation in *In Parenthesis*' in *Presenting Poetry*. eds. Erskine-Hill and McCabe. Cambridge: Cambridge University Press, 1995.

40 E.C. Hodgkin, 'A Note About David Jones' p 69.

41 Hills, 'The Pierced Hermaphrodite' p 429.

42 Alistair Hamilton, *The Appeal of Fascism - A Study of Intellectuals and Fascism 1919-45* (London: Anthony Blond, 1971) p xviii.

43 Fr. Brocard Sewell, in conversation, summer, 1993.

44 See Janet Stone's response to his reaction to a photograph she'd taken of him: 'the expression on your face couldn't possibly be LESS like Hitler's' in a letter to Jones of 11 June 1963, in the Bodleian Library, Oxford.

45 Jones, 'The Pursuit of Peace' in Georgetown University Library.

46 Stanley Honeyman, letter to Harman Grisewood 25 September 1984, in Georgetown University Library.

47 Reich, *The Mass Psychology of Fascism* p 65.

48 *ibid.* p 94.

49 Jones, letter to Tom Burns of 21 June 1941, quoted in *Dai Greatcoat* p 112.

50 See Jones, letters to Charles Burns of 25 May 1942 and 29 December 1944 in the possession of Paul Burns.

51 Doctor's Certificate, 20 November 1941, in NLW.

52 Kathleen Raine, in conversation 6 August 1993.

53 *idem.*

54 Jones, letter to Dr. Charles Burns of 29 May 1940, in the possession of Paul Burns.

55 Jones, 'David Jones: Artist and Writer' A tape-recorded commentary on his paintings.

56 In a private collection.

57 Jones, draft letter to *The Tablet* in NLW 1978 Dep. 1/1.

58 Jones, letter to Helen Sutherland of 27 August1947, in the Tate Gallery Archive.

59 Jones, notes for his doctors at Bowden House, 1947, in Georgetown University Library.

60 *Ibid.*

61 Jones, letter to Helen Sutherland of 18 July 1947, in the Tate Gallery Archive.

62 Jones, notes for his doctors at Bowden House, 1947, in Georgetown University Library.

63 *Ibid.*

64 *Ibid.*

65 Jones, quoted in 'From David Jones's Locker' Alex Hamilton, *The Guardian* 11 February 1972.

66 Freud, *Totem and Taboo* p 17.

67 *Ibid.* p 124 & for Frazer see *The Golden Bough* p 123.

68 Philip Hagreen, letter to René Hague of 1 April 1978. Photocopy in NLW.

69 See Jones, 'In Illo Tempore' in *The Dying Gaul* p 19.

70 Jones, notes for his doctors at Bowden House, 1947, quoted in *Dai Greatcoat* p 140.

71 Freud, *Totem and Taboo* pp 26-7.

72 *Idem.*

73 Jones, in conversation with Colin Hughes in 1973, quoted in *Dai Greatcoat* p 131.

74 Jane Debenham, in conversation autumn 1994.

75 Harman Grisewood, in conversation 31 October 1992.

76 *Ibid.*

77 Jones, notes for his doctors at Bowden House, 1947, in Georgetown University Library.

78 Jones, quoted in *Dai Greatcoat* pp 136-7.

79 Hugh Crichton-Miller, 'Puberty and Adolescence', a paper given before the Medical Society of Individual Psychology, London on 8 April 1937, in *The Management of Early Infancy, Puberty and Adolescence - The Psychological Approach to the Neurotic Character* (London; C.W. Daniel Company Ltd., December 1937) p 32.

80 Jones, letter to Janet Stone of 13-14 October 1959, in the Bodleian Library, Oxford.

81 Freud, *Totem and Taboo* p 86.

82 Janet Stone, in conversation autumn, 1994.

83 Hugh Crichton-Miller, letter to David Jones of 14 May 1952, in NLW.

84 See Mellor in *Class, Culture and Social Change* pp 196-7.

85 Jones, letter to Tom Burns of 14 September1940, quoted in *Dai Greatcoat* p 109.

86 See Yorke, *The Spirit of Place* p 122.

87 Jones, letter to Harman Grisewood of 7 March 1941, in Georgetown University Library.

88 H.S. Ede, letter to Kenneth Clark of 19 June 1944, in the Tate Gallery Archive.

89 Kenneth Clark, letter to H.S. Ede of 28 June 1944, in the Tate Gallery Archive.

90 Kenneth Clark, letter of 30 September 1946, to Colin Martin, in the Tate Gallery Archive.

91 Jones, letter to Helen Sutherland of 27 August 1947, in NLW 1985 Purchase, Group C.

92 Helen Sutherland, letter to Jones of 10 July 1950, in NLW.

93 See Jones, letter to Helen Sutherland of 14 August 1952, apologizing for not banking a cheque sent a month earlier. In the Tate Gallery Archive.

94 Figures given in his application for a Bollingen Foundation Grant - referees included T.S. Eliot, Stephen Spender, Kathleen Raine, and Sir Kenneth Clark. In NLW.

95 Letter to Jones of 9 May 1958, from Walters & Co. Oxford Ltd. In NLW 1985 Purchase, Group C, 14.

96 Letter to Jones of 22 July 1947 from L G Wilkinson, Tailor. In NLW 1985 Purchase, Group C, 14.

97 See NLW 1985 Purchase, Group C 14.

98 Harman Grisewood, in conversation 31 October 1992.

99 Gray, *The Paintings of David Jones* p 17.

100 Stanley Honeyman in conversation with Peter Orr, in NLW 1985 Purchase, Group B.

101 Winifred Webb, letter to Stanley Honeyman of 3 April 1978, in NLW 1985 Purchase, Group BII/8.

102 Richard Shirley Smith, 'Outline of my Contact with Jones', an unpublished memoir.

103 Harman Grisewood, 'Remembering David Jones', 575.

104 Stanley Honeyman, undated letter to Jones, in NLW 1985 Purchase, Group B.

105 See, for example, 'I have not got an ulcer so it would seem that the indigestion etc. arises from psychological causes...', Jones, letter to H.S. Ede of 7 September 1950, in Kettle's Yard, Cambridge.

106 Jones, letter of 3 August 1962, to Dorothea de Halpert, in the possession of Beatrix Dufort.

107 *Idem.*

108 Jones, letter to Pamela Donner of 28 April 1962, in the Tate Gallery Archive.

109 Jones, letter to Janet Stone of 4 April 1963, in the Bodleian Library, Oxford.

110 Jones, letter of July 1967 to Bernard Wall.

111 See 'Encephalopathy with Wernicke-Like Aphasia Secondary to Phenelzine Treatment' in *Journal of Clinical Psychiatry* (49, No. 4, 169, 1988). And see 'Parkinsonian Side Effects Induced by a Monoamine Oxidase Inhibitor' in *American Journal of Psychiatry* (141, No. 1, 118-19, 1984) and 'Myoclonus and Episodic Delirium Associated with Phenelzine: A Case

Report' in *Journal of Clinical Psychiatry* (48, No. 8, 340-1, 1987).

112 Harman Grisewood, 'A Note on David Jones's Drugs', in NLW 1985 Purchase, Group B v/15/19.

113 *Idem.*

114 Jones, letter to Janet Stone of 7 March 1965, in the Bodleian Library, Oxford.

115 'Did I tell you about my eight days of almost continuous hiccups? ... They thought it was just possibly (but unlikely) due, as a sort of side effect, to one of the drugs I was having to take.' - Jones, letter to Janet Stone of 1 February 1963, in the Bodleian Library, Oxford.

116 Jones, letter to Helen Sutherland on the Feast of St. Thomas of Canterbury 1954, in the Tate Gallery Archive.

117 Jones in news cutting in the Tate Gallery Archive.

118 Jones, letter of 17 April 1964, to Charles Burns, in the possession of Paul Burns.

119 Marked in Jones's catalogue of the exhibition in NLW and Sarah Balme, in conversation 17 October 1994.

120 Peter Orr, in conversation, summer 1993.

121 Geoffrey Treasure, in conversation 20 June 1994.

122 Nest Cleverdon, in conversation 30 March 1989.

123 Edmund Gray, in conversation 1994.

124 Jones, letter of 2 December 1961, to Janet Stone, in the Bodleian Library, Oxford.

125 Valerie Wynne-Williams, in conversation October 1994.

126 Jones, letter to Janet Stone of 27 November 1961, in the Bodleian Library, Oxford.

127 *Ibid.*

128 Saunders Lewis, letter to Jones of 19 May 1959 in NLW.

129 Jones, letter to Janet Stone of 13-14 October 1959, in the Bodleian Library, Oxford.

130 See Valerie Wynne-Williams, undated letter of 1961 in NLW.

131 Jones, letter to Janet Stone of 22 January 1972, in the Bodleian Library, Oxford.

132 Jones, letter to Colin Wilcockson of 15 September 1974, (perhaps one of Jones's last letters) in the possession of the addressee.

133 Jones, letter to Harman Grisewood of August 1962, in Georgetown University Library.

134 Jones, letter to Harman Grisewood of 27 June 1959, quoted in *Dai Greatcoat* p 177.

135 David Jones, letter to Janet Stone of 27 November 1961, in the Bodleian Library, Oxford.

RESONANT ABSTRACTIONS

1 Jonah Jones, *The Gallipoli Diary* (Bridgend: Seren, 1989) p 92.

2 Jones, letters to Helen Sutherland of 29 September and 5 November 1958, quoted in Nicolete Gray, *The Painted Inscriptions of David Jones* (London & Bedford: Gordon Fraser, 1981) p 37.

3 Jones, letter to Helen Sutherland of 8 March 1961, quoted in Gray, *The Painted Inscriptions* p 106.

4 *Ibid.* pp 106-7.

5 Jones, letter to Peter Levi of 15 June 1964, quoted in Gray, *The Painted Inscriptions* p 109.

6 Jones quoted in John Petts's *Introduction to David Jones - Paintings, Drawings, and Engravings.* Catalogue (Cardiff: Arts Council, 1954) p 11.

7 Jones, letter to Nicolete Gray of 4 April 1961, in Tate Gallery Archive, quoted in Gray, *Painted Inscriptions* p 103.

8 Jones, 'The Kensington Mass' in *The Roman Quarry* pp 87 & 89.

9 Jones, letter to Helen Sutherland of 7 October 1929, where he discusses framing his watercolours close-up without mounts which compromise the paintings as 'things'.

10 In the Museum of Modern Art, New York.

11 Jones, letter to Nicolete Gray of 4 April 1961, quoted in *The Painted Inscriptions* p 103. He had been impressed by 'the very deeply cut big inscription in the B.M. on a wall by a staircase - I think it was from Wroxeter - Uricorium' but he admired it as a 'lost art form'.

12 *Idem.*

13 See Rev. William Bushell, *Caldey: An Island of the Saints* (1911) originally printed in *Archeologica Cambrensis* (Cambridge, July 1908, rev. 1911) p 15.

14 Jones, *Epoch and Artist* p 289.

15 John Dreyfus, review in *TLS* 31 October 1980, 1229.

16 Jones, letter to Nicolete Gray of 4 April 1961, quoted in *The Painted Inscriptions* p 106.

17 Saunders Lewis, Preface to *David Jones - Paintings, Drawings, and Engravings.* 1954 Catalogue p 4 and see also, Jones, *The Anathemata*, Preface, p 38.

18 Gray, *The Painted Inscriptions* p 9.

19 John Furnival in 1964.

20 Jones, 'The Book of Balaam's Ass', *The Roman Quarry* p 207.

21 Professor Max Bense, Preface to *Concrete Poetry International ROT 21* (Stuttgart, 1965).

22 Ewan Clayton, in conversation autumn, 1994.

23 Jones, letter to Vernon Watkins of 18 October 1957 in *David Jones, Letters to Vernon Watkins* p 46.

24 Philip Hagreen, letter to René Hague 22 February 1978 pp 2-3. Photocopy in NLW.

25 Gray, *The Painted Inscriptions*, p 29.

26 Jones, 'The Myth of Arthur' in *Epoch and Artist* p 213.

27 Jones, letter to René Hague of 23 February 1972 in the Fisher Rare Book Library, University of Toronto.

28 David Kindersley, in conversation with Lottie Hoare, 21 May 1993.

29 Sarah Balme, in conversation 17 October 1994.

30 The word 'keel' was used by Ewan Clayton, in conversation, autumn, 1994.

31 Gray, *The Painted Inscriptions*, p 33.

32 See Jones, letter of 2 February 1963, in *Letters to Vernon Watkins* p 71.

33 Jones, undated draft of a letter to Peter Levi in NLW1978 Dep. Box II/5.

34 Jones, 'David Jones: Artist and Writer', a tape-recorded commentary on his paintings.

35 Muckley, *A Handbook for Painters & Art Students* (Baillière, Tindal & Cox, London, 1882) p 109 (and ticked by Jones in the r.h.m.).

36 René Hague, letter to Grisewood of 1 January 1976, quoted in *The Roman Quarry* p 215.

37 See Jones, *Letters to Vernon Watkins* p 41.

38 Jones, Preface to *The Anathemata* p 35.

39 Jones, draft of a letter to 'Miss Jones' of 20 August 1968, in NLW 1978 Dep Box II/4.

40 Jones, letter to Helen Sutherland of 10 January 1950, in the Tate Gallery Archive.

INTEGRATION AND A CHANGING WORLD

1 Jones, letter to Richard Shirley Smith of 21 April 1961. In the possession of the addressee.

2 Jones's sister in a talk with Stanley Honeyman who related it in conversation, 1994.

3 Jones quoted by Alex Hamilton in *The Guardian* 11 February 1972.

4 Jones, miscellaneous notes drafted perhaps in the 1960s in NLW 1978 Dep. Box 11 49.

5 Editorial in *The Studio* CIII, No. 468, March, 1932.

6 Wassily Kandinsky, *Concerning the Spiritual in Art* trans. Sadler (N.Y.: Dover, 1977) p 29.

7 Jones, letter to Harman Grisewood of 21 February 1942, in Georgetown University Library.

8 George Orwell, reviewing Malcolm Muggeridge, *The Thirties: 1930-40 in Great Britain* (1940) quoted in *The Spirit of Place* p 146.

9 T.E. Hulme, 'Romanticism and Classicism' in *Speculations* (London: Routledge and Kegan Paul, 1924).

10 Paul Klee, *Diaries* No. 857.

11 Jones, Preface to *The Anathemata*, p 24.

12 Donald Davie, 'A Grandeur of Insularity' in *TLS* 22 August 1980, 935.

13 Jones, 'A, a, a, Domine Deus' in *The Sleeping Lord* p 9.

14 *Idem.*

15 Jones, 'A, a, a, Domine Deus' in *The Sleeping Lord* p 9.

16 Jones, letter to Harman Grisewood of 14 November 1970, in Georgetown University Library.

17 Jones, 'The Pursuit of Peace' in Georgetown University Library.

18 Jones, *The Anathemata* p 31.

19 John Berger, *Success and Failure of Picasso* (London: Writers and Readers Publishing Co-operative, 1965, 1980) p 20.

20 Jones, 1935 Notes made for the Tate Gallery, Kettle's Yard, Cambridge.

21 Jones, 'A, a, a, Domine Deus' in *The Sleeping Lord* p 9.

BIBLIOGRAPHY

MANUSCRIPT MATERIAL

Bodleian Library, Oxford - David Jones, letters to Janet and Reynolds Stone.

Burns, John J., Library, Boston College, Chesnut Hill, Mass. - David Jones Collection.

Camberwell College Art Archive.

Harry Ransom Humanities Research Center, University of Texas, Austin.

Greater London Record Office and History Library.

Imperial War Museum Archive.

Kettle's Yard, Cambridge - David Jones, Letters to H.S. Ede

Letters from David Jones in various private collections.

National Library of Wales (NLW) - David Jones Collections: 1978 Deposit & 1985 Purchase

Royal Welch Fusiliers Museum, Caernarfon Castle.

Tate Gallery Archive - David Jones Collection; Nicolete Gray Papers; Sir Kenneth Clark Papers.

Thomas Fisher Rare Book Library, University of Toronto - David Jones Papers.

University Library, Georgetown University, Washington D.C. - Harman Grisewood Papers.

William Andrew Clark Memorial Library, University of Southern California at Los Angeles - Eric Gill Collection.

BOOKS & PERIODICALS

Aldred, Nannette. 'A Canterbury Tale' in *A Paradise Lost* ed. Mellor. London: Lund Humphries /Barbican, 1987.

American Journal of Psychiatry 'Parkinsonian Side Effects Induced by a Monoamine Oxidase Inhibitor' in 141, No. 1, 118-19, 1984.

Anon. *The Dominican Missal in Latin and English.* rev. ed. Oxford: Blackfriars, 1948.

Anon. *The Mabinogion* trans. Lady Charlotte Guest. London: J. M. Dent, 1906.

Aquinas, St. Thomas. *Summa Theologica* trans. The Fathers of the Dominican Province. New York: Benzinger Bros., 1947.

Ashbery, John et. al. *Kitaj - Paintings, Drawings, Pastels.* London: Thames and Hudson, 1984.

Atkinson, Thomas. *A Glossary of English Architecture.* London, 7th edit., 1948.

Attwater, Donald. *A Cell of Good Living.* London: Geoffrey Chapman, 1969.

Attwater, Donald. *The Penguin Dictionary of Saints.* Harmondsworth: Penguin, 1965.

Axis. London, 1937.

Ayrton, Michael. Review in *The Spectator* (London, 3 Nov. 1944).

Baron, Wendy. *The Painters of Camden Town 1905-1920.* London: Christie's, 1988.

Barrow, R.H. *The Romans.* Harmondsworth: Penguin, 1949.

Bayes, Walter. 'The Grammar of Drawing' in *The Architectural Review.* London, (Pt 1 - Jan. 1924) 12-16 & (Pt 2 - Feb. 1925) 54-57.

Beedham, Ralph John. *Wood Engraving.* Ditchling, Sussex: St. Dominic's Press, 1921.

Bell, Clive. *Art.* (1914) Oxford: Oxford University Press pbk., 1987.

Bennet, J.A.W. *Poetry of the Passion.* Oxford: Oxford University Press, 1982.

Bense, Professor Max. Preface to *Concrete Poetry International ROT 21.* Stuttgart, 1965.

Berrall, Julia. *The Garden.* Harmondsworth: Penguin Books, 1978.

Berger, John. *The Success and Failure of Picasso.*(1965) London: Writers and Readers Publishing Co-operative, 1980.

Bergonzi, Bernard. *Heroes' Twilight: a Study of the Literature of the Great War.* (1965) London: Macmillan, rev. ed., 1980.

Bertram, Anthony. *Paul Nash.* London: Faber and Faber, 1955.

Blamires, David. *David Jones.* London: Austin Desmond Fine Arts, 1989.

-- *David Jones: Artist and Writer.* Manchester University Press, 1971.

Blissett, William. *The Long Conversation.* Oxford: Oxford University Press, 1981.

Bouvet, Francis. *Bonnard - The Complete Graphic Work.* N.Y.: Gallery Books, n.d.

Burns, Tom. *The Use of Memory.* London: Sheed and Ward, 1993.

Bushell, Rev. William. *Caldey: An Island of the Saints* originally printed in *Archeologica Cambrensis.* Cambridge, July 1908 rev. 1911.

Butlin, Martin. *William Blake.* London: Tate Gallery, 1978.

Campbell, Joseph & Robinson, Henry Morton. *A Skeleton Key to Finnegans Wake.* London: Faber and Faber, 1947.

Cardinal, Roger. *Expressionism.* London: Paladin Books, 1984.

-- *The Landscape Vision of Paul Nash.* London: Reaktion Books, 1989.

Causey, Andrew 'Stanley Spencer and the art of his time' in *Stanley Spencer.* London: Royal Academy of Arts/Weidenfeld & Nicolson, 1980.

-- 'Formalism and Figurative Tradition in British Painting' and 'The Everyday and the Visionary' in *British Art of the Twentieth Century.* London & Munich: Royal Academy of Arts/Prestel, 1986.

Chadwick, H.M. et al. *Studies in Early British History.* Cambridge. Cambridge University Press, 1954.

Charles, R.L. 'David Jones - Some Recently Acquired Works' in *Amgueddfa: Bulletin of the National Museum of Wales*, 22. Cardiff: National Museum of Wales, 1976, 2-13.

Christian, John, ed., *The Last Romantics - The Romantic Tradition in British Art.* London: Lund Humphries/Barbican, 1989.

Clark, Kenneth. 'Some Recent Paintings by David Jones' in *Agenda - David Jones Special Issue.* Vol. 5, Nos. 1-3. London: 1967.

-- *Landscape into Art.* London: John Murray, 1949, new edit., 1976.

Cleverdon, Douglas. 'Stanley Morison and Eric Gill' in *the Book Collector* Vol. 32 No. 1, 1983.

-- (Producer) Transcripts of 1961 BBC Third Programme Broadcast on Eric Gill.

-- *The Engravings of David Jones.* London, Clover Hill Editions, 1981.

-- *Word & Image IV* Catalogue of National Book League Exhibition. London: 1972.

Collingwood, R.G. and Myres, J.N.L. *Roman Britain and the Early English Settlements* (1936) Oxford: Clarendon Press, 2nd ed., 1937.

Collingwood, R.G. *The Principles of Art.* Oxford: Oxford University Press, 1938, pbk. 1970.

Collins, Judy and Bennett, Nicola, eds. *Landscape in Britain 1850-1950.* London: Arts Council of Great Britain,1983.

Compton, Susan, ed. *British Art in the Twentieth Century - The Modern Movement.* London & Munich: Royal Academy of Art/Prestel, 1986.

Coomaraswamy, Ananda K. *Christian and Oriental Philosophy of Art.* New York: Dover Publications, 1956.

-- *The Transformation of Nature in Art* (1934) New York: Dover Publications, 1956.

Copleston, F.C. *Aquinas.* Harmondsworth: Penguin, 1955.

Cork, Richard. 'The Vorticist Circle, Bomberg and the First World War' in *British Art in the Twentieth Century* Munich & London: Prestel/ Royal Academy of Arts, 1986.

-- *The Bitter Truth.* New Haven & London: Yale University Press,1994.

Craig, Gordon. *Hamlet.* Cranach Press, 1930.

Cribb, Peter William. Unpublished account of the Ditchling Community, 'Joseph Cribb and the Guild of St. Joseph and St. Dominic Founded in 1920 at Ditchling in the County of Sussex'.

Crichton-Miller, Hugh. 'Puberty and Adolescence' - a paper given before the Medical Society of Individual Psychology, London on 8 April 1937 in *The Management of Early Infancy, Puberty and Adolescence - The Psychological Approach to the Neurotic Character.* London: C.W. Daniel Company Ltd., December, 1937.

-- *Psycho-Analysis and its Derivatives.* London: Butterworth, 1933.

Cross, Tom. *Painting the Warmth of the Sun.* Penzance and Guildford: Alison Hodge and the Lutterworth Press, 1984.

Cumming, Robert. *Artists at War, 1914-18.* Cambridge: Kettle's Yard Gallery, Oct.-Nov. 1974.

David Jones - Paintings, Drawings, and Engravings.

Catalogue. Cardiff: Arts Council, 1954.

Davie, Donald. 'A Grandeur of Insularity' in *TLS*. London, 22 August 1980.

Davies, Aneirin Talfan, ed. *David Jones - Letters to a Friend*. Swansea: Triskele, 1980.

Dawson, Christopher. *Progress and Religion*. London: Sheed & Ward, 1932.

-- *The Age of the Gods*. London: John Murray, 1928.

-- 'The Modern Dilemma', No. 8 of *Essays in Order*. London: Sheed & Ward, 1932.

de la Taille, Maurice. *The Mystery of Faith and Human Opinion Contrasted and Defined*, trans. by J. B. Schimpf. London: Sheed & Ward, 1930.

de Rachewiltz, Mary. 'Fragments of an Atmosphere' in *Agenda* Vol. 17-18. London: 1979-80.

Demus, Otto. *Romanesque Mural Painting*. London: Thames and Hudson, 1968.

Denvir, Bernard. *Post-Impressionism*. London: Thames and Hudson, 1992.

Dilworth, Thomas, ed. *Inner Necessities: The Letters of David Jones to Desmond Chute*. Toronto: Anson-Cartwright, 1984.

-- *The Shape of Meaning in the Poetry of David Jones*. Toronto: University of Toronto Press, 1988.

Dix, Dom Gregory. *The Shape of the Liturgy*. London: Dacre Press, 1945.

Dube, Wolf-Dieter. *The Expressionists*. London: Thames and Hudson, 1972.

Ede, H.S. *A Way of Life*. Cambridge: Cambridge University Press, 1984.

-- 'David Jones' in *Horizon*. London: August, 1943.

-- *David Jones: A Memorial Exhibition*. Cambridge: Kettle's Yard Gallery, 1974.

Eisler, Colin. *Paintings in the Hermitage*. New York: Stewart, Tabori & Chang, 1990.

Eksteins, Modris. *Rites of Spring*. Bantam: London, 1989, Black Swan 1990.

Eliade, Mircea. *The Myth of Eternal Return* trans. Trask. London: Routledge and Kegan Paul, 1949.

Eliot, T.S. 'Tradition and the Individual Talent' (1919) in *Selected Prose of T.S. Eliot* ed. Kermode. London: Faber and Faber, 1975.

Ellis, Steve. *The English Eliot*. London: Routledge, 1991.

Ellman, Richard. *James Joyce*. London: Oxford University Press, 1976.

Ettlinger, L.D. and Helen S., *Botticelli*. London: Thames and Hudson, 1976.

Evans, Mark L. *The Derek Williams Collection*. Cardiff: National Museum of Wales, 1989.

Evans, Myfanwy. *Frances Hodgkins*. Harmondsworth: Penguin, 1948.

-- *The Painter's Object*. London: Curwen Press, 1937.

Forge, Andrew, ed. *The Townsend Journals*. London: Tate Gallery, 1976.

Frank, Elizabeth. *Pollock*. NewYork: Abbeville Press, 1983.

Frascina, Francis and Harrison, Charles eds. *Modern Art and Modernism*. (1982) London: Chapman, 1988.

Frazer, Sir James. *The Golden Bough*. London: Macmillan, 1922, abridged edit. pbk. 1957.

Frèches-Thory, Claire and Terrasse, Antoine. *Les Nabis*. Paris: Flammarion, 1990.

Frescoes from Florence. London: Arts Council of Great Britain, 1969.

Freud, Sigmund. *Totem and Taboo*. (1913) trans. Strachey. London: Routledge, 1950, pbk. 1960.

Fry, Edward F. *Cubism*. London: Thames and Hudson, 1966.

Fry, Roger. *Vision and Design*. (1920) Harmondsworth: Penguin, 1961.

Fuller, Peter. *Beyond the Crisis in Art*. London: Readers and Writers, 1980.

-- *Images of God*. London: Chatto & Windus 1985, The Hogarth Press, 1990.

GK's Weekly. London, 1925-7.

Garret, Albert. *A History of Wood Engraving*. London: Bloomsbury Books, 1986.

Gasquet, Joachim. *Cézanne, A Memoir with Conversations*. London: Thames & Hudson, 1991.

Gauguin. Paris: Éditions de la Réunion des musées nationaux, 1989.

Gaunt, William. *The Pre-Raphaelite Tragedy*. London: Jonathan Cape, 1942.

Giardelli, Arthur. 'The Artist David Jones' in *Eight Essays* ed. Roland Matthias. Llandysul, 1976.

-- 'Three Related Works by David Jones', *Agenda*, 11-12 (1973-4) 90-8.

Gibbings, Robert. 'Biography of the Golden Cockerel Press' - Supplement to *The London Mercury* November 1931 Vol. XXV No. 145.

-- 'The Golden Cockerel Press' in *The Woodcut - An Annual* No. 1. London, 1927.

-- *12 Wood Engravings*. London: 1921.

Gilby, Thomas O.P. *Poetic Experience - An Introduction to Thomist Aesthetic*. No. 13 of *Essays in Order*. London: Sheed & Ward, 1934.

Gill, Eric. 'David Jones' in *Artwork* No. 23, London: Dent, 1930.

-- 'Liturgical Art' in *Orate Fratres*. February, 1927 St. Paul, Minnesota.

-- *Autobiography*. London: Jonathan Cape, 1940.

-- *Beauty Looks After Herself*. London: Sheed & Ward, 1933.

-- *Christianity and Art*. Capel-y-ffin: Walterson [pseud. Attwater], 1927.

-- *Essays*. London: Jonathan Cape, 1947.

-- *First Nudes*. London: 1954.

-- *Id Quod Visum Placet*. Waltham St. Lawrence: Golden Cockerel Press, 1926.

-- *Letters*, ed. Walter Shewring. London: Jonathan Cape, 1947.

-- *The Engravings of Eric Gill*. Bristol: Douglas Cleverdon, 1929.

Glazebrook, Mark. *The Seven and Five Society 1920-35*. London: Michael Parkin Fine Art Ltd/John Roberts Press, 1979.

Gray, Camilla. *The Russian Experiment in Art 1863-1922*. (1962) London: Thames & Hudson, 1986.

Gray, Edmund 'The Representational Art of David Jones and Ben Nicholson - An Analysis and a Moral', *Agenda* Vol 12 No. 4 - Vol. 13 No.1, Winter-Spring 1975, 126-34.

Gray, Nicolete. 'David Jones and the Art of Lettering' in *Motif* 7. London, 1961.

-- Introduction to *Helen Sutherland Collection - a pioneer collection of the 1930s*. London: Arts Council, 1970-1.

-- *The Painted Inscriptions of David Jones*. London & Bedford: Gordon Fraser, 1981.

-- *The Paintings of David Jones*. Hatfield & London: John Taylor, Lund Humphries/Tate Gallery Publications, 1989.

Griffith, Wyn. *The Welsh*. Harmondsworth: Penguin, 1950.

Grisewood, Harman. *One Thing at a Time*. London: Hutchinson, 1968.

-- Talk at the David Jones Conference, Pembroke College, 30 June 1978 - published as 'Remembering David Jones' in *Journal of Modern Literature XIV*: 4 Spring, 1988, 565-576.

-- Why Am I Still a Catholic? ed. Hoare. Oxford: Oxford Polytechnic, 1980.

Hagenblocher, Alfred and Smitmans, Adolf. *Otto Dix*. Albstadt, 1991.

Hagreen, Philip. Letters to René Hague. Photocopy in NLW.

Hague, René. 'David Jones: A Reconnaissance', *Agenda*. 5 Nos. 1-3 (1967) 57-75.

-- 'Myth and Mystery in the Poetry of David Jones', *Agenda*, 15 Nos. 2-3 (1977) 37-79.

-- 'The Clarity of David Jones', *Agenda*, 12-13 (1975) 109-125.

-- *A Commentary upon The Anathemata of David Jones*. Wellingborough: Skelton, 1978.

-- *David Jones*. Cardiff: University of Wales Press, 1975.

Hall, Douglas and Matilda unpublished 'Catalogue of Drawings and Papers in Two Outfitters' Boxes in the possession of the David Jones Trustees in 1992'.

Hamilton, Alistair. *The Appeal of Fascism - A Study of Intellectuals and Fascism 1919-45*. London: Anthony Blond, 1971.

Hanke, John W. *Maritain's Ontology of the Work of Art*. The Hague: Martinus Nijhoff, 1973.

Harrison, Charles and Wood, Paul, eds. *Art in Theory 1900-1990*. Oxford: Blackwell, 1992.

Harrison, Charles. *English Art and Modernism 1900-39*. London: Allen Lane/Indiana, 1981.

Harrison, Helen A. *Larry Rivers*. NewYork: Artnews, Harper and Row.

Harrison, Jane. *Myths of Greece and Rome*. London: Ernest Benn, 1927.

Harrison, Michael & Kimmelman, Judith eds. *Drawings by Bonnard*. London: Arts Council, 1984.

Hartrick, A.S., *A Painter's Pilgrimage Through Fifty Years*. Cambridge, 1939.

-- *Drawing*. London: Pitman and Sons, 1928.

Henderson, George. *Early Medieval*. Harmondsworth: Penguin, 1972 (rev. 1977).

Hendy, Philip. *Matthew Smith*. Harmondsworth: Penguin, 1944.

Hills, Paul. '"The Pierced Hermaphrodite" David Jones's Imagery of the Crucifixion' in *David Jones: Man and Poet*, ed. Matthias. Orono, Maine: National Poetry Foundation, 1989.

-- 'The Romantic Tradition in David Jones' in *The Malahat Review*. Victoria, British Columbia, No. 27, July 1973.

-- *David Jones*. Exhibition Catalogue. London: The Tate Gallery, 1981.

Hilton, Timothy. *The Pre-Raphaelites*. London: Thames & Hudson, 1970.

Hodgkin, E.C. 'A Note about David Jones' *London Magazine*. London: Aug - Sept 1994.

-- 'Prudence Pelham' - Unpublished memoir.

-- ed. *Thomas Hodgkin - Letters From Palestine 1932-6*. London: Quartet Books, 1986.

-- 'Helen Sutherland' - Unpublished memoir.

Holt, Ysanne *Philip Wilson Steer*. Bridgend: Seren, 1993.

Hoole, John. *Bernard Meninsky*. A Catalogue of an Exhibition, Museum of Modern Art, Oxford, 1981.

Hopkins, Gerard Manley. *The Poems of Gerard Manley Hopkins* eds. Gardner and MacKenzie. London: Oxford University Press, 1970.

Howell, Arthur. *Frances Hodgkins - 4 Vital Years*. London: Rockliff, 1951.

Hughes, Colin. *David Jones: The Man Who Was on the Field*. Manchester: David Jones Society, 1979.

318

Hulme, T.E. 'Romanticism and Classicism' in *Speculations*. London: Routledge and Kegan Paul, 1924

Hunt, Sidney, ed. *Ray - Art Miscellany I & II*. London, 1927.

Ironside, Robin, *David Jones* in *Penguin Modern Painters*. Harmondsworth: Penguin, 1949.

Jones, David, in typescripts of 1961 BBC 3rd Programme Broadcast on Eric Gill, produced by Douglas Cleverdon. In the Harry Ransom Humanities Research Centre, University of Texas, Austin.

Jones, David. *Letters to William Hayward* ed. Colin Wilcockson. London: Agenda Editions, 1979.

-- 'David Jones: Artist and Writer'. A tape-recorded commentary on his paintings ed. Peter Orr. London: British Council, 1973.

-- 'Letters to Saunders Lewis' in *Agenda - David Jones Special Issue* Vol. 11 No. 4 - Vol. 12 No. 1 Autumn-Winter 1973-4, 17-29.

-- *Dai Greatcoat - A Self-Portrait of David Jones in His Letters* ed. René Hague. London: Faber and Faber, 1980.

-- *David Jones: Letters to Vernon Watkins*, ed. Ruth Pryor. Cardiff: University of Wales Press, 1976.

-- *Epoch and Artist* ed. Harman Grisewood. London: Faber and Faber, 1959, pbk. 1973.

-- *In Parenthesis*. London: Faber and Faber, 1937, pbk. 1963.

-- Preface for the BBC recording of *In Parenthesis*. Draft in Tate Gallery Archive.

-- *The Anathemata*. London: Faber and Faber, 1952, pbk. 1972.

-- *The Roman Quarry and Other Sequences* ed. Grisewood and Hague. London: Agenda Editions, 1981.

-- *The Sleeping Lord and Other Fragments*. London: Faber and Faber, 1974.

-- Transcript of an interview for the BBC with Guy Brenton & Douglas Cleverdon, May 1961.

-- *The Dying Gaul and Other Writings*, ed. Harman Grisewood. London: Faber and Faber, 1978.

Jones, Jonah. *The Gallipoli Diary*. Bridgend: Seren, 1989.

Journal of Clinical Psychiatry 'Encephalopathy with Wernicke-Like Aphasia Secondary to Phenelzine Treatment' in 49, No. 4, 169, 1988.

Journal of Clinical Psychiatry 'Myoclonus and Episodic Delirium Associated with Phenelzine: A Case Report' in 48, No. 8, 340-1, 1987.

Joyce, James. *Finnegans Wake*. New York: The Viking Press, 1959.

Kandinsky, Wassily. *Concerning the Spiritual in Art*. trans. M.T.H. Sadler. N.Y.: Dover, 1977.

Kenner, Hugh. *The Pound Era*. London: Faber and Faber, 1975, pbk. 1972.

Kermode, Frank. 'On David Jones', *Encounter* No. 74. London: November, 1959.

-- *The Sense of an Ending*. New York: Oxford University Press, 1966/7.

Knight, W.F. Jackson. *Cumaean Gates*. Oxford: Basil Blackwell, 1936.

Kenndy, P.G. *Modern War-Paintings by C. W. R. Nevinson*. London: Grant Richards, 1917.

Lewis, Saunders. 'Epoch & Artist' in *Agenda - David Jones Special Issue*. London: Agenda, Spring and Summer 1967, 112-15.

Lewis, Wyndham. *Wyndham Lewis on Art: Collected Writings 1913-1956*. eds. Walter Michel and C. J. Fox. London: Thames and Hudson, 1969.

Lewison, Jeremy. *Ben Nicholson - the years of experiment*. Cambridge: Kettle's Yard Gallery, 1983.

-- *Ben Nicholson*. London: Tate Gallery, 1993.

Lister, Raymond. *Edward Calvert*. London: Bell, 1962.

Lucie-Smith, Edward. *Art Movements Since 1945*. London: Thames and Hudson, 1969.

-- *Sexuality in Western Art*. London: Thames and Hudson. rev. edit. 1991.

-- *Symbolist Art*. London: Thames and Hudson, 1972.

Lynton, Norbert. *Ben Nicholson*. London: Phaidon, 1993.

MacCarthy, Fiona. *Eric Gill*. London: Faber and Faber, 1989.

Malory, Sir Thomas. *The Works of Sir Thomas Malory* ed Vinaver. London: Oxford University Press, 1954.

Mandelstam, Osip. *The Noise of Time*, trans. Clarence Brown. London: Quartet, 1988.

Maritain, Jacques. *Art and Scholasticism*, trans. J. F. Scanlan. London: Sheed & Ward, 1930.

-- *Creative Intuition in Art and Poetry* (1953). Princeton University Press, 1977.

-- *Redeeming the Time*, trans. Harry Lorin Binsse. London: Geoffrey Bles, The Centenary Press, 1943.

-- *Religion and Culture*, trans. J.F. Scanlan, No. 1 of *Essays in Order*. London: Sheed & Ward, 1931.

-- *The Philosophy of Art* trans. Fr. John O'Connor. Ditchling: St. Dominic's Press, 1923.

Mathias, Roland, ed. *David Jones: Eight Essays on His Work as Artist and Writer*. Llandysul: Gomer Press, 1976.

Matthias, John, ed. *David Jones: Man and Poet*. Orono, Maine: National Poetry Foundation, 1989.

McHugh, Roland. *Annotations to Finnegans Wake*. London: Routledge and Kegan Paul, 1980.

Mellor, David. 'British Art in the 1930s: Some Economic, Political and Cultural Structures' in *Class, Culture & Social Change - A New View of the 1930s* ed. Gloversmith. Sussex: Harvester Press 1980.

-- 'The Body and The Land' in *A Paradise Lost - The Neo-Romantic Imagination in Britain 1935-55* ed. Mellor. London: Lund Humphries/Barbican Art Gallery, 1987.

Miles, Jonathan. *Backgrounds to David Jones*. Cardiff: University of Wales Press, 1990.

-- *Eric Gill and David Jones at Capel-y-ffin*. Bridgend: Seren, 1992.

Milner, John. *The Studios of Paris*. New Haven & London: Yale University Press, 1988.

Moeller, Magdalena M. et. al. *Expressionistiche Grüsse*. Berlin, 1991.

Morris, Rosemary. *The Character of King Arthur in Medieval Literature*. Cambridge: D.S. Brewer, 1982.

Morris, William. *Collected Works*. London: Longmans Green & Co., 1915 - Vol. XXIII.

Mortimer, Raymond. *Duncan Grant*. Harmondsworth: Penguin, 1944.

Muckley, *A Handbook for Painters & Art Students*. London: Baillière, Tindal & Cox, 1882.

Munby, J.E. *A History of the 38th (Welsh) Division*. London: Hugh Rees, 1920.

Nash, Paul and Bottomley, Gordon. *Poet and Painter: Being the Correspondence between Gordon Bottomley and Paul Nash 1910-1946*. ed. Abbott and Bertram. London: Oxford University Press, 1955.

Nash, Paul. *The Book of Genesis*. (A.V.) Nonesuch Press, 1924.

Neve, Christopher. 'Journey of a Soul' *Country Life - Scottish Number* (August 13th 1981).

-- *Unquiet Landscape*. London: Faber and Faber, 1990.

Newman, Sasha, ed. *Bonnard - The Late Paintings*. London: Thames and Hudson, 1984.

Newton, Eric. *Stanley Spencer*. Harmondsworth: Penguin, 1947.

Nichols, Robert. *William Nicholson*. Harmondsworth: Penguin, 1948.

Nietzsche, Friedrich. *Beyond Good and Evil*, trans. Hollingdale. Harmondsworth: Penguin Books, 1973.

Orate Fratres. St. Paul, Minnesota, 1927.

Order. An Occasional Catholic Review, ed. Burns. London: Bumpus, 1928-9.

Orr, Peter. 'Mr. Jones Your Legs are Crossed - A Memoir' in *Agenda - Special Issue on Myth* Vol 15 Nos. 2-3. London, Summer-Autumn 1977 110-25.

Ovid, *Metamorphosis*, trans. Innes. Harmondsworth: Penguin, 1955.

Owen, Wilfred. *The Collected Poems of Wilfred Owen* ed. C. Day Lewis. London: Chatto & Windus, 1963.

Pageant, The. London: Henry & Co., 1896-7.

Parris, Leslie. *Landscape in Britain c. 1750-1850*. London: The Tate Gallery, 1973.

Phelan, Gerald B. *Jacques Maritain*. London: Sheed & Ward, 1937.

Poetry Wales. Cardiff. Vol. 8, No 3 Winter, 1972, 7.

Price-Owen, Anne Louise. 'Fragments of an Attempted Painting: An investigation of the Pictorial Concepts in David Jones's '*The Anathemata*' - Ph.D. Thesis, St. David's University College, Lampeter. September, 1992.

Raine, Kathleen. *David Jones: Solitary Perfectionist*. Ipswich: Golgonooza Press, 1974.

-- *David Jones: The Actually Loved and Known*. Golgonooza Press, Ipswich 1978.

-- *The Lion's Mouth*. London: Hamish Hamilton, 1977.

-- *William Blake*. London: Thames and Hudson, 1970.

Read, Herbert. *Contemporary British Art*. Harmondsworth: Penguin, 1951.

Réau, Louis. *Iconographie de L'Art Chrétien*. Paris: Presses Universitaires de France, 1957.

Rees, Alwyn and Brinley. *Celtic Heritage*. London: Thames & Hudson, 1961.

Rees, Hugh, *A History of the 38th Welsh Division*. London: 1928.

Reich, Wilhelm. *The Mass Psychology of Fascism*, trans. Carfango. Harmondsworth: Pelican 1975.

Reynolds, Graham. *Watercolours - A Concise History*. London: Thames & Hudson, 1971.

Reyntiens, Patrick. 'The Catholic Vision of a poet-painter' in *The Tablet*. London, 25 Nov. 1989.

Richards, J.M. *Edward Bawden*. Harmondsworth: Penguin, 1946.

Ritchie, A.C. *British Contemporary Painters*, 1946. Albright Art Gallery, Buffalo, N.Y.

Rosenberg, Harold. 'The Aesthetics of Crisis', *The New Yorker*. New York: Aug. 22, 1964, 114-122.

Rosenblum, Robert. *Modern Painting and the Northern Romantic Tradition*. (1975) London: Thames and Hudson, pbk. 1978.

-- *Paintings in the Musée D'Orsay*. N.Y.: Stewart, Tabori & Chang, 1989.

Rothenstein, John *An Introduction to English Painting*. New York: W.W. Norton & Co. Inc., rev. ed. 1965.

-- *Eric Gill*. London: Ernest Benn, 1927.

-- *Modern English Painters - Innes to Moore*. London: Eyre & Spottiswoode, 1956; Arrow Books, 1962.

-- *Summer's Lease*. London, 1965.

Rowan, Eric. *Art in Wales*. Cardiff: Welsh Arts Council, University of Wales Press, 1985.

Rubin, William, ed. *Pablo Picasso - A Retrospective*. NewYork: The Museum of Modern Art, 1980.

Ruskin, John. *Lectures on Art*. London: George Allen, 1904.

-- *Unto the Last*. London: George Allen 1906.

Russell, John. *Henry Moore*. Harmondsworth: Penguin Books, 1973.

Seven and Five Society 1920-35. Catalogue with an Introduction by Mark Glazebrook. London: Michael Parkin Fine Art Ltd.,1979.

Sewell, Brocard. *St. Dominic's Press, Ditchling: A Check-List of Publications 1916-1936*. Hassocks, Sussex: Ditchling Press Ltd., 1979.

Seyffert, Oskar. *A Dictionary of Classical Antiquities* rev. & ed. Nettleship & Sandys. London: William Glaisher, 3rd ed. 1894.

Shannon & White, Eds. *The Pageant*. London: Henry & Co., 1897

Shepherd, Alan. *A Visitor's Guide to Caldey*. Cardiff, n.d.

Shone, Richard. *Bloomsbury Portraits*. Oxford: Phaidon, 1976.

Silkin, Jon. *Out of Battle*. Oxford: Oxford University Press, 1972. pbk., 1978.

Spalding, Frances. *British Art Since 1900*. London: Thames and Hudson, 1986.

Speaight, Robert. *The Life of Eric Gill*. London: Methuen, 1966.

Spengler, Oswald. *The Decline of the West*, trans. Atkinson. London: Allen & Unwin, 1932.

Studio, The. London: 1928 - 32.

Summerson, John. *Ben Nicholson*. Harmondsworth: Penguin, 1948.

Sylvester, David. *Francis Bacon*. London: Thames and Hudson. 1974.

Thirties - British Art and Design Before the War. London: Arts Council of Great Britain, 1980.

Tisdall, Caroline and Bozzolla, Angelo. *Futurism*. London: Thames and Hudson, 1977.

Valentine, Ferdinand, O.P. *Father Vincent McNabb O.P.* London: Burns and Oates, 1955.

Vaughan, Henry. 'The World' in *Collected Poems* ed. Rudrum. Harmondsworth: Penguin, 1983.

Vaughan, William et al. *Caspar David Friedrich* . London: Tate Gallery, 1972.

-- *Romantic Art*. London: Thames and Hudson, 1978.

Wall, Barbara. *René Hague: A Personal Memoir*. Wirral: Aylesford Press, 1989.

Wall, Bernard. *Headlong Into Change*. London: Harvill Press, 1969.

Waugh, Evelyn, in *Night and Day*. London, July 1st, 1937.

Webster, Grahame. *The Roman Imperial Army*. London: A.C. Black, 1969.

Weston, Jessie L. *From Ritual to Romance*. Cambridge University Press, 1920.

Wheeler, Mortimer. *Roman Art and Architecture*. London: Thames and Hudson, 1964.

White, Christopher. *Rembrandt*. London: Thames and Hudson, 1984.

Wilcockson, Colin. 'David Jones and "The Break"', *Agenda*, 15 Nos. 2-3 (1977) 126-132.

-- 'Presentation and self-presentation in *In Parenthesis*' in *Presenting Poetry*. eds. Erskine-Hill and McCabe. Cambridge: Cambridge University Press, 1995.

Wilcox, Timothy. *Eric Gill and the Guild of St. Joseph and St. Dominic*. Exhibition Catalogue. Hove: Hove Museum & Art Gallery, 1990.

Wilkinson, Alan G. *The Drawings of Henry Moore*. London & Toronto: The Tate Gallery and The Art Gallery of Ontario, 1977.

Williams, Emmett, ed. *An Anthology of Concrete Poetry*. New York: Something Else Press, 1967.

Wilson, Andrew. *David Jones and Eric Gill*. London: Austin Desmond Fine Arts.

-- 'The 7&5 Society: Modernist Activity in British Art 1919-1937' M. Phil. Thesis, University of Kent at Canterbury. Awarded 1988.

Wilton, Andrew and Lyles, Anne. *The Great Age of Watercolour 1750-1880.* Munich: Prestel, 1993.

Yorke, Malcolm. *Eric Gill: Man of Flesh and Spirit*. London: Constable, 1981.

-- *The Spirit of Place*. London: Constable, 1988.

CHRONOLOGY

1895

1 November - Walter David Jones born Brockley, Kent. The third child of James and Alice Jones. Jones sheds the name Walter when he comes to maturity.

c.1899

First visit to Wales.

1900-01

Earliest surviving drawings.

1903

The Lion, exhibited at the *Royal Drawing Society for the Encouragement of Youthful Art* and at the *Cork International Exhibition*. Another drawing, *The Bear*, wins the *Art For Schools Association Prize*.

1909-14

Student at *Camberwell School of Art* under A.S. Hartrick and Reginald Savage.

1910

Death of brother Harold, aged 21.

1913

Painting holiday in Wales with a friend.

1915

Joined the 15th Battalion of the Royal Welsh Fusiliers. Training in London, North Wales, Salisbury Plain.

December - To France to serve as a Private Soldier.

1916

10 July - Wounded in the leg during the Somme battle of Mametz Wood and returned to England.

October - Returned to France.

1918

February - Returned to England with severe trench fever.

1919-21

January - Demobilized.

Studied at Westminster School of Art on an ex-serviceman's grant under Walter Bayes and Bernard Meninsky. Taught occasionally by Walter Sickert.

1919-1928 - Pictures exhibited in the Goupil Gallery Salon.

1921

January - Visited Ditchling where Eric Gill, Hilary Pepler and Desmond Chute had formed a community of artists and craftsmen and become Dominican Tertiaries.

July-December - Visited Ditchling regularly. Made first wood engravings. Met Petra Gill.

7 September - Converted to Roman Catholicism.

1921-4 - Engraving for St. Dominic's Press, Ditchling.

1922

January - Went to Ditchling to be apprenticed to the carpenter George Maxwell.

1923

Became a postulant in Guild of St Joseph and St Dominic.

1924

24 April - Betrothed to Petra Gill.

Summer - Returned to London, using his parents' home in Brockley as a base.

Commissioned by Harold Munro to illustrate Eleanor Farjeon's *The Town Child's Alphabet*.

22 December - Arrived at Gill's new establishment at Capel-y-ffin on the English-Welsh border for the first of many extended stays. Met René Hague.

1925

February-March - Exhibited two watercolours in *Pictures, Sculpture and Pottery by Some British Artists Today* at the Lefevre Gallery.

March - First visit to Caldey Island to paint.

Elected to and first exhibited with *The Society of Wood Engravers*.

Began to paint his parents' garden in Brockley.

1925-27 - Engraving for The Golden Cockerel Press: *Gulliver's Travels* (1925); *The Book of Jonah* (1926); *The Chester Play of the Deluge* (1927).

1926

Painting at Capel and Brockley.

Met Douglas Cleverdon.

1926-32 often visits Regent's Park Zoo to draw animals.

1927

Engagement to Petra Gill broken off.

April-May - Joint exhibition with Eric Gill at the St. George's Gallery.

First visit to his parents' holiday villa at Portslade.

October - Painting on Caldey.

October - Exhibited with the *Society of Wood Engravers* at the St. George's Gallery.

Engraving for the Gregynog Press.

August - Visit to Bristol to stay with Douglas Cleverdon.

October - Visited Caldey Island to paint.

1928

January - Elected Member of the 7&5 Society, proposed by Ben Nicholson.

February - Visited 7&5 Society and *Henry Moore* exhibitions with Gill.

April-June - Visited Salies-de-Béarn in the Basque country with the Gills and went on to Lourdes to visit the Hagreens and then to Arcachon.

Engraved *Aesop's Fables* for Monotype Corporation.

Began *In Parenthesis*.

Began to meet with Tom Burns and Harman Grisewood to discuss issues facing the Roman Catholic church.

November - Exhibition at the Beaux Arts Gallery.

1929

Engraved *The Rime of the Ancient Mariner* for Douglas Cleverdon.

March - Joint exhibition with Gill at the Goupil Gallery.

March - Lunched at Pigotts with Jacques Maritain and Tom and Charles Burns.

Visited Prinknash to rest.

Paintings in Goupil Gallery *Summer Exhibtiion*.

Met Prudence Pelham who visited Pigotts, Gill's new establishment to which Jones was a frequent visitor, often staying for long periods until the 1940s.

First visit to Rock, Northumberland, the home of his patron, Helen Sutherland.

1929-32 - Painting at Portslade, Brockley, Pigotts, Caldey and Rock.

1930

May - Joint exhibition with fellow 7&5 Society artist, Ivon Hitchens, at the Heal's Mansard Gallery.

Eye troubles forced him to give up engraving.

Petra Gill married Denis Tegetmeier.

1931

January - 7&5 Society exhibition.

Beginnings of a deepening depression.

November - Group exhibition at the Lefevre Gallery.

1932

February - *7&5 Society* exhibition. Jones was the biggest seller.

In Parenthesis - main text finished.

March-May Represented in two exhibitions at The Art Institute of Chicago: *First International Exhibition of Etching and Engraving* and *The Twelfth International Exhibition of Water Colors, Pastels, Drawings and Monotypes*.

1932-3

Suffered first nervous breakdown after years of hectic work and increasing emotional stress.

1933

February - 7&5 Society exhibition.

1934

Recuperatory journey to Egypt and Palestine. Visited Jerusalem and Bethlehem.

Paintings for sale with many London galleries but a non-exhibitor at the 7&5 *Exhibition*.

Christmas at The Quay Hotel, Hartland Point.

1935

To Sidmouth as an escape from the stress of London.

A non-exhibitor at the 7&5 *Exhibition*.

1935-1939 - Divided time between Brockley, Rock, Pigotts and Sidmouth but mostly stayed in Sidmouth.

1936

Voted out of the 7&5 Society.

April - Mixed exhibition of watercolourists with Paul Nash, Ethel Walker, Arnold Gerstl and Adrian Daintrey at the Redfern Gallery.

Jones and his close friends deeply affected by the Abdication crisis.

Started to paint again after breakdown.

1937

Publication of *In Parenthesis*.

Work shown at the Venice *Biennale*.

Death of his mother.

1938

H.S. Ede lectured on David Jones across America.

Hawthornden Prize for *In Parenthesis*.

1939

Represented at the *New York World's Fair*.

Prudence Pelham married.

Started to make his mythological paintings.

Helen Sutherland left Rock and moved to Cumbria.

1939-45 Mostly spent in London.

1940

January - Successful exhibition at the Redfern Gallery.

Represented in *British Art Since Whistler* at The National Gallery.

Spent time in Chelsea and Pigotts.

Eric Gill died.

June - left Sidmouth for the last time.

1941

Represented in *Six Water Colour Painters of Today* at The National Gallery.

October - Moved to Sheffield Terrace off Kensington Church Street. First independent base.

1942

Represented in *Tate War-Time Acquisitions* at The National Gallery.

1943

October - Father died.

1944

Began to make inscriptions which became a very important means of expression between 1946-1965.

David Jones Exhibition - organized by C.E.M.A.

1945

April - Shown in a mixed exhibition of French and British artists which re-opened the St. George's Gallery.

November - *Nine British Contemporaries* - British Council Exhibition in Paris and Marseilles.

1945-6

Represented in *Modern English Painting from the Tate Collection* which toured European cities including Paris (Jeu de Paume), Vienna, Amsterdam, Brussels.

1946

To Helen Sutherland's house in Cumbria, Cockley Moor, near Dockray above Ullswater.

In Parenthesis adapted for radio; Dylan Thomas in cast.

Represented in *British Contemporary Painters* at the Albright Gallery, Buffalo and the exhibition tours North America into 1947: Cleveland, Worcester, Toronto, St. Louis and San Francisco.

Represented in *Fifty Years of British Art* which toured European capitals.

Second major breakdown.

1947

To Bowden House, Harrow-on-the-Hill for six months of treatment. During and after treatment executed a series of tree drawings.

Took lodgings at Northwick Park Lodge, near to Harrow School, Harrow-on-the-Hill.

Paintings stolen during the move to Harrow.

1948

January - Represented in an exhibition of Welsh painters at Heal's Gallery.

March and April - Represented in *Moderne Englische Graphik und Aquarelle Kunst*, Vienna.

June - Exhibition at the Redfern Gallery with Derek Hill and Bryan Wynter.

Represented in *Contemporary British Drawings* - British Council, Ottawa.

1949

November-December - Represented in *Contemporary British Art* at the New Burlington Galleries.

David Jones published in *Penguin Modern Painters* series

1950

Represented in *The Private Collector* - Tate Gallery.

Started his Calix paintings.

1951

March - Represented in *British Painting 1925-50* - Arts Council exhibition for Festival of Britain Year.

Represented in Watercolour Exhibition, Brooklyn.

Refused an invitation to become an Associate of the Royal Academy.

Represented in the Venice *Biennale*.

1952

The Anathemata published.

1953

May-June - Represented in *International Water Colour Exhibition 17th Biennial* at The Brooklyn Museum.

July - Represented in *British Romantic Painting* - National Library of Wales.

Radio production of *The Anathemata*.

Represented in *Coronation Exhibition*, Redfern Gallery.

1954

Awarded a Civil List Pension of £150 p.a.

Major retrospective mounted by Welsh Committee of the Arts Council travelled from Aberystwyth to Cardiff to Swansea to Edinburgh, ending up at the Tate Gallery in London.

1955

May - Appointed Commander of the Order of the British Empire in the Birthday Honours.

Awarded the Harriet Monroe Memorial Prize.

1956

Offered Honorary Membership of the Society of Wood Engravers.

1957

Nine paintings included in *The Influence of Wales in Painting* at the Brighton Gallery.

1958

Met Valerie Price.

1959

Epoch and Artist published.

Valerie Price married Michael Wynne-Williams.

1960

Award of £100 from The Welsh Arts Council for *Epoch and Artist*.

Awarded D. Litt. by the University of Wales.

1961

Became Fellow of the Royal Society of Literature and Member of the Royal Watercolour Society.

1962

Award of £200 from The Society of Authors Travelling Fund.

Represented in *Paintings and Drawings from the private collection of Miss Helen Sutherland* at the Scottish National Gallery of Modern Art.

Began heavy treatment of nervous troubles with drugs.

1963

Last mythological paintings.

1964

Death of Helen Sutherland.

Moved to Monksdene Residential Hotel, Harrow.

Awarded Gold Medal, Royal National Eisteddfod.

1965

The Fatigue privately printed to celebrate Jones's 70th birthday.

1967

David Jones Special Issue published by *Agenda*.

1969

The Tribune's Visitation published; awarded Welsh Arts Council Literature Prize.

1970

After a fall and hip injury - to Bethanie Nursing Home and then to Calvary Nursing Home.

Represented in *Decade 1920-30* an Arts Council Touring exhibition.

Represented in *The Helen Sutherland Collection* an Arts Council Touring exhibition.

1972

Word & Image IV - David Jones National Book League Exhibition.

1972-3

David Jones, Writings and Drawings Welsh Arts Council/ National Museum of Wales touring exhibition.

Second *David Jones Special Issue* published by *Agenda.*

1974

The Sleeping Lord and Other Fragments published.

Made a Companion of Honour.

October 28 - died in Calvary Nursing Home.

December 13 - Solemn Requiem at Westminster Cathedral.

1975

Memorial Exhibition at Kettle's Yard, Cambridge and the Anthony D'Offay Gallery, London.

1975-6

Over forty works acquired by public collections.

1976

Exhibition at the University of Stirling and at Manchester Cathedral.

1977

David Jones, Welsh Arts Council Touring Exhibition.

1978

The Dying Gaul and Other Writings published.

1979

May-July - Exhibition at Anthony D'Offay Gallery and the National Gallery of Modern Art, Edinburgh.

1980

October - November - Exhibition of inscriptions at the Anthony D'Offay Gallery.

October - November - *David Jones - Poet and Artist* Kent University Library.

1981

The Roman Quarry and Other Sequences published.

Retrospective at Tate Gallery, Sheffield and Cardiff.

1987

Included in *A Paradise Lost, The Neo-Romantic Imagination in Britain 1935-55* at the Barbican Art Gallery, London.

1989

David Jones - Paintings, Drawings, Inscriptions, Prints, a South Bank Centre Touring Exhibition.

David Jones at Austin Desmond Fine Arts, London.

Publication of *The Paintings of David Jones* by Nicolete Gray.

Represented in *The Lost Idyll* at Gillian Jason Gallery, London.

1990

David Jones and Eric Gill at Austin Desmond Fine Arts.

David Jones: Wood Engravings at Sally Hunter Fine Art, London.

1991

David Jones and the 7&5 Society at Austin Desmond Fine Arts.

Represented in *Eric Gill and the Guild of St Joseph and St Dominic* at the Hove Museum and Gallery; Glynn Vivian Art Gallery, Swansea; Usher Gallery, Lincoln.

1992

The Art of David Jones in the 1920s at Wolseley Fine Arts, London.

1993

David Jones - Celtic Mystic exhibition held by Austin Desmond Fine Arts, R.A. Gekoski, Wolseley Fine Arts.

David Jones at the Burstow Gallery, Brighton College.

Represented in *The Sussex Scene: Artists in Sussex in the Twentieth Century* at Hove Museum and Art Gallery, Towner Art Gallery, Eastbourne.

Exhibition in Edinburgh at The Netherbow Center.

1994

Included in the pan-European exhibition *La Ville* at the Centre Pompidou, Paris.

David Jones: Twenty Five Small Drawings at Wolseley Fine Arts.

1995

Publication of *David Jones - The Maker Unmade*, the first full-length major study of Jones's visual work.

Represented in *The Illustrators to the St. Dominic's Press* at Wolseley Fine Arts with Rocket Gallery, London.

David Jones: A Centenary Exhibition at Wolseley Fine Arts.

David Jones: A Map of the Artist's Mind at Glynn Vivian Art Gallery, Hove Museum and Art Gallery and National of Museum of Wales, Cardiff

David Jones: Artist and Writer at Thomas Fisher Rare Book Library, Toronto, Ontario.

1997

David Jones: Watercolour, Drawings and Selected Engravings at Wolseley Fine Arts, London.

2001

To Petra With Love at Wolseley Fine Arts.

2002

The Private David Jones at Glynn Vivian Art Gallery.

Represented in *Anthem for Doomed Youth* at Imperial War Museum, London.

2003

David Jones in Ditchling at Ditchling Museum, Ditchling, East Sussex.

Eric Gill and David Jones and the Guild of St Joseph and St Dominic at the Ditchling Gallery, Ditchling.

ACKNOWLEDGEMENTS AND CREDITS

We would like to acknowledge: the support of the British Academy for the generosity of its grant aid; The Paul Mellon Centre for Studies in British Art for its donation of a travel grant and its generous help in covering costs of photography; The Henry Moore Foundation for its grant to assist the production costs of publication; and private help without which the project would not have been possible.

We would particularly like to thank Douglas Smith who has done much of the photography for the project. Edmund Gray, Harman Grisewood, Stanley Honeyman and A.J. Hyne of the Trustees of the Estate of David Jones who have been tireless in their help and in their responses to challenging problems, Dr. Paul Hills and Professor Tom Dilworth who have also been gracious in sharing their knowledge.

We would like to acknowledge the help of Robin Vousden at Anthony d'Offay Ltd., the staff of Austin Desmond Fine Arts, particularly Robin Cox and David Archer, Rupert Otten of Wolseley Fine Arts, Philip Wyn Davies and Huw Ceiriog Jones and the staff of the National Library Wales, Jennifer Booth and the staff of the Tate Gallery Archive, The Georgetown University Library, Washington D.C., The John J. Burns Memorial Library, Chesnut Hill, Mass., The Thomas Fisher Rare Books Library at the University of Toronto, The William Andrews Clark Memorial Library, University of Southern California at Los Angeles, The Harry Ransom Humanities Research Centre, University of Texas at Austin, The Gleeson Library, San Francisco, The British Library, The Bodleian Library, Oxford, The Victoria and Albert Library and Museum.

And also:

H.M. Queen Elizabeth II, H.M. the Queen Mother, Agnews, Sir Alastair Aird, The Albertina, Vienna, The Alte Pinakotek, Munich, The Art Gallery of New South Wales, The Arts Council of Great Britain, The Arts Council of Wales, Lady Helen Asquith, Douglas Atfield, Mary Audsley, Paul Avery, Sabina Bailey, Iain Bain, Maurice and Sarah Balme, Professor William Blissett, Bloomsbury Workshop, Bradley Borum, Michael and Susan Bowers, Malcolm Brewin, The British Council, Anthony and the Hon. Alison Brown, Paul Burns, Tom Burns, The Library, Camberwell College of Arts, Kate Campbell, The Cecil Higgins Gallery, Bedford, The Central School of Art and Design, Peter Chasseaud, The Christchurch Museum, Ipswich, David Clark, Ewan Clayton, Nest Cleverdon, William Cookson, Peter Cribb, Anne D'Abreu, Reg Davis-Poynter, Tane Debenham, Winifride Denyer, The Ditchling Museum, Sussex, The Marchioness of Dufferin and Ava, Beatrix Dufort, Catherine Dupré, Elizabeth Ede, Mr. & Mrs. John Ede, Valerie Eliot, Mollie and George Elkin, Lady Elizabeth Elliott, Rosalind Erangey, J.S.K. Fairhead and University College of North Wales, Bangor, Peter Florence, Alan and Beryl Freer, Edward and Valerie Gage, R.A. Gekoski, Charles and Charlotte Gere, Arthur and Bim Giardelli, Gillian Jason Gallery, The Glynn Vivian Art Gallery, Marius Gray, Nicolete Gray, Greater London Record Office and History Library, Margaret Grisewood, Rev. John Hagreen, Ayeshah Haleem, Mariette Hall, Hampton Court Palace, Dr. Michael Harari, Heal & Son Ltd., John Heath-Stubbs, Lottie Hoare, Dr. Elizabeth Hodgkin, E.C. Hodgkin, Jacqueline Honeyman, Sally Hornby, Hove Museum and Art Gallery, Huddersfield Art Gallery, Christopher Hull Gallery, Pamela Hyne, The Imperial War Museum, Victoria Ingrams, Lucy Jebb, Hon. John Jolliffe, Dr. Brinley Jones, Ralph Jones, Margaret Kelly, Kettle's Yard Gallery, Peter Khoroche, Jenny Kilbride, Lady Lever Art Gallery, Port Sunlight, Lady Margaret Hall, Oxford University, Laing Art Gallery, Newcastle-upon-Tyne, Jean-Philippe Laporte, David Lawson, Joanna Leech, Christopher Leith, Prudence Loftus, Monique Louveau, The Louvre, Belinda Low, Eileen Lowenstein, Jenny Mackilligin, Jackie Martin, Éric Martini, Nora Meninsky, Mercury Gallery, London, Fr. Anthony Meredith S.J., Moderna Museet, Stockholm, Canon Gwilym Morgan, Helen Mosby and Alasdair MacPherson, Fr. Joseph Munitiz S.J., The Museum of Childhood, Bethnal Green, The Museum of Modern Art, New York, The National Gallery of Modern Art, Scotland, The National Museum of Wales, Cardiff, The Neue Pinakotek, Münich, The New Art Centre, London, Newport Art Gallery, Fr. Robert Ombres O.P., Peter Orr, The Earl of Oxford and Asquith, Pallant House, Chichester, Emma Pearce of Colart U. K. Ltd., June Penn, Philip and Minkey Pilkington, Portsmouth City Museum and Art Gallery, Dr. Anne Price-Owen, Prospect Music & Art Tours Ltd., Queen's College, Oxford University, Kathleen Raine, Reading University Archive, Redfern Art Gallery, London, The Regimental Museum, Royal Welch Fusiliers, Caernarfon, Michael Richey, John and Claire Rickard, Colin Ridler, The Rijksmuseum Van Gogh, Amsterdam, Dr. Miriam Rothschild, Robert Rubens, Lucienne Ruellé, Saint-Germain-en-Laye, Musée Départemental du Prieuré, Christina Scott, Jonathan Scott, Fr. Brocard Sewell O. Carm., Christina Sheppard, Lady Sidmouth, Richard Shirley Smith, Reresby Sitwell, The South Bank Centre, Spink and Son Ltd., London, The Museum and Art Gallery, Stoke on Trent, Janet Stone, Swindon Art Gallery, The Tate Gallery, London, Violet Taylor, Petra Tegetmeier, Towner Art Gallery Eastbourne, Geoffrey Treasure, Fr. Vincent Turner S. J., Barbara Wall, The Welsh Academy, Michael Werner Gallery, Köln, Westminster Cathedral, Adrian and Naimh Whitfield, Whitworth Art Gallery, University of Manchester, Colin Wilcockson, Nigel Wilcockson, Dr. Andrew Wilson, Joyce Wren, Stella Wright, Valerie Wynne-Williams.

Mick Felton has been a particularly adventurous, trusting and generous publisher. Jonathan's greatest debt is to Catherine Louveau who has been supportive, kind, lucid and creative both in her assistance with research and with her expertise in designing the book. Derek owes a debt of gratitude to Lillian Shiel without whose help he could not have completed so large a project.

INDEX

The paintings of David Jones are included if there is significant discussion in the text. For a complete list of reproductions, check the List of Illustrations. As the entire book is devoted to David Jones, indexing under his name has been selective and the whole index should be consulted for information concerning him.